**The double doors to her chamber shattered from a kick,
splintering wood into the room.**

Before the sound cleared from her ears a man in black streaked inside,
moving faster than any save a *Body* fullbinder could have managed. She
drew her saber—and thank the Gods she hadn't given up wearing it—as
he rushed toward her, wielding a pair of curved steel blades.

Assassin.

The leylines called to her, offering half a dozen energies, but *Body* was
there by reflex, and she met her attacker with steel in hand. A cutting slice
aimed at her head rattled her crossguard, and she kicked him back when he
tried a counter-slash with his other blade. The man sprang forward in a rush,
as though a *Body*-enhanced kick were no more than a lover's kiss, hacking
with a desperate fury. She turned a pair of jabbing strikes, then twisted into
him, grunting as she rammed her saber into the side of his shoulder.

White light flared through her chamber, sending her staggering back.
The man charged again, somehow uncut, and whole. Impossible. This
time she reached for *Death*, sending a tether through his form. He met
her blade again, with no sign of slowing. Blows rained against her guard,
the long reach of her sword enough to create a gap where her table and
furniture had been. They'd smashed chairs aside, shattered the table,
and sent a dozen books scattered across the floor.

The man paused, staring at her with desperation in his eyes. He had
features halfway between Thellan and Sardian, a hawk nose and a look as
though he could scarce believe she hadn't died at the first cut of his blades.

"Surrender," she said. "And I promise you a quick death."

The man stared at her, glancing between her and the window.

She tensed for another attack, and reached for *Shelter*, readying a
shield to bind him in place. Instead he bolted, taking the same route as
Tuyard, leaping through the broken shards hanging from her windowsill.

By David Mealing

THE ASCENSION CYCLE
Soul of the World
Blood of the Gods

BLOOD
OF THE
GODS

The Ascension Cycle:
Book Two

DAVID
MEALING

www.orbitbooks.net

Excerpt from *The Wolf* copyright © 2018 by Leo Carew
Excerpt from *Jade City* copyright © 2017 by Fonda Lee

Author photograph by Vakker Portraits
Cover design by Lauren Panepinto
Cover image by Trevillion
Cover copyright © 2018 by Hachette Book Group, Inc.
Map by Tim Paul

Orbit
Hachette Book Group
1290 Avenue of the Americas
New York, NY 10104
orbitbooks.net

Simultaneously published in Great Britain and in the U.S. by Orbit in 2018

First Edition: August 2018

Orbit is an imprint of Hachette Book Group.

The Orbit name and logo are trademarks of Little, Brown Book Group Limited.

The publisher is not responsible for websites (or their content) that are not owned by the publisher.

The Hachette Speakers Bureau provides a wide range of authors for speaking events. To find out more, go to www.hachettespeakersbureau.com or call (866) 376-6591.

Library of Congress Cataloging-in-Publication Data:
Names: Mealing, David, 1982- author.
Title: Blood of the gods / David Mealing.
Description: First edition. | New York, NY : Orbit, 2018. | Series:
    The ascension cycle ; book 2
Identifiers: LCCN 2018012364| ISBN 9780316552349 (paperback) | ISBN
    9780316552356 (ebook) | ISBN 9781549167867 (audio book downloadable)
Subjects: | BISAC: FICTION / Fantasy / Epic. | FICTION / Fantasy /
    Historical. | FICTION / Action & Adventure. | GSAFD: Fantasy fiction.
Classification: LCC PS3613.E157 B58 2018 | DDC 813/.6—dc23
LC record available at https://lccn.loc.gov/2018012364

ISBNs: 978-0-316-55234-9 (trade paperback), 978-0-316-55235-6 (ebook)
Printed in the United States of America

LSC-C

10 9 8 7 6 5 4 3 2 1

For Aurie

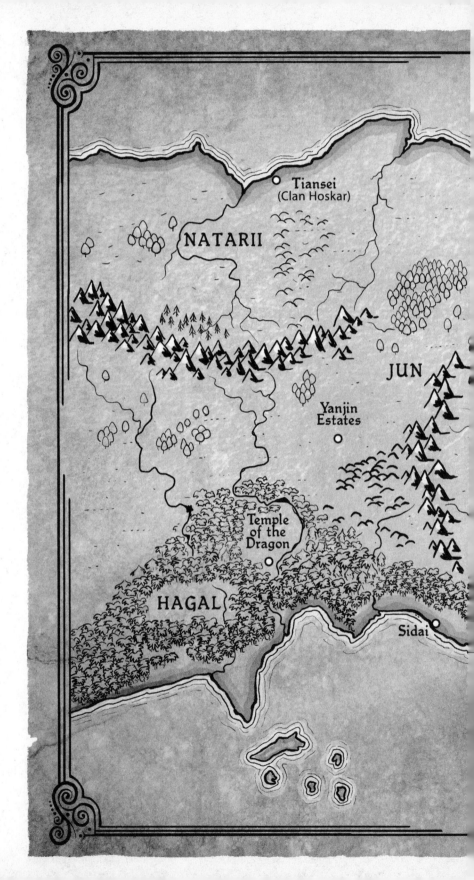

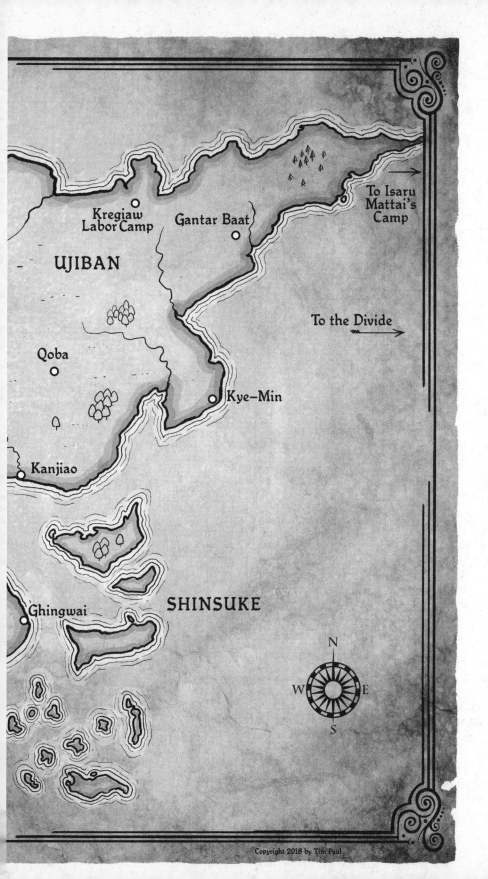

UJIBAN

Kregiaw
Labor Camp

Gantar Baat

To Isaru
Mattai's
Camp

To the Divide

Qoba

Kye—Min

Kanjiao

SHINSUKE

Ghingwai

N
W   E
S

PART 1: SPRING

ARYU | WIND SPIRITS

1

SARINE

The Belle and Brine
Market District, New Sarresant

Music drifted through the tavern's windows and into the street. Would-be drunks and revelers nodded to her as she approached, a row of red faces eyeing her as she walked through the cold spring air. She did her best to ignore them, pressing on until the signage above the tavern door was clear: a painted girl, half-naked and staring at a single wave meant to stand for the sea. The Belle and Brine, and she'd waited for sundown precisely for the cover of a crowd in case the next few minutes turned to violence.

"Anything?" she asked in a whisper directed toward her collar, though she knew Zi could be anywhere, or nowhere, and hear her all the same.

No, her companion thought back. *An ordinary night.*

She nodded, and stepped back as the tavern doors swung wide, revealing a man in a soldier's coat and a woman clearly more sober than he was holding him by the arm. Sarine stepped aside, letting them pass into the street, and wove around them before the doors could shut, admitting herself into the common room.

The music redoubled as she crossed the threshold, five players on an elevated stage and ten times as many nodding heads and drumming on tables in rhythm to the tune. No smells of meat or spices from the kitchens, only pipe smoke, sweat, and the tang of beer, wine, and ale, but those were enough to fill any space left between the music and shouted conversations carried on over top of the players' work. A few eyes tracked her as she moved through the press, but nothing to suggest they knew her, by sight or by description. She'd have Zi's warnings if any among them tried *Red*, the *kaas'* gift to move quicker than she might have seen, but she snapped a *Life* tether in place all the same, feeling green motes drawn into her to sharpen her senses as she moved toward the bar.

Taking an empty seat by herself drew attention from some of the men sitting along the counter, though it took leaning forward and a beckoning gesture to bring the barkeep.

"Wine?" he asked, already reaching for a bottle and glass.

"No," she said quickly. "Lodgings. For me, and for a few trunks of personal effects."

"This is a tavern, not a boardinghouse."

"I have it on good authority you're lodging an associate of mine." She lowered her voice, leaning in. "Along with a store of books, scrolls, and the like. Am I mistaken?"

The barkeep's doubt blossomed into a scowl, and a glance toward her hands. Any number of patrons might have worn the same white gloves, even indoors, but her question would have prodded him toward suspecting the very marques that were present on her skin. Binder's marques, blue and silver, tattooed over scars to signify her skill working with leylines and the noble blood, or the noble patronage it took to afford them.

"Fuck off, my lady," the barkeep said.

"Zi?" she said, this time not bothering to direct it to her collar.

Yellow light flashed at the edges of her vision, then green.

Yes, Zi thought to her. *Green's been used here. His thoughts are bound.*

Her heart thrummed. "Can you—?"

Already done.

"Let's start over, then," she said. "Lodgings. My friend. And more important—the books and scrolls."

The barkeep's scowl had melted, though evidently even Zi's *Green* couldn't entirely erase the man's look of suspicion and doubt.

"That's right," the barkeep said. "Upstairs, behind my offices. He rented the room some weeks past. Made a bloody right sty of it, as I see it. Papers and other such nonsense everywhere."

So, a *he*. The first confirmation she'd had that the *kaas*-mage she was tracking was a man. By now a few of the other patrons at the bar had taken notice of her exchange with the barkeep, though Gods send they thought no more of it than an exchange of business or information.

"Just as well he's come back," the barkeep was saying. "Bloody time he clean the place. I'd as soon have my quarters back, praise the Exarch for a little sense."

"He's here now?" she asked, feeling a tinge of fear. Even the little *Yellow* and *Green* Zi had used would serve as a beacon if the man was close enough to have his *kaas* give warning.

Blessedly, the barkeep shook his head. "Haven't seen him tonight, but at least he's in the city. Bloody well vanished for weeks after he took the room, though. Had half a mind to dump the whole lot of his effects in the sewers and keep the coin. Come to think on it, I've not an inkling why I didn't do it." He frowned. "Bloody well should have done."

"I'll have the key, then," she said. "If it's locked."

" 'Course it's locked," the barkeep said, fishing on his belt for a ring and producing an iron key. He hesitated for a moment, staring at his hand with a frown before another soft pulse of green light saw him lay the key on the counter.

"Thank you, good master," she said, snatching up the key as quick as he set it down. "Veil's blessings on you and your establishment."

A grunt served for a dismissal, and she scanned the room to be sure no eyes had lingered overlong on the exchange as she headed for the stairs. The gray clouds of *Faith* beckoned, but too many eyes would have seen her vanish to risk it. Instead she made do with common skulking, trying to appear nonchalant as she bounded up the steps, finally within reach of the tomes and scrolls she'd been tracking since the morning after the battle in the city. Zi appeared coiled around her wrist as soon as she'd climbed to the top, though unless he'd wanted them to see him, so far as she knew he could stay hidden from others even in plain sight. But then, her companion's oddities were his own. His metallic scales seemed to glint a mix of blue and red in the lamplight, and he'd fixated on the door behind the desk, and on the iron keyhole that stood between them and what had to be on the other side.

She tried the key, felt a click, and the door swung open.

She'd found them.

Piles of books lay stacked above her waist, with some even higher, stacked atop bedstands, tables, and chairs. Even the better part of the bed was covered in scrolls and tomes, leaving only a small corner scarce wide enough to sleep on, and a narrow walkway between the bed frame and the door. The rest was all books, loose papers, and tight-wrapped scrolls, enough to have filled a chamber ten times the size of the barkeep's bedroom. And so they had, up until she'd come to their former home only to find it empty after their owner vanished.

Reyne d'Agarre's library.

She ducked back into the office to grab a lantern, careful to be sure the oil was secure in the pan, and kept it raised as she waded through the stacks toward the bed. A thousand years' knowledge, stored in a chamber half the size of her uncle's kitchen, and it would have taken a small army to cart the contents out of d'Agarre's manor in the hours between the battle and the morning after. Yet that was what had been done; in the moment, she'd been afraid the books had somehow ascended with him, but a few inquiries had confirmed that looters and worse had been at the manor almost as soon as the battle commenced. A simple thing to reason that one of d'Agarre's people must have been charged with moving the books, and with Zi's help they'd followed the trail of *Green* here to the Belle and Brine.

She thumbed open a volume left on the bed: *Histories of Pre-Essanic Gand*, by Jean-Trant Theorain. An inkwell and quill lay beside it, with scrawled marks in the margins suggesting that whoever had rented the barkeep's room might still be engaged in some manner of research. A chilling thought, given where Reyne d'Agarre's studies had led him. But a more thorough sweep of the room gave no obvious sign of the books at the heart of d'Agarre's collection: the ones he'd called the Codex, displayed on plinths at the center of his library. No room for plinths here, and no luck in finding them among the volumes set aside near the space cleared for sleeping. With a sigh she cleared a bedside table and set the lantern down, casting enough light to work by as she settled in cross-legged on the floor to begin scanning through the stacks.

"Too much to hope you can sense d'Agarre's Codex among the others?" she asked Zi. He'd taken up a spot at the edge of the bed, lolling his head and tail together over the side while the rest of him lay coiled like a snake beside Theorain's *Histories*.

No, was all he thought.

It might have earned him a glare, had there been any point. Instead she turned her attention on the books, transferring one stack to the next as she picked up each tome and scanned its contents. *Connections to the Grand Betrayal* earned a quick discard, as did *Principles of Mathematics in Bhakal Herblore*. Some were written in the Sarresant tongue, and those she discarded easily, though more than a few required Zi to translate, and those sparked hope in the brief moment before their words became clear. The Codex had been written in a tongue unlike any other, and what little she'd seen of it had been declared pure nonsense by Zi the moment she scanned its pages. But, nonsense or no, d'Agarre had claimed that the book guided his every step; it stood to reason getting her hands on it would help her make sense of exactly what had happened during the battle, and what might be coming next.

Another stack transferred from one pile to another, and the thrill of victory began to ebb.

"They have to be here," she said to Zi as much as herself. "But if you can't help find them, this is going to take—"

Green.

She froze.

Once, she might have ignored it, dismissed the word as one of her companion's quirks. But she'd come to recognize the colors as warnings, announcements of the same powers Zi conferred on her, wielded by other *kaas*-mages. *Green* meant one of them nearby, using the gift of soothing emotions, twisting thoughts.

By instinct she snapped her eyes shut, revealing the network of leylines running beneath the tavern. She tethered the red motes of *Body* first, feeling a rush of strength in her limbs, then ran a line through a gray cloud of *Faith*, vanishing from view. A flash of panic when she looked at the bed, and the freshly transferred pile of books she'd left obstructing the walkway to the door. No time to reorder them. The *kaas*-mage would know she'd been here, which meant the books—and d'Agarre's Codex with them—would be gone if she left. Now that she was here, she couldn't back down. Whoever d'Agarre's underling was, she had to face him.

She left the lantern, and Zi, weaving through the piles of books to return to the barkeep's office, still masked by *Faith*.

Thumping sounded from below, the rush of stairs taken two or three at a time, and Zi prompted: *Yellow*, then a heartbeat later, *Red*.

A man in black leather appeared at the top of the stairs, paying her no mind—hidden as she was—and he rushed past her faster than any man should have been able to move. Even though she was expecting him, he still managed to catch her by surprise, racing to the door, bracing himself against the frame as though he feared the worst lay within.

It took a second look to register his face, and recognize him for who he was.

"Axerian?" she said, letting *Faith* drop. Zi had appeared on the desk this time, and without knowing how, she knew he'd chosen to make himself visible to her and Axerian both.

The man in black spun around, confirming it was him. The Nameless; a God, or at least he had been, before what had transpired with d'Agarre. His face was haggard, a beard's growth showing through on his jaw where he'd been clean-shaven before, his eyes carrying only a fraction of the spark of wit she'd come to expect from him during the days leading up to the battle. She hadn't seen him since.

"Sarine," he said. "Thank the hidden Emperors it was you, and not one of the others."

"One of who?" she asked. "And what are you doing here?"

He slowed down, a sign his *kaas* had rescinded *Red*, and showed her a half smile, apologetic and knowing at the same time.

"You're responsible for this," she said. "You moved the library, after the battle."

"Xeraxet moved the library," Axerian replied. "With *Green* and the help of a few dozen otherwise unoccupied militiamen." At mention of his name, Axerian's *kaas* appeared on the desk next to Zi. Unmistakably the same sort of creature—metallic scales, a narrow snout like a snake, with four short legs and long, looping coils for a body—but unmistakably different, too. Shorter, stockier, with force to his movements, whereas Zi had always moved with delicate grace.

"Why?" she said. This time it was touched with anger. "The books, and d'Agarre's Codex. You hid them from me?"

"From you? No. I destroyed d'Agarre's copy, and the others had been taken by their owners by the time I got there, more's the pity. The book is dangerous in the wrong hands, as you can well attest by now, I think.

As for the rest, a revolution is no place for a trove of knowledge. I took precautions to store it all here until I could return."

"You didn't think I'd want to read them? To find some answers, something? Or to question you, for that matter."

He gave a pained look. "I had to go. With d'Agarre's ascension there are certain matters that had to be seen to. My failure need not count for Paendurion's, or Ad-Shi's. With my help, both their places might still be secured. And even with the Veil in stasis, the block she placed—"

The world lurched.

Vision blurred, and she was in a chamber of stone, but distorted, as though she viewed it through a glass. Two faces looked up at her, faces that pulled on her memory, each connected to her through arcing strands of energy.

NO.

Zi's thought, and she heard it in two places at once.

The barkeep's office pulsed with blue light, an array of beams seeming to radiate from Zi's scales. Her companion had drawn himself up to his full height, staring at Axerian, almost trembling, for all he stood rigidly in place.

Her belly ached, and she watched as the lights receded, returning the room to amber lamplight. Bile stung her throat, and her stomach twisted, an afterimage of the stone chamber shimmering over top of the room before it faded.

"Apologies," Axerian said quietly.

Zi was shaking, his coils quivering as he stood upright on the desk. He was in pain, and Axerian had done something to trigger it.

"Why are you here?" she asked, moving to Zi beside the desk. "Why come back to the city now?"

Axerian's eyes lingered on Zi as he spoke. "I'm dying now, again, after so many years. I mean to spend my last days as I spent the last ten thousand."

"You were responsible for d'Agarre," she said. "You said as much. You manipulated him through your Codex. If you're planning to loose another monster on this city..."

"No," Axerian said. "My work here is simpler. There are two more ascensions coming. I mean to stop them, and I'd have your blessing, if you'd give it."

She has never given you her blessing, Zi thought, though his voice sounded weak, giving the impression of frailty for all she heard it directly in her mind. *Whatever you do, you do alone.*

Axerian glanced to her, as though expecting her to countermand Zi. She'd done as much before, hunting d'Agarre and his fellows while Zi suffered for it. This time she said nothing. If there was a course for her to follow, she could determine it with Zi, in a manner that didn't leave him quivering in pain.

"Very well," Axerian said. "Then I expect this will be our last meeting. I remand the library into your keeping. Take what you like; I'll see what remains stored safely against the worst of whatever comes."

He hesitated for a moment, as though he meant to say more. Instead his *kaas* vanished as he turned and headed down the stairs, leaving her and Zi alone.

2

ARAK'JUR

Wilderness, Near the Sinari Village
Sinari Land

Familiar trees marked the way home. Oaks and cedars, firs and elms. On foreign lands one was much the same as another. But as they drew nearer the Sinari village, every leaf and stem seemed to offer its welcome, coated with the drops of wet-season rain.

Corenna stepped gingerly beside him, watching where he placed his feet. He grunted when he saw it, wearing a wry grin.

"I'm almost well again," he said. "By tomorrow I will be running footraces with the children."

"As you say," she said. "Though you'll forgive me if I lay my wagers on the children in those races."

He tried to laugh, cut short by stabbing pain in his lung. It earned another bout of concern from Corenna, though she did no more than look him over when he stopped to catch his breath.

She was beautiful. He'd always known it, since their first meeting, but he saw the truth of it now. Soft russet skin, silken black hair, eyes that cut with heat that never burned. She'd accepted a place among his people with a grace he doubted he could have found within himself. And she fought like a tempest, wind dancing on water, hurling thunder and boulders with equal ease. Without her by his side, the *kirighra* would have gutted him like a fish, and instead they carried the creature's fangs as trophies to present to the tribes of their alliance.

"Wipe those thoughts from your mind, Arak'Jur," Corenna said. "You're in no state for physical exertions."

He drew her in, lifting her in spite of the singeing fire in his side. She laughed, and kissed back before he set her down.

"Later," he said.

"Later," she agreed. "Tomorrow, after those footraces."

They exchanged smiles, and pressed on at the hobbled pace they'd kept since sunrise.

It had taken five days to reach the place where Ilek'Inari had foreseen the *kirighra*, and ten to make the journey home. His leg made the difference, shattered in half a dozen places, with bruises, rips, and bite marks covering the right half of his body. The *kirighra* spirit had mocked him, full of pride, when he dealt the killing blow with *mareh'et*'s claws, and rightly so. He'd been careless, and paid with fire in his lungs. The Great Panther had journeyed north from the jungle where he made his home, seeking to kill, and it had been a near thing between him and the great beast. But now he had the right to call upon its blessing, and the people of their alliance were safe. The rest would fade in time.

The leavings of a rainstorm showed in the brush and grasses beneath the forest, and the remnants of a fire, where his people had burned away sections of the land to make way for wild berries and chestnut, maple, and cherry trees. Without his and Corenna's efforts, the *kirighra* might have sprung from the shadows on those who came to gather fruit; such was the great innovation of their people, which let them live among the bounty of the wild while the fair-skins and other folk cowered behind their barriers. Still an oddity for a woman, even a woman such as Corenna, to aid in the guardian's duties, but it was a time for change, for rebirth and renewal. The tribes would adapt, as they had always done, and survive.

The sound of falling trees greeted them at midday, shouted voices presaging each crash, with whoops and cheers when they went down. It lightened their steps, and they pushed hard in spite of his injuries to cover the final stretch of their journey.

Home.

Laughter and shouting, raised voices colored by the accents of four tribes, and the sound of woodwork ringing through the trees.

"Slow," a woman's voice called. "Let them steady the base. We must set it before we raise the outer wall."

They emerged into view, and the tribesfolk turned as one. Six men working under the woman's direction—Symara, foremost among the Ganherat—kneeling around a square frame large enough for three tents, with enough lumber and stone piled to set the stakes for twenty.

"Honored sister," Symara exclaimed, setting down a plank of wood and wiping sweat from her forehead. "Honored guardian. Run to rouse the tribes; let them know our guardians have returned!"

The last Symara said to a slight girl, who turned and ran toward the village. An apprentice, perhaps, however the women reckoned such things.

The men rose, offering warm greetings as Symara strode forward to wrap Corenna in a tight embrace.

"We'd begun to worry," Symara said. "Ilek'Inari assured us all was well, but after so many days, we feared for both of you."

"It was hard-won," Arak'Jur said, grimacing through a smile. "Yet the spirits blessed us with a victory, and we cannot ask for more."

"What is it you do here?" Corenna asked, nodding toward the wood frame.

Symara glanced toward where the men had been working. "With the snows gone, we can construct shelters in the new style. Warmer and more resilient to the wild, with stone hearths and ovens built into the walls."

"Difficult to carry a stone hearth, should it be needful to move the tribe," Arak'Jur said, thinking of the shamans' stories, of ancient times— fire, war, great beasts, floods—when tribes left the tent stakes behind and carried the hides when it became needful to flee into the wild. "Is it not so?"

"It is so, but our villages haven't moved in living memory. Ilek'Inari saw a vision of us living in dwellings of wood and stone, as the fair-skins do. It is time we build for our future, together."

The men murmured agreement, though they watched him for sign of his reaction. He misliked the look of the thing, all squared edges, and the promise of what it would become. Too close to a fair-skin house for his liking. Tribesmen didn't live in such dwellings. But then, women didn't hunt great beasts, and apprentice guardians didn't see visions of things-to-come. The proposal would have been debated in the steam tent among the elders, and he was no *Sa'Shem*, to dictate what would and would not be.

"It will be an ugly thing, when it is finished," he said. "But I will come and eat at your hearth, Symara of the Ganherat, and enjoy the comforts of your tent of wood and stone."

The men relaxed, and Symara offered him and Corenna a wry smile.

"There will be time for work later," she said. "For now, we will accompany our guardians, if they will have us, and celebrate your return."

Cookfires roared, a warmth well suited for the fire in his side. Plates of food had been served by young women, trays of smoked elk, maize, honeyed nuts, and sweet potatoes, and he and Corenna had separated, seated among the men and women at their separate fires.

The men made allowance for him, giving space enough to extend his leg while he sat, but still they crowded close, waiting for him to speak.

"A victory," he said. "And a new blessing, one no tribe has been given before."

A hush rippled through the men, and excited whispers, piercing through the quiet.

"*Kirighra*," he continued, unfastening the string on the deep pouch he'd carried fixed to his leggings. He withdrew the teeth they'd taken from the corpse, met by gasps when he produced them. Two incisors, each the length of his forearm, honed to deadly points.

"A snake?" one of the youths asked, a bright-eyed Vhurasi boy. "Like the *valak'ar*?"

"A cat," he replied. "Stronger, thicker than *mareh'et*, with fur as black as a shadow and eyes like full moons." He passed the fangs, one in either direction, and the hunters handled them with proper reverence, each man whispering the great beast's name in awe. "He is not given to toying with his prey, as *mareh'et* does, nor does he claim territory like *una're*. He stalks the land, smelling its scents, finding its secrets, until he knows the ways of every creature in his path."

"It hunts every sort of creature?" the boy asked. "Birds, fish, beasts?"

A few of the elders frowned at the questioning; it wasn't done, speaking over a guardian's recounting of a hunt. Arak'Jur met the boy's eyes, lowering his voice to just above a whisper.

"It knows them all," he said. "But it hunts one. *Kirighra* is proud; he finds the strongest, the predator who is never prey. He stalks the land until he is sure, and then he strikes. In the jungle he might choose the boa; on the plain, the alpha wolf. Here in our forest, he might choose you, if you proved your prowess and slew a bear, or some other beast to satisfy his liking." The boy's eyes went wide; Arak'Jur had timed the telling to coincide with the arrival of one of the fangs in the child's hands.

"In the west," he continued. "Five days from our lands, the *kirighra* chose me."

He gestured to the ruin of his right side, where claw marks raked his flesh, leaving a bore the size of an apple through his chest and lung, where one of the fangs had bitten clean through.

"He chose me, and stalked the shadows until he knew the pattern of my days. He waited, as patient as the *anahret*, until I slept. I woke with full moon eyes leaping at me from the brush, and the rest is between me, Corenna, and the *kirighra* spirit. Though you have the fangs, as proof of the tale."

The men laughed, those near him clapping his shoulder, offering praise and blessings for the spirits' favor. A ripple of tension broke as they took up the food, Vhurasi, Sinari, Olessi, and Ganherat sharing meat and maize together. A strange sight. Once, each tribe had their own village, their own shamans and guardians, any of whom might have told similar tales to men gathered around their cookfires after a hunt. Now the Sinari village burst with life, half a dozen fires for the men alone, and half again as many for the women, seated across the clearing, where they'd already expanded the tribe's meeting place to double its size.

He glanced to where the women gathered, where Corenna was seated at their heart, sharing whatever passed between women on such occasions, though he supposed she would be the first, the one to decide what would eventually become tradition. In all the tribe's stories, women had never hunted the great beasts, following the shamans' visions to protect their people from the ravages of the wild. But now Corenna fought at his side, and they were stronger for it. It was wisdom. Ilek'Inari received the sendings of the spirits of things-to-come unabated, though he was no full *Ka*, even now. A sign of the spirits' favor, in spite of change.

"Well done, honored guardian," Valak'Ural said beside him, a master hunter of the Olessi. "A hunt well fought, and a tale well told."

Arak'Jur bowed his head, enjoying a haunch of elk. "What passes with you, honored hunter, and with the tribes? It seems the turning of the wet season finds us in good spirits."

"It does. I led a hunt in your absence, with the spirits' blessing on our muskets, and our spears." Valak'Ural gestured to the elk in Arak'Jur's hands. "But I fear there is yet grief among us, for what passed on our lands, and the fair-skins'. The great beasts come ever more often, and yes, we are kept safe by your hand, but there is the matter of the shamans' visions, the sendings of war given to us, and to other tribes."

"Perhaps the worst of it is behind us," he said. "Our alliance is strong. Few would dare provoke us, and we lay claim to the land of five tribes, a great distance between us and any would-be enemies, with as great a distance to see the comings of great beasts."

"Spirits send it is so," Valak'Ural said, then leaned forward, his voice lowered. "But there are whispers of sightings, of Uktani warriors in the north."

"On Ranasi land?"

Valak'Ural nodded gravely.

Arak'Jur's blood chilled. The Ranasi were gone—the price of Llanara's madness, though their blood still stained his people's hands—but the Uktani, their northern neighbors, had grown cold in the last seasons. Alone they would be no threat to the combined alliance of the eastern tribes, but the thought of violence put ash in his mouth, and he lowered his elk haunch, his appetite suddenly diminished.

"Ilek'Inari will have seen it, if they meant us harm," he said at last.

"I hope you're right," Valak'Ural said. "Spirits bless us all, I hope it."

He returned to his plate, finding his maize cold. He had seen enough of death. This was a time—and a place—of joy, of changing traditions and growth. Five tribes made a home here, to think of any who might challenge it, and so soon after—

"Arak'Jur." A voice came from behind, a child's voice.

He turned, though it spread fire in his side, and met a young boy's eyes, a child of no more than five.

"Yes, little brother?" he asked. "What is it?"

"You are summoned to the shaman's tent, by the will of the spirits."

Corenna met him on the path, falling in beside his plodding steps. He hadn't seen her leave the women's circles, but she was there, and he was grateful for the company.

"It can't be another great beast," she said. "Not so soon. Even in desperate times, they never come so often."

"Better a beast than something worse."

She eyed him again, falling silent. He knew her mind, even without her speaking it. It had been no beast that ravaged her people. Corenna was the last daughter of the Ranasi, and it had been war and madness that took her father and the people of her tribe.

They crossed the village as quickly as his leg allowed, passing through a dull reflection of the laughter they'd left at the cookfires. Some few tribesfolk saw to chores or duties away from the village heart, but most feasted the return of the guardians, leaving tents and walkways empty. The child led the way toward what was still Ka'Vos's tent in his mind, though the old shaman was dead. Another stain on Llanara's hands.

"Smoke," Corenna said. "A vision, then."

She'd seen it first, but it was so: Red smoke billowed from the top of Ilek'Inari's tent, and he swallowed bile at the sight. The child darted ahead, lifting the entrance flap, and beckoned them inside.

A thunderclap sounded, with a rush of smoke, as soon as they ducked within.

"Guardian." Ilek'Inari's voice seemed to echo within the tent, an ethereal mist swirling within his eyes, strange and distant. "Our children come. You must protect them."

He fell to his knees, and Corenna beside him.

"Great spirits," he said. "I don't understand. We tracked and slew the *kirighra*. Is there another beast? What manner of spirit are you?"

"Arak'Jur," Ilek'Inari said, still speaking with the spirits' voice. "We know you. You must remember us."

Corenna met his eyes with wonder. He shared the feeling for a moment; then the voice caught his memory. A deep ache, standing tall enough to brush the clouds. The slow rush of ages, watching the world break and grow and shape itself around his roots. He remembered what it was to be the Mountain, the oldest child of the earth, the gift of liquid fire flowing in his veins.

"The Nanerat," he said in a rush. "They are your children."

An anguished wail filled the tent.

"What is it?" Corenna asked. "What has befallen them?"

"Save them," Ilek'Inari gasped. The apprentice's eyes seemed to lose focus, the brown within darkening almost to a shade of black. "The Goddess, she has gone mad, she has turned on her own. She seeks to kill us. The spirits. We are marked for death!"

"Where are the Nanerat?" Arak'Jur demanded. "Where can we find them?"

The fire burst in a wave of scorching heat, and shapes appeared in the smoke. A snake, perched on the arm of a man. A lizard, trailing beside a woman. A stag, following the pointed finger of a crone.

"What do they mean?" Corenna said over the roar of the fire.

"That's *valak'ar*." Arak'Jur pointed to the snake, as sure as he had been of any shaman's vision since he had become guardian. Even etched in smoke, he feared no other sight more. "The lizard is *anahret*, the stag is *astahg*."

"Three great beasts?" Corenna asked.

Ilek'Inari snapped toward them, quick as a viper.

"A dozen," Ilek'Inari said, and his voice had changed—a sharp, biting heat where before it had been pleading calm. "A hundred, if I have to send them. You will not ascend, whelpling of the wild. I will find you, and smother you, as the falcon hunts the sparrow."

Arak'Jur rose to his feet. This was no mountain spirit. Ilek'Inari's eyes had gone fully black.

The fire dimmed. Ilek'Inari blinked. In a rush, the smoke cleared from the tent.

"Arak'Jur," Ilek'Inari said. "Corenna. It's good to see you."

Arak'Jur took a step back. Awe rattled his senses, but Ilek'Inari's eyes had returned to normal, the tent at once no different from any other in the village.

"Honored apprentice," Corenna said. "What was the nature of that sending? It spoke of the Nanerat in danger, of great beasts in terrible numbers."

"The corrupted spirits," Ilek'Inari said. "They seized hold of me, for a moment."

Arak'Jur's heart pounded in his chest; he recognized the same in Ilek'Inari.

"A terrible burden," he said, and Ilek'Inari nodded, wearing a solemn look.

"What must we do?" Corenna asked. "The Nanerat will be coming from the north. Should we prepare to travel again, to meet them?"

"I've seen where to find them," Ilek'Inari said. "But you shouldn't join this hunt, honored sister."

Arak'Jur frowned. Corenna recoiled as if he'd struck her.

"No," Corenna said. "I've fought, as fierce and strong as any guardian. And Arak'Jur is wounded, days away from a full recovery. I see no reason I can't—"

"You're carrying his child," Ilek'Inari said.

The tent seemed to empty of air, along with his breath.

3

ERRIS

Training Grounds
South of New Sarresant

Fire!"

Musket shot belched smoke from their guns, a wall of white fog rising into the morning air, sealed off by the haze of *Shelter* conjured in front of their line an instant after the last gun fired.

"Reload!"

The command carried from officer to officer, sergeant to sergeant. Erris's vessel paced behind their line, watching soldiers pouring powder from their cartridges, filtered back to her senses through the golden threads of *Need*.

"Drop bindings!"

The command came from the colonel at the head of their column, crisp and precise. Fifteen seconds, on the tick, and the *Shelter* vanished, once more revealing the targets arrayed across the yard.

"Fire!"

Another wave of thunder, redoubling the smoke and cinders on the air. More shouted commands finished the exercise, stowing every fired gun with the same precision, leaving a thousand pairs of eyes stealing glances toward her vessel, hanging on her next pronouncement.

She let silence linger, holding them in formation without saying a word.

Finally she relented.

"Superb work, Colonel," she said.

"Thank you, sir," the regiment-colonel said, beaming though he made every effort to hide it behind a veneer of a soldier's pride. The 86th was one of the new regiments, formed in the months since the battle, given veteran officers plucked from units destroyed in the fighting. She'd expected to need two seasons at least to have the new units ready, but already the New Sarresant Army was leaner, sharper, a honed edge ready to be put to use against its enemies.

"Form your lines and report to the Ninth Division command tents," she said. "They'll have a part for you in—"

Stabbing pain roiled through her senses.

She let *Need* go, snapping back into her skin before the golden light shattered, cursing and thumping her desk.

"Sir?" Field Marshal Royens asked. He stood with two of his aides, and his counterpart, Field-Marshal de Tourvalle, ringing the large table in front of her desk in the chambers of her offices at high command.

"It's happened again," she said quietly.

The rest of the table joined her in silence. *Need* was the glue that held the army in place, binding every outlying division to her personal command, here in New Sarresant. But by now even the lowliest regiment commander had at least heard rumors of *Need* failing, since the battle. Her connections to her vessels held, but only for a time, shattering and leaving her in a daze if she held the tethers too long.

"Perhaps the rest of our training exercises can wait," de Tourvalle said. "The rest of my corps has orders to wait for your signal. A day or two of rest would not be remiss."

"No," she said. "We need to drill them on maneuver, with or without *Need*. I'll try again in half an hour. Continue your planning until then."

Her corps commanders and their aides made deferential bows, returning their attention to the papers in front of them. Gods but it was all she could do not to slam her desk with *Body*, to break it in half and send the pieces scattered into the hallway. All her preparation, all her restructuring of command, and it hinged on a binding as fickle as the southern winds. It wasn't like *Body*, *Life*, *Death*, or any of the others. When those stores ran dry, the bindings wouldn't form; simple as if she hadn't been able to see the energies at all. *Need* was different. She could sense the golden lights, draw on them, snap them into place, and share her vessels' senses, for a time. But in the weeks since the battle, the *Need* bindings shattered if she held them too long, leaving her retching and weak. Gods save them all if it happened during a battle, when all were counting on her to coordinate their efforts. And Gods save them if the enemy general's *Need* had no such weakness. She'd destroyed his forces here in the New World, but he would be coming again, and all her drilling would count for nothing if he held the threads of *Need* while she was sicking up in a basin at high command.

"Lord Voren here to see you, sir," her new aide, a young captain named Essily, said, peering through the double doors at the far side of her rooms.

"Send him in," she said. She'd sooner have ordered Jiri saddled for a long ride to clear her head. The aches of *Need* still lingered at her temples, as they too often did whenever she dared to wield its threads in recent weeks. She'd tried to pace herself, using the connections only for final drills, key orders, and confirming scouts' reports, but she had a bloody army to train.

Voren's manservant entered first: Omera, a black-skinned man who swept the room with his one-eyed gaze before nodding behind him, as though an ambush might have been planned in her chambers if he hadn't been there to spot it. Voren followed close behind, his general's uniform traded out for the fashions of the day: a slim blue coat over top of white frills and a yellow sash, calf-length boots and hose, though his gray mustaches and spectacles were the same as ever. Tuyard came behind in the same attire, never mind that he still served as High Admiral.

"Lord Voren," she said, rising from her desk despite Voren's gesture to stay seated.

"High Commander," Voren said. "Please, don't trouble yourself on my account. Gentlemen." He offered slight bows to her two corps commanders. "Could we perhaps have the room?"

She nodded, and Royens, de Tourvalle, and their aides bowed to her, gathering some of their papers before withdrawing.

"How goes recruitment?" Voren said, taking one of the chairs opposite her desk. Tuyard occupied the other, while Voren's manservant stood near the back of the room. "It's said you have them drilling sunup to sundown, and not without results, as I hear it."

"Half my soldiers were working looms or mining coal two seasons ago," she said. "They need drilling, and time to learn maneuver. But that isn't why you're here. *Need* hasn't improved. I can use it, in short bursts. Good enough to deliver orders, not to survey a battlefield or stay in command."

Voren and Tuyard eyed each other, and Voren spoke. "Would you say the army is ready to march, High Commander?"

"No," she said. "But my scouts say the enemy is quiet. Why? Have you heard otherwise?"

Voren shook his head, but reached inside his coat, withdrawing a rolled parchment bearing a wax seal and laying the tube on her desk.

"This is a signed order," he said. "Committing you to march with all haste into the provinces of l'Allcourt, Lorrine, Euillard, and Mantres."

She took up the parchment and pried the wax free. "What nonsense is this?" she said, scanning the paper to confirm its contents. Sure enough; *for the purposes of restoring order* and *committed to march forthwith*.

"Just what it seems, I'm afraid. You are ordered to invade the southern Sarresant colonies. A test of the new army, for all it tastes of bile."

"You intend us to declare war on our own people?" she said, letting the parchment fall to her desk.

"Not me, High Commander. You forget—I am no King. Reyne d'Agarre left behind an Assembly elected to represent the people. This is their will, and perhaps the first test of their authority."

"I have no intention of reaving through our own countryside," she said. "My soldiers need time to prepare to face our enemies. This is about...what? A show of force?"

Voren gave her a hard look. He seemed to have aged another five years in the span of a season, his creased skin sunk into hollows above his jaw.

"This is about taxes, High Commander," Voren said. "Not the sort of thing any government will let slip for long. Not if you want your soldiers' wages paid and your quartermasters' larders stocked past the spring. Word among the councilors is the southern lords have been slow to accept the revolution, claiming they owe taxes to the Sarresant crown, and not the New Sarresant assemblies. You are tasked with convincing them otherwise."

"I'm training soldiers, not tax collectors."

"With respect, High Commander, you are preparing this army to face the Gandsmen, or perhaps the Dauphin's soldiers, should the Old World decide to reclaim its former holdings. A few holdout lords and militias should pose little threat. And our loss of control in the southern colonies may well be the root cause of your *Need* bindings' weakening. Without a firm hold on our territory, it stands to reason the gains of our conquests would slip, not least among you and your binders."

She'd considered it, of course; she'd gained *Need* only after a season of victories against the Gandsmen, prior to their new commander taking over before the battle at Villecours. With territory came new bindings, and they'd lost all the reach of the Empire, declaring independence from the crown. But *Entropy* held, as strong as ever. Why would *Need* wane, and not the rest?

"There is an alternative, my lords." High Admiral Tuyard piped up from beside her desk, reclining against the table's edge. The High Admiral was lean, in the last years of his prime, with all the bearing of a lord and little of a seaman.

"*Égalité* is well and good, as an ideal," Tuyard continued. "But we joined ourselves to the cause of revolution as an act of preserving the colonies against the whims of a tyrant. Are we any better than the late Prince Louis-Sallet if we march soldiers into the homes of our countrymen, demanding their gold and silver as homage to a council whose authority they don't recognize?"

"Guillaume—" Voren began, but Tuyard cut him short.

"No, Voren, I am aware the timing is poor, but they've forced our hand. We here, the three of us, represent the might of the New Sarresant military. At a word we could replace these councils with a legitimate power, retaining our independence while giving the southern lords and ladies a government they can respect."

The air seemed thick with silence. Voren studied her, his thick mustaches masking any expression save the burning in his eyes.

They needed her support.

The realization struck like musket shot. Even weakened, with less than half the full strength of *Need*, she carried enough weight with the soldiers that neither Voren nor Tuyard dared to move without her. But if Voren was right, and control over territory was the key to restoring *Need*, then war was the answer, and she was positioned as well as any to dictate its terms.

"I'd as soon see this army put to the use for which it was intended," she said. "Or have we forgotten there is an enemy waiting in the south?"

"None of us have forgotten the Gandsmen," Voren said. "But the Assembly needs its coffers filled, and—"

"…and plunder from a successful conquest would do for that," she finished for him. "As sure as subjugating holdouts in Lorrine and Euillard."

"I say the time is ripe to seize control," Tuyard said. "We have the strength here to march on the city. All we have to do is take it."

"We have an enemy marshaling his strength in the south, and you propose we wade into a quagmire?" she said. "Victory against Gand would bring unity at home, and gold to supply our troops. It solves both problems, neater than any parchment from your Assembly."

Tuyard looked to Voren, who had fallen quiet, studying her.

"You are confident you could win, against the Gandsmen?" Voren asked.

"Yes," she said, putting all her resolve into the word. She'd already prepared two invasion plans, one by sea, one feinting with the ships to cover a land route through Lorrine. Springtime promised good weather for a campaign, with winter's stores left over to make for adequate provisioning. The better part of the enemy's soldiers had been taken hostage, ransomed home without horses, guns, or powder. She might seize Derrickshire, or the heights at Ansfield Crossing, before the enemy could muster a defense. A child could ride that horse to victory.

"We have the prize in our hands," Tuyard said, "and instead we pluck our neighbor's thornbush? This is—"

A deep thud cut him short, coming from outside her offices, in the high command chambers proper. Both Voren and Tuyard turned in their seats as a clamor rose, and she saw terror in High Admiral Tuyard's face.

By instinct she tethered *Body*, abundant as it had been beneath the city since the battle, and *Life*. The High Admiral bolted to his feet, dashing around her desk toward her window, overlooking the street below. Glass shattered as he hurled himself through, leaving Voren and his manservant staring after Tuyard in wordless shock. Shouts of panic rose in the halls outside her rooms, and she kicked her chair back from her desk, springing to her feet.

The double doors to her chamber shattered from a kick, splintering wood into the room. Before the sound cleared from her ears a man in black streaked inside, moving faster than any save a *Body* fullbinder could have managed. She drew her saber—and thank the Gods she hadn't given up wearing it—as he rushed toward her, wielding a pair of curved steel blades.

Assassin.

The leylines called to her, offering half a dozen energies, but *Body* was there by reflex, and she met her attacker with steel in hand. A cutting slice aimed at her head rattled her crossguard, and she kicked him back when he tried a counter-slash with his other blade. The man sprang forward in a rush, as though a *Body*-enhanced kick were no more than a lover's kiss, hacking with a desperate fury. She turned a pair of jabbing strikes, then twisted into him, grunting as she rammed her saber into the side of his shoulder.

White light flared through her chamber, sending her staggering back. The man charged again, somehow uncut, and whole. Impossible. This time she reached for *Death*, sending a tether through his form. He met her blade again, with no sign of slowing. Blows rained against her guard, the long reach of her sword enough to create a gap where her table and furniture had been. They'd smashed chairs aside, shattered the table, and sent a dozen books scattered across the floor.

The man paused, staring at her with desperation in his eyes. He had features halfway between Thellan and Sardian, a hawk nose and a look as though he could scarce believe she hadn't died at the first cut of his blades.

"Surrender," she said. "And I promise you a quick death."

The man stared at her, glancing between her and the window.

She tensed for another attack, and reached for *Shelter*, readying a shield to bind him in place. Instead he bolted, taking the same route as Tuyard, leaping through the broken shards hanging from her windowsill.

4

SARINE

The chapel doors swung inward, spilling sunlight through the atrium and into the pews. Heavy oak, almost enough to require *Body* or *Red* to move, though her uncle kept the steel hinges well oiled and polished. Carved figures of the Goddesses welcomed parishioners on the outer faces of the doors; the Oracle, her eyes glazed over, beckoning all comers forward, and the Veil, shrouded in cloth, looking away from the entrance as though she kept a secret. As a child she'd learned to draw by sketching them both, along with the other reliefs and stained-glass portraits throughout the Sacre-Lin. The thought made her yearn for charcoals and parchment, but today's proceedings would be no simple sermon. Today her uncle's chapel paid homage to the city's new master, and for all the blood it had cost, it warmed her heart to see it: *égalité*, made real, in the councils and deliberation among even the lowest of its citizens.

A line of men and women poured through the doors, shuffling steps as they gawked at the high-arched ceiling, the dazzling rays of yellow, red, and blue spilling through the windows. She held the door, though it would have stayed on its own, offering welcome and muted blessings as they passed through. Old and young, wrinkled graybeards and crones, mothers with babes in their arms, working men with soot-stained hands, and young men and women with fight still lingering in their eyes. Her uncle called out greetings from the head of the pews, gesturing for all to find a place, to sit tight together and pack every bench.

Zi appeared halfway through the procession, wrapped around her forearm, keeping himself invisible to all eyes but hers. His scales flushed gold, with flashes of crimson, as bright as she'd seen him since the battle.

"A beautiful sight," she whispered for his benefit.

It is, he thought back to her. *A rare thing, for your kind to allow it. Preoccupation with rule blinds you to the rights that uphold any regime, from tribe to city to state.*

She smiled. Zi rarely turned philosopher, but she relished his insights when he did.

"I wish Donatien were here to see it."

Zi made no reply to that, leaving her alone with the thought of her former paramour. A stolen summer, a glimpse into a world that was leaving the colonies, if it wasn't already gone. She'd been the one to break things off between them, seeing Lord Revellion safely on a ship among his peers, bound for the shores of the Old World. Given the madness that had taken hold in the city, she'd probably saved his life. Certainly she'd saved the nobles who had comprised the Lords' Council, on the night of Reyne d'Agarre's coup. She still longed to know what Donatien would have thought, watching two hundred denizens of the Maw pack into her uncle's church, ready to wield their power as part of a burgeoning republic. And she missed his arms around her, the light in his eyes when he first saw her dressed in a noble's finery, and again when he saw her in nothing at all.

She blushed at that thought, checking to be sure the last of the line was inside the chapel before she closed the doors.

"Welcome, sons and daughters of New Sarresant," her uncle's voice intoned. His usual manner, practiced from decades of service to the Gods. "We gather here as citizens of the Maw's District Council. I cede the dais to Assemblyman Gregoine for the news of the day."

Her uncle bowed, backing away from the pulpit. A calculated gesture, she knew from discussion beforehand. The symbol of the priesthood bowing in service to the Republic.

She cut across the rear wall of the chamber, angling toward the ladder leading into the lofts above the chapel nave. Zi scowled, tightening his coil around her arm, but she paid him no mind. He would make do with whatever angle she chose to watch the proceedings. A new voice boomed above the murmurs of the crowd, reciting some philosophical tenets as she climbed the ladder's rungs. The spirit of *égalité*, an affirmation of the principles of freedom and justice, of the power and duty of every man and woman to be vigilant against the sort of corruption and decadence that had ruled the colonies before Reyne d'Agarre put a knife through Louis-Sallet's back. Difficult to take such pronouncements seriously, when they'd been used to justify guillotinings and worse.

She hadn't come to this meeting to listen to men such as Gregoine, the sort that sought power enough to speak and lead, whatever their politics. She rummaged through her old leather pack, withdrawing a sheaf of paper and her charcoals, settling in against the edge of the divide between her loft and the chapel floor below. No, she came for the brightness in the eyes of the women in the crowd, for the old mothers who had lived to see the day they could cast a vote for their sons' and daughters' futures, for the men and women who longed to see their families fed for the price of an honest day's wage.

"Reconstruction progresses apace in the Gardens," the Councilman was saying. "But the parks we reseed there will be open to all; I report with pleasure I have secured the right of tearing down the old district wall for the work crews of the Maw. No longer are the poor to be trodden upon, ignored by the well-fed and wealthy."

She made the Councilman a speck in the background of her first sketch, angling the perspective to show a young mother seated at the end of an aisle, struggling to keep her son seated on her knee while she watched the speaker give his news. Narrow lines for her hair, tied back in a bonnet, and ribbons for the boy, dangling from the sleeves of his dress. Echoes of the parishioners seated around them, the rapt attention held by most, and a few disgusted looks for the boy's tantrums. A simple piece, meant to capture the struggles of the young woman's life, unchanging in spite of the momentous events around her. The nobility fallen, the battle survived, and her son wanted no more than to pluck at the collar of the man seated ahead of them.

A fresh sheet of paper, and a new subject. A ruffian, standing against the back wall. Black dirt crusted his jaw, and his knuckles; she imagined it might be mixed with blood. The sort of man who made his coin delivering beatings on behalf of men owed money by his victims. Even he seemed mollified by the aura of the meeting, looking toward the dais with a mix of hope and disbelief. She tried to capture it in his pose, quick strokes to suggest the—

Light flashed in her eyes. A ray of red and blue, shining through the central relief above the altar, and just as it had in the barkeep's office, the world lurched.

She was in another place. The same chamber of stone she'd seen before, but this time with no glass surrounding her. She stood at the center of the room, as a figure emerged from the mouth of a hallway. A titan of a man, clad head to toe in steel.

"Come forward," she heard herself say. Her voice, though she hadn't tried to speak. "Do not be afraid. This is a place of warmth, lit by the fire of the Soul of the World."

The steel-clad man pushed back his visor, eyeing her with cautious wonder.

"Is it over?" he asked. Somehow she knew him. Somehow she knew his name. Paendurion.

"It hasn't yet begun," she heard herself reply. "But you have earned succor. Come. Bind yourself to me, my champion of Order."

The man stepped forward, and the chamber shimmered. A whisper sounded in her ear, the fading memory of a song.

Stop. Enough.

Zi's voice, and hearing it snapped her vision back to the Sacre-Lin. The world seemed to spin, hard enough to catch herself on the edge of the rail. Her stomach kept turning, and bile stung the back of her throat. A few eyes turned toward her from the crowd, including her uncle, seated atop the dais. She took a breath, holding to the divide until her vision steadied.

"What of the assassin!" an angry voice called from the back of the hall.

"Reyne d'Agarre was a patriot," shouted another man. "If he's returned and struck at the army's commanders, it was in service to the causes of revolution, and *égalité*."

The rest was swallowed in a tide of angry shouts.

"Order," the Councilman shouted from the dais. "Order!"

Her breath came shallow, with a lightness in her head. The images had felt real, as though she stood in the chamber of stone, saw and spoke to the man she'd seen there. Zi still clung to her forearm, but he'd gone rigid, trembling as though he was in pain.

"Zi," she whispered. "What happened? Are you okay?"

He stared through her, his gemstone eyes as clear as black slate.

"Zi!" she hissed.

"A full inquiry will be made," Gregoine was shouting above the din. "If it is true, and Reyne d'Agarre has returned, even he must face justice. No man or woman is above the law."

"They say he scattered the officers at high command, same as he did with the Gandsmen during the battle," a voice shouted.

"Monster!" another cried.

"Patriot!"

"Zi, you're frightening me," she said. "Move. Do something. Show me you're all right."

He seemed to hear her this time, turning to look at her, and suddenly her heart raced, thundering in her ears, accompanied by a red haze at the edge of her vision.

Red. He'd given her *Red.* So he was at least well enough to hear, but he still seemed frozen, quivering and unable to speak.

"We must have consensus," Gregoine said, pounding a fist against the pulpit. "The representatives we send to the Assembly carry the will of the denizens of the Maw. But I cannot in good conscience stomach any motion other than to condemn a criminal act. The time for revolution and lawlessness is behind us. We must be ruled by justice, not emotion. I move for the Maw to voice our support for the Republic, to censure Reyne d'Agarre for his violence, if he has indeed returned."

Axerian, Zi thought to her.

"What?" she asked. "Where?"

She leaned forward, looking down into the chapel. The Councilman's words carried above the roar of the crowd, but only just. As soon as he'd finished, mutters and shouts filled the hall. She scanned the crowd for sign of Axerian's black leathers, but saw nothing; if he was there, he was hidden in the throng.

No, Zi thought. *Need…Axerian.*

Clearly something was wrong, and she'd understood enough without forcing Zi to exert himself any further. Her last vision had happened with Axerian there; perhaps he'd caused it, or done something to Zi. And if anyone in the world knew what might be ailing her *kaas,* Axerian would. He knew more of the *kaas'* nature than any living soul, as far as she knew.

"If d'Agarre has returned," someone in the crowd shouted, "he's here to sort the corruption at the Revolution's head! The generals, and all the nobles that's left."

Only then did she take note of the proceedings. An assassin, armed with magic similar enough to d'Agarre's to be mistaken for the same. But that was impossible; d'Agarre was ascended, waiting at the Gods' Seat. It had to be another *kaas*-mage, a devotee of d'Agarre's secret cabal. Or it could be Axerian himself.

"It wasn't d'Agarre," she heard herself say. A green flash at the edge of her vision swept through the chamber, and suddenly the din quieted, her words echoing through the hall.

"What was that?" the Councilman said.

He'd turned to direct his attention to her loft, along with half the eyes in the hall. A knot tightened in her stomach. Zi had used *Green* to pacify them, and so her words carried through the silence, drawing a hundred more eyes than she'd ever wanted watching her.

She swallowed and began again. "It wasn't d'Agarre," she said again.

Gregoine gave her a perplexed look from the dais, then turned to her uncle. "Do you mean to say you admit to having some knowledge of a conspiracy? Father Thibeaux?"

Her uncle rose at once. "Sarine had no part in this."

"No," she said. "I didn't. But I think I know who did."

Murmurs rose again from the crowd.

Gregoine gestured for silence, and this time he got it. "I trust you will come forward to work with the authorities? It will reflect well on the Maw, as proof we have nothing to hide."

She glanced down, looking Zi over as he clung to her forearm, and nodded, finding her throat too dry for more than a simple "I will."

It served to pacify the hall again, though her heart thrummed from nerves. She retreated from the edge of her loft, thankful when the crowd's attention returned to the dais, and grabbed her pack, retrieving her paper and charcoals. If Axerian had struck at high command, there might be witnesses, with some insight into where he'd gone or why he'd done it. Good enough for a start at finding him, for Zi's sake. And with her pack, and her charcoals, she could give them a fair likeness of the Nameless to begin the search.

5

TIGAI

The Kregiaw Wastes
Vimar Province, the Jun Empire

The scent of ice stung his nose, a sign they'd journeyed farther north than men had rights to live. In Yanjin lands the seasons would have turned. His brother would be smoking *kanju* pipes, watching children swim in the streams, eating candied plums and hunting duck. And his path led him here. A place no road traversed, behind passes buried in snow ten months of each year.

He was a fool. His own men said so.

"You're a bloody fool," Remarin said, offering a hand to help him jump the crevasse, a deep crack in the shelf of ice layered over the plain.

He grinned, catching Remarin's grip to steady himself. "I am," he replied. "But I am a rich fool. And so will you be, if you can suffer my poor wits another season or two."

Remarin grunted, offering a scowl none save a fellow Ujibari could match. The people of the steppes had a certain flair for angry scowls, especially when it came to disapproving the actions of Jun lordlings.

"Steady on," he called back to the rest of them, angling his hand as he squinted into the sun. "It's this way, another hour, no more."

Eighteen men, for this raid. A clear blue sky looked down on them as they traversed the ice, with a stiff wind at their backs. Tigai's head still swam from the exertion of the journey, but his feet were steady enough, given a few hours to rest. Once or twice a man slipped, nearly falling into fissures in the ice, but his raiders knew their shares doubled if every man made it back alive. Whatever had possessed the Imperial bureaucracy to build a prison encampment in the middle of the wastes was well beyond his reasoning. It seemed as much a punishment to the officers forced to guard the place as the prisoners sent for those men to torment.

Halfway through the hour Remarin gave hand signals to spread out, and their movements changed. Skulking replaced the menacing stride most of his men were used to. They fanned across the ice in a wide arc, spanning a half mile around the southern part of the camp. They could see it now; smoke rose from the fires that would be required to stave off hoarfrost, behind a wooden palisade silhouetted on the horizon. Kregiaw. The camp bore the name of the tundra around it, the only settlement for a hundred leagues in any direction. If he were a cautious man he'd have had Remarin order them to dig into the ice, to approach under cover of nightfall and learn the pattern of their sentries before they struck. For a palace raid he would have done the scouting himself. But one didn't become rich by cowering from the slightest risks. Speed and surprise could trump caution; he'd proved it enough to know by instinct which tool suited the moment, and his instincts hadn't killed him yet.

Remarin grunted, dropping into a shallow crevasse and going to one knee, bringing up his longbore arquebus to brace against the edge of the ice.

"Are you certain we're close enough?" Tigai asked. "I don't want any excuses when you miss the shot."

The Ujibari scowled. "You leave the distance to me."

"I shall, and the excuses, too. An extra twenty *qian* if you put one through a guardsman's eye."

"Twenty per shot?"

Tigai grinned. "Only the first."

Remarin nodded, kneeling to peer through the sight on his weapon before he nodded again.

"Good luck, my friend," Tigai said.

"You're a bloody fool."

He unslung his pack from one shoulder, slipping open a button to withdraw the banner he'd had sewn for this sort of occasion, making sure Remarin saw the flourish when he unfolded it in his hands.

"Can you see your own nose?" he asked. "So it is with all men, and what hides where they never think to look."

He sprang up from the crevasse, leaving Remarin frowning as the Ujibari tried to look down at his lip. As it happened, a man could certainly see his own nose with a little effort, but that was the point. Without cause to look closer, they wouldn't bother to try.

The banner unfurled in the icy wind, flapping behind him as he hefted it above his head. Red, the red of the Great and Noble Houses, adorned with two diagonally crossed golden stars, to signify to those with knowledge of such things that he was sworn to serve the Great and Noble House of the Fox. This far north, few would recognize the audacity of the claim, though sensible folk knew better than to involve themselves in *magi* business. He was counting on that hesitation; with luck, they'd be back at the Yanjin estates before the guardsmen could wonder as to the value of what he'd taken.

The rest of his raiders had vanished, skulking forward through the crevasses, staying low and moving slowly when terrain forced them into view. A good illusion; if he hadn't known they were there, he'd have seen no more than snow and rocks. Remarin had more than earned his commission as their teacher. In less than a season he had this lot moving like crag panthers, not that he'd admit it where the Ujibari could hear. Flattering him would only sour an already sour mood, and cost a hundred more *qian* when it came time for his brother to renegotiate his wage.

"Succor," Tigai called across the ice when he was in plain view of the camp. "Succor, for a traveler on a long road."

Movement atop the walls, but only from one shape, while four more stood menacing—and frozen—in their places. Either the guards were disciplined beyond the training of ordinary soldiers, or they were empty suits of armor strung up to deter whoever the commandant supposed might attack a prison camp in the middle of an ice field. Or perhaps they actually had frozen to death. Always a possibility, in the North.

A second figure joined the first, and Tigai raised his banner, letting it catch the wind.

"Who approaches?" the second figure called down from the wall. A woman's voice.

"Courier," he shouted back. "Bound for Gantar Baat."

"You've missed your mark by a hundred leagues to the east, courier."

"Aye, but I took a purse for a parcel of letters to Kregiaw, more fool me."

He lifted his pack, caressing it with the care due a newborn babe. By now another two shapes had joined the first, and he rolled the banner, tucking it back in place. Better if fewer eyes saw the sigil, so long as word was passed that he traveled under an Imperial marque.

"What business does a scion of Fox have in Gantar Baat?" the woman asked, her voice suddenly as frosted as the wind stinging his nose.

So much for luck.

He licked the dry sores forming on his lips. He'd hoped to avoid this part.

"Tea," he said, calling it up to them. "And I've a sample of our trade stock, if you—"

Thunder sounded from the rampart of the palisade. A tuft of powder smoke. And a stinging hole in his chest, where the force of musket shot threw him backward to the ground.

Pain seared his vision. The fucking bastards. They'd shot him, and hadn't bothered to open their gate before they did it.

Another roar from the wall, and a whistling crack where the next shot missed, chipping the ice.

Words formed on his tongue, and died. Past time for talk.

He sucked in a breath, opening his body to the strands that anchored him where he stood. Dizziness spun his eyes, the sensation of peering over the edge of a cliffside. Easy to lose himself, amid a sea of such connections. A field of stars, his mind set adrift between them. He was Yanjin Tigai, but he was not bleeding to death, shot through the chest on the ice of Kregiaw. He found another anchor point, the one he'd set moments before, and sprang back to it, feeling the rush of fresh breath through unbroken lungs.

"That was quick," Remarin said. "I take it they found your conversation stimulating."

Tigai coughed, the memory of his wounds still a reality, even if his body was whole.

"Just shoot the bastards," he said. "And give the signal to attack."

Cold eyes stared at him as he made his inspection of the dead. Cold eyes, cold winds, cold corpses. The whole bloody province was cold. Had no one told the northerners there was such a thing as springtime? A spat of wind and snow was well and good, to help one appreciate the next turning of the seasons, but a man deserved a spring and summer in his life. And now six of his men had seen their last, along with eleven guardsmen dressed in dark crimson trimmed with white. The *damyu*, the earth spirits, made no distinctions for how a man was given to the ground.

"They fought well," he said, drawing silent glares from the survivors, sitting together on the cold earth at the center of the camp. Five prisoners from among the guardsmen, and the better part of thirty who had been prisoners before the battle, neatly rounded up and put in ranks by Remarin's shouted discipline. Tigai paced the line between the living and the dead, glancing between them as he spoke. "They died in battle. For men of our persuasion, there is no higher honor."

One of the prisoners spat, loud enough for all to hear. The lone woman among them, her crimson coat a thicker, finer fabric than any of the others. Enough to recognize her as an officer, even without the stripes of rank sewn into her cuffs.

"You object to my eulogy, Captain?" he asked, pausing mid-stride to give her a sweet look.

"You have less honor than a dog," she said.

One of his Ujibari moved toward her, hand raised to deliver a bruise to match the purple already swelling beneath the woman's eye. Tigai gestured, signaling to hold.

"What would the captain of a labor camp know of honor?" he said, still holding his smile for her benefit. It was a look he'd used to charm the underclothes from courtiers in manor halls and palaces from Qoba to Ghingwai, made all the sweeter for how out of place it was amid the snow and ice. "If you had any merit, you would be captaining men of worth, not assigned to supervise the digging of holes for shit half-frozen before it leaves your asses."

The captain glared at him, the left side of her face swollen to half close her eye. A Jun woman, ambitious enough to accept a posting no one else wanted, and fool enough not to see the reason why. But she'd ordered her men to fire on a courier—at *him*—for the suspicion of being out of place, even when his banner had clearly marked him on *magi* business for the Great and Noble House of the Fox. Not a captain in the whole of the Imperial service took their duties so seriously, not when the prize they guarded was a frozen shit-heap anchored in permanent ice.

"He means to kill you all," the captain shouted. "Rush him together and you might bring him down. His men will negotiate, once he is—"

This time he didn't gesture to stop the Ujibari, and the captain got a fist to her cheekbone, hard enough to send her slumping to the ground.

"Enough," he said after the strike. "No one else need be injured today. In fact, I mean to free you. All of you, save four."

Glances passed among the prisoners, but they remained silent.

"Shanying, scion of the House of Jian. Feng-To, former seneschal to the whitesmiths guilds of Konming Province. Dhazan, former magistrate of Bijan Qan." He turned to the captain. "And you. Name Unknown, former captain of the Kregiaw labor camp."

This time murmurs rose in the assembled crowd, shared glances as though each man needed to affirm he had not been named.

"Satisfy me I have my four, and the rest of you may raid the camp's provisions and go free. There is an Imperial outpost at Gantar Baat, five days to the east, should you seek to turn yourselves in and serve the remainder of your sentences with honor. Elsewise, go south, forget your past lives, and seek employment in the hundred cities. Or come with me, and turn pirate. But first, offer up the prisoners I named, before any more of you need to die."

Remarin strode into the crowd to fetch the men who rose, or were pushed to rise by their fellows. Three men, and he would leave it to Remarin's judgment to ascertain whether they were decoys. Tigai went instead to the captain, whose glare had frosted over, a look almost akin to curiosity where there had been vitriol, before.

"I will require your name, Captain," he said, extending a hand to help her rise. She left it there, staring at him, unmoving.

"What does Fox want with these prisoners?" she asked.

"*Magi* business," he said, offering her a grin to continue his charade. She'd already shown she knew too much, but with luck she wouldn't know enough to pierce the lie.

"My name is Lin," she said, ignoring his hand and rising on her own. "Lin Qishan, and if you are a servant of Fox then I am a First Consort to the Emperor."

"Lin Qishan," he said. "If that is your real name, then I, too, am a consort to His Majesty. But it will serve, for now."

She bowed her head, and he left her there. Remarin would gather her along with the other three, and see them to him before it was time to depart.

He knelt on the ice, shifting his senses as his men came to gather around him. They'd done this enough to know it would happen without warning, between blinks or breaths, and if they weren't close they'd be left behind. The strands of home beckoned to him among the starfield, strands he knew as well as he knew his own skin. Different, when he worked in far-off places, but still a path to the comfortable and familiar.

He found the link, and the world shifted beneath his feet, the icy wind replaced by the scented breezes of the South.

6

ERRIS

High Command
Southgate District, New Sarresant

Maps of the southern colonies stared up at her as though she were the subject of their planning, and not the other way round. She knew city fighting, forests, the weathering of winter storms, amphibious landings, how to take a river crossing or set an ambush on an open plain. All the coursework at the military academies, and half again as much she'd devised on her own, fit to write her own textbooks if she managed to live to retirement. But nothing in any book or battlefield she'd ever seen prepared her to deal with an assassin armed with the same magic as Reyne d'Agarre.

It wasn't the same man, whatever foolish notions had spread through the city. One would think the eye testimony of the High Commander of the Armies of New Sarresant would be enough to dismiss such rumors, but Councilman d'Agarre had evidently embedded himself in the dreams—or the nightmares—of the citizenry. She'd seen d'Agarre's magic firsthand, when he used it to cow the officers at high command, and again through the eyes of Marie d'Oreste, driving the native invaders and her soldiers alike mad with fear and rage. No, the assassin hadn't been d'Agarre, but the man in black had used the same power to reach her through a company of gendarme police, then fought like a tempest before vanishing into the street. He'd failed to kill her, but would surely come to try again.

"High Commander, sir, I have your next appointment," her aide, Essily, said, hovering at the door to her private chamber. "Field-Colonel Regalle, here to discuss artillery stocks for the Gand invasion."

"Cancel it," she said. "Give Anchard my compliments, but see him off."

"Yes, sir," Essily said, bowing as he backed away.

"*Field-Colonel* Regalle?" Marquand asked, standing opposite her, across the table. "You give that boot-kisser a promotion, and I'm still a captain?"

She returned her attention to the maps.

"Squads of binders, perhaps," she said. "Set to patrol with the city watch. It would reassure the citizens, though I can't see us casting a net wide enough to catch someone with d'Agarre's talents."

"I'm bloody serious," Marquand said. "I'm overdue for a colonel's stripe, if not a general's star, with all this Gods-damned planning. I've never asked for it before, but I've earned it, you know I have."

She paused, taking a moment for Marquand. He'd been made foot-captain the day she made major, brevet ranks after the Battle of Talbad's Ford, during the Thellan campaign. A bloody day. He'd ignored orders at her request, taking a squad of infantrymen and binders to screen for her horse while they crossed the river. Marquand's bindings had held the line when a thousand soldiers would have broken, and lucky for them their superiors had been killed in the action. In the aftermath they'd been heroes rather than mutineers, and victory had made it all the sweeter.

"How much have you had to drink today?" she asked.

"Not a drop, not since we started this fucking planning."

"And before you came to the council hall?"

He fell quiet, and she let the question linger. No more needed be said, as far as she was concerned. The assassin was all that mattered now. Who he might be working for, and what damage he could do, left unchecked. A tool of the Gand commander behind their golden eyes, she was all but certain. A single thorn in her side, and she'd have let it fester, her personal safety be damned, if not for what it might mean in the city. Too damned many unknowns. But one certainty: They couldn't risk a campaign in the south, not when the enemy threatened to drive half the city mad. Not until she knew it well enough to counter it, or he took the field and forced her hand.

"We'll have to use binders," Marquand said. "Confirmed reports say d'Agarre's magic doesn't work against them. Not squads, though, and no patrols. Concentrated teams, prepared to respond to disturbances, and assigned to major caravans for land-based trade."

She looked him over, finding the scowl she expected as he pored over the maps, though he seemed content to let the matter of his promotion lie.

"I concur with your first point," she said. "But without patrols, we risk a slow response to a disturbance, even in the city."

"Too much area to cover in either case," he said. "And a bad precedent. Military ought not be used as police for civilians. Puts bad ideas in the wrong heads."

"Very well," she said. "We'll need to prepare deployment orders, and assign crews to each district captain. *Shelter* binders, with *Body* for support?" He nodded. "Good. Then we'll need to inform Lord Voren."

"I'd as soon leave that to you, High Commander," Marquand said. "That old fuck makes my skin crawl."

"That old fuck has the better part of the government resting on his shoulders. He's the one tasked with garnering support for our invasion of Gand; we'd best let him know, if we intend to postpone."

Marquand shrugged, returning to the maps as though the matter were settled. And perhaps it was.

"See to preparing the orders," she said. "I'll sign and seal them when I get back."

He nodded, offering a belated salute as she donned her coat, and left her private chambers behind.

The Lords' section of the council hall had been retooled for war before the battle for the city, and had grown into its purpose in the weeks and months since. She'd as good as moved in, sleeping in the cot in her office often enough she wouldn't be at all surprised if her rooms in the Tank & Twine had been let to merchants in her absence. Voren had urged her to use the not-inconsiderable sums of the High Commander's pay to purchase an estate in the city, to staff it with cooks and servants and use it to host lavish parties or whatever other nonsense the former nobility did with their coin. A waste of time and money, in her view.

This was home. The salutes of aides as she passed, officers making way, or so lost in debating a point of strategy they didn't notice her presence. She'd converted the Lords' Council into a war college to rival and exceed any academy in the world, and all the more so since her students were in position to wage the wars themselves. Tables covered with maps dominated the central hall, decorated with painted figurines and piles of books, texts on strategy, military theory, mathematics, and more. When it worked, her *Need* connected them to units in the field, but every one of her commanders would be trained to think, to fight as she did. The enemy was out there, and when they met again she would be ready, Gods damn her soul.

Sentries bearing field muskets stood guard at the mouth of the long hallway bridging the Lords' Council with the rest of the council hall, offering a last pair of salutes before she left her world behind. Blue velvet carpet cushioned her steps as she strode toward the other half of the building, where the Council-General, the elected estate of the commonfolk, had met before the revolution, and continued on as the government entire in its wake. She'd had the carpets torn up and removed from high command; it seemed the councilors of the Republic were content to remove only the paintings of the de l'Arraignon Kings, leaving discolored spots on the walls where they'd hung before. The rest of the hall was empty for the moment, though couriers came and went across both sides of the building, attending to governance and military matters as the need arose. The twin pillars of the Republic: *égalité* and honorable service, so her recruiters said when they went to drum up fresh levies. Clear enough, at times, to see which way power flowed. If not for Voren, the Assembly could bugger itself for all she cared, so long as they provided the coin to feed and equip her soldiers.

"High Commander," Omera greeted her when she stepped across the threshold into the outer hallways of the Council-General. "His Lordship awaits."

Groups of men and women in plain clothes exchanged conversation up and down the hall, taking note of her with no more than raised eyebrows, for all she represented the power of the military. And somehow Voren's servant had known to be here, waiting for her, or had been set to watch in case she arrived.

The Bhakal servant led her swiftly through the chambers, where her uniform—freshly tailored, cut to include five stars on her sleeves and collar—stood out as a gentleman's suit or lady's dress would have done on the opposite side of the building. Yet they gave way for Voren's servant, noticing him first and her second, leaving whispers behind as they passed through the hall.

"High Commander d'Arrent for you, sir," she overheard Omera announce when they arrived in the foyer of an office twice as large as hers, with fresh paint and moldings suggesting they'd made it by tearing through walls of two—or three—lesser chambers.

Voren appeared in the doorway moments later, as though he'd sprung from his desk, or already been standing. An old man by the time she'd met him, but with a tireless energy, and fire in his eyes today.

"High Commander," Voren said. "I hadn't thought you would come so soon. A delight, truly."

"Sir, I'm afraid my visit is not—"

He cut her short with a gesture, inviting her inside. "Let us speak of it shortly. First, I must reintroduce you to an acquaintance I believe we both hold in high esteem."

She entered the chamber ahead of him, and found a young woman seated in one of the cushioned chairs opposite the desk. A pretty enough girl, in a plain-looking way, dressed in an undyed tunic and breeches that wouldn't have been out of place among the workers of Southgate or the Maw. Little enough to note about her, save for the blue and gold tattoos on the backs of her hands—a royal marque, sanctioning the use of the leylines, which marked her a priest, a noble, or a cat's-paw for one or both.

"Erris d'Arrent," Voren said, closing the door behind them. "I have the honor of presenting the hero of the Battle of New Sarresant."

Nerves were writ large on the girl's face. Not a face she recognized, but for Voren to call her that, she had to be…

"Sarine," she said, the memory coming to the fore. The strange girl who had appeared at the height of the battle, standing at the fulcrum point of the enemy's position, fighting alongside the 11th Light Cavalry until she vanished in the moment of victory.

"Commander d'Arrent," the girl said. "It's an honor to meet you in person."

Erris stared. It was as though a specter had arisen from the fog of war, a dream she had never more than half believed, suddenly confirmed as real.

Voren beamed, returning to his seat behind the desk. "We ought to defer our pleasantries for now. Madame Sarine brings us news of great import, pertaining to the identity of our mysterious assassin."

"His name is Axerian," Sarine said. "I worked with him to oppose Reyne d'Agarre, during the battle. He's a *kaas*-mage. I need to find him, before Zi—"

"Hold," Erris said, taking a seat opposite the desk. "How can you be certain of his identity? And what is a ... *kaas*-mage?"

Voren furnished a sheet of paper, handing it to her across the desk. She glanced and found a perfect likeness of her attacker, rendered in black lines. The hook nose, the tired intensity of his eyes, the blend of Sardian and Thellan blood in his face.

"Sarine offered this drawing without description," Voren said. "Unless you gave her the description yourself, I'm sure you will agree it proves her claim."

"It's him," Sarine said. "I'm certain of it. And a *kaas*-mage is..." The girl trailed off, seeming to listen to a voice before she paused, and started over. "It's what Reyne d'Agarre was. The tribesfolk had one among their number." She swallowed. "And I have the gift as well."

Without further warning a four-legged serpent materialized from nothing, coiled on the edge of Voren's desk.

Body snapped into place before Erris could think, battle instincts propelling her to her feet, a hand placed on the hilt of her saber, ready to draw. Voren leaned forward, intent on the creature, as though Erris hadn't reacted at all.

"Fascinating," Voren said.

"Don't worry," Sarine said. "Zi is harmless, and he's sick. I need to find Axerian, before he gets any worse."

"What is this creature?" Erris asked, keeping hold of her saber's hilt as she met its eyes. Twin rubies, flickering like fire.

"This is Zi," Sarine said. "He's a *kaas*. We form a bond that gives us their gifts, but he isn't dangerous."

Erris listened as Sarine explained, though she wasn't about to relax her guard. Certainly the descriptions of strength and speed, the white shield conjured when her saber had struck the assassin's shoulder, all matched with her experience and the terror inspired by what the girl referred to as "*Yellow*." But how to countenance the claim that such magic had existed alongside the leylines, separate and secret, kept hidden for hundreds—thousands—of years? Even though she had seen it firsthand, it begged an explanation within the frame of what she knew: leylines, Skovan hedge magic, Bhakal herblore, or even the terrible beasts native to the New World. Yet the girl claimed it was something else.

"I trust you share my assessment," Voren said when she was done. "With Sarine, we've found a weapon that can counter this assassin."

"That was the purpose behind my visit," Erris said. "I'd been weighing options with Marquand. With another d'Agarre to threaten us, we'd considered postponing...our plans."

"Sarine changes the situation," Voren said. "With her aid, we can find this Axerian, and keep your armies marching south."

Erris eyed the girl—Sarine—with a dubious suspicion. Voren had as good as entrusted her with secrets the Gandsmen would sacrifice a dozen spies to hear, and with no effort to show proof of trust.

"Are you willing to help us?" she asked the girl.

"Yes," Sarine said. "I have to find him, for Zi's sake. And whatever he's planning, if it involves assassinations, he has to be stopped."

"You see, High Commander?" Voren said. "A stroke of luck, for once. With your permission, we can deploy Sarine with your binders here in the city and continue the invasion, both at once."

She nodded as Voren finished. Too much to consider it luck, but it was at least an opportunity. With *Need* waning, she could ill afford to let it pass; however, trusting unknown magic turned her stomach. Her enemy was using an assassin armed with one of these serpents—one of these *kaas*. Just as well to have one on her side again, to counter it.

"I'll assign you to the gendarme corps, then," she said to Sarine. "As for the rest, I intend to ride south with the army. If you can prevent anything the assassin might try here in the city, our binders can counter an attempt to strike at us in the field."

"Is it necessary to ride to the front in person, given the resources here at high command?" Voren asked.

This time she let silence stand as an answer to Voren's unspoken question. Her *Need* had grown no stronger. And it was good to see there were limits to his trust, even with would-be saviors.

"I leave in the morning," she said, earning a solemn nod from both. A dubious thing, to place so much on the head of an unknown girl. But then, she'd done it before, and been proved right. Gods send it would be enough again.

7

ARAK'JUR

Wilderness
Uktani Land

The forests had given way to plains of long grass some days before, marking the boundary between what had been Ranasi land and the land claimed by the Uktani, their northern neighbors. He'd come this way before, with Corenna at his side, on their first journey to reach the Nanerat, the tribe that called themselves the earth's most peaceful children. They'd been full of hope then. Now every step on Ranasi land was a step on cursed ground, all the joy of her people snuffed out by the treachery of his.

He'd tried to argue against Corenna's coming before they departed the village. A daughter grew in her belly, or a son. His child. Too soon for it to show, but the visions of things-to-come did not err on such things. He might as well have shouted at the tide. Their people were in danger, and she would be at his side to face it, and that was the end of their argument as sure as it had been the beginning. He loved her for it, even as he pleaded for the sake of their unborn child. Yet here she was, walking ahead of him, weighing their surroundings and planning for what might come when they arrived.

"It was here, near this field," she said, making it a question and a statement, both. "I saw it in the smoke, though I can't say how I know."

"It was," Arak'Jur replied. "We're getting close now. Such are the ways of the shamans' visions."

She showed him a smile, at once a token of humility at her lack of knowledge and a prod to ask for more.

He returned it. "We're left with an impression, after a shaman tells us where the spirits wish for us to go," he said. "An imprint in our memories as though we had traveled to the place too often to need remember the way. When we draw near, we know."

She nodded, savoring the knowledge in her expression as she might have done a sweet fruit. Spirits, but she was strong. He knew the carrying of a child was a delicate thing, but even knowing the seed grew in her belly, he could never see her as fragile. She had faced the horrors that haunted his worst imaginings—her people broken, dead, scattered to the wind—and pressed forward with a resolve he wouldn't have found in her place.

"I wonder how much we've missed," Corenna said. "How much our separate ways have cost us, dividing knowledge between men and women. Can we be certain the spirits intended it? We tread on ground that unnerves me, even now, but—"

She came to a halt a step too late, giving him a questioning look.

The wind had changed.

A tingle on his skin. A scent beneath discerning in his conscious mind.

Corenna's eyes frosted over, her feet set before he could speak a warning. Too slow. The space around her shimmered, and Arak'Jur howled, charging forward as a mighty stag stepped through a shadow ripped in the fabric of the air. Blood ran from the sockets where its eyes should have been, rivulets staining the sides of its elongated face, pooling over teeth too sharp for any plant eater.

Astahg.

The beast lowered its head, thrusting with a rack of antlers half as tall as a man, twice as sharp as any spear. A cracking sound rang out, ice shattering where Corenna had put a wall between them, and he crashed into the beast's hindquarters, drawing on *una're*'s strength to lift the creature and throw it away from Corenna's shield.

Corenna turned on the beast as he rushed after it, icicle spears sailing through the air from another angle as he ran. Neither strike landed. Shadows gathered around the creature, swallowing it before it crashed to the ground, leaving them standing alone on the plain, as though the beast had never been there at all.

"It will come again," he said, his breath coming hard from the sudden exertion. "Be ready for—"

He dropped prone by instinct as antlers gored the space where he had been. Tendrils of shadow licked the air as *astahg* appeared, and he rolled into it, grabbing hold of one of its forelegs as the rest threatened to trample him on the ground. A flurry of hoof and grass surrounded him. The creature reared, thrusting downward with its antlers as it convulsed to shake him free, and pain shot through him where one pierced his skin, ripping a gash down his back like dried husk. Still he kept his hold, drawing on *una're* to send shocks up its joints. If he could keep it pinned long enough, Corenna could finish the beast.

Shadows replaced the sinew and bone in his hands, and the creature vanished.

"I wounded it," Corenna called to him. "Are you hurt?"

Before he could call back, a howl sounded nearby. Not the *astahg*. Men.

He sprang to his feet, feeling loose skin and blood hanging on his back. A searing pain, drowned to a dull throb as he found his footing and saw a group of hunters running toward them across the plain.

"I am," he said, "but I can fight." It sufficed to keep Corenna's attention on the men, and on the *astahg*'s next reappearance.

He squinted toward the hunters, trying to discern their tribe while keeping a watchful eye in all directions.

"Down!"

Corenna shouted it, and too late he saw that the hunters had stopped, dropping to a knee to level their muskets, three hundred paces away.

Belching fire roared over the plain. Corenna conjured a shield of earth, broad enough to shelter them both from the hunters' shots, but he drew on *lakiri'in*'s speed and *ipek'a*'s power, leaping toward where shadows had appeared behind her.

Stone chipped as the shots impacted her shield, and he sailed through the air, *ipek'a*'s scything claws connecting with the antlers, hard enough to scrape bone on bone. *Astahg* gored with his antlers; Arak'Jur sliced through, catching an eye socket with a bloodied hand. He yanked, twisting the creature's neck as its jaws snapped, and he ducked under its rack, striking the beast in the chest hard enough to shatter its ribs, piercing it through the heart.

YOU KILLED HIM.

No, Arak'Jur thought back to the spirit. *No, Corenna is in danger. I must return. The hunters, the men, they approach, and mean us harm.*

YOU ARE CHOSEN, THOUGH NOT BY US. WE BOW BEFORE YOUR STRENGTH. WE BOW BEFORE THE MOUNTAIN, WHO HAS CLAIM ON YOUR ASCENSION.

Great Spirit, Arak'Jur thought. *I honor you, and the scion of your form. But—*

YES. HE WAS A MIGHTY STAG.

He had no body, here, communing with the spirits, surrounded by formless void. Yet he felt the sensation of a pounding heart all the same. The hunters had fired on them; that much was clear, even if he had no notion of why. The Uktani had been reserved, cold, and distant on their last journey north. If they had turned hostile, while he was trapped within the spirits' realm, it would leave Corenna to face them alone. Hunters she could handle, but if a guardian were among them, or a spirit-touched woman...

Great Spirit, he thought. *I must refuse your gift. Please allow me to return to my place.*

THAT WOULD BE UNWISE. THE TIME OF ASCENSION IS CLOSE AT HAND. WE CAN FEEL IT NOW. YOU MUST GATHER OUR GIFTS, ENOUGH TO STAND BY THE GODDESS WHEN THE DAY ARRIVES.

No, he pleaded. *My woman is in danger, and my unborn child.*

A POWERFUL THING.

Silence fell between them, enough to kindle warmth in the empty space surrounding his senses. He felt as though a dozen eyes watched him, whispers sounding at the edge of his hearing. Faint voices. *No*, and *Let him go. The Wild*, and then, stronger: *She comes. The Goddess is waking. He must bring her to us.*

IT IS DECIDED. A WOMAN AND CHILD DO NOT OUTWEIGH THE COMING SHADOW. YOU HAVE EARNED OUR BLESSING, AND YOU WILL HAVE IT.

No.

He put all his will into the thought, and found instead a shining light, faded through glass. A woman's face. A song echoed in his mind, of sadness and loss. She was dying. Then the light flared around him, and his senses bled away.

He sprang across the grasslands, feeling the bounding rhythm of the plain. The cool water of a stream, the joy of pausing to drink, a splay-legged fawn at his side. He was accepted among the plant eaters, a mighty rack of antlers promising strength, wisdom, protection from the predators that stalked them all. He basked in their tranquility, rightly proud of the place he was given in the eyes of the elk, the beaver, the squirrel, and the hare. Yet he was of two worlds, a prince of predator and prey, and the shadows set between them. He stepped through one world and emerged in the other, donning the mask of the hunter, devouring the creatures of peace. He was *astahg*, prince of plain and forest, and he alone was master of the space between his worlds.

REMEMBER HIM, the spirit's voice intoned.

A bitter wind seemed to blow across his face, and Arak'Jur thought of Corenna as the blackness twisted away, returning him to his skin.

———————

He expelled a breath, still surrounded by darkness.

The smell of blood pierced his nose, the tang of raw iron and flesh. Still dark, but the void was gone. A soft moon hung in the sky above, and a sheet of stars. *Astahg*'s corpse lay beside him, eyeless sockets empty and lifeless, though he remembered what it was to wear that form. Corenna. He snapped to his feet, legs aching from the strain of kneeling.

"Arak'Jur, thank the spirits."

Corenna's voice, warm and desperate. He turned, met by the force of her arms wrapped around him, and relief melted the knots in his chest.

"Corenna," he said. "I pleaded for the spirits to release me. I left you alone. If you had been hurt, or—"

She shushed him, holding tighter. They hadn't moved from the place where *astahg* had set upon them, clear enough from the presence of the creature's corpse, but also from the outline of dead men in the grass, bodies twisted to face the sky, holding muskets, arrayed as though they'd tried to charge Corenna, and failed.

"What happened?" he began, and she shushed him again.

"More are coming," Corenna whispered, finally relenting her embrace. "I tried to warn the first of them, but it took killing to drive them off. The rest ran, cursing me, cursing us, swearing they would return. Uktani warriors, struck by madness."

She gestured northward across the plain, and he saw what he should have noticed first: lights, winding through the grass. Torches, or lanterns, though they were still a great distance away. Strange, for hunters to announce their presence. Yet they were not hunters now. If they had embraced the mad spirits, the Uktani men would be *Venari*, warriors, carrying spears and muskets, and bound for war.

He signaled for Corenna to follow, and spared a last look at the body of the *astahg*. Ilek'Inari's vision in the smoke surfaced in his memory; the stag tied to men, with more and deadlier beasts to come. Had the spirits sent the beast to attack, ignorant of the Uktani warriors, or was there a deeper link? He couldn't forget Arak'Atan, the Jintani guardian, who fought with *ipek'a* at his side atop the peaks of Nanek'Hai'Tyat. A frightening thing. The beasts had only ever been unknowable, terrible forces of death and destruction. If they were more, now, instruments of the mad spirits, weapons to be used against his people...Chills ran through his blood, imagining horrors that could too easily become real.

He and Corenna tracked through the grass, heading west across the plain. He set a cautious pace, careful to stay low. No time to hide their trail. But so long as they kept below the horizon line, men blinded by lanterns would see nothing of their passage until morning.

"How long was I speaking with the spirits?" he asked when they'd covered enough ground to satisfy caution.

"The better part of a day," she said.

He gritted his teeth, torn between reverence and anger.

"I am well," Corenna said. "It was only men; my gifts are strong enough to deal with them."

"And if it had been more? Another beast, a guardian, a woman with gifts to equal yours?"

She fell quiet, keeping pace behind him. He hoped she would have left him behind, entrusted him to the spirits, for the sake of the people of their alliance. In his heart he knew it was the right thing, just as he knew he would never have left her, were their places switched.

"They're moving," Corenna said. "The lights."

She was right; the warriors had changed course, heading farther west. Toward where they would be, in an hour's time.

"East, then," he said, leading back the way they'd come. Corenna followed in silence. He might have asked for more, pushed her on the decision to stand and fight while he communed with *astahg*. But she would not bend; he knew it by now. She would listen, acknowledge wisdom where she heard it, give him the respect he was due, as guardian, lover, and companion. But she wouldn't abandon him, and he loved her for it, even as he thought it weakness, and recognized that he shared the flaw.

"Arak'Jur…" Corenna said, pointing, and this time he saw it when she did. The lights had moved again, changing course as they pivoted across the plain. "How can they hunt us? We are too far to sight, without light to give us away. They have no trail to follow, and the wind favors us, does it not?"

He nodded, staring toward the lights. No hunter in any tribe could have marked them so swiftly, not until morning, after intercepting their trail in the last place they'd been known to be. No hunter, but in light of *astahg*'s attack he couldn't rule out something worse, something more.

"*Munat'ap* could do it," he said, his voice solemn as he guided them to a halt, crouching in place.

"*Munat'ap*?" Corenna said. "Another great beast. Working with the Uktani."

"The Great Timber Wolf. He runs with a pack of ordinary wolves, hunting the scent of his prey across rivers, forests, lakes, and mountains. If he stalks us, he won't be deterred by darkness, distance, or terrain. It might explain the lanterns; the Uktani wouldn't need to sight us to give chase, only to stay in step with the Great Wolf."

The lanterns changed course again when they stopped, this time heading directly for them, instead of on course to intercept their chosen path.

"Then we fight," Corenna said.

He nodded, rising to his feet. Corenna matched him, shedding the cover of the tall grass.

Night sounds echoed around them. Cricket song, and a distant owl, hooting beneath the cover of the stars. The lanterns kept on course, a shining light growing brighter as they moved toward where he and Corenna stood. Minutes passed, and he kept the spirits' gifts ready, every gift he had been granted the right to wield. The powers of the beasts: *valak'ar, mareh'et, una're, anahret, juna'ren, ipek'a, lakiri'in, kirighra,* and now *astahg*; the blood of the mountain, the woman's power he drew from the sacred place at Nanek'Hai'Tyat. He kept his eyes low, watchful from the corners of his vision for the flanking tactics employed by wolves and men alike.

"They're here," a voice called from across the field ahead. "At last; we've arrived."

Memory sparked through his senses, a ripple in the still water of calm before a fight.

"Arak'Jur," another voice shouted. A woman's voice. "Corenna. Is it you?"

"Asseena," Corenna called back, exhaling a breath she'd held too long. "Yes. By the spirits, yes. We are here."

Corenna pushed past him, and he followed in her wake, dispelling a fog of battle fury he'd held too close to let slip easily. Asseena. Foremost among the spirit-touched women of the Nanerat, as good as a *Sa'Shem* in the aftermath of her tribe's near-destruction at the hands of their enemies. The very people Ilek'Inari had sent them to find, and bring into their fold.

Asseena met them halfway across the field, wrapping Corenna in her arms. A weary man followed at her flank; Ilek'Hannat, the apprentice shaman, whose connections to the spirits must have been the means by which they tracked his and Corenna's movement. A dozen more men and women trailed behind, gaunt faces cast by the shadows of the moonlight. No more.

"Brothers, Sisters of the Nanerat," he said, extending a greeting to them in formal tones. "We came at our shaman's behest, to bring an offer of alliance before the representatives of your tribe."

"And we mean to accept it," Asseena said, her eyes haunted by a mix of vigor and regret. "But this is all that is left of our people, now."

Corenna's expression mirrored Asseena's, a deep sympathy born of the same pain.

"They hunted us," Asseena continued. "The Uktani. With great beasts among their warriors, their guardians gone mad, even their women joining in the chaos." She turned back, finding cold iron in the eyes of her fellows. "They broke us, when they came to know we had treated with the southern tribes. And now they are coming."

"We faced *astahg*, and ten Uktani warriors," Corenna said. "But we've gathered great strength at the Sinari village. They will find us standing together, the remnants of five—and now, six tribes."

"Honored sister," Asseena said. "They're not coming to break your alliance." She looked to Arak'Jur, her eyes glazed with pain. "They've listened to madness, and madness has told them your name. No, they are not coming for the Sinari, Arak'Jur. They are coming for you."

8

TIGAI

Yanjin Palace
Jun Province, the Jun Empire

Uncomfortable silence seeped into the hallway, and Tigai waited, hidden from view.

He'd spent the better part of the morning being fussed over by his brother's servants, primped and preened like a show hound, short only a dangling ribbon to mark him a prized specimen for the benefit of their guests. He wore a paneled skirt over too-wide hose dyed Yanjin colors, yellow and red. Knee-length leather boots swallowed his trousers like cobras, puffed out at the head, and he wore his shirt fastened with rubies set in gold, with the same in bands around his neck and upper arms.

It had taken twice as long to don the costume as it had to get drunk on potato vodka, waiting for his brother's summons. Now the seconds ticked past on the mechanical clock in the first receiving room—only the best, for Lord and Lady Han—and he delighted in listening to his brother run out of things to say.

"We've had an orchid harvest," his brother offered after a lengthy pause. "The seedcrafters labored through the winter to bring it about. The first blossoms in spring, as early in the season as any at court."

"Delightful," offered a woman from a chair beyond his vision. A pruned voice, like month-old cabbage dipped in vinegar, that could only belong to Lady Han.

"Yes," said Lord Han with a grunt. "A delight. As will be the sight of your brother, Lord Yanjin. I do so hope our visit has not inconvenienced your house, or burdened you past the limits of hospitality."

Tigai stifled a laugh, though not before the sound made it halfway to his nose.

Shit.

The room shuffled, expensive robes and dresses shifting in their seats. His brother tried a cough to hide it, but the damage was done. Ah well. All pleasures had to end, in time.

With a flourish, Tigai pushed the cracked door open wide, bowing as he made his entry.

As he'd expected, Lady Han sat in the chair in the far corner of the room, her hair pinned into an elaborate piece dyed green to match her dress, with enough cosmetics on her face to coat the walls in fresh lacquer. Her husband had the seat beside her, a narrow couch, with their daughter, Huame, occupying the same place as her father. Both wore green; the father a tight-fit robe pinned with the chain of the office of Second Chancellor, the daughter in a dazzling sheen of silk trimmed with emeralds, the very height of court fashion, last he'd been aware of the trends. His brother had the place of honor beside the hearth, befitting the Lord of Yanjin Palace, though Dao lacked the weight and gravity their father had possessed, in more than his demeanor.

"Lord Tigai," Lord Han said. "You will forgive an old man, if I do not rise to greet you. My bones grow weak when left to sit overlong, even on cushions as fine as these."

"It is past consideration," Tigai said, offering a bow for Lord Han's sake and making a point of slurring his words. "I can only offer my humblest apologies, and hope you find our meager palace up to your inflated standards of grace and propriety."

If Lord and Lady Han were frost, their daughter was jagged ice. Tigai affected not to notice, lowering himself with aplomb into an empty seat at his brother's side.

"Yes," Dao said. "Well. Now that my brother has arrived, we can address the business at hand. A sponsorship for Tigai to the Magistracy of Lingzhou, and the hand of the Lady Huame. As fine a pairing as there has been at court, since—"

"No," Lady Han said. "No, I think not."

The matron of the Han bloodline rose from her seat without further word, sweeping the train of her green silk behind her as she left the room.

Lord Han coughed, watching his wife pass through the doors and vanish into the hallway beyond. "What Lady Han meant to say..." he said. "That is, she meant to intimate that I have suffered from a flux, and we must send for my doctors at once, which will require a return to our estate."

Dao rose, keeping his face a mask of smooth stone. "Of course, Lord Han. Your health must precede all other concerns."

Lord Han coughed again, affecting a stiff bow as he accepted his daughter's help to rise. Tigai made a point of staring at Huame's chest, enjoying the curves suggested beneath the neckline of her dress until she glowered steel at him, guiding her father from the room.

Dao sighed when they were gone.

"You are becoming far too adept at that," Dao said, slouching back into their father's chair.

Tigai laughed, plucking a sugared date from a tray left half eaten by Lady Han. "The other families expect a reason why your brother and heir remains unwed. What better excuse than if the court itself rejects me? Besides, you would do well to whelp a few sons in the interim. This is far from my burden alone."

Dao glowered, running a hand across his shaven scalp. "*Koryu* know I've tried. Mei has grown distant, of late."

"Make more time for her. And buy her a necklace of Ghingwai pearls, next you go to market."

"This is serious."

Tigai nodded. With Dao, everything was serious. His brother had been the reason they inherited anything at all, after their father died with debts to half a score of creditors tied to thrice as many banks. Unraveling the knot—and keeping one set of promises weighed against the others— had preserved their status long enough to establish Tigai as a bachelor at court, little as he had any desire to be snared by a creature like Han Huame, or any of the dozens of simulacra that could be found among the other noble houses.

"You want me to talk to Mei?" Tigai asked.

"If you would. And put a child in her, if she'll let you."

Tigai laughed, and got a grim expression in return. "You treat your wife like a sentence to a labor camp," he said. "Mei is sweet enough, even if you prefer sour ale to spiced wine."

"Easy to say when it isn't your cup being filled," Dao said, pausing to gulp down the remnants of a crystal wineglass from the table beside his seat. "How goes your preparation for Kanjiao?"

Here it was. The true question, hiding behind a veil of gripes and pleasantries.

Tigai reached for a glass himself, left behind by the Lady Huame. No sense letting good drink go to waste.

"It goes well," he replied. "If slowly. Remarin has them drilling on the floor plan for the vaults, and I've found my ironcrafter for the keys. With the prisoners of Kregiaw in our keeping, we're days away. Not weeks."

"I need not remind you—"

"No, you need not."

Dao glowered, and Tigai met his brother's eyes. Almost, the knot of their father's debt was untangled. But the men in black hoods whom Dao had seen three weeks prior at the opera would have been in the employ of the Bank of Shinsuke, and neither of them had any illusions why the Yanjin gardener's villa had been torched, even if they couldn't be certain which of their creditors had set the fire.

Dao broke off their stare, rising to his feet.

"Quickly, little brother," Dao said. "Or next time I will let Lady Rin, or Lady Bilong into your rooms before you've had time to drink."

Tigai answered with a long draw from his wineglass, but his brother had already vanished into his private study.

———

Lamplight flickered across the walls, casting shadows as he descended into the crypts. A hundred generations of Yanjin corpses, and room for a hundred more. So their father had said. He'd never have believed Dao would take up the mantle of chastising him on the family's behalf. Still, Dao was right. Tigai's plans at the Emperor's Kanjiao Palace would decide whether another generation of Yanjin boys would walk these crypts. He only wished he could do it for Dao's sake, and not his father's.

Their father's statue greeted him in the first chamber, a likeness hewn from granite, as hard and cold as the man himself had been. Propriety demanded they honor him, commissioning the statue and making it available for all to come and offer their respects, not that anyone would. A delicious irony, that the *magi* training that his father had secured for him in secret would be used for thieving and piracy, headquartered in his very tomb.

"You're late," Remarin said gruffly, holding a lantern in the tunnel beyond the main passage. "I've had the prisoners naked and wondering at your perversions half the morning now."

"Apologies, my friend," he said. "I was enchanted by the beauty of the Han heiress, and had to stay to offer my respects."

Remarin snorted. "Enchanted by wine and potato liquor, by the smell of you."

"That, too."

Remarin shook his head, producing a silvered key from his coat and offering it on his way out of the crypt.

"They're your problem, then," Remarin said. "*Damyu* know the price we paid to get them."

"Are we ready, otherwise?"

"We are. Another month of drills and we might do it without leaving any men behind; another past that if we want to do it without killing. But we're ready now."

A few weeks' efforts, weighed against the lives of his men, and a few weeks more to balance the lives of guardsmen who'd committed no more crime than taking the wrong posting at the wrong time. But it was no consideration at all. The banks would have their due, in gold, or blood and steel.

"We don't have a month," he said, and Remarin nodded.

Tigai took the key, and let his master-at-arms vanish up the stairwell leading back into the keep.

Remarin had been with them from the beginning, hired by his father to instill the hard-edged iron of the frontier into boys who might otherwise have been softened by the silks and pillows of the Imperial court. More fool him that Ujibari clansmen took bonds of stewardship as heavy as they took their liquor. Remarin hadn't balked at piracy, nor at kidnapping or murder, if that was the price for his charges to survive. A good man, more a father to him and Dao than Lord Yanjin had ever been, and worth every bar of gold they'd promised to pay him, when it was over.

The lock clicked as he turned the key, and he pushed the door inward, stepping inside.

Four pairs of eyes fixed on him. The prisoners of Kregiaw, reduced to nakedness and shivering in spite of the southern heat. Three wrinkled men clapped in irons, and the enigma, the captain who'd called herself Lin Qishan, who stood out as much for her smooth skin and supple breasts as the fact that she should never have been anywhere near the wastes.

A shame about the manacles. They'd interfere with his purpose almost as much as clothes would have done.

"A fine morning to you, my guests," he said, offering the same bow he'd given to Lord and Lady Han. "I trust your needs have been seen to, and I apologize for the necessity of your present condition."

The men regarded his words with a varying mix of fear and false pride, while the captain's eyes smoldered like a doused fire.

"What do you mean to do with us?" one of the men asked—he couldn't tell which, by sight. Feng-To, Dhazan, and Shanying, each of varying talents and ancestry, though they could have been any three naked old men, but for the connections between them.

Tigai shifted his vision to the strands before he replied. A starfield, as rich as the night sky, superimposed over top of his sight. It had come as a shock to learn that none of the other boys could see those stars, or the strands between them. His father had hired expensive tutors to visit the Yanjin estates in secret rather than pledge him to the *magi* for placement and training. Not an uncommon thing, for a family to keep a few of its most talented from the Great and Noble Houses. But he'd since gone further than any of them dared, and he meant to go further still.

"I mean to use your blood to summon demons," he said. "A dark ritual, fed by darker offerings, and mysteries long missing from this world."

A pause let their faces go ashen white, even by torchlight.

"He's no sorcerer," the woman, Captain Lin, said. "He wants you for your connections to the Emperor."

Tigai's smile dimmed, but held as he examined the starfield. There. A pulsing star that signified the first of the three men, with strands of light connecting him to the others by proximity. And yes, a pale tether linked to strands far in the distance, echoed between the three of them by the common thread of their experience. If they'd been clothed he might have found shared connections in their tailors, or the flax seeds or sheep that contributed to make their garb. Naked, he sensed only *them*, the true, raw essence of their experience.

"My lady is quite correct," he said. "Though it is unfortunate for you she said it aloud."

The chamber fell silent, and he traced the strands again, following each line far enough to be sure they led to Kanjiao Palace, and not to some quarry or forge where their manacles had been smithed, or to an academy where they might once have schooled together by happenstance. Good enough. When the time came, he could use their connection to shift Remarin's men into the secret chambers of the palace vaults, where Shanying had performed for His Majesty in his youth, where Feng-To had served as a coinsmith for the better part of a decade, and where Dhazan had been a lesser aide at the start of his career. He'd need to bring the three of them along, more to their pity; there wasn't time to spend weeks making a solid connection for himself. But it would serve.

"How is it a scion of Dragon has turned pirate?"

Captain Lin met his eyes as he dismissed the starfield and the strands. This time he frowned, in spite of her nakedness. A pleasant surprise, to find such a well-shaped body beneath the furs she'd packed over her uniform in the snows. But for her to mention Dragon—or more properly, the Great and Noble House of the Dragon…he'd never heard of the house, not that his knowledge of the monastic orders was anything close to exhaustive. But she spoke as though she was sure he belonged there.

"Are you a Dragon yourself, to be so sure?" he shot back, intending it to settle the issue.

"I know your mind," she said. "You've betrayed your order, in service to Isaru Mattai."

Inwardly he winced. *Magi* politics. He had no idea who Isaru Mattai was, or why serving him would count for a betrayal. He'd been a bloody fool to take this one along with the others. He'd expected a noble ingénue, a seed planted in the far north, perhaps a part of some scheme he might unravel to sell the information for gold. But if whatever she was involved the *magi* and the Great and Noble Houses, he would have been better off leaving her in the ice.

"You will go free," he lied. "All of you. After our purpose is done, we will—"

The captain moved, faster than her manacles should have allowed. Only she wasn't wearing the irons; they lay behind her, piled as though they'd never bound her wrists or feet. A glass dagger shone in her hand, polished enough that it seemed to drink the light of the chamber's lantern.

Impossible. Remarin would never have bound a prisoner loosely enough for them to escape, nor missed a weapon, even concealed in clothing, and this woman had been naked.

He stepped back as she lunged, springing like a coiled snake. Glass streaked, and he felt the lancing pain of cuts across his forearms.

By reflex his mind reached for the strands, finding an anchor point he'd set some weeks before.

Dao gave a start, looking up from a ledger he'd held open across the desk between them. His brother's study. Good. At least he was still on the palace grounds.

"Tigai?" his brother said. "What are you doing here?"

"Summon the house guards," he said, his breath short from the exertion of the shift. "We have a problem."

9

SARINE

Gendarme Corps Headquarters
Outside New Sarresant

Dust blew on a northbound breeze outside the city walls. She'd watched the bulk of the army departing under clouds of the stuff, brown, dusty fog rising where men and horses filled the trade roads in columns eight across. The army was disciplined, and quick. They'd uprooted a small city's worth of stakes and canvas faster than she could sketch the work, and now she stood, waiting for her adjunct among the High Commander's staff.

A company of soldiers wearing the purple armbands of the gendarmes eyed her as they strode past. Military police, the army's answer to the city watch. Raised eyebrows and muttered words proved enough for one of their number to peel off, returning to where she sat outside a building that had surely been a stableyard, in better times.

"Are you lost, my lady?" the young soldier asked.

"I'm waiting for a liaison from the gendarmerie," she said. "A liaison I was assured would be here half an hour ago."

The soldier frowned. "Your pardon, my lady, but this is a military camp. I'll need you to move along, if you please."

She said nothing in reply, weighing between *Faith* and Zi's *Green* to make him go away.

"Madame, I'm certain you aren't looking for trouble," the young man continued. "But unless you comply at once, you will—"

"Belay that, Corporal," a woman said from the path behind them. "Or you'll be the one with more trouble than he's fit to handle."

Sarine turned, and beamed at the sight.

"Lance-Lieutenant Acherre," she said, rushing to stow her pack. The other woman waited for her to rise, then met her with a tight embrace, doubtless at odds with military decorum. The young soldier who'd been about to accost her wore a look of bewilderment, but made no move to retreat.

"The High Commander didn't tell me it would be you," Sarine said when they separated.

Acherre grinned. "It's Captain, now. As of twenty minutes ago. Gendarme-Captain, after I insisted I be given this assignment."

"Sir," the corporal said. "Forgive me, sir, but she's out of uniform, and this is a military camp..."

A sizzling pop sounded in the air, hissing smoke between Acherre and the young man.

"Bugger off, Corporal, and consider that a direct order."

The young man yelped, offering only a last look at Sarine before retreating farther up the path.

"Lance-Lieu—er, Captain," Sarine said. "That was *Entropy*. You could handle only *Body* and *Mind*, during the battle, no?"

"The High Commander finally found a use for my ability to see *Need*," Acherre said. "She showed me an *Entropy* binding through the connection, and suddenly I could see them for myself. Quite a thing. Though I hear you've been associating with assassins and criminals, since we fought together."

Sarine smiled, in spite of the weight she'd felt since the chapel. She'd been expecting some grizzled sergeant or veteran infantryman when High Commander d'Arrent instructed her to report to the gendarmerie for an attaché who could keep her connected to the army's high command. Lance-Lieutenant—no, Gendarme-Captain—Acherre was as friendly a face as she could have hoped for, given they'd all but bled together, side by side during the battle against the Gandsmen.

"Let's head into the city," Acherre said, brandishing a sheaf of papers bound by a leather cord. "I have the reports on citizens who've seen our nameless assassin, or at least claimed to recognize the man in your sketches. And I do believe I promised you a hard drink, during the fighting."

———————

Her throat burned from the rye liquor as Acherre repoured their glasses. A stronger bite than any wine she'd tasted, and quicker to leave her senses wrapped in cotton, though the other woman seemed unfazed. Papers spread between them on a chest-height round table near the back of the tavern they'd chosen, the first they'd come to after entering through the southern gates. The rest of the room was as empty as the army camps had been, most likely for the same cause.

"So you know the man," Acherre said, setting a now-full glass on Sarine's side of the table. "What do you think his aims are? We start there, if we're to try to piece together what he might do next."

"His name is Axerian," she said. "He's...ah..."

What was she to say? That their assassin was a God—and might still be; she wasn't sure how that sort of thing was reckoned. That he was behind the madness that drove every *kaas*-mage who touched his Codex to murder, and worse. And she still wasn't certain why he'd come here at all, or where he'd gone in the months since the battle.

She took a drink from her glass and told what she knew. The heat from the liquor helped to mask the color in her cheeks, speaking of Gods and grand plots as though they were more than religious allegories or children's stories. To her credit Acherre listened with gravity well beyond what Sarine felt her words commanded, and by the end she was nodding along, giving full credence to the tale.

"We know at least that he's attacked the High Commander," Acherre said when she'd finished. "Even if the why of it is a mystery. D'Arrent is surrounded by binders while the army marches south, with decoys posing in the council hall. The greatest danger is the use of the...*kaas*... powers"—she swallowed the unfamiliar word—"to stir the people to the same sort of madness we saw during the battle for the city."

Sarine nodded. "If he uses *Yellow* with any strength, Zi will alert me to his presence."

"Good," Acherre said. "Then we can focus on finding our man here. If he's marching with the army, Marquand's people will handle it. We just have to piece this together and find a pattern of where he's been sighted. All of this is fresh, gathered by the city watch using your sketches in the last two days."

Sarine took another drink from her glass. A daunting prospect, given the enormity of finding a single man in a city of almost a million. And he might not even be in the city, no matter what its citizens claimed to the city watch. More than a few commonfolk would lie for the thrill of it, enough to lay a false trail through any quarter where the people were like to mistrust authority, even now. And Zi had gotten no better, still quiet and sluggish, even days after her episode at the Sacre-Lin.

Acherre laid a hand on her forearm. "It's all right. Half the watch and as many gendarmes are looking for him. We're there to take him at the end as much as aid the search. This isn't our burden alone."

She met Acherre's warmth with a grim expression. Better to have the help than not, but she needed to find Axerian, before Zi got any worse.

———————

The city sang with the sound of builders as they walked the streets of Southgate. Not two months had passed since the Gand army tore the city apart, and already the roads and buildings were a strange half-breed of fresh construction and reminder of what had been. New paint covered a wood fence beside a barren garden; glass so clear it might have been air adorned a shop window beside a thoroughfare pocked by artillery shells; men laughed and joked, climbing scaffolds as they laid the framework of a new building overlooking a cemetery.

Zi had appeared nestled on her shoulders like a shawl, his serpentine head lolling back and forth as she walked. Much as she appreciated Acherre's company—and all the more so when her attaché could as easily have been some gruff soldier who two months prior had been a ruffian from the Maw—it still felt passing odd to have the notice, and approval, of the city's ruling class. All her life it had been her, her uncle, and Zi. Acherre, in her blue uniform, with a captain's knot on her collar and the purple armband fastened around her sleeve, represented the sort of men and women she'd always taken pains to avoid. Though it appeared she'd traded in her old enemies for new ones. Gods, this time. The Nameless himself, in the literal flesh rather than the abstract of her uncle's sermons. He was alone, for now, while she had the strength of the city watch and the army at her back, though she would never mistake the traitor of Jukaris San for anything other than a red adder coiled around her leg. She'd made that mistake already, and paid in sixteen cycles of stasis, frozen in her prison at—

The world lurched, and pain lanced through her. She stopped mid-stride, the image of an underground city shimmering into view, superimposed over top of the street. Jukaris San, jewel of the Amaros Empire, though she had no idea where the words, or the memory, had come from in her mind.

No, Zi thought to her, a blue light flashing to blur the image of the city before it could fully engulf her senses.

"Sarine?" Acherre asked. "What was that light? Is he nearby?"

Breath came ragged through her throat. She saw lingering images, of Axerian, of a school built from crumbling marble, of a glass enclosure in the now-familiar chamber of smooth stone.

No, Zi thought again. *It's too soon.*

"No," she said. "Not another vision. Zi, please, hang on."

"Sarine, are you well?" Acherre asked, still on alert.

An echo of pain reverberated through her mind, and she urged herself to calm. She was hurting Zi, but the vision seemed to pass, before it could materialize into more than the first few images.

"We have to go," she said. "We have to find Axerian, quickly."

Acherre stayed still, eyeing her with a questioning look.

It took a forced march through the pain for Acherre to follow behind. Zi tightened around her shoulders, coiling the loop of his tail around her upper arm while his head quivered against the other.

"It's okay, Zi," she whispered. "We'll find him. Soon."

His scales were ghost white, almost translucent, and he said nothing as she stroked his neck. An odd visual, for her to be patting the air where others couldn't see him, but the Nameless could take their comforts when Zi was in pain.

"Gods above," Acherre said from behind. "Is that your . . . your *kaas*?"

Sarine pivoted mid-stride. "You can see him?"

Acherre nodded, eyes wide. "He appeared a moment ago."

From a glance it was clear Acherre wasn't alone in seeing him; passersby and builders took notice of her, squints and frowns for the sake of the crystalline serpent coiled along her shoulders. Dread turned over in her stomach. This was wrong. Zi had never appeared to so many; she'd done something to make him lose control, pushed him too far in spite of his warnings.

"We have to get him to the Maw," she said. "Back to my uncle's church. Something is—"

No.

"Zi, you're sick. I know you never wanted me to tell uncle about you, but you need help."

No.

She frowned. Zi had never needed food or medicine or anything of the kind before. He just *was*. A part of her, like a thought or daydream. But she wasn't about to push him now. If he said no, she'd find some other way to help.

Emotions. That was the key. He'd always fed on strong emotions.

A flicker of gold showed along his scales, glinting in the sun. Fear? It had to be, if he was collecting the dread pooling in her veins.

"What do you need?" Acherre asked. "The horse doctors perhaps?" She said it with a dubious cast, and rightly so. No other beast was quite like Zi.

"We need to find strong emotions," she said. "A bar fight, an execution. Something intense. Follow me. I'll know when we get close."

Acherre fell in step as she increased their pace, striding up the streets of Southgate toward the river. The Market district at the center of the city might do, if its usual denizens were there, haggling and shouting and insulting each other over prices.

She kept a hand on Zi's neck to steady him as she unslung her pack from the other shoulder, cradling his body as she lowered him inside. Already too many whispers followed them, pointed fingers and curious looks toward the girl and her crystal serpent. Zi couldn't have chosen to appear to them; whatever he'd done with the blue light and the visions had caused him to appear, and for his sake she'd keep him hidden in her pack. She left his head and neck poking over her shoulder, with the rest of him tucked alongside her sketches. Enough to stay the whispers, but she kept him pressed against her skin to let him feel her fear, her concern, her love and determination, every emotion more intense for his sake, knowing he needed them now as he never had before.

A flicker of red colored his scales as they drew near the river, and she shifted course toward the nearest bridge.

"This way," she said, and Acherre kept pace as she pressed forward.

Warmth pulsed from Zi as his scales flushed red. A good sign. Some of the thickest fighting during the battle had been here, on the west side of the river. Chipped bricks and broken glass patched by cheap wood gave truth to the horrors of the battle, but the stalls and merchants were as alive as they'd ever been, divvying up the prizes seized in the months since the founding of the Republic. Gold and jewels, silks and spices, but more important: food. If there was a commotion worth stirring Zi's scales to crimson, it surely devolved to the price of bread. Thank the Gods if the market found cause for argument today.

They passed a knot of foot traffic moving away from the central square in a hurried rush, and she turned down a side street that would end at the very heart of the district. Another pack of citizens crowded the street, and she wove through them, trusting Acherre to keep pace. Zi's pallor had improved, his head lifting on its own as she cradled him against her shoulder. It seemed the worst of it had passed. If he was still visible to others, they were preoccupied enough not to notice or stare, and from the lack of attention they received it seemed Zi had regained control of his faculties. Not that she understood the workings of what he did. But he'd always—

"Sarine."

Acherre's voice, filled with alarm.

She didn't slow her pace, only turned to find Acherre staring ahead as they drove toward the central square.

It took a moment to see it: The people around the fountains weren't rushing away on hurried business, or preoccupied with some discomfort they'd sooner avoid. They were running. Panicked.

Screaming.

Acherre's form blurred, the sign of a *Body* tether as the gendarme-captain surged forward. By the time Sarine found her own strands of *Body*—and had a *Faith* tether ready by reflex—Acherre had split into three copies of herself from a *Mind* binding and reached the end of the street.

Sarine ran, careful not to jostle Zi, and caught up before Acherre had moved again.

The market was full of death.

A dozen men and women lay at all angles, draped over the fountain's edge. Three times that number were scattered like seeds across the square, each of them charred, leaking green liquid instead of blood.

Acherre moved, and a heartbeat later Sarine saw the thing that had drawn her attention: a snake, shrouded in mist and haze, rearing up to hiss beside the waist-height stone ringing the fountain pool. An ordinary serpent, but for the black mist around it, a ghostly shroud that made the creature seem half-transparent, like fogged glass.

Acherre roared some unintelligible battle cry as she charged the creature, billowing the smoke and flame of *Entropy* from her gloved hands.

Lakiri'in granted his blessing to go with *Body*, and Sarine rounded the serpent's flanks, keeping clear of Acherre's gouts of flame. If somehow the creature proved resilient to Acherre's attack, she could be in position to strike before—

Acherre's fire passed through the snake as though it were no more than a shadow, scorching the cobblestone behind it, melting and fusing the street into slag, without touching the serpent's ghostly scales.

The snake hissed, and charged.

It flew toward one of the three copies of Acherre, passing through twisted corpses on the ground as though they, too, were made of light. Acherre's *Entropy* sputtered out, replaced by a wall of *Shelter* at the last moment. The snake flew through it as though the swirling blue haze weren't there, snapping its jaws through Acherre's thigh.

Sarine screamed.

The copy blinked and faded, collapsing into the real woman, before Acherre shimmered, projecting two new copies. The snake pivoted, knifing its head toward the new trio.

Lakiri'in's blessing held as Sarine leapt across the square. Zi granted *Red* to go with it, and she paired *mareh'et* with the rest of her gifts as she cleared the space between them, striking where the snake leapt and finding her spirit-claws shearing through air where the creature's hide should have been, clanging as she struck the stone.

Another darting attack, and the center copy of Acherre blinked out. But before the images could reset, the serpent struck again, leaping faster than Sarine could have seen without her gifts of speed.

She called on the Storm Spirits, and discharged lightning into the creature as it struck.

Streaks of blue energy leapt between her and the snake, wrapping themselves around its body and Acherre's together as they entwined.

White light surrounded her, and she slipped away.

———————

YOU KILLED HER.

Panic flared.

No. I never meant for it to hit Acherre. I can't have—

The sensation of laughter enveloped her, though she had no body to hear it.

FOOL GIRL. THE ORDER MAGE IS NO CONCERN OF OURS. YOU KILLED MY CHILD. *VALAK'AR.*

Acherre lives? she thought to the entity.

IT IS OF NO CONCERN. YOU ARE A WHELP AND A WEAKLING. YOU SHOULD NEVER HAVE MANAGED TO KILL ONE OF MINE. I SHOULD END YOUR LIFE, AS RECOMPENSE.

Anger rose in her. Last time she'd conversed with these spirits they'd been curious—distant, perhaps, but never threatening. And whenever she'd come to this strange place it had been hours before she returned to her body. She couldn't lie here talking to a spirit while Acherre might be dying, struck by thunder loosed by her own hand. Acherre needed a chirurgeon's attention at once.

VALAK'AR IS NOBLE, DEADLIEST OF ALL BEASTS. FEW HAVE SLAIN ONE OF MY CHILDREN, AND YOU ARE A WOMAN. THIS IS AN OLD THING. STRANGE TO US. YOU USED THE STORM SPIRIT'S GIFT. A COWARD'S ATTACK. YOU ARE NO GUARDIAN.

Shut up, she demanded.

YOU ARE NOT WORTHY OF OUR GIFT.

Enough!

As she sent it she found the power nestled in her gut, the strange blue sparks she'd used to set wardings, at Axerian's instruction. Somehow the power wrapped itself around her words, and what had been a forceful thought turned into a cacophonous roar, tearing through the emptiness like the peal of a bell.

MOTHER, the spirit sent, suddenly humble where before it had been full of pride.

Release me at once, she thought to the spirit, amplified by the blue sparks. *I have to see to Acherre.*

IS IT YOU? WE THOUGHT…ANOTHER'S VOICE. WE BELIEVED. IT TOLD US TO COME HERE, TOLD US A WEAKLING OF A MAN WOULD HELP US THROUGH THE BARRIER. WE FOLLOWED, AND—

Let me go!

YES, MOTHER.

The void faded.

———

Acherre coughed as Sarine's senses returned, a sputtering sound that could as well have been sweet music.

Sarine scrambled to her side. The captain's uniform was torn, smoke rising from her chest and limbs where seams had been blackened and frayed.

"Don't move," she said, cradling a hand under Acherre's neck.

"I'm fine," Acherre said, coughing again. "The damned snake. It singed me. But I'm fine."

"That was my doing," Sarine said. "And you're not fine."

"Bah," Acherre said. "I'll be the judge of that. And whatever you did, at least you killed the fucking thing. Never seen anything like it. Whichever priests let the barrier fail long enough to let that little bastard into the city are going to get a hard whipping, and that's the least of their worries."

Memory sparked. The barrier. The spirits had said a man had let them through.

"I know where he is," she said. "Axerian. Or, at least where he's been."

10

TIGAI

Yanjin Outer Courtyard
Jun Province, the Jun Empire

N
o sign of her, my lord," his brother's guardsman said, offering a snap to attention that did little more than waste a precious second of his time.

"How is that possible?" he demanded. "She was bloody naked; Remarin confirmed it, the clothes still piled..." He trailed off, shaking his head. Pointless to spare breath for men inclined to duty, instead of results. "Redouble your search. Every man-at-arms. Secure the perimeter of the courtyards on close watch. Wherever she is, we can't let her escape the grounds."

"Yes, my lord," the guardsman said, wasting another second with a salute before he went to deliver the order.

The woman Lin Qishan—if she was a woman at all; who could be sure, with the Great and Noble Houses and their *magi* trickery—had revealed herself for a thorn in his sandals, accusing him of *magi* politics when he only intended to game for gold and wealth. He'd been a bloody fool to take her. And the heavens help them all if she turned out to have the same gift he did for the starfield and the strands.

He climbed the pathway toward the terraces, broad steps requiring a running leap to take two at a time. No, the *magi* captain had to be on the grounds. Whatever talent had secured her a place among the Great and Noble Houses, if she'd had his gift with anchors and the strands she'd have had no need to attack him to flee. The worst possibility—that she meant to attack him, and now had been at Yanjin long enough to recognize it among the starfield—didn't bear consideration. An assassin armed with his talent would succeed no matter their defenses, and as the gamblers said: One played toward one's chance of victory.

"Lord Tigai!"

The shrill demand stopped him when he reached the top of the steps, and he suppressed a groan.

"Lady Mei," he said, forcing himself to stop and make a bow. Precious seconds, wasted. "I passed instruction to your guard. You are to—"

"Stay cooped in my rooms, practicing my calligraphy and memorizing steps to the wind spirits' dance. Yes, I know. I chose to ignore it."

"Mei, it's serious this time. We have a prisoner escaped on the grounds. You need to go somewhere safe, and stay there."

Mei's eyes flashed. "I can think of no safer place than at the side of my husband's brother and champion."

No time to waste talking her down. He took the dirt path outside the inner wall, careful to keep watch for skulking movement among the hedgerows. Two pistols dangled against his leg as he moved, slung on a silk strap hung from his belt, with a shortblade sheathed against his other hip. Poor fare against a *magi*, if whispers of their capabilities were to be believed. He'd never faced one, nor paid especial attention when his tutors had warned him not to interfere in the business of the Great and Noble Houses. Any fool knew as much. *Magi* politics were kept separate from the concerns of the Empire, and if it was not strictly legal for him to practice his art outside the confines of their monastic schools, he'd always taken pains to conceal his gifts from anyone who might report him to their orders. It had worked; his talents had only ever been an edge over mundane soldiers and lords. Apart from his tutor he'd never even seen a *magi* in person, until now.

"So, who is this prisoner?" Mei asked as she kept pace behind him. "No one I know, I hope."

"Would we deploy the full retainer for a lady of the court? Wind spirits, Mei, would we even imprison a lady of the court?"

"With the company you keep, I can scarcely imagine what you would or wouldn't do. And don't presume to know with whom I spend my time, when you spend most of yours abroad."

He gave her an exaggerated look, then swept a glance across the herb gardens. Two men-at-arms were walking the paths making a cursory examination of the shrubberies, as though this were just another patrol.

Mei stood a pace behind, watching him rather than help scan the grounds. A tiger among lilly-flies; so his father had called her, before he arranged the match to Dao. She'd grown up here at Yanjin, his mother's ward, before Lady Yanjin died of pox, and in her absence Mei had taken to courtly politics instead of the dances and poetry expected of her as a dowress of a noble family. Their marriage had been a snub to Dao—an improper wife for an improper son, so had been their father's reasoning, of a surety. But Mei was pretty enough in spite of it. A pity she was doomed to unhappiness, given Dao's predilections, though that couldn't be his worry today.

"This prisoner is a *magi*, isn't he?" Mei asked.

This time Tigai winced.

"You wouldn't have so many ants scurrying about otherwise," Mei continued. "Unless you'd captured a *jinata* assassin, you wouldn't need so many to fight him."

"It's a her," he said as they crossed the path toward the water gardens, past the shrubs and herbs. "And keep your voice lowered."

Mei laughed. "What bloody fool decided to bring a *magi* here?"

His ears stung, but he said nothing. She was right; he should have known better. This close to their assault, the last thing they needed was a show for the sake of impressing a captain assigned to guard a block of ice.

A troop of men-at-arms rounded the outer wall, with Remarin in the lead. They sighted each other at the same moment, and Tigai raced toward him, as thankful for the reprieve as he was for the prospect of news.

"We've found her," Remarin called as he approached. "She's pinned down on the opposite side of the grounds."

"Excellent," he said, then, "What are you waiting for? Kill her and have done with it."

Mei gave him a look as though she'd taken a mouthful of fresh seaweed. Remarin only grunted.

"Can't get near her, and not going to risk my men for it. Not unless you want to wait a month to train another team."

"You want me to do it."

Remarin nodded. He sighed. Mei laughed.

"I'm taking an extra share for this," he said, and unslung his pistols as he led the company back the way they came.

––––––––

A semicircle of men kneeling behind marble colonnades greeted them when they rounded the yards, sighting their arquebuses together on what appeared to be a glass statue hiding behind a rock.

"Is that…?" Mei said.

"Stay down, *please*," he said. Remarin would make her obey if anyone could.

Shards of glass lay strewn across the green, glinting in the sun. One of his men—Remarin's Ujibari, not Dao's worthless peacocks—moaned and clutched his belly, curled over ten paces from the silent form of a guardsman.

"Wait, is that her?" he said. "She's *armored* in glass, and she's throwing it at us? Of all the bloody stupid—"

A boom sounded where one of his men took a shot, loud enough to sting his ears even halfway across the green. The glass-armored hulk thudded to the ground where she'd been struck, chipped shards flying off the faceplate and regrowing before she could pick herself back up to hide behind her rock.

"Too much to hope you know the workings of whatever she's doing?" Remarin asked.

Tigai gave a helpless shrug. His education had focused on basic principles said to be common to every talent. His tutor had been skilled with potato plants, a former scion of the Great and Noble House of the Ox. The man could graft potato vines out of dirt, the most luscious, succulent potatoes served this side of the Kanjiao Palace. His tutor couldn't do a damned thing with glass, and neither could Tigai. But if the principles were the same, the *magi* would have a source, something she converted into glass. Wind spirits save them if she used dirt like his old tutor, or if she used physical exertion, like Tigai.

"No telling what she can do with it," he said. "But she's got to have a source, and that means she can exhaust her supply."

"So we keep her pinned here until she runs dry," Remarin said. "And hope she doesn't skewer us in the meantime?"

"Apologies, my friend. If you hoped I could swoop to the rescue, I don't mean to disappoint, but—"

"*Magi*!" A voice cut across the green. "Come out, and my guards will not fire. I swear it on the Emperor's life."

Mei. His stomach lurched as he pivoted from his hiding place to find her standing clear as day on the grass.

Laughter came back in reply, muted by the glass covering the *magi*'s face.

"This house has less respect for the Emperor than I have for leavings from the pig trough."

"My life, then," Mei shouted back. "I'm as good as offering it to you, standing here, am I not?"

"Mei, get back here at once!" he hissed.

No reply from the *magi*, and less from Mei for his sake. She kept still, facing the stone and the woman in glass, ten paces from the nearest cover.

"My husband's brother erred in bringing you here," Mei said. "House Yanjin has no quarrel with the Great and Noble Houses, and I have no wish for more of my loyal servants to die for a simple mistake. Rise, and let us speak of what we can do to make amends."

A moment passed, and he half considered running to seize Mei and hook them both to the strands in Dao's library. Dangerous, to try to force it. They might end up at the bottom of the Sidai Bay, if he slipped in haste. But it was better than seeing her stuck with glass shards.

"Very well," the *magi* called back.

"Hold fire," Remarin called as the *magi* rose from behind her stone. A fearsome sight, sculpted glass thick enough to plate every part of her body, colored green and blue where it caught the light. It had to be heavy as a load of pig iron, but the *magi* moved smoothly as she stood.

Then she turned and ran.

"Oh bloody fuck," Tigai said. "Shoot her!"

A half-dozen roars filled the green as Remarin's men set off their guns. Chips of glass broke and shattered where their shots struck home, enough to send her sprawling face-first into the grass. But she pushed off the ground and kept on, racing toward the wild forest at the edge of the gardens.

Tigai vaulted the waist-high colonnade he'd hidden behind, pausing to sight his first pistol and fire as he ran. He struck her in the back, sending her down again. Fifteen seconds before Remarin's men reloaded. Maybe less. He let the pistol fall from his hand, taking up the second for another shot. This one went wide, pelting the grass in a rain of dirt.

The *magi* scrambled back to her feet, this time running in a crooked pattern meant to confuse the arquebusiers as she put range between them. Another volley rang out; this time only a single burst of glass shattered from her shoulder, but she kept her footing, angling toward the tree line.

Fuck. He ran after her, but stuttered to a halt after a hundred yards. Suicide to chase her into the woods. He was a fair hand with his shortblade, but he had no desire to try himself against a glass monstrosity. And he'd earn no more than a mouthful of glass if he tried to close on her when she had brush and foliage to hide behind.

He watched as she disappeared into the woods, taking far too much knowledge of his plan with her into the trees.

Dao scrawled a note as he and Remarin sat opposite the desk. Mei hovered, standing beside a bookshelf, turning a half-black globe that showed the territory of the Everlasting Empire of the Jun.

"Fifty *qian*," Dao said as he wrote. "The least I can spare. Did you know the man the *magi* killed was married? A wife and son, left behind in Zhouxing."

Tigai kept a wince in check.

"I've tried to recruit young men, my lord," Remarin said. "But even young men marry."

"So they do. This one did."

"The son will get his father's share," Tigai said.

"You still mean to go through with it?" Mei said, stopping the spin of the globe with the dark side facing him. "I thought we were here to prepare for the ruin of this household, now the *magi* know what we're about."

"The *magi* have never troubled themselves with house politics," Dao said.

"We have no choice," Tigai snapped back. "Whether the *magi* come for us or no. They might be dissuaded by gold, but unless we go through with it we'll have to pay them in promises. I expect that would work as well for the *magi* as it has for the banks."

Dao's study fell quiet at mention of their creditors. Mei pursed her lips, making a point of trying to bore a hole in him with her eyes. Never mind that she'd gifted his prisoner an opening to break from cover, with her grand gesture of bravery on the green. Unfair to blame her; she'd likely saved a life or two, and maybe his, if fortune had frowned on him. It didn't change that she'd acted without his approval, or Remarin's, when either was the natural choice to lead in the context of violence. She wouldn't appreciate him taking up her webs of politics and lies and declaring himself spymaster. Not that she would see it that way.

Remarin coughed.

"Yes?" Dao asked.

"We have another problem, my lord, where our plans are concerned. The three prisoners—Shanying, Feng-To, Dhazan. All are dead."

"What?" Tigai said. "You assured me there was no sign of them, in the cells."

"And so there wasn't, when I reported it. The *magi* led them out, perhaps intending to escape with them, before she encountered my men. We found the three of them slashed with glass, throats and wrists cut, left to die in a passage beneath the inner yard."

"Fuck," Tigai shouted, perhaps a touch louder than propriety dictated in a lord's study. "Fuck, fuck, fuck, fuck."

"What does that mean?" Mei asked. "Hadn't you already had a chance to examine—where are you going?"

Tigai had already risen and was halfway out the study before he remembered he didn't know where to find the bodies.

"Take me to them," he said. "And, Dao, rouse the rest of Remarin's men and get them into the tunnels."

Dao frowned. "What? What's going on?"

"Now!" he shouted. "We have to go now, before the strand connections fade from the corpses. It may already be too late."

His brother went pale. "You mean... tonight?"

"I mean right this bloody instant. Provided we're all still comfortable with the plan."

He meant it as an irony. They'd been preparing for this since his father's death revealed the depth of their debt. But Dao considered it in solemn silence, taking entirely too long to nod, as though they needed a final blessing.

Mei gave a bitter laugh. "And so we become thieves, from no less than the Emperor himself."

11

ERRIS

Village of Salingsford
Devon County, Northern Gand Territory

Jiri held her head aloft as their column made its way through the village square. The 9th Cavalry had the honor of carrying her flag today; it would be the 11th, tomorrow. Vassail's old brigade, though Vassail had the 3rd Division now. Always upward mobility, during war. Empty places around the campfires meant majors became colonels, colonels became generals, and too many became corpses, making way for those pushing ever upward through the ranks.

The Gand villagers had turned out to watch the column pass, women in drab colors and foreign-cut dresses standing by the roadside. Sullen eyes, there, and far too few men. How many brothers and sons had died already, or already wore the Gandsmen's red uniform, marching elsewhere to meet her soldiers in the field?

"That's d'Arrent," she heard the women say in the Gand tongue, passed between them like gossip on a trip to the village well. "It's her. Their High Commander."

She kept her eyes level as they stared. Jiri alone was enough to give her the stature she knew the enemy expected from the commander of the armies of New Sarresant, nineteen hands of horseflesh and snow-white coat and mane where she herself was nothing exceptional. A woman of below-average height and well-below-average birth, no matter the five stars pinned to her collar. Though the Republic meant her lack of landed title counted for nothing, anymore. Strange.

She reined Jiri to a halt outside the largest building in the village, where her aide waited beside a portly man in finer clothes than a farmer's wage could buy.

"High Commander, sir," Aide-Captain Essily said, offering a salute she returned before he continued. "I present the Honorable Master Cormack, Mayor of Salingsford."

"Master Cormack," she said, remaining seated on Jiri's back. Better if the man had to look up at her. "My quartermasters tell me I have you to thank for the rashers of bacon and fresh-cooked wheatcakes we enjoyed this morning."

She spoke the Sarresant tongue, waiting on her aide to translate.

"Your servant, High Commander," the mayor said, the cold glare in his eyes a poor mask for the politeness in his words.

"They also tell me they suspect your people have some knowledge of the Gand army's position, owing to the recent depletion of your granaries. Unless you folk stored rather poorly against the winter, you quartered the army here, and recently, too."

The mayor said nothing as her aide translated the words, remaining silent when he'd finished.

"You have the good fortune of entertaining me personally, Master Cormack," she went on when it became clear he wouldn't speak. "One of my generals might not prove so patient."

"We're simple folk," the mayor said. "Not the kind to pay attention to soldiers' comings and goings."

"Have you heard of a village called Fantain's Cross?"

The mayor's face went ashen white as Essily translated the name. Of course he'd have heard; in better times the northern Gand villages would have traded across the border. Little chance the papers would be able to suppress news of a slaughter on the order of Fantain's Cross. Erris had been there herself, and personally seen the chapel doors the Gandsmen had barricaded to keep the villagers in place as they burned alive.

"No," the mayor said. "Please, no. We're farmers; we've given you what food we have, and freely. We'll not obstruct your march, nor burn our fields."

"The Gand army passed this way," she said. "And you had best cease denying it, and start convincing Captain Essily you know their strength, composition, and where they intended to march. If my aide is satisfied, I am satisfied. Else your people will face the Exarch's justice, and I'll leave it to you to consider what that might mean, in light of Fantain's Cross."

She said nothing further, heeling Jiri to ride as her aide stayed behind to finish the interrogation. The mayor's reticence was confirmation enough, whatever else Essily managed to pry from him. The enemy had come this way. Her army had stolen a march southward, and found the Gandsmen already marshaled to meet them in the field. Just as well. The better part of the Gand survivors from the Battle of New Sarresant had been ferried back to the Old World on Tuyard's ships, ransomed for the coin that now equipped her soldiers. Fresh levies wouldn't stand against battle-hardened veterans, no matter the prowess of their commander. That the Gandsmen fell back from their border suggested he knew it, as well as she.

All that remained was to find them, and pin them down. And now she'd found the trail. This would be a simple victory, momentum against the inevitable marshaling of the Gand forces across the sea. For now she had the initiative, and she meant to press it.

———————

A cloud of pipe smoke greeted her as she made the *Need* connection to Voren's aide. She suppressed the urge to cough, though it seemed the aide was more accustomed to the sting of it in her lungs than Erris was in hers.

"Ah, High Commander, a pleasure," Voren said, bristling his mustaches above the stem of his pipe as he smiled.

The other two men in Voren's office turned toward her with wide eyes.

"This is...?" the one to her left began.

"It is indeed," Voren replied. "The power of *Need*, wielded by d'Arrent herself. High Commander, I have the pleasure to introduce Assemblyman Gregoine, first representative of the Maw district, and Master Humbert, a newspaperman and pamphleteer who has been most generous to us in his writing."

"Time is short," she said. "As you well know, my lord."

Voren withdrew his pipe again. "Indeed, gentlemen. You'll have to excuse us."

The newspaperman, Master Humbert, leaned forward, giving no sign of rising to leave the room.

"Is it a report?" Humbert said. "From the front?"

"Master Humbert." Voren smiled. "I'm certain you know you cannot print the disposition and intent of our soldiers in the field."

"Yes, of course," Humbert replied. "But this…this *Need*…this is how—?"

"This is the secret to our High Commander's victories," Voren said. "This and the most brilliant military mind I have encountered in fifty years' service to the crown."

Already she could feel the strands of *Need* wavering; precious seconds wasted with their gawking. It took Voren rising to his feet for them to move, shuffling out the door into the company of his manservant.

"Sir," she said when they were gone, "you know *Need* is in short supply. And I'd prefer our movements not be printed in the dailies, if it's the same to you and your fellows."

"He'd have done it, too," Voren said. "Then begged forgiveness, promised to make amends with a story of my choosing." He smiled, and took a draw from his pipe. "So it is, with the newsmen. You can be sure he's already making note of my aide's features—gold-lit eyes and all— for a wood press in tomorrow's morning run."

"We've crossed the border, sir," she said. "That's the essence of my report. Gand has fielded a new army against us, but from what little we've scouted thus far, we believe it to be fresh conscripts, not more than fifteen, perhaps eighteen thousand strong."

"Excellent," Voren replied. "How are the maneuvers? Will there be a battle soon?"

"I expect their main body will be dispositioned to check a southward move toward Covendon and the ports at Lynnstown. It leaves us to seize the crossing at Ansfield and the junctions around the town."

"I recall similar tactics were used eighteen months ago, by your predecessors."

"Yes, sir," she said. "The strategy is sound."

She omitted the part where the former high command had blundered away their position at Ansfield, spreading the army too thin to hold a single crossroads, let alone the key shipping lanes for the rivers that cut across the northern Gand colonies. She wouldn't be so stupid. Taking the crossings meant her men could range and reave across the countryside, within easy reach of resupply while the enemy had to expose his wagon trains to her cavalry, coming up the central trade roads. No amount of brilliance from the enemy commander would save him when his supplies were being torched and stolen before he could feed his troops.

"Any surprises you might expect?" Voren asked. "We've been burned by this enemy before."

"He might try for an attack from the west, but I have cavalry screening our movements there. Tuyard has ships blockading their northern ports to cut off an attack by sea. Brilliance only counts for so much, sir, when the enemy lacks materiel for the campaign. Thus far he's been conservative, as I would be in his position. His best strategy is to slow us, but he can't hope to stop us with what he has in the field."

"Very well, High Commander. Gods grant you speed on your march. Give my regards to—"

The *Need* binding snapped, as though a hand had reached for the tether and strangled it, leaving sputtering gold flecks dancing in her vision.

She gasped, the world seeming to spin as her senses returned to her body.

"Sir? Is everything well?"

Her aide's voice. Essily.

Breath came hard, and she steadied herself against a lamppost.

It didn't matter. She had an army to lead. *Need* had lasted longer than she'd expected, with Voren. Perhaps she could manage one more connection, before she had to rest.

She reached out, and smoke burned her throat as soon as she made the tether.

"Down!" Chevalier-General Vassail shouted. "Reload!"

"Report!" she yelled over the din. A *Shelter* barrier deformed the smoke clouds a few paces ahead of where they stood, while heavy guns barked behind them, sending the low whine of canister shot over their heads.

"High Commander," Vassail said. "Lovely to see you, and damned fine timing. We're engaged, sir. At least one brigade of enemy cavalry, with infantry support coming fast up the roads to the east."

For Vassail to be engaged in the east meant the enemy had anticipated their attempt to seize Ansfield, and positioned himself for a fight rather than trying to goad them into a chase. A baffling maneuver, when she had strength of numbers and the advantage of veteran troops. It had to be a trap.

"Hold them here," she shouted. "And get cavalry on the move. We can't be blind to his numbers. If this is a feint, we—"

Once again, *Need* ripped itself from her grasp.

The world splintered into fragments, re-forming like glass broken in reverse.

Clouds and sunlight shone on her eyes. She was lying on her back, with a face peering down at her overhead.

"High Commander," Aide-Captain Essily said. "Sir, careful. Stay still."

"Gods damn it. Get the staff ready to ride. Vassail is engaged. I have to be there, have to see it for myself."

"Easy, sir," Essily said.

"Now, Captain!" she said, offering a hand for him to grab and pull her to her feet. The ground seemed to come with her, threatening to heave her stomach into her throat, but she rose, propelling herself toward Jiri to rise up into her saddle. If *Need* wasn't going to work properly, she could bloody well lead the old-fashioned way, with spyglasses, couriers, and scouts.

"We ride east," she said. "And I need cavalry headed south. Get de Tourvalle's best in their saddles. If the enemy is committed to an attack in the east, we need to know whether he's abandoned the roads to Covendon."

"Yes, sir," Essily said, passing the order to a woman who saluted and ran to deliver it.

"I sent for the doctors, sir," Essily continued. "You seemed unwell, after your last connection. Then you fell, a moment ago."

"I'm fine," she said. "Just get us moving. The enemy is here, in the field, and we're half-blind. No time to be fussed over by medics. I need cavalry riding south at once, to know if the enemy has abandoned the roads to Covendon."

Essily gave her an awkward look. "Sir, you gave that order already."

Memory blurred. But yes, she had.

"Good," she said. "Then get me an update from Field-Marshal

Royens. I need the First Corps ready to reinforce the east, but I don't want them to commit to the action until I have a better view of the field."

Essily lingered for a moment, watching her.

"Move!" she barked, and he nodded, turning to fetch a lieutenant to deliver the rest of her orders. She didn't dare use a *Need* connection again, after the last two. She felt seared and brittle all at once, as though she'd been dipped in fire and left to cool.

Not surprising, for the Gandsmen to offer some resistance. But she had to know what they risked with this feint to the east. A full-strength attack would be madness, offering her a clear route to seize their capital at Covendon and all but end the war. The sort of blunder an utter novice would make, and the enemy commander was no one's fool.

Her head swam. She knew better than to be confident against this enemy. He'd beaten her soundly before. Yet even with *Need* hamstrung, leaving her sick and dazed when she used it, every sign pointed to an easy victory, whether at Ansfield or the campaign at large. There had to be more. Some other ploy or tactic designed to bait her, entrap her, goad her into an ill-conceived attack. But even working through every contingency, she couldn't find it, and dread crept into her belly as they rode toward the front.

12

ARAK'JUR

Outside the Steam Tents
The Sinari Village

Cold air passed through the elders as they stood beneath a moonless sky. An ill omen, on a night when they needed no portents of shadows over their future. Already too many stood waiting, gathered near the heart of the village. When the shamans arrived, the deliberations would begin in earnest, crowding the steam tents past the point of breaking. But for now they waited.

Corenna stood at his side, dressed in the full regalia of a Ranasi woman, the white dress and blue paint on her skin, the thick braid bound by cord for her hair. Asseena wore a similar style, though her furs were thicker, her hair bound but not braided, the designs painted on her face showing different markings. Ghella wore the Sinari women's dress, and Symara the Ganherat's. The rest wore fine clothing, as fine as they possessed, but the spirit-touched were few, even among the remnants of six tribes. Four women. Two apprentice shamans. One guardian. A frightening thing, for their people to be so near the loss of any of the three lines of the spirits' magic.

A small boy approached the throng, and every head turned as he made his way up the path.

"Honored sisters," the boy said when he arrived outside the tent.

"Elders. Honored guardian. The shamans bid you wait as they listen to the spirits. They will come soon, to speak of what they have seen and heard. But not yet."

Murmurs followed the boy as he wheeled and went back the way he came, and another gust of cold wind carried the words through the crowd. But none showed any intent to leave. The elders had gathered at sundown, having heard the news of the Nanerat's arrival, wishing to be present for the formal induction of a new tribe into their alliance. But it was well past twilight now, and still they waited.

"What do you suppose it means?" Corenna asked in a low voice. "I've never known a vision to take so long, in all the years witnessing my father's gift."

He eyed Asseena before replying. The Nanerat woman stood alone, only she and Ilek'Hannat serving as elders among the remnants of their tribe.

"The Nanerat are a strong people," he said. "They have endured much. We must give the spirits time to find a path for all of us, together."

Corenna nodded, though he saw worry under her veneer of calm.

Another hour passed, and sleep threatened to take some, though most remained standing. And when Ilek'Inari showed himself, clad in white furs pristine as untouched snow, even Arak'Jur couldn't have said whether the shaman appeared from nothing, or he had blinked to rest his eyes, and missed the apprentice's approach.

Relieved sighs passed through the crowd, and the youngest, who had situated themselves at the entrance, opened the tent flaps, prepared to light the fires that would steam the rocks within.

"No," Ilek'Inari said. "It is not the spirits' will, for us to meet in council tonight."

Silence fell behind the apprentice shaman's words, and Ilek'Inari met Arak'Jur's eyes as he spoke again.

"Gather the folk of every tribe," Ilek'Inari said. "Men, women, children. Tonight we sit in judgment."

"Judgment?" Ghella said, pushing forward from among the women of the Sinari. "Judgment for what? Who among us stands accused?"

Ilek'Inari held Arak'Jur's gaze.

"Arak'Jur," he said. "If he is being hunted, we must decide whether exiling one man is preferable to war."

———————

A greatfire raged by the time the village was emptied, a sea of tired faces roused from sleep, sober and unbelieving. The smallest children cried out, but the rest were quiet, a mix of wonder and whispered speculation as they filed into the meeting area where Ilek'Hannat tended the flame.

Six places had been made at the head of the gathering, on log benches between the audience and the fire. Four for the women, two for the shamans. The seventh place was his, standing at the center of every eye between the benches. He waited in silence as the tribes were roused to take up places on the grass. He had done nothing. The spirits could be inscrutable, but until the last year he had never known them to be unjust. Ilek'Inari seemed to wilt when Arak'Jur looked to him for answers, and Corenna simmered with cold rage in her place as judge. It was their way to honor the shamans' spirits, and so he did, but if the corrupt voices had taken hold of Ilek'Inari or Ilek'Hannat, the night could well end in blood. A sorrowful thought, and a blasphemous one, but he was past such concerns. Or, he could be, for his people's sake. For now, he waited to see what would come of the shamans' visions, until the last of the tribes were gathered, and Ilek'Inari rose to speak.

"We have gathered at the spirits' behest," Ilek'Inari said, his voice ringing clear over the crowd. By now the night had deepened, closer to sunrise than the day before, and stillness hung over the village, amplified by the gravity of the apprentice shaman's tone and the weight behind his words. "They have shown us the way forward, for our people."

A hissing bang sounded from the fire, met with gasps from the crowd. Arak'Jur turned to watch as billowing red smoke rose into the sky. Another surprise; he had never seen shamans work ritual magic so openly, the smokes and powders of the divining ritual used to find the great beasts. Yet here it was, displayed for all to see.

The red smoke rose to form shapes writ against the night sky. A cat. A bear. A stag. More. Wolf and dog, lizard and beetle, toad and bird and crocodile. A dozen shapes, until they ran together. An army of beasts. And still they grew, more and more forms taking shape before they blended into the mass arrayed against the stars.

Fear and awe stirred in Arak'Jur's belly, given voice in gasps and screams from the crowd.

"We are coming," another voice said. Ilek'Hannat, standing beside the fire, though the apprentice shaman's words seemed to rise with the smoke, forming from the mouths of the beasts as he spoke them. "We seek the Ascendant of the Wild."

"See what we face," Ilek'Inari shouted, directed to the assembled six but loud enough to carry through the crowd. "The great beasts. And more."

As he said it the smoke rippled, shifting from beasts to men. A thousand shapes of men and women, raising weapons, charging forward until they burst into wisps of red vapor. Screams rose from the crowd at the moment of impact, turned to sobbing as the images faded from the sky.

"How can we trust these sendings?" Ghella demanded from beside the fire. "The spirits have whispered of doom too long for us to believe it now."

"It is true, honored sister," Ilek'Inari said, sadness in his voice. "Some among the spirits of things-to-come are corrupted. But their corruption is a power unto itself, and on this, we have heard both kinds speak as one."

"Death," Ilek'Hannat said loudly, his words still echoing from the clouds of formless smoke in the air. "We demand it. The Wild is ours, and we will not surrender lightly. We see you, and we are coming."

"We can fight," Symara said. "Our people are strong. If these malign spirits seek to challenge our alliance, they will not find us cowering in fear."

"Not us, sister," Asseena said. "They are not coming for us."

Corenna was already staring at him when the rest turned to where he stood.

"Arak'Jur," Corenna whispered.

"Arak'Jur," Ilek'Hannat repeated, the same whisper seeming to come from the smoke, a thousand miniature voices echoing his name.

Dread settled on him like a fog. An Ascendant of the Wild. He'd been named as much, at Nanek'Hai'Tyat. He hadn't understood what it meant then, but hearing it now, with all the trappings of judgment, it stung deep. The crowd took up the charge in whispers, giving voice to their fears by speaking his name. An omen of fear, and death.

He'd believed it of himself since he became guardian, unforeseen, the mark of a curse. Now every eye of their alliance confirmed it. He'd wondered why Ilek'Inari had summoned every member of the tribes. Now he knew. They meant for him to leave, and they needed every tribesman to see the cost if he refused.

"Go," Ilek'Hannat whispered. His voice before had been dark and terrible, booming like thunder through the shapes writ in smoke above the crowd. Now it was changed—different, somehow. Softer. Almost a woman's voice. "Arak'Jur. Go and seek your strength, while you might still become my champion. Do not fear. You are—"

"—marked for death," Ilek'Hannat finished, his voice returned to how it had been before. "We are coming."

Ilek'Inari went to Ilek'Hannat's side, and laid a hand on the other apprentice's shoulder. The greatfire returned to an ordinary blaze, and the smoke cleared from the sky, its red hue dissipated into gray wisps swallowed by the light of the stars.

"We call for judgment from our elders," Ilek'Inari said. "You have seen what the spirits foretell. But the decision falls to us, as leaders of these tribes."

Tears ran down Corenna's face, as she was the first to rise from her seat. "I won't," she said, first softly, for his benefit, then again, louder. "I won't pronounce judgment, no matter the threat he brings on us by staying. He is our guardian. We couldn't survive without him."

He longed to go to her, to wrap a hand around her, to draw her close enough to feel her belly pressed against him, where his son or daughter grew within. Instead he rose out of turn to speak.

"Is this the spirits' will?" he asked. "Is it their will for this alliance to be left alone, without a guardian, defenseless against the wild?"

The unspoken accusation ran beneath his words: that the apprentices had misunderstood, or been deceived by the corrupt spirits. He wished it were so, even as he recalled the memory of *astahg* fighting alongside the Uktani, or older, of *ipek'a* fighting alongside Arak'Atan. The great beasts were roused to the causes of men, or men were roused to theirs; the fact of it was plain, though the cause lay beyond his understanding.

"The foul spirits seek men and women of power," Ilek'Hannat said, his voice returned to normal, without the influence of the spirits. "They demand that these men and women surrender to their will, or die."

"Ascendants," Ilek'Inari said. "Those with the beast magic of the guardians and the war-magic of the land. They are unsure why these gifts have merged, but they speak of a Goddess, who has need of their power, in times to come."

The Goddess. He'd heard the spirits speak of her, of her need. He'd never understood, before.

"If you stay among us," Ilek'Inari continued, "the beasts will come, and the warriors sworn to their cause. We may be weakened without your protection, but we have the women's gift—"

"No," Corenna said. "I won't stay behind. If Arak'Jur is hunted, I will be hunted with him."

Arak'Jur winced. He hadn't yet considered what Corenna would do. The shamans fell quiet, glancing between each other, and the women. Symara had a single gift of the land, the weaving of stone from Ondan'Ai'Tyat, and Ghella had only the visions of Ka'Ana'Tyat, the Sinari sacred place. Neither would be enough if a great beast threatened their people. Even Ilek'Inari's gift from *una're* would fall short if *valak'ar* or *kirighra* came near the village.

"Honored sister…" Ghella began.

"Don't ask it," Corenna said. "My people were slaughtered, and I forgave it for the madness it was. But I will not abandon Arak'Jur to die, not when his child grows inside me. You cannot expect me to do this. You cannot."

She showed ferocity in her expression, but he could see her trembling, and knew it for more than anger boiling in her veins. Madness had cost her every comfort in her life, all save his company. He understood; even faced with the prospect of banishment for the good of the tribes, he would not want to face the wild alone. Duty compelled him to go, and her to stay, but weighed against the death of a wife, a husband, a child, all other concern gave way to desperation. And from desperation, clarity.

"We are not the only people with the strength to survive in these lands."

The words sounded foreign to his ears, even as he spoke them. The rest of the men and women around the fire looked to him with a blend of curiosity and confusion.

"I will not stay among our people," he continued. "Not when my presence draws such strength arrayed against us. Nor will I ask Corenna to stay behind. I mean to face our enemies, to find the source of their corruption and root it out. For that I will need her strength. But I will also need surety of this people's safety. And for that I turn to the fair-skins, whose barrier is proof against the creatures of the wild."

13

SARINE

Approaching Lavendon Abbey
Near the Great Barrier

S unset streaked behind them, painting the clouds a blend of purple and blue. Zi's scales seemed to mirror the hues, flashing as he lay draped across her saddle. His pallor had recovered after the slaughter in the market, but he'd remained visible, sickly, and weak as they'd followed the roads north. For the twentieth time she questioned the decision to chase Axerian, and redoubled her conviction as she clung to her gelding's reins.

The barrier had grown in the time they'd spent on the road, from a blue line shimmering in the distance to a towering haze, consuming half the sky in either direction. Hard to fathom the barrier could be real, seeing it so close. A marvel of engineering, and it ran unbroken from the coastline here to the tip of the Thellan colonies in the south, beyond even the Gand territories. She might have appreciated it more if not for Zi, and for feeling like her backside had been beaten with reeds after two days in the saddle.

"That's the abbey's spires," Acherre said, pointing to a dark shape silhouetted against the barrier's haze. "Shall we make a race of it, the rest of the way?"

"No," she said. "Zi does best under a steady walk."

The reminder seemed to sober the captain's mood, and Acherre nodded as she and her mount fell into step beside Sarine's gelding.

"We'll have to get you a proper mount," Acherre replied. "A well-trained binder's mount is worth a company of muskets, in the right hands."

Acherre stroked her horse's mane, and the creature whickered without missing a step. Their movements were as fluid as Sarine was sure her own were not, and if Acherre had any sores she hadn't needed *Life* when they'd put in at a farming village the night before. Horses and riding had always had a certain appeal, a majestic cadence to it when teams of four or six drove carriages through the Gardens. She'd imagined riding one couldn't be all that different from being driven by them, more fool her.

Another quarter league and the abbey resolved from silhouette to wood and stone. Her uncle's chapel was a lavish affair in comparison, the Sacre-Lin's stone and stained glass cutting a sharp relief against the dull brown rectangles clustered around the abbey's spire, but any comfort would be welcome after a few days on the road. There were a dozen such abbeys placed along the barrier, charged with maintaining the *Shelter* bindings that kept it standing against the wild. With luck the priests would recognize Axerian from the drawings she carried. And surely even priests had to keep warm water on hand for a bath.

Acherre called something to her, muted and lost on the wind as the captain charged her horse forward.

Her gelding skittered to follow, caught between obeying her hold on the reins and charging alongside Acherre, but Zi was in no condition for a gallop, let alone a run, and for a moment her attention turned to struggling not to fall.

"Dead," Acherre called back. "The priests. Their bodies...my Gods."

Acherre had dismounted in the outer yard, and now hovered over what appeared to be three brown-robed figures sleeping beside a stone well. Sarine scooped Zi into her arms, careful to cradle him against her chest as she swung a leg over her gelding's flank, dropping the reins as she all but jumped from the saddle, her mount as eager to be free of her as she was of it.

"The snake we saw in the market," Acherre said. "It must have come through the barrier here."

"I don't think so," Sarine said, nestling Zi into place across her shoulders. "It might be the snake, but the ones it killed were sickly, covered with rot. These are different."

She pointed toward a man in priest's robes, with pale skin, cold and gray, but where the man's eyes should have been there were empty sockets, as though carrion birds had come and pecked them clean while leaving the rest alone.

Acherre nodded, pacing between the bodies. Another two shapes lay on the path from the well to the inner yard, and no doubts there would be more.

"Could it be the assassin?" Acherre asked. "These priests have been dead for days. If it was his work, he'll have moved on. We should check the rest of the abbey, then do the same."

She shook her head. "It isn't like Axerian to kill innocents, not unless he sees no other way."

Acherre raised an eyebrow. "You know him that well?"

"I . . ." she began.

The world lurched.

She stood on a field of ice, a rolling tundral plain beneath a darkened sky. Armored figures lay dead around her, piled deep and caked in snow and frozen blood.

Worry for Zi surged, and panic. But her emotions counted for nothing here; she tried to move, to shout, to fight and make it go away. Instead she stood, as frozen as the corpses, and heard a voice roaring with the fury of battle beside her.

Paendurion.

Fire crackled around him as *Shelter* shielded him from the heat, and he danced forward, toward the last man standing on the Regnant's—her ancient enemy's—side of the field.

Shelter dissolved the moment before impact, and Paendurion's longblade clanged as it met his opponent's folded steel. Her champion shifted his massive girth behind his shield, and his enemy twisted, evading his attacks, weaving purple lines in the air with the dessicated remains of his free hand. A sheet of glass turned Paendurion's attack, conjured and shattering at the last instant, and the other man darted forward, striking with the sword in his hand and four new glass shards conjured in the air. *Death* tore them apart as they flew, and Paendurion rushed into the man, bashing through another sheet of glass with his shield.

Paendurion's enemy staggered backward, weaving a barrier of light between them, and Ad-Shi gored him from behind. Spectral claws emerged from his belly, and the Regnant's final champion died, gasping for air as Ad-Shi twisted her hands, rending his flesh to pulp.

A voice sounded in her ears: *FOR THIS ONE, IT ENDS.*

Paendurion dropped his sword.

"It's done," her champion of Order said, emotion welling in his voice as tears mixed with blood and dirt on his face.

It was.

Power flowed into her, a torrent of energy. A sea of possibility, already changing the face of the world.

"Forgive me," Axerian whispered, and black claws tore into her from behind. Sorrow and shock overpowered her senses, and she screamed. Betrayal. The world shuddered, and she rushed to complete what she'd begun.

Air choked from her lungs, and tears soaked her cheeks. Sunlight burned on her skin.

Blue light flashed, and a sensation of... sobbing?

I can't stop it. Zi's voice, and she recognized the sobbing as coming from him, a tide of emotion and despair.

"Sarine?" Acherre asked.

A hand propped her up, steady on the small of her back, with another around her arm to brace her.

Her vision returned, shimmering from moisture in her eyes.

"No," she said, rushing to cradle Zi from atop her shoulder. "Not another one. I'm sorry, Zi. I don't know what's wrong with me."

Zi writhed in her arms, constricting his body to dig his claws into her skin. She reached to shelter him by reflex.

"That's what hurts you, isn't it?" she asked. "Each time... each time I see these things."

Yes.

She hadn't expected otherwise. But hearing it tore her through the heart.

"I'm sorry," she said, barely above a whisper. He felt brittle against her skin, like cold glass on the cusp of breaking.

Acherre walked a few paces away, giving her and Zi space as she inspected the priests' bodies.

"I count seven, in the yard," Acherre said quietly. "There may be more inside. And I need to check the barrier."

Sarine said nothing, cradling Zi as she walked to sit atop the well. Emotion hadn't helped him after all; his color had refreshed after the murders in the market, but he was still languid, as infirm as any poxy child. She needed answers. Without knowing what was wrong, she couldn't begin to help him recover, or stop the visions. If the answer lay there, perhaps she could piece together what had triggered them. That was something at least.

NO.

The thought roared in her mind, as fierce and strong as Zi had ever sent, and a white shield flared to cover her left side, where a tiny lizard had clamped its jaws around her finger.

She leapt to her feet, shaking her arm to fling the lizard into the dirt, but Zi acted first, a wave of purple light flaring in her vision as the creature exploded into ribbons of gore and paste.

Shock glazed over her senses. The lizard had bitten her. Zi would never have reacted so strongly against a common reptile; it had to be one of the terrors native to the New World. She stared between the empty-eyed corpses and the stain of brown and red Zi had made of the lizard in the mud beneath the well. He'd saved her life. Not that he hadn't done the same a hundred times over with his gifts of *Red* and *Green* and *Yellow*, but it was something else seeing him act directly. And now he was frozen, quivering as he coiled around her forearm.

"Zi," she said. "I..."

"Gods," Acherre said, coming around the side of the abbey. "There are holes here all right, bores through the barrier wide enough to drive a cart through. Clean made, too, no sign of fraying or...what's wrong?"

Sarine wiped tears from her cheeks, cradling Zi against her chest with her other hand. She was doing this. Her inattention had caused him to overexert himself, as sure as these Nameless-cursed visions were responsible for his sickness.

"A...a lizard. A beast. It attacked and Zi killed it."

"A lizard?" Acherre asked. "Like the snake in the market, or something else?"

She stood, keeping Zi close to her skin. She wanted to cradle him there, hold him and assure him she'd find a way to make things right. But tears and weeping wouldn't bring her any closer to Axerian.

"You said there were holes in the barrier," she said instead.

Acherre nodded. "That's right. Like nothing I've ever seen. Even with these priests dead, it should have taken longer for the *Shelter* to decay, and no binding unravels as clean as this."

"Show me," she said, and let Acherre lead the way.

They went around the abbey, where weeds had already started breaking through what had been well-tended grass and gardens. A wheelbarrow had been left full of mud, now leaking rainwater into a puddle in the dirt. Signs of well-tended grounds, interrupted by whatever terrors had come through the barrier that had been their most important charge. No chance the priests had let the stretch of the barrier right behind their abbey fall into disrepair. Yet as soon as she and Acherre rounded the main building, she saw the holes, clear as she saw the barrier itself. Two gaps in the blue haze, made with clean, fine cuts, as though the pearls of *Shelter* had been split with a razor's edge.

"*Black*," Sarine said. "It has to be. It was him. Axerian was here."

"Black?" Acherre asked.

She cradled Zi closer to her chest. Even with the horror of what Axerian had done here, knowing they were following his trail put a spark in her belly. "A *kaas* power. Like *Yellow*, or *Green*. It disrupts magic."

"Like a *Death* binding?" Acherre said. "Though I've never seen a *Death* binding cut this cleanly."

"It's similar, in some ways. But worse. And not without its costs." She almost shuddered, remembering the waves of pleasure when she killed, the barest taste of Zi's harvest from death and murder. A foul thing, made worse for her bond to Zi making it feel sweet. "*Black* disrupts magic, like *Death* does, but it takes it in, allows its wielder to borrow..."

"Hm?" Acherre asked. "To borrow what?"

Words slid away from her. The barrier towered overhead, and it should have turned her stomach to see any hole in it at all. Instead she caught a movement, something faint and out of place.

"Sarine?" Acherre asked.

"This is wrong," she said. "Axerian...he did something, here. More than *Black*."

And suddenly, she saw it.

Blue sparks, the same color as the swirling haze above the holes, but different. They'd been woven into the fabric of the *Shelter* itself. Axerian had called it a warding, when he'd first shown it to her: the blue sparks that allowed her to set anchors and channel leyline and *kaas* energies from somewhere else, somewhere far away, even if she wasn't there in person. She'd seen that same energy around Reyne d'Agarre's Codex, and again in the sewers, guarding the place the strange spirit voices had named Tanir'Ras'Tyat. And now she saw it here, dancing among the strands of *Shelter* in the towering haze of the barrier, a mesh of blue sparks woven as far as she could see in both directions.

She reached for it, the same as she'd done before, and the blue sparks obeyed. A slow trickle at first, then faster. They'd been woven into the barrier itself, but they unknotted at her touch, as though she picked apart a knitted pair of stockings or a rug.

"He set wardings here," she said as the sparks pulled toward her. "Gods, Acherre, he wove wardings into the barrier. They'll let him channel the *kaas*' gifts as though he were here in person. If he has enough of them, he could—"

Black.

The warning sounded like a bell in her ears.

Holes appeared in the barrier, a hundred at once, as far east and west as she could see. In an instant the towering haze shimmered, all hundred handspans of swirling blue film seeming to wane like the last slivers of a sunset. Then it was gone.

The barrier was gone.

Trees and grass stretched to the horizon. Bushes rustled where squirrels or rabbits might have nestled against the barrier before it vanished. Otherwise the land was quiet, as still and calm as any ordinary wooded plain.

14

ERRIS

Atop an Unnamed Hill
Near Ansfield Crossing, Gand Territory

Musket fire sounded in the distance, popping and rippling across the field. She reined Jiri to a halt and the rest of her retinue followed her lead, planting her flags atop the hillside behind the 3rd Division's supply line. Gods damn the stars on her collar; she'd as soon have been in the thick of it, feeling the rhythm of the fight as it unfolded around her. Instead she made do with a spyglass, panning to see the lay of the battle that had found them here, unexpected but not unwelcome, given the ground.

Vassail had taken the initiative, seizing a ring of hills and fortifying them with a screen of infantry between the town of Ansfield and the best approaches to her line. Long guns were coming up the hillsides now, nine- and twelve-pounders pulled by teams of half a dozen horses each. They should have had to bleed for this position; the Gandsmen should have been the ones with artillery in place to shell every inch of the fields surrounding the town. Instead the red and white flags of Gand decorated lines that seemed timid, rows of infantry slow to deploy and slower to grasp the importance of the terrain.

"High Commander, sir," Vassail said as she rode up the hillside, offering a salute beneath a wide-brimmed hat she must have donned for the sake of the southern heat. "They only just told me you'd arrived. My apologies for my absence, along with my compliments."

She snapped the spyglass shut. "Fine work here, General," she said, and meant it. "Any guesses as to why the Gandsmen made it this easy for you?"

Vassail grinned. She was young, no more than thirty, but with a hardness in her born of years' experience with wartime command. "A simple blunder, sir," she replied. "We arrived to find them fortifying around the crossing, as if we'd up and ford the river without securing our flanks. The heights were empty. I sent skirmishers to pin them down while the rest of my division pulled back and dug in here."

Another wave of artillery sounded, four or five leagues distant, enough to dim the sound to tiny pops, and obscure altogether the screams that would go with them. Erris raised her spyglass again, pivoting southward to scan the tree line near the river. It made no sense. Ceding the choicest ground on the battlefield was a fool's mistake, the sort made by novice commanders pushed into action by bureaucrats and newspapermen.

"Are those guns with Royens's corps, sir?" Vassail asked.

She nodded. "He has orders to drive south-southwest, and hold the junction there."

"Sir, we have the initiative here," Vassail said. "If you order Royens up the roads, to flank the enemy's line while we hold the heights—it could decide the battle today, push him off the rivers and secure the crossings."

"Field-Marshal Royens has orders to hold back, not to engage." She snapped the spyglass shut again. Good enough for a firsthand look; the scouts would have detailed reports for the rest. "You've done fine work here, General. But your orders are to hold this position. Check the enemy's ability to redeploy his forces here, against an attempt to flank us on the route to Covendon. You are not to attack."

"Sir, we can press our advantage. Even if the enemy is holding back, trying to trap us in the south, he's weak enough for us to break his line before he could bring up a reserve."

"You have your orders, General."

Vassail's boldness had earned them an easy victory, there for the taking, if Erris had been willing to order the attack. Another handful of brigades might decide this battle, and she had eight divisions uncommitted between her three corps. But the Gand army had to be out there, hiding some reserve, part of a ploy to offer her a plum at Ansfield, then swallow her whole when she took it. Vassail could be the daring mouse, snatching cheese from the trap when they knew it had been set, but she couldn't order the full strength of the army to follow the example.

"Sir," Vassail said. "If I do this, I do it under protest. We can break them, here. Today. If we give the enemy time to fortify, it may cost a thousand lives to push them out of the town. Give me two divisions, and I will hand us a victory."

"I put my flag here, and came here in person, to judge it for myself. If circumstances change, so will the orders. Until then, see to your division, General. Dismissed."

Vassail's eyes flashed a bare hint of the fury Erris was sure was hiding under the surface. She'd been given stupid orders often enough to recognize the look; but this was no blunder on her part. The enemy commander was out there, the man behind the threads of *Need* who had almost beaten her twice. A novice's mistake could be a master's gambit, and until she knew which was which, she had enough strength to hold back and force his hand.

"Good at hiding her anger, that one," Foot-Captain Marquand said after Vassail and her aides were riding down the hillside. "You sure she's not right?"

"No," she said, and nudged Jiri toward Marquand, offering a hand to help him up into the saddle behind her.

"Going to use *Need* again?"

"I have to. Vassail's doubts are a pale shadow next to mine. I need reports from the south to be able to piece this together."

"Aren't we stopping here? You can use *Need* without risking falling off the bloody horse, and leave me out of it."

"Get up here, Captain. I need you to hold me in place. And no; we're moving toward the front. The enemy is going to spring this trap, and soon, and I intend to see it the instant he does."

Marquand grunted and accepted her hand, swinging up to hold her around the waist. She relayed the order to reposition her flag to her aides, and made sure Jiri was moving and Marquand was in place before she slid her eyes shut. A sea of gold greeted her, dim awareness of hundreds of vessels and the golden threads between them. She snapped a tether in place to one stationed leagues to the south, somehow knowing precisely whom she'd chosen, though she still didn't understand *Need*'s workings in depth. Enough that her senses shifted, giving her precious minutes—or seconds—before the binding shattered.

Her vessel was in a tent filled with pipe smoke, a cloud thick enough to wrap its occupants in a dim haze. Field-Marshal de Tourvalle, commander of her 2nd Corps, stood opposite a long table with the offending pipe in hand, accompanied by a woman and two men, each bearing a colonel's insignia. It took another instant to recognize them as de Tourvalle's cavalry commanders, including Brigade-Colonel d'Guile, her former second with the 14th Light Cavalry, now promoted to her old unit's command.

"Respectfully, sir," d'Guile was saying, "this proves it, beyond any questioning. Why would their papers print the thing, if it weren't true?"

"Perhaps precisely because they suspected you'd find it and bring it here." That was Brigade-Colonel Valerie de Montaigne, commander of the 11th and General Vassail's handpicked successor.

"And the six hours my men spent among their tents?" d'Guile shot back. "Not a single instance of their golden light. Not one."

"What's this?" Erris asked through her vessel—a young woman with a voice pitched almost low enough to be a man's. Always disconcerting, when her vessel's characteristics differed sharply from the familiar.

"Ah, High Commander," Field-Marshal de Tourvalle said. "We were just entertaining debate over Colonel d'Guile's latest field report."

"They've lost it, sir," d'Guile said, beaming like a schoolboy who'd nicked his neighbor's pie. "They've lost *Need*. I led a team from the Fourteenth into their camp. Five others can confirm it: None of the Gand officers have the golden light behind their eyes, not anywhere in the camp. And I intercepted this."

He indicated a newspaper lying atop the table at the center of the tent, bearing a simple headline: *Chamberlain Promoted to Command; Promises Swift Action Against the Enemy.*

She reread it. "Chamberlain?" she said. It could only mean Major-General Marianne Chamberlain, who'd had the 1st Corps of the Gand 3rd Army the year before. A blind fool of a commander, with a propensity to order her divisions to sit waiting for hours while she wheeled long guns into immaculate positions for where the battle would have been, had she engaged at once instead of dithering for artillery support.

"Chamberlain." D'Guile nodded. "Two of my scouts confirmed it with spoken rumors, and one by sight. The old bitch has the command, sir."

The maneuvers around Ansfield replayed themselves in her mind. Yes, Chamberlain was fool enough to expect an exact repeat of the Sarresant invasion from the previous campaign. A new commander, under pressure from her peers to attack, when prudence dictated caution. The resulting haste might explain bungling the trap the Gandsmen had meant to set at Ansfield, ceding the heights while they set up batteries at the river crossing. And most importantly: Chamberlain could have been fool enough to miss the importance of the roads south to Covendon, or at least to expect her to miss it, too.

It was too neat. It had to be a trap.

Was the enemy's true commander that good? Not Chamberlain—the man behind the golden light. But to refrain from using *Need* anywhere her scouts could see, to maneuver his army in the precise manner of a novice, a feint to trap her in the northern colonies while leaving the way to their capital undefended... It would require sheer brilliance, perfect execution from the highest levels of command down to the line officers, the quartermasters, sentries and...

No.

Fear bloomed in her stomach, but instinct overpowered it. This was no trap. This was exactly what it looked like, and she was wasting the initiative with indecision.

"South," she said, meeting d'Guile's eye with a look of approval before she wheeled toward the others. "I want every corps on the march. Send riders for Royens and Etaigne, and get the Second Corps marshaled on the double. We move for Covendon. The objective is to seize the Gand colonies' capital, imprison their Parliament, and end this war before the campaign begins."

"Sir," Brigade-Colonel de Montaigne said. "We can't be certain of their numbers. If they have reserves in the west, they could pincer us between their force at Ansfield. They could cut us off from home."

"I have no doubt that's exactly what General Chamberlain meant to try," she said. "But that leaves the Gandsmen a seven-hundred-league march to reach anything of value north of Lorrine, and we're days away from their capital."

"What of Vassail's division at Ansfield?" de Tourvalle asked. "We'd be sacrificing her position to entangle the enemy. Casualties would be heavy."

"As it happens, I am there in person at present. Vassail can hold, and Chevalier-General Perand has Royens's Ninth Cavalry nearby for support. I'll ride west and take personal command of the reserve. If you and Field-Marshal Etaigne can—"

Her senses splintered, the golden light shattering like a pane of glass.

"Gods fucking damn it!" she roared, making Jiri miss a step. Marquand tightened his grip around her waist, and she stayed in the saddle, for all she might have otherwise tumbled down in anger before her senses cleared. *Need* had shattered again, and she was once again on Jiri's back, riding down a steep slope toward the sounds of musket fire through the trees.

"Steady, sir," Marquand said. "Are you all right?"

She grabbed hold of the reins, pivoting Jiri around into her column of aides.

"Send a rider for General Vassail," she said. "And turn our column around. We ride west, on the double."

Her aides snapped into action at once, asking no questions before they moved to execute her orders. Gods bless their discipline, and Gods damn the shortcomings of *Need* breaking before she could fully deliver a plan to move the army. It meant couriers, delays, and putting trust in her field commanders. After a season of *Need* the old way felt cumbersome, but just as well she'd uprooted the old command structure and put men like Etaigne, Royens, and de Tourvalle in charge of her soldiers. They'd need to be swift to make the turn south toward Covendon, but she could do this. It felt right. D'Guile's revelation that the man behind the Gandsmen's golden light of *Need* had been removed from command had been the last piece she'd needed to understand the shape of this campaign. The time for planning was over. The time for action was here, whether they were ready or no.

"First east toward the front line, and now we're riding west?" Marquand said.

"Just hold tight," she said as Jiri wheeled around. "Keep me in place and we'll be in the thick of it soon enough."

"Wait, you mean to use *Need* again?" Marquand asked. "Didn't it just bloody shatter in your face?"

"No choice, Captain. If my guess is right, the enemy has a force in the west, waiting to strike Vassail as soon as she's engaged. General Perand needs to know it before we arrive in person. Now hold on."

Need glimmered as she shifted her sight, but this time the golden light seemed sharpened to points, each one like a shard of glass ready to break at the slightest touch. She had to be quick.

"High Commander," a ragged voice said as soon as she made the tether. "Thank the Gods."

Her vision shifted into focus. Quiet; no sounds of musket fire or artillery shot. Only open plains, clear to a strange line between rolling grass and thick brush a hundred paces off, as though some overzealous gardener had cut wild forest like a nobleman's hedge maze.

"It's gone, sir," the voice said. Chevalier-General Perand, commander of the 9th Cavalry, though he sounded more a worried graybeard than a seasoned commander. "Bloody curse us all for fools, it's gone."

"Slow down, General," she said. "Report. What's gone?"

"The Great Barrier, sir. I swear to the Gods themselves, my scouts saw it vanish; one moment it stood, the same as ever. The next..." He gestured toward the break between the grass and the trees. "Gone."

Her stomach lurched, and she stared. She'd been expecting a trap, even if it had been a trap set by a fool. But this...

The enemy had beaten her again. She couldn't yet piece together why, or how the barrier's collapse would lead to her defeat. But she saw his hand in it, and that was enough to be sure. Despair clawed through her, and before she could reply the golden light shattered, throwing her senses back atop Jiri's saddle.

15

TIGAI

A Dark Room
Somewhere Near the Emperor's Palace

The starfield faded, and the air changed from southern wind to a stale, cloistered calm.

"Wh—" a man began, and Remarin knifed him in the throat.

The servant's body slumped forward as the Ujibari chieftain pressed a hand to his mouth to stifle any cries. Tigai's head reeled, the smells of dust and sour wine hanging in the air. He'd shifted them halfway across the Empire, and it left him haggard, breathing hard and seeing double until the strands cleared from his eyes. Darkness helped; a hooded lamp rolling on the ground where the servant had dropped it was the only source of light in the otherwise windowless room.

Remarin's men moved at once, fanning out among barrels and casks stacked in neat rows up and down the chamber.

"Where have you taken us?" Remarin asked, holding the dead or dying servant tight in his arms as blood ran down his shirt.

Tigai shook his head. No way to be sure, and Remarin should have known better than to ask.

Remarin scowled as one of the Ujibari stooped to pick up the lamp, casting light on the servant's last struggles before the man went limp in Remarin's arms. A poor omen to have a servant here at the moment of their arrival. Then again, the starfield could as easily have put them in the throne room with the Emperor in state, surrounded by sentries shocked to see a company of armed men appear without warning. Just as well they'd appeared somewhere free of sentries, and remote enough, judging from the quiet in the halls beyond.

One of Remarin's men returned, wearing a stone look without a glance for the dead servant.

"We're in a cellar beneath a kitchen," the soldier said. "But it isn't the Imperial palace proper."

Both the soldier and Remarin gave him a withering look.

"Never promised I could get us there precisely," he said, trying for a smile that ended in a grimace through the pain in his head. "Not when my subjects are fresh dead."

"If the wind spirits smile on us, we'll be in one of the adjoining palaces," Remarin said. "The magistrates' estates, or the servants' manor. Anywhere else and we call this off. You can return us to Yanjin, yes, my lord?"

"We won't have time for another attempt," Tigai said. "It took six weeks to find those three."

"And the same amount to get accurate maps of the Emperor's palace. But if you've put us somewhere else, even somewhere close, those maps won't count for the ink they're drawn with."

Wit soured on his tongue before he spoke. Remarin was right. Their plan hinged on quiet movement through the Kanjiao Palace, with force enough to overpower any sentries and avoid undue attention before they could escape. A half league in the wrong direction and his magic might as well have put them in the sand seas. Even if they were within the Imperial City proper, scaling the outer walls that ringed the palaces of the Imperial gardens would all but certainly end with their heads parted from their necks by a headsman's blade.

Remarin led the way through the cellar, the lamplight flickering shadows of the casks against the walls as they passed. The room was dank but wide, with rough stonework on the walls and enough wine and barreled foodstuffs to feed a thousand lords and keep them drunk and laughing. A hundred casks at least, and as many crates and boxes. A good sign that they were at least within *a* palace, if not the Imperial one. And just as good that Remarin's men hadn't yet doubled back with warnings of sentries or other such trouble; a dozen had gone ahead, climbing the stairs at the end of the chamber to clear the rooms above and report their whereabouts as soon as they discerned them.

Blood pooled on the floor at the top of the stairwell, close enough that he almost stepped in it before he saw its source. Three dead cooks, servants with the same misfortune as the man who'd gone to fetch the wine. The rest of the room was quiet. Open flames sizzled beneath iron pots, where cabbages half chopped with onions, peppers, meat, and spices made a pleasant smell that promised dinner, though it would never be finished now. The rest of Remarin's men arrayed themselves about the kitchen, flanking the entrances in case another servant had the misfortune to join his fellows.

"We're done here," Remarin said. "Lord Tigai, prepare to take us back."

Remarin's words lanced through him. He'd scarce had time to survey the room. "No," he said. "Where are we? We have to be sure."

"Those are eunuchs, my lord," Remarin said, a pointed gesture directing his meaning to the bodies leaking blood toward the stairwell.

Tigai gave them a second look. Yes, he could see it, as much as one could tell anything from the shape of a corpse's face. Soft features, hairless like boys. Eunuchs made fine servants, so it was said, though they didn't come cheaply. To have three—four perhaps, if the first man they'd encountered shared their affliction—meant the owner of this palace was at least a wealthy man. And who would waste eunuchs on kitchen fare, when uncut cooks could be had for a tenth their price?

"Oh, fire spirits fuck me in the eyes," Tigai said. "We're in the harem."

"We're in the harem's kitchens," Remarin said. "And we need to be well on our way back home before His Majesty's guards come looking. We're not prepared for this."

Tigai kept his head down, skirting toward an open window. Tranquil gardens blossomed on the grounds outside, the sort of idyllic pasture he might imagine building, if he owned a score of women devoted to giving him pleasure. Tall reeds stood beside a winding stream, with purple and orange flowers, and gold banners—the Emperor's colors—hanging from stone walls ringing the enclosure. Great palaces for each consort would be built around the common ground, places for their denizens to lie idle until they were summoned by His Majesty.

Remarin was right; they needed to get out of here. Setting foot in the harem was death, for him, his men, and any girl they came close enough to have had a chance to ruin with their non-Imperial seed. But leaving was death, too, in its way. Leaving meant the banks would have their due. The Yanjin family would be ruined, Dao tried and sentenced as a debtor, Mei auctioned to an end no better than the girls imprisoned here.

"You're right, of course," Tigai said.

"Good. There will be another day for riches. I'll rally the—"

"You're right, but even if we're not on the Kanjiao Palace grounds, a eunuch-led escort from these manors can reach the Emperor's chambers unmolested by the palace guards. If we convince the sentries we've been summoned, the rest will follow, simple as a tumble in the hay."

His words hung in the air for a long moment, Remarin staring at him in disbelief.

"I know," Tigai said, forcing a grin through his exhaustion. "I'm a bloody fool."

The already-dead eunuchs' clothing provided their first set of disguises, four of Remarin's men donning the bloodstained tunics and robes to scout ahead and signal that the way was clear. Lucky for them a small few wore no beards or mustaches; the Nikkon and Hagali favored clean-shaven looks, though none among them would stand a close inspection, if it came to it. They crossed the grounds without such a disaster, wind spirits be praised, and on his orders made for the nearest consort's palace, a small manor house adjoining a garden split by a slow-running stream.

His false-eunuch soldiers fanned out as they took the steps leading to the consort's palace. Tigai and Remarin came last, making for the central chambers while their soldiers swept the side halls for eunuch servants and any attendants in residence. He tensed as Remarin followed behind, waiting for the cries that would signal their discovery. None came. Instead they tracked across a wood floor polished almost to the point of reflection, past banners hung with characters signifying *Peace, Joy, Happiness*, and came to a paneled door, sliding it open to reveal the mistress of the house.

A young girl, closer to birth than to thirty, stared at them—and, more pointedly, at the full beard that made it all too clear that Remarin had never been a eunuch—showing them a panic in her eyes as though they were death itself. She sat on the floor reclined against a bed, flanked by two maidservants seated atop it, each with half their lady's hair in their laps and ivory-inlaid brushes in their hands.

"Don't move, or cry out," Tigai said as Remarin stepped into the chamber beside him. "To do either is death; nod to assure me you understand."

Neither maidservant moved so much as a quiver of their lips, frozen as though they'd been cast in stone. Their lady held her stare, but her expression had hardened, whereas her servants wore only fear.

"You're here to rape us," the girl said.

"I'm here to steal from you," Tigai said, "and nothing so precious as that. I need your garments, your cosmetics, and your servants' spare dresses as well, if there are any on hand. After, I'll leave you tied and bound but otherwise unharmed, I swear it on my ancestors' blood. Cooperate in silence and none of you will be hurt."

The girl held her stare, this time touched with confusion. "My... garments?" she asked.

"Her garments?" Remarin repeated. "Do you mean to bloody dress up as a princess?"

Tigai turned back to Remarin. "Of course. I said before, an entourage from one of these palaces can enter the Emperor's chambers unmolested, but that'd be bloody hard to do without one of his prizes at the heart of it, no?"

"I thought you meant to take her with us, or one like her. No one's going to believe the Emperor chose you for a concubine, no matter how many layers of paint you bathe in."

He hesitated a moment. "I'll need their help," he said, nodding toward the still-frozen maidservants.

"Their help, and an hour or more of preparation we don't have. Even for you, this is bloody fucking mad."

"Don't hurt them," the girl said, reaching to lay a hand defensively across one of her maidservants' laps. "My maids go free, untouched and unspoiled. For that price, I will do whatever you ask."

Tigai looked between Remarin and the girl. Yes, he'd thought to masquerade as a concubine himself, imagining the rest of their soldiers putting enough distance between him and any prying eyes to cover for any inadequacies in his disguise. But Remarin was right. It would take time to don the costume, and any moment might herald sentries come to check the kitchens, or the outer wings of the manor they'd stormed.

"All right," he said. "Get up. And show us where they keep the palanquins, or whatever other conveyance you use for transport to His Majesty's bed."

————————

As it happened, the conveyance of choice was her own feet. Product of their having chosen a Second Consort to His Majesty the Emperor, rather than a First Consort or a recognized Empress, of which there were apparently six. A little-known fact outside the walls of the harem's palaces, but evidently one of significant weight, judging by the way their captive phrased the titles when she gave her name. Second Consort Zhaoling Xia, a niece of General Zhao himself—not that Tigai knew one military officer from another. He guessed it was right to act as though he knew the name, and judged from her satisfaction he had squarely hit the mark.

The rest of Remarin's men split the costumes available to them within Consort Xia's apartments, and now walked in stately procession through the gardens toward the Kanjiao Palace. Six dressed as eunuchs—freshly uniformed, without the blood-torn clothes they'd left behind—with four more as sentries carrying decorative halberds draped with the Emperor's sigil in gold and black. For Remarin they'd managed a black magistrate's robe, lending an air of dignity to their party that served doubly well as a means to avoid fitting the Ujibari chieftain into gray-gold eunuch's attire.

It was more than a Second Consort deserved, according to Xia, and all the more fortunate they'd managed to secure the magistracy for Remarin. With luck the Kanjiao sentries would see no more than two parties collided on their way to His Majesty's chambers, opting to make common company as they traversed the grounds.

"Scribe Dan, you must share the source of the tonic you procured for First Concubine Liao," Xia said suddenly as they approached the first gate. Her tone was even, measured as though they'd been engaged in light conversation for the last hundred paces. "Her maids say it has done wonders for her health during the pregnancy."

Remarin walked forward a few steps before Tigai *tsk*ed to get his attention. "What?" Remarin began, then recovered himself. "Oh, yes. A tincture of…moss water and goat's blood. From Ghingwai. Helps ease…back pain."

The sentries outside the Kanjiao gate made no move to suggest they'd heard the conversation, nor even that they'd noticed the procession approaching up the stone-laid path. Two spearmen that he could see, with another two armed with muskets atop the walls, looking down, standing at attention. Simple enough to assault the grounds, if it had come to it. He had a pistol and a long knife tucked under his gray-blue servant's tunic, and most of Remarin's men carried similar fare hidden beneath their disguises. But where he saw four guards, there would be forty more within shouting distance once they got inside the Kanjiao walls, and four hundred more could be summoned if an alarm was raised that His Majesty was in danger. Consort Xia had only to shout to bring them all, and Tigai had his knife at the ready to silence her if she tried. Perhaps they could claim a fainting spell, a need to visit an infirmary, if he was quick with his cut. Still a better chance than they'd have gotten without her, though it made his knuckles white on the hilt of his blade as they walked.

"Liao speaks highly of your acumen with trade," Xia said, giving no sign anything was amiss. "She hopes you will carry her compliments to her uncle, in Kongzhen."

"Yes," Remarin said. "Of course. The…ah…governor?"

Xia laughed as though he'd made a joke, and Tigai tittered along with a handful of Remarin's soldiers. Was it possible the consort spoke in some sort of code known only to the sentries that would have half the palace take them before he could shift vision to the strands? Curse him for a bloody fool.

"Second Consort," one of the gate guards said as they approached, bowing his head slightly. "Master Scribe." He repeated the gesture for Remarin's sake.

With that, their party passed through the gate, earning no more than bored looks from gate guardsmen paid to stand and stare for more hours than they spoke to anyone, coming or going.

Tigai's heart thumped in his chest, and he spared a second glance backward to be certain no sentries hid in the shadows. That was it? For months they'd planned this attack, and he'd botched the arrival by putting them in the concubines' quarters, and evidently all it took to get them on the grounds was a half-befuddled scribe's costume and a concubine's airy laugh.

A limestone walkway as broad as any thoroughfare extended from the wall through gardens twice as lush as those surrounding the harem, and they followed it toward a building rising from the maze of vines and hedges. Here Remarin's preparation took over; they knew the way from any point in the Emperor's palace to the vaults, and at once Remarin's soldiers seemed to recognize where they were. Remarin barked a quick order and two of the eunuch-dressed men split off, trotting ahead to scout the way.

"Is my part done, then?" Xia asked, her tone suddenly sharper than before.

Remarin gave her no notice, delivering orders and scanning the grounds as they approached a side entrance to the palace proper. The sort of gate that would have been used for consorts, small and nondescript for all its surrounding gardens were lush and green. Tigai hadn't put in the same hours studying the maps they'd procured, but he trusted Remarin's judgment and the training instilled in their men. He'd intended to stay quiet and out of the way while they moved through the grounds, there to get them in and out again once the Emperor's vaults had been breached. But Xia provided an opportunity for him to help: to keep her quiet, under watch, and ensure she gave no sign to the palace guard.

"You are with us to the end, my lady," he said, according her the respect due a scion of a noble house. Which she was, technically, though it was hard to see one of forty women kept for one man's pleasure as anything more than a whore.

"And what end is that? You abducted me to enter the palace; whatever you imagine your escape will be, I assure you, it is not so easily done for consorts to leave the palace grounds."

Consort Xia gave no outward sign of the heat in her voice; to observers she would appear no more than a woman on her way to do her duty, a jewel in red silk surrounded by servants in gray and gold. A beautiful girl by any measure, with honey-milk skin, eyes like almonds, and a mouth caught between a pout and a too-inviting smile. A treasure the likes of which could not be found if a man searched half the cities in the Empire, and he supposed the Emperor had done just that to find her. A travesty, for so much wealth to be held in one man's hands. Enough by itself to assuage any remaining guilt over planning to steal the Emperor's gold, had there been any left for him to lose.

"We have our ways," he said. "But I promise you again: comply with our direction, keep your promise, and you will not be harmed."

They climbed steps to the doorway, entering into a narrow hall, and Remarin sent scouts left and right while he held out a hand for Xia. She ignored it, hissing a whisper under her breath.

"You are supposed to be a servant, and a eunuch, not a gentleman out courting."

He retracted the hand, following along as Remarin led them down the left passage. The smell of fresh-polished wood lingered in the air, with paper screens letting in light from the courtyard beyond. Gold inlays came alive with scenes from a mathematician's dream, intricate patterns echoed on the walls and on carpets laid at the center of the smooth wood floors. Difficult to reconcile the opulence with what had been simple lines on paper, when he and Remarin had first reviewed their maps. So far it seemed Remarin had his bearings, directing them down passages the scouts had pronounced secure—free of sentries or watchful eyes, or made free with quick bladework. As a consequence, the palace seemed asleep, though he knew it was the sleep of a tiger, and their company dared to sneak close enough to fix the bell in place around its neck.

"Why do you do this?" Xia asked in a soft whisper when they made another turn. "Do you not fear for heaven's wrath?"

"My father taught me to fear the wrath of the banker, and the envious neighbor, before the celestials," he said. "Coin and treachery; these we can touch, and feel. The rest..." He grinned. "Only dust."

Remarin raised a hand to halt their progress as they came to an intersection between two halls. A jade statue of a half man, half tiger on a plinth marked the only difference between one way and another, though Tigai had to trust that Remarin knew the way.

"Blasphemy is unbecoming of a nobleman," Xia said in a low voice.

"What makes you think I'm a nobleman?" Tigai said in reply, huddling alongside their consort at the back of the line.

"What makes you think you can hide it?"

The exchange drew Remarin's notice, a frown and a look that made clear what the Ujibari chief thought of Xia's inclusion in their company.

"My man should have returned by now," Remarin said. "We need to know which way is—"

A clang and shout rose from deeper in the palace, and Tigai froze along with the rest of Remarin's men, craning to listen for an awful moment, as though they might have misheard.

Xia spun and ran back the way they'd come.

Tigai made a belated grab for her and missed, two steps too late, uttering a curse as the shouts from within the palace sounded again.

"She's running—" he began, and Remarin cut him short.

"Move!" the Ujibari barked. "Fuck the whore, we move now."

Tigai took another moment, caught between wanting to chase after the woman and follow Remarin's lead. She'd made him as a nobleman, and if she had any skill with inks she could draw a likeness of his face, or give instruction to someone who could. And she knew their intent—to breach the vaults—if not the method of their escape or entry.

"Now!" Remarin said as the last trace of color from Xia's red silk disappeared around the corner from which they'd come.

Tigai shook his mind free of her, and joined the company as they moved.

Remarin took the opposite fork from where the shouts were sounding, an infectious cry spreading through the palace walls. No mistaking it now. Soon the first forty guards would be weaving through the palace chambers, with four hundred, or more, close behind. At best they had a handful of minutes while the sentry-captains prioritized the Emperor's person over his wealth, but the gold would come to mind soon enough. Sooner, with Xia to help them see.

They took another left down a winding hallway before bursting through a door to a chamber where three guardsmen stood on alert, keeping watch over a stone stair leading down beneath the palace foundation.

Remarin produced a pistol from beneath his magistrate's robes, leveled, and shot the first guardsman in the head.

Powder and smoke flooded the room, and a ringing whine filled his ears, muting all other sound to a dull thrum. Two more puffs of smoke erupted forward, though he heard nothing in the calm that followed the first shot. The rest of the company rushed forward through the smoke, some with blades drawn, others with single-shot pistols held ready. He cut through it in their wake, finding the three guardsmen's bodies fallen beside the mouth of the stair, and followed as they descended in a rush.

The Kanjiao basements were a pale mirror of the grounds above, rough-cut stonework and dusty floors in place of smooth-polished wood and ornate gilding. He'd meant to bring them here at the start, or as close as the three dead prisoners' connections to this place would allow. Impossible to think three midlevel servants and apprentices might have had access to the harem and its palaces instead, but not beyond reason that they'd separately daydreamed of it enough to anchor the place in their memories. He might have been able to suss out the distinction between lived experience and imagination had he been given proper time to work the strands.

Once more Remarin's preparation took hold, only this time no scouts went forward to clear the way. They moved as one, a company of seven where they'd begun as over a dozen, the rest sent out to do their work aboveground and now caught in the rising tide of the guardsmen's alarm.

A wide chamber gave way to a passage spiraling in left turns around ever-tighter arcs. He recognized the way now, the last steps before the stairway leading down into the vaults themselves. A long hallway decorated with lanterns, made to trap any would-be thieves with a long trek in or out, though its designers had no more knowledge of the starfield and the strands than his tutors had done. A rare gift, and rarer still if he could get them out of the palace alive. Driving footsteps from the ceiling gave accompaniment to the thought, though his ears still rang from Remarin's shots in the antechamber of the first stairwell.

"Stop there," a man in gold-dyed leathers said when they rounded the hallway's final curve. "His Majesty's soldiers are—"

This time Tigai had enough warning to brace himself before the shot went off, and he clamped hands over his ears as smoke and powder discharged from one of the Ujibari's guns.

The gold-clad man emerged from the smoke, and Tigai might have figured Remarin's man had missed, if not for the shimmer of silver coating the sentry's skin.

Tigai blinked and set an anchor, feeling the familiar sense of dread sending tingles up his spine, then drew his long knife and attacked. Metal for skin meant the sentry was House-trained, a *magi* the same as he was, and more than Remarin's men could hope to handle.

"Go," Tigai shouted. "Secure what we came for."

If Remarin made a reply it was lost as the sentry whirled a shortsword from a scabbard at his hip, a folded steel blade as smooth and polished as the fingers that gripped it, each joint wrapped in metal as though the man were a statue come to life. Tigai shoved the man backward with his free hand, slashing at the sentry's chest with the other as a counterattack bit into his shoulder. Stinging pain lanced through him, numbed by adrenaline, and he'd done no more than dent the coating over his enemy's rib cage.

His vision blurred as the sentry staggered back from the force of his push. Remarin's men had followed his commands, fanning around them and making for the stairs. All he had to do was hold the sentry off until they returned, laden with gold.

The sentry lunged toward him, sweeping his blade overhand as though he expected to make short work of the intruder, then turn his attention on those who had slipped past. Instead his cut met only air. The strands swallowed Tigai, shifting him back to his anchor, standing at the mouth of the room, his shoulder uncut, his knife in hand.

A look of shock passed over the sentry's face, and Tigai set another anchor as he darted to the side, rushing to attack again.

This time the sentry met his cuts with a clanging parry, smoke from the pistol shots swirling around them as it rose to pool along the ceiling. Blood spattered on the stone floors from the first cut, and soon the sentry added a second, a wicked slash that bit through the tendons on his wrist before he could score a blow through the sentry's silver skin.

Wind spirits take him for a fool. He could hold his own in a fight, all the more so with the aid of the strands, but he was no soldier, and from the way the sentry carried his blade, the man most certainly was. Tigai staggered back, once more feeling an adrenaline surge from the pain, and snapped back to his anchor, blinking halfway across the room.

"How is it a *magi* comes to be posted as a mere guardsman?" he said, a haze of pain putting an unintended tremor in his voice. *Koryu* but he hoped the man could be baited into an exchange of words rather than steel.

"I might ask you the same," the sentry said, holding a defensive posture with his shortblade raised. "But it would be enough to note Dragon plays at politics, after all, no?"

Dragon, again. The same house to which the captain from Kregiaw had accused him of belonging.

Before he could form another reply, the clamor of footsteps rose from the spiraling hallways behind. He spun, and a squad of twenty guards came into view at the mouth of the chamber, pouring into the room.

He dropped his knife, letting it clatter to the floor, and held his hands out, open and empty.

"Too late to surrender?" he asked.

It served to stall the guardsmen's advance, which was all he needed. Another minute, at most. Remarin would be quick.

"Take care," the sentry called to his fellows. "This man is a *magi*. Leave him to me."

"Stay back, then," Tigai said, waving a hand in a threatening gesture toward the door. The guards flinched as though he'd thrown fire, or conjured a demon, or some other child's tale of what *magi* could do. Not that he was certain some among the monasteries *couldn't* do those things, but the illusion served him well enough for now. Thirty more seconds.

"You intend to submit yourself?" the sentry said, taking a step toward him, his blade still raised in a warding stance.

"There is no retreat," a voice from among the guard called to him. "We have the vaults encircled."

Tigai raised his hands, settling them atop his head. Ten more seconds, if Remarin was at his best.

"It's more than him alone," the sentry said. "Another squad went down into the holdings; no more than ten. Wait for another company to take them. I'll secure this man until more arrive."

Tigai held his pose, waiting for the sentry to approach. One cautious step, while the man fished for a knot of cord to bind his hands, then another. A final feint served to bait another step, and Tigai lowered his hands as if he meant to submit meekly to having them bound.

He blinked, and the strands snapped him to his anchor, ten paces to the left.

Shouts followed him as he darted past the sentry to the mouth of the stairs, where Remarin and the rest of them were already climbing. He rushed to meet them, his eyes closed, seeking the pattern of their stars and the familiar comforts of Yanjin. More bulk than he was used to, for transporting seven men. The bulk of gold, in coins and bars, jewels and jade and ivory. A smile creased his face as the starfield enveloped them, and they blinked between places with a blast of rushing wind.

"Lord Tigai."

The voice was wrong; it should have been Dao's, or Mei's. His vision cleared, and panic gripped his heart.

Lin Qishan. The captain of Kregiaw, the glass-*magi* who had murdered his three prisoners and fled the grounds of his brother's palace. She stood alone in his brother's receiving room, its familiar cushions and mats somehow warped by her presence.

Remarin's men took a moment longer to register the shift, milling into one another behind him where seconds before they had been racing to climb a stairwell from the Emperor's vaults. Tigai prepared to disorient them again; whatever else had happened, he could abscond from here as easily as he had from the Kanjiao Palace.

"Don't flee," Lin Qishan said. "I have your brother, and his wife. If you value them, you and your men will leave behind what you have stolen, and come with me."

The strands went to ash, fading as he blinked them away. Remarin gripped one of his pistols as though he meant to raise it, but Tigai reached out, gesturing for him to submit.

16

ARAK'JUR

Wilderness
Sinari Land

The men and women of five tribes flowed around the trees, cutting new paths as they trampled grass and brush by the thousands. Most carried parcels and packs, or drove horses, with some animals lashed to carts small enough not to hinder the beasts on uneven terrain. He carried nothing, as befitted the way the guardians traveled. His tent had held nothing of consequence; it had never been his way to keep mementos, art, or other such fare worth preserving on this sort of journey. The Sinari people were his treasure, and the rest of their alliance. Where others took caches of bead necklaces, stores of food, or woven rugs, he took the blood of six tribes, bonded to him as sure as any girl child's favorite doll.

"The hunters say we will arrive at the fair-skins' barrier today," Corenna said, keeping pace beside him.

Arak'Jur squinted into the sun, as though its rays might confirm the end was close. "They know the distance better than I," he said. It sounded cold to his ears before he said it.

Corenna seemed to notice, offering him a look of sympathy. "I'm frightened, too," she said. "Even after the assurances the fair-skins gave during the battle, it's one thing to promise peace, and another to ask for..."

"Charity?" he asked.

"Protection. And it was your words that convinced the elders to take this course."

The reminder stung enough for him to drop the pretense of anger. She was right. The Uktani were coming for him with their army of men and beasts, and that meant his people were in danger unless he found a way to leave, to find the source of the spirits' corruption and cleanse it away. They needed the fair-skins' barrier to shelter them from the beasts of the wild, but it hurt his pride to acknowledge it, even knowing it was the wisest path.

Another break in the trees gave a second glance at the sun, and this time he frowned, studying the horizon. It was already well past midday, three days from the Sinari village. The tribe traveled more slowly, encumbered by their burdens, than the hunters did alone, but even so they should be close enough to see the fair-skins' barrier by now.

"This course was wisdom when you spoke it," Corenna said. "And it remains so now. With the spirits' blessing we will return within a season, and find ourselves—"

She cut herself short as a figure emerged from the trees. A man in black, garbed in fair-skin clothing, and coming toward them whereas every other man or woman in sight walked the other way. The man passed by a family, a man carrying a child on his shoulders and a woman carrying a babe in a wrap on her chest, and neither gave him a second look, though he was a fair-skin by his clothes, an oddity enough to merit more than the indifference he seemed to be receiving.

"Who is that?" Corenna said. Arak'Jur didn't wait for her to finish the question. The man in black sighted them, and steel glinted from sunlight reflected through the trees. Swords, one in either of the man's hands, drawn from scabbards on his belt.

Mareh'et gave his gift, and Arak'Jur roared a warning as he charged.

The man sped up, enough to match the Great Cat's agility, and they raced toward each other over the open grass. Fear pulsed in his veins: fear of the unknown, of what this man might represent, a manifest attack on his people when he had feared its coming for so long. Instinct dwindled those concerns to an ignorable knot in his throat. For now, he faced one man, whatever else he signified.

Steel points flicked like snake's tongues, and he ignored them, punching through the guard of his enemy's blades. Searing pain took his shoulder and side where the blades cut his skin, but *mareh'et*'s claws connected with the man's torso in a brutal thrust. Only instead of goring through his flesh, a flare of white enveloped the man, hissing as it threw Arak'Jur back.

He skidded through a bough of leaves and brush, feeling his skin rip further as he scrambled to his feet.

"Llanara's gift," he shouted. "He has Llanara's gift."

Corenna had already sent out two of her tendrils of shadow, the gift of the swamp spirits from the far south. The man in black darted around them, moving with a viper's speed as the smoke twisted, a hairsbreadth from enveloping his legs and snaring him to the ground.

Then Corenna's smoke vanished, and the man leapt for her, impaling her chest with his left-hand blade.

Arak'Jur staggered as though he'd been the one to receive the blow. His throat went raw, and the clearing filled with howls that could have been his; he had no way to be sure. An image of Rhealla, his dead wife, tore through his vision, smothering the comforts he'd had at Ka'Ana'Tyat. Corenna's legs gave out as the man in black withdrew his blade, and she folded like cloth, dropping to the grass.

Lakiri'in's blessing gave him speed. He wanted to break the man with his hands, to rend and tear his eyes from their sockets, his nose from his skull, leaving the man's jaw unhinged and loose as he pounded his enemy to pulp and gore. But the man fled as soon as his blade was withdrawn, at blinding speed rushing west, away from the clearing, and Arak'Jur instead ran to Corenna's side, cradling her head as he lifted her to rest within his arms.

Her skin was cold, though it had to be a trick of the wind, a chill on the air. Her mouth moved, caught between a breath and a gasp, until blood came to her lips, leaking into her throat.

She seemed not to register that he was there, her eyes distant as she fought for breath.

"You will heal," he was saying; he heard the words in his own voice, as though some other man were speaking. "You will heal and heal quickly. It is part of the women's gift, the same as it is part of mine. Our son or daughter will grow in your belly, and you will heal. You can't die. You will heal."

A rasp of wind escaped her lips, gurgling where blood seeped in. Finally she met his eyes, and hers were full of fear.

"Arak'Jur!" a voice called from behind. Ilek'Inari. "There is a terrible problem. The fair-skins' barrier; we approach it now, or where it should be. But instead of their magic, there is nothing. It's as though the barrier has vanished."

His apprentice's words washed through his ears without touching him. Blood leaked from Corenna's chest where the man in black had stabbed her, staining her clothes and his hands where he held her. A finger's width shy of her heart, though it would have shattered ribs and punctured a lung. But she couldn't die. He repeated it in his head. She wouldn't die. She would heal. She wouldn't die.

A curse sounded next to him, and Ilek'Inari appeared in a flurry of motion. The apprentice knelt beside her, peeling Arak'Jur's hands from Corenna's head and lowering her to the ground. Herbs appeared, and quiet words, her clothing torn away from the wound, exposing her chest to the cool air. It was right. Ilek'Inari had been trained with medicine. She would heal. She couldn't die. He wanted to reach for her, to comfort her as Ilek'Inari worked. Instead he heard his voice turn hot, felt his belly roil with anger.

"How could you miss this?" he said. "A fair-skin, come to murder us, passing through our camp as though he were no more than the wind. And you saw nothing! Between two shamans, you and Ilek'Hannat, you saw nothing of his coming!"

Ilek'Inari spared him a pained look. Part of him wanted him to focus on Corenna; part wanted to strike Ilek'Inari for his failure.

"The spirits of things-to-come cannot see all things," Ilek'Inari said. "Especially so where men are concerned. And I was only ever an apprentice."

Quiet hung between them. Ilek'Inari had turned Corenna's head to the side, looking away from them, but he heard her cough blood, spattering the leaves and brush. As strong as she was, she looked frail, like a fallen child crying from a bruise.

In the back of his mind, his apprentice's words played again. The fair-skins' barrier, gone. The promised safety for his people, gone, though it should have run a length greater than the boundary of all land claimed by the Sinari, Ranasi, Ganherat, Vhurasi, and Olessi together.

It should have mattered, but it didn't. He stared, sure of nothing, only that Corenna couldn't die, that she would heal, that she wouldn't leave him alone.

17

SARINE

Wilderness
Near Lavendon Abbey

Oaks and elms twisted away from the space where the barrier had
been. A natural growth over hundreds of years; touching the
barrier meant a violent shock, same as coming into contact with any
Shelter binding. The wilds had responded by making a wall of wood and
brush, while most of the land to the south had been cleared for farming.
No one had ever seen the gap between them, the space between worlds,
save in controlled areas where the barrier was opened for trade. She'd
seen illustrations of those, if never attended such a meeting in person.
And now she was among the first to see the wild—the true wild—since
the first colonists had drawn the lines in collaboration with the native
tribes and engineers from Thellan and Gand.

Though she supposed that wasn't strictly true. The native tribes *lived*
in the wild. It wasn't fair to say she was among the first to see a place
thousands of people called home. And of course, the traders caught their
glimpses, and the priests. But thought came slow in the wake of what
she'd seen. Axerian had torn it down, using *Black*, and the wardings.
He'd brought down the Great Barrier, and every league of the colonies
was now exposed.

"How?" Acherre said. One word, enough to capture the horror and
wonder of what they'd witnessed.

"*Black*," she said. "It's like *Death*, but it only comes from killing. He used *Black*, and the wardings—the blue sparks. That's where he must've been, since the battle. Traveling the length of the barrier, setting wardings, preparing to do this."

Acherre paced toward the tree line, her hand on the hilt of her saber as though she might draw and charge the open sky. "He," Acherre said. "You mean Axerian? The assassin?"

"Yes. It has to be."

Quiet fell between them, and numbness. She wanted to act, to do something, to find him, force him to undo what he had done. Zi's weight rested on her shoulder, whereas before he had never been even the slightest of burdens. She could feel him now, sick and pale, flickering yellow in the midday sun. Once she might have thought his coloring a reflection of the light; now she knew better. Yellow meant emotions— strong emotions, and negative ones. Shame, guilt, and fear. She felt them all. This was her fault. She should never have trusted Axerian, should have listened to Zi's promptings and warnings against helping him. And he was still her best hope of finding a cure for whatever was afflicting Zi. The thought of using Axerian for anything was like oily filth coating her skin, but she hadn't lacked for reasons to search for him before. Now she added a new one: justice for what he'd done. For the thousands that would die to the beasts of the wild before a new barrier could be put in place.

"Gods damn it," Acherre said. "I need High Commander d'Arrent to make a connection. She has to see this. Is there any chance it's a localized thing? If the barrier went down here alone, it could mean an attack coming, but I'd as soon chance that over...the alternative."

"I...I don't think so." She'd felt the blue sparks in the moment before Axerian had triggered *Black* through them. A network of wardings as far south as the barrier ran, from New Sarresant to the swamps and marshlands of the Thellan colonies, with the southern plains of the Gandsmen in between. "I think he took it all. I think—"

Acherre snapped her fist into the air. A sign for quiet.

A moment passed, with no more than birds chirping in the trees.

"What is it?" Sarine asked.

"Movement." Acherre hissed it, just above a whisper, though they were standing in a cleared field, with nothing to use for cover short of the

twisted trees neither had been eager to approach. "Tether *Life* to be sure."
She pointed. "There, and there."

Sarine followed the instruction, finding the green pods of *Life* on a
nearby leyline. A tether between them made the spring breeze cooler on
her skin, light enough to feel every current of it, and sharpened the tones
of the birdsong sounding nearby. She looked where Acherre had pointed
and saw nothing, only copses of thick foliage. Not even a rustle from a
beaver or a deer.

"I don't see anything," she said.

"Shake me if there's danger," Acherre said. "I'll use *Mind*."

Sarine nodded, but Acherre's eyes had already gone blank, a fogged gray
covering pupil and iris together. Strange. Was that what she looked like
when she used *Mind*? A power with two uses—like *Life*, which could heal
wounds or sharpen senses, depending on how it was tethered. *Mind* would
split Acherre into a set of perfect copies if she bound it into herself, but
bound into the distant foliage it would shift her senses forward, to see and
hear as if she were there in person.

As suddenly as Acherre's eyes had fogged, she returned. "They're
there. Tribesmen. Three at least, by my count, and likely more."

The wind seemed to bite colder than it had. The last time she'd
seen tribesmen, they'd attacked the city, spurred by Reyne d'Agarre's
madness.

By the time she'd processed the warning, Acherre was already walking
back to their mounts, retrieving the reins they'd dropped to let the
animals graze in the field behind the site of the barrier.

"What are you doing?" Sarine asked.

"You're heading back to the city. Full gallop for a league and a half,
then you dismount and walk half a league before you gallop again. Can
you measure distance by the movement of the sun? Never mind if you
can't."

"Kiss the Nameless if I'm riding back to the city."

Acherre halted mid-stride, holding the reins to both mounts. Evidently
direct refusal of an order wasn't a thing commonly experienced in the
cavalry.

"One of us has to carry word of this to high command," Acherre said,
still keeping her voice low. "And you're not suited to scouting whatever
these tribesfolk are doing."

"Axerian could be out there. He has to be close, if he's the one the spirits said opened the barrier for *anahret* and *valak'ar*. And with Zi's help I can speak the tribesfolk's tongue. Can you say the same?"

Acherre frowned, showing signs of piecing together an argument before she spoke. But there wasn't time. They had to reach Axerian before Zi got any worse. He was already coiled around her shoulder, clutching her and trembling. His scales were pale white, almost pink.

"You there," she shouted, gesturing toward the twisted growth of forest, trusting to Zi to translate her words to the tribesmen's tongue. "I need your help. Show yourselves."

"What in the betrayer's damnation do you think you're doing?" Acherre strode forward to grab her by the upper arm.

She felt Zi pulse *Red*, strong enough to rebuff Acherre's grip and keep her footing. "I'm known to your guardian," she shouted. "A man called Arak'Jur. Show yourselves and help me!"

Acherre let her grip loose in disgust. "Fool! Those could be advance scouts, or did you forget what happened last time the barrier was breached?"

"Anch'a bi ulav. Arak'Jur orai dhakai dan Sinari. Q'ana il cha'be?"

Zi translated the words in her mind: *You are a fair-skin. Arak'Jur is the Sinari guardian. How can you know him?*

She grinned, forgetting for a moment that Acherre wasn't likely to know one word in three, if she knew any at all. Still, vindication was vindication.

"I brokered a peace with him, when you last came into our city. Is he with you?"

"No," the tribesman called back in their tongue. "But he is close. If you speak for your people, I can lead you to him."

"Let's go," Sarine said to Acherre, offering a hand to take her horse's reins, though the thick foliage wouldn't allow for easy riding. "They say their leader is nearby. If anyone has seen Axerian, the guardian will know."

"You're bloody mad. I'm not—"

"Either you're coming, or you're not."

She tugged the horse's reins, the animal's reticence somewhat spoiling the gesture of her striding away toward the wood. But she was pleased to see Acherre and her mount following behind a few paces later, enough to outweigh the tingling fear of passing through where the barrier had been, hours before. She raised a hand to signal to the tribesmen. For Zi's sake she could brave the wild, and worse. For him, she would face the Nameless himself, and whatever chaos he'd sown in his wake.

The tribesmen stood from where they'd hidden in the brush, and she waved again. Tall men, bronze-skinned, dressed in a mix of sewn coats and fur-lined breeches of the sort the trappers favored in the south. The men returned her greeting with cautious eyes, directing her to follow as one went ahead, and two more flanked them on either side. One stole a glance at her, then looked again, pivoting his gaze to Zi, resting on her shoulder.

"*Gan'cha il'si Llanara! Ana kar'ka, dommat—*"

He shouted it, too fast for Zi's translation to register in her mind. But *Green* flared, and the man went docile at once, all sign of his alarm quelled as they returned to quiet among the trees.

Sarine froze, waiting for more, a lashing out that never came.

"What was that?" Acherre said from behind.

They mistook me for another of my kind, Zi thought back, and somehow she knew he'd made himself heard in her thoughts as well as Acherre's. *Follow, and I will be sure none are troubled by the sight of me.*

His words sent a pang of sympathy through her. He would have vanished, as he always did, if he could. Instead she fished for a saddlecloth in her horse's bag, withdrawing it to wrap around him as she cradled him to coil around her forearm. They had to be close now. Axerian would know what to do. The tribesmen would know where to find Axerian. It would work out, and Zi would be fine. But no matter how she wished the tribesmen would rush as she followed them through the trees, they kept a steady pace, and she led her horse close behind.

———

The forest broke in small clearings, and it was clear at once this was no hunting party. This was a people on the move.

She'd seen wagon trains of refugees, villagers displaced and relocated to the city by the ravages of war. The ragged hunger, and the shame of being uprooted and made reliant on others' charity. This was different. Tribesfolk watched her pass with pride burning in their eyes, though from the presence of children and wrinkled elders this was no army on the march. Something had driven these people to move toward the barrier, and for the first time she began to wonder what else had been done, alongside Axerian's taking down the *Shelter* ringing the colonies.

Their guides stopped twice to converse as they passed through the trees, quick directions given to where the guardian had last been seen, and questions for her sake, and Acherre's. She tried to look as docile as she could, unthreatening and calm, though Acherre wore full military dress and couldn't help but look a soldier. It seemed to serve, and soon they broached a clearing following an elder's sure direction that he had seen the guardian and his woman walking the outer edge of their company, to the north.

The guardian, Arak'Jur, sat on the far side of the clearing, resting on his heels but leaning forward, watching another man perform some work as they kneeled over the grass. No mistaking him, though—he was the same bull of a man she'd seen in the city, when he'd brokered a peace between the tribes, Lord Voren, and Erris d'Arrent. He was bare-chested, as he had been in the city, and still muscled like an ox, with russet skin decorated by scars. A dangerous man, but one who spoke of peace and reserve and caring for his people. He would listen, when she asked for help.

"Honored guardian," their escort said in the tribes' tongue. "There is a fair-skin here who claims—"

At mention of her skin, Arak'Jur snapped a look of fury in her direction, though he hadn't deigned to notice their approach. It gave their escort a start, just as it revealed the subject of the guardian's attentions, and the man's at his side: a woman's body, blood-smeared and lying flat in the grass.

Sarine dropped her horse's reins, rushing forward without thought.

Arak'Jur sprang to his feet, surrounded by a shimmering image of a birdlike creature, all leathery skin and feathers and claws.

"It's all right," she said, stuttering to a halt and feeling half a fool for her hasty approach. "I can help, if you'll let me."

Arak'Jur weighed her a moment before recognition dawned in his face. "Sarine," he said. "The girl. Yes. Yes!" He gestured to the woman's body. "We were attacked by a fair-skin. Corenna took a wound to her chest."

The man who'd been tending the woman Arak'Jur had named Corenna moved aside, making way for her. Sarine knelt, shifting her sight to the leylines as she placed both hands on the woman's skin. *Body's* red motes sprouted like weeds through the clearing: a sign of violence, and recently done. The woman's chest corroborated it, her skin opened to the cool air around a gash still seeping blood, just shy of her heart.

"A fair-skin did this," she said, working strands of *Body* through the woman's form. A tether to strengthen her one working lung, and another for her throat to swallow the blood without choking. One more for the heart itself, to calm it and give it strength through the shock. "Dressed in black, with a hooked nose and curved swords on his belt?"

Arak'Jur nodded, a feverish agreement. "Yes."

Her heart raced. Axerian was close, close enough for the woman not to have died yet from the blow he'd struck. She blinked again, this time finding *Life*, the green pods that would heal the wounds, rather than simply giving the woman the strength to handle her pain. Tethers formed as quick as she could think them into being, a strand for the skin and ribs, another for the ruptured blood vessels, another for the punctured lung. At best she could stop the damage, let the wound regenerate faster and do in a few days what might have taken weeks, but it was better than—

The woman coughed, a spat of blood sprayed over Sarine's hands and chest, and she opened her eyes.

"Corenna!" Arak'Jur said, coming to kneel on the opposite side, clutching her hand as though he held a treasure.

"Arak'Jur," the woman—Corenna—muttered weakly. But she seemed to grasp his hand back, more firmly than should have been possible.

"How did she recover so fast?" Sarine began, though neither the guardian nor the woman seemed to pay her any mind. Instead it was the other man, the one who had tended to the woman first, who laid a hand on her forearm with a gentle smile.

"It is part of our magic, for those touched by the spirits to recover quickly," he said. "Whatever you did, you were aided by that gift."

A glance at Corenna's chest confirmed it; the blood still soaked her clothes, streaming down her sides, but the wound itself was half knit shut, with pink swelling and raw flesh of the sort she wouldn't have expected to see for a month of healing.

"Can you examine her belly?" the man continued. "She is pregnant. If you can sustain the child..."

He left it unsaid, but she nodded, reaching again for *Body* and *Life* and laying hands on Corenna's stomach. This time both Arak'Jur and Corenna turned to watch her in silence. She tethered lines into Corenna's belly, finding a small spark stirring within. If it had dwindled, there was no sign of it now; the child embraced the lines she tethered like a fish swimming in a stream. Warmth pulsed through her, and she fixed the bindings in place, withdrawing her hands from Corenna's flesh.

"The child is healthy," she said, feeling almost embarrassed at the beaming looks shared between them.

"Thank you," Corenna said, her voice reduced to a croaking rasp.

"Thank you," Arak'Jur repeated. "You have restored to me all that I value most, and I owe you a debt."

Sarine reclined back on her heels, taking a moment to loosen the saddlecloth wrapped around her forearm to check on Zi. "You can repay it," she said. "By helping me find Axerian—the man in black, the man who attacked you. My companion is sick, and I need him to lead me to a cure."

18

ERRIS

The Grand Promenade
Covendon, Capital of the Gand Colonies

Her field-marshals flanked her atop the platform—Royens and Etaigne on the left and de Tourvalle on the right—with a dozen more generals at attention to their sides. There hadn't been time for dress uniforms; instead they made do with field colors, disparate shades of blue and gray, with a mix of stars, epaulets, pins, and stripes for rank. Opposite her commanders, the Gandsmen were immaculate on the other end of the stage, each one in a matching red coat with white undershirt, breeches, and hose. It stung her pride to see her army so mismatched. An error in judgment, perhaps, not to insist on ceremonial dress before the signing. But if her pride was wounded, the Gand generals' would be limping to its grave. At the center of the stage, under the open air of a park the size of more than a few trade villages, the Gand aides laid out inks and pens, half for the officers of New Sarresant, half for the politicians and generals of Gand, intended for the signing of documents offering the Gand colonies' unconditional surrender.

An audience of five thousand ringed the stage on all sides, a sea of eyes watching as the final preparations were made. Civilians' dress for half the crowd, and blue uniforms for the rest. Soldiers from Royens's 1st Corps, given the honor of being the vanguard for taking the city, while representatives from among the Gand nobility, priesthood, and merchant classes watched with wide eyes as the Sarresant soldiers formed ranks at the center of their promenade.

"Her Ladyship the General Marianne Chamberlain, Commander of the Armies of Gand in the Reach and the Far Side of the World, hereditary Countess of Verben and Devonshire."

The crier made the announcement with no pomp, no formal introduction or statement of purpose. That had been Erris's doing, the swift ceremony a nod to the fact that Etaigne and de Tourvalle's corps were already on the march along the northward roads. Even with the Great Barrier's collapse, she'd made the call to finish this campaign first, and finish it she had. She was too late to stop whatever was happening in the north. If they were to have any hope of standing against what was coming, it meant establishing a hold over as much territory as they could claim, and it started here, with an almost bloodless victory over an incompetent fool.

That fool trundled forward from their side of the line, a too-fat woman who nonetheless shone as though she had servants employed full time to do nothing more than polish her boots and the gold buttons on her coat. General Chamberlain made a show of her signature, taking up a pen and scanning the document as though she meant to read it again before she signed. A quick turn made for her name, and an aide offered her wax for the seal that followed, pressed firm on the Gand side of the document's line.

"Erris d'Arrent," the crier called. "High Commander of the Armies of New Sarresant."

She strode forward to the table that had been prepared at the center of the stage, feeling the weight of ten thousand eyes on every step. A knot rose in her throat, but she forced it down. Now she doubly regretted not waiting on the ceremony until Voren could arrive, at the very least. But she was here, the Gandsmen were here, and defeat smoldered in their eyes as they watched her, doubtless already seeing provocation in her soldiers' ragtag attire. Gods but she had no skill at politics, or at giving speeches.

"Sons and daughters of Gand," she said in the Sarresant tongue. Enough of them spoke it, and one of them would translate as she went on, she was sure. "For two years you have been my enemies. You've fought hard, and claimed the lives of many good men and women of

Sarresant. I have never faced an enemy more cunning, more dangerous, more deserving of being called my equal."

Never mind that the sentiment applied to their onetime commander, the beast behind the golden eyes, and not to the overdressed woman now standing at their head. It served to stir them, the Gand soldiers shifting in their places, and she heard her words translated and carried from their line down into the crowd. She paused to give them time to translate, then spoke again.

"I accept your surrender today, not because I wish to see you subdued, beaten, and brought low. No. I wish to lift you up, for your lands to be merged with ours as part of a representative, united colonial government. Our Great Barrier has come down, the shelter we've shared from the hostile wilderness native to these lands, and we will need our combined strength to rebuild it, to face whatever power engineered its collapse."

A risk, to share the information, when the first reports about the barrier were only just being confirmed. But she'd seen it with her own eyes, and a shared struggle was good as anything to make men and women come together.

This time a buzz rose, with a hint of panic.

"Forces align against us," she continued. "A great evil you have already foresworn—the man behind your use of the golden light. I have confronted this man, I have faced him and can confirm: He was no friend of Gand. I know you will see us no better—as conquerors, not liberators—but I propose for you to see us as peers in the struggle placed before us. Red coats and blue, side by side against the wild, and the unknown. Dark times are ahead, and we must all of us be strong, together, before the end."

She finished, and once more let the translators pass her words from ear to ear. It would have to serve. She couldn't even be certain of the true cause of the Gandsmen's rejection of the golden light. But the man was evil. He'd butchered thousands, sacrificed Gandsmen like chaff in furtherance of a plan to find *her*, not achieve any military objective that she could see. Even the barrier's collapse was surely another ploy, another angle to draw her into the field.

When her words were finished propagating through the crowd, she paused at the center table and offered the Gandsmen a salute, fist-to-chest. She held it as they stared, until General Chamberlain herself offered a countergesture in the Gand fashion, bladed hand to forehead. The rest followed, her officers in the Sarresant style and the others following Chamberlain's example. Good enough for now. She let her hand fall, and the rest did the same. Then she turned to the document, took up a pen, and signed her name.

———————

"Their wine tastes like boot piss," Field-Marshal Royens observed, taking care to keep a brave face as he took light sips from his crystal glass. The finest wares, prepared in a rush to host a fête for a thousand guests, the sort of propriety that wouldn't have occurred to her without noble-born aides to ensure that the New Sarresant High Commander acted the part. Gods damn her if she wouldn't rather be on the march. But Aide-Captain Essily had insisted on staying at least the night, to abide Gand traditions and Sarresant ones alike. She'd acquiesced, if only for the comfort of a goose-feather bed before the Oracle knew how many weeks she'd be spending in the field.

"Give the old country one thing," Field-Marshal Etaigne said. "They can tend a grape, and press it without slipping loose their cocks and pissing in the vat. Ah—begging my ladies' pardon."

Vassail snorted, caught between a laugh and a sip from her own glass. Erris raised hers in a mock salute. "You don't know the women of the general corps, Field-Marshal, if you think you need a pardon for that."

"Careful praising any aspect of Old Sarresant," Royens said. "Don't let them catch you speaking ill of the Republic, or you're like to kiss a guillotine."

Across the room a group of Gand officers laughed in unison, where one of their number appeared to be gesturing to emphasize the better part of a story.

"We ought to mingle," Etaigne said. "Send the right message to our troops."

The notion soured their group, even as the Gandsmen redoubled their guffaws. If Voren were there he'd doubtless have them all dancing the latest gavotte step by now.

"Bugger that," Vassail said. "I woke up this morning intending to kill as many of the red-faced bastards as I could put in the ground. We're the victors here, and the guests. Let them come to us."

"No," Erris said. "Etaigne is right. We'll need their loyalty, never mind what the politicians and diplomats work between them. Power comes from musket shot and cannon fire. All the rest is window dressing."

Vassail fell quiet. It was the simple truth, as far as she saw it. Let the scholars quibble over legitimacy and cultural pressures and the rightful boundaries on the map. The fact was, if a commander fumbled their attack, if a flank collapsed when it should have held, any nation in the world could fall, bend its knee, and start looking for justifications for how it could have been no other way. As with battles, histories went to whoever put the greatest numbers on the choicest ground.

"Royens, Etaigne, with me," she said, pausing to fetch a fresh wineglass from a servant meandering through the hall. The stuff did taste like piss, though she'd never made it a habit to drink in the field.

Her field-marshals walked with her as she approached the still-laughing group of Gandsmen, where General Chamberlain stood surrounded by majors' stripes, colonels' hawks, and generals' stars.

"High Commander," General Chamberlain said, sobering at last, from the joke if not the wine. "It is the giving me great pleasure for you to be joining of us." The woman's command of the Sarresant tongue was thick with the chopped, harsh accents of Gand, but she noted the gesture, and spoke slowly in reply.

"My corps commanders," she said, indicating to her left and right. "Field-Marshal Reginald Royens, and Field Marshal Marcél Etaigne."

Both men bowed, precisely low enough to avoid giving offense and not a hairsbreadth lower. Chamberlain effected the same gestures. "These are being the generals and command staff of the Gand Third Army." She recited names Erris had known only from scouting reports; passing strange, to match names and faces for commanders whose men she'd killed by the score if not the hundred.

"A fine speech at the signing, High Commander," a Gand officer said, a cavalryman by his uniform, one Brigadier-General Wexly, a tall man with the bearing of a soldier, through and through. "Did you mean what you said?"

The rudeness of the question snuffed any remaining mirth among the group. Shuffling steps served as a proxy for the instinct to withdraw among the Gandsmen, and her field-marshals went stiff, just shy of snapping to attention.

She took a moment before replying, imagining Voren standing behind her, watching and weighing her movements like her father had done, when she'd first learned to stalk and skin a kill. Socialites at a party were as foreign to her as beavers had been, when she was five. She knew soldiering, not politicking. But she needed their support, and they stared at her, expecting her to fail.

"Which part, General Wexly?" she said at last. "My praise for the Gandsmen's skill at arms, or my condemnation of the commander who led you all astray?"

"You will not to be finding supporters of that creature here," Chamberlain said, still half butchering the Sarresant tongue as she spoke. "My officers retook our army from his hands, and right it is to have done it. The general refers to your promising to bring Gand's colonies into your Republic. Into governance. We were discussing it, a moment ago."

"I meant it," she said. "The colonies are stronger together, strong enough to challenge the Old World. Strong enough to rebuild our barrier, and stand against the forces that engineered its collapse."

"What do we know of such things?" Chamberlain asked. "Could it have been the natives, perhaps? Are we to be deploying our forces to invading of their lands, now we've submitted to your rule?"

"Forgive me, General," Wexly cut in. "But I would know whether Commander d'Arrent is in position to promise a political union. Or, more likely, whether we're to see our peoples reduced to table scraps while Sarresant lords gorge themselves on our estates."

Once more the group went quiet, and all eyes turned to her.

This was the heart of it, and the place she knew she'd overstepped. Voren would upbraid her for such loose talk, absent any vetting from the diplomatic corps. She didn't care.

"The Old World is all but in the hands of the man behind your golden light," she said. "And every instinct tells me he's behind the Great Barrier's collapse. We've been enemies for eighteen months, but I need unity if we're going to face him. I need strength. I need your armies, and I need you."

"With respect," Wexly said, "that is not an answer, High Commander."

Wexly took a sip of his wine, and she saw a hint of the gambler in his eyes. Chamberlain was a fool; her tactics had proved it at Ansfield if Erris hadn't known it before. But even the Gand army had its men and women of skill. One more burden to bear, reorganizing their chains of command to promote soldiers daring enough to cut to the heart of a challenge.

"I have the loyalty of the armies of New Sarresant," she said. "And I have it for a reason. I need not tell men or women of our nature that a throne—or a Republic—is only as good as the armies at its command. So I say yes. If any think to oppose your equality under our laws, they will face me, and the army at my back."

"A good answer, High Commander," Wexly said, returning to sip his wine.

Murmured agreement passed among the Gandsmen, and an introspective silence. She might have made an attempt to turn the conversation to lighter fare, but instead she fought down the urge to gasp.

The golden light.

It shone like a beacon at the edge of her vision, on the opposite end of the chamber.

"Excuse me, ladies and gentlemen," she said. "I must withdraw for a moment. Field-Marshals Royens and Etaigne will carry on in my absence."

There would be a water room or some other contrivance for privacy. She could have jumped into the nearest broom closet, for even the slightest sign *Need* might behave differently, now she'd conquered the Gand colonies. It had been weeks since the light appeared unbidden.

A door latched behind her, the first empty chamber she found away from the main hall, and she tethered *Need*, shifting her senses into the far north.

"Ra'ni amanai chuqu'an, niral a'rai'et, qu—sa che si?"

The tribesfolk's tongue sounded in her ears before her vision cleared, enough to set her on edge by the time her vessel's sight resolved into a forest clearing, surrounded by men, women, and the scent of blood.

No officers that she could see, nor soldiers. Two tribesmen kneeling beside a tribeswoman opposite a woman in civilian's clothes. Recognition dawned a moment later.

"High Commander," the civilian said. Not just any civilian. The girl. Sarine. "Thank the Gods."

It meant she had to be connected to Rosline Acherre, and it took only another moment to recognize one of the tribesmen: Arak'Jur, the man she'd treated with at the height of the battle, and his woman, the one now injured, though she seemed to be moving without concern for the blood caking over her fur-lined dress.

"What passes here?" she asked. "And where are you?"

Sarine pivoted where she knelt. "We're just outside the Great Barrier; or rather, we're beyond where it used to be. It's fallen, Commander. The barrier has fallen."

"I know. Is the city in danger? What can you tell me of the situation in the north?"

"*An'ni kepai dan di sur?*" the man—Arak'Jur—asked. "*Di Erys d'Aru?*"

"Yes," Sarine said, giving him her attention and using her trick of speaking in both tongues at once. "It's her, the High Commander. Erris d'Arrent. She asks whether there is danger here, for the city—"

"My time may be limited," Erris snapped. "I need to know the situation here, girl. Now! Were these tribesmen responsible for bringing down the barrier? Have you been captured? What are their intentions?"

"Captured? No. And no, it wasn't the tribesfolk who brought down the barrier. It was—"

All three tribesfolk spoke at once, raising a protest, gauging from the tone, though she couldn't understand their words.

"Slow down," Sarine said. "It wasn't them, High Commander, and they want to be certain you know it. It was Axerian—the assassin, the man Acherre and I were tracking. I don't know why he did it, but he attacked them as well." She gestured to the tribeswoman, and the blood. "The tribesfolk had nothing to do with the barrier coming down."

"Then what are they doing here?"

She wasn't about to trust the judgment of a novice girl. She'd hear it for herself and form her own conclusions about why exactly one of the most powerful men among the tribes was at the barrier at the moment it went down.

Sarine paused, then relayed the question. Evidently she hadn't asked it yet herself.

The tribesman—Arak'Jur—listened, then replied in solemn tones, meeting Acherre's eyes as he spoke.

"They're in danger," Sarine translated. "All of them. They've left their village, and traveled here, fleeing what he calls an Uktani army—men and beasts, the great beasts of the wild, working together."

Arak'Jur spoke again, still locking eyes with her. She stared back, weighing him.

"The Uktani hunt him," Sarine said. "He says he is marked, as an Ascendant of the Wild, that they mean to..." She trailed off into silence.

The stares broke between her and Arak'Jur, both of them looking to Sarine to continue.

"Zi says it's true," she continued, just above a whisper. "He says Arak'Jur is on the path to ascension, and you are, too. The golden light, *Need*; it's a sign. It's why they're hunting you. Axerian, Paendurion, and Ad-Shi."

"What under the Nameless are you talking about, girl?" she asked.

Arak'Jur spoke at the same time, a forceful insistence behind his words.

"No, Zi, don't say any more," Sarine said, and only then did Erris notice the snakelike creature she'd seen in Voren's office, coiled beneath a blanket around Sarine's forearm. Sarine appeared to be crying; tears streaked down her cheeks as she stroked the creature.

Arak'Jur spoke again, repeating whatever he'd said a moment before.

"Yes," Sarine said for her benefit. "Yes—he says his people wanted to shelter here, behind our barrier, while he goes in search of the cause of the evil that has driven his people mad. And I'm going with him. I have to find Axerian."

"His...people?" Erris asked. "How many are there? And a tribal army, marching south, while we have no barrier to protect us?"

Sarine translated her words, and then the other tribesman rose to his feet beside Arak'Jur, speaking with an earnest passion in his voice.

"Ilek'Inari says their people can offer better protection than our barrier. He is a shaman, he says, and gifted with visions of things-to-come. He says he and another man, Ilek'Hannat, will use their gift to tell our soldiers where the threats are. He says this is how the tribes survive, in the wild. Their visions, and our bindings, to protect both peoples from the beasts of the wild."

She cast a dubious look at the speaker, the so-called shaman. Superstition at best, and no easy matter to convince Voren and the other members of the Assembly even if she had believed. But the tribes did have their magic, there was no denying it, and she had no inkling what forms it took. Perhaps it was true.

"How many?" she asked again. "They ask for refuge; how many are they?"

"Fewer than we were," Arak'Jur replied in the Sarresant tongue; his command of it was broken, but she understood it well enough. "But we are strong. Help us, and we help you."

She needed more time, more information. Even the most foolish general couldn't make a tactical decision with so little to work from. *Need* had already exceeded her expectations, allowing a connection to go on so long without shattering in her face. But even then, her supply wouldn't last forever.

Gods, but Voren would be less than pleased. First her promises to the Gandsmen, and now this.

"You'll have my protection, then, so long as you speak true. Move your people onto our land. I'll ride north to meet you in person, and we can settle terms."

ELSEWHERE

INTERLUDE

DON GONZALO

Bartoleme Plantation House
Felipa-Tuscaigne, the Thellan Colonies

The sting of Dalusian tea warmed his throat. He'd learned to tell the difference between authentic Dalusian leaves and their imitators, more to the detriment of his grandchildren's inheritance. True Dalusian Gray grew only on the heights of the Kastaandr ranges, and it cost fifty times its weight in gold to import it here, across the Endless Ocean. A luxury, one of the few his gold could buy that gave him any true satisfaction.

"Don Bartoleme," his visitor said. "My sincerest thanks for granting the audience. I know you are a busy man."

"Call me Gonzalo, and please, sit."

He didn't rise to greet his visitor, nor did he gesture with the magnanimity he might have done, twenty years before. Certain allowances were made beyond the bounds of etiquette for men of advanced age, and he took full advantage. The Veil knew there were plenty enough drawbacks, in aching bones and a reflection that bore only token resemblance to the man he still thought of as himself.

"I'd heard of your travel to our island, Don Revellion," he said as his visitor took a place opposite him, overlooking the waves rolling in, where children splashed and played below. "What business can the Sarresant ambassador have visiting an old man waiting to die?"

His visitor, the Marquis de Revellion, cleared his throat. Was the man nervous? A strange affectation, for a diplomat, though he supposed the political situation was uncertain, at best. A rebellion, or a revolution, if the new Republic stood, to the north. Enough to put even the most steadfast man on shaky ground.

"You have heard tell of my overtures to the Cadobal families, the Ruiz and Lugo-Aviera."

"I suspect you think me better informed than I am, Don Revellion. I am a grandfather twice removed. I have more pressing concerns weighing on my soul than any affairs of state or trade."

"Nonetheless, you have surely heard of my attempts, and my failures. They say no ship docks at Porta Fernanda without the Don of Bartoleme's approval. I am here at the end of my ventures, and only now do I suspect I should have come here at the beginning."

Don Gonzalo hid a smile behind another sip of his tea. "The Don of House Bartoleme is my grandson, now, Don Revellion. If they say such things still, it is a point of pride to him, not to me. Tell me, do you have children?"

"A son," the Marquis said. "He fled the madness in New Sarresant, and arrived safely on Sarresant shores. A better fate than many got, faced with the prospect of rebellion."

"Tragic, so I hear it told." And telling. He noted that the Marquis made no mention of the two bastards all but certain to be his. A point as to the sort of man he was. Not worth dwelling on it now.

"Beyond tragedy, if you will permit me the correction, Don Gonzalo. A lawless bloodbath, and I have been rebuffed in my attempts to persuade His Majesty my King to act on behalf of my claims. But I have been given assurances. A Thellan contingent alongside fresh conscripts from the southern Sarresant colonies would be enough to find victory against a New Sarresant Army worn and weary from fighting against Gand. Gand herself might fall—and His Majesty has suggested we would return our claims and fivefold more, if it is a Thellan hand that tips the scales toward us."

"Politics, Don Revellion. As I have said, I am too old for such fare."

"Please. It can be done, Don Gonzalo, I'm certain of it. Two fresh armies in the field, against two depleted by better than a year of fighting. At your word, the right men and women will be brought to reason. They say yours was the voice that rebuffed Prince Emerich, that kept Thellan neutral in the Old World. I give you my assurance: Gand is weakened, and the time to strike is now. First here in the New World, to secure what Sarresant lost to these rebels, then across the sea. We are natural allies. Do not let yesterday's politics shape the future."

The last dregs of tea went down his throat, as sweet and pungent as every sip that came before. A latent magic in the leaves, he would swear it, though Thellan's binders insisted the plants had no especial connection to the leylines.

"What you say may be of interest to my family," he said at last. "I will speak with my grandson on your behalf."

"Thank you, Don Gonzalo." Revellion rose. "I cannot ask for more. I will remain here on the island another two weeks. I sincerely hope I will depart as your ally, in this and all other things."

"I hope you will find time to swim on my beach, Don Revellion, and sample my granddaughter's polvorones. She bakes them for me, and insists she be allowed to kiss my cheek as the price of each batch."

Revellion showed him teeth—he'd never call such a gesture a smile— then bowed and withdrew from the balcony.

The waves crashed below, and children squealed. A reminder of what it was to be young. He'd imagined old age would bring a return to carefree convalescence, a doddering excuse to pinch pretty girls' bottoms and say crass things at parties. But the world went on, unchanging, and if his body had long since failed him, his mind had yet to slip.

A sad truth, that Don Gonzalo in his ninety-fifth year had more wits than most men of position and influence a quarter of his age. He'd already treated with representatives of New Sarresant, and accepted Anselm Voren's bribes to stay out of the conflict, in the New World and the Old. Trade to enrich his grandchildren, levers over the right men and women, in his and other houses. Fools such as the esteemed Marquis de Revellion imagined they could implore him with grand dreams, of rightness and future gains. The world was run by ten, perhaps twelve men and women who understood the subtleties of power, and not one of them styled themselves an ambassador, minister, or King.

Would it serve him, to string Revellion along with promises, or was it best to let the man down firmly? The ambassador would continue his crusade with Don Portega next, or perhaps Portega's daughter, if he had sense enough to know whose hand held those strings. An undecided question. He could leave it for tomorrow.

"Don Gonzalo"—his manservant bowed, hovering in the doorway leading to the balcony—"I have three more visitors, come to see you. They claim the utmost urgency."

"Not today, Enrico." Fatigue crept upon him with little warning, at times, but he had an inkling of it now. "Brew me another pot of Dalusian Gray, and I will watch the children until sundown."

"Of course, sir."

Enrico left the balcony, to settle in the latest visitors to become tomorrow's business. A true luxury there, the sort more precious than gold: Time. Every second was precious, at his age. He relished the brine on the air, the whooping cheers as a brave boy dared to race the tide. He had been that boy, once. He'd run harder, farther than any others, and returned to kiss Donna Marchesa when he was sure the grown-ups weren't looking. What a fool he'd been. What a joyful, glorious fool. All the gold in his estates couldn't buy that sort of foolishness. Now there were half a dozen Marchesas on the beach, so named for their late great-great-grandmother, an honor deeper than they could know. She would have loved to watch them play.

A crack and thud startled him.

It was a sound that didn't belong in the Bartoleme house. He tried to twist in his long chair, to catch sight of the door to the balcony and what might have produced the noise. Instead his hips ached, the pillows tucked against him all but confining him in place. He stopped and fought for a breath, and heard footsteps broach the wood of the deck. Three pairs.

"Don Gonzalo, I'm afraid we must insist you see us now."

A Gandsman came into view midsentence, sandy-haired and blue-eyed, with a neat-trimmed beard and clothing of their latest styles. Just the sort of ambitious young man who frequented his balcony, the sort who thought themselves alone in daring to pit their fortunes against the world. But his companions were different.

One was a man, tall and thick-muscled, with long black hair shaved at the sides. He wore Gand styles, too, but he was no man of the isles. A tribesman; Gonzalo knew their look. The third, a woman, had it as well, though she made no attempt to hide it in her dress. She wore furs stitched into something he might have described as formal wear; he'd certainly never seen the tribeswomen wear anything like it, in the times they'd come to treat at his estate. She was older than the other two, but with a timeless ripeness he'd come to recognize as the peak of a woman's beauty.

"You have injured Enrico," he said, feeling a pang of guilt. It was ill done, violence. A thing for lesser men and women. Yet he feared he'd have to order these three skinned alive, perhaps burned or impaled for their imprudent act.

"A regrettable thing," the Thellan man said. "But your servant insisted we not be admitted to see you, and this simply will not do."

"Do you plan to do violence to me, sir, if I likewise do not grant your wishes?"

"Not to you," the woman said.

The children squealed as another wave hit the beach, and his blood went cold.

"You will be leaving now," he said. "And praying I forget this insult. I hope for your sake Enrico recovers, or you will find my family to be most unpleasant enemies."

"We are here for your loyalty, Don Gonzalo Bartoleme." The Gandsman walked to the edge of the balcony, looking down on the sand below.

Don Gonzalo laughed. "Do you imagine this is how loyalty is won? Shows of muscle, threats? Fools who think so will rise to be lords of a city block, never dreaming their associates plot to kill them when they leave a room."

The woman came to sit on the edge of his chair. It felt like an invasion, a gesture of familiarity when her garb suggested she should be foreign and strange.

"I have found obedience serves," she said. "When loyalty is not attainable."

He went quiet. "What is it you want?"

"A simple thing," the Gandsman said. "Accept Arak'Inu into your service." He nodded toward the third of their number, the tribesman in Gand clothing. "He will remain behind, and aid you in things to come."

"And what is to keep me from ordering him strangled while he sleeps?"

This time the Gandsman laughed. "You are free to try, Don Gonzalo. I suggest you employ an assassin you consider expendable, for that task."

"Do we have your agreement?" the woman said. "Arak'Inu may remain behind, in your service?"

His mind worked, trying to untangle the puzzle they'd put in front of him. He could make little sense of it. Coming to his house to threaten him would do little more than engender his wrath, whether there was some tribal warrior sleeping under his roof or no. They couldn't possibly imagine their efforts would bear any fruit. At best they would kill him, or do some other sort of violence. Neither would spur him to act in furtherance of their goals. But there seemed little choice for what must happen next.

"By all means," he said. "Your thug will be provided the finest chambers I can spare."

The woman stared at him, as though waiting for something more.

"Is there more, then?" he said. "Are you not satisfied with—?"

Golden light flooded through him, and his senses wrenched themselves from his grasp.

A line, a thread of gold, binding him to someone else, someone far away. He'd never understood the mysteries of the leylines, no more than he'd had to know for politics' sake, but now a terror gripped him that should have had him retching, screaming for help. Yet no sound came from his lips. It was as though another pair of eyes had conquered his, forcing his vision to step back, though he could still see. His ears, his nose, his skin, all redirected elsewhere, while his consciousness fell into darkness. He felt it all, every sensation, but somehow knew he was no longer in control.

"Ah," he felt himself say. "You took too long. It may be too late, even with the old man's influence behind our cause."

"Forgiveness," the woman said. "It took time to find the right lever to move the mountain."

"Don't quote Axerian to me. I've heard it all."

"There is time, Great Ones," the Gandsman said. "Even with our influence waning in Gand, Thellan is ripe to rise."

"I am not here for your ascendant, Paendurion," the woman said, meeting his eyes. "I offer this one service; the rest must be your doing. I mean to travel north, and west."

"Time is short," he said. "And already you risk too much. See that you succeed."

"I know what is at stake."

"Be well, Ad-Shi."

"You as well."

INTERLUDE

BAVDA

The Starfield and the Strands
Soulless Eternity

P ain still lingered behind her conscious mind. Part of her could feel
the needles boring holes in the base of her skull, piercing through
the tissue of her chest between her ribs. She'd ordered her attendants to
suspend her body by leather straps, and she hung there, leaking blood
down her naked skin. But her mind was elsewhere. Her mind was here.

She'd done it. She'd returned.

The old man reclined in his reed chair, his form blurring as her senses
recovered. Behind him an endless void stretched, as though the night sky
had swallowed them both, blackness filled with thousands of points of
light. He wore simple garb, the sort a fisherman might favor, gray linen
tied by hemp rope, and his skin was pruned and dry, with wisps of a
pale white beard growing from his jaw. The first time she'd come here
she'd expected splendor: a jade throne adorned with gold, a mighty King
floating on golden clouds and flanked by celestial dragons. Yet now she
knew the old man for what he was, and she wept, falling to her knees to
be in her God's presence once again.

"Lady Khon," the old man said. "It brings me great joy to see you."

"My lord," she said, struggling not to mumble. For reasons unknown
to her she wore her robes here, though she'd been naked in the physical
world. It gave her the comfort of her veil to hide her emotions. She'd

scarce gone without it, and certainly not in meetings with outsiders, since her induction into the Great and Noble House of the Heron.

"You are in pain," the old man said.

"Great Lord," she said. "I return bearing news of victory. You bade me secure a place close to the Imperial Throne, and I have succeeded. The Emperor listens to my counsel, and I have urged him along the path you have ordained."

"This is good," the old man said, showing her a sorrowful look. "Yet I fear for you, and all of yours, in what is to come."

She remained silent, keeping her eyes level with the blackness below their feet. She'd never call it the ground—it appeared to be empty space, extending downward as far as she could see.

"Your desire is still the same, is it not?" he asked.

"It is, Great Lord," she replied.

"Power," he said, and she nodded, keeping her eyes low. Power. All she'd dreamed of, since she was a girl. She'd been five when her father had tried to strike her, and she found the gift within herself to turn the force of his blow, to magnify it, shape it, redirect it into a strike of her own. The news of his death had carried far enough from her village to bring the *magi* in the orange veils, to see her tested and taken away. And she'd clawed for it since, for every scrap of her potential. It had brought her to the top of the Tower of the Heron. It had brought her here, into the presence of God.

"You will have it," he continued. "The Herons are promised a place in this cycle, and so long as you serve, I will keep faith."

"Anything, Great Lord," she said, and meant it. "Guide my hand, and I will serve."

"Our world is dying, Lady Khon," the old man said, his voice filled with sadness. "You have secured your House a place in the Emperor's Councils, and this is good. But we have need of more. The time has come to set aside secrecy, and act in the open. Your order must prepare for war. Raise an army, and see your acolytes placed at its head. The time will soon be upon us, and you must be ready to pay whatever price is asked, when it arrives."

Her heart thrummed. War. The Great and Noble Houses had abstained from politics for generations, yet here was God himself telling her to violate that taboo.

"Yes, Great Lord," she said. "I will."

He seemed content. "You have great skill," he said. "Ascension may be yours, if you seek to claim it."

She struggled not to show emotion. Even the most ancient texts spoke of such a thing only in rumor. And here it was.

"Ascension," she said.

"Yes."

"What is it, Great Lord?"

"A chance," he replied. "A chance to stand at my side, when the moment arrives to cleanse the world. If you are worthy, you will be granted power enough to see it done."

"How will I know, when it comes?"

He smiled. "You will know. The Soul beckons to all those worthy of the Master's call. You will hear His voice, and be judged. You will…"

She waited for him to finish, almost daring to look up.

"Ah," he said instead. "It appears you are waking."

Panic filled her veins. "No, Great Lord," she said. "I gave them strict instructions."

"Nonetheless. It was pleasant to see you, Lady Khon. Be well."

The stars shimmered, and anger flooded away her panic. Fifteen minutes. She'd been assured at least fifteen minutes, and this was scarcely five. The fabric of her dress melted as the stars bled together, the darkness seeming to drink their light. The old man smiled, untouched by what was happening around them.

The pain returned in full.

She screamed, the leather bindings chafing her wrists as she convulsed. She was back in the Tower Apex, a chamber of rough-cut stone, suspended over drainage already soaked red with blood. Steel needles protruded from her chest, though it appeared the needles in her temples and jaw had already been removed. Her muscles ached, raw and sore where they'd been punctured, and burning pain lanced through her at her slightest movement.

"Grandmaster," one of her attendants said breathlessly. "Thank the earth spirits you've come back."

"Too soon," she said, her voice hoarse and cracking. She wanted to find anger, to summon the gift of Force and smash her attendants to blood and pulp. Instead she whimpered, tears shaking her body. God but it hurt.

"Remain still, Mistress," a man's voice said. It took a moment to place it through the pain: Master Wen, her Master of Commerce and Coin. She'd trusted him to oversee this affair, which meant he served as Grandmaster, however temporarily, in her absence. "You are here, among friends. You will be whole again soon."

"No," she said, trying to shake her head and finding the pain too raw to move. "No."

Wen nodded to the adepts, who reached for the needles in her chest. She understood their purpose an instant before they yanked the steel from her body, and she screamed again.

"Loose her restraints," Wen said when they were finished. The adepts complied, and she sobbed as the leather was undone. Blood smeared as it ran down her skin, and pooled beneath her, trailing into the steel drains in the floor. She'd had this chamber made, when she came to understand the nature of the ritual needed to commune with God. She'd never shied away from the price of her ambition, and she wouldn't now. But pain shook her senses, the colors around her seeming to dim, until her blood ran gray.

"You are well, Mistress," Wen said, dismissing the adepts to stand back as he cradled her body down from the harness and straps. "We acted in time."

"No," she said. The word was a comfort. She'd lost something of great value. Perhaps protest could bring it back.

Wen held her, and her body shook with each sob as she pressed herself against his shoulder.

"Fetch the Bhakal healer," Wen said to one of the adepts. "We must be certain she survives."

Footsteps shuffled from the room, and she, Wen, and the other adept were alone. He carried her to the cushions they'd prepared for this moment, and laid her down gingerly, though every motion sent pain wrenching through her limbs.

"I saw him," she said, her sense still clouded by fog. Reverence descended on Wen and the adept both, a sudden silence in place of her screams.

"There will be time to speak on it when you are recovered, Mistress," Wen said after a moment. He'd knelt at her side, dabbing a linen cloth in water and pressing it against her skin. It stung, though the memory of what she'd seen had returned enough to dull the pain.

"No," she said. "He spoke of war, of ascension. We are to be scholars no longer. War is coming. We must be ready."

Wen froze midmotion, though the other adept continued to dress her wounds.

"His words will need interpreting, of course," Wen said. "We cannot be certain he intended us to—"

"We can," she interrupted. "He spoke it plain. It is time for us to come out of the shadows."

This time even the adept stopped in place.

"Pardon, Mistress, and forgive this poor adept for speaking out of turn," the boy said. "But are we truly meant to make war?"

"We are," she said, letting resolution fill her voice. "We are to be captains at the head of a great army."

"But, Mistress, the *magi* have not warred in a thousand years," the adept said.

She maintained her composure for the boy's sake. Inspiration would be the least of her duties in the months to come. And he was, strictly speaking, incorrect, though only those with access to the House's secret histories would know the truth. It put a double burden on her. *Magi* were forbidden from the very sort of thing she had to drive them to do. But God had spoken. Her purpose was clear.

"We must change," was all she said; all she had strength to say. Her body shook, trembling from the pain. She had survived the ordeal. There would be time to rest.

Instinct warned her before the attack came.

She'd worked with Force too long not to notice it in another. Wen's eyes had closed for the barest fraction of a moment, and a tremor rippled through the stone floor, through the cushions, through the pain-enhanced senses of her already fragile wounds. Wen absorbed the pressure of his body's weight against the floor, magnified and redirected it into his hand, imbuing a strong arm's punch with the power of an anvil dropped from the sky.

It should have smashed her to pulp where she lay. But she was Grandmaster. None alive knew the workings of Force as she did.

He struck her, and the blow landed with the strength of a child's.

"No," Wen said, his eyes suddenly desperate. "Lady Khon, I...I only meant to...Our order is peaceful. If we give the rest of the world cause to fear us, they will—"

The energy of Wen's attack reverberated inside her, rattling an already fragile frame. It surged through her limbs, coursing through her fingers as it sought release. It would destroy her if she tried to keep it contained. Instead she turned it on Wen, and tore his body apart.

She felt his attempt to turn the energy, as she had with his attack, and for a moment their wills collided. Hers was stronger, the relentless hunger that had driven her since she was a child. Wen's body sheared itself in two, flung across the chamber in a rush of blood and tissue. His head struck the wall, his legs contorted and bent as his spine shattered, leaving a red stain across the stone.

The adept stared between her and the wall, his jaw open in shock.

"M-M-Mistress...I...I..." the adept said, muttering as he stared. "I...I d-don't..."

"He won't be the last," she said, as a wave of fatigue rushed through her. Always the price of working with her gifts, and doubly so now, with her body already on the cusp of death. But even as she felt it, she found strength. She was Bavda Khon, Grandmaster of the Great and Noble House of the Heron. Her God had called, and she had answered. He promised power, and for that price, she was his tool, to whatever end.

INTERLUDE

REYNE

Library
Gods' Seat

Boredom.

He thumbed through a volume on economics; an ancient tome by a man called Smith. A Gandsman, from the name, though he'd never heard of such an absurd practice as naming oneself for one's trade. Were there men named Cooper, Miller, Baker, too? He tried to refocus his mind on the arguments, a point about measuring wealth from production and trade, rather than stocks of gold and specie. The thread carried for another half page before he realized he hadn't been reading its words.

He sighed, and set the volume on his desk. Impossible to focus when the hunger struck.

"How long?" he asked out loud. "How long am I to remain here?"

You must have patience.

Saruk's voice grated on his skin. He needed a kill. Or at least some passion, some intensity. Something. Instead the days droned on, blurring one into another. There wasn't even sunlight, or any indicator of nighttime beyond snuffing the lamps that relit themselves when he was ready to wake. He was a God, so said every precept of the Codex. So far it felt rather like being shut in, under house arrest. He wasn't even certain where he was.

He rose, cracking his neck and shoulders as he stretched. Another walk would have to settle it. The library would be here when he returned, all his lesser tomes left open if he intended to read them or shelved if he was done. Strange beyond reason, how the room seemed to be able to anticipate his will. But if that was the only manifestation of Godhood, it was a poor trade from a life spent leading men and women in pursuit of *égalité*.

He turned toward the doorway, and almost jumped back. Paendurion loomed there, unmoving. Watching him with coal-black eyes, sized to fit three men within the width of his frame.

"You," Reyne said. "Are you going to speak to me today?"

Ad-Shi had sworn Paendurion could speak as well as any man, but he hadn't heard a word from the so-called champion of Order since his ascension. He'd hardly seen the fellow, only heard him smashing furniture in the part of the Gods' Seat Ad-Shi had told him to avoid. Yet now he was here, in the library, or at least hovering on the cusp.

Reyne held his place for a long moment. "Can you speak at all, you dumb brute?"

If the insult bothered the man, he gave no sign.

"Why are you here?" Reyne said. "Why am *I* here? What is this place?"

More silence.

Ordinarily he'd have composed himself. It wasn't of any use, betraying your emotions to men who might be your rivals. But the hunger ached beneath his skin. Saruk was no help. Even Ad-Shi, who had tried to burn him to cinders and only begrudgingly offered any company at all in the weeks since his coming, had been absent. He hadn't seen her at all for days.

He pounded a fist atop the table, cracking the book he'd left open there down the spine.

Paendurion gave him a half smile, but said nothing.

"Amusing, is it?" Reyne demanded. "Either tell me why you're here or leave off. Or did you finally snap and kill the tribal woman in one of your tantrums? Are you here to finish me as well?"

"Ad-Shi is Vordu, not one of your tribesfolk."

The words stunned him. He took a step back, rubbing at his forearm where he'd struck the table, and waited for more.

Nothing came.

"Where is she?" he asked. "Have you injured her?"

"She is gone."

Once more the reply surprised him; until now the giant had given him dark looks and little else.

"Where has she gone? Are there places we can go, from here? What is the nature of this place? Saruk tells me only to wait; Ad-Shi promised more would be made clear with time."

"Time has passed," Paendurion said. "Come."

Paendurion turned, leaving the library entrance behind.

Reyne followed, trailing through the halls. They strode past the living quarters Reyne had claimed, and another fork in the hallway leading to the meditation chambers, and the stone passage whence he had come after his ascension. If there was some other way he'd never found it, and he'd explored the twists and turns of this place half a hundred times since he'd come here. Only the wings of Paendurion's chambers had been declared off-limits, and perhaps that was the reason why. If there was some means to leave, some way the tribeswoman had taken, perhaps the secret lay there. But they didn't veer toward that section of the halls. Instead they went toward the center, the wide circular room covered over with stone and ringed with pulsing light. The Goddess's chamber, with her crystal enclosure running floor to ceiling at the center of the room.

He shivered, crossing the threshold into her presence. Pain leaked through the glass, the dull ache that kept his hunger from becoming madness, a slow drip to charge Saruk's stores of *Red*, *Yellow*, and *White*. More emotion than any one person could hold.

Sarine.

The girl who had been a thorn in his shoe, whom Saruk had always cautioned him to avoid. Somehow she was here, trapped within crystal, covered by ribbons frozen in patterns around her half-naked form. Had the ribbons moved, since he saw her last? Ad-Shi had refused to speak of her, as firmly as Paendurion had refused to speak at all. Yet here he was, in her presence, at Paendurion's side.

"Ad-Shi has told you your place," Paendurion said. His voice was as deep and booming as one might have expected, from a man the size of a bear.

"She tried to kill me," Reyne said. "And never told me much of anything, beyond that this was the Gods' Seat, and our place is here, waiting."

"The waiting is almost finished. Soon we return to the world, to reclaim the Soul."

"And what is that? What does it mean?"

Paendurion eyed him with loathing, but said nothing, returning to face the Goddess's crystal.

The gesture stung. It felt as though his hold here were precarious, as though the wrong move might send the giant back to ignoring him. Best to try a different tack.

"Why do you two seem to hate me so?"

The question drew Paendurion's attention again, but with a look as hard as the one he'd given before.

"Because we two were once three. Your presence here was a mistake, and it cost us more than you could know."

"I'm sorry for your loss," Reyne said automatically. "But I had nothing to do with it."

"You have no idea of what you speak. Axerian is not *my* loss. It will fall to you, to stand against the champions of Death in his stead. What will you do, when the skinchangers of Fox appear as your closest allies, knifing you in the back? Will you face a blade-dancer of Crane, or a Force-*magi* of Heron? Heavens help us if a Dragon ascends this time, or a Lotus."

Paendurion's words slid past him, beyond his understanding. He knew enough to recognize the threat behind them, but the Codex had promised nothing past his ascension. He had followed its path here, expecting Godhood, the power to effect a better world, and found only bitter solitude, and waiting. Yet to hear Paendurion tell it, there would be more.

"You're right," he said. "I know nothing of this. But I can learn. Will you teach me?"

Paendurion barked a sharp laugh, full of scorn. "Not for your sake. But yes. Where the enemy's Houses have had thousands of years to pass down their traditions, I will teach you the ways of Balance, and the *kaas*. I, who have never held one of their bonds. Surely my tutelage will lead you to greatness, when I know nothing of your gifts."

"I know some part of what Saruk can do."

"You know less than nothing."

The dismissal cut him short. Fair enough to suppose he was ignorant of whatever conflicts Paendurion seemed to take for granted. He hadn't risen to power through arrogance, and proximity to the Goddess was enough to sate his hunger and have him thinking clearly. He could be humble, and learn whatever the giant had to teach. The first part of mastering a new mode of thought was recognizing that there were patterns to know—that much he had from the Codex—and the second part was admitting to ignorance, to avoid anchoring bad habits and false knowledge in the way of progress.

"I know less than nothing," he repeated. "Teach me, and I will learn."

Finally Paendurion gave him a look without scorn, or at least, with less.

"It starts here," he said. "From the power of the Goddess you know as the Veil."

It took a moment to realize he meant the girl. "Sarine. The girl from—"

"Be silent," Paendurion interrupted. "First, you must learn there are many systems. Order, Balance, Wild—these are only three. There are many, many more. Over time they develop affinity for one another, some grown subservient to others, and others given mastery over the rest. Life and Death are the apex; all systems serve one, or the other. Do you understand?"

Reyne kept silent. Paendurion would know he couldn't have given enough information for Reyne to understand. But the patterns would reveal themselves, if he listened and waited.

It seemed to serve. "The Veil holds the reins of Life magic," Paendurion continued, "and through it, she calls Order, Balance, and Wild to be her champions. The enemy wields Death—he is known as the Regnant, and he in turn calls on the strength of the Great and Noble Houses of his lands. There will be time to study their strengths, to attempt to prepare you not to die as soon as you meet one of their ascended. First, you must learn to wield Life magic for yourself."

"*Life?*" he asked. "The bindings the priests use to heal?"

"A perversion. The proper name for that tether is *Growth*. Life is beyond the leylines. Life stems from the Soul of the World, channeled through the Goddess herself."

Paendurion took a step toward the crystal enclosure at the center of the room, raising a hand toward it. In an instant an arc of blue light shot out from the crystal, meeting his fingertips. Reyne stared. The same energy had bound him here, after his ascension. The energy coursed and sparked, dancing between the crystal and Paendurion's fingers.

"This is the essence of Life magic," Paendurion said. "It is everywhere, but we gain its power here, from—"

The crystal cracked.

A ripping sound, like metal torn in half, with shards of glass shattering and falling to the floor.

Paendurion whirled to face the crystal, and the arc of blue light vanished. Liquid flooded from the crystal as it broke at the center, spiderweb fissures tracing outward from the focal point of the break.

"What's going on?" Reyne asked. "Is this part of your demonstration?"

The Goddess remained suspended as her prison shattered around her. Chunks and shards of crystal broke, falling around the ribbons, somehow still hanging in the air.

"No. No. Please." Paendurion's voice, odd as it was to hear his thundering baritone making pleading sounds.

The Goddess opened her eyes.

"Zi! They can't...Where are...d'Agarre?"

A ray of light erupted from her body, a blinding flash so bright he had to raise a hand to block it out.

A thud sounded, and he opened his eyes to find the Goddess's body fallen amid the broken crystal shards. Her eyes were open, but lifeless, her mouth half-open in shock. The ribbons fell around her, painting her body with strips of black cloth.

"No. No," Paendurion continued. "Not yet. Not now."

Reyne strode past him, kneeling amid the rubble at the Goddess's side. Her skin had already gone a bluish pale; a touch confirmed it was cold, though her eyes remained open, unblinking, frozen in a look of permanent surprise. He reached to close them. It seemed the right thing to do, for a corpse.

PART 2: SUMMER

KORYU | FIRE SPIRITS

19

SARINE

A Campfire
Wilderness

Blackness surrounded her. She heard a heartbeat, but saw nothing. Pain came rushing like water poured into her.

She screamed, and jolted up from her bedroll.

Acherre snapped up from where she'd slept, instantly awake. "What is it? Are we in danger?"

The tribesfolk roused themselves slower, but reacted in the same manner to her scream. Arak'Jur, Corenna, Ilek'Inari. Words came pouring in her ears, mixed in two languages and sorted by Zi. She didn't listen.

Something had changed.

Her heart thundered in her chest, giving rise to a sense of dread. Something terrible was coming. Her belly ached, a raw pain echoed from her dream.

"Sarine," Acherre said, laying a gentle hand on her upper arm. "Sarine, are you all right?"

Sparks flickered at the edge of her vision. Something out of reach.

"I ..." she heard herself say. Her voice. Hers. The same she'd always used. "I must have ..."

"A dream," Arak'Jur said. "Not an unexpected thing, as we draw closer. Ka'Ana'Tyat is a place of great power."

"I'm sorry I woke all of you," she said. "It was nothing. Only a dream."

Arak'Jur and Corenna offered her looks of sympathy, then returned to their sleep after a cursory check of their surroundings. It was black outside, a deeper darkness than she'd ever known in the city. Stars shone through the trees by the ten thousands, brighter even than the nights she'd slept in the woods outside Rasailles.

Ilek'Inari lingered by their fire, adding a new branch and a handful of dry leaves. He'd been the one keeping watch for the midnight shift; Arak'Jur had taken the first, and Acherre offered the last.

"Are you sure you're all right?" Acherre asked. The captain had seemed alert, instantly awakened, but she'd returned to the edge of sleep, now that the danger had passed.

Sarine nodded, and that seemed the only cue Acherre needed to let sleep return in full.

Quiet fell, thick as the darkness. Her belly still ached, and she stayed seated, pulling her knees into her chest from beneath her blankets. Zi lay coiled around her arm, and she checked him, running a finger over his scales. He seemed to be asleep, too, though until recent weeks she'd never seen him do more than a light nap, alert, or at least aware of her at the slightest attention. His long body rose and fell with each miniature breath, a strangeness unto itself. It seemed wrong for Zi to breathe—she couldn't recall having ever noticed him do it before. Perhaps she hadn't paid enough attention.

"Would it help to talk it through?"

Ilek'Inari kept his voice quiet enough not to disturb the others, but it still startled her.

"It was just a dream," she said.

"Dreams can still keep us awake. I find it helps, to shift your thoughts, to do something else until your body remembers it needs to sleep."

With that he offered a stripped tree branch, gesturing for her to come and help him tend the fire. Well, why not. She wasn't likely to unravel any mysteries sitting in her bedroll. She rose, careful not to make noise, and joined him.

He poked the fire after handing over his spare stick, prodding the wood to belch cinders into the air.

"There is a story of a man who had vivid dreams, if you would like to hear it."

"Please," she said. Still an oddity, that Zi could translate her speech as easily as others speaking to her. To her it seemed as though she spoke in the Sarresant tongue, and she heard them speak in the same, despite Zi being asleep. Even a week traveling in the guardian's company, with his woman and the apprentice shaman, hadn't wholly erased the strangeness, though it was slowly becoming familiar.

Ilek'Inari stoked the fire again. "In the days of my grandfather's grandfather's grandfather, when the Sinari tribe made war against the Tanari, there was a man called Venari'Dan." He paused. "*Venari* means he is a warrior, a soldier." When she nodded, he continued. "One morning, Venari'Dan came before the steam tents, interrupting the elders with a tale of his visions. He'd seen a flute in his dreams, a flute of petrified wood and *mareh'et* bone, a flute so soft and pure it could make any who heard it—man or woman—think only of love, forgetting all thoughts of war, all notions of anger, sadness, or despair. Venari'Dan had lost a brother, to the Tanari, and all Sinari in those days knew the pain of that sort of loss.

"The elders listened as Venari'Dan told them of his dream. They reckoned it a fine thing, imagining music could settle feuds of blood, or salve the sting of death, or sadness. They lauded his dream, and thanked him for sharing it. But Venari'Dan was not finished. He swore his dream could be real, that the spirits had chosen him to seek the materials to carve his perfect flute, to be the one who ended war between the tribes. The elders gave wise counsel: He should let the idea rest, and see if the spirits sent him the dream again, before he went off in search of the wood and bone to make his flute. He listened, and set the idea aside for some weeks. But after the turning of the next moon, he had the dream again.

"This time he took his vision to the tribe's shaman, coming before the ritual fires to ask the guidance of the spirits of things-to-come. The shaman again gave him wise counsel, urging him to first learn to play the flute— since Venari'Dan was a hunter and a warrior, and had never made a note of music in his life. Venari'Dan listened to the shaman's words, and took up a simpler instrument of reed and elk bone. He practiced for the turnings of six moons, morning to nightfall, until he could carry a tune so pure and soft it would make you weep to hear it.

"He believed himself ready, and so he sought counsel from his mother, a venerable elder among the women of the tribe. She cautioned him to be grateful for the spirits' gift, that his dreams had led him to learn the making of beautiful songs. This time he did not listen to wisdom, and he set out in search of the ancient tree and *mareh'et* he had seen in his dream. He was sure he knew the way, many moons' journey westward, to the land where the sun meets the sea at night.

"Venari'Dan packed his implements for the hunt, and enough food and water for a long journey. On the night before he left, he had the dream again, the same dream. He left in the morning, confident the spirits guided him on his path. He left, and he never returned."

Ilek'Inari smiled and went quiet, returning to prodding the fire.

"And?" she asked. "What became of him, and his flute?"

"As I said, he never returned to Sinari lands."

"That's it? That's the whole story?"

"It is."

"What's the point of telling a story like that? If you don't know how it ends?"

"Ah, but we do know. Has there been an end to war and sadness in the world? If there has not, then we know the end of Venari'Dan's tale."

She frowned, turning her attention back to the fire. Doubtless any number of her uncle's parables would be baffling to tribesfolk. Better not to insult with her lack of understanding.

She kept quiet, but Ilek'Inari leaned forward, and spoke.

"Sometimes dreams are only dreams."

The rest of the night passed in relative quiet. Croaking toads and humming insects took the place of late-night wagons or drunken revelers, the sounds of the wild replacing those of the city. The city's noise would have been louder, but she could have slept through the market at midday before feeling comfortable beyond the barrier. She hadn't returned to sleep in spite of Ilek'Inari's company, or Acherre's, when it was the captain's turn at the watch. Ilek'Inari was right, she was sure. Her dream was just a dream. But something had changed.

The blue sparks still danced at the edge of her vision, as though she could turn her head suddenly and catch sight of them. In quiet moments between the hooting owls and rustling branches, she could almost swear they formed a pattern, pulling her attention deeper, as though they lurked behind everything she saw. A new sense, paired with sight and sound and touch to suggest a different reality than she'd ever known before. The world seemed to be a reflection of the sparks, shadows cast by things' true nature. Even her own flesh seemed to hide a pattern, a spiderweb of blue lines suddenly more complex than she had ever seen or noticed. She traced it in her mind, following the impulse of the strange new sense in an idle haze between waking and sleep.

She was beautiful.

An embarrassing thought, and more than a little self-absorbed. Her uncle would have chided her for pride. But it was true. A network of blue lines, twisted to form shapes that echoed her limbs in etchings of pure light. How had she ever missed this side of the world? It seemed so obvious now. She followed the sparks without knowing what she was doing. A curve, for her spine, another that reflected her bond with *mareh'et*. Two burning embers were her eyes; somehow she saw them from another vantage, looking into herself. *Mind* lay there, coiled at the base of her skull. *Mind*, and a knot, where a hundred strands ran together. Having found it, she couldn't look away. The sparks became twisted loops upon each other and themselves, a tangle of light and heat that seemed out of place. It was out of place. The rest of her was elegant and well-formed; the knot was ugly and cold. She reached for it with a different sense, nudging it toward warmth. It should obey, and—

A shrieking sound thundered through their camp. A screech, so loud it burned in her ears, like a falcon's cry, a lion's roar, a small child's scream.

Arak'Jur was on his feet instantly, surrounded by a halo of light in the shape of a bear. The rest followed within seconds, but the screech was gone, returning the camp to a dull quiet beneath a cold blue sky.

The sound still rang in her ears as the rest of them darted about, seeking a source. She'd done something to provoke it. But the sound hadn't come from outside the camp. She hadn't opened her mouth, but it had come from her.

No. Not from her.

"Zi," she said. "Oh Gods, Zi."

She unwrapped her forearm, revealing Zi's metallic coils looped around her skin. He was shaking, clinging to her, his eyes wide, staring at her in silence.

"Zi, are you all right? What's happened? What have I done?"

A thin trickle of hurt passed into her thoughts. No words, only a sensation of pain. She clutched him to her chest, feeling his claws dig into her skin. He was clinging to her. He was alive.

"Traveling with you is lively, Sarine Thibeaux," Arak'Jur said, returning to stand beside the firepit.

"Is all well with your...companion?" Corenna asked. The tribeswoman had been distant from her since making her recovery, and it showed in her stance, hovering a few paces behind Arak'Jur.

"I don't know," she said.

"The sun is due soon," Arak'Jur said. "We can start early, and reach Ka'Ana'Tyat by midday, if you are fit to travel."

"The perimeter is clear," Acherre said, coming into view through a thick copse of oaks. "Nothing more than wildlife out here, and no sign of whatever made that shriek."

Zi still clung to her collarbone, but he was breathing, his heart beating a tiny rhythm against hers.

"I'm sorry," she said. "For my nightmare, and for Zi. I think he's well enough. At least he's alive."

"We can rest, if you require it," Arak'Jur said.

"No," she said. "We can go."

"The sooner we reach Ka'Ana'Tyat, the sooner the spirits can prompt us where to find this fair-skin, this Axerian. Provided you are still sure you can clear the way?"

She slung her pack up to her shoulder, cradling Zi with her free hand. From the sound of it, Arak'Jur's sacred place had been cordoned off by the blue sparks, the same as she'd seen in the sewer. If it was so, then she could get them in. She'd at least sworn to try.

"I can do what I promised."

Arak'Jur nodded, and the rest set to disassembling their camp, untethering the horses, rolling blankets, and preparing to start the day.

She checked Zi again. Whatever she'd done, it seemed to have left him in shock. "Stay with me," she said, just above a whisper. "We'll find Axerian soon. He'll know how to make this right."

20

ARAK'JUR

Wilderness, Approaching Ka'Ana'Tyat
Sinari Land

He eyed Corenna as she and the fair-skins secured their horses. He and Ilek'Inari had opted not to use the animals to speed their journey, a matter of pride for the guardians, and of practicality. Trained beasts were too precious to risk, if it came to fighting, and it would all but certainly come to fighting, before his journey was at an end. A single mount between him and Corenna would serve. Provided he couldn't convince her to stay behind.

She caught him looking as she swung into the saddle, and gave him a knowing smile, a spark in her eyes that promised more, when next they were alone. He'd already failed to leave her with the tribes as they settled onto the fair-skins' lands. Incredible how quickly she'd healed. Strong enough to plant her feet and talk him down at the mere suggestion that she might remain behind. The sight of her with a blade in her chest had cut him to the ground, but he hadn't found the words to convince her. There might be one more chance, after Ka'Ana'Tyat, and he held out hope for that, rehearsing different arguments in his head as they kicked dirt over their fire, and pressed on into the woods.

"Are you well, apprentice?" he asked, pulling even with Ilek'Inari, just ahead of the rest. "Sarine didn't trouble your sleep overmuch?"

"No, honored guardian," Ilek'Inari said, a shade too quickly.

Arak'Jur grinned. He might have expected to find his apprentice nervous, uncertain as to whether the spirits would accept him as *Ka*, in spite of every tradition that should have made him *Arak* rather than shaman. Instead Ilek'Inari stole a glance behind them, toward where Sarine sat atop her horse.

"A fine-looking woman," Arak'Jur said. "Even for a fair-skin. Though I would be cautious of the power she carries, tied to that serpent."

Ilek'Inari flushed. "I didn't... I don't..." He fell quiet, and Arak'Jur held his grin. "Spirits, but is it so obvious?"

"You have to have been smitten to see it in another. But I meant what I said. I speak from some experience on matters of the gift Llanara carried, and Reyne d'Agarre."

"They say Sarine used that gift to fight against them both, during the battle."

"That she did. She saved our warriors' lives, and I will praise her again if her claim holds true today. But I need not remind you of your importance to our people. Have a care with her, should she prove receptive to your advance."

"I will, honored guardian, of course." They walked a few more paces before Ilek'Inari stole another look over his shoulder. "She hasn't said anything...?"

He laughed, clapping his apprentice on the back as he walked past.

A simple thing, to find such interests blossoming even here, in the midst of chaos and uncertainty. It brought a smile, thinking of attraction and wooing instead of violence, and proved a welcome distraction, remembering the steps he'd taken as a youth to catch Rhealla's eye. He'd made himself look more than half a fool, trying to lift a ritual pole alone and almost lodging it in Ka'Vos's backside while the shaman told a story to the rest of the hunters. Rhealla had blushed on his behalf, rushing to quell the laughter that erupted at his expense. It had always been her way, to protect the ones she saw as hers. It was why he'd loved her; she'd been fearless and iron-spined, unflinching against the slightest threat to what she knew was right.

No small part of what he had with Corenna, now. It was good to be reminded of the simple things, on their way to something else. From the look of it Sarine wouldn't be easily interested, no matter how delicate Ilek'Inari's approach. Her crystalline serpent raised every warning instinct in him as a guardian, but she seemed engrossed by the thing, and by its apparent sickness. It would be just as well if their paths diverged, after they made their pilgrimages to Ka'Ana'Tyat.

The forest turned from dense foliage to too-thickly spaced trees, one trunk almost atop the next. A subtle sign as they walked and rode, easy to miss. But soon the trees would intertwine, blending into the walls of growth that marked the path to Ka'Ana'Tyat.

"Keep alert," he said to the rest of them. "There will be a great beast here, guarding the way."

They fanned out, as much as they could manage through the dense wood. He kept his senses sharp, listening for rustles in the leaves, looking for sign, trusting instinct to warn him if anything at all was out of place. His mind receded into a thoughtless hum. His muscles stayed loose, relaxed, but ready to tense at the first sign of danger.

The wood grew darker in spite of the midday sun beating down overhead. The seasons had turned, while the tribe collected its belongings and set down on fair-skin land. Heat rose, and with it, insects buzzed past his ears, birds chirped their greetings, lizards and rodents scurried for a place to hide and wait out his passing. All of it faded into a tableau of normalcy. There would be more. A wisp of smoke, trailing from a lizard's eyes. A bellowing roar, when they crossed a threshold of a great bear's claim. A flickering shimmer, to reveal an illusory piece of bark on a tree. A pack of feathered birds, walking upright with scything claws. Something.

Instead they reached the opening, where looming blackness swallowed the sky, the branches of the trees grown together to suggest a passage into darkness.

"This is it," Sarine said, her voice touched with awe.

Their horses skittered back, and Sarine dismounted, passing the reins to Acherre.

"We've reached the entrance," Arak'Jur said. "But stay alert. There have been great beasts guarding our sacred places for six turnings of the seasons. I have no cause to believe it would have changed."

Ilek'Inari unslung his pack, kneeling in reverence as he withdrew the pouch of implements he'd prepared almost a full year before.

"I saw nothing on the way in," Corenna said, joining Sarine in dismounting, though Acherre stayed on her horse. "And I see the way unblocked, now, where before it was walled over by the trees. Perhaps...?"

"It's still blocked," Sarine said. She stepped toward the opening with a hand outstretched. "It was like this in the sewer, but bricked over instead of blocked by wood. It isn't real. Ad-Shi can only use the blue sparks to weave a barrier against those not chosen by the spirits to enter. There are limits to what can be done, even for me."

Sarine's voice seemed to echo with a surety he'd never heard from her before. Almost as though someone else spoke with her voice. Before he could dwell on it, a rush of energy sucked through the air around them, a snapping sound as blue light flashed, draining from the air around Ka'Ana'Tyat's opening to absorb itself into Sarine's fingertips.

"Spirits' blessings," Ilek'Inari said, staring into the darkness. "She's done it. The way is clear."

To Arak'Jur's eyes nothing had changed; it had been a passage into darkness the first time he'd escorted Ilek'Inari and Corenna here, and it remained so now. But Ilek'Inari rose to his feet, his eyes wide with awe, and walked toward it slowly, one step at a time.

Sarine waited for him to approach before she strode forward at his side.

They reached the edge of the darkness, and Ilek'Inari vanished, swallowed into the spirits' presence. Sarine remained behind.

It took a moment to realize she hadn't intended to stay back.

"Why?" Sarine demanded, directing her question into the opening. "Why not me?"

The wind shifted, and his instincts sharpened. Something was wrong.

"No," Sarine was saying. "You have to let me in. I have to find Axerian. Zi is dying!"

A chittering noise. Approaching from the south. Distant, but drawing nearer too quickly to be rustling, or the wind.

"Caution," Arak'Jur shouted. "Something approaches."

It was all he needed to say for Corenna to be on alert. The soldier, Acherre, responded as well, to his tone even if she wouldn't understand the words.

The noise grew louder, and he saw a black figure in the distance, vanishing as it moved between the trees.

"I know this beast," Corenna said. "*Sre'ghaus.*"

Two more black shapes appeared, swirling masses, almost-man-shaped, crashing through the trees toward the clearing around the passage into Ka'Ana'Tyat.

Not one beast. Not two, or three. Thousands. A roiling mass of insects, beetles swarming toward them, clouds of fluttering wings and gnashing jaws.

Corenna struck the first blow with a gale of wind, scattering the creatures into the upper boughs of the trees as she smashed apart one of the man-shaped figures. Acherre split into three copies of herself and her horse, each one drawing its saber as they charged. Arak'Jur stayed back, hovering near the entrance to Ka'Ana'Tyat. Corenna had told tales of facing *sre'ghaus*: long hours of fighting, with an uncertain end. The spirits' gifts would have to be conserved as long as possible.

"Please," Sarine said behind him. "I was promised you could show me visions of where Axerian is, of how I could make Zi well. Please don't let him die."

A fist-sized cluster of beetles descended from the trees, flying with chittering wings as they formed into a bird shape. He struck, and a stinging pain bit his forearm. The beetles came apart, dashed against the forest floor, but they raked with their teeth where they touched him. Foam rose from the tiny crosshatched wounds, and hissing, leaving a burning sensation on his skin. Acid.

Trails of beetles flew between the trees, and he lost sight of Corenna and Acherre. The creatures seemed to take their time swarming, forming shapes and masses before they struck. Buzzing drowned out all other sound as they arrived in full. His instinct was to retreat, to flee and return prepared for what they faced. Without the shamans' counsel he couldn't know the beast's weakness. But Ilek'Inari was already inside. If they left, the apprentice would emerge alone against the chittering mass.

He called on *ipek'a*, and leapt.

A cloud of beetles flew together overhead, gathering like a beehive on the edge of a branch. He grappled the tree with one hand, cutting through the center of the insects with the other, dispersing them like stinging smoke. He leapt again, passing through a formless stream of the creatures as he fell back to the earth. He braced himself for more stinging wounds, but none came. Instead the mass broke apart, flowing around him before re-forming into smaller shapes, each going a different direction than before.

Black specks decorated the ground, some skittering together, more smashed and leaking green ichor over the boughs and grass.

"Strike before they form," he shouted into the buzzing horde. Corenna had to be close; spirits send she was close enough to hear. "They attack only when they join together."

A stabbing pain took his shoulder from behind, and he whirled to smash a cat-shaped mass, *ipek'a*'s scything claws fending them off as they tried to bite. He leapt again, toward another cloud hovering at waist height behind a tree. Fluttering wings enveloped him as they burst apart, and he shielded his face. They seemed to multiply, engulfing the clearing in a deafening roar.

Acherre rode through a cloud, cutting with her saber as she wove to dodge the trees. Then another copy of her dashed past going the opposite way, parting the beetles like ribbons dropped to the forest floor. Both were swallowed by the beetles as soon as they rode through, more clouds forming as quick as they could be dispersed. He leapt into one, cutting with *ipek'a*'s gift, feeling the creatures' blood spatter as their bodies fell. Still they came.

Worry rose with every shape he cut, until he found Corenna. She held her ground, hurling ice, needlepoint barrages casting whole swarms into the grass. *Mareh'et* came when *ipek'a* faded, and for a time he fought at Corenna's side, until a man-shaped cloud danced between them, forcing them apart.

His limbs ached with exhaustion and pain as he fought. *Mareh'et* gave way to *lakiri'in*, and then *kirighra*, and the war-magic of fire. It seemed *sre'ghaus* fought with attrition, losing thousands of their number to score a single blow on their enemies, and he'd taken a score of their cuts, acid-drenched teeth marks ripping lines across his skin. He tried to shout directions to the women, in the tribes' tongue and the fair-skins', but his words were swallowed by the buzzing and clattering as the beetles flowed between the trees. He lost sight of the entrance to Ka'Ana'Tyat, and worried what would come when Ilek'Inari emerged, if they lasted long enough to wait through the rituals. Of Sarine there was no sign; he reasoned she'd been granted her plea, and must have vanished into the depths of Ka'Ana'Tyat's shadows.

But it was her voice he heard, when the chittering dimmed.

"Stop," Sarine shouted. "Stop fighting them. Let them leave."

He struck through a horde, splitting what was on the cusp of forming an elk shape, earning another searing cut slashed across his arm.

It took the beetles falling to the ground like the patter of rain on snow before he registered that he'd heard her voice.

"Stop," she said again. "Show them they can trust us."

This time he paused, only a moment of lowering his guard, and the beetles receded at once, backing away as though they were cautious of him. They withdrew through the trees, a cloud of black withdrawn to reveal Corenna, and Acherre. Both women stood, on their feet but haggard. Corenna's wraps were torn, hanging open to reveal skin cut and bleeding. Acherre was reduced to one copy, her military uniform in tatters, her saber scored black and green. Her horse was dead, a half-eaten corpse with rib bones protruding through flesh burned by acid, fifty feet from where Acherre stood. The captain ran to the beast as soon as the swarm retreated enough for it to be visible. He ran to Corenna.

She saw him at the same moment, and met him with strength in her arms. A tight grip, full of life, thank the spirits.

"How did you do this?" Corenna called to Sarine when finally he let her go, though she kept an arm around him for support, and he did the same.

Sarine walked toward them, stepping gingerly around the blanket of slain beetles draped across the ground.

"*Sre'ghaus* didn't want to be here," Sarine said. "They were compelled by Ad-Shi."

Sarine turned to Acherre, and he and Corenna turned to look along with her.

"Are you well, Captain?" Sarine asked.

Acherre made a reply in the fair-skin tongue, too fast for him to understand, though her voice was hoarse and ragged. Tears soaked her cheeks, and she clutched her fallen horse's body, though whatever she'd said must have satisfied Sarine as to her well-being.

"Honored...Sarine," Corenna said. "Would you...?"

She motioned to her belly, but left the question unasked. He tensed as Sarine laid a hand on Corenna's skin.

"The baby is fine," Sarine said, and once again the world lifted from his shoulders. "Better than you, from the look of it."

Corenna wiped a tear from her eyes, thanking Sarine as she tightened her grip around his lower back.

"Spirits curse my soul," Ilek'Inari said from behind. "What happened here?"

Arak'Jur turned to see his onetime apprentice hobbling over the corpse-strewn ground, picking his steps gingerly as he regarded them with awe.

"A great beast," he said, at the same moment Sarine said, "They wouldn't let me in. I didn't get the answers I needed."

"I know," Ilek'Inari said. "It was never your place, to speak with the spirits of visions."

Sarine swore, taking a challenging step toward the dark opening. "Ilek'Inari, I need your help. Convince them to permit me. I need to—"

"I am Ilek no longer," he interrupted, and for a moment a chill wind seemed to blow around him, a haze that blurred the edges of his form against the shadows behind. "The bond is complete. I am Ka'Inari, and I have sworn an oath to aid you on behalf of the spirits of things-to-come."

21

TIGAI

A Hidden Temple
Deep Within Shanshin Jungle

One of his escorts shoved his lower back, sending him staggering forward. He kept his footing, spinning with a glare for the spearman. Both guards showed him a mocking smile—he couldn't be certain which of them had done the pushing. They stayed back, hovering in the doorway he was unceremoniously made to enter.

"Put it on," the woman said from a dark corner of the room. Lin Qishan, the captain he'd abducted from the prison camp. The *magi*. His jailor, so long as she held Dao and Mei and Remarin.

He squinted to see through the dark of the chamber. After ungodly weeks marching through the jungle, being indoors felt alien and strange.

When he saw what she'd pointed to, he laughed, making it as scornful as he could manage. A hauberk of metal plates, a half helmet, and a short, curved blade, lying together in a pile atop a wood bench. Old weaponry. The sort used by soldiers centuries ago, and for entertainment today.

"Am I to be a pit fighter for you? After all this trouble?"

"You are to do as you are told. Put it on."

"No."

She gave him a cold glare, weighing him as though she tried to discern how seriously to take his refusal.

"You've had me on the road long enough to have tracked halfway to Nikkon," he said. "I'd expected a bath waiting at the end, perhaps a warm meal. At worst a prison cell. But if you think I'm donning pit fighter's gear for you without seeing Dao, Mei, and Remarin alive and untouched, your wits are as soured as your manners."

He'd practiced a better speech in his head, but circumstances dictated a certain amount of improvisation.

She held her glare as his speech gave way to silence.

"Pick one," she said.

Well, it was progress at least.

"Mei," he said. "Let me see her. If she can confirm everything is—"

"Kill the woman." Lin spoke past him, for the benefit of his two guards.

"What? No!"

Lin nodded, and the guardsmen showed him wicked grins, the leftmost one wheeling to deliver the order.

"You carry that out and I leave this place, returning only to murder you and everyone who dwells here in their sleep."

This time Lin gave a signal to hold.

"Our time together will pass more easily if my commands are obeyed," she said.

"We have no time together without Mei, Dao, and Remarin." It helped to say their names. Remind her they were people, not merely hostages. "If you hold them, show me, or I will assume they are dead."

"Do you imagine I am ignorant of the workings of a master Dragon's gift? If I bring them to you, you are gone, and they with you."

Flattering, for her to give him such a lofty title. He'd never mastered anything, so far as he knew. But she knew well enough the workings of the strands; he'd been planning to do precisely that, to anchor himself to his family and escape.

"Then we are at an impasse," he said.

"Only if you don't believe I have them, and I think you know I do."

For the thousandth time he weighed the truth behind her words. It would be a trivial thing, to hook himself to the starfield, to return to any place to which he felt a strong enough connection. Doing so meant a last farewell to his brother, to Mei and Remarin. It would be like cutting off a leg. Unthinkable. Easier to follow instructions, to let come what may.

He eyed the pit fighter's gear again. "I won't kill for you." A lame stand, but he needed at least a sliver of defiance after too long spent bending his pride.

"You have killed many men, Yanjin Tigai. Do not expect me to accept that you will blink at violence."

"I said I won't kill *for you.*"

This time she smiled. A cruel, strange gesture. It seemed out of place on her, though she would have been pretty enough to court, had he met her in a different world.

"Very well," she said. "Now put the armor on. We're already late."

———

He shuffled onto the dirt of what had to be a training yard, encumbered by the unfamiliar weight of steel. Not a pit fight, at least, or not one with an audience. He'd attended the pits at Qoba once. Nasty affairs, with blood and crowds trained to scent it. But those arenas were towering walls and rows of staired seating, constructs of clay with iron gates, roaring crowds, vendors hawking wares and taking bets amid the chaos. This was an empty ring of dirt surrounded by stone buildings nestled in the jungle. The only watchers were a pair of men on the far side of the ring, each dressed in white robes with saffron belts around their waists. His two guards completed the audience, and Lin Qishan, waiting at the center while he trotted into the ring.

"He moves like a boy in his father's armor," the elder of the two men said, a pruned figure with a thin white beard. Hagali, from the look of him, or one of the coastal peoples. The other robed man said nothing, a young, bald, well-muscled man with a Jun look, holding a staff almost as tall as he was.

"I assure you," Lin said, "he is everything that was promised."

"We shall see."

Suddenly Tigai felt like a horse at market. "Why am I here?" he demanded. "You've given me arms, am I meant to fight for your amusement?"

"You are here to answer for Captain Lin's wild tales," the younger robed man said, then turned to the elder. "Master, with your leave?"

The elder gestured toward the center, and Lin Qishan bowed, retreating to the edge of the ring, leaving him alone on the dirt.

"Hold on," Tigai said. "I never agreed to this. I told you, I won't kill for you, or for them."

"No one expects you to be the one doing the killing, Lord Tigai," Lin said.

Shit.

The younger robed man strode onto what had suddenly become a dueling ground, working his staff in both hands. His opponent had a familiar grace, the sort of lightness on his feet Tigai had come to recognize in Remarin, and the best of the soldiers Remarin had trained. Hardly fair to give him unfamiliar weaponry against a man clearly trained to the implements at hand. Then again, he had armor on his chest and head, where the monk didn't even have the luxury of hair to shield his scalp. His enemy had the advantage of reach, whereas he had a sharp edge to his weapon. And of course, the starfield and the strands.

He set an anchor where he stood, then fell back, brandishing his sword in a two-handed grip at waist height. Pistols were his preferred implement, but he'd spent enough hours to know a stance or two with the blade. As soon as he set his feet, the monk spun his staff into a different grip, nested beneath the crook of an elbow.

Without warning the monk snapped forward, darting the butt of his staff in a jab aimed at Tigai's head. He brought his sword up in time, shoving it away, and found the staff withdrawn and jabbed again as quick as he could blink. This time it caught his helmet with a ringing thud, and the world rushed out from beneath his feet. Pain crunched along his side, and air left his lungs.

The elder laughed from the edge of the ring; if he said anything it was swallowed by the ringing in Tigai's ears.

The monk shuffled forward, a cautious step with the staff extended like a spear, pointing at him. No sign that his enemy intended to allow him to yield. Of course not. Why would it be easy?

He groaned to sell the pain, letting his sword drop from his hand to clatter into the dirt. The monk still prowled toward him, legs spread wide. Another jab from the staff connected with his ribs through the hauberk, and he howled with unfeigned agony. The monk shuffled forward, raising his weapon for another strike.

Tigai reverted to his anchor, appearing—sword in hand—beside the monk, all injuries vanished, as whole as he had been when he set the strands in place. Even the exhaustion was manageable—it was worse, the farther he traveled, and here, blinking less than a stone's throw away did little more than wind him. He pulled his blade upward in an arcing cut, and the monk spun to block the strike, a step too slow. Steel bit flesh, splitting the monk's silk robes like paper.

The monk's eyes rolled back in his head, and the young man collapsed, going limp while his staff fell into the dirt.

"Fuck," Tigai said. "I didn't mean to—"

The monk vanished, and another splitting pain struck him from behind, this time a blow landed to tangle his legs. He went down around the staff, and the monk struck again, landing a thundering hit to his helmet, hard enough to bounce his head off the ground. His senses faded out, blackness pouring into his vision. But first, the strands. By reflex he tied himself to another anchor, set by instinct when he walked onto the yard, and snapped back to health.

Rage flooded through him, and wonder. The monk had his gift. He'd all but killed the man with his cut, and the monk had reappeared behind him, healthy and whole as Tigai himself. He'd never seen anyone else do anything like it.

"Enough," the elder said, all sign of mirth vanished from his voice.

"With respect, Master Indra, you see I told it true." Lin Qishan preened like a child proven innocent; her guards came to stand behind her, and once more all of them looked at him as though he were a prized horse. "He has a master's skill, untrained. Enough to take twenty men from Vimar to Liao. And perhaps more, if you push him."

"Sixty thousand *qian*," the elder—Master Indra—said. "If you can provide leverage that will keep him here, when the training grows hard."

"What the bloody fuck are you talking about?" he said.

"Done," Lin Qishan said. "And done. His brother, his brother's wife, and a childhood mentor, safely away from anywhere they might have had a connection he could trace."

"No," Tigai said. "I won't have any part of this."

"Be silent, boy," Master Indra said. "Let Captain Lin have her gold. I'm offering you a chance to learn to use the power you've been stumbling over like a drunken fool. Shut up and recognize fortune when it falls at your feet."

22

ERRIS

Assembly Hall, Hearing Chambers
Southgate District, New Sarresant

A trio of faces looked down on her, a man and two women seated atop elevated plinths that evoked the Exarch, Oracle, and Veil. An oddly religious overtone, for an otherwise secular assembly, but then the power of three was a pattern repeated without thought, even outside the priesthood. A ring of observers watched from a gallery running the length of the circular room, and she stood alone at the center, as though she were a criminal set to face her trial.

"High Commander Erris d'Arrent," one of the women said, the one seated in the middle chair. "You've been summoned before the Assembly to discuss the matters of the treaties brokered at the height of the spring campaign. Thank you, for your swift appearance."

"Three weeks' delay," a man said, seated to the chairwoman's left. "Hardly appropriate to call it swift."

"Assemblyman Lerand, please," the chairwoman said, and the man relented at once. An unfamiliar sort of combat, verbal sparring with even the rebuke and retreat an almost-scripted part of their affair. Erris's full dress uniform added to the separation she already felt, setting foot within these walls. Gold epaulets on her shoulders, her knee-length coat lying open, five stars pinned at her collar, five stripes slashed across her sleeves. Every other soul in the chamber wore civilian clothes: slim dresses paired with corsets, or knee-length hose with lace-trimmed collars and cuffs.

"Our first matter must be the Gand treaty," the chairwoman said. "More properly, the Treaty of Covendon, signed Fourteenth Apollinaire, and drafted in the field, without review by this assembly. Assemblywoman Julée, you have a copy of the text?"

The third of them, seated atop the lesser of the three elevated daises, held aloft a sheaf of papers for the benefit of their audience. "I do, Chairwoman Caille."

"High Commander d'Arrent, would you summarize the key points of the treaty for us, if you please?"

Every eye turned to her. Gods but she'd stared down half again as many muskets, at shorter range, and felt no less apprehension. Easier when she remembered that words and poise were the weapons of this battlefield. She'd show them no more than she gave the enemy.

"I maneuvered against General Chamberlain at Ansfield, enticing her to commit her forces to a defense of the river crossings. This left the way south open, and we executed a forced march to seize the Gand capital, leaving a harrying force to pin their army in the hills of northern Gand country."

"High Commander, I'd asked for—"

"And I'm giving it," she snapped back. "Total surrender. Those are the terms of the Treaty of Covendon. I rendered General Chamberlain's army powerless to stop us razing the capital, if we had so desired. Their materiel had been depleted in the summer and spring campaigns. They were in no position to mount a siege, or an attack, with us in possession of their seat of power. Chamberlain sent riders to sue for peace, and I received them personally."

"And what of the barrier, High Commander?" The man, Lerand, leaned forward over the edge of his lectern. "You expect us to believe you had no forewarning of the enemy's capabilities, that the Gandsmen had nothing to do with its collapse?"

Murmurs sounded from the gallery.

"That issue is not under consideration by this hearing," the chairwoman said.

"She's ducked two summonses on the matter already," Lerand shot back. "If we're to trust her with command of our armies, she must be held to account. She's here, now; let us hear what she has to say."

Erris weighed the three of them. The chamber's design prevented her from seeing the faces of those in attendance ringing the podiums. Voren had urged her to make this appearance, insisting she had nothing to hide. The barrier had been a machination of an unknown power; she believed the Gand generals when they insisted it was no doing of theirs.

Eventually the murmurs fell silent, a hundred eyes resting on her, waiting on her every breath.

She wheeled about, a gesture fit for any parade ground, and marched toward the exit.

"High Commander!" Chairwoman Caille said at her back. "This hearing has not yet concluded. You must return to your place."

It was a mistake to come here, to cede even the slightest authority to fools. How many had suffered for it already?

Two guardsmen flanked the double doors, dressed in the blue cloaks of the city watch rather than the uniforms and armbands of the military police. They wavered as she approached, and she came to a halt in front of them.

"H-High Commander," one of the guardsmen said, "the ch-chairwoman says—"

"Do you mean to stop me?"

Neither man reached for his musket. Little wonder why such men had joined the watch, rather than answer the call to arms in wartime. She pushed past them, swinging the doors wide to spill a tide of gossip into the hall.

It followed her as she strode the length of the council chambers, buzzing voices and curious eyes watching as she climbed the stairs. Her ears burned the whole way.

Voren's doors swung wide as she approached, and his manservant, Omera, fixed them in place. His one-eyed glare unnerved her as much as it ever had, but he bowed, greeting her as she strode into Voren's receiving room.

"High Commander," Voren said from behind his desk, blinking and reaching for his spectacles. "Are you finished already?"

"It was a bloody witch hunt. Or due to soon become one. My decisions are not going to be held up for point-scoring for the sake of some cowards who've never held a musket."

"Slow down. Do you mean you walked out? Midway through the hearing? It can't have been more than ten minutes since it was due to begin."

Her ears burned hotter. Just as well for the cosmetics or it might have shown on her cheeks.

"Oh Gods," Voren said, slumping back in his chair. "You did."

"Sir, I apologize if I've let you down."

"Let me down?" he said. "D'Arrent, this isn't some bloody parlor game. You weren't summoned to that meeting to satisfy my expectations."

"They meant to pick apart my decisions."

"And what of it? Did you expect anything less, wearing those stars on your collar?"

She resisted the urge to snap to attention as Voren continued.

"This is your sphere now, High Commander. Like it or not, you are playing at politics as well as war. And you've blundered here today, not least for coming here directly after."

"Sir?" This time she didn't see the harm; what was done was done.

"If we don't put distance between ourselves, the Assembly will see my influence as little more than an extension of the army. We must at least play at service to the Republic, or we'll be forcibly conscripting farmers to feed our soldiers before we're through. They do have power, whether it's power you choose to recognize or no. And their power means we engage in politics, unless you mean to put any man or woman who disagrees with you to the sword."

"Sir, I do see the need for politics, but if it hampers our ability to wage war, we can't—"

"The High Admiral for you, sir," Omera said, suddenly hovering five paces behind her, though she'd neither heard nor seen him approach.

Tuyard burst through the outer doors a moment later. "Voren, you'll never believe what—ah. High Commander."

Silence descended on the room. She offered Tuyard a nod, though she could have done with nigh anyone else's company over the High Admiral's.

"Just the three of us, if you please, Omera," Voren said. "Turn the rest away, for now."

The Bhakal servant bowed, shutting the door behind them.

"One question," Tuyard said, seeming as though he struggled to contain a laugh. "You walked out after one question, from a hearing scheduled to take the bulk of the afternoon."

"I'll not have my orders questioned by fools," she said, and this time her ears burned right alongside her cheeks. "What right does some farmer or baker's boy have questioning my command? I wouldn't waste time telling that assemblyman how to bake bread, and expect him to listen or benefit from my insight."

"Guillaume, Erris, please, be seated," Voren said, gesturing to two open chairs across from his desk. They paused to take the chairs, Tuyard with a relaxed confidence, where she sat as though she were still at attention. No mistaking she was due to be questioned here, if not beneath the three lecterns in the hearing room. At least Voren and Tuyard had some semblance of military training.

"Now, High Commander," Voren said, "some would say the Assembly's right to question you derives from the people who elected them, through whom you and all of us rule through representative consent."

Tuyard snickered.

"A system for fools," Tuyard said. "They've lived their lives eyeing plates at our tables, thinking it's taught them how to cook. As though governance were a thing for amateurs, instead of men and women trained to it from birth. But it's what we endorsed, I suppose, signing on to depose Louis-Sallet."

"Peace, Guillaume," Voren said. "High Commander d'Arrent knows well enough the cost of what we did."

She stayed seated upright, and found herself longing for Jiri's saddle, and the open country. She'd never wanted more than to command soldiers in battle. Politics was meant for men and women like Tuyard. He was right; corrupt and decadent the nobles might be, but at least they'd been born and trained to rule. A new system should have been based on merit, as she'd implemented with the army. The Assembly should have been organized from experts in every role, set to craft policy and review proposals with careful wisdom. Instead the people had elected representatives skilled at getting the people to vote them into office, and not much more.

"What was it they asked to set you off, d'Arrent?" Tuyard asked.

"The barrier," she said. "I had no way of knowing it would happen. The Gandsmen themselves had no inkling of it—they swore off *Need* and met us without it in the field. No general could have predicted it. I'd had patrols sweeping its perimeter since the summer campaign. They swear there was no forewarning, even when it went down. No *Death*, or sign of any disruption."

"Neither Guillaume nor I are questioning your abilities in the field," Voren said. "If you couldn't have planned for it, no one could have. But you need to build a similar rapport with the Assembly. If they don't trust you, they become an obstacle where they should be a tool on our side."

She nodded. His words went at least some way to salving her pride. But she'd been beaten three times now by the man Sarine had called Paendurion. Even if the Gandsmen swore they'd cast aside his influence, it didn't mean the man was dead. He'd engineered the barrier's collapse, she was certain of it. And it meant she'd been beaten, sure as if he'd flanked her in the field.

"How bad has it been?" she asked quietly. She'd had only cursory briefings on the road, marching the army north to fan out and defend the borders where the Great Barrier had stood before.

"Better than it would have been, without the assistance of Ilek'Hannat. Seven sightings of beasts, four of which we put down or drove away before anyone was killed."

Four driven off, in three weeks, with three they'd failed to reach. He'd left the number unsaid, but she couldn't. "How many dead?"

"Two hundred and eight, as of this morning."

She felt sick.

"And we've only seen sign of the beasts?" she said. "Arak'Jur was convinced there would be more, accompanying an army of tribesmen, active in the north."

Voren shook his head. "Nothing. Only the beasts, so far as we've heard here in the city."

She nodded. Her scouts had confirmed the same; quiet, all along the remnants of the barrier, with no sign of tribesfolk, save the ones that had come with Arak'Jur.

"Arak'Jur and Ilek'Hannat were convinced a tribal army had gathered," she said, "and if I know our enemy—Paendurion—at all, I can't see it as a coincidence. They'll be part of his attack. Now that I'm here, the reports will be better, leveraging *Need*. I have more regular use of it again, with the Gand colonies' surrender."

"Good," Voren said. "And I trust the rest of the army is soon to deploy here in the north."

She nodded, though the why of it—why Paendurion wouldn't have attacked already, with the bulk of her forces tangled at Covendon, cut off by the Gandsmen—was a mystery as sure as any of the surprises he'd sprung before.

"There's still the matter of the Assembly, then," Voren continued. "And the promises you offered the Gand leadership."

"I meant them," she said. "And it's imperative we honor every word. Without *Need* at full strength we're doomed the next time Paendurion takes the field. We must secure their loyalty, not only their lands. You were right, my lord—*Need* seems to stem from territory claimed and held. We'll need the full extent of the Gand colonies, and with the right concessions we can turn them to our side within a season or two."

"Political union," Tuyard said. "And we wonder why the Assembly has been foaming over."

"You promised them full representation in our government," Voren said.

"And why not?" she said. "Isn't this Republic founded on principles of fairness and *égalité*? Is a man less a man, a woman less a woman, because they're born a hundred leagues too far south? If we've claimed their territory, we must allow them a voice in our government, or they'll be plotting rebellion within the year."

"Try that line in tomorrow's papers, hm?" Tuyard asked, grinning as though he'd made some private joke.

Voren nodded, looking more weary than she'd seen him before, the lines on his face bending around his gray mustaches. "We might," he said. "But for now, we need you to get back in the field. A show of force, aligned against this native army, if it exists, or at least a victory against one of these beasts. Something we can print to drown the story of your storming out of the hearing."

"Sir? Do you really think anyone will care that I left a simple hearing?"

"You don't read the colonial papers, do you, d'Arrent?"

"I read scouting reports, sir."

"Change that, High Commander. Papers and pamphlets are the scouting reports for this battlefield."

The truth of it stung her. Voren was right, though she'd never intended to fight in this sphere.

"I will, sir."

"Very good, d'Arrent. Gods' speed on you, and I mean that. Better if you're back with the army, marching north before sundown."

23

ARAK'JUR

A Thunderstruck Tree
Near the Western Boundary of Sinari Land

Ka'Inari embraced his forearms in farewell. Arak'Jur's apprentice—former apprentice, now—was a full shaman, blessed with visions of things-to-come. If Ka'Inari saw that their paths wouldn't cross again, it would be so. He couldn't bring himself to ask it aloud. It was enough to see the distance in the shaman's eyes, the lingering grip of his hands before they let go.

"This is the place," Ka'Inari said. "Your path turns south from here."

"Yours should return to the east," Arak'Jur said. "Back to our people. They need you, Ka'Inari. Ilek'Hannat's gift is strong, but he is no full shaman. Even with the fair-skins' magic to protect them, if your visions should falter, and the Uktani choose to attack them . . ."

Ka'Inari showed him a weathered look. There was weight there that had never graced the young man's eyes before. A certainty, and a sadness.

"The Uktani pursue you, Arak'Jur," Ka'Inari said. "Much as I wish our visions had been wrong, or our interpretations flawed. They know you, and they are coming."

Corenna came to stand beside him, having finished whatever passed between her and the fair-skin women. Sarine stood opposite them, flanking Ka'Inari, with Acherre at her side. The husk of wood from Ka'Inari's vision loomed beside them, a blackened char rent by lightning, split and cracked, overlooking the grassy valley beyond. A fitting portent for the exhaustion he felt, for the broken paths set in front of him. It was wrong, for a shaman to leave their people. It was wrong, for him to be forced to do the same.

"Spirits favor you, honored sister," Ka'Inari said as Corenna approached, and the two of them stepped aside, sharing an embrace, leaving him to face the fair-skins.

"Are you certain you can't come with us?" Sarine asked. "Your magic is strong, and we'll need everything we can manage, when we catch up to Axerian. We have to confront him with enough strength that he won't even try to fight."

He eyed the serpent coiled around her forearm, sickly white, though it seemed to be watching him with its onyx eyes. The creature triggered memories of Llanara; he'd as soon have it far away from his people, even if it meant Ka'Inari going with her.

"Thank you for what you did at Ka'Ana'Tyat," he said. "You returned a great gift to us. But my path leads elsewhere."

"Where will you go?" she asked.

"Ka'Inari has seen a glimpse of the corruption's source, far to the south. A woman. We seek her, and we seek the gifts of the spirits along the way."

"A woman," Sarine said. "Ad-Shi? It can't be. It isn't time yet."

Arak'Jur frowned, eyeing once more the serpent coiled around Sarine's forearm. Llanara's creature, too, had led her to give cryptic assurances of things-to-come. An unnatural thing.

"If it is her," Sarine said, "you must be cautious. She can set wardings in the minds of beasts and the land itself. But it's never been her way, to come to the world before the appointed time. It isn't like the *kaas*—she can't just collect enough energy to re-ascend. If she's here, she…"

A blue light flashed, emanating from Sarine's coiled serpent, and Sarine staggered, stumbling forward. He darted to catch her, and Acherre did the same. Both of them propped her up, but Sarine had gone limp, unconscious as though she'd been struck in the head.

"What's happened?" Ka'Inari said, turning from where he'd been speaking privately with Corenna a few paces away. "Is she well?"

"*Elle est tombée,*" Acherre said, moving to lay Sarine's head on the grass while Arak'Jur lowered her body. The woman had gone cold, enough so he reached for her wrist to feel her blood flow. Alive, but weak. She'd been healthy and vibrant mere moments before.

"She's fallen," he said. "But she gave no warning sign anything was amiss."

Her eyes came open, expression returned to her face so suddenly he might have questioned whether she had ever been otherwise.

"Another vision," she said, pushing to sit up before he or Acherre could suggest she might do better lying down. "I'm sorry, Zi. I didn't mean to."

A moment of silence passed, and she spoke again. "I'm fine," she said. "I'm fine."

Acherre said something too quickly for him to follow, and Sarine looked down at her serpent, caressing the creature's scales with a mother's care.

"We have to go," Sarine said. "We have to find him now."

Sarine rose to her feet, using his arm as leverage though he hadn't meant to do more than support her when she fell. A strange woman, and all the more unnerving to leave Ka'Inari in her company. Only after Sarine rose did he notice Corenna's face was slicked with tears, that she was still standing where Ka'Inari had been speaking with her.

He made sure Sarine was set on her feet, and he went to Corenna's side.

"I'm well," Corenna said, betraying the sentiment in the tears she tried to wipe away. His worry sprouted, not knowing. Had Ka'Inari given her counsel, or shared some vision pertaining to her, to him, to their unborn child? She gave no answers, only accepted a proferred hand to stand by his side as they returned to face Sarine, Acherre, and Ka'Inari.

"We go, then," Ka'Inari said. "Care for her, and for our people, Arak'Jur. The spirits offer both of you blessings in your tasks."

"Blessings to the three of you as well," he said, and once more wished he were bidding Ka'Inari farewell on a journey to the east, back to their people, instead of west into the unknown. But the fair-skins and Ka'Inari turned and started down the valley, leaving him and Corenna behind.

They tracked along the valley's edge, where the tree line broke enough to see the three specks of their former companions. The way south was still obscured by foliage, but he knew it well enough. They meant to keep to the east until the *sukhrai* river, the old boundary between Olessi and Vhurasi lands. It shouldn't have been possible to track one man or woman over such a distance, but something had changed. Somehow his path was revealed to the Uktani shaman, and first they needed to see whether greater distance could throw off their pursuit.

"A strange farewell," Corenna said when they were away. "What happened with the fair-skin woman?"

"Sarine fell," he said. "And before that, she seemed to speak with great knowledge, in another voice. Not madness—not of the sort Llanara and Reyne d'Agarre brought to us—but some affliction beyond my understanding."

"She frightened me," Corenna said. "To think she dismissed *sre'ghaus* so easily, by asking it to leave. Asking it! In all the women's stories, I'd never heard of such a thing."

"Nor I, from the hunters, or the shamans. But I sensed no malice in her, and she helped us open Ka'Ana'Tyat."

Corenna seemed to concede the point, and they walked a few more paces before she spoke again.

"I worry for what we face," she said. "The wilds were never meant to be tamed. Yet Sarine appears, and she can do it. The woman in the south, the one from Ka'Inari's vision, she must be able to do the same. How many more sources will there be of this corruption? How much more will we face, before our lands pass from under this shadow?"

He had no answers, and so he gave none, only a grim acknowledgment as they continued on their way. Almost he asked after Corenna and Ka'Inari's private word before their farewell, but it was her place to share; if Ka'Inari had meant it for him, he would have been brought into the telling. It didn't stop him from worrying over what might have been said.

They made camp on what felt like the first night of their journey, since it was the first night alone, without the fair-skin women and Ka'Inari for company. He urged Corenna to sleep first, and kept watch over her while she did. They'd picked a hilltop covered with trees for their camp, giving him vantage over the approaches without revealing his silhouette against the sky for those looking up toward him. There could be eyes out there, Uktani warriors driven to give chase. He almost hoped there were; the shamans had promised him the Uktani pursued him alone, but their assurance would not put to rest his fears for their alliance, left behind on fair-skin land far to the east.

He'd meant to leave the Alliance behind the fair-skins' barrier, and instead brokered a deal between Ilek'Hannat and Erris d'Arrent: the shamans' visions for the fair-skins' arms and magic. Strange to think their Great Barrier was down. It had always been there, in his mind, though he knew the stories of its origin fifteen generations before. But now if he walked east he would arrive in one of their villages. No small part of him worried it was some fair-skin ploy, some trick to expand their claims and remake their barrier westward. Erris d'Arrent had seemed terrified enough to believe the crisis genuine. But if it was a trick, they would find his people ready to fight.

Corenna woke on her own, before he would have roused her. She came to sit beside him against an oak tree, a welcome respite from his worries. She nestled under his arm and laid her head against his chest, looking northward over treetops lit by moon- and starlight, still some hours before dawn.

"All is quiet?" she asked.

"It is," he said, holding her against his skin. She smelled of sweat and dust. A sweet smell, uniquely hers.

"You should rest," she said. "If the Uktani are following, it will be hard days ahead."

She left unspoken the threat of what would follow if the Uktani gave no sign of pursuit. It could mean they'd abandoned the chase, their shaman's vision blurred by great distance. But it could also mean they followed the Alliance onto fair-skin land, or that they tracked Ka'Inari and the fair-skin women instead.

"Corenna, if the Uktani aren't following us, we would need to go back, to help the tribes, or—"

"Shh. Even guardians need sleep. Ka'Inari said they would follow you. That is what they will do. Trust in his gift, and rest while you can."

His instinct was to protest. The horizon was clear as far as they could see, treetops blanketing the hills with boughs of dark leaves. No signs of fire or smoke against the sky.

Instead he rose. Corenna ensnared him with a kiss before she took his place resting against the tree trunk, and he made way to the pallet of grass and leaves they'd made for her to sleep on. Dark thoughts set in at once, visions of what might happen if an Uktani army of men and beasts descended on the fair-skins without their barrier. He'd seen Acherre fight enough to know a grudging respect for their magic, and their powder and steel were strength, too, in their way. Unless the Uktani shaman could see him with perfect accuracy, there was always a chance they would believe him there, with the Alliance. He should have been there. Running was a coward's path. Rhealla would have stood and fought. Even his dead son had found the courage to take up a spear, when *valak'ar* threatened their home.

Fatigue washed his thoughts into darkness, and then dreams. Most nights he discounted the images he saw there, and this night was no better than most. He stood alone on a street in the fair-skins' city, looking for Llanara. He heard Ka'Vos's voice, but couldn't see the old shaman's face as he gave a warning against another new beast. A pack of hunters appeared, carrying pelts, offering to let him shoulder the burden, but no matter how he tried he couldn't lift even the lightest fur. They laughed and went on their way. The fair-skins' city was suddenly the Sinari village, where his feet were rooted in place. The tribe was packing their belongings, gesturing for him to come and join them, but he couldn't move. Reyne d'Agarre appeared in his red coat, and urged the same: Go, join your tribe, leave the beasts to me, but again he couldn't move.

Sunlight warmed his eyelids, and his senses snapped into place. The sun had already crested the horizon, a few degrees above the tree line, lighting a blue, cloudless sky.

His muscles tensed to quiet. Something was wrong.

He rose to his feet quietly, scanning the view from atop their hill. Movement caught his eye, through a break in the trees. Men. Distant, but there. Either they had camped a few hours' journey to the north, or they had traveled through the night. Heading south, toward his and Corenna's camp.

"Corenna," he said in a low voice. "The Uktani. We must go, now."

No answer.

He turned and found the hilltop empty, no sign of Corenna where he'd left her. He cursed, loping over the hillside toward the nearby stream. She must have gone for water. But when he arrived there were only birds scattered at his coming.

"Corenna!" he called, louder than he should have dared. But if she was nearby, she should have heard. He tried again. "Corenna! We must go. Corenna!"

Another flap of wings, a bird frightened to flee now, where it had tried to hide before.

He strode back up the hillside, scanning for sign of her passage. At their camp he scoured the dirt, seeking bootprints in the soil, crushed leaves or grass, snapped twigs, brush bent or scraped or out of place.

He searched until the sun had made its way clear of the horizon. He searched until fear over what might have befallen her gave way to certainty she must have hidden her tracks. He would have been roused, if a beast had come, or a man had taken her. She would have fought, or raised a cry to wake him from his sleep. Instead she'd stolen away, covering her trail, leaving him alone to face the day.

24

TIGAI

Training Yard
Temple of the Dragon

Dirt scuffed as he sidestepped, keeping a wary eye on his opponent. The monk, Jyeong, was apprentice to Master Indra, and had been careful to remind him he hadn't yet been accepted to their temple, as though he'd come here willingly and gave a shit about his rank.

Jyeong tried a feint with his ji, whipping the blunt end of the polearm up as though he meant to strike before he came down with the bladed edge. Tigai saw it coming, spinning his own ji in his hands to block the attack. Wood struck wood, but Jyeong pivoted, sliding the bladed edge of his weapon down to shear Tigai's fingers from his hand clean as cutting a flank from a slab of pork.

Tigai shifted to an anchor before the pain could hit, though phantom echoes of it shot through him all the same.

"Good," Master Indra said, watching them from the edge of the ring. "Your form was good, though you erred in locking weapons overlong. But you were trained well enough."

"Trained well enough to stop this façade and tell me what the fuck I'm doing here?"

The old man ignored him, pacing around the side of the training yard, eyeing him and Jyeong as though they were horseflesh come to market.

"Again," Master Indra said. "This time use an anchor to strike from two directions."

Tigai scowled. His days had begun with precisely this sort of nonsense since the woman—the bounty hunter, he supposed—Lin Qishan had delivered him here. Jyeong stood motionless, holding his ji level, knees bent and legs spread wide. Was the old man's direction meant for him, or the monk? Before he could ask, Master Indra raised a hand in the signal to begin.

Jyeong shouted some sort of battle cry as he charged. Tigai made a face and echoed it back to him in a mocking tone. Bloody ridiculous, fighting to the death over and over as though their magic were made for spectacle. He stabbed wildly, hooking to his anchor and blinking to Jyeong's left side. He thrust again in a quick motion, then anchored, blinked behind, and stabbed again. The world shifted beneath his feet, so quickly it threatened to make him sick, but this time the sharp point of his ji found its mark, impaling Master Indra's apprentice through his shoulder, sending him forward into the dirt.

Jyeong snapped back to his feet an instant later, made whole by passage through the strands. "That was not what the master said to do," the monk said, gripping the haft of his weapon as though it would add emphasis to his words. "You were told to strike twice."

"I'm not in the habit of letting my enemies know how I mean to attack them."

"I am not your enemy, you bloody fool. We are here to practice, to learn and hone our skill."

"*I* am here because you stole away my brother—"

"*Paryaapt*," Master Indra said, his tone making clear it was meant to be an end to their exchange. "Drop weapons. It's time to eat."

Jyeong's polearm clattered to the dirt at once. Tigai's grip lingered for a moment before he let his do the same.

The old man led the way between the ruined buildings, toward the brick ovens where their cookpots were stored, along with parcels of rice and herbs and meat. The temple seemed to be empty, as far as Tigai could tell. Cracked stone and missing roofs spoke of a once-grand complex, storerooms and twisting hallways, sleeping chambers and feast halls. Vines had long since claimed it, jungle overgrowth making it more a home for wild beasts than a strange old man and his apprentice.

Only one building in ten had a roof to keep out the constant stream of warm drizzling rain; thankfully they'd let him sleep beneath one, though in a separate chamber from where the master or Jyeong resided. An unusual sort of prison, but then, they knew he could anchor himself away whenever he chose.

"Sit," Master Indra said, pointing to a pair of straw mats laid out beside the oven. Jyeong sat in a rigid pose, legs folded so his heels propped beneath his buttocks. Tigai stretched and opted for comfort. The old man would have told him if he wanted him to try to sit like a stone.

"A well-struck maneuver, in the yard," Master Indra said as he rummaged through stone shelves, withdrawing pots and rice to cook in them, a handful of vegetables and what looked like fresh-cut beef. He hadn't seen any livestock on the grounds. But then, of course—the old man could take a jaunt to Ghingwai market and back here before he roused from sleep. Strange, to live with people who had his gift. "Two anchors so quickly speaks to your skill with the Dragon's gift, though you need work, with the implements of war."

Was he supposed to banter with the man? "I prefer pistols," he said. "No point getting close enough to stab a man when you can shoot him twenty spans away."

Jyeong snorted, but otherwise kept still.

"Firearms have their uses," Master Indra said. "But the precepts of our order teach harmony in the union of self and tool. Work done with one's hands is better, closer to revealing the true self."

"Why use blades and polearms, then?" he asked. "Why not punch your enemies to death?"

Master Indra paused to inhale atop his cookpots as he sprinkled spices into his rice. "If you would prefer to face Jyeong unarmed, I am certain my apprentice would welcome the challenge."

"I'd as soon you let my family go. I might well choose to stay and learn what you have to offer. You could have kept your sixty thousand *qian*, or split the lot with me as a bounty."

The old man only smiled, adding another handful of spices in with the rest of his ingredients.

"Time is drawing too short to leave such things to chance. You are something of a surprise, Lord Tigai. What you can do should not be possible. We set a snare for Isaru Mattai and caught a true Dragon instead. I am not so foolish as to let you escape before I've had a chance to teach you why you should stay."

"I've never wanted anything to do with the Great and Noble Houses. Your politics can keep, along with your games and trickery."

"Great and Noble Houses indeed," the old man said. "You know once, the *magi* ruled in the open? Emperors and Queens, a legacy of lordships to make what passes for nobility among the unordained seem no more than the parlor game it truly is."

"Every child knows those stories. The Emperor sealed the pact of heaven when the Jun Empire was formed. The *magi* are forbidden from holding the keys of power, on pain of doom if—"

"—if they seek the loyalty of men," Master Indra finished. "A sweet tale. And the governors and magistrates preach it like disciples of the Way. But tell me, Lord Tigai of Yanjin House, do you suppose a prohibition on sitting a throne or holding a title keeps us from wielding power, when we can break the ones who do with a shard of glass, a whiff of poison, a knife transported to their chambers at night?"

"I'd never thought about it," he said, affecting a bored tone. It wouldn't have made a difference whether some *magi* blackmailed the Emperor; politics was Mei's, or Dao's concern, if it was any concern at all.

"Quite right," Master Indra said, pausing for a moment to sip his broth before pinching another handful of spices into the mix. "And the truth is, if the *magi* were motivated by worldly power, we'd have found a way to have it, celestials be damned. But we aren't. We have a more pressing concern. And it will be yours, too, once our training here is finished."

"Master," Jyeong said. "Is he ready to know these secrets?"

"No, he is not," Master Indra said. "But as I said, we are running out of time."

Master Indra scooped a bowl of rice and broth, setting it in front of him, with another for Jyeong. Then he sat, taking up his own bowl, opposite the straw mats.

"Do you have questions, Lord Tigai?" Indra asked.

"I really don't," Tigai said. The broth was warm and well-spiced, an unfamiliar blend of flavors, but not an unpleasant one. "You're holding me here because you have my brother, Mei, and Remarin, or at least because you claim to. I wouldn't trade the attentions of a dockside whore for your secrets."

Jyeong made a sound as though he was choking on his rice.

"I see," Master Indra said. "This is disappointing."

Tigai raised his bowl in a mock salute. "It's what you get for making friends at knifepoint, or recruiting apprentices or whatever it is you're doing here."

"I would have hoped you could acknowledge power, when you see it. What we have here—"

"What you have here is a ruined temple in the middle of the fucking jungle, an obsession with learning modes of fighting made obsolete when the first powder tube spat out the first ball of lead, and a half-assed command of a gift I learned better from a potato farmer. Or do you think I hadn't noticed your apprentice struggle to hook a simple anchor and binding I could do half-asleep and more than a little drunk? Either you're shit as a teacher, he's shit as a student, or you have somewhat less wisdom to impart than you think you do."

By the time he was finished, Jyeong looked as though he was struggling not to leap to his feet and tackle Tigai into the dirt. Master Indra laid down his bowl and stared.

Tigai's ears burned a bit, as silence stretched and the old man didn't speak. Well, what did they want him to say? It was all true. The hidden temple in the jungle, the fighting with sticks and swords, speaking in cryptic phrases as though they had preserved some hidden truth. It was the exact sort of thing people expected from the *magi* of the Great and Noble Houses. They existed, true enough, no one disputed that, and they had power of a sort everyone feared and knew was real. But they lived in a world apart from his, from Dao's, from anyone who built cities or governed people or really lived at all. They were monks in monasteries atop mountains or hidden in some other remote locations, dedicated to practicing magic they never actually *used* for anything. And if Jyeong's skill with the strands was any indicator, they hadn't even practiced it very well.

"We are finished for the morning, Lord Tigai," Master Indra said. "Take your soup and go."

He hadn't expected to feel sorry for the old man, but he did. It seemed as though his words had cut deeper than he'd meant them to. Jyeong's eyes were full of hate, but even he seemed content to stay where he was. Not that it would matter. If the apprentice tried to kill him, he'd just blink away. Wasn't that the point of their magic, the gift they shared? Life without consequences, violence without any permanent damage. He'd murdered the apprentice a hundred times since coming here, and been murdered as many more.

But then, there was Dao, Mei, and Remarin.

They flashed in his thoughts as he took up his bowl of soup and retreated to the worn-down building where he'd slept.

Rain fell from the sky, making leaves glisten, forming puddles in the dirt walkways between the ruins. This was the first time they'd left him alone during the day. He could walk the grounds, contemplate his fate, wonder at whether the seneschals at Yanjin had used the Emperor's stolen gold to pay off their debts or run away with his prize. Instead he kicked a particularly offensive bush that grew outside his building's door. What was he doing here? Remarin would have written him off as a loss the moment Lin Qishan showed up at his door, instead of playing along with their games. Dao would have made the same decision, coldly calculated and no less a brother for it. Mei would have fought, and that was why he loved her.

His soup tasted flat, soured by rainwater. He should leave. Indra and Jyeong be damned by demons, their ancestors' bodies dug up and burned. He wasn't even sure what they'd meant, with their cryptic allusions to his gift. As near as he could tell, they had the same power he did—the starfield, the strands, anchors and reversions. He did it better, with less forethought and exertions for its use, but there was nothing worth paying sixty thousand *qian* for the hope that he loved his brother more than his freedom.

He finished his meal and retired to rest in his chambers. They'd furnished the room with a stone bed and nothing else. He'd have paid sixty thousand *qian* for a feather mattress and a pair of down pillows, and maybe a palace serving girl to bed down alongside him. But even a stone bed was a comfort after a week of solid sparring. The strands could preserve his body, keep him from bruises or any other need for healing, but the strands imparted an exhaustion all their own. He slept almost as soon as he lay down to try, and for a time the world went quiet, finally at peace.

Shuffling footsteps woke him, and he sat up in time to see Master Indra looming at his door.

"Sleep while the sun is out is a poor habit, Lord Tigai," Master Indra said, unslinging a bag from around his shoulder and letting it fall to the floor. "I've brought you a gift. A reminder, of why you are here."

He kept his eyes on the old man's face. "I know why I'm here."

"Do you?"

His heart pounded. Blood scented the air of his chamber. A metallic tinge he wouldn't have noticed, but for the satisfied smile creeping across Master Indra's lips.

"What have you done?" he asked.

The smile bloomed in full. "Open your gift, lordling."

He slumped off the side of his bed, kneeling on the floor. Fumbling with the drawstring on the bag was torture, a hot poker pressed against his spine. Red liquid stained his fingers as he reached inside, and his stomach put bile in his throat hard enough that he turned his head to the side and vomited onto the stone.

"She screamed, when I removed it," Master Indra said. "And it took three men to hold her for the cut."

A hand protruded from where he'd dropped the bag. Five fingers, a palm, a wrist, and a severed stump. A woman's hand. Mei's hand.

"I'll kill you," Tigai said, not bothering to wipe the bile from his chin. "I'll stuff charcoal in your throat, put needles through your eyes, peel your fingernails back until they break and feed them to you, one by one."

"No, you won't. You'll come with me, now, and since your gift is already so strong, it is time you begin your service against our enemy. We go to Ghingwai. You will find Lin Qishan there, and do precisely as she says. If she is harmed in any way, or if you fail to return to me within three days, I take another hand. Then a foot. Then another piece, for every day you are late in carrying out your orders. Do we understand each other, Lord Tigai?"

He bowed his head and forced himself to look. Delicate fingers, with the nails painted red and yellow. Yanjin colors, marred by blood, blurred by tears.

Somehow his bow became a nod, and he rose to follow Master Indra into the rain.

25

ERRIS

Sinari Encampment
North of New Sarresant

Their company's horses kicked dust clouds as they stuttered to a halt. Makeshift paths and trails had already formed between the tents, strange constructions of hides and long poles leaned together in conical designs. She'd never considered before whether the natives had built permanent settlements; the ease with which they'd erected this one suggested a certain familiarity with uprooting their people, or at least a readiness to do it on little notice. Not altogether unlike a military encampment.

Hitching poles had been placed on the edge of an open green at the center of their camp, and she handed Jiri's reins to an aide as she dismounted. Eight thousand tribesfolk, if she had to guess. She might be off by half in either direction, if they'd packed tents that went unused. But this was a division's strength, if she'd been scouting it in her cavalry days. She'd ordered Royens's 1st Corps into the north, now deploying near the banks of the Verrain with enough numbers to check the tribesfolk should it come to that.

Five tribesfolk seemed to be waiting for her on their green, four men and one woman, each dressed in hides, furs, and sewn fabrics. Her company was twenty strong, but she nodded for most to stay behind.

"Marquand, Essily, Wexly, Savac, with me."

The named riders came forward, sliding down from their mounts. A binder, her aide, the Gand attaché, and a translator perfectly fluent in Sinari, Sarresant, and Gand. Voren wouldn't have come to treat with the tribes, and she'd wager a month's pay none among the citizens' assembly would have been so bold. It meant hers was the highest-ranked visit to date, and that meant standing on ceremony. Even Marquand had agreed to a buttoned-up, fresh-tailored coat before they rode.

"High Commander," the woman among the tribesfolk said, directing it her way. "I am Tirana, of the Olessi tribe. It is our great honor to welcome you among our tents."

The words had a crisp inflection despite the heavy accent; clearly the woman had practiced her lines.

"The honor is mine," she replied. "I hope our haste has not inconvenienced you."

"The shaman foresaw your arrival some days ago, High Commander. He is eager to speak with you, if you will follow us to his tent."

"Of course."

Their welcoming party turned and gestured for them to follow across the grassy field. The tribesmen flanking Tirana gave no outward sign of discomfort, and thank the Gods her soldiers showed the same restraint. Talk of seeing the future roused all the skepticism she'd learned in eleven years campaigning with the army. No denying the shaman's abilities when it came to the great beasts—already his missives had warned four villages and townships in time to flee, and predicted three more. Gods send the shaman proved himself equally capable, where this supposed tribal army was concerned.

They cut through rows of tents, passing by solemn tribesfolk keeping emotions from their faces but staring all the same. She might have reacted just so had a squad of tribesmen come marching down the streets of Southgate. Even their children had halted their play, watching the uniformed soldiers striding behind their guides and doing a worse job of masking their stares than the adults.

"I will accompany you inside, Erris d'Arrent," Tirana said when they came to a halt in front of a tent no different in kind than the others around it, save for tufts of orange smoke billowing from its apex.

"Aide-Lieutenant Savac will accompany me as well," she said. She wasn't about to filter her words through a translator she didn't know and trust. Wars had been started for less.

It seemed to serve, as Tirana bowed her head, and Marquand, Wexly, and Essily joined the tribesfolk in watching them enter the shaman's tent.

The sting of incense bit her nose, an unfamiliar scent like birchwood mixed with fresh meat. The tent's interior was wide and open, with only a fire burning at its center and animal skins thrown like carpets a safe distance from the flame. The shaman stood opposite the entrance, clad in a pale white bearskin draped over his head and shoulders. Not the sort of reception she'd expected. The tribes' shaman seemed prepared for some kind of ritual, rather than a formal greeting and diplomatic exchange. Had he met Voren's people like this? It would have ended up in the papers, scaremongering and suspicion-raising over the foreign ways of a foreign people, now living in proximity to their city. Then again, she still hadn't bothered to read much of the colonial press. Perhaps those stories had already run.

"*Erys d'Aru,*" the shaman said, butchering her name through a thick accent. "*Qu'iluru shi n'iral, ahn dhakron, Ilek'Hannat, niris Ka di Nanerat, alain ti'ana lanat dal ahn qirat.*"

Tirana and Savac spoke together: "He says—" before each paused, and Savac bowed to let the other woman speak. Two words before their first gaffe. Bloody lovely.

"He says he is pleased you have come to this place, and introduces himself," Tirana said. "He is Ilek'Hannat, apprentice shaman of the Nanerat people, wielder of the gifts of the vision spirits and elder of the alliance of six tribes."

Erris glanced at Aide-Lieutenant Savac to ensure that there was no disagreement on the translation. None. Good.

"I am equally pleased," she said. "I've come as a gesture of peace between our peoples, at the head of a division of my army, ten thousand strong and set to deploy along the northern frontier at your direction. I want to ensure that you understand our soldiers are here as a check against the army Arak'Jur called the Uktani, not to threaten your people."

"He understands," Tirana said after her words were translated, and the shaman offered his reply. "He has seen your heart, and wishes to offer you communion with the spirits, if you wish it."

She suppressed a sudden desire to tether *Body*, an old reflex. Communion? With his spirits? Walking alone into a village of a foreign people was trusting enough, but she'd never expected to be put into some sacred ritual. The shaman seemed to be studying her, the white paint on his face making him appear to be some kind of apparition, hiding behind his fire.

"What does it mean, to commune with the spirits?"

"He cannot say," Tirana translated. "They will speak of what they will, once they have hold of him. He says only that they wish to speak with you."

"They *must* speak with you," Savac said in a low voice, angling to try to mask the correction to Tirana's translation.

Erris met Ilek'Hannat's eyes. Yes, there was urgency there. A need she could almost sense. No denying the tribesfolk's spirits had power; she'd seen it firsthand, watching Arak'Jur reave through the Gand lines during the battle of New Sarresant.

"Very well," she said. "So long as you can promise my safety, and that of my aide."

"He cannot promise it," Tirana said. "The limitations of *Ilek*, instead of *Ka*. He cannot be sure what will happen."

She looked to Savac for translation of the two strange words, *Ilek* and *Ka*. "Apprentice," Savac said. "And shaman. She means he is not fully trained."

Not fully trained. But then, he'd introduced himself as the elder among their six tribes. And his visions had worked, so far, for predicting the beasts.

"Very well," she said again. "Tell him to go ahead."

The shaman nodded before the translator gave him her reply, striding out from behind his fire as though facing her for the first time. A shadow seemed to stretch through the tent; Ilek'Hannat's form cast against the fire, but writ larger, until it occupied every empty space on the walls. It could have been a trick, an artful positioning of the man against the flame, until shadow seemed to swallow the light. There was magic here, of a form unlike anything the leylines had ever produced.

"Erris d'Arrent," Ilek'Hannat said, in what she heard as flawless Sarresant, all traces of his accent vanished. "You are different from the ones we know."

"I am she, High Commander of the armies of New Sarresant," she said. "To whom—to what—am I speaking?"

Ilek'Hannat had adopted a cautious pose, the sort one might use to survey an intruder.

"You wield magic, but you are not a spirit of mountain, grass, or sea. Your powers are known to us, though we had forgotten them. You are… Order."

Ilek'Hannat reached into his vest of hides and withdrew a powder he dusted over the fire. The flames fought through the shadows, cracking as smoke rose and formed the image of a man in armor, holding a long sword and shield. Strange to see such an image here, when no knights in plate armor had ever walked on the soil of the New World. Muskets and cannonfire had long since replaced such arms by the time the first colonists sailed across the sea. The smoke was almost a religious image, as though the shaman had conjured the Exarch into being at the center of his tent.

"This was Order when we saw it last," Ilek'Hannat said. "Though it has been many ages since those days."

"I came to you as an offering of peace," she said, ignoring the armored figure in the smoke and speaking directly to Ilek'Hannat. "To ascertain the source of threats to our Republic, and to bind our peoples in uncertain times. We had word of an enemy army, of warriors and great beasts, and with our barrier fallen, we are at the mercy of both. With your aid, we can discern where they will come, and drive them back."

The shaman seemed to be looking through her, his eyes gone milk-white. If he'd listened to her he gave no sign, studying her face as though she were in the way of something fascinating on the tent walls beyond.

"Paendurion," the shaman said.

Her enemy. The girl, Sarine, had so named the enemy commander, the man behind the golden light.

All pretense of diplomacy splintered. "How…?" she said. "What do you know of him? Where is he? What is he preparing?"

"You are not Paendurion," the shaman said. "But you work the golden threads; we sense it, in your form."

"No, I am bloody well not that monster. Please, whatever you are, tell me what you can of his doings. Is he preparing another attack? Are these Uktani involved?"

"Yes," the shaman said, nodding as though understanding dawned from far away. "Yes, this is a thing. We remember. Once, there were other champions. The knights of Order, with Paendurion at their head. And the serpents. Other powers, magic our children cannot touch. Order. And Balance."

Fury rose, and frustration. She needed a plain answer. Instead the shaman dusted another powder into the fire, and without further warning a boom shook the tent, spewing cinders in a fountain that threatened to bathe the hide walls in flame.

"Yes," the shaman said. "There are dangers lurking in the things-to-come, but not from the Uktani, who have been called toward another path. We see three. Three threats to your Republic."

She raised a hand to ward away the heat. Was the shaman mad? She'd bloody well placed their fate in the hands of a man who would kill her, and himself, standing at the center of a tent he'd set aflame.

"Ad-Shi," the shaman said. "She is known to us. The spirits of the marsh speak of her presence in the south, among the Lhakani."

Cinders fell from the tent's conical ceiling, where its wood beams had caught fire, a rush faster than any natural spread of flame.

"Paendurion. He moves among the ones called Thellan, in your Old World and here, on our lands."

The words stung like ice amid the heat. They had to get out of the tent, but she hesitated, since neither the shaman nor Tirana had made an attempt to move. Paendurion was among the Thellan. The enemy commander had taken root there, among the third of the great powers.

"And a final threat, from one not yet ascended. Nestled at the heart of your Republic, entrusted with its protection, but—"

The fire bellowed again, a roar of smoke and cinders, and the shaman's figure blurred. *Body* came as quick as she willed it, and she moved, weaving *Shelter*, though the blue haze dimmed to a pale white as soon as she set it in place. She grabbed hold of Ilek'Hannat as Tirana shouted something indiscernible at her, and Savac followed her lead, heading for the tent's entrance, leaving them all singed and smoking in the dirt as they emerged into the sun.

Marquand was at her side at once. Coughing sounded around her: her lungs expelling smoke, or the shaman's, or both.

"No," Tirana was saying. "No, High Commander, this is a grievous offense. You have disrupted the ritual. This will anger the spirits."

Savac began speaking the Sinari tongue as Marquand tethered *Life* into her, the normally red-faced captain's expression hardening as he loomed over her, working the leylines.

"What do you mean?" she asked. "Your spirits meant to let Ilek'Hannat burn, and us with him? I saved his life."

A tribeswoman in red-dyed cloth had come to kneel at Ilek'Hannat's side, and Aide-Captain Essily was shouting at Savac and the native translator both, with more voices adding to the din on both sides. It seemed as though a company had formed around the burning tent, her four escorts surrounded by tribesfolk who now converged on their wounded shaman even as the tent collapsed behind them in a pillar of fire.

"No, High Commander," Tirana said. "The spirits would protect us from the flames, and you and your aide as well. Now you have offended... what are you doing?"

She'd moved to kneel beside the shaman, still lying flat where she'd dragged him, no more than a handful of strides from the fire. The shaman was a bloody madman, but he held the key to their protection from the wild. She found *Life* and bound it into Ilek'Hannat, along with a strand of *Body* for strength. Black streaks marked his flesh where the fire had bit deepest, but his right side was deep red from forearm to the side of his face. He was a dead man without her intervention. She worked threads of *Life* into his lungs to keep him breathing, with more to bolster his heart while the bulk of her tethers soaked into his skin.

"High Commander, you cannot do this," Tirana said. "It is the spirits' way, to tend to their own. We do not interfere."

"We do not leave people to die!" she snapped back, finding a full-strength *Life* binding for the shaman's scorched windpipe, using the force of the tether to prop open his throat.

The shaman coughed, and the milk-haze drained from his eyes.

Impossible. The red splotches on his skin seemed to recede, his burns bubbling with a white foam.

"*Ilan ti ennikat, Tirana*," the shaman said, and he sat up, unaided.

The man should have been close to death, and apart from a rasp in his breathing, he could have been no more than winded from a run or a hard day's exertions. "*Shi n'at quiral, t'a kapek ni ana.*"

"He was never in danger," Tirana said, her tone still touched with indignance and anger. "Though he insists we should bear you no ill will for your ignorance. You have brought him a powerful vision."

"Paendurion," she said. "Thellan."

The shaman met her eyes, and he spoke again.

"He says our tribes will be safe here, that the Uktani have followed Arak'Jur into the south."

"You're certain," she said. "You're certain the Uktani pose no threat here in the north?"

The shaman nodded, and Tirana translated: "He says the spirits would not err in this. He is sure."

Plans took shape in her mind. Taking down the Great Barrier would pull all her attention to the north, and west, to protect the city from beasts and tribesmen in equal measure. Was Paendurion bold enough to make such a grand gesture, only to cover his true intentions, to attack with Thellan armies from the south? She knew the answer already.

26

SARINE

A Sacred Pool
Tsassani Land

Steam rose from the surface of the water, as though the whole stream had been put to a boil. White silt seemed to pool along the edges and around rocks in the stream, and the whole area stank like a soapmaker's shop, pungent chemicals stinging the back of her throat and nose.

"Is it safe?" Acherre asked. "The horses won't drink it."

Acherre's mount stood beside her, shying back from the bank of the stream. Sarine's own horse had taken to grazing as soon as they'd arrived, but it, too, seemed to be avoiding the water.

"It's not safe to drink," Ka'Inari said, after she'd relayed Acherre's question. "The animals are wise. But it is a sacred place, and safe to enter, if you can stand it."

"This is the place from your vision?" Sarine asked, and Ka'Inari nodded.

She didn't wait for more. Her boots came off as quick as she could free her feet. Her leggings followed, and her smallclothes. No sense dousing her garments in water that smelled like the leavings from a munitions factory. She took care to cradle Zi as she lifted her shirt, easing the sleeves around his fragile coils. She held him tight against her chest as she waded into the water, leaving her clothes behind on the shore.

The water was hot to the touch, enough to sear her skin. If not for Zi she might have held back, but the beast spirits' gift of ignoring temperature made it bearable. The soreness in her feet and legs melted away as she submerged them, blisters from walking and riding salved by the heat. It took lowering herself at the center of the pool for the water to reach her chest and shoulders, but she did, careful to keep Zi's head above the water as she soaked the rest of him in the spring. Zi's scales flashed red and gold beneath the water, and he met her eyes, though he said nothing.

"I take it that means he said it was safe," Acherre said dryly.

"Yes," she said. "Sorry."

Translation had been the least of her burdens since they'd set off from Ka'Ana'Tyat, though the need for it had made Acherre and Ka'Inari stranger company than they might have been, if the two of them had shared a tongue in common. The burden of walking had been tempered by the discovery of a pack of horses still wearing saddles and tack; Acherre had claimed the lead horse for herself, and roped down two more, with no sign of who their owners might have been, or why the horses had been left to the wild. With the horses they'd ranged across the span of two tribes' land and not seen another soul. If not for Zi she would have let Axerian go. She'd never imagined traveling so far from New Sarresant, so far from her uncle and the city and every comfort she'd ever known. But for Zi she would find out whether the earth had an end.

Sarine. Zi's thoughts felt frail, as though he struggled to form her name.

"Shh," she said. "It's all right. Ka'Inari said this place has healing magic. It will help."

During blinks she caught sight of the leylines twisting in strange patterns beneath the springs, leaving afterimages of green pods swarming where the water bubbled up from the ground. She'd tried tethering *Life* into Zi a dozen times without effect, but perhaps a different power was at work here. There had never been a healing spirit among the creatures of the wild, though it was always possible this was an older place, predating the spread of her influence in—

Zi tensed, tightening his grip on her forearm, and she smothered her thoughts. "I'm sorry," she said, and felt a rush of shame. She hadn't had a vision in days, but intrusive thoughts sprang up like weeds in the chapel garden. Thoughts she shouldn't have, memories from no life she'd ever lived, and even pondering their mysteries seemed to hurt Zi beyond what he could bear.

"Exarch's balls, that's fucking hot," Acherre said, and withdrew her foot from the water quick as she'd dabbed it in. Only her boot was off, piled near Sarine's clothes, but the captain hastened to get it back on rather than shed the rest. "I think I'll leave the bathing to you, if it's all the same."

A fog of steam rose all around her. Perhaps it was hot, but her skin took it in stride. "Sorry," she said. "I should have warned you. It was only, Zi needed..."

"Don't trouble yourself," Acherre said. "I need time to work with my mount. We'll patrol around the spring a ways, make sure none of the natives are taking an interest in us."

Ka'Inari had removed his footwear as well, thick leather slippers set beside a rock he'd sat atop, dangling his toes into the steam.

"You seem troubled," Ka'Inari said as Acherre walked her horse away, leaving her and Ka'Inari alone beside the pool. "Is all well between you and the captain?"

"Yes. Acherre means to watch for anyone approaching while we bathe here."

"Your companion, then."

Sarine nodded, returning her attention to Zi. He was still quiet, clinging to her forearm as the heat from the pool seemed to lap streaks of red across his scales.

"I don't think it's helping him," she said. "This is the place from your dream, isn't it?"

"It is," the shaman said. "The Tsassani pools. Not a place of the spirits, but it is known to them."

"You said it was a place of healing."

"Yes. But there are many sorts of wounds. Who can say, for your companion..." He trailed off, and seemed to stop himself. "That is, I'm sorry. I'd hoped this place would help."

Zi's eyes had closed, though his claws still held him in place. Asleep, perhaps, or resting. Best to let him linger. Perhaps the waters took time.

"What's it like," she asked, "hearing the voices of the spirits of visions?"

The question seemed to surprise the shaman. But it was better if they spoke of other things, something besides Zi's sickness. If the pool was going to heal him, it was going to heal him. Dwelling on it wouldn't help.

"It's something I've known since I was a boy," Ka'Inari said. "And not something spoken of, except to other *Ka*, or *Ilek'Ka*."

"Oh." She hadn't meant to offend, but it appeared she had.

"It's all right," the shaman said. "I only meant I'm not used to describing it. The spirits of things-to-come speak differently than we do. They send images and sensations, memories sometimes. Dreams. It falls to us to interpret what they mean."

"So it's different than the others?"

"Others?"

"I spoke with spirits, when I killed *mareh'et*, *lakiri'in*, and again at Tanir'Ras'Tyat. They were cryptic, but they spoke in words, not emotions or images. Not so different from Zi, actually."

The shaman had rolled his hide leggings up to his knees, submerging his calves into the pool, and he leaned farther forward at her mention of Zi, studying the serpentine head poked above the surface.

"I know nothing of your companion," Ka'Inari said. "But yes, the spirits of beasts are different. More direct. As different as beasts are from the concepts of time and possibility."

"Is that why they wouldn't let me enter Ka'Ana'Tyat?"

"They only told me it wasn't your place," he said. "Typically they refuse entry to any who hasn't performed the rituals and been foreseen by another shaman. I'd suspected it might be different, for you, given your blessings with the other spirits. But it appears it was not."

"They said it wasn't..." She trailed off. They'd said it wasn't her place. Perhaps they'd only meant what Ka'Inari had said, that she hadn't been chosen or performed the proper rituals, but it came dangerously close to the sort of talk that had been hurting Zi. Better if she changed the subject.

"Your visions," she said instead. "When they send emotions, memories. Do you ever worry about getting them wrong?"

"Always. Even the best of us make mistakes."

A painful reminder that they were two hundred leagues from anywhere, on little more than Ka'Inari's promise that he saw a shadow in the west.

"You're worried over our journey together," he continued, and she nodded. "Don't. One or two sendings could be misinterpreted, but I've had many, pertaining to you."

"The spirits speak of me?"

Ka'Inari's eyes seemed to flash, but he looked away again quickly.

"They are fascinated by you," he said.

Silence passed between them. She wasn't sure how or whether to ask for more. Strange, to consider how close Ka'Inari and his people lived to her city, yet neither knew the other's ways. Suddenly her nakedness came to the forefront of her thoughts. Neither the shaman nor Acherre had reacted when she strode into the pool, but it was far from polite to shed one's clothing in the presence of strangers. Was it similarly forward among the tribes? Now she felt like an ass—she hadn't considered anything beyond the need to try to soak Zi in the pool.

She turned her attention back to her companion, stroking his neck below the water's surface. He was getting worse. He'd hardly been able to string two words together since Ka'Ana'Tyat. His eyes seemed to be full of pain, and he spent most of the day asleep or comatose—she couldn't tell which. She'd seen him dozing a thousand times, lazing about on whatever surface was at hand while she drew her sketches. This was different. She wasn't even sure he would tell her if he knew what was wrong, or how to fix it. It had always been his nature to protect her, and who could say what would qualify as a thing from which she needed saving? The inequality of it burned, doubly so in light of the searing pool. It was her turn to protect him, and she came up short for her ignorance of how to do it.

Light flashed in her eyes, and she was somewhere else.

An empty place.

Her body floated in the water, but even the shape of her seemed a foreign memory. She had no form, no weight, only consciousness.

She wasn't alone.

Another spark of light, a deep purple where she was blue.

IT SHOULD BE EASIER, IN LIGHT OF THE BREACH IN THE DIVIDE, AND YET I HAVE STRUGGLED TO SPEAK WITH YOU OF LATE.

What?

The words resonated in her mind, and seemed to project outward, until she wasn't certain whether she'd spoken it or heard it from another source. The void around her was similar to the spirits' place, but it was different. Calmer, somehow. More empty.

YOU ARE RESTORED. IT'S DONE, THEN. MY PART IN YOUR REBIRTH.

This was hurting Zi, she was sure of it. Her thoughts again seemed to reverberate with sudden force, and she formed them into words.

Please, stop. Let me go.

SO LONG AS YOU DO NOT FORGET OUR PACT. I HAVE TRUSTED YOU BEFORE, AND BEEN BETRAYED.

Air and water sputtered through her lungs, and she coughed, lying on her back in the sunlight.

"Sarine!"

Ka'Inari knelt over her, his image seeming to blur between the man and a shimmer of blue sparks before it settled on his face, full of concern and alarm.

She coughed again, tasting spoiled eggs in the back of her throat, and sat up, her lungs burning raw where water had gotten into her chest. She was on the bank of the pool, a trail of water splashed across the rocks where Ka'Inari must have dragged her out.

"Are you all right?" he asked.

She tried to nod and coughed again. Zi was still coiled around her forearm, but her skin stung where his claws dug into her. Red droplets trickled from where he clung to her arm.

"Zi," she managed. "Zi, are you okay?"

Zi clung tighter in reply, squeezing blood from her skin. She ignored the pain.

"You slipped under the water," Ka'Inari said. "I was afraid you'd passed out from the heat."

"No," she said. "Something... I'm not sure what happened."

The Regnant, Zi thought to her. *I've tried to hold him back, but he grows stronger as we travel west.*

"Zi!" Surprise touched her voice—it was more than he'd said at once in days.

I'm sorry. It wasn't supposed to happen so soon. We needed time. Time for you to grow.

Ka'Inari sat back, surveying her as if to be sure she was all right.

"Zi, it's fine. Don't exert yourself. I'm fine. I didn't—"

You must change. If you inherit too many of her memories, you will be lost. I tried to hold it all back, but I've failed. You will have to be strong now, Sarine.

"What do you mean? What's happening?" Tears came to her eyes. Zi's claws still stung where they dug into her skin. He wasn't suddenly healed. He was using the last of his strength.

It's time. I'm sorry. I tried to do better than this.

"Stop it," she said. "Stop this, please."

Don't repeat her mistakes. You are not her.

Tears flowed, and she whispered something indiscernible. Begging. Pleading. But Zi had gone cold as suddenly as he'd seemed to find his strength, and his claws released their hold on her arm. His body uncoiled, leaving dead, scaled loops lying across her lap, the light in his gemstone eyes faded to a dull gray.

27

THE VEIL

A Sacred Pool
Tsassani Land

She heard screaming, wailing from a girl's throat.

She was the Goddess.

She remembered dying. Accepting the Regnant's poison through the crack in her prison. Axerian, Paendurion, Ad-Shi; doomed to be defeated, as the first price of her ancient enemy's assistance.

"No," the girl was saying. "No, Zi, wake up. Wake up!"

A *kaas* lay dead in her lap, the shell of a four-legged serpent in its molting stage, devoid of a spirit to forge its bonds. Grief washed through her. Was this her emotion? She had no especial cause for grief.

A man sat beside her, cross-legged and leaning in closer than he should.

"*Ah'ske ni Sarine*," the man said. "*Hana tur qu'ela.*"

Zi was dead. The thought struck her senses with terrible force. She'd failed him. She could have pushed harder, run faster, killed her horse and found a dozen more to die to track Axerian down. Zi would have done it for her. She sobbed, and repeated the thought. He would have done it for her.

"Zi, no," she said, her voice already breaking. "Please don't be dead. You can't leave me alone. I can't do this without you."

The weight of his body suddenly felt heavier than a stone, lifeless and draped across her legs. His now-gray eyes had lolled back as his head sagged, his limbs hanging loose, claws open. All color had drained from him like flows of blood, making puddles of green and red and gold on her skin and on the rocks around them.

Kaas were easy to bond, once you knew the way of it. So much grief over a single incarnation seemed unwarranted, but she couldn't stop the flow of emotions raging through her body. Stronger than they had ever been; too strong to control.

She picked up Zi's body and held it to her heart. He'd always relished making her blood pump double with *Red*. He'd saved her more times than she could know. Sobs shook her hands, but she kept hold of him. He was dead.

Ka'Inari reached a hand to comfort her, laying it atop her knee, and she recoiled. It was wrong for him to see Zi. Zi had never wanted to be seen, had almost never appeared to anyone but her. It was only when he was sick, only at the end of his life that he couldn't stay hidden. And even then he'd preferred to stay beneath her saddlecloths, wrapped close to her skin. She twisted away from Ka'Inari's gesture, turning her torso to hide Zi's body from view.

"*Ah'ske,*" Ka'Inari said. "*Ki in uluru dan.*" It took a moment to register that she was hearing the Sinari tongue, and didn't have Zi to translate it for her.

She sobbed again, a racking cry that doubled her over on the rocks. She was on her side somehow, the world spun on its end.

She had to find Axerian; from all she'd gathered so far, he was the nearest of the Three. Ad-Shi and Paendurion had yet to snuff out their ascendants, and Axerian had already been replaced by the one called Reyne d'Agarre. He would be here, while the others were cloistered in the Master's Sanctum until the appointed time.

She tried to stand, and her body refused to obey.

She needed to stay here, lying on the rocks. She needed to sob, until her eyes ran dry and her belly had emptied and she'd shown the world the barest measure of her grief.

She tried again, and stayed in place.

Her blood mixed with the colors leaking from Zi's scales. Good. She deserved to bleed. Whether from the small cuts he'd traced on her skin, clinging to her in the last moments of his life, or scrapes from the rocks, or a searing poker through her belly to mirror the pain of Zi's death.

A tinge of frustration coursed through her. She was supposed to be reborn. The knot tying off her memories should have faded when the prison collapsed. Perhaps that was the answer. Yes, she would have to block the memories of this girl who had kept her body warm during her imprisonment. If she failed to honor the bargain, the Regnant would come for her with more than his chosen Three. It would mean war, war of a kind they hadn't seen since the Master's passing had left them the keys to Life and Death.

She drew a deep breath, pulling Life in with it. That much still worked. Blue sparks danced in her vision, painting images in thousands of points of light. She wove fibers around her mind, slipping from the physical world into a world of pure form.

Goddess.

The thought came to her from all sides, echoed in a hundred voices, great and small, male, female, and more. The *kaas* served every aspect of creation, and yet stood apart from it; two worlds, existing side-by-side.

"I have need," she said, more a projection than a vocalization, but it passed here. They stirred like a hive at her words, a skitter of claws and tails.

Zi is dead.

Confusion. That thought hadn't come from the *kaas*, but it hadn't come from her, either.

You wish him returned to you?

The collective perked their heads, looking at her with curiosity from a thousand angles, above, below, from every side.

"No," she said, at the same time another voice shouted *YES.*

She was surrounded by images drawn from the blue sparks, as though a whole world had been painted with dots of light. A world of strange shapes, with more *kaas* than she could count draped from platforms suspended in the air, cubes and pyramids floating endlessly in every direction. Fear coursed through her. Had they truly offered to return Zi to her? Nothing else mattered. *Yes,* she thought again, as forcefully as she could manage.

He is not ready to return, a dozen voices echoed in her head. *He is weak.*

Zi, she thought. *Are you there? Are you alive?*

"No," another voice said in frustration. "I need a full-strength *kaas* suited to managing another bond. A weakened incarnation will not serve."

It is agreed.

Good. The Zi soul had served her well for some time, but a fresh bond would prove pliable, and she needed raw strength if she meant to face Axerian. His bond with Xeraxet was strong, an old power he had reinforced with stolen Life. A perversion, to prolong the connection so long, but that had always been his great failing: He had never bothered to understand power before he seized it.

No. The girl projected the thought. *Zi, if you're out there, come back to me!*

Irritation flared, smothered by hope and desperation.

Sarine?

His voice. Zi's voice. He was alive.

Zi!

A presence parted the waves of light, shapes and serpents bowing and bending as they made way. Zi trundled through the crowd, hobbled and weak. But it was him. Even washed out through a million points of blue light, she knew his form anywhere.

"No," the other voice said. "I won't accept this bond. I require a soul suited to my command."

Yes. Zi's thought. *I am not strong enough to return.*

It is agreed, the chorus chittered all around them.

No it isn't, Sarine thought. *I need you back. Please don't leave me.*

I submit my daughter, Zi thought to them all. *She will go, and serve in my stead.*

His daughter. Was it a trick? *Kaas* weren't meant to take interest in the world, but the girl inside her body seemed attached to Zi beyond the limits of a natural bond. She hadn't acquiesced, but the chorus murmured acceptance, skittering over top of their shapes and coils as they pecked each other, a transmission of doubts and assurances beneath the layer of conscious thought.

It will serve, the chorus seemed to say. *Will it serve?*

Zi, please, the girl thought.

Accept, Zi thought back. *Accept my daughter and care for her. Let her guide you. I must watch, for now.*

Panic. The *kaas* would always overreach, if it was allowed. A firm hand was required, to keep them in place. Accepting a new one as a guide was a poor beginning.

"I will not accept," she said. "This *kaas* is flawed. I demand—"

All right, the girl's thoughts sounded. *If she is your daughter, I accept. It is done.*

No. This body was hers! But a new presence formed between her and the girl, a cold light seeming to scan them both in the depths of their minds. Warmth sprang from elsewhere, beckoning the presence toward it.

The points of light seemed to blur, revealing color splashed between them. A pool, covered over with steam. A man sat nearby, torn between wanting to help and keeping away. She lay against the rocks, covered by blood and emotion.

She could feel a new presence coming toward her. Zi's daughter. Her body had been sobbing, and now it cracked with a new emotion, born of joy. Zi wasn't dead. He needed to rest, but he was alive.

Who are you?

The voice was new, and full of fear. It quavered, afraid to show itself. She welcomed it with love.

"I'm Sarine," she whispered. "I loved your father, and he asked me to care for you."

The presence drew closer, a curiosity in the way it approached her thoughts, though it hadn't appeared yet in physical form.

Who is the other?

"I...I don't know," she said. Memories ached in her head. A prison of glass. An insistence that Zi be refused. Suddenly she heard a voice, speaking faintly, from a great distance. *I am the Goddess, Wielder of Life, Mistress of the Soul of the World. I am the Veil, and you will obey!*

The voice cut off, suddenly quiet.

I bound her, the new presence thought to her. *She is full of anger.*

Sarine sat up on the rocks, feeling a weight she hadn't known was there melt away. The world seemed brighter, full of new energy. Ka'Inari looked to her with confusion and curiosity, but she could laugh and kiss him. Zi was alive. His daughter was with her. The memories were gone.

"What's your name?" Sarine asked. "It's all right. You can trust me."

A crystal serpent appeared on the rocks, an arm's length away. She'd seen Zi do it countless times, yet it almost made her gasp. This *kaas* was different. Smaller than Zi. A narrower point to her snout, a softer line for the curve of her neck and head. Longer limbs, relative to her body, and finer claws. The same metallic scales, shimmering silver and gold in the sun.

I am Anati. I think we are bonded. Can you see me?

"Yes," she said, wiping the tears from her eyes. "Yes, Anati, I can."

28

TIGAI

Market Square
Ghingwai

Three days.

Master Indra's warning stuck in his head, as it had every sundown since he'd been given Mei's hand amid the ruins of their destroyed temple. Three days until Mei suffered again for his failure, and two had already come and gone.

An Imperial crier pushed through the throng, calling the sunset as he used a long pole to light the lanterns draped from roof to roof. Few seemed to take notice of the hour, continuing their shouts and haggling over carpets, sugared figs, incense sticks, bed slaves, silks, and whatever else was on offer. Tigai stood at the center of it, the eye of a monsoon as it swirled around the heart of the square. He'd placed his back against the plinth of General An's statue of horse and rider, proof against pickpockets, and a means to avoid being judged by the gold-lacquered eyes of the woman seated atop her cast-iron horse. An Ling was the daughter of an ancient general, who took up her father's standard midway through a battle to save the Empire. He couldn't help but see Mei in her face.

This was the third night. Anger had given way to fear and desperation hours ago. Indra's promise of a second hand as the price of failure flashed in his thoughts as he scanned the crowd. Desperate. Three days wasn't enough to forge the sort of connection that would let him hook himself to a man's bedchamber. But it had to be tonight.

He saw Lin Qishan before he was meant to, he was sure. She made no especial attempt at subterfuge, but neither could she have expected to stand out among the crowd of merchants, buyers, and thieves. Soldiers and mercenaries flooded the streets in all three capacities; she blended in among them in her tunic and breeches, shambling through the press with a purpose, where most were content to consider some ware or another, or leer at whoever looked as though they wouldn't put up a fight.

"Master Anji," Lin said when she took a place beside the statue, affecting the air of a chance encounter with an old acquaintance. "A pleasure to find you here, in Ghingwai of all ports."

His heart thumped in his chest. Three days, Indra had said. The third wasn't finished. She couldn't mean to deliver the news yet.

"You as well, Sergeant Hui," he said. The need for false names was absurd, as far as he saw it. The name Yanjin Tigai meant nothing to the soldiers assembled here to buy salt pork and sex. But he'd call her the *aryu* of the west if it meant reprieve from the direst sort of news.

She leaned in to kiss his cheek, and her tone changed. "Tonight," she said in a low voice, but sharp as the glass he knew she could summon at a whim. "Now. You've already dithered too long."

They switched cheeks. "It isn't like buying a ticket to a bloody circus," he said, and she withdrew, cutting him short.

"Master Anji, I'm afraid any business would have to be discussed over tea, and time is short. Perhaps I will run into you again tomorrow, if the wind spirits are favorable."

"I'd be inclined to take that tea tonight," he said, but she was already pulling back, fixing him with a heavy look before she faded into the crowd.

He had half a mind to go after her. None of it made sense. Indra had anchored them to Ghingwai, only to find the city overrun with mercenaries. A reaction to his and Remarin's attack on the Emperor's palace, perhaps, only why would they mobilize here, and not the Imperial City? Indra had said something about a rebellion, led by someone called "Isaru Mattai" as though the name was meant to hold some significance. All it meant to him was a city on the brink of war, with enemies or with itself, and him tasked with shadowing one of its commanders.

On the opposite side of the square, where crimson-sashed soldiers formed a makeshift phalanx around a whore-seller, lay the object of Master Indra's interest, and by extension, of his. Boisterous laughter rose from among their number. He'd been shadowing the inner circle of Priva Ambiyyat's company for three days now, slowly letting strands fall away where they had no connections in common. Just as he'd done with his prisoners and their connections to the Emperor's chambers, so Lin Qishan and Master Indra expected him to be able to do with Priva Ambiyyat. But it wasn't so simple, with men who ate and drank and fought and fucked together. They had two dozen strands in common; he was as likely to hook himself to some distant battlefield as the inner sanctum of wherever their company kept the contracts Lin Qishan had charged him to steal.

Tonight. It had to be tonight.

He pushed off from the statue, angling around to make it look as though he were coming from the west. The whore-seller's stall was broad enough to occupy the space for two lesser merchants, with as many bare-chested guardsmen as bare-chested women on display. Even so, Ambiyyat's men outnumbered the guards, swarming around the stall to make clear the goods were reserved for men in crimson sashes. He ignored the implied warning, edging toward the stall as he pushed through the crowd, eyeing the girls with lust he wouldn't have had to feign if not for the doom hanging over him, and his family.

"This one is a sweet brown, half-Bhakal and bred to please," the whore-seller was saying, an Ihjani man done up in an exaggeration of his people's traditional style, colorful silks and patterned turban wrapped tight around his head. "Pair her with a white-skinned Natarii from the north, and both will leave you drained as a fresh-molt snakeskin, I swear it on my mother's heart."

One of Ambiyyat's men took note of his approach, gesturing to his fellows as they turned to block the way.

"Move along, friend," the mercenary said to him. "These slaves are spoken for tonight."

Tigai affected a humble posture as the whore-seller moved on to a different stall, this one featuring a Nikkon girl bound in chains around a post. "This one is fresh, but fierce," the Ihjani man was saying. "Still unbroken, but you may find pleasure in the breaking, so long as you agree to waive any claims against me, should she do you or your men harm."

"Come now," Tigai said to the mercenaries. "You've had claim on these the last two nights already. Surely there are plenty to go round."

"Move along," the mercenary repeated. "Return tomorrow and you can have your pick of our leavings."

"By tomorrow I'll be half a day's journey to Hagong. I'd saved enough *qian* for one of the Ihjani's girls to see me off. All the men of my guild say they're the best."

The mercenary made a face between a leer and a grin. "You'll have to spend your seed in the dirt along the road, tradesman. Or find some lesser whores."

"The slave girls are only for men with your sashes?"

"Men of Ambiyyat's company," the mercenary said. "Fighting men."

"Very well, then," he said. "I'll fight you for your sash."

Laughter roared from the mercenary's fellows, and the man who'd spoken gave him a second look, as though Tigai had already struck him across the eyes.

"What did you say, tradesman?"

"You heard me, my friend. I mean to wet my cock tonight. If that means trading blows with you before I get my hands on a girl, so be it."

He knew at once he'd judged the situation aright. The man's fellows wore skull-splitting grins, looking back and forth at him as though they couldn't believe what they knew they'd heard. The mercenary had spoken truly enough; they were fighting men, tall and broad-chested where Jun lords were seldom renowned for their height or girth, and Tigai was no exception. But he'd been trained at arms by an Ujibari clan chief, hopefully enough to hold his own. It might end with his face in the dirt, but these men respected strength, so strength was the tool he had to employ. And the mercenary couldn't refuse such a challenge, not and share a drink with any fellow of his company for weeks to come.

"You're a gnat," the mercenary said. "Fuck off before I swat you."

Tigai replied by dropping into a fighting stance, setting his weight between both legs and relaxing into a half crouch, allowing his opponent the first attack.

The laughter turned to a buzz that passed through the crowd, their eyes turned from within the Ihjani's stall and from within the press of the square. Space appeared around them, though anyone would have sworn the press was packed tight a moment before.

The mercenary gave him a look of equal parts confusion and scorn, and offered the same to his comrades. Tigai waited, lowering his eyes to watch all parts of his enemy's body at once.

Weight shifted to the mercenary's front leg, and gave away the strike before it came.

The mercenary grunted, lunging to throw a punch across his body with enough force to crack a stone. Tigai ducked, jabbing into the mercenary's abdomen as a feint while he sent a kick to the side of the knee on the mercenary's front leg. Simple. Remarin had drilled him on it a hundred times: Disrupt your enemy's balance and he would fall, no matter the size advantage in your opponent's favor. Only instead of falling, the mercenary staggered forward, carried by the force of his own swing.

Tigai tried to shift his weight and turn aside, but the mercenary caught hold of his shirt, wrenching them both into the street. Pain stung his forearm where he landed, scraped against the stones and dirt, and his breath burned as it left his lungs. The crowd roared, and the audience seemed to blur as the ground spun beneath him.

He kicked to free himself, landing a solid blow on something he hoped was the mercenary's torso. Then the world shook and he tasted blood.

The mercenary hit him again. His head ached and his teeth hurt. Instinct hovered over the strands like the fibers on a weaver's wheel. But no; leaving that way meant questions, and questions meant heightened alerts, knowing a *magi* had taken an interest in Priva Ambiyyat's band. The mercenary wouldn't strike to kill. They lay tangled on the street, and he flailed and kicked between the mercenary's punches, landing a fist in the other man's jaw, and another in his eye. The crowd roared, laughing and shouting until rough hands grabbed hold of his shoulders and dragged them apart.

He staggered to his feet, hefted by a Hagali man a full head and shoulders above him. Another who could be the Hagali's twin held his opponent, and Priva Ambiyyat himself stood between them, a man attired tenfold as grandly as his soldiers, with a scabbarded shamshir blade tucked in the folds of his gold and crimson sash.

"What passes here?" Priva Ambiyyat said. "Almost I think I have taken a wrong street, and ended at the fighting pits, instead of the flesh market."

"This man tried to fight me," his opponent said. The man's lip had split, his eye already turned a soft purple that promised to bloom before the night was out. Evidently Remarin's training had counted for more than he'd thought, when instinct took over.

"This is true?" Ambiyyat said. "You have assaulted one of my company?"

"I challenged him for one of your sashes, and the right to bed one of these whores," Tigai said, ignoring the throbbing pain in his head and the trail of blood running from his nose. "He accepted the challenge when he threw the first punch."

"Summon the guards," the Ihjani whore-seller said from behind a line of mercenaries. "This sort of disruption is intolerable, and around my delicate night-flowers, who know nothing of these cruelties."

Ambiyyat grinned, looking between him and the mercenary he'd fought. "It seems to me you have earned yourself a night in a cell, my friend."

"I wanted nothing more than the honor of having what you have already had, my lord," he said. "They say Priva Ambiyyat's company is generous in victory and honorable in defeat. Do they have the right of it?"

Desperation strained his voice. He could hear it as the words left his lips, as Mei's face flashed in his memory. But the captain paused, looming between his Hagali bodyguards as though deciding what to have for supper.

"No man says that of my company, not in any port of call I have visited."

"Perhaps they will start, when you grant me my whore."

Ambiyyat laughed. "I have never seen a man so desperate for fucking. Yes. Let them go. For your zeal, and the unexpected entertainment. Did you have a particular slave in mind?"

Tigai suppressed the urge to exhale in relief.

"I am a humble man, my lord. Would it do you homage, if I chose whichever girl you had last night?"

This time the crowd laughed along with the captain, and he nodded agreement, clapping Tigai across the shoulder hard enough to rattle his teeth a second time.

Their tea service had been prepared in the Emperor's kitchens, ferried to Ghingwai on the backs of sea turtles, then left to steep under moonlight for the length of an owl's song. Or so it bloody felt.

Lin Qishan, still wearing the costume of a mercenary sergeant, insisted they keep decorum, which meant tea before business, no matter how late the hour. She reclined in an oak chair carved with dragons for armrests, looking for all the world as though her tea was the most important thing in the world. She lifted the cup, inhaling the steam, and he resisted the urge to knock it to the floor, to yell at her to read the fucking papers he'd delivered before they'd even entered the teahouse.

The slave girl he'd won the right of bedding had led him straight to Priva Ambiyyat's tent. Her strands had been unmistakable, and thank the Gods the captain hadn't shared her yet with his lieutenants. A look at her had made clear why: a beauty from the southern jungles, done up like a Jun court haremite, but with a boyish figure and a penis to match. She'd reacted with confusion when he spent more time with his eyes closed, sensing her connections to the starfield, than staring at her figure. Gods only knew what she'd thought of him excusing himself in haste once he'd made the connection.

"Do you not find your tea agreeable, Master Anji?" Lin Qishan asked.

He glared at her. The servants had poured him a cup, too, of course. He hadn't looked at it. Lin Qishan seemed wholly intent on their useless charade, as though they were actors playing for the sake of an audience who'd paid to watch their every dalliance. Fine.

He took up the cup and downed its contents in a single gulp, regretting the decision quicker than he could lower it back to the table. Boiling water seared his throat, and he coughed, loud enough to turn heads and spoil the scene.

Lin Qishan only sipped her tea, ignoring his display.

"Very well," she said after an eternity. "Let us see what business you've put before me."

Priva Ambiyyat's mercenary contracts. He'd read them through twice to be sure, and grabbed three extra sets of documents, governing the company's employment history for their prior four campaigns. Ambiyyat's company had been hired to garrison Ghingwai for the season, paid by the magistracy itself. Before that they'd been fighting striking workers on behalf of a mining company, doing patrols in the jungles of Honjin, been armed escorts for the wool merchants' guild's caravans, and fought Ihjani tribesmen for a Jun march lord in the far west. Lin thumbed through them all, seeming to pore over every word.

"It's all there," he said, straining through his scorched throat. "You must give me whatever token will suffice, to stop Master—"

She hissed before he could say the name. Oh for the *koryu's* sake.

"...to stop our *mutual acquaintance*, then," he finished.

"Yes," Lin Qishan said. "In due course. First I will need you to murder the owner of these documents, then do the same for each of the other five mercenary captains in Ghingwai."

He nearly coughed again. She insisted on the pretense of a masquerade, then spoke openly of murdering a half-dozen men? And not just any men, the very captains employed to defend the city?

"Of course," he said. "Naturally you want them dead. Shall I deliver the Emperor's wives to you as well? Then the heads of Zan House, the Jiyuns, and perhaps their firstborn daughters to keep you entertained while you wait?"

"No," she said, as though he were perfectly serious. "Only these six, to send a message. Then you wait for the reply."

"No. I won't do anything of the kind. Not without assurances that Mei and—"

Once again she hissed to cut him short.

"You'll have your assurances," Lin said. "Our mutual acquaintance will not act without my word. Do this. Do it tonight."

"What? I can't—"

She slammed the table. "You can. You will."

Patrons from across the house were eyeing them, and Lin seemed not to care.

He leaned forward, lowering his voice to just above a whisper. "You mean for me to walk into their camps, strike them down, and hook an anchor to the next tents? Half the city will be in an uproar, screaming about a *magi* gone mad."

"Yes, yes they will."

She was half-witted herself. No other explanation fit. Her and Master Indra and his apprentice and all of them. Even with Dao, Remarin, and

Mei in their keeping. They were asking him to start a war, to declare that the Great and Noble Houses intended to interfere in politics again. He wasn't even associated with the monks or their temples, and Lin Qishan was asking for the sort of incitement that would send half the Empire into a panic.

"Why don't you do it yourself? Go throw glass at them until you stir the hornets into a frenzy."

"I wouldn't survive. You will. And it is imperative you do, so take no chances with the soldiers."

"You're asking me to weigh three lives against what, how many? A thousand? How many will die in the panic alone?"

She said nothing to that, giving him a cold look in place of argument. Mei's face flashed again in his memory, and the terrible image of the hand in Master Indra's sack. All his better judgment screamed to run, to write off his brother, Remarin, and Mei as casualties of whatever insanity prevailed among his captors. Instead he could feel the decision being made, and hated himself for knowing what it would be.

29

ARAK'JUR

A Fetid Swamp
Lhakani Land

Light touched him, and he swallowed it. Thick wood loomed overhead, draped with moss and vines, blacking out the sun. Water and mud coursed through him, mixed with peat and tar. Upright animals came and went, and birds perched on branches above the carcasses of beasts that stayed too long. Yet though he welcomed death, he was a wellspring of life. Mushroom caps bloomed from the morass of dead flesh and trees. Flies and larvae crawled on branches, nesting on any surface that could hold their tiny bodies. Ensnared animals hosted infections as they died, and sprouted rot when they fell still. He was the swamp, cradle of decay, and his was the gift of death before rebirth.

REMEMBER US, the Great Spirit thought into the void. DEATH STIRS, AND THE GODDESS HAS NEED OF OUR GIFT. REMEMBER US, WHEN THE DAYS OF SHADOW COME AGAIN.

I will, he thought back, and the void slipped away, replaced by the emptiness of life.

———

His muscles ached. *Ipek'a* had guarded the way into the swamp, a pack of ten with two alpha females, one aged matron and a daughter soon primed to challenge for the place. He hadn't bothered with subterfuge, attacking the pack at sunrise after he'd stalked them to the edge of the bog. Claws and beaks had raked him for his hubris, but the beasts had fallen to his rage. A temporary relief, fighting with the spirits' gifts against a flurry of feather and claw. It had distracted from the pain, the dullness that had been his companion in the days since he'd turned south.

Corenna had abandoned him.

Had she come to him and reasoned against continuing on their journey, he would have called it wisdom and found the first safe haven for her to shelter against the storm. But instead she'd gone. Was it fear of letting him down? Never cowardice. Never abdication of her duties. A thousand explanations ran through his thoughts, each more empty than the last. But the fact remained: She was gone, he was alone, and the mantle of Ka'Inari's visions fell on him like a shadow.

The bog stank, but he rose to his feet amid the thick mud and peat. A squelching sound accompanied his footfalls, each step yearning to keep him there until the tar had hold of him. Moru'Alura'Tyat, the spirits had named it. The place where death sleeps. A carrion bird crowed through the fog, and insects buzzed a welcome as he trudged through the slime. He went out the way he'd come, a turn northward in case the morass extended farther south than the entrance to its sacred heart. Corenna had to have come here, once, to learn the secret of the black tendrils, the secret the swamp spirits had granted him when they'd judged him worthy. She'd never spoken of it. A reminder there were parts of her he hadn't known, parts that could abandon him with the Uktani mere hours behind. Spirits send she had veered far enough to escape their scouts. But if she had been taken, it hadn't stopped their pursuit. He'd spent hours inside the swamp; days, perhaps, if the spirits had willed it. He might well find the Uktani waiting, when he left the murk behind. It was vulgar to hope for it, for the release of violence, but still the feeling came, slowly burning hotter as he trekked toward solid ground.

The fog thinned before he reached the corpses of the *ipek'a* pack, but the tar and peat was still thick around his feet. Impossible to move stealthily, or easily conceal one's passage, when the ground tried to swallow his steps and left open maws behind when it failed to keep him. He moved in the open, leaving a trail to show where he had gone. A trail that had been followed.

He saw their silhouettes drawn against the thinning fog before he saw them in the flesh, but no mistaking the count, or the nature of what he saw. Two figures had climbed into canopies of dead branches, the desiccated husks of fauna that passed for trees near the heart of the swamp. Four more waited in the open, beside the corpses he'd left behind.

Not Uktani. Or if they were, they'd taken to wearing different markings. He stepped forward, until the fog lifted enough for sunlight to illuminate them. They'd smeared themselves with mud and peat, until their skins were almost black, and shorn their heads clean of hair. They waited for him, though it was clear from their stances he'd been seen, and they made no attempt at surprise.

"Who are you?" a man called when he drew near enough to hear it. A short, thin man who stood at the center. The words had been spoken in a thick-accented dialect, but close enough to one he knew from travel and trade with the southern tribes.

"I am Arak'Jur, guardian of the Sinari," he said in the same tongue. There was danger here; he'd entered a sacred place without the host tribe's blessing, and invoked their wrath, if they chose to give it. Corenna's departure had left him beyond caring. If they chose to try to take him, they would find him no easy prey.

"You tread close to a sacred place, Arak'Jur, guardian of the Sinari," the man said. "Is it a thing for northerners to violate such sanctity?"

"I have come to treat with the spirits who dwell here. It is not my intent to treat with men."

"This is not a place for you, or any man," a woman among them said. "Your presence offends us, and you will not draw any nearer the heart of the swamp."

Violence loomed behind her words, and a tinge of shame passed through him that he almost welcomed it. A vulgar spark against the blackness of Corenna's absence.

"I've been there already," he said. "I've spoken with the spirits."

"You lie!" the same woman said, and the man raised a hand between them, as though he meant to block her way.

"The *ipek'a* pack," the man said. "You fought them?"

Wisps of fog rolled between them over open ground, finally solid, though the stink of peat hung in the air. He wasn't close enough to read the man's expression, but there was disbelief in his words, and a glimmer of something else—hope, perhaps, or awe.

"I did," he said. "And I passed through the corruption sealing the entrance to Moru'Alura'Tyat. I spoke with the spirits there, and earned their gift. And now I mean to go, and leave your people in peace."

"He lies," the woman said. "He is a man. The swamp spirits would never—"

"They would," Arak'Jur interrupted. "They have already, whether you accept it or no."

"Prove it," the woman said. "Show us their gift, or we strike you down for your blasphemy."

The spark struck, and almost caught, in the stances of the warriors arrayed behind her. The rest were men, he was almost sure, though they were thin and slight enough to make it uncertain. Yet they seemed to take the woman's lead.

"I wish no violence here," he said.

"Then show us the truth of what you claim."

A vulgar display, but less so than unnecessary violence. He expected hostility from foreign tribes; part of why he hadn't tried to secure their approval before venturing into the morass. But if he could have it now, for one misuse of the spirits' gift, it was well worth the price.

He closed his eyes, opening his body to the spirits' touch. Images flooded through him, sensations of death and rot. Black fog rolled through his eyes, staining the world a deeper and deeper shade of gray. Then it spewed from his hands, billowing clouds, inky tendrils rising like snakes, seeking life to kill, obeying his will as he commanded them into being.

"It is," the woman said, almost making it a curse. "It is the swamp spirits' gift. It is not possible, it could not be."

He let the tendrils fade, feeling a stinging rebuke in his mind. Their power was to be used for killing. The spirits' anger rippled through him as the ink-clouds faded, a vestige of their disapproval.

The small man stepped forward, as though he'd triumphed in whatever passed between him and the woman.

"Arak'Jur, guardian of the Sinari," he said. "Our shaman will wish to speak with you. Will you come, and listen to what we have to say?"

The better part of him wanted only to journey onward. The shadow from Ka'Inari's vision was elsewhere; the spirits of Moru'Alura'Tyat had known nothing of it, only repeated their insistence that the time of the Gods was coming, that the Goddess had need of her champions, that he must possess their gift, if he meant to fight at her side. But the corruption of his people had been delivered through the shamans of each tribe. If these people had a shaman speaking visions of his coming, he might find direction there, guidance toward the source of the madness that had driven him from his home.

"I am hunted," he said. "So long as you know there are men tracking me, who might threaten your village and your shaman for treating with me, then I will listen."

———

They left the darkest parts of the swamp behind, but traveled through long grasses and wetland pools as they angled around to the south. He'd been wrong as to the composition of their hunting party; three of the six were women, with clean-shaven heads and slim bodies caked with mud as though it were meant to be *echtaka* paint. They carried bows and short spears rather than muskets, with clothing that looked as though it had survived too many seasons without repair.

"Not far," the man said when he asked after the location of their village. "A half day's journey south and east, where the woodland meets the riverbank."

"He is Hanat'Etak," the woman said after, when he'd fallen in line. "I am Yinala. We are Lhakani."

"Lhakani," he said. "I've traveled south before, but never met a member of your tribe." The woman's manner seemed different, curious and eager where before she'd been full of disbelief. She paced alongside him while the others fanned out, two ahead and three behind, as though they were escorting a prisoner.

"We are hunters, by nature, not traders. Our neighbors know us well enough to respect our claims. The Sinari lands are far to the north, are they not? Why are you here?"

"As I said, I am hunted."

"You were driven to exile, for crimes?"

The audacity of the question struck him. "No," he said. "A neighboring tribe came for me, unrelenting. I left to spare my people a war."

"You were marked by the spirits."

"What does that mean?"

"Marked. Shamans granted visions of your passage, warriors promised power at your death, women threatened with loss and suffering, so long as you remain alive."

"What...? This is a thing not known to my people."

"Then the Sinari are fortunate," she said. "The Lhakani were given such a quarry in our shamans' visions, and the spirits have been terrible in their wrath, for our failures."

"This is a thing for the shaman to speak of, Yinala," Hanat'Etak said, having slowed enough to listen.

"He will learn of it soon enough," she said, but fell quiet as they walked.

"This is a thing born of the spirits' corruption?" he asked. "Their calls to war? Our shamans have heard these things." He refrained from speaking of their alliance; too early to predict how a strange people might react.

Yinala and Hanat'Etak shared a look. "Ka'Urun will speak of it," Hanat'Etak said. "We will reach him by the day's end."

The exchange weighed on him as they walked. A mark, or a quarry, given by way of the shamans' visions? In all his people's stories there was no mention of such a thing. Yet the Uktani had pursued him without pause, beyond the skill of any hunter to track without a shaman's guidance. The spirits' hand was in it, he'd been sure before the Lhakani woman's prompting. Now he was certain. But the shape of it would come from their shaman, whether or not they had recognized the split between the vile spirits and the pure.

The swamp thinned to a murky plain, dead trees replaced by live ones and then none at all, only light brush and long grass as they veered south and east. A sparse, thin land compared to the bounty of the northern forests, but it suited his mood, as did the relative quiet that passed between them as they traveled. A strange people, the Lhakani; he found himself wondering at what their village might look like, if the women shaved their heads to the scalp and carried bows and spears to mimic hunters. Yet soon they drew near a raging river, a soft roar in his ears through the whole of the approach, with no sign of tents or longhouses by the time they reached its banks.

"He's here," Hanat'Etak said. "Ka'Urun will receive you within."

Arak'Jur frowned, looking up and down the banks. Only grasses and rocky hills, and the slow rush of a river a hundred spans across.

"Where is your village? Your people?"

"We are all that remains of the Lhakani," Yinala said. "We six, and Ka'Urun."

Hanat'Etak pointed with his spear, toward a rocky overhang he'd missed in his search for sign of settlement or life. "The shaman hides here," Hanat'Etak said. "A cave, where he shelters from the wild." He unslung a pouch from across a shoulder, offering it up. "Take this to him, if you would. Water, and food. We don't enter unless summoned, and he doesn't leave. But he will want to speak with you."

Arak'Jur eyed the pouch, but made no move to take it. "You seek to trick me?" he asked. "Six of you remain, and your shaman, who will not leave a cave?"

"Not all of those marked by the spirits are so strong or brave as you, Arak'Jur," Yinala said.

Hanat'Etak held a hand to forestall her, and turned toward him. "Please, honored guardian. I swear by the memory of my people, no harm will come to you by any Lhakani hand."

An earnest look, and a deadness, hung behind the tradesman's eyes. He recognized that look; he'd seen it on Corenna's face, when she resolved to seek revenge for her people. He took the pouch, and turned toward the cave.

The river's roar muted to a dull echo as soon as he stepped within. He'd entered a hundred such caves in his travels, sheltering within them from rain or snow, but the air was thick here, dense enough he felt no need for more than shallow breaths. Moss grew on rocks slicked by dampness, and the way within was dark after twenty paces, though the downward-sloping ground suggested a path that fell below the river's waterline.

Yes, a voice seemed to whisper as he reached the edge of the shadows. *Come to us.*

Still he wavered on the edge. He'd expected a shaman, sheltering in the shallows of a hidden alcove. But this was more.

He took a step forward, and a light appeared in the distance. Fifty paces, straight and down along the slope the path had suggested before it disappeared.

Arak'Jur, the voice whispered. He took another step, slow and sure, using his hands to feel along the wetness of the rocks jutting up from the surface. *Chosen of the Sinari. Chosen of the Wild. You who would fight to become a champion. Come to us.*

A man's voice sliced through the haze of the spirits, and a silhouette appeared against the light.

"Who is it?" the man asked. "Is that you again, Yinala? I told you not to risk coming here."

"You are the Lhakani shaman?" he asked.

Laughter rang through the cave. "A stranger. Here I am, last seer of my tribe, living my days in the shadows of a wellspring of the vision spirits, and still I am surprised by your coming."

Arak'Jur stepped close enough to see the speaker, a man seated beneath a torch on the floor of the cave; but no, not seated. He was legless, shorn stumps where his upper thighs should have extended into legs. The man's left eye was a ruin of warped flesh, his torso pocked by bite or claw marks where he could see the skin beneath a wrap of albino furs.

"I am Arak'Jur, guardian of the Sinari. I met your people in the swamp. They guided me here."

The man laughed again, a bitter sound, old and cracked, though his skin had no wrinkles from age.

"I am Ka'Urun, and yes, I am the Lhakani shaman. You went to Moru'Alura'Tyat. I was right. You did it."

"You...? Did you not say you were surprised by my coming?"

"Bah, I didn't say I saw you in particular. I saw that *someone* would come, a man who could wield the woman's gift, or the reverse. And now you're here, and you can help me track her down."

He spared a glance at the shaman's missing legs, and once again the shaman replied as though he'd given voice to his doubts. "No, no, I don't mean to go with you ranging into the wild," Ka'Urun said. "Only that we can flush her out. She'll never expect another chosen when I show myself. But you'll have to strike quickly—she's as cunning as you'd expect."

"What are you speaking of?" he said finally.

The mother, the voices whispered in the air. *The false mother, who has whispered madness through our bonds.*

The shaman grinned into the torchlight. "You can hear them. They'll tell you. She's here. She's here in person, in the flesh."

"Who?" The shaman was half a madman, as far as he could see, but the spirits had echoed the truth of it, and he was sure this was their place, as sure as he had ever been at Ka'Ana'Tyat.

"Ad-Shi," the shaman said. "The False Goddess. She's come to the world to die, and you and I are the instruments that will kill her."

30

ERRIS

Overlooking the 17th Thellan Infantry Encampment
Northern Thellan Country

A sudden wave of heat struck her as *Need* slipped her senses into place. A moment before she'd been in her chambers at high command, far enough north for the occasional cool breeze through open windows, even in the dead of summer. Those comforts were replaced in an instant by humid, searing heat, the acrid sting of dust in her vessel's throat, and the smells of horses, sweat, and dung.

She wore yellow, a Thellan cavalry uniform, as did the soldiers at her side. A copse of trees surrounded them, thick birchwood atop a hillside overlooking a flat plain, where yellow flags hung limp in the absence of wind. Thellan flags. Enough by itself to raise suspicions—why had the Thellan mobilized an infantry brigade so close to the Gand border? But a pale shadow next to the answers she expected to find, as soon as her company braved the distance between their trees and the Thellan lines.

"Colonel," she said, and stirred the men and women around her.

"High Commander, sir," Brigade-Colonel de Montaigne said. She was dismounted with the rest of her soldiers—a handpicked unit from among the best of the 11th Light Cavalry. Most among them had spyglasses, either pressed to their eyes or lowered to acknowledge her arrival.

"Has there been any sign?" she asked.

"None, sir. No golden light that we've seen, but this brigade is small, scarcely a regiment and a half, and idle here along the border. It's possible the enemy wouldn't have needed to deliver them any orders since we arrived."

"How long have you observed them?"

"Four hours," de Montaigne said. "I sent two of my soldiers to approach their line with false reports and they've already returned. They're ripe for you to go, sir, if you're still inclined to do it."

She nodded, unlimbering a spyglass from her vessel's belt and edging forward to the tree line. The soldiers of the Thellan 17th were down there, milling about in a valley a good two leagues below de Montaigne's trees. The colonel had done a fine job picking a vantage point, as fine a job as the Thellan commander had failed to do in picking where to muster their brigade. With the spyglass to magnify her vision she saw the rope lines holding their tents in place, specks of campfires under clouds of black smoke, and the soldiers milling about in yellow coats that matched the ones de Montaigne had stolen for her soldiers. No sign of any alert in the Thellan camp, nor of any particular haste. If de Montaigne's 11th had been noted crossing the border, she suspected an active infantry brigade would have had a somewhat different demeanor. Always possible for it to be a trap. But for now, she was inclined to believe it was what it appeared to be.

"How soon can you be ready to ride, Colonel?" she asked.

"Now, sir. It's only the six of us. A small force, but enough for a convincing retinue. We even stole a proper flag."

She glanced to where de Montaigne was pointing, where two of her soldiers were already unfurling a battle standard. Yellow, with a red cross, seven stars, and the design of a lion rearing on its hind legs.

"You stole a general's flag?" she said.

De Montaigne grinned. "Yes, sir, and, if you'll permit me…" She gestured to Erris's vessel's collar, and only then did she notice the cut of her stolen coat. Three stars on the lapels. A Thellan major-general's uniform.

"We figured it best, sir," one of de Montaigne's sergeants said, "seeing as you and the colonel don't speak Thellan. It was Renauld's idea. He figured you wouldn't need to speak with the golden eyes, then Lieutenant Daréne could take up the deception playing the general's role, once you're finished. That's…ah….you, sir. Daréne speaks Thellan almost as well as Renauld."

"Fine thinking, then," she said, directing a nod toward the man the sergeant had called Renauld, then another toward Colonel de Montaigne. It was bloody mad, the whole exercise. Precisely the sort of thing she used to do with the 14th. And she needed mad brilliance here today.

"Twenty minutes, to make the camp?" she said.

"Better if we approach in some haste, I think," de Montaigne said. "Make it fifteen."

"Fifteen, then," Erris said. "I'll reestablish the *Need* bond then. And we'll see the proof of it, one way or another."

De Montaigne saluted along with the rest of her soldiers, and Erris let the *Need* binding go. It had been Brigade-Colonel de Montaigne's idea, to save days of scouting by approaching a Thellan camp directly. They might have spent a week watching for sign of the golden light behind an officer's eyes—or they could approach using one of Erris's vessels and see the Thellan officers' reactions firsthand. If they recognized *Need*, then Paendurion was in command, and Ilek'Hannat's vision was confirmed. If not…there was a reason she'd insisted de Montaigne's company be composed entirely of volunteers.

Fifteen minutes. She would have made the ride with them, but she had to conserve *Need*. It was stronger now, with the conquest of Gand, but it had never been infinite. She settled into the cushions of her desk chair, content for a moment alone, to wait.

————

"Lord Voren for you, sir," Essily said. "Arriving shortly—his people just sent word."

"He'll have to wait," she said, a sliver of guilt rising in her belly. Voren should have been among the first to know of her plans. Too much to do, not enough time for the doing. Only natural for some things to be missed, though she suspected Voren wouldn't see it that way. "Tell him a sensitive operation is under way. I'll see him in…two hours' time?"

She made the last a question; Essily knew her schedule better than any man or woman alive. "Very good, sir," Essily said. "Can I bring you a pot of tea in the meantime? Perhaps have the cooks send up a plate?"

No mention of the tray already sitting atop the side table near her chambers' entrance, long since gone cold.

"Thank you, Essily. A fresh pot of black, if you will."

"Sir," he said, bowing as he left the room.

She rifled through the papers and maps on her desk to pass the time. Another few minutes and she could resume the connection to de Montaigne and her company, and settle this with a certainty she already expected to find. De Montaigne's 11th had ridden ahead of the main body of the army, but the rest of de Tourvalle's 2nd Corps was already on the march, with Etaigne's 3rd and the Gand soldiers, under command of the freshly promoted General Wexly, trailing in a long line, all pointed toward the Thellan border. No need to commit them until she was sure, but she already had a plan. High Admiral Tuyard's ships would blockade the two largest port cities, and de Tourvalle would march for the third, while Etaigne and Wexly postured on the Thellan side of the border, seeking to draw Paendurion into the open and provide cover for de Tourvalle to strike. With their shipping cut off, Thellan's colonies would be unable to resupply, and be denied fresh levies from the island plantations to boot. A neat plan. Too obvious to work as stated, but open and flexible in the face of the enemy's response. All she needed was confirmation it would be Paendurion on the other side of the field.

Raised voices in the outer chamber were her only warning.

Lord Voren swept into the room with Essily trailing a pace behind, protesting as her old commander stormed to a place in front of her desk. Voren's old military uniform had been traded for an immaculately tailored coat and breeches in patterned green and gold, his spectacles tucked away as he brandished a rolled-up paper in his hand.

"What is the meaning of this, High Commander?" Voren snapped. He slapped his newspaper on her desk.

"Apologies, sir, I've told him you were—" Essily said.

"Let it be, Captain," she said. Voren's eyes smoldered with a heat she'd rarely seen, glowering over his newspaper as though it were a warrant for his—or her—arrest. "Give us the room."

"Sir," Essily said, backing away.

"Well, d'Arrent?" Voren said. "What do you expect me to make of this?"

"You'll have to excuse me, sir," she said as Essily retreated and closed the door, leaving her and Voren alone. "I haven't had time to read this week's papers."

"An invasion!" Voren said. "They're reporting you've given orders to the Second and Third Corps to march southward, with supply wagons already dispatched to follow down the trade roads. Either you mean to resecure the Gand holdings or you're aiming for Thellan, and there are equal measures of speculation on both sides in the presses."

She cursed. "Why should the enemy bother with scouts, when the papers will print our fucking movements for him?"

"It's true, then. *Koryu* burn it, you ordered this without consulting me? This is reckless and stupid, d'Arrent, even for you. Do you have any inkling of the state of the citizenry, with the bloody Great Barrier vanishing and you doing not nearly enough to convince them you take the issue as seriously as they do?"

"I've ordered Royens's corps to remain in the north, and the whole purpose of the tribal alliance was to leverage Ilek'Hannat's visions to—"

"The tribes. Yes, there's another thorn you've wedged in my foot. High Commander, do you understand that the people of this Republic are *terrified*, and your response is to broker a peace with the very people the barrier was meant to protect them against?"

She felt her own anger rising to match his. It was past time to make the connection to de Montaigne's aide. She didn't have time for this sort of second-guessing.

"The barrier was built to protect us from the beasts, not the tribes," she said. "The natives have power of their own, power we can leverage to keep us safe. I'll not discard a tool for the sake of fear and superstition, newspapermen be damned for their fearmongering."

A quiet fell between them. Her position relative to Voren had never been made explicit; he had been her mentor, and she his protégé, but command of the army was hers, for all his work in the political sphere.

"Now, sir," she continued. "I'm afraid I'll have to ask you to wait."

"What could be more important than this, d'Arrent?" Voren said. "This is the political future of our Republic. No less than your—and my—positions are at stake here."

"Confirming Ilek'Hannat's vision," she said. "A field operation in the south, to confirm Paendurion—the man behind the enemy's golden eyes—is in command of the Thellan armies in the New World."

Voren pulled back as though she'd struck him.

"Wait," he said after a moment. "Ilek'Hannat...the tribesfolk's leader?"

"Their shaman," she said. "He saw it, and I ordered the army to move. If the information is accurate, we have a chance to surprise Paendurion, to turn the campaign before it begins."

Voren sat on one of her cushioned chairs, the tension finally slipping from his shoulders.

"You'll have to excuse me, sir," she said. "It will take only a moment."

He nodded, and she closed her eyes, shifting her vision to the leylines.

Need shone like a beacon as soon as she did. A glowing light, far to the south. Hopefully no more than a sign she was late.

The tether snapped into place, and her senses shifted back into blazing heat.

"*Ah, aquí está él*," one of de Montaigne's soldiers said—Renauld, the one who spoke fluent Thellan.

The quiet of the trees had been replaced by the bustle of an infantry encampment, and this time she was mounted, along with the other five members of de Montaigne's company. The colonel herself was on the horse beside her, while Renauld had the lead, opposite four Thellan soldiers standing in front of a row of orderly white tents. Dozens of soldiers were in view behind them, and some few had begun to take notice of their exchange. The general's flag de Montaigne had procured flew over their rearward horse, though the Thellan soldiers seemed to be aloof, eyeing Renauld and the rest of them with suspicion—until they turned eyes to her at Renauld's direction.

"*Mis Dioses*," one of the Thellan soldiers said, making it halfway between a curse and a prayer.

The rest snapped to salute at once, all sign of sloth dispelled, and a ripple ran through the encampment, words passed in haste from one tent to the next.

"*Tenemos órdenes de su comandante*," Renauld said.

"*Sí*," the lead Thellan soldier said. "*Sí, por supuesto.*"

De Montaigne met her eyes with a knowing look as the Thellan soldiers rushed to admit them into the camp, any pretense of suspicion vanished as they were led into the sea of tents.

It was already enough. They recognized the golden light in her vessel's eyes. They thought she was Paendurion, which confirmed it. He was in command.

She gave de Montaigne a hard look in return. The next hours would decide whether the colonel and her soldiers survived the ruse, but that was down to their skill at playing their chosen roles. Better if her vessel took over from here.

She held *Need* another moment, long enough for a few more Thellan soldiers to see and confirm her suspicions. Then she released it, and returned to her desk.

Voren had calmed, but stared at her as intently as he had when raging over his unfurled newspaper.

"They recognized the golden light," she said. "Paendurion has the command."

"Gods save us all," Voren said.

"Just as well I ordered the bulk of the army southward."

Voren gave a bitter laugh. "You don't make this easy, d'Arrent."

"Sir, I've done what I've known to be right."

"Best pray the press doesn't make the connection between your visit to the tribes and the order to start another war. Fuel to an already burning fire, if they do."

"Damn them all, sir. I have no interest in the bleating of a council full of fools. I'm taking action to keep us safe, and if you'll pardon me, sir, I've been proved right today. I won't shy away from my duty for the sake of popularity, or favorable pamphlets among tradesmen too frightened to pick up a musket."

"All right," Voren said. "All right. Damn it, but we can see this through. The enemy—Paendurion—won't be content with a few islands and marshlands in the south; he'll be marshalling his power in the Old World, like as not aiming to pin you here. But there is time, if only just. I'll leave the military campaign in your hands, of course, but we must begin laying plans to consolidate a Thellan conquest into the new Gand holdings, if we're to establish and maintain control."

"Sir?" Strange to hear him reverse his anger so quickly, though she could never fault her old commander for being slow to accept the new realities of a battlefield.

"Proceed with your attack, High Commander. I will sell this to the Assembly. But you mustn't leave me out again. The next months are as crucial to your place as any waters we have navigated so far."

"We have a chance, here, sir. He won't be expecting so much of our strength in the south. We can win, and unite all the colonies, if we do."

"Politics for another day, High Commander," Voren said. "Just see to the victory, and leave the diplomacy to me."

"Yes, sir."

He rose, and they exchanged a salute. Odd, to see him do it in civilian clothes, but a small relief to see him leave the room, though he'd left his unfurled newspaper behind on her table. A reminder that the political sphere was always there, looming over her affairs. But for now, the way was clear for her to proceed.

She returned to her desk, leaving the newspapers there as a reminder of Voren's work. Maps, ledgers, logistics, dispositions, and *Need*: The rest fell to her.

31

SARINE

Wilderness
Erhapi Land

Anati crawled forward on the branch, shaking loose leaves as she made way toward a ripe, purple fruit.

"I don't know," she said. "I never saw Zi eat. I assumed he couldn't."

Her *kaas* reached the prize, and darted another look toward her, full of curiosity.

It looks right, Anati thought to her. *Will it hurt me?*

"It's a plum. I can't imagine it will poison you, but then, I don't know what your kind will find edible."

Anati clamped her tiny jaws into the plum, rending a gash through the skin, and immediately spat it out, raining pieces of fruit from the tree into the undergrowth.

It is foul!

Sarine laughed and plucked a low-hanging plum for herself, taking a bite and relishing the juices as they ran sweet on her tongue. "We can sample all manner of fruits when we get back to the city. But if you're anything like Zi, I expect you'll prefer bar fights and public tribunals to anything that grows on a tree."

A bar fight. Is that . . . red?

Again she smiled. Anati seemed to know nothing of the world, whereas Zi had come to her fully formed. Maybe a bar fight *was* red—or somehow tied to *Red*, as Zi had understood it. Dust-ups and fisticuffs certainly seemed to produce *Body* on the leylines, and those were red motes; it stood to reason the *kaas* might see things in a similar vein.

Thinking of Zi still hurt, though the pain had dulled, since the springs. She wouldn't think of him as having died; she'd spoken to him, seen him move, watched the rest of the *kaas* give way for him as though he were a conquering hero come home. But now he was beyond her reach. Whatever the strange consciousness that had taken hold of her had done to shift their senses to the *kaas'* world, she couldn't find a way to replicate it. And teaching Anati had been a joy unto itself.

A knot of anger rose in her stomach, and an image passed through her thoughts: Axerian's face. The anger wanted to direct itself toward him, paired with frustration and need. The emotions were strong, but not hers. She felt them through pinpricks on her skin, the same as she might feel an arm after lying on it too long.

Anati draped herself from the branch overhead, coiling her tail tight enough to hang her body in the air. Strange; she'd never seen Zi do that.

She's pushing again, Anati thought.

Sarine nodded. The anger rose harder, a storm of needles, but she fought it down. She wasn't angry. She was content. Acherre's mission had been to prevent assassinations in New Sarresant, and Ka'Inari had sworn only to go with her. Now, without Zi's sickness driving her, there was no need to keep pursuing Axerian halfway across the continent. Better for them all to turn back, and go home. She focused on that, to quell her emotions. Her uncle would be overjoyed to see her. They would embrace and he would lecture her on the virtue of love: third virtue of the Veil, second parable, "*duty to family is born of the deepest bond, higher than blood or honor.*"

The rage subsided. Calm returned. Breath came hard, as though she'd been running through the trees, but it was hers, slow and steady.

She keeps doing that, Anati thought. *I wish she would stop.*

"Who is she?" Sarine asked. "I still don't understand any of this."

Anati let go with her tail, dropping to the ground with a rustle of dry leaves. She skittered toward Sarine's foot and climbed it, coming to perch on her shoulder as quickly as Zi might have vanished and rematerialized there. It startled her, but the *kaas* affected not to notice, keeping her hind legs steady on her shoulder while the rest of her loomed into Sarine's view, hovering mere inches in front of her face.

She is you, Anati thought to her. Her eyes were amethysts, the color of the plums, and her *kaas* seemed taken with a deadly seriousness, planting her two forelegs on the sides of Sarine's face.

"Anati, what are you doing?"

You must know this. She is you.

She fought the urge to pull away. Instead she took another calming breath—no easy feat, with a *kaas* perched to loom across her face—and moved to sit cross-legged on the leaves.

"Can I have you rest on my arm? It isn't comfortable to speak with you when you're so close."

Oh. All right. Sorry.

As quickly as she'd darted up Sarine's side, Anati retracted herself, skittering down to take a place in her lap, coiled in a tight loop but still with her head raised, intent as she had been before.

"Now what did you mean, 'she is me'? These surges of emotion, these memories, they aren't mine. I remember, after Zi…" She swallowed. "…I remember someone else taking control of me. The emotions are hers, right?"

No. You're her. Like the Soul of the World, split in two halves between light and shadow, she used a trick to keep your souls apart, but now you're back together. She's stronger, but I like you. My father liked you. You'll do better than she did.

"Sarine!" Acherre's voice rang through the trees.

"Here," she called back, then rose, brushing dust and leaves with one hand while she cradled Anati in the other. "We need to speak more on this," she said to Anati. "Who is she? She called herself the Veil, just before you quieted her. She can't mean—?"

Yes. The Veil. The Goddess. You are her.

Anati said it as though it were the plainest fact, like stating the tree's bark was brown, its leaves green. Her *kaas* seemed content to coil around her forearm, just as Zi had done, lowering her head to rest against her skin. Numbness washed through her. She wanted more, and wanted none of it at the same time. What was she supposed to think, a *kaas* telling her she was something other than the girl who had grown up on the streets of the Maw, who learned to sketch by stealing charcoals and paper until she realized the shopkeep knew she was doing it and was letting her get away with her thieving? She was Sarine, not anything or anyone else.

Acherre led her horse through the brush, dry leaves cracking under its hooves. "Where is the shaman? We've got riders coming from the west, straight on to our position."

"He's nearby; the smoke, the fire. He went to commune with his spirits."

"Good." Acherre paused, looking at her again. "Are you all right?"

"Yes. I'm…I'm fine." She heard the numbness in her own voice, but Acherre seemed to be content to let it pass.

"Lead on, then. Those are tribesmen coming our way. They know we're here, and if they're half as prickly as the eastern tribes they'll be none too pleased to see us."

A chant hummed through the trees as they drew near; two voices at least, a low harmony and a haunting echo above it.

"Ka'Inari," she called ahead. It felt as though she were walking in on him bathing, or attending to other personal needs. "Apologies, but Acherre has sighted riders. We need to move."

"To move, or at least to be ready for it," Acherre added, though she still hadn't managed to learn enough of the Sinari tongue to speak it to Ka'Inari directly. A consequence of her being ready to translate whatever was said, and a blessing from the Gods that whatever else Anati needed to be shown, she still seemed to possess Zi's gift for language.

The chanting ceased, but in a slow fade that seemed to linger in her ears. She came to a place where the brush grew thick enough to block her vision, and tingles on her skin sufficed as barrier to any impulse to push through. It was wrong to go farther; the surety of it hung in the air. Even Acherre seemed suddenly content to halt, and the horses lingered behind, skittish as they approached the brush.

"Ka'Inari," she called again. "I'm sorry, but we have to go."

"The Erhapi," Ka'Inari finally replied. "Those are the riders you saw." He emerged from the brush a moment later, a pack slung over his shoulder, but with red rings around his eyes and white paint on his face.

She looked down. It was wrong for her to see him like this; he hadn't said anything to bar her following, only picked up his materials and distanced himself from the camp. He'd done it a handful of times, though it had never been needful to intrude prior to his being finished, before.

Did the vision spirits see where Axerian went?

Anati had made herself heard by all three, somehow Sarine knew it, though she couldn't have said how she knew. Her *kaas* hadn't vanished either, though Anati was certainly capable of it, and instead chose to be visible to them all, her head perked with interest as Ka'Inari appeared.

The shaman gave her and Anati a rueful look. "Such things are sacred."

No, they aren't. The vision spirits will tell you if you ask.

Color rose in her cheeks. "Anati!" she whispered. At the same moment another well of anger surged through her, accompanied by a sense of agreement, and an image of Axerian's face.

"Time to speak later of the spirits' sendings," Ka'Inari said. "For now the Erhapi have been alerted to our presence on their land. A great ill has befallen their tribe. I can't say whether they will be enemies; we must decide whether to hear them out."

He seemed to be looking to her for guidance, but the sensation of rage was still flooding through her veins. Terror accompanied it, blending two more images: one of her going home, meeting her uncle on the steps of the Sacre-Lin, with another of a black sky and a great army, a host of men in strange armor beneath red banners marching toward a city's gates.

She almost fell, staggering forward as the images raced through her mind.

"Sarine?" Ka'Inari caught her.

"Are you all right?" Acherre asked. "The riders will be here any moment, at the pace I saw. If we're going to try to run, we need to mount up and ride now."

"I...I'm..." she said. "I don't know. I can't..."

She wants you to listen to her.

"Something is wrong. Sarine isn't fit to try to outrace mounted hunters," Ka'Inari said, accompanying it with gestures for Acherre's sake. "We stay, and meet them here."

Blood pounded in her chest. The sun vanished in her vision, a red disc that soured to purple before it went black. Three figures stood at the head of the horde of strange-armored soldiers. One wearing a mask of flesh; one whose hand was withered, covered in a purple aura; and one whose form blurred, seeming to occupy a dozen places at once.

"Sarine." Ka'Inari dropped his pack, moving to grip her by the shoulders. "Look at me."

She did, feeling herself exist in two places at once. Her body stood next to a tangled wall of brush, but the rest of her felt the terror of watching the three figures marching toward her, and suddenly where there had been three, there were nine. A man who could cloak himself in glass; another who could dance on water with a sword in his hand; another with skin of iron and great claws for hands. More.

"This is a vision," the shaman said. "You are receiving a sending from the spirits of things-to-come. How can this be?"

Not the vision spirits, Anati thought to them both. *They won't talk to her. It's just the Goddess's memories. Should I make her stop?*

"Yes," Sarine said, hissing it through clenched teeth.

"They're almost on us," Acherre called out. "Three coming straight on; more, sweeping around to flank."

Sorry, Anati thought. *You are bonded to her. Sometimes, she will want to speak.*

"I want nothing to do with her," she said. "Keep her quiet, as much as you can."

Cracking brush and pounding hooves drew her attention back toward the way they'd come, and three riders appeared. Each man's head was shaved save for thin strips of hair running down the center; two strips for the riders to the left and right, and four for the one at their head. They were bronze-skinned, dressed in cured hides sewn into tunics and breeches, and they carried carbines of the sort the cavalry used, half muskets leveled toward where she, Acherre, and Ka'Inari stood together with their horses.

"What passes here?" The lead rider looked as though he'd changed his mind as to his planned greeting, looking back and forth between Ka'Inari in his shaman's regalia and Sarine.

"Honored warriors," Ka'Inari said—though to her ears, before Anati translated, it was plain Ka'Inari spoke a different tongue than the riders. "We come to your lands under the guidance of the visions of things-to-come."

The lead rider gave him an empty look, keeping his weapon leveled toward them.

"We came chasing after an evil man," Sarine said. "Now we're returning home."

The rider lowered his gun a fraction. "How is it a white-skinned demon speaks our tongue better than one who pretends to the garb of the spirits?"

"He is a shaman," she said. "Ka'Inari, from the Sinari tribe. My name is Sarine, and this is Gendarme-Captain Acherre; we're from New Sarresant, far to the east."

The riders conferred, speaking in low tones to each other. At the edge of her vision she saw another pair of mounted warriors converging from the north, keeping their distance but still close enough to fire their weapons, if it came to it.

"Their shaman has been slain," Ka'Inari said to her. "The spirits showed me great suffering among these Erhapi. If they believe we are connected to the cause, they will not hesitate to—"

"You seek evil," the lead rider said abruptly. "A man, you said. Speak of him."

She glanced toward Ka'Inari. If he'd had a vision portending danger for them, she'd as soon know what it was before she spoke. Yet it seemed the riders wouldn't afford them the opportunity to confer.

"A man in black," she said. "A man who carries two swords, and has a companion, of the same sort..." She trailed off, realizing Anati had vanished from around her forearm. "...a serpent companion, with great power, though it is not a thing of your spirits."

"You spoke of pursuing this man, and yet now you mean to return home?" the Erhapi tribesman said. "What sort of evil did he commit, that you are so content to give up your pursuit?"

"He was—" A rush of foreign anger flooded through her again, and she fought it down. "One of our companions...fell, to a sickness. We'd sought the man in black as much for his knowledge of a cure as a desire to be sure he was far away from our peoples. And his evils are many. Too many to list."

The riders conferred again, but snapped attention back to her before she could turn to Ka'Inari for more insight.

"You will come with us, Sarine of the New Sarresant. If this man is as vile as you say, you will have the chance to speak of it before the Erhapi elders. Convince us, and we will be in your debt."

Another surge of emotion welled in her chest; this time she wasn't certain whether it was hers. "You've seen him? He's passed through your lands?"

"We have. He has laid a heavy burden on us, in a time of loss. But if there are reasons not to trust his words, our elders would know it, before he guides us to war."

"Guides you to war? You mean he's still here?"

"Yes. Your quarry is among the Erhapi. Come with us, and you may confront him for all to see."

32

TIGAI

Numbness settled in behind his eyes. He'd seen Mei's face behind the first score of men he'd killed. She would have understood. Dao was the one who would judge him, aghast at the violations of propriety in his use of magic, to say nothing of the shock of outright murder. Mei was harder, for all her softness.

"What manner of devil spawn are you?"

The captain's bodyguards stood a few paces apart, each square in their stance, spears leveled in a grip at their midsections. Both stared at him with horror in their eyes, as though they'd drained feeling from him and stolen it for themselves.

He attacked wildly, rushing forward with his knife extended, and took one of their spears in the gut. The impact wrenched him backward, but not before he opened a gash on the leftmost guard's lower torso. A kidney strike; death, without a surgeon's intervention.

He snapped back to his anchor, standing in the doorway, where he had entered the chamber moments before.

The man he'd wounded dropped his spear, clutching at his belly as though he could repair the damage and keep his innards in. The rightmost guard stepped back, muttering something to the wind spirits and eyeing his partner without looking away from Tigai.

"Run," Tigai said. "Run, and I won't kill you."

The guardsman held his ground for a heartbeat, then turned and fled for the doors. The Daisheng Bank had six: double archways, propped open by dead men struck down by Tigai's knife.

Tigai let him go, entering the room at a slow walk.

"Your master," he said to the leftmost guardsman, the one still clutching his belly. "First-Captain Grazh. Where is he?"

The guardsman's face twisted with a mix of shock, pain, anger, and defiance.

Tigai sighed. "Just tell me which chamber he's hiding in. He's not paying you enough to die, and die you will if you don't have that cut looked at."

"Go back to hell, you *magi* son of a dog."

"My father *was* a bit doggish, now you mention it. I'll give you one more chance. Directions to where the captain is hiding, and you can walk out that door. I don't even care if you lie. Just tell me something to keep me from having to kill you."

The guardsman spat.

Tigai slashed him across the eyes, spraying blood across the chamber as the guardsman howled and crumpled to his knees.

Outside the banking house the city had long since erupted into chaos. Boots pounded in the streets, more disorganized clatter than the lockstep marching of the Imperial police. Women and men screamed, no few of them wounded by his blade. If there was a secret exit from the banking house—and surely there was—he had to hope the bankers had used it prior to First-Captain Grazh converting the building into a makeshift fortress. With luck he'd frighten the mercenary lord into making a dash for the main exit before Grazh chanced on any secret passages.

He shoved a lamp through a paper screen in a crash, and picked a hall at random to race down, kicking doors and thumping against the walls. Jade and porcelain vases shattered as he kicked their plinths, scattering shards across hand-woven Hagali carpets, and he raced past doors that opened to reveal gilded armoires, cabinets, scroll racks, and tables. First-Captain Grazh might have chosen any of them to hide in, and he didn't have hours to properly comb through its rooms.

"Show yourself, coward!" he shouted into the halls. "Death comes for you."

With that he threw a wood bust down a stairwell at the end of a hallway, and kicked in the plinth for good measure. Then he closed his eyes, hooked himself to the starfield, and found the same anchor he'd used a moment before, leaving him standing in the doorway of the banking house lobby.

Breath came hard as he waited. He fought to keep quiet, preserving the impression that the main floor had been sacked and left behind in his rage. Another minute, perhaps. He waited, unmoving, watching the halls.

Footsteps sounded quietly, and First-Captain Grazh emerged, creeping into view from the farthest passage, aiming to make his escape while Tigai's attentions were elsewhere. Tigai had never seen the mercenary captain before, but it was simple enough to place him, judging from the gold-silk shirt, the gold earrings, and the gold-hilted tulwar blade sheathed through his gold-studded belt.

Grazh met his eyes for a moment before panic dawned.

"I can pay you," the captain said. "Please."

Tigai charged.

The mercenary spun, but Tigai was faster, racing across the lobby before Grazh could make ten paces down the hall. He threw the knife and missed, whipping it past the mercenary's ear and sending him crashing off-balance into the side wall. Tigai drew his pistol and fired before Grazh could find his footing, and this time he struck true, pitching the man forward through a haze of smoke.

He couldn't hear the sound of the last captain's body smacking into the floor through the ringing whine left behind by the pistol, but emotion flooded through him at the sight, bathing over his numbness with relief.

––––––––––

"That's it," he said, and reached into his blood-soiled coat pocket for his prizes. Four ears dropped to the center of the teahouse table. "I only thought to take a token after the first two were done, but I swear to you on my brother's name, they're all dead."

Lin Qishan picked up one of the ears, handling it as though it were a gold coin before depositing it back among its fellows.

"Fine work, lordling. I believe you, though you'd best hope Master Indra does the same."

"He's here, then?"

"He's on his way."

A serving man brought their tray before Tigai could say anything more, a steaming kettle with rice cakes dabbed with sugar ringing the base. If the man thought it odd to see four bloody ears decorating the center of his table he showed nothing on his face, and said less, only laid the tray down and poured their first cups, offering crisp bows to each of them in turn.

Lin Qishan seemed content to drink and eat in silence, and he obliged her. The shock of the night's events had put gauze through his senses. He'd lost count of the men he'd killed long before tonight, but it was still a horror to do so many at once. All his upbringing had taught him *magi* didn't move in the open. They existed, of course—he was one of them, in a manner of speaking—but the founding of the Empire had exiled them to their monasteries, and to his knowledge the only violence done by magic was done by house retainers, and even they had the shame to do it in private and cover up its consequences. His pirating was among the more egregious violations of that taboo so far as he knew, though he'd always been careful enough not to draw the attention of any Great and Noble Houses. Until tonight.

"They're coming, you know," he said abruptly. "The *magi*."

She smiled behind her teacup, taking a short sip before lowering it again. "Yes, I expect they are."

"You must have been House-trained, no? Do their taboos mean nothing to you?"

"I could ask you the same, Lord Tigai."

"So you mean to start another war?"

She shrugged. "I mean to do whatever Master Indra's coin pays for."

"You're a mercenary. No better than the fat fools I killed tonight."

"You're a pirate. A touch worse, by most people's reckoning."

He glowered at her; she returned to her tea.

The innards of the teahouse seemed immune to the alarms and shouts that reigned elsewhere in the city. He'd set an anchor here, and returned as soon as the last of his marks was dead; the building had already been emptied, save for Lin Qishan and the service staff.

He tried to think of another means of challenging her and came up with nothing. Whatever the shape of their plan, it would end with thousands dead, if the city-lords took it on themselves to take revenge on the *magi* and storm the local monasteries. No telling what sort of magic would be practiced therein; perhaps nothing more deadly than his old tutor's potato farming. Then again, they could be skilled with iron, silver, steel, or glass, and stories spoke of methods far more frightening and dangerous. The Empire had been founded on the promise of the *magi* to govern themselves, to withdraw the gift of magic from public life as an answer to centuries of strife and war. There were always going to be exceptions, but not so the public killing of every mercenary captain hired to defend one of the six greatest cities in the Empire. He'd done a terrible thing. Even Remarin would chastise him for it. But it would be worth having done it, to hear Remarin tell him he was a bloody fool again.

"Is it done?"

Master Indra's voice sent a jolt through him, a mix of hate and surprise. He turned to see Indra and his apprentice standing behind the table.

"Not yet," Lin Qishan said.

His hate flared to rage. "Not yet?" he said. "I bloody killed them all, just as you said. I swear it, if you've harmed her again, I will murder the lot of you if it takes following you to the world's end."

"Calm yourself, Lord Tigai," Lin Qishan said. She hadn't stirred from behind the table, though he'd risen from his seat to face Indra and Jyeong without realizing he'd done it.

"Our lordling has kicked the hornet's nest," she said. "It remains to be seen whether the hornets will respond."

"It was supposed to be done already, *before* I came to the city. You promised it would be done."

"I can only make promises for myself. If you give me inferior tools, I get the results you allow me to deliver."

"Am I the *inferior tool* in this situation?" Tigai said. "I don't even know what you're doing here. How am I supposed to accomplish anything, without knowing what I'm doing?"

Master Indra showed him a cruel smile. "You'll know soon enough." He turned back to Lin Qishan. "You're absolutely sure the rebel *magi* are in the city?"

"I'd hardly have summoned you if I wasn't."

"Rebels?" Tigai said. "What did you have me do? Is this some ploy to seize power? Is that why you abducted me? Am I to take you all to the Emperor's vaults, now that you've lopped the head off the armies here in Ghingwai?"

Lin Qishan looked annoyed, Jyeong looked smug, and Master Indra looked him over coolly. None of them spoke.

"You can't mean to do this," Tigai continued. "For two centuries we've had peace in the Empire, precisely because the *magi* accepted their place in exile. If you unseat the Emperor, the noble families will resist. Can you say how many *magi* lurk among their retainers? You're dooming half the Empire to die for your hubris."

"The assassin has a conscience," Jyeong said, but Master Indra raised a hand to cut him short.

"Put your fears to rest, Yanjin Tigai," Master Indra said. "You know nothing of events unfolding here, but I assure you, we do not stand in opposition to the Emperor. Quite the contrary."

A thundering boom sounded from outside the teahouse, loud enough to shake the building frame. The teapot went so far as to rattle off its serving dish, spilling hot liquid on the floor.

"You see," Lin Qishan said when the boom died down. "They're here."

———

Lin led the way toward the boom, with Jyeong taking up the rear. The streets of Ghingwai were as clear as Tigai had ever seen them, and he'd done his share of carousing there in the small hours before dawn.

"This will be your final task, Lord Tigai," Master Indra said as Lin gestured for them to cross the street ahead. "Do this, and you will be released from my service."

"Do *what*?" he asked. Another boom rumbled through the buildings on both sides of the street, louder than it had been at the teahouse.

Lin held up a fist to halt them at the mouth of an alley. "Here," she said.

Tigai recognized the place; the market square with General An's statue, where he'd come to kill the first of the six mercenary captains.

Master Indra laid a hand on Tigai's shoulder, squeezing in an approximation of a gesture of familiarity, the sort of things fathers did to their sons, though Tigai's own father had rarely displayed such affection.

"There will be a man in white, in the square ahead," Master Indra said. "You are to hook him to the strands. Bring him to the Temple of the Dragon."

Another boom sounded, this time close enough to be mere paces away. Gravel and dirt sprayed into the alley in a cloud of dust, and voices cut through the silence of its aftermath.

"Show yourselves, dogs," a voice shouted from the square. "You strike from the shadows—now strike in the open, if you dare."

Jyeong stood by the mouth of the alley, wearing a hard expression. Lin and Master Indra had stepped back, both looking to him.

"That's it?" Tigai said. "Reach a man in white and bring him to your temple?"

"That's it," Master Indra said. "Do it, and you're free. Fail, and your family will not wake tomorrow."

"Cowards," the voice in the square shouted. "Assassins."

"What are you not telling me?" Tigai said. "That man is a *magi*, is he not? Why is he raving in the middle of a market? And how is he making those—"

Another boom sounded, swallowing Tigai's words, a violent tremor shifting the ground enough to set them all off-balance, forcing them to lean against the building to steady themselves.

"You know all you need to know," Master Indra said. "Go, perform your task, and earn your freedom."

Tigai hesitated, tasting the dust scattered by whatever the *magi* was doing in the square. Was the man's talent to convert blood to earthquakes? He tried to make sense of what had happened in Ghingwai, and came up short. Remarin would have chided him for his lack of vision. *Always see the shape of the battle*, Remarin would have said. *Know what your enemy wants; find a way to give it to him that still results in victory.* Fine advice for facing a sparring partner in a practice ring. Less practical here.

He stepped forward to the mouth of the alley, keeping his body pressed flat against one of the buildings. Jyeong stood beside him, evidently intent on coming along, while Master Indra and Lin Qishan stayed behind.

The square was strewn with dead bodies, no few of which he'd put there with his knife, an hour before. General An's statue still stood, a bronze and cast-iron horse-and-rider seeming to point the way forward to the heart of the city. The rest of the market stalls had been collapsed and scattered, with figs and nuts and slaver's chains sent rolling in the dirt. Three figures stood at the center. A man in white, surely the man Indra had marked for him to abduct, wearing a strange tight-fitting garment that covered him from head to toe, even wrapping his face so only his eyes were visible. Another man stood beside him, a swordsman from the look of him, with lamellar plate armor and a long curved two-handed blade strapped to his back. And the third was Mei.

He stared, to be sure. But it was her. She wore a blue silk dress, cut loose to let her move freely, with her hair pinned back and the same defiant look he'd come to know through all the years of watching her be married to Dao. She surveyed the square as though she were thinking of buying it, and she had both her hands, each one ungloved, showing naked, unbroken skin.

"Go, you coward," Jyeong said behind him. "And know if you don't reach him, I will. It will be sweet to watch you suffer for your failure, after I succeed."

Mei's face flashed in his memory, and he compared it to the woman in front of him, across the square. It was her. But if she was here, it had to be as a captive, or a pawn. She'd never have chosen to aid or ally herself with *magi* willingly.

He ran forward.

The buildings and dirt around him blurred together as he covered the ground. He had the sense of Jyeong following behind, running the other way but both converging on the center of the square.

The man in white raised a hand, his forearm suddenly enveloped in a purple glow, and Tigai felt his lungs constrict.

It was as though someone had shoved a branch of stinging nettle down his throat and torn it out. His chest burned, a searing pain burning in his neck and mouth.

He snapped back to an anchor and ran forward again. Jyeong was coughing, hunched over on all fours. Tigai set two more anchors as he crossed the square, running zigzagged toward the center. The man in lamellar armor drew his blade, hefting it over his shoulder and lowering into a guard alongside his waist. Mei had gone wide-eyed, staring at him as though she couldn't believe what she saw. And the man in white pivoted, his hand once more enveloped by a soft purple glow.

This time the ground exploded, and pain lanced through him as his feet were ripped apart.

He blinked to an anchor and ran forward.

Wordless shouts came from the center. A flash of light illuminated the square, and a sucking wind, and he snapped to another anchor before the rush of fire could consume him. Instead he saw the fireball from the other side of the square, sailing past to detonate against one of the market buildings and send torrents of sparks and ash into the air.

The swordsman reached him, slicing a broad arc with his blade. It cut him, and he blinked a few steps to the side. Mei screamed, calling out in words he couldn't discern.

Fear touched the eyes of the man in white, and he was close enough to see that the man's hand was no hand at all: It was blackened, rotten pink and blue and green. Purple surrounded it, and Tigai blinked again.

He reached Mei.

She was still shouting as he hooked her to the strands, carrying her as far as he could take them, the chaos of the square replaced by cold wind through long grass.

33

SARINE

The City of Hokhan
Erhapi Land

The path around the hillside ended abruptly, and it was all she could do not to stare. She'd expected tents, perhaps, or houses cut from logs and stone, as the tribes living close to New Sarresant used. Instead a score of buildings had been chiseled into the cliffside, as though a sculptor had cut away the mud and rocks to reveal a city waiting underneath. And it was a city in truth; hundreds of men, women, children, and animals wandered its streets, with tamed dogs pulling sleds, goats and sheep, terraced plots filled with corn stalks, beans, and tomato plants decorating the side of every building, as far up and down the canyon walls as she could see.

"You have not been to an Erhapi city before, have you, Sarine of New Sarresant?"

Her guide, who had been the lead rider from the party that accosted them, had given his name as Kurinchanakaya—a name she'd never have remembered, had Anati not translated it in her mind as *Leaping Wolf.* It took her aback almost as much as the city itself; neither Zi nor Anati had ever translated a Sinari name. But she tested it, opting to call their guide Leaping Wolf instead of the Erhapi name, and so far it hadn't given offense.

"No," she said, attempting to guide her horse out of Leaping Wolf's way. The Erhapi warrior grinned at her, wedging his horse between hers and Ka'Inari's. The shaman seemed as ill-at-ease in the saddle as she was, while the Erhapi riders sat atop their mounts with an easy grace. "I've never traveled so far from home."

"You have more than one city such as this?" Ka'Inari asked. He seemed full of disbelief.

Leaping Wolf laughed. "We have many. We are a great and numerous people." He gestured to the carbine slung from his mount's saddle. "And we are fearsome warriors."

"But how do you survive, when great beasts come?" Ka'Inari asked.

Leaping Wolf shrugged. "They rarely trouble us; an advantage of a city cut into a cliffside. And if needs be, we flee. The city is waiting when we come back."

The cityfolk noted their arrival by clearing a path for them through the swarm, packs of horses and dogs being herded away as Leaping Wolf called out their intent. They climbed a steep path switchbacking up through the city, and she found a dozen questions coming to mind, though Ka'Inari voiced them first.

"How would you build this," Ka'Inari asked, "with the threat of beasts? It must have taken generations."

"We did not build it, Ka'Inari of the Sinari Tribe," Leaping Wolf said. "As I said, we are fearsome warriors."

Odd.

It took a moment to register that the thought had come from Anati. Leaping Wolf had taken to bellowing for a dozen horses to make way, exchanging what seemed to be good-natured words with the women who were tending to them, while she, Ka'Inari, and Acherre waited for them to pass.

"What's odd?" she whispered quickly.

Color. Green. It's here, among their buildings.

"You mean you can feel *Green* being used?"

Hmm. Yes. It would be the same, if I did that. Green.

Her heart raced faster than it had before.

"Is it Axerian's *kaas*? Can you tell how he's influencing these people?"

He's making them content, happy about something he did. Something bad. That's wrong. They shouldn't be feeling that way.

"Wait, Anati, where is he? Can you find him here in the city?"

A yellow haze flared at the edge of her vision, and suddenly the buzz of the cityfolk quieted in a wave of silence rolling between the streets.

Yes. There.

The horses trotted out of their path, and Axerian emerged from a stone building fifty paces ahead.

No mistaking his black garb, the curved swords at his side, or the bemused expression he wore, scanning through the crowd. He settled on her almost at once, and the mirth on his face died.

No. Not now. He mouthed it; she couldn't tell if he'd spoken it aloud. He ran.

She tried to kick her horse forward, but the beast shied back, and she cursed, pulling the reins. The horse reared up, and Leaping Wolf was there, making calming sounds as he reached for her mount's bridle. Acherre raced past them both, horse and rider seeming to blend together as they wove through the press, streaking toward where Axerian had vanished down the opposite path.

"Easy," Leaping Wolf was saying, as the silence from before melted into curiosity, the Erhapi cityfolk turning their heads to question what was going on. Sarine cursed and lifted a leg across her horse's saddle, trying to free herself, and only succeeded in tangling her feet, falling sideways to the ground in a thud.

He's using Red, Anati thought to her. *The same way he did Green, but different. It's wonderful. I could—*

"Not now!" she snapped. "Give me *Red*, too."

Her heart beat double as soon as she asked for it, and she blinked to find motes of *Body* beneath the buildings, tethering strength into her limbs as she pushed up to find her footing. Leaping Wolf was still eyeing where she'd fallen, and Ka'Inari as well, but she sprinted forward at a run, twisting to avoid the animals and people in her way.

Within a hundred paces they'd left the city behind, following a path down the cliffside that mirrored the one they'd taken to climb into the city from the opposite side of the plateau. Acherre streaked toward Axerian, thundering downhill on horseback where Axerian was on foot.

Acherre had almost caught up to him when a flare of pale energy appeared in front of her mount. *White*, came the thought from Anati, and Acherre turned her horse's head to the side at the last moment to blunt the force of the impact. A sickening crunch sounded as the horse ran shoulder-first into Axerian's shield, throwing Acherre from the saddle. Acherre's body recoiled from the collision, sending her sailing backward as fast as she'd been riding, then skidding through the dirt before she ground to a halt.

Smoke rose from the dirt where Acherre landed, and Sarine raced toward her. A tranche thirty paces long had been cut through the earth, terminating with Acherre's body jutting up at angles it wasn't supposed to make. A broken leg, for sure, and maybe an arm.

She slid to kneel beside Acherre, whipping *Life* connections into place. Frustration and rage rose, strong enough to almost overpower her work with the tethers. Yes, Acherre's leg was broken in two places. The *Life* lattice revealed a fracture in her thigh and a much more serious break below her knee, though the knee itself was—

"NO."

Acherre snapped the word through clenched teeth. Sarine ignored her, continuing her work with *Life* and *Body*. She bound a small tether of the latter, using it to strengthen the tissues as she poured healing energy over the rest.

"No," Acherre said again. Her face was caked with dirt and already red and swelling where bruises would be formed, later. "Sarine, don't you dare. Don't stop for me."

The frustration in her belly seemed to flare along with Acherre's words, adding a sentiment of agreement.

"I can't leave you here like this," Sarine said.

"No," Acherre said. "You chase him down. Now."

She hesitated, glancing up to see Axerian already almost descended to the floor of the cliffside, a silhouette getting smaller as he reached the valley floor.

"Go." Acherre made it an order, of the sort she'd heard officers give during the battle for the city. Coupled with the surge of foreign emotion in her gut, it served to pull her away from Acherre. The woman could handle *Body* and *Life* on her own, and Axerian was getting away.

She called on *lakiri'in*, the spirit of the crocodile from the sewers, and ran.

Anati appeared coiled around her wrist, her serpent head perked into the wind, eyes half narrowed as though she were enjoying the brisk run. *Red* surged through her limbs, and a crimson color flashed in Anati's scales.

Axerian had grown from a shadow back to a man, running faster than anyone could have managed, unaided, but still far from her equal. She closed the distance. He pivoted away and she followed, *lakiri'in* giving her speed enough to overmatch his pace. Glances over his shoulder revealed terror in his eyes, each look surging the sense of justice and rightness in her chest.

He tried *White*, set through a warding, the same trick he'd used to bring down Acherre. She ripped the blue sparks away before she knew what she was doing, unraveling his use of Life magic and passing through his shield as though it were no more than wisps of harmless smoke.

She blinked to search for *Shelter* and found none at the base of the cliff, instead opting to copy Axerian's trick, opening herself to the blue sparks. She set a warding ahead of him and Anati flared *White*; Axerian countered instantly with *Black*, siphoning away her shield as easily as she'd pierced his.

"Do that to him," Sarine shouted toward Anati on her wrist. "Take his *Red*."

But we can't use Black. We've never killed anyone.

Frustration bloomed, doubly so with half of it coming from her. *Lakiri'in*'s gift wouldn't last; she remembered what it was to be the reptile, lounging in the sun to store the energy for a single burst of speed. She added *mareh'et*, and found enough stray motes for a quick jolt of *Body*. Axerian had already spent his *White*; it would take a few moments for it to return. All she had to do was catch him.

Four gifts combined to boost her speed, and she shot forward. Axerian pivoted, juking left, and she matched him. He turned again, and she caught hold of his torso, wrenching his body off-balance, sending them both tumbling to the ground.

Anati had spent her *White*, too; she fell along with him, each of them rolling and bouncing through the dirt. *Red* made her resilient, and *Body*, but still pain shot through her limbs, her breath forced from her lungs in a stinging gasp.

"Stop," she managed, her voice rasping in her throat. "Stop running."

Their bodies were still entangled, close enough that she could feel his heart thundering, the same as hers.

"You didn't kill me," Axerian said. "I'd expected you would."

Another surge of emotion in her chest swelled with vindication, justice, rage. Not her emotions. The Veil's. She fought them down.

"No," she said, pulling their bodies apart to rest on the grass. She didn't think anything of hers was broken, only bruised and covered with dirt. She took another deep breath through a searing pain in her chest. Maybe a rib was broken after all. "Though Acherre might, after what you did to her, and her horse. I only wanted answers."

Axerian seemed to be testing his body, rising to sit, his legs extended, propping himself up on his arms.

"You wanted answers," Axerian repeated.

"Why," she said. "Why you attacked High Commander d'Arrent, and Arak'Jur and Corenna. Why you set off wardings to collapse the Great Barrier. I wanted to know what was wrong with Zi, too, but he... well..."

Anati had uncoiled herself from Sarine's wrist, stepping gingerly onto the trampled grass.

"You've bonded a new *kaas*." There was caution in Axerian's voice, his usual knowing mirth replaced by a guarded distance.

"Axerian, I..." Another wellspring of emotion flared in her chest, with images of Axerian standing over her, watching her as the world around her filled in with glass. "I don't..."

"You're still Sarine." He said it with awe.

"You knew," she said, her emotions mixing with the foreign ones churning inside her. "You knew I was the Veil."

"Yes," Axerian said. "But also no. You were never truly her."

"Anati said I was. And I can feel her. Her emotions, locked inside me."

"You are the Veil as she might have been, a thousand cycles ago. That doesn't make you her. It doesn't mean you have to do what she would."

She drew a deep breath, feeling another spike of hatred she knew couldn't be hers.

"Axerian, I need to know the truth behind all of this. You've done terrible things. I need to understand why."

"Satisfy your justice, or you'll kill me after all?" He said it with a half smile.

She said nothing, only fixed him with a serious look as she fought down the rage rising inside. Her chest felt hollowed out from too much emotion, but there was a thread of hope. She had no desire to kill him, but had no other means to stop him. He'd threatened the lives of every man, woman, and child in the New Sarresant colonies. He'd as good as killed the people in the square, when she'd faced down the *valak'ar*, and the priests with *anahret*, and who could say how many more since. But there was more to him than mindless violence. The prospect of understanding frightened her, but she had to know.

He seemed to sense her gravity, and bowed his head before he spoke.

"Very well," he said. "Where do I begin?"

34

SARINE

At the Base of a Cliffside
Erhapi Land

I first ascended to the Seat sixteen cycles ago, from the Tenadaan schools of the Jukari. Back then the path was different. Smoother. We knew the precepts and studied the mysteries of the *kaas* before we even knew to whom they would grant a bond."

"Hold on," Sarine said. "What is the 'Seat'? And a cycle?"

Axerian reclined against his hands, sprawled out on the trampled grass. "I still forget you aren't her. It's strange, to me, speaking to you of such things when she was my teacher."

"So the Veil was a master at your school?" The question felt odd even as she shaped it—thinking of a Goddess as a schoolteacher—but they had to start somewhere.

"Not that sort of teacher. Let me start over. It's been ages since I delivered this lecture, so I'll need your patience if I am out of practice."

She waited while he made a show of gathering his thoughts, and he leaned forward, tucking his legs into a crossed position.

"It begins with darkness," Axerian continued. "A world where the sun struggles to shine through clouds of ash and smoke. Plants die. Fire rains in place of water; the seas roil with storms. Caves and dwellings belowground are the only refuge, and they are never safe, between magma leaks, ash vents, earthquakes, and fumes rising from the depths.

"One child in a hundred lives to die of age and infirmity. Most breed as soon as they've flowered, and count themselves blessed to meet their grandchildren. Philosophy and religion are preserved only by dedicated schools: The greatest luxury of every civilization, and no few peoples go without. A terrible world. Can you picture it?"

She nodded, not wanting to interrupt. He gave her a wry look, and spoke again.

"Understand," he said, "I don't have to imagine what that world is like. I was born into it. I remember the last days of shadow. Only two others living can say the same—three, perhaps, if you count the Regnant."

"I don't understand," she said. "You mean the world was once as you describe?"

"Yes," he said. "In some ages, it has been as you see it now. Light, and life. Knowledge, growth, succor from the wild." He held his hands up, cupped together, and rotated them, moving one hand below the other. "In others, Death holds sway. A 'cycle' is all the years between the choosings—at the end of each age, when the time is right for ascension, champions are chosen to fight for Life, or Death. Then whichever is victorious makes the world in their God's image: poison, gas, and blight if the Regnant's champions win. And this"—he gestured to the grass and dirt around them—"if the Veil's do."

She weighed his words in her mind. It sounded more like a creation fable, the sort passed down by provincial elders outside the earshot of any Trithetic priests. But then, d'Agarre had vanished at the height of the battle in the city. And she'd heard Axerian—and the native spirits— speak of ascension, and Gods, before.

"Ascension," she said. "Champions. What precisely are they?"

"There are three ascendants on each side. The God and Goddess each bond three warriors to fight for the Soul of the World. For the Veil, they are champions of Order, Balance, and the Wild. The Regnant preserves more schools, and settles things in his own way. Last cycle his champions were Crab, Crane, and Fox. They could be entirely different this time. No way of telling before the day arrives."

She nodded slowly. "That's what happened, in the city. When d'Agarre vanished."

"That's right," Axerian said. "He gathered enough power to ascend, and take my place. For sixteen cycles I was champion of Balance. And now no longer."

"How many years in a cycle?"

A sudden weariness appeared in his eyes, and grief, mixed with his usual mirth.

"Thousands," he said. "Too many to count."

The emptiness of it stretched in front of her. Too vast to consider. He was sixteen thousand years old, maybe older? But Axerian spoke again, leaning toward her as he did.

"We spent most of it sleeping. No need for champions to watch as civilization sprouts from ashes. We wake to guide the world into the next war. But I'm still technically old enough to turn the head of your most ancient graybeard. And now I'm mortal again, picking up life where I left it, after my first ascension."

"So what happens? The champions face each other. Then what?"

"The God and the Goddess abide by the victor. I've only ever witnessed a transformation once, from one state to the other. It was beautiful. The clouds cleared, the seas calmed, the sun flared gold and bright in the sky."

A surge of hate wrenched her gut, foreign for all it felt as though she'd summoned animosity for his words.

"The three of us," Axerian continued, "the Veil's champions, decided that day we would never again see the world transformed back into shadow. It was her intent to see us discarded, left to die as mortals once our fight was over. We refused. We knew we had the skill to best whatever the enemy sent to face us. We used her power to preserve ourselves, and for sixteen cycles, we fought the Regnant's champions, and won. We kept the Death God from ever remaking the world into the nightmare we'd destroyed with our first victory."

Memory sparked, to one of the first visions she'd seen. Those visions hadn't been her memories; they were the Veil's. A battlefield, with three champions victorious. The world transformed by her power. A betrayal, and her imprisonment.

"You imprisoned her," she said.

A sober look passed through Axerian's eyes. "Yes. No more than you and your *kaas* have done to contain her now. I used the *kaas'* powers to bind the Goddess, and we drew Life magic from her. Enough to sustain ourselves, and keep the champions of every age suppressed."

Another flare of rage from deep within her gut. Another emotion from the Veil. She fought it down.

"So why am I here?" she asked. "If she's the Goddess, what does that make me?"

"I don't know. None of us have ever understood the full extent of her power. But her prison was destroyed some weeks ago, and so far as Paendurion could tell, the Veil was dead. I expected it meant she'd taken control of your body."

"I think she tried to," she said. "Zi protected me. And Anati."

Axerian nodded. "The *kaas* are strong. But the Veil will try again. She was ancient long before I ascended. I can't think she would let herself be defeated so easily. Even our attempts at containing her were temporary; I think we all knew it, even if we feared this day would come."

"So what happens next? You're trying to hunt down the...champions? Is that why you attacked Erris d'Arrent, Arak'Jur, Corenna?"

"Yes." He said it unflinching. "And why I've been using *Green* to help Ad-Shi with the Vordu people. I know what we do is terrible. We all know it. But the alternative is the world returned to shadow. None of us are willing to let that happen."

Quiet fell between them, and she watched as Anati climbed a blade of long grass. Her *kaas* raced up its stalk, almost sniffing the grain heads before skittering back down. She knew from experience the *kaas* were lightweight, perhaps even weightless, but it was strange to see a creature of Anati's size balanced on a stem no thicker than the nub of one of her charcoal pens. And Anati was evidently all that stood between her and a Goddess, trapped and roiling inside her belly.

It was too much to keep in her head. She almost laughed at the absurdity of it. The Veil, a Goddess, and not only a Goddess in the manner her uncle might have taught. Axerian revered her as something else, some primal force responsible for sunshine and blue skies and kindness and damn near everything good in the world. She wasn't that. She wasn't anything more than an artist gifted with enough tools to survive the Maw, to stay hidden and avoid getting herself caught up in the wrong kind of trouble.

"What happens," she asked abruptly, "when the champions fight and win and suddenly I'm expected to keep the sun shining? I don't have her memories or her knowledge. She's nothing more than a stomachache as far as I can tell."

Axerian let the quiet linger a moment more, studying her.

"I'm more afraid of what happens if we lose," he said. "If the Regnant claims the Soul of the World. Will you survive until the next age, to be there to change it back? I know this is the last cycle for me, but I'm terrified it will be the last cycle for all of us."

"What are you saying? I should let her out? Let her be in control?"

"She'd kill me at once, if you did. But wouldn't that be a price worth paying, if it meant preserving this?" He gestured to the plain, to the cliffside, the city above them, the summer sky and the sun shining overhead. "I don't know if it will come to that. But I've already been unseated, and we have a madman championing Balance for this cycle. Ad-Shi has given in to despair; she's left the Seat early, and all but sealed her fate to join with mine. Paendurion alone might not be enough. Everything is at stake, Sarine. This isn't some miniature battle for the fate of one people, of one city. *Everything* you know and recognize as this world will be gone if the Regnant wins, and it might well be gone forever, if you take the Veil with you into death."

He took a breath.

"So yes," he said. "It may be prudent for you to at least prepare yourself to make that sacrifice."

"No," she said.

Axerian gave her a pained look. Even Anati seemed to have gone still, watching, her balanced atop a wheat-stalk blowing in the wind.

"No," she said again. "You said you were trying to assassinate the ascendants from this cycle, right? Arak'Jur, Corenna, High Commander d'Arrent? To keep your places as champions?"

"They're not the only prospects, but yes."

"Why limit it to the Veil's champions? Why not attack the other ones, the ones fighting for... the Death God, or the Regnant, or whatever you called it? Aren't they just as vulnerable?"

Axerian frowned. "I'm sure they are, but we have no way to reach them, prior to the last ascensions."

"Why not?"

"There's a Divide, between East and West. Your maps show it, in this age: the blackness on the far side of your globes. We'd thought the Regnant's champions might have found a way through, but it turned out to be your influence. So far as we know, it is impenetrable."

Her mind worked quickly, chewing on the idea like she might have planned to sketch a difficult angle or form. She'd seen globes marked with blackness on the far side, but that was no more than undiscovered country, as the New World had been, waiting for explorers to sail and find what lurked there.

"It can't be," she said. "If the Veil can bring the champions together, then she can find a way through. Or at least she has the power to do it, and that means I do. I'm not going to surrender myself to her. But I'd rather start with the problem of breaking through some artificial Divide than the problem of keeping the sun shining, if I'm going to learn to use her power."

"It might work," Axerian said slowly. "Killing the Regnant's ascendants, before they're ready. If you could get us through the Divide."

"Why not?" she said. "If the Veil's power is responsible for all creation, it's responsible for this Divide, too. Better to win this war, or whatever it is, before it starts. I can do it. I can learn. And I won't give in to her."

A violent lurch of anger spiked through her, as fierce as she'd felt since Anati was bonded. It only redoubled her resolve. Zi had been willing to die to keep the Veil from taking control, and seen to it Anati was put in place to continue what he'd started. She could trust in that, even if every word Axerian said terrified her beyond any conception she'd had of the world.

Zi had believed in her. That was enough.

35

ARAK'JUR

A Rock Overlooking the Swamp
Lhakani Land

B leak nothing extended to the edge of his vision. Gray haze settled over the top of the peat, broken trees looming through the fog with branches like teeth of a predator, circling him from all sides. It felt wrong to be here, so long in one place, exposed, when the spirits had warned him of the Uktani's intent.

"Mushrooms," Ka'Urun said, climbing up the side of their rock looking almost like a beast himself. Wrong to think it; he was still a man, whatever his deformities. "Yinala found a patch, growing with those bushes over there. Want some?"

Arak'Jur waved him away, and the shaman shrugged, spread himself atop a rock, and began eating.

No other sound made it through the bog, and so he listened as the shaman bit and chewed the caps and stems of his meal. Even the usual hum and croaking of toads, beetles, and birds was absent, leaving near-total silence as they lingered close to Moru'Alura'Tyat. That was Ka'Urun's plan. They would linger close, but not so close that the sacred place would blind the vision-spirits' glimpses of where they were. To a hunter gifted with a shaman's power, it would appear as though they had tried to use the sacred place for cover, and made a mistake, leaving them exposed. Then, if the hunter came, they would fall into the Lhakani shaman's trap.

The shapes of the six Lhakani warriors were visible through the fog, but only if he already knew where to look. One of the men pressed himself against the branches of a tree. A patch of moss and debris floating in the bog masked another hiding under the surface. The Lhakani tribe knew the secrets of their marshland home, their shaved heads and black *echtaka* paint serving to blend them into the wild. Only their shaman shattered the illusion, sucking hungrily as he devoured another handful of white-capped fungi.

"What do you see?" he asked the shaman.

"Patience, guardian," Ka'Urun said between bites. "She's coming."

"And what of the Uktani?"

"Again you ask of them, and again I say they are not here, Arak'Jur," Ka'Urun said. "Only her. Only the nightmare."

He fell quiet again, returning to watch the haze pooling over top of the marsh. He'd meant to leave Lhakani land, and instead found its bleakness suited to his mood. Corenna was out there, somewhere. Perhaps she'd drawn the Uktani away. A sacrifice he'd never asked her to make, but then, Ka'Inari had spoken to her at length after Ka'Ana'Tyat. Perhaps that was why she'd stolen away, saying nothing, fading into the morning. Emotion burned in him at the thought, at the dreams of their child's future and all the love he thought they'd still held between them. Stolen by the spirits' whims. Cursed.

A hissing sound went through the bog, like a snake. Yinala. They'd agreed to make such a call when there was sign of danger.

His senses cleared, and he lowered himself closer to the fetid water's surface.

"She comes," Ka'Urun said, whispering loud enough to sound like a snake himself. "She comes!"

The other Lhakani were shifting in their hiding places, visibly readying spears and arrows now that he knew where to look to find them. He stayed low, near the shaman's rock. The ways of moving quickly through the marsh were foreign to him, but *una're* or *ipek'a* wouldn't care for subtleties. He prepared to draw on both, leaping strength and electrified claws outweighing unfamiliarity with the swamp.

A silhouette cut through the haze, approaching.

Then another.

Two. Before he could weigh what it might mean, spears flew through the mist. A gurgling sound, caught between a startled yelp and a scream, and both figures went down.

Yinala stood, revealing herself, and he joined her in moving toward where they'd fallen. The rest of the Lhakani stayed hidden.

"She is dead," Ka'Urun said. "They've killed her!"

Yinala reached the bodies first, hefting them from the surface of the peat.

"Not women," she called in quiet tones. "These are men. Foreigners."

Arak'Jur forced himself to scan the horizon as far as he could see through the mists, satisfied nothing else was approaching by the time he reached her side.

A spear protruded from one man's chest, a clean strike through the heart. The other throw had punctured the second man's jaw and neck, careening off to land in the peat but no less sure a killing blow. He took no time admiring the precision of the Lhakani's attack. Feathers and paint showed on both corpses, stuck with tar from where they'd fallen but no less clear in their origins.

"Uktani," he said. "These are Uktani scouts."

He rounded on Ka'Urun, the shaman still in the throes of celebration despite Yinala's call that neither slain attacker could be the woman he'd foreseen.

"You swore the Uktani were not here!" he said in heated tones, only the need for caution keeping him from bellowing it across the swamp.

"She is dead," the shaman repeated. "Ad-Shi is dead. We are saved."

Disgust overpowered his senses. This was no true shaman. He'd been deluded by the ravings of a fool.

He turned, heading west, away from the shaman's stone.

"Arak'Jur!" Yinala called to him.

He ignored her and the shaman both, though she took nimble steps where his were slow and trudging, and soon appeared beside him.

"Arak'Jur," she said again. "What are you doing? Why do you leave?"

"The Uktani are coming," he said. "Your shaman's visions are clouded, if ever they were true."

"No," she said. "Ka'Urun's gift is strong. He foresaw our people's destruction."

"Ka'Urun saw it in the waning of his own gift," he said. "Your tribe is broken. Leave here, Yinala. Find a man to make children with. Find another tribe."

"Arak'Jur has fallen under her control," Ka'Urun said behind them, his voice raised and cutting through the swamp. "She has him. She made him lure us here."

"Ka'Urun saw your coming," Yinala said. "His gift is still strong."

"How long would you have waited in the swamp, for someone to come? It is no vision, to claim someone would visit a sacred place. If not me, it would have been another."

"Kill him," Ka'Urun shouted. "The Sinari guardian is her creature. He must die!"

The remainder of the Lhakani warriors had risen along with their shaman's cries. Spears rose from the bog, though none had yet been leveled toward him.

"I will go in peace, if you let me," Arak'Jur said, loud enough to cut through the shaman's commands. "Your shaman is a broken man. The spirits have deserted him, and cursed the rest of you. Leave him. Go and find peace, where you can."

The shaman's ravings continued, but the Lhakani spears stayed pointed toward the sky. Only the thick slurp of mud and peat around his boots accompanied him as he trudged away from where they'd thought to set their trap.

Guilt stung him, conflicted emotions running through his veins. If the woman, Ad-Shi, was truly coming, then he was leaving them to die. But the Uktani were here. He might already have drawn them too close for the Lhakani to survive. How many more tribes needed to perish, for the spirits to be sated? The Ranasi had already been destroyed. The Uktani corrupted by some malefic vision, driven to hunt him with strength enough they must have abandoned their homes to do it. The Nanerat, reduced to a husk of their former pride. And the Lhakani. All around him, civilization collapsed. And yet if he had his way, he would join Corenna wherever she had run. He would retreat to some corner of the wild, find a lush piece of land, and raise their child, with his magic to keep them safe from the comings of beasts, great and small. The spirits bade him seek their gifts, but he was tired. Weary of death and killing.

A yearning for life burned deeper than any charge from the spirits. If Corenna had only asked, he would have gone with her anywhere.

Instead he left the Lhakani sacred place behind, walking until the shaman's ravings dimmed to nothing on the wind. The fog lightened as he left Moru'Alura'Tyat, and he walked in twilight, though there should be hours yet to go before nightfall. How many had been corrupted? How many had fallen to the madness of the hunt that drove the Uktani, the destruction of those foolish enough to wish for peace? The answer seemed to stretch in front of him, the land itself seeming soured by heat and lack of color. Perhaps the next tribes he met would be unfettered by the calls to war. Not enough hope to lift the burden from his mind, but enough to keep him walking, one step and then another, until the sky turned black, and he made camp.

———————

Instinct woke him hours before dawn.

A subtle jolt, enough to bring him to his senses without disturbing his body, even leaving his eyes shut, his breathing steady. Better not to reveal he knew he was being hunted.

His other senses cast out, searching for whatever had triggered him awake.

He'd lit a fire and given it enough fuel to burn through most of the night; a ward against predators, and needed warmth against the nighttime cold. He heard it still crackling, felt its heat against his skin. Nearby leaves and grass rustled in the wind, with no telltale scraping if they blew over a predator's back. The smell of mud filled the air. Insects buzzed their song, but no birds. Nothing to give warning of something approaching, save a warning tingling on his skin. Eyes were on him, from somewhere. He remembered what it was to be *kirighra*, burning with the ferocity of perfect stealth, the sure knowledge of the unseen killer.

Better to meet it on his feet, whatever had come for him. He made slow, deliberate movements. Open his eyes. Roll to put his back away from the wind. Rise to his feet. No few would-be predators would retreat against such a display: confidence and strength where they'd expected fear. But this one didn't move, and hadn't moved since it came close enough to provoke his instinct. A silhouette drawn against the night, twenty paces from where he'd slept. A woman.

She waited for him to set his feet, then bowed her head, only a slight incline.

He said nothing, keeping his body still, but not rigid. Thoughts simmered beneath the surface. For now, instinct reigned, until he could be certain she was not a predator.

"Guardian," she said, "or shaman?" The accent was foreign, unlike any tongue he'd heard before.

"Who are you?" he said. "Why have you come on me in the night?"

She stepped forward, enough to add color to her form. She was short, even for a woman: Corenna's height, and almost of an identical frame. But Corenna had never worn garb of fox hides sewn together and fringed with red and gray fur. Where most would travel with a cloak or coat, this woman's arms were bare from the shoulders down, with no sign of pack or pouch. Mud seemed to cake her legs and hands, until she took another step and he saw the stains were a deep crimson, not the dull brown of dirt.

"You are the woman from Ka'Urun's visions." Instinct still reigned, strong enough to suppress the fear that went with the realization, and the guilt. He hadn't truly believed the shaman could see anything more than his own terror.

"He must have had a powerful gift, to see the coming of one woman."

Her voice was chilled, but flat, absent emotion. The same as his; the voice of a predator given over to instinct in the moment of the hunt.

"Ad-Shi," he said, and for a moment she paused, looking to him as though seeing him for the first time.

"The spirits of things-to-come know my name," she said. "Are you a shaman, to hear their whispers?"

"No," he said. "I am no shaman. I am guardian of the Sinari, and if you mean to strike at me as you slew the Lhakani, you will know what it means to claim my tribe."

She changed direction, pacing around the fire as though she meant to see him from another angle. He pivoted with her, keeping the fire at his back. A small edge, if she attacked; the fire would dim her night vision, and his would be sharper for looking away.

"Sinari," she said. "The tribe Axerian touched. They are far to the north, are they not? Why are you so far from your people?"

He said nothing, hardening his stance. She meant to unsettle him with her words. It could precipitate an attack.

Instead she came to a halt.

"There is much you do not know, guardian of the Sinari," she said. "But if you were strong enough to weather Axerian's influence, I have great hopes for you. It would be a disappointment, if you were to die."

Mareh'et beckoned at the edge of his awareness, and *valak'ar*. He held back, watching her.

"You mean to kill me?" he asked.

"I mean to try. This is the way of things, among the Vordu. For too long, our ascendants have gone untutored, learning by grasping at weeds instead of firm instruction. We are meant to learn from our betters, from those who have gone before."

Fear again spiked below the surface of his conscious mind. A thought of Corenna's face, of his unborn child, mixed with Rhealla's, and Kar'Elek's, his slain wife and son.

"I hope you survive, guardian of the Sinari," Ad-Shi said.

Sadness seemed to touch her eyes. Then they filmed over with ice, at the same moment a nimbus of a strange creature—a winged serpent, spined and surrounded by fire—shimmered into place around her.

He let *mareh'et* give its blessing, and thought fled before the instincts of battle.

36

TIGAI

A Lush Green Field
Somewhere Far from Ghingwai

They fell together, tumbling in long grasses under a burning sun. The exertion of using the strands coupled with the feel of her in his arms set his mind swimming in a fog.

"You bloody fool!" Mei shouted. "You can't...you didn't..."

He wrapped his arms around her, squeezing to make certain she was real. She was.

"Why are you laughing, you oaf?" she said. Mirth crept into her voice, over top of indignation. A blend that suited her perfectly. She'd always been at her best chiding the Yanjin brothers while reveling in his and Dao's schemes.

Her hands tightened around him when he didn't relent, making it a mutual embrace. He buried his head sideways against her chest, and her fingers gripped the back of his head, pulling him close. He felt tears in his eyes. She was alive. He was free, and they were far away from the horrors he'd had to perform to try to make it so.

"It's really you," he said.

"Yes, it's really me."

He let the moment last long enough to push the bounds of propriety. But then, they were alone, and far from the watchful eyes of any house servants inclined to gossip.

"Where have you taken us?" Mei asked when he finally withdrew. He leaned back on his knees, surveying the field as she propped herself up. The field was a lush green, a place that had to have its fair share of rainwater, even late in the summer. The sun was halfway to the horizon, either making its descent before nightfall or its ascent to its apex at noon. He couldn't be sure which, only that night had long since fallen in Ghingwai before they'd left.

"Somewhere far to the east, or the west," he said.

"A comforting thought, that you have no idea which."

He grinned, though just as likely he only noticed the expression he'd doubtless been making since their arrival.

"I thought you had to know a place," she said, "before you travel there? Is this field somewhere you've been frequenting in secret, Lord Tigai?"

"I have to know a place to pick it out among the strands, but I can see thousands of *possible* places."

"You mean you could have put us under the ocean? Had us falling from the clouds?"

"Either would have been a possibility," he said, ignoring her stare. Yes, it was dangerous to hook himself to strands he didn't know, but he had enough of a sense of things to know the difference by feel. Most of the starfield were places like that: deep underground, deep water, empty air. He'd learned to avoid those sorts of memories and connections by instinct. Evidently that knowledge had carried over for the purposes of panicked flight.

He took another look at their surroundings, trying to remember a connection if in fact there had been one, and he'd taken them somewhere he knew from childhood, his raiding, or his travels. A wide plain of rolling grass, but it was neither the long brown stalks of the Ujibari steppes or the low, rolling hills and farmlands at the heart of Jun. He could guess they were somewhere in the north by the chill on the wind, though it could as easily have been no more than an unusually cold day.

"Your hand," he said abruptly. "You still have it."

She gave him a curious look. "I still have my feet, too."

"The men who took me...they threatened to hurt you, Dao, and Remarin. When I didn't comply, they presented me with...a severed... I could have sworn it was yours."

Her expression softened.

"No," she said. "After you left, Dao and I were attacked by assassins. They seized control of the estate, but we escaped. Dao's soldiers sheltered us until Lord Isaru arrived."

"Lord who?" he asked.

"Lord Isaru Mattai," she said, a sudden fervor in her voice. "He contracted the Yanjin legion, and paid enough *qian* to hold off our creditors for at least another year."

A ruse. He'd been deceived. Suddenly the image of him returning to Ghingwai and discharging his pistols in Indra's face surfaced in his thoughts, and it felt damn good, even to think it. But it soured just as quick.

"Remarin," he said. "They still have Remarin. He was with me, when Lin caught us coming back to Yanjin from the palace."

"Lord Isaru will know what to do," Mei said. "They're his enemies— he was certain they would bring you to Ghingwai. That's why he had me come along, in case they used you."

"What? Mei, that makes no sense. How could he know? I still have no idea what Indra and Lin were planning, or why they wanted me to attack the mercenary captains there."

"Isaru is leading a rebellion," Mei said. "A *magi* rebellion, against the Great and Noble Houses. That's why Lord Isaru paid so highly for Dao's contract. He's doing the same with other houses all across the Empire. And he's gathering *magi* like you, free *magi* unsworn to the monasteries. He'll pay triple if you join us, for your services alone, and maybe more. This is the answer to everything. We have to head back to his camp and wait for him there."

"Slow down," he said. "What under the heavens would possess us to involve ourselves in a rebellion, let alone a fucking *magi* rebellion? Are you and Dao both mad?"

"Lord Isaru can explain it better than I can," she said. "And he will, if you'll hear him out. But I heard him talking about you as if you were something enormously important. A 'True Dragon,' he called you. Do you know what he meant? It must have been related to your gifts, with your stars."

Dragon. The name resurfaced his fancies of blasting powder into Master Indra's face. The name for the Great and Noble House of fools who could use the starfield and the strands.

"I think I do." He held out his hand. "But there will be time to talk about all of…whatever this is…later."

She grasped it. "Good," she said. "We'll have to travel to Isaru's camp as quick as we can."

"Mei, we're not going to any camp. I'm taking you somewhere safe."

He blinked, still holding her hand, and tethered them both to the strands. The chill air vanished, replaced by the musty smell of the dead.

Darkness enveloped them both, and his head pounded, a trail of blood leaking from his nose. Evidently he'd taken them farther than he'd intended; coming back took a harder toll than he was used to, though he had more travel to do, before he was done.

Mei sputtered a cough, spilling dust and a puff of wind in his direction. "What the…where are we?"

"Keep your voice down," he said in a whisper. "Please. I only need to leave you here for a few hours."

She responded by clinging to him, latching both hands around his arm. "Don't you bloody dare."

He growled, trying to wrench himself free. She collided into him, sending them both backward into the side of the crypt. Dirt scraped along his back, and she pressed forward, pinning him against the wall.

"Mei, we're in Yanjin Palace. In the crypts. You'll be perfectly safe here. Just let me—"

"Perfectly safe? Last time I was here one of my own retainers tried to knife me in the rib cage. I thought it was debt collectors then and I still fled; I know it's worse now."

"No one will look for you here. I have to find Remarin before they kill him."

"No one will think to look in your *ancestral home* now that you've escaped the Great and Noble Houses' influence? Are you bloody serious?"

He relaxed, though she still kept a cold iron grip on his arm. She was right. It was stupid to bring her here.

"I have to get back to their temple," he said. "Remarin has to be somewhere close, somewhere they could reach."

"Their reach is anywhere in the Empire," Mei said, her voice suddenly soft, but still sharp enough to cut through the darkness of the crypt. "And they won't keep him anywhere you have a connection. Remarin is dead."

He tensed, and she held him harder, pressing him into the wall.

"Remarin is dead," she said again. "Unless you listen. You've never cared about politics, or anything beyond your brother. And maybe me. But if you value either of us, you'll understand. More is at stake here than just your master-at-arms' life. We have to go to Isaru Mattai's camp. You'll hear it from Dao, if you won't listen to me. And if there's any chance at all to save Remarin, Isaru will know of it."

"Why should we trust this Lord Isaru?" he asked, and finally Mei loosened her grip, though she still held to him. "How is it he seems to know all there is to know?"

"Don't be jealous. It doesn't suit you."

"What? I don't—"

"Shh," she said, cutting him short. "I'll leave it to Dao to explain. You never trust me anyway."

"That's far from true," he said, then paused. "Dao is well? He's at this camp?"

"He's fine, and yes, he should be there, if Isaru doesn't have him in the field. Now, can we go? I meant what I said, that this will be among the first places they look for you."

He sighed, feeling a pain in his chest over the thought of Remarin, alone and held in some cell somewhere. They wouldn't kill him. They'd be throwing away whatever leverage they might have had, if he encountered them again.

"All right," he said. "You've been living in this camp for the past few weeks?"

"Yes," Mei said. "But you can't take us there directly. It's on the other side of a wall of shadows, something Lord Isaru calls the Divide."

"...What?"

"You'll have to see it to understand. He says it keeps the *magi* from being able to track him. It can't be safe to try to travel through it."

"Well, I think I have the strands for the camp," he said, his eyes closed, feeling Mei's light blending into his among the stars. One light shone brighter than the rest, the soft glow of recency; the place she'd last thought of as home. "Should I take us, or not?"

"No," she said. "It's too dangerous. How close can you get us?"

"It doesn't work like that," he said. "I can't just pick a different route. Either I have a connection to the place, or I don't."

"Somewhere in the north, then," she said. "We traveled across the ice fields north of Gantar Baat to get there."

"Oh for the *koryu*'s sake..." he said.

"We have to go there," she said. "Even if we have to walk the whole way. Lord Isaru will have the answers, and the coin to keep our family out of debt."

It felt wrong. A sudden savior, when they'd never trusted any outsiders before, and a *magi* war mixed in for spice. It was a relief beyond measure to know Mei and Dao were safe, that Master Indra had lied about having them and lied when he'd presented the bloody trophy of her hand. But Remarin had been taken; barring an escape, they had him somewhere. Without knowing this new *magi*, this Lord Isaru, for himself, he couldn't have any degree of confidence in the man's ability to help him find his master-at-arms. But he couldn't see any other course. And he could trust Mei. It would have to serve.

"Let's fetch coats, then," he said. "The thickest you have. Kregiaw is the closest I can get us without going there directly, and that shithole might as well have been hewn from ice."

37

ERRIS

Grand Foyer
Outside the Assembly Hall

O nly the barest moment, if you please, High Commander," the orderly said. "They are preparing the chamber for you now."

She gave a nod that sufficed for acknowledgment and dismissal together, then glanced toward Marquand, standing in a relaxed pose to her right, after the attendant had given them the chamber.

"Fifteen minutes by my count," she said, and Marquand nodded his agreement. "Past the bounds of propriety, wouldn't you say?"

"Far be it for these assholes to make you wait at all," Marquand said. "If it were up to me."

Aide-Captain Essily coughed. "Sir, the attendant said it would be only another moment."

The three of them stood alone in the hall, with all the power of the Assembly of New Sarresant buzzing on the opposite side of the doors. Marquand was right. It was past time for waiting.

"Marquand, if you please," she said, squaring herself in front of the door. He obliged, pushing through ahead of her, holding it open long enough for her to follow.

The roar of the chamber greeted them at once, a swelling tide of shouts and bedlam that should have threatened to burst the heavy oak inward. Good. Let them see military discipline in a moment of disarray. Voren had promised her a favorable outcome in these proceedings, but she'd come to understand the importance of appearances in Voren's world.

Essily formed up on her left, and Marquand fell in on her right as they marched toward the rostrum at the center. A tide of shouting surrounded them, a dozen clusters of ten or twenty men and women each, standing among the chairs and desks that ringed the room in concentric half circles. She led the way toward the empty dais at the heart of the chamber, welcomed by stares and the silence that followed. First one group's conversation died, then another, but she was already at the base of the steps before the bulk of the room noticed the three uniformed soldiers among them.

The Assembly stared, but it was the same silk-and-lace-covered orderly who came scurrying toward where she stood, his head tucked low as though his presence were an apology.

"It isn't time yet, High Commander," the attendant whispered, still loud enough to carry through the last sputtering remnants of debate. "The hall hasn't yet issued its summons."

She ignored him.

For a moment, the spreading quiet prevailed. Like the last moment before a charge, when what would become a battlefield was still given to calm.

"High Commander," a voice called from the crowd. A man, one she recognized from her farce of a hearing some weeks before. Assemblyman Lerand, dressed in an imitation of factory workers' clothes, but cut too finely and kept too clean for her to have confused them for the real thing. "The chamber isn't yet prepared to receive you. I move the Commander be escorted from the hall while we conclude debate."

"Second," came a cry from circles nearby the speaker, carried by multiple voices at once.

"She's here, we knew she was coming"—another voice interrupted, and then another—"let her speak. We intend to settle—" And then cacophony as a dozen more sentences began and ended midway through.

She stayed in place, briefly scanning the room for faces she knew. She saw a handful she'd met in Voren's chambers, scattered among the various circles, and a small knot of familiar faces seated around High Admiral Tuyard, who seemed to be grinning at her with a knowing smile from one of the rearward benches.

Voren himself was nowhere in sight.

The realization hit her hard. He'd been the one to urge her to make this appearance, the one who swore he could deliver a majority of support for the Thellan invasion on the floor.

Nothing for it now. She swallowed, took a deep breath, and began.

"Assemblymen and women of New Sarresant," she said. "I've come before you to make plain my intent to make war on the Thellan colonies, and by extension, on Thellan itself. I stand before you as High Commander of our military, land and sea. My aim here today is to secure your support for the invasion, on grounds of the essential need to defend our nation through preemptive action against an enemy bent on our destruction. I invite you to join me on the right side of our nation's history. Without this action, our country will have no history at all."

Voren had composed the speech for her; it sounded foreign to her ears, for all she was the one giving it. At first the chamber had continued its cacophonous debate, but quickly fell silent as she spoke. When she said the last words of the short speech, the silence lingered for another beat, as though she might continue, before Assemblyman Lerand stepped into the aisle.

"Is that a threat, High Commander d'Arrent?" Assemblyman Lerand asked. "Do you mean to tell this Assembly you mean to snuff us out should we fail to accede to your warmongering?"

"She means there are military matters that should be beyond the purview of nattering fools who aren't fit to command a textile loom." High Admiral Tuyard rose to his feet on the opposite side of the chamber. "This is the danger of democracy, my friends. This council holds its positions by way of cajoling citizens with false promises, if not outright bribery. Not a one of you is suited to tell High Commander d'Arrent how to dispose her army."

"Forgive me, Admiral, but this is an outrage, against our very principles." This came from Assemblywoman Caille, the pruned elder who had chaired her hearing. She rose from a cluster of chairs between the factory worker and Tuyard, speaking softly but somehow managing to project it through Tuyard's tirade and echo through every corner of the hall.

"Assemblyman Lerand is quite correct," Caille continued. "This council cannot exist as a governing body with the threat of military force hanging over our heads. Without question there are matters over which we do not presume to vote, but expertise cannot be confused for sovereignty. And so the question is: Can we allow a military officer to draw us into war? Are there not factors we must consider that run well beyond the needs of soldiering, and, if so, do we not rightly claim purview over them?"

Lerand was nodding in time with her words, with the rest of his coterie of supporters following along.

"Assemblywoman Caille has seen to the heart of it," Lerand said. "I, and my supporters, embrace her vision of the matter at hand, and propose the submission by High Commander Erris d'Arrent to this Assembly a detailed accounting of the military concerns of her invasion, to be considered in due course alongside the trade and taxation concerns, as this chamber deems appropriate."

Tuyard's laugh filled the room, like a stage actor cutting above the audience. "You would have our brigade-colonels give you a detailed accounting of the ground before they dispose their troops. Were you fools not listening? D'Arrent claims an imminent and certain threat from Thellan. This is a simple question of existence: Do we fight the inevitable war, or do we wait to vote on what to call it when we surrender?"

Caille and Lerand both spoke at once, but Erris stopped listening before they resolved the issue of who would command the floor. It was clear the three of them represented factions with broad support clustered among the seats in the chamber: Tuyard with his group on the left, Caille in the center, and Lerand on the right. The center group seemed the largest by a fair margin, and Assemblywoman Caille, inasmuch as she spoke for them, seemed to balance the viewpoints of the two more extreme men on either side. She couldn't have said where Voren would have stood; a second scan of the chamber confirmed he was nowhere in sight. Whatever subtle politics were at work here, she didn't trust any of them. Voren had been her guide through hostile ground, as valuable as a turncoat scout native to her enemies' lands. Without him, this trip was like to be wasted, with consequences she couldn't foresee, except that they were likely to be dire.

"I am prepared to concede the need for swift action under threat," Assemblywoman Caille was saying. "And I accept it may illumine the need for an executive within our government. But the point must stand that no such executive exists today, and therefore whatever action is proposed by High Commander d'Arrent must be considered in due course by this Assembly before it can be considered legitimate."

"You use my own words against me," Tuyard replied. "But I argue we must have a leader, empowered to act without deliberation. Without such a figure, we will be paralyzed while our enemies move against us. This is a time for bold leadership, not dithering and debate."

Caille affected a look of consideration, as though she hadn't before considered the idea. She had the look of an elderly grandmother, the sort depicted in village folktales as a stern voice of reason when the local magistrates pushed the bounds of common sense. Yet for all that, the woman had iron in her voice, a sound Erris recognized from her own commands, and the circle of Assemblymen and women at the center looked to her with nodding heads, as though her contemplation counted for theirs.

"A King," Lerand said, sneering as though he'd been the first to see it. "You mean to give us a King, before our hands are dry from de l'Arraignon blood."

Erris stepped forward, drawing eyes from across the room. "We must make war," she said. Voren hadn't prepared this part of the speech, but she sensed weakness, as sure as if her lines had been stretched too thin at the critical juncture of a battle. "I led our army against the Crown-Prince because he meant to order us to abandon our homeland. He put our people in jeopardy. I tell you now, the enemy mustering in the south represents a threat no less dire. My soldiers do not fight for freedom, *égalité*, or the glory of your revolution. They fight for their homes and families. If it takes a King to allow them to do it, they will put this council down for cowards who lack the nerve to act, and swear allegiance to whatever crown will let them fight."

Silence returned to the chamber.

"There it is," Tuyard said, at the same moment Lerand took a step away from his supporters, toward the dais.

"I will never swear to another King," Lerand said, "who makes liberty his enemy, nor a Queen, who would commit us to foreign entanglements anathema to the ideal of *égalité*. I name any man or woman who tries to take us down that path a traitor, owed the lawful punishment for treason, the same we gave Louis-Sallet de l'Arraignon."

Murmurs sounded through the chamber, from the balcony above through the rows of benches situated below. It appeared she'd said precisely the wrong thing, and Assemblyman Lerand the right one. Hot eyes fixed on her, and Marquand pressed closer than he had before. Easy to find comfort in his presence, as she'd done on battle lines in her younger days. The main halls connected the Assembly Hall to the army high command, but this chamber had started to feel like hostile ground. No chance of making a retreat without displacing some among the crowd. Gods send they could do it without resorting to *Entropy*.

"Time to go," she said under her breath, low enough for only Essily and Marquand to hear. Both men adjusted to cover her flanks, watching her for the cue to move. It had been a mistake to come here. Voren had promised a resolution supporting the invasion, and the tax money to fund her quartermasters. Instead she stared down vipers in thrall to ideas wholly distinct from the realities of war. Fools, but powerful fools, and Voren had abandoned her to—

"High Commander d'Arrent is right."

Once again Assemblywoman Caille's voice cut through the chamber, though somehow the woman seemed to be speaking in measured, even tones.

"Our people must be kept safe," Caille continued. "The sanctity of the state begins there. It is not treason to suggest our soldiers—our people—would follow any government that could provide safety, and reject any that failed to do so."

"Well enough, and so do we propose," Lerand cut in. "This Assembly will serve to—"

"No." This time Caille's voice was sharp. "We need the counsel of experts empowered to govern their respective areas. And we need a leader to preside over them. Not a King. A First Minister, accountable and beholden to this Assembly for their authority, but placed at the head of an empowered executive arm of our government. And given the nature and imminence of the threat presented by High Commander d'Arrent, we must settle the matter swiftly."

"A First Minister?" Tuyard said, and laced the title with cynicism, as though the words themselves were meant to be amusing. "I suppose you'd nominate yourself for this post, Assemblywoman?"

If Tuyard had meant the charge to resonate, it seemed to have the opposite effect, with voices raised in agreement from among the chairs at the center of the room.

Lerand seemed confused for the moment, conferring with councillors among his supporters on the far side of the chamber while still more voices stirred at the center. Erris raised a hand to stay Marquand and Essily. Where before the chamber had seemed volatile, on the edge of erupting into shouting if not outright violence, now it simmered with a different sort of heat. She could see Voren's hand in it, an echo of a battlefield strategy played out in front of her, though she couldn't guess the precise nature of the moves it had taken to set it in motion.

"We could accept Assemblywoman Caille in such a role," Lerand said at last. "But only so long as there were strict limits established. A matter for extended debate, past the point of settling the question the High Commander brings before us."

"I am flattered, of course," Assemblywoman Caille said. "But if a leader is selected from among our number, their constituents would be necessarily raised above all others. First among equals is no *égalité* at all. No—I move our First Minister be chosen from outside our halls. Empowered to act in matters of state, but ultimately beholden to a majority among this Assembly."

Tuyard leaned forward, looking like the lead wolf from among his coterie of similarly wolfish compatriots. Voren had planned this. She was sure of it now.

"There is wisdom here," Tuyard said. "But I ask again, do you have a name in mind, Assemblywoman?"

"I do," she replied. "A man who has been instrumental in the formation and constitution of our republic. He has made his share of enemies—and I might have counted myself among them, once. But for the good of our country, I urge all inclined to trust my judgment to join me in putting our support behind Anselm Voren for First Minister, with a term to be deliberated by this Assembly."

Voren's name percolated through the chamber, repeated in whispers by those who needed to be certain they'd heard aright. Erris stood at its heart, watching as those seated in the center—the largest group, and from the look of things a group disposed to trust neither Voren or Tuyard—whispered his name, and looked to Caille for confirmation. It was a rout, as certain as if Voren had broken an enemy's best-reinforced flank and now swept around to take their center from behind. The Assemblywoman stood tall, confident, and proud without an overbearing air. Erris had seen entire companies rally to a lone soldier holding a flag, firm and steady when it seemed all hope around them was lost. She'd held such a flag herself. Caille did it now.

"A former lord," Lerand said, echoing a sentiment stirring among his fellows on the right-hand side of the chamber. "This alone should disqualify him."

His complaints drowned beneath a hum of activity. Voren's name continued to be repeated, and smaller bouts of conversation sprang up between seats and benches with varying degrees of fervor. Tuyard reclined in his seat, wearing a knowing smile as his fellows exchanged excited looks.

Caille raised a hand, gesturing to calm the chamber. For a moment, the seats nearest the dais seemed to obey, while those in the rear of the room still buzzed with a thrum of energy. Men and women rose to their feet near the exits, and the wave of excitement seemed to pass through the room, replaced by quiet, and anger.

It took a moment to realize why.

Omera, the Bhakal man Voren had retained for his private service, had entered the chamber through its doors at the back, carrying a woman in his arms.

"What is the meaning of this?" Assemblywoman Caille said, then paled as the crowd rose to its feet, craning to see Omera reach the center, only a few paces from Erris's entourage, before he turned to address the room.

She recognized the woman Omera held the moment the rest of the chamber seemed to do the same: an elderly matron with iron-gray hair. A perfect copy of Assemblywoman Caille, for all the woman herself stood twenty paces away, as though she'd used a *Mind* binding to make a copy and place a perfect replica in Omera's keeping.

"The man called Voren is not the man you believe," Omera said to the hall, then turned to Caille as though addressing her directly. "He has done evil, and he must meet justice for his crime."

By now the front ranks could see there were two Cailles—one standing, ashen-faced and full of panic, and one seemingly dead, lying in Omera's arms.

Erris's mind reeled; the chamber seemed to do the same, meeting Omera's words with open mouths and expressions caught between shock and fury. Assemblywoman Caille darted frantic looks around the chamber, but managed no more than a stuttering step into the aisle before her eyes rolled upward and she collapsed.

Marquand caught the assemblywoman—or, the copy of her—before she fell to hit the floor. He made as though to lay her down, and recoiled with a burst of profanity over top of the growing roar among the Assembly.

Where Assemblywoman Caille had been, a man lay instead: young, olive-skinned, with a neat-kept beard and high-set, narrow eyes.

"That is him," Omera said. "That is Voren, as he is when he thinks none are watching."

ELSEWHERE

INTERLUDE

REMARIN

Dungeons
Tower of the Heron

Damp air and windowless walls gave the only sign he was anywhere but in a palace. Not even Dao's father would have permitted such waste. He was a prisoner; the pistoleers posted to his door made clear of it, if the *magi* who headed their detail didn't. Yet he slept on silk, in a four-post canopy bed the likes of which he would expect for Princes' consorts, or perhaps their daughters. Scroll racks stocked with texts of great poets, philosophers, mathematicians, and generals lined the walls where tapestries left them bare, with ornate vases and miniature fir trees decorating the corners not occupied by sitting tables and matching redwood chairs. Servants brought him boiled goose eggs, stuffed pheasant, deep-sea fish steaks, fermented mare's milk, and any number of other such delicacies. All the coin he'd earned in his life wouldn't have sufficed to live in it for a month, and now he'd been here for three.

Sweat glistened on his forehead as he began his daily routine. No true Ujibari man could live like this. Pampered luxury was a thing for Jun lords. He'd as soon have taken all the *qian* spent to imprison him and bought a fort on a hilltop, built on good, defensible ground, with farmland enough to staff a company of men-at-arms he'd use to raid his neighbors' holdings. That was a man's life. *His* life, or it would have been, if the Yanjin brothers' scheme had paid him what he was owed.

Raps sounded on the door. The familiar interruption, on the half hour past the delivery of his morning meal. He paid them no mind, continuing a set of body presses, one arm at a time before he sprang to the opposite side.

"A fine morning to you, good master Remarin," the usual voice said, in the same polite, even tones. "This servant hopes you passed the night well, and find yourself in good spirits to greet the day."

A slight smile creased the corner of Remarin's mouth as Huni Song stepped through the door. Bruises covered the side of Song's face, swallowing his eye in a purple knot, and though the attendant's greeting hadn't wavered from the same he'd delivered every morning since Remarin's capture, today a second figure came behind him as they entered the room.

Remarin sprang up to his feet as Song came to a halt in his entryway. Song was a slender man, but still twice as thick as the woman at his side, who might have hidden among bamboo stalks and not been seen head-on. Both were dressed in the slim-fitting orange robes Remarin had come to associate with his captors, with white cords belted around their hips and hoods covering them from hair to jaw. Yet where Huni Song's hood left his face exposed, the woman wore a mesh veil that left only her eyes—a cutting blue, with the too-wide look of the Natarii tribes of the northern plain.

"You are here to punish me," Remarin said, "for taking offense at yesterday's line of questioning."

Song flinched; a slight movement, but one Remarin's eyes were trained well enough to see.

"No, good master," Song said. "The insult was given without intent, which requires your humble servant to apologize doubly for failing to see how his words would be received. It is far from this servant's place to mete out punishment. This one is here only to see you well attended and comfortable, and in failing that, this one aspires only to your forgiveness."

The saccharine tone was almost enough for him to put Song on the ground again, but it would be no more satisfying than kicking a dog. Worse, since the dogs Remarin favored had at least some measure of pride. And there was the newcomer, the woman behind the veil.

She regarded him coldly, though he couldn't help but wonder if all

Natarii seemed cold, given the unfortunate pigment of their eyes. Hers were a pale but lustrous shade of blue, like ice reflecting fresh water.

"This is the Lady Bavda Khon," Song said, bowing toward the waif. "She is highly placed, and deserving of the utmost deference and respect."

"You've learned by now what Ujibari men think of deference and respect," Remarin said, wearing a wolfish grin.

"This servant has had great fortune in learning from you, good master. But this time, for your sake, this one hopes you will see the value in propriety. Now. Might we avail ourselves of your chairs to sit, share tea, and discuss the matters the Lady Khon has brought to hand?"

"They are your chairs," he said.

Song smiled as if Remarin had instead given him praise, leading the way to a set of four matching chairs arrayed around a glass table at the near end of the long hall that passed for a chamber. The woman, Bavda, sat at once, keeping her eyes on Remarin as Song returned to the door for a fresh tray of tea.

"What are you here to discuss?" Remarin asked at last.

The woman raised herself to her full height in the chair—still a full head shorter than him, even seated—but managed to make it look as though she were standing. Her cheeks were gaunt, her skin too pale a shade of white, though the full contours of her face were hidden behind the veil.

"You were the Yanjin family quartermaster," she said. Her voice was deeper than he'd expected, only lightly colored by the accents of the north. "In service first to Yanjin Gaido, and then Yanjin Dao, when the father passed inheritance to the son."

"Would you believe this is only the second time I have been asked about my service to the Yanjin family since being brought here?"

He made a pointed glance toward Song's purple cheek, as the servant made to prepare their tea. Song had been standing just there when he mentioned Lord Tigai, and earned himself a cuffing for it, more for Remarin to see how his captors would react than any malice for the servant. He'd expected far more brutal questioning in the days immediately following his arrival, and been met instead with only kindness and civility.

If she took his meaning, she didn't show it.

"You conspired with Lord Dao," she continued, "to steal the sum of two hundred eighty thousand *qian* worth of gold, artifacts, jewels, and antiquities from the Kanjiao Palace."

He nodded—no point trying to deny it when they'd caught him with the gold in his hands—and she went on. "You oversaw the training of one Lord Yanjin Tigai, the younger son."

"You've been misinformed," Remarin said. "I taught the boys the arts of war and fighting, yes, but you know as well as I do his training was—"

The world lurched, and pain lanced through his neck and shoulders, followed by a dull ache at the back of his head.

He scrambled to his feet. "What the—?"

Another ringing crack staggered him.

Song had a knowing smile on his face, shaking his head ruefully as he poured the tea. The woman hadn't moved.

"What is this?" he managed, bracing himself for another blow that didn't come.

"Please be seated, good master Remarin," Song said. "This servant hopes you will answer our lady's questions to her satisfaction, to avoid any unnecessary discomforts."

He stayed frozen in place, until Bavda raised an eyebrow, somehow making it both a question and a threat.

"Thank you, good master," Bavda said. "It will be appreciated, if you do not speak to me as though I am a fool."

As she spoke she removed her gloves, pulling each off to reveal skin as pale as the visible part of her face, with tattoos of a long-legged bird— a heron—marked from the backs of her hands up the length of her forearms.

"You have been given every courtesy, in accordance with our law. But you must know Lord Tigai has fallen under the influence of Isaru Mattai. The time for pretense is finished. The time of our God's choosing approaches, and the order will not be disrupted for the sake of whatever scheme you think to put in play."

Pain still throbbed in his head, and he had to think doubly hard to be sure he'd heard her words correctly. He understood not a word of it. All he knew for certain was this woman was a *magi*. Enough on its own to dictate caution, and fear.

"I...I'm not sure what you expect from me," he said at last.

"Heron *will* have a champion at the end of this cycle." She said it fiercely, with a sudden passion that had been absent before. "If Dragon means to take a place, it will be from Crab, not from me. I know you have agents with Isaru Mattai. Activate them. Kill this Lord Tigai, or Isaru himself, if you must. I will provide the means to send missives, and remand our other captive into your company, as a sign of good faith. I have no designs to usurp Fox's seat; only promise me my rightful place, and I will be your faithful ally."

Remarin steeled his features to calm. She'd taken him for someone and something he was not, someone who deserved apartments like these, even in captivity. In three months it was the first sign of a means to escape.

"Very well," he said, trying to sound as though he were relenting a long-held façade. "I can agree, but I grow tired of these surroundings. Our pact is sealed, if you permit me leave to wander the tower under guard."

She laughed as though he'd made a joke.

"Yes," she said, "and I will leave the chamber with you, arm in arm." Sarcasm drenched the words, and snuffed his easiest route to freedom. But there would be others, unless he misread the change in his circumstance.

Bavda took up her gloves, rising from her seat as she put them back in place, and spoke again. "It is well to have you among us in the open again, Master Fei."

With that she offered him a deep bow before she and Song withdrew from the room, leaving him still smarting, from the upheaval of her words and from whatever *magi* trick she'd used to strike him.

What had he just agreed to? Who the bloody fuck did they think he was?

———

He gnawed on the questions as the day passed, replaying the Natarii woman's visit in his mind. In the moment, the nature of his captivity had changed, but after, it was back to empty hours in his apartments alone with a scroll rack and a view of windowless stone. There would be no answers in Li Sun's *Treatments of War*, nor in Kotamaru's *Siege Weapons and Tactics*, but they served as a distraction when he could empty his thoughts enough to read. The Lady Bavda had spoken as though he were a *magi*, privy to the endless plotting of the Great and Noble Houses; that much, he could be certain of, if the force behind the woman's strike wasn't confirmation enough. He was a captive of the *magi*, and they thought him not only a piece but a player in their game. He'd been called raider, warrior, chieftain, prisoner, tutor, master-at-arms; never Master in their sense of the word. Never *magi*.

He should have seen it coming. He'd been a bloody fool to involve himself in Lord Tigai's work. He'd known what the boy was from the first moment Tigai had blinked back to the kitchens when Remarin caught him plundering the crust of a stolen pie. Gold had blinded him. The thought of a raider who could move himself and his men behind the most stalwart walls and defenses, unseen, unheard, unknown, had been too tempting. There was never a chance Tigai's story ended in any way other than bloodletting and death at the *magi*'s hands. He'd thought Tigai would get him his keep, his company, and his retirement. It had seemed a grand adventure, little as he might have admitted it in the moment. Now he was finished, unless he could find the means to play the one card they'd given him. A gamble. Tigai had been the gambler; Remarin was a warrior, a sergeant at best. But life hadn't killed him yet.

"Midday, Master Fei." Song's voice accompanied a rap on his door. The usual ritual, but somehow different. Some factor of the status the Natarii waif had given him.

"Enter," he said, as though his permission were required. And perhaps now it was.

The door swung wide, and Song bowed twice, placing the broad silver tray he carried atop the entry table.

"This one has the good fortune of presenting your acolyte," Song said. "The Lady Khon regrets that certain liberties were required by the Dragons before she was remanded into our keeping, but hopes you will not hold such matters against Heron, in light of your newfound understanding."

Remarin tried to mask his confusion as to the meaning of Song's words, and felt his efforts melt as Dao's wife was ushered into the room. She wore patterned blue and white silk cut in the fashion she'd always favored at the Yanjin Palace, but her hair was matted, her face absent cosmetics, her cheeks streaked with tears.

"Lady Mei," he said.

Song gave him a knowing smile. "This servant will leave you to your reacquaintance, and return in due course to escort her to her own chambers."

With that the servant was gone, the door locked and latched, and they were alone.

"Lady Mei," he said again. "I never expected to see you here. Are you...?"

She met his eyes with a mix of fear and hurt, an alien look for a girl he'd always believed the proudest, the fiercest between her and Dao and Tigai.

He took a step toward her, and she took five to close the gap, burying her head in his chest.

Her body shook, and she trembled as he held her.

"It's all right," he said, not knowing what else to say. "Whatever they've done, we can set it right."

A bitter laugh escaped her throat, and she pulled away. "No, master-at-arms. There is no means to set this right."

She tugged the long sleeve covering her right arm away. Where the right hand should have been, there was scarred ruin, severed just below the wrist, the flesh sewn together in misshapen knots belying any semblance of health.

"We have to find a way to escape," she said. The fear and hurt still lingered in her eyes, but now there was passion, too. "We have to escape and run as far from these monsters as it is possible to go."

INTERLUDE

CORENNA

Approaching Jati'Ras'Tyat
Jatasi Land

Twin kicks to the walls of her stomach drew an unconscious hand, rubbing her belly as she walked. The sensation had grown familiar as the seasons changed. A child moved inside her. Everything from flaring moods to swollen nipples and sleepless nights could be laid there. Love stirred along with it. A dull ache, accompanying the pain of loss, the reminder of all she'd done to bring herself here. And still she hesitated.

"*Kirighra* will come," Ka'Yiran said. "Make yourselves ready. He will not allow us to enter the sacred place; nor will he strike at us when we are together."

One of the Uktani women turned to her as Ka'Yiran began the work of splitting the company into teams of twos.

"Have you faced *kirighra* before, honored sister?" Irinna asked. A girl, only a few years younger than Corenna herself. Irinna eyed nearby great beasts as she said it, the *ipek'a* and *munat'ap* wandering freely among their warriors, as though they were no more than domesticated dogs and horses. A dire wolf—*munat'ap*—stalked ten paces from where they stood, eyeing her and Irinna together, and nothing Ka'Yiran said could convince her it wasn't weighing them both for suitability as prey.

"Yes," she said in reply. "A new beast, but I faced one in the company of a guardian, during my travels."

"So it is best, to hunt them in twos?"

"It is. *Kirighra* will strike the stronger of the pair; it will be up to the weaker to finish the beast before it can kill."

Irinna's face paled. A heartening word might have softened the task, but she hadn't come to the Uktani to befriend them. As hard as her days had been among the Sinari, the weeks she'd spent here were harder, smothering her emotions and waiting for Ka'Inari's visions to manifest themselves.

"Irinna," Ka'Yiran said, finally approaching where they stood. "You will travel with Arak'Utai. Corenna, our Ranasi sister, you will come with me."

The words froze and echoed in her mind, and she fought down the nerves that came with them. Now, finally, she and Ka'Yiran would be alone.

Irinna spared her another glance, perhaps hoping for the missing words of encouragement, before the Uktani girl went to find the *Arak* to whom she'd been assigned. Ka'Yiran watched the younger girl go before he turned to Corenna, snapping two fingers to signal her and the *munat'ap* both to follow. She felt her growing belly in every step now. It took an effort to keep pace with the shaman, who made no allowance for her frailties—just as well, since she would ask for none. The *munat'ap* strode beside her, hovering a step too close as they moved deeper into the wood.

"You are certain, honored sister, that the women have blessed your coming with us today?" Ka'Yiran asked.

"Yes," she said, fighting to keep her composure. Close, now. So close. "I am fit to travel, and to fight. These are not times for mothers. If I lose my child, I lose it. The strength of our tribes is too important to do otherwise."

It hurt her to say it, a feigned callousness she feared could all too easily become real. But Ka'Yiran only nodded along.

"That is the last Ranasi in your belly," Ka'Yiran said. "Your words do your tribe great honor, but it would be an ill thing, for the Ranasi to pass altogether from this world."

Memories of burnt bodies, broken tents stirred deep within. A simmering anger she had to force to quell. "I will fight," she said, and left it at that.

They walked together, a trio of man, woman, and beast, deeper into the wood that marked the location of Jati'Ras'Tyat. She could hear the other pairs assigned to draw out *kirighra*, but more dimly with each step. Two dozen hopefuls, more than she had ever seen in any tribe. She could almost hear Ka'Inari's voice, sounding in her memory, and fought it down. Who could say what the Uktani shaman's gift could see?

"Your father," Ka'Yiran said abruptly after they'd walked no more than five hundred paces into the wood. "He saw the coming of these troubling times, didn't he?"

"My father's gift was strong," she said.

"This is why you wield so many of the spirits' gifts," Ka'Yiran said.

She said nothing, tracking close as the *munat'ap* paced beside them.

"I have watched you, Corenna of the Ranasi," Ka'Yiran said. "You came to us in need, but not weak. I have watched for sign of a man to claim the child growing in your belly, and seen nothing."

What was this? If he'd seen some hint of her purpose here, he wouldn't waste breath on words. "The father is gone," she said.

"Dead?"

She feigned calm over top of hate, but made no reply. Better not to think on Arak'Jur, for fear of drawing the shaman's visions too close to the truth.

"I have seen promptings from the spirits," Ka'Yiran continued. "A guardian's child grows in your belly."

Fear spiked through her, and she prepared the gift of ice.

"The father is Arak'Doren, isn't it?" Ka'Yiran said. "Before he was slain by Sinari treachery."

"We are meant to be hunting *kirighra*," she said, turning away to hide her relief. "Why do you ask me these things?"

"As I said, I have watched you," Ka'Yiran said. "If the father is Arak'Doren, I am sure he would give his blessing for your child to be raised by a fellow guardian. I was Arak'Yiran before I became *Ka*."

She turned back, finding an earnest look from Ka'Yiran as he'd stopped to face her. She'd come here as an assassin, keeping her distance until the time was right, as Ka'Inari had instructed her at the Sinari sacred place. She'd been prepared to give everything—her life, her unborn child—to stop the Uktani, to kill the shaman who hunted Arak'Jur. And Ka'Yiran had asked her to consider taking him as her man.

"I hope you will consider it," Ka'Yiran said. "We have placed great trust in you already, but it could be more."

"I've told you what I want," she said. "Revenge for my people. Perhaps when that is done . . ."

He nodded, a solemn gesture she hoped would put an end to this line of talk. "This is good," Ka'Yiran said. "It is just, and right. But the spirits see more for you, Corenna, and for me. Vengeance is a hollow salve; your father will have taught you as much. Even now they whisper to me of things-to-come. I see you, alone, with a child at your breast, in need of a protector in spite of all your strength."

Her heart pounded, suddenly all the more aware of the *munat'ap* and the forest around them. If he called on visions of her, it could draw all too near her secrets.

"I see you leading an alliance of many tribes," Ka'Yiran was saying. His voice had grown distant, too distant, as her father's had done when he received a prompting from the spirits. "I see a great battle, at the walls of a fair-skin city. I see a reunion, between you and . . ."

He stopped, pausing to look at her with disbelief.

". . . the Sinari guardian," Ka'Yiran said. "Arak'Jur. You come to us, claiming sanctuary, and yet the spirits see the two of you, together."

She conjured ice before he could react, spears to impale the *munat'ap* through the jaw, sending icicles through the roof of its mouth and into its brain.

A shield of earth sprang up around Ka'Yiran before she could turn on him, exploding outward with force enough to throw her to the ground. Raised voices sounded through the trees, shouts warning of the sounds of fighting that would draw the Uktani hopefuls toward them. Ka'Yiran had turned toward her with fury in his eyes, the truth of her betrayal made plain by her actions, and by the spirits' visions. She saw it as gray slate encasing his eyes, the gift of stone preparing to conjure earth to strike.

Ice formed again, flung from her fingertips in a desperate salvo. He had to die. Ka'Inari's vision had been clear, delivered to her where Arak'Jur hadn't been allowed to hear: feign her way among their enemies, kill the Uktani shaman, and their pursuit would end. The Sinari people and their alliance would be left at peace. Ka'Inari had promised it, seen the truth of it from the vision spirits at Ka'Ana'Tyat. The very spirits who had given her assurance it had been Llanara, and not Arak'Jur or any of the other survivors, who had been behind her people's destruction. Her faith and hope for peace and goodness had overpowered guilt; they all came back to her now that the moment had arrived.

"Betrayer," Ka'Yiran said, a mix of shock and anger in his voice. "You throw your life away for nothing."

Her ice had shattered on his shield of earth, leaving splinters of cold melting in the grass, and she rose to her knees, flinging a last salvo of ice before she drew on the gift of stone herself, conjuring earth to collide and crack against Ka'Yiran's barriers. Yet he seemed to know her strikes before she did, shifting his shield to break her attacks before she made them.

Raised voices drew closer. She had to strike.

Inky tendrils from the Lhakani sacred place at the heart of the swamp rose from her hands, creeping around Ka'Yiran's stone. He stepped back, his earthen shield collapsing as a wind rose to scatter her attack. He did it with a snap gesture, as though he were impatient to see her strikes through to an inevitable end. Contempt showed on his face as he conjured wind to knock her back to the ground, dispersing another attempt to summon the shadowy tendrils before they materialized as more than wisps of smoke.

"A waste," Ka'Yiran said. "A waste of so much strength and beauty. I would have been better for you than—"

His face lit with understanding, and he spun in time to dodge *kirighra*'s mauling attack from behind.

The Great Panther had materialized from nothing, a cat made of pure shadow. It swiped down with its claws, raking the air where Ka'Yiran had stood an instant before. Her conscious mind knew she should feel terror, the same instinct she'd had when a *kirighra* had savaged Arak'Jur's shoulder and side. But she felt only relief.

Wind came to obey her call, the blessing of Hanat'Li'Tyat, the sacred place of the Ranasi tribe, and she formed a tempest into a cutting blade of air. Ka'Yiran had squared himself to face the *kirighra*'s attack, and she brought it into the shaman's side, ripping through his skin in a rain of red and gore.

The Uktani shaman screamed. She struck again, whipping lashes of air toward his head, and he fell silent.

We know you.

The voice came as a whisper, sounding inside her head. *Kirighra* had turned, leaving its now-dead prey and eyeing her instead.

Come to us.

Kirighra sprang toward her. Wind sheared through the beast, slicing wisps of shadow in a furious gale. For a moment the cat hung in the air, the forward momentum of his leap stalled by the upward force of her summoned storm. Then its body broke, a forward leg severed by cutting wind, its head twisting as its body collapsed into the dirt.

The world faded.

————

YOU KILLED HIM.

Her consciousness fell away into the void, the voice sounding all around her. It was as though she had entered a sacred place, though she had not moved from where she'd struck at Ka'Yiran and the *kirighra*, lying on the forest floor.

Great Spirit, she thought back. *How is it we are speaking? Did I enter Jati'Ras'Tyat unknowing?*

NO. THAT IS A PLACE OF STORMS. YOU SLEW A GREAT BEAST, AND SO NOW WE COMMUNE. THIS IS THE WAY OF THINGS, THE WAY OF THE GUARDIANS.

But I am a woman.

The shock of it coursed through her.

YES, the voice responded. BUT WE REMEMBER. THOSE WHO PREY ON THE SPIRIT-TOUCHED ARE WORTHY OF MORE.

Ka'Yiran. She'd killed him.

He's dead, she thought back to the void. *The Uktani shaman. Arak'Jur is safe.*

THIS NAME IS KNOWN TO US. ARAK'JUR. THE SINARI CHAMPION. YOU WISH FOR HIM TO BE MADE YOUR QUARRY?

Horror rose in whatever passed for her gut here in the void. *No*, she thought.

ALL ASCENDANTS MUST PROVE THEMSELVES. THIS IS OUR WAY: TO SEEK THE STRONGEST. *KIRIGHRA* HUNTS THOSE WITHOUT PEER, AND SO SHALL YOU.

No, she thought again. *I want no part of the madness that has driven our people to war.*

YOU ARE ON THE PATH TO ASCENSION. WE GRANT YOU OUR GIFT, TO SEAL THE WAY. IT IS NOT YOUR PLACE TO DENY US.

Light flashed, and visions came, of stalking her kill, melding into shadows, hunting men and beasts alike.

She let it pass through her, accompanied by a growing certainty that was no emotion of hers. Violence, somewhere to the south. A nagging drive compelling her to seek her prey, stronger than any sense of love or duty. To hunt and kill, as *kirighra* did, the strongest of the champions among men.

INTERLUDE

AD-SHI

Wilderness
Lhakani Land

Life stirred around her, in the thrumming of cicadas, the chirping of newly hatched songbirds, the parents caring for their young. Even the grasses grew longer in the hot months, when the winds blew air laden with moisture from the east. It was sweeter, knowing the impermanence was finally more than an illusion. She had seen hundreds of summers, lived for the passing of thousands, and this would be her last.

Thinking it was a release unto itself. She was dying, finally surrendered to the cycle that consumed all life. There was fear in her; she recognized it as an old companion, long forgotten in all the years of her Godhood. But without the fear of death, the brush of the grass against her legs, the smell of the pollen in the air, the whirring of insects and birds and smaller creatures all amounted to no more than the dust that made them. There was beauty in being a part of the decay.

"You missed our last meeting."

Paendurion's agent approached, climbing the small rise upon which she'd sat to wait for him. Ad-Shi opened her eyes to see him, the sort of pale-skinned, blue-eyed man Paendurion had always favored for his vessels. This one wore the military uniform of one of the Imperial powers of this cycle, his yellow-trimmed jacket an absurdity in the southern heat. The golden eyes marked him for what he was, light spilling out as though miniature suns had been implanted in his sockets.

"Apologies, honored brother," she replied. "I was in recovery."

The gesture with her right arm toward where her left should have been soured Paendurion's vessel's expression. Ad-Shi's arm had been torn off, a clean slice only *mareh'et*'s claws could manage, leaving a severed stump where her shoulder ended. It would regrow in a few weeks' time, but not before the rest of her body had healed its lesser wounds in preparation.

"How close did you get to dying this time?" Paendurion asked. His voice was laden with bitterness he made no attempt to hide. Once, the rebuke nestled there would have stung; now, she felt it as no more than the summer breeze.

"Close," she said. "Closer than I had in many, many years."

"Ad-Shi…"

"What news from your would-be ascendant?" The interruption was rude; they had long ago learned to respect one another in conversation, as the least part of learning to live eternity together. But there were limits to her appetite for scolding, when so few moments remained to her before the end.

Paendurion's vessel remained standing, towering over her as she sat among the grass.

"My enemy waits," Paendurion said, "dithering with politics. Axerian's plan to pin the Sarresant forces in the north has succeeded, and I have consolidated enough reserve to snare them here in Vordu lands for the remainder of the time before ascension. If all continues as it has, I will again champion Order when the moment arrives."

"A fine turn, for you," Ad-Shi said.

"And with you? Your injuries were at least fruitful, I hope?"

"It remains to be seen."

No point raising his hopes before she was sure. But he seemed to detect the note of confidence she knew would be there. The Sinari guardian had slain another spirit-touched man or woman, and drawn on more than enough gifts to secure ascension. All that remained was to nurse him back to health and find in him the drive to defend the world. An easier thing, if he were a younger man. But not beyond her ability.

"You'll never find someone to match you," Paendurion said. She might have taken it for praise, had that been Paendurion's way.

"Nonetheless, it is decided."

Suddenly his anger turned hot. "What am I to do with that? With your decision? You've chosen to abdicate your duty. You doom me to face the enemy with a half-mad fool and a half-trained pup at my side."

"There is some time, to train him."

"How much time? A season at best? Two? You've doomed the world with your cowardice. You must think beyond your emotions. See reason. See your folly for what it is, and return to me, or you are no better than all the false ascendants we have slain together, or all the failures who came before us. Do this, or you are a coward, and a fool."

His words rolled off her like morning dew from a falcon's wings.

"This is the last time we will speak," she said. "Do not send another of your vessels into Vordu lands, and do not expect me to tell you where to find me."

"Wretch," he said. "Craven. After all this time, you run when I need you most. Do you imagine the shadow will ignore you, or your people? The Veil is *dead*, Ad-Shi. If we lose now, there may not be another cycle."

"You were a true brother to me, Paendurion. Do not soil it in our last moments together."

"You can go to your spirits. Beg forgiveness; plead their understanding. They will let you re-ascend. It's always the apex predator with your kind, is it not? None can stand against you. Act, and see reason for once in your bloody life."

He glared at her, as though he waited for her to speak, and she met him with silence.

"You truly were the weakest of us," he said. "I always knew you would break, though I'd hoped you were stronger than this."

Valak'ar gave his blessing, and she moved with the wraith-snake's speed before she'd had time to process the thought.

Paendurion's vessel gagged, *valak'ar*'s venom spreading in black spiderwebs from where she struck him in the stomach, reaching his face above the rise of his collar. His skin bruised and bubbled into open sores, and he fell forward on his knees before he collapsed into the grass.

Quiet returned, in the birds' songs and the low hum of insects on the wind.

She closed her eyes, letting the rage coursing through her dissipate. All of this was hers: the sunlight and the warmth on her skin, the smells of the grass and trees and swampland. She'd fought to make it so, to change the world from ash and poison to lush beauty. But she'd never been fool enough to believe it would last forever. She'd paid every price that had been asked, until now. If it made her weak, so be it. But even the mightiest fire guttered out in time. Even the strongest beasts had to lie down and die.

She left Paendurion's vessel there to seep into the ground, and rose to return to where she'd left Arak'Jur's body. He would wake soon, after his limbs had regrown and repaired themselves. And she had not truly abdicated her duty. Always, with the Vordu there was a master and apprentice. Life was finished with her, but she could pass on what she knew before the end.

PART 3: AUTUMN

DAMYU | EARTH SPIRITS

38

SARINE

A Coastal Bluff
Chappanak Land

She sat atop a small rock, just high enough to elevate her legs to serve as an easel. Pressed white birchbark sufficed for paper, and if her coal hadn't been refined into a pencil to avoid blacking her hands while she worked, it was similar enough to what she was used to. She drew the coastline, the evergreen trees that grew so thick it seemed they might encroach into the ocean itself, given enough time. She drew her companions, gathered together on the shore. She drew the waves, crashing toward the base of the cliff in steady rhythm. And she drew the Divide.

She'd never have believed it was real without seeing it. Even Axerian's accountings—of a black, billowing cloud stretching from the sea to the sky, swallowing the ocean's currents not more than a quarter league from the shore—had defied her imagination. She'd pictured a second Great Barrier, but next to the Divide the barrier was flimsy, a thing made by men and women, like comparing the majesty of a cathedral tower to a mountain. The Great Barrier was a wall, with a clear base and a fixed height and width. The Divide was the land itself. Blackness, as far toward the horizon as she could see. A place where maps would end, and the place she meant to take them, once Axerian finished bartering for a boat.

Ka'Inari's footsteps announced his coming before she'd finished the sketch. She glanced up to greet him, but he seemed in no rush to disturb her work, and so she returned to her bark to finish adding details to the coastline while he sat atop a rock a few paces away, staring out at the sea. She made quick strokes to add definition to the pine and fir trees' needles, and broad, slow ones where the waves broke into the base of the bluff. She'd been able to barter for only a single sheet of white bark—evidently it was precious, used to line the interior of boats and longhouses—and with only one sheet, she meant to capture the coastline in as much depth as her lack of practice would allow.

"May I see?" Ka'Inari asked when she paused to consider whether she was done. Bless him for waiting; he'd kept still, seated and looking over the ocean while she'd worked. She gestured him over, giving him a full view of what she'd done so far. It was a scene more inspired by her view than a literal translation of the view itself, sketched from a perspective slightly above where they sat, as though a bird perched atop a tree behind them, looking down to see them standing at the edge of a cliff, overlooking the shadows of the Divide.

Ka'Inari stayed quiet too long, until she worried he was searching for the right words to tell her he hated it. She almost moved to continue working, to apologize for showing it in a half-finished state, when he spoke.

"There is truth here," he said. "You have a great gift. Perhaps you will make a drawing for me, someday."

"I'd let you keep this one," she said, feeling a rush of relief, "if I had any sediment to fix the drawing. As it is, it will smear within a day or two. But I hadn't had a chance to practice in weeks." She lifted the birch-paper gingerly, offering it to him as she rose to stand. He took it with reverence, and she stowed her lump of coal in a belt-pouch before clapping her hands to remove a hundredth part of the black dust caked across her palms and fingers.

"Thank you," Ka'Inari said. "I will treasure it, for as long as it lasts."

She felt a touch of heat in her cheeks, as she always did when anyone complimented her work. "What word from Axerian?" she asked. "Has he finished his negotiation?"

"He says he has, though the Chappanak shaman did not look pleased to me, when I left. Axerian sent me to find you. He says it will be settled in time for us to leave today."

"Good," she said, and felt a flare of emotion in her chest. Too strong to be hers; she fought it down as she always did when the Veil showed herself, and kept outward sign of it from showing in her face. "Let's not keep him waiting."

————————

The Chappanak had greeted them with nocked arrows when they'd first arrived. Now they stood arrayed like diplomats in the Rasailles palace gardens. Two rows of men in ornately stitched tunics and necklaces of clamshells and what looked like animal teeth stood on either side of the shaman in the center, with a single woman observing, standing halfway between the men and the heart of their village. A hundred more pairs of eyes not officially part of the shaman's retinue watched her and Ka'Inari approach, hovering near boxlike wood houses not altogether unlike those in the residential blocks of the Maw. Axerian stood among them at the center, and Acherre, who held the reins of their horses twenty paces back.

Quiet hung in the air as she came forward, the men in the shaman's retinue watching her with looks that made her aware of every step.

"We have an agreement," Axerian said when she approached. He was dressed in his usual black leathers, though he must have found time to clean them before the day's business. "The shaman has agreed to exchange our horses for one of their war canoes, though he wishes to assure us we are fools, and he laments the loss of their boat when we sail to our certain deaths."

The tribesmen nodded, eyeing the shaman at their center without looking toward her or Axerian. The shaman—who'd refused to give his name, so far as she was aware—was the only one to meet her eyes, though he stayed silent, watching her with a wrinkled glare that reminded her of her uncle when she'd come home well into the small hours of the morning.

"He also insists on one further condition, before we make the exchange," Axerian said. "You must speak privately with one of their women. So far as I understand it, the deal is final only when the women approve."

"That's it?" she asked. The men seemed uncomfortable as soon as she spoke, taking shuffling steps away from her, still avoiding her eyes.

"That's it. I managed to convince them of the value domesticated horses might bring—they'd heard of the beasts, but thus far no herds have made it this far west." He said it with a glimmer in his eye, as though there was some joke nested there, though she didn't understand where it would be. "As to the rest, they value their boats as highly as you might value a chapel or a ship-of-the-line. So imagine my having negotiated the sale of Paendurion's Basilica, or the flagship of the New Sarresant Navy, if you want a sense of what I've managed here."

"Fine work, then," she said, and Axerian gave an almost-mocking bow. She ignored it, looking through the assembled tribesmen to where the lone woman stood, watching from higher ground. She had to assume the woman was there to meet the terms of their deal, strange as it was. "May I?" She directed the question toward the shaman and Axerian both, gesturing to make clear her intent to pass through their line.

The shaman looked offended, and broke eye contact with her at once.

"Tell her she may pass," the shaman said, delivering it to the rocks instead of her or Axerian.

Axerian maintained his grin. "By all means, my lady, you may pass."

Sarine trudged up the hill toward where the tribeswoman stood, unmoving. Clearly she'd managed to violate some taboo, though beyond a prohibition on Chappanak men speaking with women at all she couldn't fathom what it was. Perhaps it was only speaking to foreign women; to hear Axerian tell it, the coastal tribes here had never seen anyone from the Old World. But it wasn't as though she was all that different from Ka'Inari—certainly his ways were at least as divergent from the Chappanak as hers were from his. Then again, Axerian alone among their party had been welcomed to speak with their hosts, and she'd been sure *Green* had played no small part in that.

"Your man claims you speak our tongue," the Chappanak woman said when she reached her, blunt and clipped, with nothing in the way of introduction.

"After a fashion," Sarine said. She intended to stay deferential, but there was no reason to cower. "He and I possess a gift, a bond that allows us to—"

The woman hissed. "Keep your secrets, girl. Is your man using you here? Are you in distress, in need of rescuing from his keeping?"

"I'm not in his keeping, first of all. And second—no. Traversing the Divide was my idea, not his. Your shaman said we had to speak, in order to finalize our exchange."

"You are a fool, then."

She felt the stirrings of anger and fought it down by reflex. Whether hers or the Veil's, this was no time for emotion.

"Why?" she asked instead. "Why does it make me a fool?"

"This is a thing young men do," the Chappanak woman said. "When a lover scorns them, when an elder refuses to apprentice or teach too quickly. There is only death waiting for you there, foreign woman. Whatever gift you think you have, whatever magic has befouled your skin to turn it pink, there is no spirit that can traverse the shadows. To reach them is death. To touch them is death. All women know this, and any man who is not a fool knows it as well."

"I've watched the sea since my coming," she said. "You have tides and waves and currents, the same as there are in the East. Fish come and go, and birds; I've watched gulls fly into the shadows of the Divide, and emerge again from it."

"Are you a fish? A bird?" The woman paused for a moment, as though the question was more than rhetorical, then spoke again with disgust in her voice. "Think better of this foolishness. You are young; you should be thinking of suckling children on your teats, of lying down with pretty men, if they will have you. I will find you a place in my house, if needs be. Only—do not take one of our boats and sail into death."

"I don't mean to die," she said, and another surge of emotion came; this time she was certain it was the Veil's. "I mean to fight. There is evil there, across those shadows. I mean to find the way through."

"And just so, the man who leaps from the cliffside means to fly."

Quiet fell between them, and the Chappanak woman's face returned to stoic calm, touched with mild irritation.

"May we make our exchange, then?" she asked when the woman offered nothing further.

"For one more price," the woman said. "Your name."

"Sarine."

"Sarine," the woman repeated, making a thorough butchery of the syllables of the Sarresant tongue. "Sarine." She tried it again, no closer. "Sarine. I will remember you, when you are dead."

With that, the Chappanak woman turned and hiked up the hill toward the village, leaving her to retreat back down the hill.

"Come," the shaman said. "We will deliver you our part of the exchange."

Sarine fell in line as they walked toward the shore. The path traversed the cliffs to end at a rocky beach, where a row of boats lay with the bottoms facing up. Each canoe seemed to have been cut from a single massive tree; the evergreens and redwoods surrounding the Chappanak village made clear the potential for such scale, though the largest of their canoes must have weighed as much as a building, broad enough to seat forty and taller than any tree in sight of the shore. They stayed well clear of those, coming instead to a smaller craft perhaps five armspans in length, situated at the end of the line.

"You will require aid in launching the craft?" the shaman asked, and Axerian waved him off.

"No, honored friend," Axerian said. "Your part of the bargain is fulfilled. Go in peace, with the blessings of the *Ka* spirits to guide you to plenty."

The Chappanak eyed him with distrust, but backed away, the three men retreating as swiftly as they'd come back up the winding path toward the village, leaving Sarine, Axerian, Ka'Inari, and Acherre alone on the beach.

"What do you suppose they would do," Acherre asked, "if we tried for one of the bigger ones?"

Axerian laughed. "Rain arrows on us, I expect, or stones at least." He gestured above.

Faces were already visible, peering out over the cliffside. More than just the men who had gathered to make the exchange; there were dozens, perhaps a hundred or more lining the bluff, watching them.

Sarine glanced between the Chappanak and Ka'Inari. "They're a suspicious people, aren't they?"

"What did the woman speak to you about?" Acherre asked.

"Warnings of doom, I'm sure," Axerian said cheerfully. "Seeing as we are more than likely about to sail to our deaths."

"Why are you coming along, then?" Sarine said.

Axerian strode to the head of their boat, single-handedly gripping and turning it over on the beach, accompanied by a prompting of *Red* from Anati.

"Because," he said after the boat had lurched over, faceup, "I'm dying already. And you may well be right. There's hope here, if we can breach the Divide and suppress the Regnant's champions. Paendurion would call me a fool, but that's never stopped me before. In dire times, sometimes boldness is required of us all."

"None of you have to come with me," she said, turning to face Acherre and Ka'Inari while Axerian hopped inside their canoe, working to fix the wood pole in place at the center to hoist the cedar slats that made the sail.

"You're as mad as Reyne d'Agarre if you think I'd miss a chance to see what's on the other side of this Divide," Acherre said. "I've already seen half the world since leaving the city; the Nameless take me if I'd pass up a chance to see the rest."

Axerian snicked loudly at her invocation; it took a moment to remember he *was* the Nameless, or at least the basis of the myth.

Ka'Inari faced her with a serious expression on his face. "We will survive the crossing," he said. "The spirits of things-to-come have seen it. And beyond it lies a greater shadow. I will be at your side to face it."

Me too, Anati thought to her, materializing already coiled around the mast as Axerian hoisted the sail. *I swore to protect you. My father wouldn't like it if I left you behind.*

"A finely built craft," Axerian said. "Sturdy and swift to launch, by the standards of any age." He stepped outside the canoe, gripping the side and bracing himself against it. "Assuming we're all coming along, now's the time to go."

Acherre took a place opposite Axerian, and Ka'Inari did the same, suddenly enveloped by an aura of a great bear as he hefted the canoe's mass. *Red* flowed through Sarine from Anati, and she helped roll the boat down the smoothly polished stones toward the shore.

The water stung like ice as it lapped against her calves, then her knees and thighs before they jumped inside together. Axerian distributed oars to row while the wind was calmed by the cliffside, and soon their tiny craft was pushing through the waves, slicing a path atop the water toward the roiling black fog stretching out on both sides of the horizon.

39

TIGAI

A Private Tent
Isaru Mattai's Warcamp

An arm stirred him from sleep, draped across his chest when he'd drifted too close to waking. His sleeping pallet lay opposite the fire burning in the center of his circular tent, and the whole of it smelled of sweat and sex. He reached a hand in reciprocation around his partner. He couldn't remember her name, but she'd smiled at him sweetly over milk-mead the night before. Now she lay entangled in his limbs, the Natarii clan tattoos running the length of her temples and cheekbones giving her an exotic look in the dim firelight. He studied her for a moment, gently gathering her straw-colored hair and pulling it back to reveal her face. Almost Perasi or Hagali features, though her skin was pale where it would have been dark as coffee beans if she'd hailed from either of the southern provinces. The Natarii were from the far north, farther even than the Ujibari clans, and this one had made love with the wild abandon of the beasts from which he knew their clans took their names.

After a moment studying her, and another spent caressing her lower back in hopes she might wake with an appetite for more, he eased himself free of her grasp and knelt closer to the fire. His teapot still had water from where he'd filled it with snow the night before, and he hung it over the fire as he rummaged for leaves to both fill his cup and scent the air.

The warcamp's tents were built in the Ujibari style, circular yurts with raised centers of their roofs to allow smoke to vent, but the space was still confined, and scents tended to linger, bad and good, unless replaced by something fresher.

His tent flap lifted before his tea was done, blasting cold wind across his skin, enough to wake his Natarii lover and almost to douse the fire, if Tigai hadn't been hovered over it with his cooking.

"Mmm," the Natarii girl said, at the same moment Mei pushed through the layers of hide, spattering snow across his entryway.

"You could have given a signal," Tigai said. Wind spirits but it was bloody cold outside; the sting of ice hung in the air even with the thick hide flaps closed behind her.

Mei paused, looking between him and the girl rousing herself in his furs. "I wouldn't have been offended, if I'd come in while you were…" She gestured with her head, letting the innuendo finish her sentence.

"I'd have invited you to join us," Tigai said, keeping any sign of wit from his voice. "Only, it's bloody cold out there. Your delicate parts would likely be frozen shut."

Mei gave him a disappointed look. "Really?"

"Who's this?"

The Natarii girl had risen, half-seated and half-awake, and blessedly less than half-covered by his sleeping furs, in spite of the cold.

"I take it her parts were in working order," Mei said.

"Ignore her, ah…my dear," Tigai said. "This is my sister by marriage. Harmless as a garden snake, however much she looks the part."

"Oh but you must introduce us," Mei said.

Tigai suppressed a scowl, and the Natarii girl pulled up a blanket to cover her chest.

"I am Yuli," the girl said, sparing him the ignominy of having forgotten her name. "Twin Fangs Clan Hoskar."

Mei lowered herself without invitation, folding her legs into a seated pose beside his fire. "Forgive me, Yuli Twin Fangs Clan Hoskar," Mei said, "but I am ignorant of how talents are reckoned among your people. Which Great and Noble House had claim on you, before you came here?"

"I was sworn to no Jun house," the girl said. She had a thicker accent than Tigai remembered from the night before, slow and drawling. "My clan pledged me to Lord Isaru at the turning of the season, and so I came here, for training."

"Then you'll be as delighted as Lord Tigai with my news," Mei said.

"What news?" Tigai asked.

"He's back. The Divide has opened again. By midmorning Isaru will have returned, and Dao along with him."

She said it as though she'd proclaimed the Yanjin House debts settled with the Shinsuke Bankers, and he knew he should have received it with at least a spark of unfeigned delight. Yet he'd found it hard to rise to more than drink and sex since coming here, to this camp as good as chiseled from ice. They'd made the passage from Kregiaw and been waiting here since, with no sign of Mei's new supposed liege, or of his brother. Perhaps it was only the anxiety of waiting, and all would be well once the wait was done. He'd have his answers as to what was going on here, and begin the search for Remarin in earnest.

"Good news," he said finally, and Mei echoed it back with vigor.

"Yes, it is good news. Now dress yourself and let's go to greet him. Lord Isaru will head for the common hall as soon as he's in. I mean for us to be first to receive him."

The sun was still sleeping by the time he and Yuli were dressed, and they emerged into a fresh sheet of frost encrusting the camp, the tents and ropes all draped with miniature icicles that would be broken up as more men and women woke to begin the day. Mei led the way in snowshoes lashed to her boots, wide wicker nets that dispersed her weight across the permanent layer of knee-high snow. He and Yuli wore the same; standard issue at the camp, though, blessedly, new layers of snow had been rare since his coming. The one storm he'd survived had been a night of blackness and howling gales, and a morning of digging out pathways and resituating tents atop the ice. Wind spirits knew what awaited them when the seasons grew colder, though he meant to be gone long before then.

The common hall was no larger than four yurts jammed together, but devoid of sleeping furs the space seemed wider, enough to accommodate the revelers that gathered there to drink and begin the process of pairing off for the night. It seemed wrong to be there before nightfall, but Mei stopped at the entrance, kicked the snow from her shoes, and removed them before stepping inside. Tigai let Yuli go next, intending to follow behind. First he paused, looking west to the horizon, where Isaru Mattai and his brother would be coming through the hell that marked the separation of this warcamp and the rest of the world. Amazing how the terrifying could become commonplace, sleeping in its shadow.

Mei already had a pot of cider simmering by the time he'd removed his shoes and stepped inside the common hall. She'd stayed bundled in her coat, and well enough for it, given they were alone apart from one of Isaru's lieutenants. Absent a crowd, the tent lacked its usual heat, and even the two fires being tended near its center were far from adequate to warm the space.

"How long?" he asked when he came to sit next to Mei and Yuli by the larger of the two fires.

"Four hours since the Divide opened," Mei replied. "They're past due, though if Isaru has new recruits, who can say how long he will take, to ensure they make it through."

"Four hours?" he repeated. "And you were the first to see it? Have you slept at all?"

"I miss my husband," she said. "Not all of us have the pleasure of your diversions."

A Jun girl might have blushed at the aspersion; Yuli only looked to him with a subtle smile, a slight crack in an otherwise stoic exterior. But it was an odd thing for Mei to say. He was sure no few of the better-looking Yanjin serving men could attest to Mei's need for diversions, as she put it, and to Dao's, too, for that matter. An open secret on their estate, but not often touched on directly, especially in the company of outsiders.

"It will be good to have him back," Tigai said cautiously.

"It will," Mei said. "Dao has become essential to Isaru's plans. He'll secure a place for you, before the campaign begins in earnest."

Tigai looked askance at Yuli, and at the heavyset lieutenant tending the other fire on the opposite side of the tent, before leaning in close.

"Mei, I'm not here for your war. I want to find where Remarin is being held and find a way to get him back. Whatever else Dao has us committed to, it's well and good for him, but it's no part of why I followed you here."

"It isn't *my* war, Yanjin Tigai," she said. "Any more than it's yours or your Natarii friend's. Do you think I've stayed here because I yearn for bloodshed and violence? The *magi* backing the Emperor have their fingers in the dealings of every house in the hundred cities, or do you believe it was an accident for the Shinsuke Bank to have amassed such leverage over your father? They meant to conscript Dao's company to pay off the debts. Opposing them is the only way we remain free to control our destinies, instead of being dragged into the wrong side of their war."

"War with *whom*?" Tigai said. "Yes, there is corruption throughout the Empire—who would believe otherwise? But I've seen nothing that would suggest—"

"Neither had we!" Mei said. "Until Isaru showed us the proof. They've been manipulating the accounts of any house not stolidly in support of the Great and Noble Houses. Ours were only one of many. The *magi* mean to seize power, and purge any faction they suspect of disloyalty. The why of it doesn't matter, only the when. And we are past the time of needing to swear our resources to Isaru Mattai's cause. We can't fight *magi* without *magi* of our own."

"It's true," Yuli said in a quiet voice, a stark contrast to Mei's heat. "The *magi* came to us, threatening our homes, demanding we relinquish our children. When Isaru Mattai came, my father offered me up to him instead."

"Ask around the camp," Mei continued. "You will hear half a hundred stories, the same as hers."

"It isn't my fight," Tigai said. "Not when Remarin is still being held."

"Then fight for Remarin, if Dao can't convince you to see reason. The Yanjin have to come forward against the Great and Noble Houses. Doing it to rescue our master-at-arms from our enemies' keeping is as good a reason as any."

A thud sounded outside the tent, forestalling his reply and bringing Mei to her feet.

A figure emerged through the entrance flaps, one he recognized if only from a distance. A man dressed in white, head to toe. Last Tigai had seen him, his left hand had been uncovered, a desiccated ruin surrounded by a purple glow. Now the hand was covered by a glove, but it wasn't so easy to forget the man had choked him, and would have killed him if not for the starfield and the strands.

Mei ran to the man in white, throwing arms around his neck and stopping just shy of kissing him. Tigai almost recoiled, seeing it. If mentioning her and Dao's diversions was taboo, he'd never known Mei to show any affection at all where others could see. Yet she embraced this man without a care for him, Yuli, or the guards.

Isaru Mattai's laugh was soft, but deep, a resonant voice that filled the space without trying. He seemed to heft Mei off the ground, though it was more likely her springing up to wrap him in her embrace, before he set her back down, looking past her, surveying the rest of the tent.

"You're back," Mei said. "And whole, from the look of you."

"Whole in the ways that matter," Isaru said.

The lieutenant who had tended the fire delivered a bow met by a nod of acknowledgment, then Isaru turned his attention to Tigai and Yuli.

"Yuli Twin Fangs Clan Hoskar," Isaru said, this time offering a deeper nod, almost a bow. "I hope the camp has treated you with all the honor your father's daughter deserves."

"The new moon's blessing on you, son of Dasui Clanless," Yuli said.

"And you," Isaru said, turning to Tigai. "Our latest prize."

"Where is my brother?" Tigai asked.

"Regrettably, Lord Dao has been delayed in his return," Isaru said. "The Yanjin retainers were needed in the field; your brother insisted I return with his deepest regrets. But he wouldn't leave his men in command of any of our lieutenants."

Mei's look soured for a fraction before recovering. "In the field?" she asked. "Then...?"

"Yes," Isaru said. "War has begun in earnest. We lay siege to the cities of Buzhou, Sidai, and Kye-Min."

"I'll rally the camp," Mei said. "You need to rest. You shouldn't have come back; they will need you. We're three weeks from Buzhou, at the fastest we can march. If the Great and Noble Houses respond, we'll be too slow by a week or more."

"You forget," Isaru said. "We have a true Dragon now."

Mei seemed to take a moment before she remembered Tigai.

"We can leave today then," Mei said.

"And be fighting by nightfall," Isaru finished for her. "Has he joined our cause?"

"He isn't sure what to make of you," Tigai replied for himself. "He doesn't appreciate being spoken of as if he isn't present. And the lack of his brother here has done nothing to help persuade him."

Isaru showed him a patient smile, the sort his father had used in the moments before a whipping. "Allow me to rectify that," Isaru said. "No man's destiny is certain, but for someone in your position, it's only logical to have doubts."

"I don't know you," Tigai said. "If I help you, it won't be because of anything you've said."

Mei glared at him. He turned to face her.

"Give me the tent alone with my sister-in-law, if you please."

Isaru looked him over for a moment before offering him a bow, and gesturing for Yuli and the lieutenant to join him in leaving the tent.

"You bloody fool," Mei said when they were alone. "Do you have any idea how serious this is? Dao and I have worked for months to secure our place with him, and you jeopardize our standing with rudeness."

"Mei," he said, "I meant what I said: Words aren't going to convince me. If I fight, it will be for my family."

"And what am I, if not for that? What is Dao?"

"Do you remember how my father died?"

She looked at him coldly, but suddenly curious. "Of course."

"Do you remember the pledge we made to each other?" he said. "You mixed the poison. I put it into his wine. Dao served him, and watched him choke, with Remarin at his side. All of us complicit, and any could betray the others. We're bound tighter than blood. Our fates in each others' hands."

"Your father had to die," Mei said. "Why relive this now?"

"I need to know you remember what we owe each other," Tigai said. "They have Remarin. Whatever we do, I have to believe you mean to get him back. The rest doesn't matter."

"I haven't forgotten," Mei said. "And I do. I promise."

He did his best to look relieved. "Then that's enough for me. Tell your Lord Isaru or whatever he calls himself that he has my assistance."

She stepped toward him, cupping his cheek in her hand. It was all he could do not to flinch away.

"Thank you," she said.

"Anything, for my family."

She lingered for another moment before showing him a wistful smile, turning and going in pursuit of her lord.

Agony tore through him as soon as she was gone. His and Dao's father had been many things, but poisoned to death wasn't one of them. The old Lord Yanjin had died in his sleep after a week's worth of coughing, shitting, and vomiting anything they'd tried to make him eat. Mei had held the bedpans, and commiserated with him and Dao when the old fuck had finally died. Whoever had just claimed to have poisoned him, it wasn't Mei. Which meant the real Mei was elsewhere, probably a prisoner, the same as Remarin. He was being used again, and no closer to finding any of them.

40

ERRIS

First Prelate's Study
The Exarch's Basilica, Gardens District

I would hope, High Commander, that you know you can always count on the priesthood."

First Prelate Casanne said it with a crisp, almost bored tone, the sort used by academy lecturers, no few of whom were priests themselves. Never mind the long hours spent arranging this meeting, and never mind the pitfalls still ahead of her if it went poorly.

"It's settled, then?" Erris said. "You can deliver a majority in the Assembly?"

Casanne smiled. Enough powder had been caked over the First Prelate's weathered skin to give the expression a foreign look on her face, as though two sets of wrinkles fought for control. The rest of her was immaculate, dressed in pure white, with the same motif carried through the décor of her study. White-painted wood for the furniture, white tapestries on the walls, with only a single stained-glass relief of the Exarch in blue-painted steel for color.

"I prefer you, I think, to Voren," Casanne said. "Your directness is refreshing. You know neither I nor any of my priests have been elected to the Assembly, yet still you assume I can deliver you support."

"Isn't that what we've been discussing?" she said. "I've already promised you control of the Thellan monasteries, when the conquest is done."

"So you have," Casanne said. "As is our rightful purview, as the true expression of the faith here in the New World."

She waited for Casanne to continue, yet the woman said nothing. The silence served to heat her blood—which was almost certainly the point. Tactics for a battlefield for which she was not prepared. This sort of meeting had been Voren's purview, before his exposure, and she could curse him twice over for leaving her to face it alone. Yet this was the battle in front of her, and she wasn't about to surrender for lack of knowledge of the ground.

"Look," Erris said. "I know you have some leverage with Assemblywoman Caille's former block. No fewer than three of them suggested I arrange this meeting. But if I've wasted my time, so be it."

"Stay seated, High Commander," Casanne said before Erris could rise.

Another moment passed, a silence too long for comfort, before Casanne spoke again.

"You have Voren imprisoned, in the Citadel," Casanne said. "Or rather, the creature that was our former colleague."

"Yes." She'd seen to it at once, and stopped short of executing him only for the shock of his betrayal. Though, so far, none of her interrogators had managed to pry loose his secrets.

"I wonder, perhaps, whether a kind word from the priesthood would—"

"Out of the question."

Casanne showed no reaction, only maintained the knowing smile the Prelate had worn from the start of the meeting, as though she intended to have her way, no matter the means it took to reach the end. But Voren knew too much about her—her plans, her tendencies, and, loath as she was to admit it, her weaknesses. She might lack knowledge of political strategy, but she knew enough to keep him to herself, at least until the mystery of who—and what—he was had been settled.

This time she stood.

"Thank you for your time, First Prelate," she said.

"Very well, then," Casanne said, rising along with her.

Erris gave a stiff bow. A failure, then, with no time for anything shy of success. She'd have to go back to Tuyard and plan to chase a different thread. Perhaps a meeting with—

"You'll have your votes, High Commander," Casanne said.

She almost missed a step.

"You'll have your votes," Casanne repeated, "but I will require your support for my gaining purview and control over the Thellan priesthood, and expanded influence in the Gand colonies. If it's directness you require, then I'll be direct: I intend to see the New Sarresant church in control of the spiritual life of every soul on this side of the ocean. So long as our goals are compatible, then we will be allies."

"Agreed," she said. It was as though she'd ordered a cavalry charge into a line that folded and broke before her soldiers fired their first shot. No, she understood this battlefield not at all. Damn Voren. Damn him into the Nameless's arms.

Casanne came around her desk, offering kisses on either cheek.

"A word, then, from one ally to another," Casanne said. "I respect your desire to keep Voren's secrets close, for now. But we have reports from the incident in the Assembly, reports of what he could do. A binding to change one's face would be a powerful tool indeed. See to it I don't find any agents using this binding to infiltrate my orders. And remember me, when the time comes to share knowledge of the gift. It would be unfortunate, if some accident were to befall him before we had time to extract his secrets."

It took all her discipline to keep from nodding, or revealing more than she intended. Enough that Casanne had promised support for her preemptive war against Thellan. The threat against Voren, and against her, if she understood Casanne's meaning correctly, would go unanswered, for now.

———

Jiri followed the turns toward the council hall almost without prompting, and Erris let her horse guide the way, relaxing in the saddle and keeping the reins slack as they rode.

De Tourvalle's 2nd Corps would be crossing the Ansfield river junctions today, and thank the Gods Casanne had agreed to lend her support with the Assembly. It meant an official declaration of war, with the supplies and taxes to fund it, and not a day too soon if they passed it within the hour. Another week and de Tourvalle would cross over into Thellan territory, and then the dance would begin in truth. She'd have

ridden south already if not for Voren, and the political mess his exposure
had left behind.

Essily waited for her at the entrance to the stableyard, taking Jiri and
leading her away without asking for more details than Erris ventured to
give.

Casanne's warning about Voren was no idle threat. A skin-shifter, or
whatever the fuck Voren was, carried real danger to her, to Casanne,
to anyone with pretentions of power anywhere in the colonies. What
was to stop such a creature from posing as her, delivering an order that
would lead her army to its doom? She'd scarcely formed an outline of the
problem in her mind when she opened the doors to her receiving room,
and found Foot-Captain Marquand already seated at one of the chairs
across from her desk.

He snapped to his feet when she entered, offering as clumsy a salute as
she'd ever seen.

"Foot-Captain?" she said. "A bit early for you, isn't it?"

"Sir, I made an appointment with Aide-Captain Essily."

"You made an appointment?" She almost swallowed the words.
"You?"

"Yes, sir."

She'd made it only halfway across the room, but came to a slow halt,
staring at him. "What's going on, Marquand?"

"Sir," he said with an air of starting over. "High Commander, sir. I'm
here to formally request a promotion. I've been foot-captain for two wars
now, and we're about to start a third. I've led troops in battle. I've helped
you plan this campaign. I've earned it."

She almost laughed out loud. "Gods damn it, Marquand, I was sure you
were about to tell me the city had broken out in riots, or there were signs
of plague, or food rot in our stocks. Instead . . . you want a promotion."

"Sir." He saluted again. "Yes, sir."

"At ease, Foot-Captain." It seemed wrong to have to tell him of all
people to relax, though he still hadn't moved by the time she took her
seat behind her desk. "I said *at ease*. Sit down."

He did, though not without averting his eyes enough to make her
think there was some prize hidden in the corners of her office. She might
have confused it for him wanting to be anywhere but here, save that he'd
been the one to arrange this audience to begin with.

"Tell me where this is coming from," she said. "Are you wanting to be in the field, with the army on the march?"

"No, sir," Marquand said. "I'm no coward, if you want to put me on the front, but I'll serve wherever I'm needed."

"You want to try your hand leading a company? A regiment?"

"No," he said. "Or, I mean, I would, if you thought it best."

This time she did laugh. Marquand's cheeks went red, as flushed as they'd ever been when he was drunk.

"Tell me what you want, Foot-Captain," she said.

"I want...rank," Marquand said. "You don't see how these assholes at high command are. When you're there they bow and salute and say your name like it's a bloody fucking prayer. They see my collar and think I'm a fucking aide, there to fetch your tea and groom your horse while you're sleeping. I planned half the action if there's a battle in the Vulmannes. I know the use of binders' companies better than any damned officer in this army, including you, sir, if you don't mind my saying it. I want the half pricks here to salute and bloody *listen* when I talk, instead of needing to route every idea in my head through you."

"You've been a captain for four years," she said, and he nodded. "Has a double bar on your coatsleeve made a lick of difference, when it came to men listening to you in a fight?"

"We're not in a fight here," he said. "We're in a bloody debate chamber."

"I know," she said. "And I've tried hard, with this army, to ensure that the best ideas rise." Marquand leaned forward as though he wanted to speak, but she cut him short. "I haven't always been successful. People are people, and for the most part, people are shit."

He snorted.

"But Marquand, I have to ask: When was the last time you had a drink?"

"Fifty-eight days ago," he said. "And not a drop since."

He said it with a glow, beaming as though he'd just led a charge that shattered an enemy line. The quick admission stunned her. She'd been too wrapped up in planning and politics to notice, but now, racking her memory of the past few months, he was right. He hadn't been drunk in weeks, or at least not where she could see. It was clear from his expression he thought that alone was enough. And perhaps it was.

"Typically rank comes with responsibility," she said, and saw him shifting in his seat, as though he'd prepared a sermon on the topic. She forestalled him with a glance. Her meeting with Casanne had provided an opening. An opening Marquand could fill, so long as he was sober. "We might one day see what you can do with a brigade, but for now, I think a colonel's pin will suffice. No attendant unit assignment—a strategic officer, posted here, to high command."

"So, an aide-colonel?" he asked.

"Call it just a colonel, no appellation for line of duty. Similar to the lords-general under the monarchy, and my field-marshals now. Can you be satisfied there?"

"Thank you," he mumbled, then again, louder. "Thank you, sir. Yes."

"It does come with a few added layers of duty," she said. "First, the higher you are in this army, the more you reflect its character, both outside our ranks and within. You say you haven't had a drink in two months—good. Make it two years, and we'll talk about a generalship. I make full allowance for social drinking among my officer corps, for those who can handle it. For you, a glass of wine is like to see you pissing yourself and sleeping in a horse trough, before you're through. So make it abstinence, or you can resign your commission and find work in a taproom somewhere. Am I understood?"

"Yes, sir," he said, and, by some miracle, looked as though he actually meant it.

She continued. "Next, while I expect and even encourage you to call me a fucking idiot in private—so long as I end up being wrong—I insist you keep a certain decorum in others' company. This army will be a place where ideas trump their source. I'll not have anyone holding back truth for fear of a browbeating, nor do I want my officers to be the loudest, most persuasive voices without concern for the underlying strength of their positions. You are a forceful man, Marquand; see to it you invest effort in learning to be humble when you're wrong, and learning to keep anger from inhibiting your ability to recognize it."

By now he'd sat up straighter in his seat, almost at attention by the time she finished. "Yes, sir," he said. "I won't disappoint you. And I'll hold you to your word, about that generalship."

"Good," she said. "Congratulations, Colonel. Your first order—and your first test of the decorum I just mentioned—will be one I should have seen to weeks ago."

"The Vulmannes campaign?" he said. "I've got a bloody good idea for the fords there, around—"

"No, Colonel. Voren."

"Voren," he repeated.

"That's right," she said. "He's been held at the Citadel since the Assembly. I'm ordering him moved here to high command, and placed in your personal custody."

"What? Are you bloody fucking mad? Why would you...?"

She raised an eyebrow, and he paused, seeming to draw a steadying breath.

"That is," he said, "if the High Commander would please explain the rationale behind her decision."

"You know, Marquand, most of the time I expect you to follow orders without needing to hear my reasoning. This time I'll make an exception. I met with First Prelate Casanne this morning; she made a threat I should have known was coming. Voren has some sort of magic, something we've never encountered before. So far the gendarmes haven't gotten anything out of him, but you saw the truth of it as plain as I did. We need to know how he can do it, whether there are more like him, and we're not alone in wanting answers as to his nature. So your assignment is twofold. First, learn what you can of his magic and his purpose. And second, protect him from those inclined to do him harm."

"Yes, sir," Marquand said. "I won't let you down."

She paused, but the glib remark she expected never came. Instead she nodded. "Dismissed, then, Colonel," she said. Just as well if she could leave that piece to Marquand. The bigger puzzle lay ahead of her: two wars, one she knew how to fight, unfolding in the Thellan foothills, and a second, far more deadly, in back rooms and hidden meetings here at home.

41

SARINE

A War Canoe
On the Edge of the Divide

Salt water sprayed around the bow of their canoe as it cut through the waves. The horizon was gone now. From the shore it had looked as though the shadows of the Divide were close—a quarter league, perhaps. But in the hours since they'd pushed into the water the blackness had grown taller and wider with each stroke of the oars. Courage had flagged beside the need for rote movements to propel them forward. Now the shadows swallowed the sky, and silence prevailed aside from the splash and pull of creaking wood.

"I wonder if it's cold in there," Acherre said between strokes. "It looks bloody well like it would be."

"No one's lived who's been fool enough to try it," Axerian said. "A memoir after we pass through would make you a legend, if the text survives."

Anati skittered along the edge of the canoe, darting over top of the oars with each pull. Sarine watched her, only half listening to the exchange at the front of the boat. Ka'Inari held the seat behind; the war canoe was wide enough for a person-and-a-half at best, and they sat in a row staggered two to a side to preserve a forward view for all. She'd had to crane her neck almost behind them to see anything but shadows for some time now.

"Is it always here?" she asked. "Has there always been a Divide?"

"It renews itself," Axerian said. "When the moment of ascension arrives, the Divide vanishes for a time. I know some measure of what we can expect, on the other side."

"And?" Ka'Inari asked.

Axerian affected a shrug before he made another pull on his oar. "Men. Women. The same as anywhere. Tall, short, brown, black, and pale. Rare for either side to progress much further than the other, but we've been surprised before. They'll have ships, likely gunpowder by now, though we'd best hope they haven't yet progressed to steam or rail."

A cold wind rose ahead, lifting the canoe high on the chop before slamming it down. Sarine's heart spiked, but nothing else had changed; only the wind.

"What of their magic?" Acherre asked after they'd settled. "You'd mentioned before, about their Houses."

"Yes," Axerian said. "Always the Houses retain their names. Rather like the Veil, on our side, and none of us can puzzle why. Properly they are the Great and Noble Houses, named for the flora and fauna of the East. Badger, Dragon, Lotus, Crane, Crab, and many more, each with their own gift."

Another jarring landing scattered his words to the wind. Even Anati paused as the boat righted itself, seawater lapping over the sides and soaking them with wet spray.

"Not too late to turn back," Axerian said.

"No," Sarine said. "We can't—"

Roaring sounded in her ears.

On either side of the canoe, the shadows had gone from an endless stretch of horizon to tangible black strands, as though twisted vines ran from the clouds all the way beneath the waves.

She screamed, and heard the same sound from different mouths.

"We're in it," Axerian called out. "Heavens protect us, but we're in it."

The canoe's prow slammed down hard, pitching them forward into one another's backs. Axerian braced the front of the boat, but Sarine could feel the tail end of the canoe listing, and pushed off to resettle her weight.

A rushing sound thundered around them, and more shouting. Too loud to discern any words. *Red* spiked through her, or if it didn't then her heart had doubled speed of its own accord. She gripped both sides of the canoe; her oar had gone over the side without her noticing, and the prow bucked again, this time skyward, hurling Axerian and Acherre into her.

"Use *Red*, and *Body* if you can find it," she shouted, but might as well have been screaming into the wind. A shimmering bear-spirit enveloped Ka'Inari, and he seemed to be holding the canoe as though he could will it to stay upright. She blinked to try to find *Shelter*, and saw nothing, no leylines at all, only coal-black empty space as far as she could see.

"Gods," Acherre was shouting. She couldn't make out anything more, though the captain seemed to be pointing straight ahead.

Hm, Anati's voice sounded in her head. *It falls.*

She hadn't had time to process the words when the prow of the canoe plunged forward, and they fell.

Water showered around them, soaking through her clothes as the sea drained itself into nothingness. The peak of the falls vanished above her, leaving them plummeting together amid a spray of salt water as high as a mountain, growing taller with each passing moment. Her stomach lurched and she vomited, gagging as the shadows raced past on their descent.

Minutes passed, or moments. Adrenaline coursed through her. Death was coming. She'd blundered, and any moment they would strike the bottom of wherever they were. Her body shouted it, sent every signal of certain doom.

Axerian was the first to laugh.

She hadn't realized the roaring had subsided enough to make out any other sound until she heard it, a mad glee over top of the water's raging hum.

Acherre added her laugh to his, and soon all four were joined in. They were falling—and her stomach had turned in on itself, reminding her of certain death—but they were still together, even still in the boat, somehow, each of the four of them having gripped the sides and kept themselves attached to its frame.

"What now?" Acherre shouted. She had to lean in to make herself heard, but they clustered together, and it seemed the water had cascaded far enough apart to dim its roar.

"You might consider giving in," Axerian said.

"What do you mean?" Acherre shouted back, but the comment had been directed toward Sarine.

Axerian pointed to her chest. "The Veil," he said.

"No!" she shouted. She took his meaning, though she wasn't even sure how to do such a thing, even if she could. The Veil had memories, and power; she could vaguely remember her body being used in ways she hadn't conceived possible. The terror of falling had masked the torrent of emotions roiling in her belly. No few had to be hers, but she couldn't account for the cold hate, or the indignant rage. The Veil was there, and she might well know some means of escape.

"It's that or fall until we go mad," Axerian said. "Or starve, unless you think there might be fish somewhere in the water. And thirst will claim us, even then."

Sarine closed her eyes, muting his voice as easily as she'd learned to ignore the Veil's emotions.

"What can I do?" she whispered. "Anati, help me."

My father might know. I've never fallen through an abyss before.

"Sarine?" Ka'Inari's voice. "Can we do anything, to help?"

"No," she said, sharper than she'd intended. "No—I'm not going to surrender to her. Just let me figure this out."

If they'd been on land she might have gone elsewhere, left the room or walked a few paces away. Instead she stayed within arm's reach of each of them, tumbling alongside water that had begun to more resemble raindrops frozen in the air than the drained ocean she knew it was.

"Anati, is there a way to reach Zi?" Her memory stirred, recalling that the Veil had done something, before. "He was somewhere surrounded by *kaas*, but we didn't travel there. It just…was."

Of course. Anati materialized standing atop the canoe next to Ka'Inari, then blinked across it, vanishing and reappearing beside Acherre. *Like this.*

"Is there a way for *me* to reach him?"

Anati seemed suddenly cold, staring at her with smoldering black in her eyes.

"Can you speak to him, then?" she asked.

Yes, of course, Anati thought, and vanished.

"Trying to reason it out with the *kaas*?" Axerian said.

"Yes. Wait, Axerian—the Veil, when she had control of me, she took us to a place where I saw Zi, and others. Other *kaas*. Do you know where it is, or how I can get there? Anati thinks Zi might have answers."

Axerian gave a grim look. "Bonding a new *kaas*, you mean. It might work, but Xeraxet would doubtless frown on trying."

"We have to do something," Acherre said. "I don't know if you see the same, Sarine, but I can't find anything on the leylines here, not even the damned lines themselves."

She nodded, realizing too late that the gesture was likely to be lost in the state of perpetual falling through the air. "Yes," she said instead. "It's the same for me."

Anati reappeared.

"What did he say?" Sarine asked. "Could you reach him?"

He says you're not ready to know about it.

A spark of her old anger kindled. Yes, that sounded like Zi.

He also says you're close enough for the Regnant to hear your thoughts. If you project to him, you'll draw his attention.

"If I project my thoughts...?" she asked, then bit back the rest of the words. Try as she might, Anati wasn't like to offer meaningful instruction. But she could figure it out.

"Sarine, be careful," Axerian said. "The Regnant is our enemy—*your* enemy."

"Better than starving, or dying of thirst, or madness," she said. "And better than giving in to her."

Axerian shook his head. "You can't. There has to be another way."

She braced herself, stilling her mind to calm.

I'm here, she thought, trying to focus the words outside herself. *We need help. Can you show us—*

Ka'Inari shouted at her, a wordless yelp, grabbing hold of her shoulder and wrenching her around.

"No," he said. "No, Sarine, whatever you did. It is certain death."

The shaman's eyes had glazed over, a look of horror on his face.

"I didn't..." she began, then said, "I don't know what to do." She turned to the others. "Help me think of something."

Before either could reply, a low rumble sounded in the distance.

In a surge of panic she looked down. It had to be the ground, or some terminal point, where the water was impacting at last. She saw only blackness, but the rumble grew, until she realized the blackness was moving.

YOU COME HERE TOO SOON, IN BREACH OF OUR TRUST.

The voice thundered louder than the ocean when it fell, coming from a place below them.

"It's him," Axerian said it, a shouted cry above the roar. "Veil protect us, it's him."

A monstrous shape shifted in the darkness, and though her stomach insisted they were falling, they didn't seem to move relative to the shadowed form. It was spherical, but massive, large enough to lie down next to mountains and dwarf them. Without light she couldn't see more than a silhouette where the water below them struck against its shape.

No, not a sphere. A head.

The seawater traced a face the size of a city district. The eyes were each the size of the Exarch's Basilica, the nose a ridge as high as Courtesan's Hill. Its mouth moved when it spoke, making a gaping pit of shadow the size of the harbor. And below the head, the water began to outline a body: shoulders, arms, torso, all covered in shadow.

HELP, the voice said, full of contempt. YOU COME BEFORE ME WITH A WIELDER OF LEYLINE ENERGY, A SPIRIT-BLESSED, AND ONE BONDED TO THE *KAAS*. THREE CHAMPIONS. AND YOU ASK FOR HELP.

Terror coursed through her. If there was an answer from the *kaas*, Anati wouldn't know it, and Zi was beyond her reach. The spirits would talk to Ka'Inari before her, and she didn't know how to force contact outside one of their sacred rituals or places anyway. The leylines had vanished. All that was left were the blue sparks. The Veil's power, Axerian had called it. All she knew how to make it do was anchor one of her other gifts, but there had to be more.

IS THIS HOW OUR WAR BEGINS? AS YOU BETRAYED OUR MASTER, SO NOW YOU BETRAY ME?

She reached for the blue sparks, feeling its power envelop her. Blue energy streaked along her fingertips. Axerian shouted something at her; she couldn't hear it over the roar of the water crashing against the shadowy colossus below.

The sparks could set anchors in the world; perhaps if she set enough, she could pry open the blackness in front of them. She tried it, hooking the energy to four points, applying force to each in a different direction.

I REJECT YOUR CHAMPIONS, the figure was saying. NONE OF

THESE THREE HAVE MET THE MASTER'S REQUIREMENTS
FOR ASCENSION. NONE OF THESE WILL—

Light flashed.

Her anchors tore a hole, and sunlight spilled into the darkness like
rays shone through cut gemstone. Smoke billowed in, too, and water,
leaking down into a tiny version of the waterfall that had accompanied
their fall.

"Go!" she shouted, but somehow she could move them herself, the
blue sparks arresting their fall and propelling them toward the opening.
All four of them gripped tight on the sides of their canoe, and in an
eyeblink they were through.

The roaring vanished. The monstrous shadow was gone. In place of
darkness there was light: sunshine as bright and pure as she'd ever seen.

They were back in their canoe, all four seated upright as it cut
through the waves toward the shore. Land was close, and not the cliffside
wilderness they'd departed from. The spires of a city stood where the
water ended, ringed by a great harbor. Ships unlike any she'd seen filled
the bay, great square behemoths with square sails and shouting figures
swarming over their decks.

It took another moment to register the smoke clouds rising from the
city, and still another to realize the ships were exchanging fire, pounding
cannon shot alongside flaming arrows launched from one deck to
another.

They'd escaped the abyss, and dropped straight into a battle.

42

ARAK'JUR

The Mouth of a Cave
Lhakani Land

Sizzling meat filled the air with smells of home and comfort, pulling him back from the edge of sleep. Rhealla used to bring him fare from the cookfires, after a grueling hunt. She would have been proud of him, though the prospect of a guardianship had never entered into their plans together. He had aspired to be Valak'Jur, to share a hunter's life with her, to raise their son in the Sinari tradition, to make him a good man, and to try to be one himself. He could live the rest of his life and never forget her, nor be free of the chord of sadness her death still struck, however he'd learned to live with its melody.

He gasped and lurched forward. He was seated, but his hands were held in place, suspended over his head.

A fire burned at the mouth of the cave, venting smoke into a darkening sky, and a woman sat on the opposite side, staring at him through the flames. He tried to move again and found the same resistance, his hands held in place against the cave wall. His body ached, with heaviness in his eyes when he tried to look and see what bound him.

The woman said nothing, watching him struggle.

He tried again. His muscles were raw, a deep pain when he strained his shoulder, and another in his chest. Finally he fell still. *Una're* could aid him, if his body was too weak to break free.

"No."

The woman's voice, though she hadn't moved from behind the fire. He met her eyes.

Memories flooded in, of the moments leading up to his long sleep. The image of a winged creature, of talons and fangs. He'd landed a savage cut with *mareh'et*'s claws, ripping the sinews of her left arm free of its socket, dangling veins and gore as they fought. She'd screamed, more fury than pain, and redoubled her attack. More images came, of brutality without elegance or grace. Fire had been exchanged, and earth. Then without warning, blackness. He never saw the blow that put him down.

"Call upon the spirits and I will renew my attack," the woman said. Ad-Shi. She said it flatly, without sign of malice or anger. "We are too close to the end to waste more time on recovery."

His throat burned from thirst, and his arms throbbed from the exertion he'd already put them to. A lesser instinct demanded he call on *una're* anyway, burst himself free of whatever prison she'd made in the stone, and run. The greater instinct won out. He was exhausted, on the barest edge of waking, where she'd had time enough to regrow the arm he'd severed, her left now a perfect mirror of the right. If she'd wanted him dead, he would have been dead long since.

When the moment had passed, she rose from beside the fire, retrieving a skewer he hadn't noticed was there.

She approached, holding the stick to his mouth. Rabbit meat, still sizzling, giving off the scent that had awakened him.

"Eat," she said.

Hunger overpowered defiance, and he tore a chunk loose with his teeth. His jaw ached after a single bite, but he forced his teeth to work the meat, chewing as simmering juices ran down his throat. Warmth spread through him, and he took another chunk before he was done with the first.

She stayed until he'd cleaned the skewer, then offered a skin of fresh water. More ran down his chin onto his chest than made it in his mouth, but every drop was sweet and cold. When it was done she stepped away, this time sitting closer, directly opposite where he was bound.

"Why?" he asked. One word, but enough to carry his meaning. Why had she attacked?; why had she let him live?; why nurse him back to health now?

"It was once our way, to recognize strength," Ad-Shi said. "I have done many things, destroyed many things. Once, the Vordu were one people. One tradition. Now we are many, and we have forgotten. I am dying, but I do not mean to be the last to remember."

It wasn't an answer, at least not any he recognized.

"You murdered Ka'Urun," he said. Better, perhaps, to try directness.

She nodded.

"In his ravings, he said you were the root of the spirits' madness, of their drive to war."

She nodded again.

"Why?" This time the question burned hot.

"I was once like you," Ad-Shi said. "Though never as ignorant. I knew it would be my place, to kill. I trained for it. After the first *Arak* fell by my hand, *rin'ji* spoke to me, told me I was chosen, that I might ascend to serve the Goddess. I proved myself, and became her champion. I fought to protect my people, to protect our way of life. We created paradise, and you live in it with no understanding of its price."

He shook his head. Answers he couldn't understand were no answers at all. Whatever this woman was, she had a great many gifts. Easier to think her power-mad, her mind driven too far from what made men sane. It wasn't unheard of, in the shamans' stories. An *Arak* blinded by power, believing the spirits' gifts set him too far apart from ordinary men. Perhaps the women told similar tales, for the war-spirits. Seeing her in such a light inspired pity in spite of her strength.

"May I free myself?" he asked.

She went back to staring at him. "I will kill you, if you run."

He nodded, slow and deliberate as he called to *una're*. Strength surged through him, and the crackling energy of the Great Bear's thunderous claws. Earth and stone broke over his head, raining dirt on him as he pulled his hands free of the enclosure she must have used the earth spirits' gifts to make.

He flexed his hands and forearms, turning them over to inspect that they were whole.

"How long has it been," he asked, "since you encountered a man, or a woman, you didn't have the ability to kill?"

She gave a bitter laugh, and he saw again the pain behind her eyes.

"I did what was necessary," she said. "Would you do any less, to protect your people?"

He found himself wishing Ka'Inari were here, or any shaman. It was never the guardians' place to deal with troubles of the heart or mind.

"Attacking me doesn't protect your people," he said. "It is evil. Holding me here on threat of death is evil."

"You know nothing of good and evil," Ad-Shi said. "I am tired. I have endured enough. I am ready to die. I meant to pass my knowledge to one strong enough to wield it, to give this world a chance when I am gone. Testing you was right. It was needful. To let Godhood pass to one without the proper strength would hand this world to the shadow. That is evil, guardian. The rest doesn't matter."

Tears had risen in her eyes; they reflected the firelight, even as the night sky darkened around them. Again he felt pity for her. Whatever had unhinged her mind, she had clearly been a powerful soul, blessed by the spirits' favor.

"May I go?" he asked. "I wish you peace on your journey, but I see no reason for you to hold me here."

"You think I am a wretch," she said. "You see none of what approaches. You know none of it! The Regnant is an Eastern dream to you, if he exists at all. Do you not see the nature of our magic? Do you not sense the threat?"

She searched him with a piercing gaze, but he could offer no more than he understood.

Blue sparks enveloped her hand, and she closed her eyes.

"See, then," she said. "Remember."

The world faded to blackness.

———————

A small girl bounded through a cave, humming a song she had heard her mother sing, before she died. She carried a stick meant to scrape lichen off the walls, but no firelight, leaving the passages black and sightless. Too dangerous to carry fire. She knew these tunnels well; she was no foreigner, to need to risk attracting *astahg* or *valak'ar*.

Fifteen paces carried her to the place, and she was careful to adjust for the way her stride had lengthened in the past year, since the last time she'd come here. It took time for the best patches to regrow. She reached through the blackness with her stick and found it right where it should be. A patch of soft, moist food almost as valuable as the stick itself. They'd eat it in the glowing room, where the mushrooms grew bright with colors, casting light—real light—as bright as Mountain's gift. Her brothers would beg her to tell them where she found it, but they were cowards. She could give them all the paces and they'd never make it past the outlying rooms. If not for her, they'd have been sold off a dozen storms ago, deemed too frail to make their contributions to the tribe.

She rolled the lichen strip into her basket, fingering it closed in the dark.

A right turn led to a narrow passage, and she was careful to keep her balance as she crossed the windy place. She'd tested its depth with pebbles once, and they'd taken ten heartbeats to make their first *clack*. Any wind was dangerous, and she knew better than to breathe as she made the crossing. One skittering step in front of another, until she dropped down twenty paces later, lowering herself past the five rocks that led up to the windy place's passage.

The last rock was smooth, a sign it had been near water once. That was a secret she had yet to explore. Not for today, though. She'd never been more than five paces from it, and there were at least two more smooth rocks leading away to the left, if she was facing home. A source of clean water would be a treasure, enough to put her name up for consideration the next time the *Ka* met to decide who got a chance to speak to Wind. Food first, though. If her brothers hadn't come up short again she wouldn't even have been in this tunnel, so far from the outlying rooms.

Twenty-six paces brought her through a narrow crack, two steps down and thirty more to the left. Another one hundred eighty-one paces weaving through the stalactites of the hot room, careful to pause and take a different route when the air grew too warm. Twenty paces down, using her hands to dig in to keep her from falling too far. Forty-nine down the tunnel where Makas had become an *Arak*, when the *ipek'a* pack attacked the tribe. Ten more to the left, then a short climb to the ledge where her brothers would be waiting. They were cowards, but they would come this far. She was careful to make the approach in silence, one slow shuffling step at a time. Her brothers couldn't hide their breathing forever, and she wasn't about to let them ambush her again, jumping out at her and making her howl while they cackled with delight.

She slowed even further for the last seven paces. Nothing yet. Even if they'd been practicing, they couldn't hold their breathing for more than three hundred heartbeats. Not even Nok-Ta could hold her breath so long, and she'd once survived an ashstorm that had burned all her hair to cinders.

She reached the ledge, and it was empty. No sign of her brothers, though they'd promised to meet her here.

Ninety-six paces brought her to the winding tunnels, and another two hundred five took her through them. Her steps had quickened. She didn't care if her brothers surprised her again. Yes, she'd yelp like a cornered fox cub, but it meant they'd be there. Fifty-three more steps across the shallow pools and she would have welcomed their laughter.

She took the leftward passage into the glowing room and dropped her basket, spilling her lichen on the ground.

Tears came before she knew what she was seeing.

Dead bodies, huddled together in the corner. Rows of them, piles. The glowing room cast its iridescent light as high as the cave ceiling went, bright enough to sting her eyes after her journey's long darkness. She would have come here with them, if she'd been with the rest of the tribe. The glowing room was supposed to be safe. That was why the mushrooms grew here, old enough for the toadstools to be taller than her waist. Ashstorms and poison winds never reached it. She walked forward thirteen paces, counting the dead. Their skins were blackened, streaked with pox and sores, and rivulets of blood traced from their bodies into narrow channels, until it seemed as though a hundred riverways carved a path through the glowing room.

A new kind of storm. It had to be. Something the *Ka* hadn't been able to see. And now her tribe was dead.

She cried.

The Yurani tribe would take her in, if she could get to them. It would mean burning fire to light the way, but she wasn't going to die for fear of meeting the wraith-snakes in the tunnels. And Wind was on the way, the sacred place at Hanet'Li'Tyat. With fire she would find it, even without the *Ka*'s blessing. Her people might be dead, but Ad-Shi had no intention of dying with them.

———

Arak'Jur's vision cleared, and he coughed out the blood and phlegm built up in his lungs. His body still healed itself, and the night sky was full darkness now. He'd been out for some time, and it took a moment for his senses to return.

When they did, he saw Ad-Shi sitting by their fire, unmoving. She watched him with redness around her eyes, sign of tears staining her cheeks, saying nothing.

"What did I see?" he asked. "And how did you show me?"

"It is part of the Veil's gift, to impart one's will to others. You saw my life, as a child. You saw the world as it will be if the Regnant wins."

He moved closer to the fire, welcoming its warmth. The vision had been bleak, but it was the way of things, to fear nature's wrath. He'd seen villages destroyed in his lifetime, peoples scattered and broken. Surely Ka'Vos's visions had been at least as dire, or Ka'Hinari's, before they were slain.

"You lived belowground," he said, searching for understanding.

She glared at him. "You did not understand," she said. "All things lived belowground. There was no light we did not fear. Winds carried poison. Dust and tremors meant storms, of ash and gas and fire. One child in three lived to make children of their own; one in thirty lived to see their children's children."

"Your people endured a great blight," he said. "But you survived."

"No," she said, shaking her head. "You still do not see."

He fell quiet.

"You were strong, guardian," she said. "Strong enough to face me and survive. But you must know what awaits. You must know." She raised her hand, and again he saw it outlined in the blue sparks. "You must see."

———

Thunder cracked through black clouds as she struck the killing blow. The Crane champion had failed to defend his flank, and she cut him down with *mareh'et*'s claws. Blood soaked her forearms as she rent his flesh, throwing his body into the stone. A voice sounded in her head again, for the third and final time: *FOR THIS ONE, IT ENDS.*

A man had appeared, dressed in a white robe. His face was creased with age and worry.

Paendurion dropped his sword, facing the man in white. "It's done," he said, in the heavy accents of the Amaros. "Accede, now, and honor our victory."

The Veil stood behind, and she stepped forward. The old man met her on the rocks.

Ad-Shi flinched as a cold wind blew through the darkened sky. Clouds as thick as any cave ceiling hung overhead, but they were still outdoors, aboveground. The space was too broad. The wind was here, and even now she couldn't escape the desire to run, to find shelter, even in their moment of triumph.

"My champions are defeated," the old man said. "I acknowledge your right, to hold the Soul for this cycle. Let it be done."

The Veil bowed her head, and the old man vanished.

The world changed.

The clouds' color melted, falling to the ground like thick ink. Blue light shone overhead, an expanse of blue as wide as any underground sea. A ball of fire seemed suspended in the sky, radiating warmth. Heat touched Ad-Shi's skin, and she stared in wonder. There was no danger here.

The change spread. Rocks crumbled to dust before her eyes, and what had been barren waste sprouted green. It spread like waves of fire, covering hills and mountainsides with plants thicker than any moss or lichen. Mighty sticks like hardened vines grew from the earth, covered in green, rising until they were taller than ten men. What had been a basin littered with corpses became a lush carpet of color. The darkness was gone, and the wind blew strong and sweet, coursing over her skin with a delicate warmth.

Ad-Shi trembled, daring to test an indrawn breath. Heat was a sign of ash; wind a sign of gas or noxious fumes. But she was safe now. The Regnant's champions had fallen. She filled her lungs with clean air, staring over the basin with awe. It was done. The world was healed.

A faint scream echoed in his ears as the vision faded.

"Now do you see?" Ad-Shi asked. "This is the price of failure. This is what you fight to preserve, if you are strong enough to follow my path."

His mind reeled from what he'd seen. It hadn't been a blight. To his eyes the scene was no more than any lush valley, but through hers he had felt the wonder, the awe of seeing life in abundance for the first time. Of not believing it was possible for horrors to fade.

"I offer you the choice," Ad-Shi continued. "If not you, then I must move on. Time is short. Will you follow me, and learn what you can, before the end?"

He thought of his people, of the Alliance and the dream of six tribes come together as one. He thought of Corenna and the child she would be bearing soon, if she still lived. He found himself nodding before he could consider the whole of it, the implications of the visions he'd seen shaking the foundations of what he knew of being *Arak*, of being Sinari, of being a man at all.

"Yes," he said. "I would know more. But yes."

A great tension melted from her face, and fresh tears escaped before she could close her eyes.

"Then we go," she said. "We seek the guidance of the spirits. They will tell us where to begin the hunt."

43

TIGAI

An Icy Shore
Across the Divide

Tigai's furs caught enough flakes of snow to wreathe his face in white. Around him, the leaders of the warband wore the same: thick coats, hoods ringed with white-speckled fur. But for differences in height he couldn't have told them apart.

"Sixty-two," one of Isaru's lieutenants said as another pair came trudging across the frozen river. Or perhaps it was a narrow sea; difficult to tell, in the bank of thick fog clinging to the shore. Isaru nodded and repeated the count, with Mei and four more lieutenants standing at his side. Tigai and Yuli stood a few paces away, but close enough to hear the numbers each time new faces were spotted. It served as a mundane distraction, after the horrors of the morning.

The Divide loomed through the fog, a low hum emanating from its shadowy mass. Behind him, the tundra extended as far as he could see, a flat wasteland of snow and ice. Ahead, where the rest of Isaru's warband had appeared one at a time through the fog, there was only shadow. They'd lived on the other side for weeks, lodged in tents in plain view of its jet-black heights. It felt different, here. More deadly, more present in his thoughts, after he'd spent the morning traversing the jagged turns and crevasses joined together to make the passage through. Sixty-two meant there were two more yet to finish the crossing. They'd set off from the warcamp with a firm count beforehand—repeated twice to be certain of their numbers—and after being among the first through, Isaru and his closest had stayed here, accounting for the rest.

"There." Mei's voice, pointing into the fog.

"Sixty-three," the same lieutenant said, as a lone figure shambled into view.

"Another quarter hour," Isaru said. "If the last hasn't come through by then, gather us and make a count to determine who we've lost."

Murmurs of agreement, then Isaru left their circle toward Tigai, laying a hand on his shoulder. He managed not to recoil as Isaru used the gesture to guide him a few paces away, toward the frozen shore.

"Your brother's wife has the utmost confidence in you," Isaru said. "Do you feel ready?"

"I know my part," Tigai said.

Isaru smiled; a false, easy expression born of confidence and power. Men like the warband's leader were common enough at court. Schemers, who imagined their attentions were uniquely suited to any listener's circumstance. Little wonder how the man had convinced threescore *magi* of various persuasions to join him, even here in the wastes.

"Humor me, then," Isaru said. "How does the Dragon's gift function? I know it only from observing our enemies; the workings remain a mystery."

A lie, almost certainly, designed to give them a connection that flattered Tigai. No surer way to charm one's way into a mark's smallclothes, proverbial or otherwise, than to get them talking about something they knew well. But for the moment he had to play his part.

"I've read your aura, among the strands," Tigai said. "You have strong connections to three stars, which means you visited them recently, or have a strong need connected to your time there. As I understand, in this case it's both. A child with my gift could take us there."

"I see," Isaru said. "And how do you know one from another? Which 'star' is Buzhou, which Sidai, and which Kye-Min?"

"I don't know," he replied. "That's up to you. The strongest will be the one you visited most recently, or the one you have a stronger connection to, or both. Rank them for me, and I can guess which will be which."

"The strongest will be Kye-Min," Isaru said. "Next, Buzhou. Sidai last."

He nodded. "Simple enough, then."

"And how long must you recover, between uses?"

Tigai shrugged. "If I use the strands too often, I'll get nosebleeds, headaches, or worse, but I can use them again immediately if I have to. It's worse the farther I travel, and the more I bring with me."

"Our enemies seem to need rest, sometimes for days between their shifting. It's been our one advantage—goading them into committing the Dragons, then striking elsewhere."

"It's not like that, for me."

Isaru clapped him on the shoulder. "We are fortunate, to have you joined with our cause, Lord Tigai."

This time Tigai showed him teeth, though he was spared the need to reply.

"Sixty-four," Isaru's lieutenant called out. "That's it—all accounted for, my lord."

Isaru and the rest of them turned to see a silhouette cut through the fog. Exhalations and relief spread across the riverbank. A count of sixty-four meant none had been lost to the shadows during the crossing, a difficult enough feat when touching the wrong wall or stumbling a pace in the wrong direction meant vanishing into its depths. But they'd come through, and Isaru was already beaming, calling for the rest of them to gather around him and his lieutenants.

Mei—no, the creature wearing Mei's face—approached him with a look of determined pride. The look Mei herself would have worn, giving Tigai an opportunity to showcase his worth.

"Dao will be there, in the city," Mei said. "We'll be together again soon. And we'll take up the hunt for Remarin's captors."

He made a noise he hoped would pass for tempered excitement, and forced himself to wear a grin. A thousand times harder with her than with Isaru, but he did it. He'd told lies enough to know how to make them feel like the truth. Yuli, strangely enough, was the weakest point of his façade. He barely knew the northern clanswoman, but she'd been finding excuses to hover near him, to be there, when he'd been too long alone.

"My people," Isaru bellowed over the cutting wind as his followers assembled. "Gather here." Then, as an aside to Tigai and Mei, he said, "How close must we be, for the Dragon's gift to work?"

"Close," Tigai replied. "I've never tried at greater than twenty or thirty paces away."

Isaru nodded, gesturing for all to approach. They came with a mixture of battle-hardened and wide-eyed faces, all stung and reddened by the ice and snow. Not all *magi*, but the better part by far, at least among those whom Tigai had met and shared revels. Easier to bond with them when he'd believed them to be Mei's cohorts. Easier to see them as more than tools of a man who intended to tell him lies.

"We go," Isaru said once they were assembled, "to the city of Kye-Min, the jewel of the peninsula. We will find it already under siege. Our first true strike, to test the arm of our enemies. We have trained for this! We are ready. Follow my lieutenants, once we are there. They know our objectives, and will guide you through the action to come. Do not shy from using your gifts—we are there to remind the populace that the Great and Noble Houses do not have sole grasp of *magi* powers."

Tigai watched as the crowd shuffled together into smaller cadres. No one had given him any direction on whom to follow, so he stayed near Isaru and Mei, with Yuli at his side. Isaru turned to him when they were finished.

"We are ready, Lord Tigai," Isaru said. "Take us into battle."

A deep breath served to center him, and he closed his eyes. The starfield presented itself at once, a million points of light, surrounding him like a sphere on all sides. Faint strands extended outward as he pushed the sphere, projecting his will to envelop the company. Most of the strands were pale, thin streams of light extending out to wherever home would be for each of them. Isaru's three points shone brighter, for his three cities of Kye-Min, Buzhou, and Sidai.

He pushed, snapping the strand into place. Isaru had packed his sixty-four *magi* close enough that Tigai didn't have to strain. He enveloped them all, then chose a star as far from Kye-Min as possible, a blinking redness far, far to the west. He hooked them through it, and the icy chill on the air vanished, replaced by a furnace blast of parched heat.

A wave of nausea racked his body, and he fought it down, blinking for the barest fraction necessary to reset the strands, catching a glimpse of where he'd taken them. A vista of empty sand dunes, extending toward a shimmering horizon as far as he could see.

A purple light flashed, and a shout of anger. Breath constricted from his lungs, accompanied by burning pain.

He found another star, hooked a strand around himself and Yuli, and shifted again.

Thunder boomed, rattling the frames of nearby buildings. Jun construction, with Jun paved streets, lined with shattered glass and quiet corpses, caked in blood.

"Where are we?" Yuli said. "How did... what did...?"

Tigai retched, doubling over as the strands took their toll.

"What did you do?" Yuli demanded at last.

"Come on," Tigai said, struggling back to his feet, taking her arm and pulling her toward the husk of a nearby building. Cannon shot had struck and collapsed it on one side, leaving a heap of rubble where the upper floors fell through.

"What is this?" Yuli said as she staggered behind. "Where is Lord Isaru?"

"Somewhere far the fuck away from here," Tigai said. "And you're better off for it, I promise you. He wasn't what he seemed. None of them were."

Yuli snatched her hand back from his grip. "What's going on? I saw, for a moment, sand... You took us somewhere, then..."

"That's right," he said. "I took them to the desert and I bloody left them there."

"You betrayed Isaru Mattai?" she asked. "You betrayed your own sister?"

"No. She wasn't my sister. Or, my sister by marriage, but—look, never mind. She wasn't Mei. That fucking bastard used her face, tried to lure me into supporting his cause, but that was never Mei in his camp, only some *magi* trickery. That meant it was all lies, do you see what I'm telling you?"

"My father pledged me to his cause," Yuli said. "We were meant to fight against the Great and Noble Houses, and now I am run away like some dog. Where was this desert? Where are we now?"

"Technically you can still join the fight, if you insist," he said. "We're in Kye-Min, unless he played me false there, too. I don't have a clue where I left Isaru and his people. Somewhere far from any water, if the *koryu* are good."

Yuli's skin had paled to a shale gray; he hadn't noticed before, but now her eyes seemed to be bleeding, tracing droplets of blood down her cheeks.

"Yuli, whatever he told you—are you all right?"

Her limbs had grown thinner, and longer, elevating her above him by a few inches, where he'd had the advantage before.

"You tell me he played you false," Yuli said. Her voice had thickened somehow, seeming to come from all sides, though her mouth still moved to form the words. "Explain how my clan's sworn lord is my enemy, and not you."

By now she was a full head taller than she had been, her arms and legs elongated to form a stooping posture that was difficult to see in full beneath her heavy furs. Her face had grown longer, more angular, exaggerating her already-too-prominent nose and jaw, and when she spoke it revealed her teeth had been replaced by jagged points. Her skin was full gray now, as though her too-thin body had been wholly carved from stone.

"Oh bloody fucking fire spirits," he said. "I took you with me to save you from a fate you didn't deserve." He took a step back into the rubble, and she followed, leaning toward him like a hunting hound sighting a fox. "You didn't bloody—though I suppose, for you to be a *magi*, too..."

Metal points had pierced the fingers of her gloves, long and thin as knives.

"Look," he continued, "my brother, Dao, and his wife were captured by the *magi*, when they took me. Isaru's Mei wasn't her. I tested her, used something she should have known. It meant the whole thing was lies. His Mei wasn't mine. Some kind of skinchanger, or illusion. If he was lying, then I wasn't going to help him do a damned thing. I don't give a fuck about his war, or the *magi* or anything else. I just want to find the prisoners they took. My brother, his wife, and our master-at-arms."

He blinked by reflex, looping a strand between Yuli and somewhere far away in case she took another step.

Instead she stopped.

"Hyman Three Winds warned me," Yuli said. "The day my father came back from the hunt, with Isaru Mattai at his side. He claimed my father would never pledge a Clan Hoskar warrior to a foreigner. He insisted some devilry had bewitched our chief; that it could not be the same man."

Tigai exhaled sharply. "It probably wasn't," he said. "It was probably the same creature that made me think Mei had gone over to support him."

In an eyeblink Yuli was back to how he'd known her at the camp: tall, but only almost of a height with him, blond-haired with a too-large nose, her face covered with tattoos, with no sign of the ash-gray skin, jagged teeth, and metal shivs for hands.

"You say your family, they were taken as prisoners?" Yuli asked. "How can you be sure?"

"I can't," he said. "But what other choice is there? If they might be alive, I have to find them."

Yuli nodded, and the building frame shook again, this time from thunder landing closer, spilling dust from the half-collapsed floors above.

She stepped away, looking upward with a mix of uncertainty and awe.

"I've never been to any of the hundred cities," Yuli said. "Where should we begin?"

"There are two armies here," he said. "And one of them is expecting *magi* reinforcements. Let's be what they expect, and see if we can learn whatever they might know."

44

SARINE

*S*helter sprang up around them as the war canoe slid onto the rocks. Acherre was out first, with Ka'Inari close behind. They'd veered away from the harbor using a combination of *Shelter*, *Red*, and *Body* in lieu of lost oars, pushing off against miniature barriers to propel them through the waves. Only a few shots and arrows had come their way; the strange, square-sailed ships had seemed intent on hurling projectiles at each other, or trying to ram their enemies, and hadn't shown interest in pursuing the tiny war canoe materialized from nothing in their midst. Though now their canoe had reached the shore, and drawn soldiers out of hiding to face them.

"Stay down," Acherre shouted. *Shelter* hissed between the roars of gunshots, sending up wisps of smoke where it dissolved projectiles into heat. The beach where they'd made landfall had seemed no more than a plot of gardens and villas overlooking the sea, but soldiers swarmed from its buildings as soon as their canoe ran onto the rocks. They wore painted armor in reds and blacks, their domed metal caps reflecting the sunlight as they took up firing positions on the far side of a waist-high stone wall.

"*Magi*," Sarine heard the soldiers shout, a cry raised from twenty voices at once. "*Magi* on the shore."

"We shouldn't—" Ka'Inari began, his words drowned into a thundering roar of smoke from their guns.

Acherre had loosened her carbine, somehow still slung on her belt, even after their fall through the void of the Divide. Her back was pressed against *Shelter*'s blue haze, and without warning two more Acherres sprang into being, exact copies, each one seeming to be preparing to fire.

Sarine blinked to add her *Shelter* to Acherre's. The leylines here shone like glittering gemstones, seemingly endless reserves of every energy, from the green pods of *Life* to *Faith*'s shimmering haze. The bellows of gunfire shattered thoughts before they could form. They'd stumbled into a battle, but there was nothing to give an inkling of who was fighting whom, or why.

Acherre shouted something, perhaps no more than a wordless cry, and the soldiers along the villa wall threw down their guns and ran.

Axerian stepped from the boat, wearing his familiar grin.

Yellow, Anati thought to her. *That was Yellow.*

Sarine blinked. She should have thought of that. Damn if the crossing hadn't muddled her senses.

"Trouble with the landing?" Axerian said. "We shouldn't let—"

A cocoon of white energy flared around him, and he staggered backward, knocked off-balance into the rocks.

"Axerian!" Sarine shouted.

All three Acherres leveled their carbines, belching a shot over top of the *Shelter* barrier, and the lone soldier left manning the villa wall snapped his head back, his helmet flying backward as a spurt of blood fountained into the air.

A high-pitched whine sounded in her ears as Sarine rushed to Axerian's side, tethering strands of *Body* and *Life* into him, probing for sign of injury. He waved her away, and she read his lips and gestures before she could hear him say, "I'm fine. Bloody heavens, I'm fine."

"You missed one," Acherre said, rising from behind her barrier and reloading her carbine. The rest of the beach had cleared in an instant, all sign of the enemy soldiers scattered by the terror of Axerian's *Yellow*.

Sarine pulled Axerian to his feet. "We need to move," she said. "Even if only to get away from here."

"Wholeheartedly agreed," Axerian said. He spat for emphasis. "Just my sort of luck, to meet a *magi* in the first detachment of their soldiers."

"More coming." Ka'Inari pointed behind them, toward the harbor. Sarine turned to see three of the massive ships converging toward them, their decks swarming with men in yellow and white armor, lowering boats already rowing toward the shore.

"What did we stumble into?" she asked.

Axerian turned back, scanning the harbor as though it were no more than a minor object of interest. "A war, I expect. Though who can say which side these soldiers think we're on."

"What can you tell us about them?"

He gave an exaggerated shrug. "Too many differences each cycle for there to be anything reliable. But if there are *magi* on the field, that means the Great and Noble Houses are here. Just the sort we came looking to find."

"Ka'Inari?" she asked.

The shaman shook his head. "Things are clouded here...I need time to consider what the spirits' sendings mean."

"A guess, then. Anything at all."

"Danger. Hope. A woman in a tower. A mesh, dark with points of light, like a pattern woven from the night sky."

"Inland, then," Sarine said, and the others nodded along. The provisions they'd stored in the canoe were still tumbling through the Divide; it meant scavenging for food, water, and shelter, and the villas were as likely a place as any to start, even in the middle of a battle.

"Arquebuses," Acherre said when they traversed the garden walls, stepping over the soldiers' discarded weapons. "A hundred years behind Sarresant's arms. Maybe two hundred."

"Best pray their knowledge of the Regnant's magic is equally stunted," Axerian said. "*Yellow* can protect us from their foot soldiers, but it will draw attention from the *magi*, if they're here."

"Let's move," Sarine said. The estate they'd landed on was deserted, built in a combination of familiar and strange. Vines covered the stone walls, hanging from a canopy draped over top of a curated garden. Long boxlike halls extended out from the main building, with redwood framing under curved-tile roofs. Inside the main hall the furniture could have been from Sarresant, albeit from a distant, foreign era of art and decoration. Cabinets and armoires lined the walls, ornately carved and patterned with gold, with tapestries above them sewn depicting scenes of men and women in ankle-deep fields of water. Chairs were missing; the tables were situated at knee height, with cushions laid beside them in long rows.

"This way," Acherre called when they reached a fork in the hall, and the rest followed into the kitchens. Again the implements and décor echoed home without confirming it: three stone bowls dominating the space, with spice racks and a pile of neatly stacked firewood laid beside the hearth. Acherre vanished into the pantry while Ka'Inari descended down wooden steps into a cellar, leaving her and Axerian to pore over the spices.

"It always seemed wrong, to me," Axerian said, "that the Regnant's people would enjoy the fruits of our victories. Shouldn't they live in shadow, gas, and ash? At least as a form of homage, one would think."

"We need to decide what to do," Sarine said. "Provisions first, but we have to find where their champions are likely to be."

"Not as easy as it sounds. On our side of the Divide, the moment of ascension is different for each line. No telling which Houses are chosen for this cycle, and even if we knew that, they will guard their prospective champions from us, all the more so if the Regnant has the means to tell them we're here."

"They have pigs, Oracle be praised," Acherre called from the next room. "Ham shanks, rashers of bacon—and beef! Cows, too!"

"We'll need sacks, or bags to carry it in," Sarine said, rummaging through the kitchen in search of something fitting. "You called them Houses, are they physical places? Temples or such?"

"Likely not," Axerian said. "The Great and Noble Houses are schools of power, not unlike the Vordu spirits or the *kaas'* bonds. Collections of people who share a certain affinity for magic. In some ages, they've ruled an Empire; in others they warred between themselves until the end. From the look of things I'd say we're in the latter—too close to the end at this point for city fighting to be coincidental. But which side is which? Which do we want to aid, or oppose? Who can tell?"

He said it as though it were a joke. Sarine frowned, midway through upending a sack of what looked like radishes to repurpose it for carrying jars of spices, smaller sacks of grain, and iron pots. "You agreed to follow me through the Divide; didn't you have an inkling of what we'd do once we passed through?"

"I expected us to die," Axerian said. "When hope is exhausted, one accepts risks one might otherwise eschew."

"Well, we're here," she said. "If Ka'Inari can see threats, we can follow his spirits' guidance. That's something."

Axerian nodded. "Reassuring, if the Vordu gifts aren't impaired by the Divide."

"You didn't know...?"

"How could I have? The Divide was always down when we came to face his champions."

She stuffed a few more jars into the bag, shaking her head in disbelief. Had he really expected them to die? The enormity of the task loomed in front of her. From the sound of it, they would have the spirits' visions to guide them, and they had the *kaas'* gift with language, to say nothing of their collected prowess at protection and, if it came to it, fighting. Four of them against an entire world, equal in the depth of its nations and magicks to the one she knew. She could solve it one step at a time. Food first, then a bearing on which armies were fighting here, and why. There would be civilians caught in it, or soldiers to capture. They would have the first kernels of information, and offer a path to find the next. She could do this.

Ox, Anati thought to her.

She frowned, as Axerian darted his head around, peering through one of the kitchen windows.

"Where?" Axerian asked.

"Wait," she said. "What does that mean?"

"*Magi* coming," Axerian said, then again, louder, for Acherre and Ka'Inari's benefit, "gather here—it's time to go."

Acherre came around from the pantry holding two sacks slung over her shoulder. "What is it?" she said, at the same moment Ka'Inari came trotting up the stairs from the cellar, carrying three glass bottles in either hand.

A roaring crash struck the house, shattering glass, blasting apart the walls from the pantry. Screams sounded as stone and mortar scattered through the kitchen, and a boulder the size of a tree stump came to rest in the hallway. The outer wall hung open like a wound, letting sunlight stream into the wreckage of the pantry, where Acherre would have been standing had it struck a moment before.

This time Sarine put up *Shelter* by reflex, a barrier as thick as she could handle. Thundercracks sounded immediately following the boulder, and more glass shattered, though the bulk of it impacted on her *Shelter*, dissolving into hissing smoke.

"Out," Acherre shouted, leading the way through the breach created by whatever had thrown the rock through the wall.

"Careful," Axerian called after her. "There will be a *magi* with them. An Ox."

The rest dimmed as Sarine followed behind Acherre, *Red* and *Body* giving her the speed and agility to keep her footing through the rubble. They emerged into the outer courtyard of the estate, where a fresh line of red-armored soldiers had dropped to their knees, busily reloading their guns after delivering their volley. Anati gave her *Yellow* as quick as she could think to ask for it, and she felt the tableau of the soldiers' emotions: steadiness, fear, exhilaration, obedience. She pressed on fear at the same moment Acherre tore into them with *Entropy*, a ripping explosion engulfing the leftmost part of their line in billowing flame. The rest broke, save for one man among them, already hefting another boulder when his fellows deserted their line. He looked toward her and Acherre with bewilderment, then threw his rock as Acherre tethered another binding, enveloping him in a cloud of fire.

A fresh *Shelter* barrier absorbed the boulder's impact, sprung up moments before it hit. Ka'Inari emerged from the hole in the pantry wall as the rock exploded into fragments against the white haze, and he cowered back before he had time to realize it was safe.

"I'd almost forgotten how lovely it was fighting at your side," Acherre said to her, grinning.

"Careful!" Ka'Inari cried out.

Acherre's *Entropy* had left behind a cloud of black smoke where it must have caught the soldiers' powder, but a creature emerged through it, a silhouette suddenly made real. It was as though the man had been replaced by a creature of gray stone, or perhaps he'd conjured armored plating, a thick layer of it covering him from head to toe. Another boulder formed in his hands, and he threw it before he cleared the smoke, a splintering crash where it struck the *Shelter* again, making a ripping sound where the barrier drained from a rich blue to a pale white.

Lakiri'in added its blessing to *Red*, and *Body*, and she surged with speed.

Stone formed in the *magi*'s hands, and the rock-armored man raised it midformation to ready another throw. She struck first, *mareh'et*'s claws growing from her fingers as she slammed them through the *magi*'s armored neck. Stone cracked, and the skin beneath it split clean, a single heartbeat's worth of blood staining her hands as his head fell to the ground.

Pleasure spiked through her in a rolling wave.

She felt her blood thrumming in time with her breath. Sweat dripped from her forehead.

No, Anati thought. *Fight her. Don't let her have control.*

She muted the upstart *kaas*. She was the Veil; it was never her place to be told what to do by such a creature. The storm spirits granted their blessing at her demand, and rage burned through her body. She whirled to face the traitor, Axerian, and the other two fools who had accompanied him on this deadly-stupid foray into her rival's claim. The Regnant would offer no quarter, if he took them here. Even the *kaas* could not grant them passage back through the Divide, and the enemy would have his revenge for coming here at all. Killing them first might be the start of penance, if she could entreat the Regnant to listen.

She discharged lightning toward them, and Axerian moved, leaping to intercept the bolt.

The energy tore through him. He fell, covered in wisps of smoke.

No, Anati thought to her as she readied another strike. *This body is not yours. I am not yours!*

The pleasure receded, and Sarine sucked in a hard breath, her hands shaking as her senses regained control.

"Sarine!" Acherre shouted. "What the bloody fuck are you doing?"

The memory of what she'd done played again in her mind before she registered the cause. Not her. The Veil. Killing had triggered *Black*'s waves of pleasure, and let the Goddess escape. She raced forward, dropping to her knees beside Axerian. Ka'Inari already held his hand, rolling him over to face the sky.

"The Veil," Axerian croaked. "You lost...you let her..."

"I didn't mean to," Sarine said. "*Black* came, and I lost control. Axerian, I'm sorry. I didn't mean to."

Axerian managed a rasping laugh. "Forgot I'd already used *White*," he said. "Should have let the girl die."

Life obeyed her as she wove it into his body. His lungs had charred from the inside; she fought to repair them. Blood poured through rips in his organs. *Red* and *Body* coursed through her as she worked, slowing each blood vessel as it burst. She sealed them shut, bolstering him with as much energy as she could handle.

He'd gone quiet, and pale, staring at her with sadness in his eyes.

"More coming," Acherre said. "We have to move."

Axerian's heart stopped, and suddenly *Life* went sluggish as she worked the strands into his body, the same as if she'd tried to bind them into a stone.

The pleasure of death, of killing, came again.

She recoiled from it, fought it down as soon as it rose.

Cheers filled the manor garden as soldiers in yellow-painted armor streamed onto the grounds. Acherre moved to put herself between them, but the newcomers greeted them with shouts of welcome and relief.

"Lord Isaru's *magi*," the nearest ones said. "They've arrived!"

45

ERRIS

A Trench Overlooking a Hillside Fort
Cadobal Highlands, the Thellan Colonies

Artillery bellowed behind their line, sending tremors through the ground. Mud spattered from the sides of their trench, painting most uniforms shades of brown rather than the usual deep Sarresant blue. Spades lay discarded for the time being, and the smells of piss and excrement had yet to be washed away by the late-season rain. If the sun was shining, it was hidden behind a layer of clouds and gun smoke. The regiment-colonel in command of the 16th was the only bright spot, meeting her *Need* with a crisp salute and thick mustaches unstained by soot or grime.

"High Commander, sir, it's an honor," the colonel said. "A true honor, straight from the stories."

"Thank you, Colonel," she said in her vessel's voice, a deeper, harsher tone than hers, though still a woman's. "Report. How is your line disposed?"

"Dug in, sir. The Thellan are cowards, hiding behind walls we've no need to risk assaulting. I ordered us dug in to ring the hills here, with support from Calenne's artillery. We're spread thin, but with Brouard in reserve on the left, we can react to any enemy movement if they try to leave the fort."

She translated the words into materiel in her mind—Calenne had the

22nd Battery, and Brouard the 41st Cavalry. Nine guns, with some seven hundred soldiers surrounding the fort.

"What strength does the enemy have here?" she asked.

"Not more than a half-strength regiment, sir," the colonel said. "Four, maybe five hundred. Easy enough to crack, if we assault the walls, but I valued my soldiers' lives over a swift attack. Our guns will push them out in short order. Unless you think it better, if we press our advantage?"

"No, Colonel. Hold this position. Send word to Major Calenne to conserve as much ammunition as she can, but drive them out. Bombard them through the night, if you have to. And keep a clear eye for any attempts to flee."

"Sir, yes, sir."

"Do you have a spyglass, Colonel?"

He patted his coat before an aide produced one.

She panned the glass along the walls. Thellan soldiers in their mustard-yellow coats were visible behind the palisade, hunkered down where Calenne's battery hadn't torn holes in the fresh-built wood-and-mud-brick barricades. A dozen more forts like this one had sprung up in the Thellan march, as though the enemy had planted a garden of nettling bushes in her path. None were any better defended than this one, nor had there been any sign of reinforcements set to break her sieges. The enemy had stationed just enough soldiers in each to threaten her with raids if she ignored them, but not to offer any serious defense. A few weeks' delay, at best, before she'd taken them all, if these forts continued into the Thellan heartland.

She'd almost given up and collapsed the spyglass when she found what she'd been searching for.

A Thellan officer, standing proudly in plain view, holding a spyglass pointed straight back at her. It took a second look to recognize the golden light of *Need* spilling from the end of the enemy's glass tube, the same as it would be for hers. They held each other in view for a moment, until the enemy lowered his glass, raising his fist to his chest in what she could only read as a mocking imitation of a salute.

She collapsed the glass, handing it back to the aide.

"Keep morale up, Colonel," she said. "We have the advantage, on the fields to come. This fort is only the beginning."

"Sir, yes, sir," the colonel said.

She let *Need* fade.

"Any updates, sir?" one of the aides asked.

"Nothing new," she said. "The Sixteenth is where you have them, still besieging their fort."

Another aide reached to add a token to the map near the 9th and 16th, signifying a freshly reported position. She left the table, heading for another group of officers standing nearby.

"Sir," they said collectively, moving to make way as she took a place overlooking their work. Brigade-General Vassail headed the table, though she did it sitting down, her leg raised atop a second chair, lashed with wood splints and linen wraps from the break she'd suffered while drilling her troops, some days prior to the southward march.

It took a moment for her eyes to focus on their maps. Her days had become an endless chain of tabletops and planning, one theater in sequence with another, while her nights had been spent with more of the same, only with politics and the concerns of state thrown in for seasoning. These maps were hand-drawn, and freshly done. An approximation of the tribes' lands beyond where the Thellan part of the barrier had fallen, far to the south.

"Report," she said. "Where do we need updates?"

"We're well enough situated, for now, sir," Vassail said. "The western front is quiet; I was preparing orders for Wexly to move in support of the Second Corps. But it can keep till morning."

Thank the Exarch for small graces. "Very good, then," she said.

Vassail grabbed wooden crutches and rose to her feet as Erris turned to leave. "Sir, may I accompany you for a moment?"

"Of course, General," she said, and paused while the cavalrywoman hobbled forward, falling in at a lopsided gait as they moved toward Erris's private offices.

"You're finished with the morning reports, sir?" Vassail asked.

"Yes. And you're interrupting my downtime, General." She said it with a smile to take away any malice, but there was truth to it. Conserving her energy while the army was active was imperative.

"Yes, sir," Vassail said. "Apologies. I'm concerned as to why the enemy is throwing his soldiers away with these makeshift forts. It doesn't make any sense to me, sir."

"What do you think he's up to?"

Erris pushed through the double doors leading to her office foyer, holding them open while Vassail swung her crutches through. Aide-Captain Essily greeted them, rising from behind his desk in the receiving area; that much she'd expected. But Marquand was there, too, already on his feet by the time she'd cleared the door, and Omera, the servant who'd attached himself to Voren.

"High Commander, sir," Essily began, while Marquand said, "About bloody time," and Omera said nothing, merely stared at her with his unnerving one-eyed glare.

"What's this about?" she asked.

"The colonel insisted he be allowed to—" Essily began.

"I Gods-damned need your attention, d'Arrent," Marquand said.

"Enough," she snapped. "Did you forget our last exchange? I asked for decorum, Colonel. I expect to see it here, waiting for me when Brigade-General Vassail and I are finished."

Marquand smoldered, but said nothing.

Vassail went ahead into her private offices, ushered through the door by a smug-looking Essily.

"This is about Voren, isn't it?" she asked Marquand, pausing halfway through the room.

"Of bloody course it is."

Lovely. Precisely what she needed right now. Her body was sore enough to have been riding for days, her eyelids heavier than an hour's midday nap could hope to cure. But then, she'd put Marquand to the task of divining the creature's secrets. Too much to hope he might have taken longer to do it.

"I'll be quick, Colonel," she said, sparing a nod to acknowledge Omera. The Bhakal man still hadn't said a word, only watched her as she strode the rest of the way into the inner chamber.

The exchange with Vassail took the better part of an hour. All they concluded was that the enemy's forts made little tactical sense, which made them a part of some strategy neither she nor Vassail understood. Whatever Paendurion intended, it began with throwing away thousands of his troops solely to slow her down. She knew from the last campaign that Paendurion wouldn't balk at such sacrifices—and worse, worse by far—but for now it meant hedging while maintaining a strong front line to her advance. By the time Vassail left they'd laid the groundwork for the next phase of the campaign, though it would fall to the remainder of her staff to flesh out the broad strokes of her plan.

"Colonel Marquand and Master Omera to see you, High Commander," Essily said after Vassail departed. "Shall I send them in, or will you be retiring for the afternoon?"

"Send them in, Captain," she said.

Marquand strode through her door quietly, stopping to stand briefly at attention while Omera came and stood beside him. She couldn't help but brace for the inevitable storm of cursing, or at least a muted effort to still himself for her benefit. Instead he kept his features smooth, staying in place without a hint of his usual insubordination.

"Sit," she said, gesturing toward her couches. "Now, what news from our prisoner?"

Once again she expected Marquand to show signs of cracking under the weight of her forced etiquette. He didn't. His eyes were gaunt, with a look of fatigue she hadn't noticed in the foyer, and his hands trembled; signs of withdrawal from a man accustomed to drink, perhaps, but paired with the seriousness in his expression they suggested something else. Fear.

Omera startled her by speaking first. "The creature Fei Zan is a thing born of lies," he said. His voice was touched with an unfamiliar accent, though he handled the words of the Sarresant tongue cleanly enough. "We know of his kind, in the Bhakal countries. You would do well to learn from what he is, not what he says."

"All right," she said. "Care to start a few steps earlier? What brought this on?"

"He's...not a binder," Marquand said. "Or at least, not susceptible to any of the usual tests. I tried binding through him, leaving the tether open. I tried watching the leylines while he performed his...trick. Nothing."

She nodded, waiting for more.

"He's not a bloody binder," Marquand finished. "But he can do magic, sure as I can shit myself watching it."

"And what's the significance of that?" she said. "The leylines are far from the only sources of power in this world. The Skovan have their folk-magic, the New World tribes have theirs, the Bhakal have at least three different kinds on record, bound up in their herblore..." She nodded toward Omera for the last. He only watched her, unmoving and calm.

"I'm not a fucking idiot, d'Arrent," Marquand said. "And neither am I some ignorant schoolboy. I studied the basics of every type of magic there is, at the academy. The point isn't that Voren, Fei Zan, or whatever the fuck he is can change his face without a binding, the point is that he can do it at all. It isn't something recognized in any school, anywhere in the world."

"Omera just said—"

"Let him tell you the whole of it," Marquand said.

They both turned to the Bhakal servant.

"It is not a thing of the West," Omera said. "But the West is not the world."

"Go on," Marquand said. "Tell her where Voren's power is from."

"Fei Zan told the truth on this," Omera said. "He is a man of the Jun, the great power beyond the Divide. How he came here, I cannot guess. But he is here for evil, of this you can be certain."

Erris weighed Omera's words without understanding. "Explain," she said. "What precisely did the prisoner claim?"

Marquand stood and went to a globe on a stand in the corner; it had come with the office furnishings, so far as she knew.

"It means our maps are wrong," Marquand said, spinning the globe to indicate the far side of the world. All blue, between where the Skovan reaches ended on the far coasts of the Old World and the best guesses of the cartographers supposing where the end would be of the new one. An older style; some of the newer maps and globes would show black for unmapped territory rather than permit the mapmakers to guess. "It means there's something out there, something our best explorers never found. Or maybe those were the ones who didn't come back, Nameless take me if I know the difference. Ask Voren yourself, if you doubt it. He claimed to be from the people on the far side of the world, and I believe it. He spoke tongues you've never heard, recited place names and ranks and titles that might as well come from some invented folk-tale."

She spared another glance for Omera. There was more to the Bhakal man's understanding of this than he was revealing; Marquand had reacted with shock, while Omera kept a cool composure no servant's training could explain. Omera had known something of this before Voren's revelation, and unless she misjudged, it meant the Bhakal people had kept secrets, even in the face of the Empires of the Old World.

"Why are you revealing this now?" Erris asked, directing the question to Omera. "Your people knew of it before, didn't they?"

"It is not a secret, High Commander d'Arrent," Omera said. "It is the way the world is."

"That isn't the half of it," Marquand said. "Though you'll need to hear the rest from Voren himself. He claims the Thellan campaign is doomed to fail, that the enemy—Paendurion, he calls the man by name—is trying to snare you there while he completes the conquests required for 'ascension.' He said this 'ascension' has already happened, with the man called Reyne d'Agarre. And he says if we don't stop Paendurion, it will mean the Divide between our two halves of the world will collapse."

She leveled a look of skepticism at him.

"I know," he continued. "I know, it sounds absurd. But I half believe him, Gods damn me for a fool. You need to hear it from him personally, High Commander. I'm bloody well sorry to have to drag you into it. I know you have enough on your back without my adding more, but I wouldn't have brought it to you if I didn't think it was worth hearing him out."

Fatigue burned behind her eyes. She had a campaign to manage, with the strings of political power in the Republic sapping any strength she tried to keep in reserve. But Marquand wasn't the kind to jump at shadows. She'd given him this command. She owed it to him to take him at his word.

"All right," she said, rising from her chair and buttoning her coat. "Let's hear what Voren has to say."

———

Marquand led the way, though she kept Omera between them as they descended steps past the first basement and into the second. Warm carpets and tapestries gave way to cold stone. Soldiers in uniform still paced the halls, with sign of work being done in every corner, every space that might be utilized, no matter how remote from the main levels. It seemed more fitting for a dungeon than an office, and all the more so when they reached a steel-plated door, for which Marquand reached into his coat to produce a key.

A soft light greeted them as they stepped inside, with a crosshatch cast on the floor from iron bars covering the window well. So, a dungeon in truth, then. And a prisoner, though where her mind's eye had expected the wiry frame and weathered skin of the man she'd known as Anselm Voren, instead something, and someone, else stood in his place.

The prisoner's features were strange: a broad, flat nose, skin a dark honey color that might have marked him as a Sardian or northern Bhakal, if not for the face. Cuts and bruises marked the rest of him, starting above his cheekbones and winding down his naked back, where lash marks and welts crisscrossed down below the waist of his trousers, the only clothing he'd been allowed. He stood firm in spite of it, with a soldier's tightly muscled form that gave no sign he was in pain.

"It's you, High Commander," the prisoner said in an unfamiliar voice. "At last, you've come."

"She's here for what you told us," Marquand said.

The prisoner turned, rattling the chains attached to the manacled cuffs fixed around his wrists and ankles as he met her head-on.

"I never acted other than in your interest," he said. "I swear it, High Commander d'Arrent. I swear it on the four winds, on the Trithetic Gods, on any other symbol you require."

"You lie," Omera said.

"No," the prisoner said. "I came here to aid her, not to—"

"Enough," Erris said.

Both men fell silent.

"I'm here for answers," she continued. "Swift and clear, without evasions. Give an indirect answer, or tell me a lie, and I will leave, and you will be executed. Am I understood?"

"Yes." The prisoner said it crisply, and fell into a relaxed pose that remained firmly upright. The look of a man prepared to die.

"You were the man I knew as Marquis-General Anselm Voren."

"I was," he said, "and am."

"You possess some magic, some trickery, that allowed you to take his form."

"I do."

She almost flinched at the admission, but he made it boldly, with no sign of caution.

"Had I ever met the real man, before you took his place?"

"I can't be sure," the prisoner replied. "I believe you may have met him once or twice in passing, between his arrival from the Old World and your promotion to command the First Division. But I murdered him and took his place after the Battle of Villecours. I was behind your promotion, and all the affairs and planning that have gone between us since."

Her hand might have shook if she held it up, but otherwise she gave no sign of the rage coursing through her.

"What is your true name?" she asked. "Where are you from, and why have you come to New Sarresant?"

"I am Fei Zan, Grandmaster of the Great and Noble House of the Fox. My Lord guided me to the breach in the Divide created when your Goddess made her pact to be reborn. I am here to guide you to ascension, to uphold the pact between Life and Death, and to depose the treacherous Three, who have perverted the cycles of the Soul of the World since their first and only honorable victory."

"Cryptic words are as good as an evasion," Erris said, and made a show of turning to go.

"Wait, High Commander," Marquand said, at the same moment the prisoner—Fei Zan—pleaded, "It's true, every word. I swear it."

"Then explain," she said. "No more chances. Make it clear, now."

The man who had been Voren took a deep breath. It was impossible not to see it, now: the slightest similarities, in the angle of his head, the way he looked at her, the way he stood. It was as though this man had been a puppeteer in Voren's body, with the curtain now torn away to reveal the player's hand.

"Our world is divided," the prisoner began. "Sarresant mathematicians have proved the world is round, yes? And yet every globe is marked black on the far side. Sailors on the eastern oceans have reported reaching the end of the world—a towering shadow, through which nothing can pass."

"Sailors have reported dragons and merfolk living beneath the waves," Erris said. "It doesn't mean any of it is true."

"The Divide is real, High Commander," Fei Zan said, as Omera nodded in time with his words. "I have passed through it, where a seam was torn by the Goddess—your Veil—in her haste to be reborn."

"You expect me to believe the literal truth of the Gods and Goddesses, too? Even the staunchest priests deny they ever walked among us, no matter the parables in the Holy Virtues."

"They are wrong, then!" Fei Zan said. "Yes, High Commander. The Gods are real. I have seen mine, spoken to him as clear as you speak to me now."

She eyed him with an eyebrow raised. He was earnest in the telling, but then, she'd believed he was a seventy-year-old soldier for too long to feel anything but a fool at his behest.

"It is truth, Commander d'Arrent," Omera said. "This Divide falls in the ocean, for your people. But for mine, it is a shadow that cleaves my country in two."

She turned to the Bhakal man. "Your people are split by this… Divide?"

"They are," Omera said. "Though only our oldest stories speak of what happens when it falls, and none with any surety."

A silence fell between them. Half the world, bound up by Gods and Goddesses. Too much to be believed.

"There is also the matter of my gift," Fei Zan said. "You must acknowledge I have a magic unknown in your half of the world. Surely that counts for something?"

"Likelier by far that you've discovered a new binding, and thought to use it to gain power."

"No!" Fei Zan said. "I sought to manipulate you, but only toward your greatness. The Three—Paendurion, Axerian, Ad-Shi—they have commandeered the natural order. You had to be strong enough to challenge Paendurion, before the time of ascension. Already we are close to the moment of choosing, too close. If he succeeds again, and takes up the mantle of Order, my Lord has made clear he intends to shatter the pact, to invade at his full strength. It means no more champions, no more epochs of peace. There will be only war, to the last, to decide the fate of the Soul."

This time she pivoted toward the door.

"I said no more cryptic evasions," she said. "I'm finished here."

"Please," Fei Zan said. "No. You can't."

"You can make him prove it," Marquand said.

"Prove what?" she said.

"*Need*," Marquand said. "If he's truly loyal to you, you can bind him and have done with questioning it."

For a moment Fei Zan's eyes went wide. Then he nodded. "Yes," he said. "Yes! Tether it through me, and you will see."

Erris glanced back toward him. "A trick?"

"It isn't. I swear it. I've served your cause more faithfully than any of your soldiers. If you think my gift to be no more than a new binding, bond me as a vessel and see."

She nodded slowly. *Need* required loyalty for a first binding. Unfeigned, true loyalty—else what was to prevent her enemy from using it to subvert her commanders? If it could be done, Paendurion would have done it.

Her eyes snapped shut, and a font of gold appeared in front of her. Always before her connections had been mere figments, tiny flakes that flowed into the leystream. This creature oozed golden light, as though she'd pierced an artery of hope and desperation.

The connection snapped into place, and she saw the now-familiar sight of herself through foreign eyes. A flick of the eyelids revealed a gray and lifeless grid beneath the room, the inert sight of a vessel without the gift to touch the leylines.

It was true. Fei Zan's gift had no connection to the leylines. And he was bound to her now, as sure as any of her other vessels, with all the surety that entailed. She released *Need* as soon as it was clear.

"You see," Fei Zan said. "I am loyal to your cause, and have ever been. Allow me to explain in detail, before time grows too late."

"Too late for what?" she asked.

"Ascension. The moment will be on us soon. You will hear its promptings, and be judged. We must be sure you are the one to ascend, and not Paendurion."

"And what precisely does that mean? I've already discerned that Paendurion is in command of Thellan's armies in its colonies, and ordered my soldiers south."

Fei Zan shook his head. "Not just Thellan, High Commander. Ascension will be granted to the one who commands the greatest empire, the one who blankets your side of the world with loyalty, and control. Paendurion has tried to snare you here in the New World, but to challenge him, you must contest his holdings across the sea. You must conquer Thellan's colonies swiftly, then sail for the Old World, and prepare for war upon its shores."

46

ARAK'JUR

Eras'Ana'Tyat
Eratani Land

N O.

The spirits' sending crashed into him with the force of a storm, and he felt himself pushed back.

YOU HAVE HAD OUR GIFT ALREADY, SON OF THE SINARI. IT IS NOT YOUR PLACE TO COME TO US AGAIN.

He tried forming an image of himself victorious, a proud hunter standing over a kill. Ad-Shi had insisted the spirits would bend to him, if he applied enough force. Yet if this was strength, it was a strength beyond his understanding.

Vision Spirits, he thought to them. *I have need of knowledge. The Goddess's choosing approaches. I would know what path I might take, to prove myself worthy to ascend.*

This, too, Ad-Shi had told him to say. But scorn filled his mind as soon as he'd formed the words, a sensation of indifference and spite.

YOU ARE NO CHOSEN OF OURS. GO.

Once more he attempted to fill himself with pride, and felt it falter, the blackness of the spirits' void shimmering around him. Color leaked through where reality seemed to twist, and he saw images of the trees grown together in a dark thicket, where he'd stood before entering the Eratani sacred place.

GO. DO NOT COME AGAIN.

The void shattered, and color flooded to fill his vision. He coughed and staggered back, sucking wind into his lungs as Ad-Shi caught him and kept him on his feet.

A black haze pulsed at the edges of his vision as he tried to take his bearing. He was outside the sacred place, standing among the trees. Its opening loomed ahead, but he was on solid ground, surrounded by thick branches, grass, and fallen leaves.

Ad-Shi took a step back, watching him as he recovered his breath.

He shook his head when he could manage it.

"They refused," he said.

"They are willful," Ad-Shi said. "I have made them so. You must be stronger. Try again."

Determination fought with sense, the latter bolstered by the exhaustion of hard travel and communion with the spirits. They'd traveled through two tribes' lands, heading west, with no more than a few hours' rest each day. Of his companion he'd learned little more than he already knew: She was small-statured and reserved, with a temperament like ice, though she was prone to bouts of biting anger. And above all, she could run *munat'ap* himself to tiring before she gave up on a pursuit. She'd given him nothing more than the words he was to say, the postures he was to take when they reached Eras'Ana'Tyat. Now she stared at him as though catching his breath was a distraction they could ill afford.

"They were clear I was not to try again," he said. "That I was no chosen of theirs."

This time she cocked her head, a gesture more like a falcon than a woman.

"What else?" she asked.

He drew a hard breath, grateful for a moment to compose his thoughts.

"They said I had their gift already," he said. "Though that is not possible; I have never ventured to Eratani lands. Perhaps they mistook me for another."

She clicked her teeth. "No. This place is *Ana*, bound to Visions. Your Sinari sacred place is *Ana*, too. You have been there, yes? But then, they said you were not one of theirs."

His mind reeled even as he suppressed the urge to wince, the old taboo of shamans' and women's secrets coming to the fore of his thoughts. He knew the similarities between sacred places' names—Ka'Ana'Tyat in Sinari land, Hanet'Li'Tyat for the Ranasi, Nanek'Hai'Tyat for the Nanerat. But he had never guessed the names might reveal their natures. And this place, the Eratani sacred site, was called Eras'Ana'Tyat—having *Ana* in common with the Sinari sacred place, just as she'd said.

Sudenly Ad-Shi turned her gaze at him, as full of fire as she had been before their duel.

"Where did you first receive word from spirits you were chosen?"

He almost started away from her. "It wasn't at Ka'Ana'Tyat," he said. "I remember, the *ipek'a* spoke of it, or perhaps..."

She gestured to cut him short. "It would not have been a guardian spirit," she said. "It would have been after a great victory, and it would have been a war-spirit, judging from..." She trailed off for a moment. "You used fire. The Mountain. It was *Hai*, wasn't it?"

His memory flashed to Arak'Atan, and the floating stones outside the Nanerat sacred place. "Yes," he said. "At Nanek'Hai'Tyat."

She uttered something sharp, halfway between a guttural rumbling and a hiss.

"You knew I was taking us to *Ana*," Ad-Shi said. "Why did you say nothing of this? We've wasted days, when every hour is precious."

"I didn't know..." he said, but she'd already blinked to glaze her eyes in the milk-white haze of the spirits.

He fell quiet, feeling his ears burn. Not since his first days as a trapper had he felt so out of step with the path in front of him. Then, it had been the rebukes of Valak'Ser and Hanat'Ran and the rest of the traders he had feared. The worst they would have done was scold him, send him to find his way back to the village alone. And no more had ridden on his learning than the day's hunt. It paled beside the future Ad-Shi had painted, and it tore at his sense of duty to have failed. It was a thing for young men to worry over excuses or blame; he knew the end was all that mattered.

"Fortune smiles on us," Ad-Shi said, her eyes returned to their deep brown. "There is *Hai* close to us, perhaps five days north and east."

He turned, at the same moment she did. Awareness of direction was among the first senses honed, by hunters and guardians alike.

Even through the trees, he could see that the horizon showed no sign of mountaintops akin to the great peaks of the far north. There were hills at the eastern edge of Vhurasi land, but none broke into mountains, unless...

He looked up at the horizon again. She meant to take them beyond where the fair-skins' barrier had stood, onto the lands of their cities. And she meant to cover in five days what had taken him and Corenna three times so many, even traveling at a pace fit to flee from the Uktani's pursuit.

Ad-Shi had already started running through the trees.

He followed, feeling his heart thrum in time with his breath.

———

"Rest," Ad-Shi said.

He'd almost crashed into her, finding her suddenly still when the day had been a struggle to keep her in view. Even *lakiri'in* and *mareh'et* hadn't proved enough to keep close; as soon as he'd used their gifts, she'd done the same, leading him through wooded plains without pause for food or sleep. The spirits had found the uses vulgar, taking longer and longer between granting their blessings. But after the first bursts of speed, Ad-Shi had called on them in sequence, rotating through any gift that might hasten their journey. *Ipek'a* had been used to leap from hillsides, *astahg* to blink from shadow to shadow as often as the spirit would listen to their call. Now his body screamed with pain, his calves and back and lungs sore, still not fully healed from his time in recovery.

He staggered to a halt, lowering himself beneath a canopy of elms, and Ad-Shi paused to look at him. The sky had darkened past twilight, closer to dawn than sunset, but still he could make out the curiosity in her eyes. Shame blossomed under her gaze, but he was past the point of being able to conceal his fatigue. If she thought less of him for being willing to drive himself to the point of exhaustion, so be it.

He expected some comment or rebuke; instead she turned and ran onward, vanishing into the wood.

He half sat forward, intending to follow, but his body would not obey. Aches lanced through him, redoubled for the comfort of having finally come to rest.

Thoughts were fleeting as he listened to his breath come heavy beneath the trees. He'd never pushed himself so hard for anything, even at the direst need, even in fighting beasts or men. In a way it was refreshing to find his limits. Ad-Shi seemed to revel in it, though he still had yet to fully grasp the meaning behind their journey. Enough that he was on a course to protect his people.

Ad-Shi returned as suddenly as she'd gone, crashing through brush with a renewed bout of *lakiri'in*'s speed.

She sat as quickly as he'd registered she'd come back, holding two slain raccoons by their tails. She slipped a bone knife from her belt, set to skinning them in quick strokes that took no care to preserve their pelts.

"Food?" he asked. It would mark the first they'd eaten, since they began.

She nodded, handing him the first skinned carcass as soon as she'd finished it. Blood ran over his hands, accepting the freshly slain animal. No part of him wanted to gather sticks for a fire; instead he called on Mountain's gift, scorching the meat to a crisp char before he pulled it loose from the bone.

She did the same a few moments later, blackening her meat with a burst of fire, then setting to eat it in the darkness.

"It is customary for hunting duties to be shared," Ad-Shi said suddenly. "You provide in the morning, I provide at night?"

The question took him by surprise. From her he half expected a challenge to lift a mountain, or outrace the sunrise; nothing so mundane as shared hunting on a journey.

"Yes," he said. "We share the same custom, between master and apprentice."

He couldn't make out her expression in the dark, but he saw the small nods that indicated satisfaction as she returned to her food.

He watched her eat, the warmth of food in his own belly enough to bring back curiosity. She knew more of the spirits' ways than any shaman, even spoke of the spirits themselves as equals, if not inferiors, for all she drew on their power. Yet she was alone, a quiet reserve and fragility in her manner he'd seen even in their first exchanges. It was clear she didn't intend to venture unprompted answers, but that didn't mean he couldn't ask.

"Your people," he said. "They followed the spirits' ways as well?"

"They were our ways," Ad-Shi said. "Vordu ways, shared by men, women, beasts, and spirits."

"And this was long ago."

She set the last part of her meal on her lap.

"Yes."

"How long?"

"More days than there are stars in the sky," she said. "More days than there are men and women in this world."

"There are stories of shamans grown old," he said, "pruned as cracked leather. Older than mighty oaks. And yet you do not have the look of age."

"What do you wish to know?" she asked. "Ask only what you need, to motivate you to take my place. The rest is unimportant."

Her directness again surprised him. Even with Corenna, sharing had come slowly, a push to shed taboos together. And now, having the chance to ask, his mind worked to find the right words.

"Being chosen," he finally said, "does it mean aging as you have done? Outliving your people and customs, while the world grows old around you?"

She gave a soft laugh, subtly shaking her head as she spoke.

"Twice wrong," she said. "Chosen is nothing; chosen is the spirits taking note of your potential. Ascension is what you seek: to become the paragon of our ways, the embodiment of the Wild in service to the Veil. And ascension carries no promise of age. That was Life, the Veil's power. Unless she invests it in you, you will age and die in your rightful time, whether you are champion or no."

"And she invested it in you?"

"No. I took it."

"Why?"

This time she glowered at him, hard enough that he could almost see the fire in her eyes.

"Ask another question," she said. "Or sleep. It is no matter to me; we move with the sun, whether you are rested or no."

Her words bit sharp, but he sat straighter, invigorated with the potential for knowledge.

"What can I expect from the Mountain spirits?"

"They will set you a task, or help you divine one for yourself. *Hai* are protectors by nature, given to nurture and growth. Other chosen will have different tasks; the ascendant will be the greatest among you, at the end."

"You were the ascendant, before."

"Sixteen times before, yes. None have achieved so great a deeds as I have." She said it bitterly, almost mocking in tone.

He frowned. "How will the spirits choose another, if you are so accomplished?"

"I will not be alive, when the moment comes. I will find a high cliff, and leap from it, when I am satisfied you have learned enough."

The stillness of night crept between them, stretching the silence too long for new words.

In the face of that admission, any further questions soured on his tongue. There would be time for more, after the next day's grueling pace. But now a fire kindled in him as he prepared for sleep, the first since Corenna had left. The spirits would confirm Ad-Shi's words, and confirm the threat behind them. If it was true, it would fall to him to understand, to rise to protect not only himself and his tribe, but all peoples of all tribes. He had never sought status as a warrior or a leader, but he couldn't deny the power Ad-Shi held. If it was the spirits' will for it to pass to him, even in part, he would strive to be worthy of it, to find a way to still his doubts and champion their cause.

The admonition cut through his fatigue, filling him with warmth in spite of the cold, and sleep came swiftly, carrying him through the last hours before dawn.

47

SARINE

A Collapsed Temple
The City of Kye-Min, the Jun Empire

Their guide flinched as cannon shot rattled the building frame, shaking loose dust stored on rafters overhead. Fifty-odd more soldiers dressed in yellow dyed leather and wool beneath their scale hauberks did the same, shuddering as the building shook, huddled together in clusters beside small fires burning around the room. Trade their armor for the finery of the old nobility and they could have been in her uncle's chapel at the height of the battle of New Sarresant. The sight struck a chord of longing mixed with grief. Her uncle would be worried for her, serving soup unaided to anyone who asked for charity, alone with only the Gods for company. A fine lot that had turned out to be, between the Nameless and the Veil.

"My lady," their guide said, bowing twice to her and then again to a soldier standing near a horse-sized idol of some strange creature she didn't recognize, a serpentine figure crossed between an elephant and a snake. "I present Captain Hashiro, of the Company of the Golden Sun."

The captain wore armor of the same quality as his soldiers, stained by dirt and dented by fighting, with only a golden cord bound at his shoulder to indicate his rank. He had a few days' growth in his beard, and leveled a weighing glare, first on her guide, then on her, Ka'Inari, and Acherre.

"You are the *magi* Isaru Mattai promised us?" Hashiro said. "Three?"

"That's right," she said. "Your men promised us there were leaders of the *magi* among your enemies. We're here to deal with them."

The captain looked askance over his shoulder, toward a pair of soldiers in the same attire standing at his flank.

"They are most effective fighters, sir." The soldier who had been their guide spoke up. "With their aid we repulsed two companies at the waterfront, and drove through the center of the city to reach your headquarters here."

"My men have counted over twenty *magi* arrayed against us here in Kye-Min," Hashiro said. "And Lord Isaru sends me three. Yet I have word some number of your fellows have reinforced Captain Ugirin's White Tigers. Why would he not send you together? Does Isaru intend us to work with the Tigers?"

Sarine swallowed a knot before it could form in her throat. Here was the risk of the masquerade she'd adopted in the moments after Axerian's death, when a rush of soldiers had come on them praising their gods for their deliverance. They were here to kill the would-be ascendants of the Regnant's lines; what better way to do it than to have soldiers point them out on a battlefield? But if the others—the ones these soldiers in yellow were truly waiting for—were to show themselves, it might well mean their ruse would fold. Still, her uncle had lectured her often enough on the virtues of pragmatism and adaptability. Best to use what she could, while she could.

"I wasn't given any information on Lord Isaru's plans for the battle," she said. "Only—"

"Wait," Acherre interrupted. "Translate for me. If he's their captain, I can use him to understand what to expect in the rest of the city."

Captain Hashiro eyed them with suspicion. "I speak the Natarii tongue," he said, changing the inflection of his words, though Anati still translated them for her perfectly.

"Acherre doesn't speak Natarii," Sarine said. "But I can translate between you. She's a...a captain in her army. Tell her what you know of the battle, and we can aid in planning our next attack."

"Our next attack...?" Hashiro said. "Forgiveness, my lady, but I must have misheard. I just told you we face a score of acolytes of the Great and Noble Houses, to say nothing of the Emperor's soldiers at their backs.

My men have been slaughtered here. If we survive the night, I intend for my company to withdraw into the field, to make an escape along the Songye river, if we can secure the northside docks."

"Tell him to give us a full accounting of their numbers and disposition," Acherre said after Sarine managed a hasty translation. "His men, any friendly troops, and the enemy."

The captain went along with her requests, though she couldn't dismiss his distant demeanor as merely an artifact of a foreign culture, much as there was plenty of that. Still, as Acherre began to understand enough of the battle's layout to contribute to planning their next steps, the captain's suspicion seemed to fade. Strange to think they could be ten thousand leagues from anywhere familiar and still share the common bond of a struggle for survival.

It became clear in their exchange that Captain Hashiro's Golden Sun was a mercenary company, hired by a lord named Isaru Mattai to attack the city—which she learned was called Kye-Min. Two rivers cut through the city, emptying into its harbor from opposite directions, and the temple they were holed up in sat in the district situated between them, with the enemy holding the banks on both sides. A second mercenary company, Captain Ugirin's White Tigers, was reported to be besieged in the east, surrounded by soldiers in red.

"So you see," Hashiro said after he'd described his latest scouts' reports. "The situation is without hope, even with three *magi* to bolster our line."

"He mentioned more friendly *magi* with the White Tigers," Acherre said after Sarine had translated. "Ask him how many, and what they can do."

"The *magi*'s secrets are beyond my knowing, my lady," Hashiro said when she posed him the questions. "I am a simple warrior and general. I will honor my contract with Lord Isaru, but there is a time to fight, and a time to withdraw. If my lord demands my head as price for failure, then I will give it, but not before I see my men to safety."

"Bloody odd attitude for a mercenary," Acherre said after she'd repeated it.

"I'm not going to translate that," Sarine replied, and Acherre grinned, both for Hashiro's sake and hers.

"Well, he's not wrong, under ordinary circumstances," Acherre said.

"I'd judge he's got maybe twenty thousand, and not more than thirty. Even if his friends on the other side of the river have the same number, the enemy has to have at least twice so many. Judging by the fighting we saw in the harbor, the sea isn't going to be an escape route, which leaves him the rivers. That's his one advantage; he has control of both waterways, and the enemy will have the Nameless to pay if he wants to try an assault across the bridges."

"All right," Sarine said. She'd followed the thrust of Acherre's analysis if not the specifics. "But I'm sure he knows this. What do you want me to tell him?"

"Just trying to think what High Commander d'Arrent would do," Acherre said. "I bloody wish she had her *Need* bindings back. I could do with a connection right about now."

If it was meant as an invocation, nothing came of it—the captain and his soldiers watched them as Acherre spent a moment in thought.

"Do you think there's a chance we could find the *magi*'s leaders in the field?" Sarine asked. "Between *Faith*, the blue sparks, and Anati, I can break up just about any line of battle unseen, I'm sure of it."

"Right," Acherre said. "That has to be the main thrust of our plan. But we need to know where to look; if we use your magic too openly, we're going to scatter them and send anyone of any significance on their side into hiding. There's just too damned much we don't know about this place, and these people. I can't plan an attack without information. And it's a mistake to assume their *magi* won't have powers of their own."

"So…what's the plan? You agree with the captain that we should help them withdraw?"

A moment of tension passed among Captain Hashiro and his soldiers. Frustrating, that she had no means to stop Anati from translating her words into the native tongue of anyone who could hear.

"Maybe," Acherre said. "I think a probe first, to show the captain what you can do. We spend the night here, see if Ka'Inari can find another way. If he doesn't, we get the captain to try an attack across the eastern bridges, small enough that we don't frighten the enemy, but enough to show Hashiro he doesn't need to fear them, so long as he has you. Maybe we try to link up with the other company, if we can cut through the center of the enemy's line. If it works, we decide from there. If not, then we help him withdraw, and save as many of his company as we can."

She nodded, wishing Acherre could speak it for herself. At least the mercenaries hadn't questioned the *kaas*'s gift with languages. Perhaps it meant the *magi* here had a similar trick. Either way, Anati had earned her gratitude a hundredfold, and would surely prove herself a hundred times more, before they were done.

The captain listened as she explained Acherre's plan, grunting with some deference, though he gave no sign of being willing to abdicate his command. Still, Acherre's orders came with descriptions of *Shelter* and *Entropy* bindings, Anati's *Yellow*, and the guidance of Ka'Inari's visions of where they might find the enemy. Given even a cursory explanation of what the three of them could do, and the assurance that if they were pushed back, an escape up the river was the secondary plan, the captain relented, even joined in with Acherre in structuring the finer details. It took a few more rounds of translation to see the orders polished to Acherre's liking before Hashiro bowed and pronounced it would be done come morning.

Acherre vanished toward the temple's makeshift stable as soon as they were done, having somehow earned her pick of any save the captain's own mount during their exchange. Sarine found herself suddenly alone after a day spent at the center of a storm. Grief flickered at the edge of her thoughts, touched by steady flares of rage she knew belonged to the Veil. The latter she had learned to dismiss, though the grief was hers in full.

Ka'Inari had found a place in a corner of the temple's main chamber, given wide berth by the soldiers of Hashiro's company. In her uncle's chapel there would have been pews; here the cold stone floors were empty, save for fires built indoors, vented through places where the temple roof had been shattered and broken by artillery rounds. Ka'Inari had a small fire burning by himself, and she approached without thinking whether she should disturb him until she was already at his side.

"May I?" she asked belatedly.

The shaman blinked, looking up from his fire to meet her eyes.

"Sarine," he said. "Yes, yes, of course."

She sat, too late realizing he must have been consulting with his spirits. It would have been better to follow Acherre, or take a place by herself, but neither choice seemed available when she'd already lowered herself to sit cross-legged beside his fire.

"What news from their leader?" Ka'Inari asked.

"An attack, come sunrise," she said, "though it depends on you. Have you...? That is, are the spirits able to see anything here?"

"They are," Ka'Inari said. "Though I suspect the spirits of things-to-come are more awed by this place than even we are. They give me much to consider."

"Oh," she said, now fully aware she'd disrupted him. Better to wish him well and excuse herself. Food would work to explain it; she hadn't eaten since morning, though she felt no especial hunger in spite of the already darkened skies.

"You knew him well, didn't you?" Ka'Inari said. It took a moment to realize he meant Axerian.

An unexpected rush of grief put tears in her eyes.

"I didn't mean for..." she began, and heard her voice break.

Ka'Inari moved without her noticing, and suddenly he was beside her, offering a shoulder, and a comforting arm.

"I didn't know," she said. "I didn't know what would happen."

Soldiers around them turned to watch as Ka'Inari held her; she felt their eyes, her shame temporarily suspended by the memory of the terrible moment. The surge of lightning from her fingers, the white flash as it lit the courtyard, the smell of sizzling meat and fabric as Axerian crashed to the ground.

"It was the Goddess, wasn't it?" Ka'Inari said when they separated.

She nodded, wiping her eyes. "Yes. The Veil. She's still inside me. I didn't know *Black* would let her loose."

"I can't claim to understand all of what you endure," Ka'Inari said. "But I know something of unwanted voices pleading for terrible things. For us, for the shamans of my people, it's a constant struggle. Any moment might carry a dire threat, a terrible image or vision of things-to-come. It is a great burden."

She saw softness in him, a look she knew all too well from her uncle, when he'd shouldered his parishioners' burdens. A strange realization, that Ka'Inari might have played a similar role with his people. He searched through her with his eyes, as her uncle would have done, seeking some place for his words to still her grief, and it was no less welcome for knowing what he was trying to do.

"Anati has her bound," she said, though the reassurance sounded hollow even to her. "Yet I feel some measure of what the Veil feels. When

I slipped, she seized control, and..." The memories returned, and she winced, lowering her head.

"Are we in danger, traveling at your side?"

"I...I don't know," she said. "I'm sorry. I dragged you here, as good as into another world, and now I can't even control myself. You're right not to trust me. I should send you back, and Acherre. I should..."

Ka'Inari wore an amused smile, and she trailed off, watching him turn it on her.

"Think about what you're saying," he said. "You're trying to contain a Goddess, one for whom even the spirits themselves have reverence. You do wrong to expect too much of yourself. These are dark times, and there are risks to standing in the path of darkness. I know this, and I am here. Captain Acherre knows it. Axerian knew it, too."

"I came here because I'm frightened," she said. "I don't know what will happen, at the end of all this. I thought if we could find the other side's champions, we could cut it short. That I wouldn't have to use the Veil's power. But now we're here, and it isn't a city, or even a country. It's a whole bloody world, and I'm still frightened. I don't know where to go, or what to do."

"Tell me of the plans you made with Acherre and the captain," Ka'Inari said. "Perhaps the spirits can help."

She did, grateful for a moment to recover her composure. By now the soldiers around them had returned to whatever they were doing, but it still stung to think she'd wept openly in front of people who were going to need to look to her as a protector come morning. She dried her cheeks on her sleeve as she laid out the situation in the city: the two forces in red enveloping the mercenary companies here and on the other side of the river, the score of *magi* on the enemy's side and the handful reported to be trapped with the other band of mercenaries in the east.

Ka'Inari listened as she spoke, nodding along with each point.

"It is difficult," he said at last, when she'd finished. "I don't believe the *magi* among the enemy's lines are significant, for all the spirits seem fascinated by what they can do. I see two images that draw my attention. First, a tower overlooking the sea. A great evil dwells there, connected to shadows I see around you, the shadows of the Veil. And now I think I understand the second set. A traveler, come from far away, trapped by yellow spears, with a wolf at his side. These are the *magi* with the eastern band; our course should lead us there, if I understand the spirits aright."

"I'll tell Acherre, and Captain Hashiro," she said. Ka'Inari nodded, and reached a hand to bar her before she could rise.

"Sarine," he said, his voice taking on a harder edge. "The spirits… they know your strength. You must know it, too. But it will be tested, again and again, before the end."

She pulled back, halfway between curiosity and a sudden anxious fear. "You've seen more visions about me?" she asked, realizing belatedly the stupidity of the question. Of course he'd seen visions about her, if he was trying to divine the future of their travels together.

"Yes," he said. "Enough to know none of this will be easy. But you have my strength, such as it is, and the strength of the spirits whose gifts I carry. You are not alone in your burdens, nor will you ever be, so long as I draw breath."

The assertion took her by surprise, and she stammered a belated thanks before he withdrew, returning to focus on his fire.

48

TIGAI

Line of Battle
Eastern Markets, the City of Kye-Min

White-armored soldiers braced ahead of him, their spears thrust forward, impaling the red-armored soldiers as they charged.

Howls and grunts sounded, and Tigai watched, ten paces back, as men rushed to plug the gaps where red spears and poleaxes had cut bodies down trying to break through. Arquebusiers worked in a fury on the sloping hills behind the line, ramming balls down their barrels, pouring powder into their pans, locking burning rope in place to aim and fire.

Yuli stood beside him, scanning the enemy lines unflinching as they crashed together. Captain Ugirin's orders had been clear: Stay back, watch for enemy *magi*, and kill them. The rest, the captain had claimed, would fall to the White Tigers. So far the captain's bravado had proven itself in full. Daybreak had found the enemy army attacking from six sides at once, though if there was a plan to do more than bleed them for every inch of ground, the captain hadn't shared it with him.

"No *magi* here," he shouted for Yuli's benefit. It took saying it twice over the roar of the guns before she nodded. He extended a hand, and Yuli grasped it firmly. A blink revealed the five other anchor points he'd set the night before, and he tethered them to the strands, shifting from the din of heavy fighting to a muted quiet, five hundred paces down the line.

Here the soldiers were arrayed in the same lines—pikes, spears, maces, swords, pistols, arquebuses—but with no enemy in sight.

"Lord Tigai!" a heavy voice boomed. "How goes the fighting? Have you any trophies to show me yet?"

Captain Ugirin could have been Remarin's twin, from a distance. A hulking man, who eschewed heavy lamellar plate for the boiled leathers of an Ujibari horseman, with a shortbow on his shoulder and quiver on his belt, and never mind that his place was as a general, not a soldier.

"None yet, Captain," he said. "If the enemy has *magi* on the field, they're waiting to see where you deploy."

Ugirin's manner turned from boisterous to sober in an instant. "Be sure of it," Ugirin said. "We faced two yesterday. But White Tigers do not die easily." With that the captain placed a thumb behind his belt, showing off a fresh ear that had been sewn in place alongside a dozen more in varying stages of decay.

"Your flank, there, is under heavy pressure," Tigai said, inclining his head back toward where they'd been moments before.

"A feint, Lord Tigai," Ugirin said, smiling. "If there are no *magi*, it is not the main attack."

He nodded, extending his hand again for Yuli.

"Good hunting, *magi*," Ugirin said, and Tigai bowed before blinking to find the next anchor point on the line.

According to the captain the battle had been going for two days already, but for all Ugirin's bluster, Tigai couldn't see how it would last to see another sunset. Isaru Mattai had promised them *magi*, and those *magi* weren't coming. He didn't care at all in the abstract; Isaru had dug the grave for anyone fool enough to support him, so far as he could see. But Master Indra and the *magi* who had taken him had been Isaru's enemies, and that meant Remarin, Mei, and Dao were being held by the soldiers in red, or whoever pulled their strings. Finding his family started with taking one of their puppeteers alive, someone who might know where prisoners would be held. A flimsy beginning, but it was all he had.

This time they shifted into smoke and chaos.

Powder stung his nose, and a man lunged around him, stumbling sideways as another man grappled the first to the ground.

Tigai drew a pistol from his belt, and ducked as another pair came crashing past. A quick thumb set the match and he pulled the trigger, belching smoke into the swordsman's gut and knocking him into another mêlée, five paces down the line. A cloud of fog rolled through the street, obscuring most of the fighting and filling his nose with the tang of powder and ash. Thunder boomed overhead where guns were firing, but he saw no shells exploding here—at least, not yet.

"We have to get back," he shouted for Yuli's benefit. "Back toward the guns."

A gamble, since he couldn't see enough to tell one rank of troops from another. He had to hope those were Ugirin's guns, situated behind the line of battle, where the White Tigers had fallen back behind his anchor.

He spun, looking for Yuli to be sure she'd heard, and tried to duck as a spearman came screaming for him, thrusting a metal point into his leg. A ripping pain shot through his body, and he blinked to set himself back to where he'd first appeared, a few paces to the left. The spearman held his weapon steady for a moment, recoiling in a momentary confusion before Yuli sheared the man's head and shoulder from his spine. Blood sprayed in a wide arc where her claws sent the man and his spear clattering to the street, and she sprang toward where he was standing. A yelp escaped his throat, and he almost tethered himself to a different anchor before it became clear she was bounding for a target behind him. He spun to see three swordsmen cut to ribbons under her claws, slicing through steel, armor, and skin as though they were shields of paper.

She was at her full height now, as he'd seen her when they'd first arrived in Kye-Min, head and shoulders taller than any soldier in the line. With the smoke clouds spilling over her she appeared as a feral silhouette, her limbs long and thin, her face narrowed almost to a muzzle, with fingers sharpened to claws that raked the soldiers in red in a rain of blood and gore.

"Yuli!" he shouted, trying again. "Back!"

This time she snapped around, meeting his eyes for a brief fraction before she turned back the way she'd been headed, bounding in the opposite direction, into the red soldiers' lines.

"Oh for the *koryu's* sake…" he said, and charged after her.

This time there was an empty path through the chaos, carved by streaks of blood and mangled limbs lying across the street. He rushed after her, enjoying the momentary panic in the red soldiers' eyes. The smoke and powder cleared enough to see glimpses of the enemy's ranks, extending well past the edge of the market, and he chased Yuli, calling after her to turn back, wishing he'd asked after a few more of the details of her Natarii magic. If she had some sort of blood-craze beyond her morphing into some fucking horror from a children's tale, he'd as soon have known about it before he chased her into oblivion.

Yuli stood hunched forward in a clearing when he caught up to her, her claws stained a dark red where she held them out, as though she were brandishing ten knives at once. A hulking figure of polished glass stood facing them. Thick crystal armor encased the enemy *magi* from head to toe, making for a creature of equal height and a hundred times the girth of Yuli's long, thin limbs.

"Wait," he said. "Fucking wait. I've seen this sort before; they can—"

His words were swallowed in a rush of cracking glass as Yuli charged. The soldiers on both streets backed away in awe, no few chanting and calling for blood, while just as many scrambled away from the spectacle. At the center, Yuli rained her claws on the *magi*'s armor, shattering fragments of glass into the crowd. The *magi* shoved off, pivoting to throw her down with a jarring crunch as her body impacted the stone street.

Tigai had freed his second pistol, taking aim for a quick shot at the *magi*'s head. The ball struck home, spiderweb breaks appearing in the armor as the *magi*'s neck snapped to the side. Just as quickly a salvo of glass peppered Tigai's hand as he raised it to block his face, searing pain shooting up and down the side of his body. He blinked to return to his anchor, shifting his body back to the mouth of the junction. He drew his pistol again and fired, the same ball he'd used before, reset by the anchor. This time he missed, sending a shot into the crowd of soldiers with accompanying howls of pain from whomever he'd hit. He blinked and fired again, this time moving to make new anchors in case the *magi* pursued toward the first he'd set.

"Yanjin Tigai," the glass-*magi* said, snarling it through the layers of her glass. Still, no mistaking the voice. Lin Qishan. Of all the *aryu*-twisted coincidences…

Yuli had rolled back to her feet, though her body showed signs of a limp, and cuts from where salvos of glass must have stricken her when she was down.

Lin seemed to balance her attention between him and Yuli. No time to think, if he wanted to prevent Yuli from taking another volley of shards. Tigai charged, howling as he loosed a final shot toward Lin's glass-covered torso. It served to put her off-balance, and he connected, laying a hand on Lin's forearm. In an eyeblink he tethered them both to the strands, sending them somewhere far to the south, past the point of any stars with any connection to dry land.

Water splashed around him, a light spray where he impacted the surface and a powerful gulp where the ocean swallowed the glass-armored *magi* at his side.

For a moment the surface of the water was clear, the brief interruption of their arrival forgotten as waves rose and fell around him. A soft breeze blew over the crests, and he treaded water to stay where he was, at the center of a horizon filled end to end with ocean, as far as he could see.

The water broke as Lin Qishan swam to the surface, her familiar features having replaced her now-discarded glass.

"You fucking madman," she said. "Where have you taken us?"

"Where does it bloody well look like?" he said. "We're in the middle of the ocean, and you know if you try a damned thing here, I'll leave you to drown."

She stayed in place, all the chaos of the fighting left behind in quiet paddling to keep her head above the surface.

"What do you want, Yanjin Tigai?" she asked.

"Answers," he said. The water was calm enough they could speak, though his words were chopped, alternating between treading water and gasping for air. "Make me believe you know exactly where Mei, Remarin, and Dao are being held. Make me understand why any of this has happened. Do it and maybe I'll take you with me when I go back."

"I'm only a mercenary," she said between waves lapping around them.

"Not good enough," he said. "If you don't know where they are, then you're useless to me." He closed his eyes, preparing a tether to take him back to Kye-Min.

"Wait," she said.

He opened his eyes.

"I know where your master-at-arms is," she said. "He might have the girl with him; I can't be sure."

Remarin. Tigai's heart skipped at the prospect, and if Mei was there, too...

"Go on," he said.

"He's being held at the Tower of the Heron, in Kye-Min," Lin Qishan said. "Bavda Khon believes Remarin is Master Fei Zan, of the Great and Noble House of the Fox."

"Who? And...who?"

"Is he?" she asked. "But then, you likely wouldn't know."

"What are you talking about?"

"Take us back to the city," she said. "I swear I will explain in full."

"Like fucking hells," he said, spitting a gulp of water before it could wash down his throat.

"If you don't believe me," Lin said, "then I'm doomed no matter what I say."

More than a little truth to that. He watched as she kept her head above the water, her usual calm confidence fraying. She believed he would leave her; it was the only leverage he could hope for.

"Tell me exactly what I'm up against," he said.

"Please," she said. A surge of water almost swallowed her head, and she fought back to the surface. "This isn't...take us back to the city. I swear on my House, I will be your prisoner."

He shook his head, or tried to, between the rise and fall of the spray. She was right. In her place, he would have told any lie he could think of to get back to freedom. It made it impossible to believe her—even the prospect of Remarin being alive, and in Kye-Min no less...all too convenient, for the sake of her release.

"I know you put no stock in honor," Lin said. She gasped for another breath, this time with real panic in her movements. If she was going to try an attack, it would come soon. "But please believe me: My honor means more to me than my life. Take us back, and I am yours."

He wouldn't get any more here. Without a sign that he might trust her, she had no incentive to say anything more. It fell to him, then. Either trust, or leave her to die. For all he hated her—and he did, for her smugness as much as the nightmare she had put him through in service to the Dragons—he loved Remarin, Mei, and Dao more. If she betrayed him, he wouldn't be any closer to finding them than he was now.

He held out a hand through the waves, and she took it in a firm grasp.

The strands took them back to Kye-Min, to his second anchor, with Captain Ugirin's line.

Once more they were surrounded by soldiers. This time the spearmen had uprooted from their lines, marching in a flurry around where he and Lin Qishan now stood at the base of the hill.

"Thank you," Lin said, offering him a bow, surprisingly with no hint of mocking. "I am in your debt."

"Forward, Tigers!" Ugirin shouted. "Move! Leftward wheel to the line, go!"

The command bellowed above the chaos of the spearmen and reserve redeploying their line. No sign of any soldiers in red, but the men around him moved as though they had enemies on their heels, those nearest him and Lin Qishan giving them looks of surprise at finding two people unmoving in their way.

"Let's go," he said, reaching to grab her by the arm again. "If you meant what you said about being in my service, then we move with these men."

She went along with him, thank the wind spirits, and doubly thank them she'd worn ordinary clothes beneath her glass armor, rather than the red uniform of the Imperial army. They cut through the ranks together, aiming for the mounted figure bellowing orders at the mouth of the westward street.

"Captain!" he shouted as they approached. "Captain Ugirin!"

The mercenary commander pivoted in his saddle, his eyes brightening as he focused on Tigai.

"My *magi*," Captain Ugirin said, grinning. "Have you taken a prisoner? One of theirs?"

"What's the situation here, Captain?" he asked.

"We're marching out to meet the enemy," Ugirin bellowed, making it half an answer, half a rallying cry for troops near enough to hear. "Hashiro's Golden Sun have lived up to their name. The enemy's line is breaking, and we have reinforcements coming from the west, with *magi* at the head. *Magi!* Isaru Mattai may well be a dog-faced bastard, but I'll be damned if he didn't keep his word."

49

ERRIS

Private Chambers
High Command

Her temples ached, a deep pain no amount of kneading seemed to be able to cure.

"This is bigger than a bloody campaign," Marquand was saying. "And why did you order the army south in the first place? You knew the enemy commander is more than an ordinary man; we all bloody knew it, even before the battle at Villecours."

"I can't do it alone, Marquand," Erris said. "This decision is outside the purview of my command."

"It's a mistake. They'll see it as weakness, because it bloody well *is* weakness. I've never known you for a coward, d'Arrent."

"Careful," she said.

"Why? Should I fear speaking the truth to you now? You believe Voren, or Fei Zan, or whatever the fuck he's called. You know it's true."

"And since when has that ever been enough? Without the priests, the Assembly, the fucking *navy* at the very least—"

"You know what they'll say!" he snapped back. "They'll call you a second Louis-Sallet, and put a knife in your back, sure as he got. You'd do better to take this invitation as an excuse to put them all under guard until our ships are fifty leagues past the horizon. Anything else is cowardice, pure and plain, and I won't stand here and watch you deliver yourself into their hands."

"Where do you think you're going, Colonel?" He was already halfway to the door. "You turn around at once. That's an order."

He pushed through, all but slamming it shut as he stormed into her foyer. She had half a mind to follow him, and call him to answer for the insubordination. But he was right. Gods damn him, he was right. She'd called this meeting hoping Marquand would stand behind her, help her convince High Admiral Tuyard, Assemblyman Lerand, and First Prelate Casanne of the rightness of their cause. She didn't have the words to do it on her own. Gods bind her to the Nameless's soul, she couldn't do it alone.

"Sir, is everything well?"

Aide-Captain Essily appeared in her doorway, eyeing her with his usual attentive care. She nodded without looking up from her desk, back to massaging her temples in Marquand's absence.

"Yes, Captain," she said. "I could do with some hot tea. Otherwise, send in my guests as soon as they arrive."

"Of course, sir."

Maps lay open on her desk, and her attention drifted to studying them. She knew the forested valleys of the southern New Sarresant provinces, the hills and flatlands of the Gand colonies, even the Thellan islands as well as she knew the twisting streets of Southgate or the Harbor. Better, for some stretches of ground. But the maps she'd requisitioned today were new, for all they were the very oldest and best-laid-out among any maps drawn anywhere.

The Old World.

Mountains, the Capallains, stretched along the border between Old Sarresant and the Thellan home country. But how high did they rise, and which passes frosted over in wintertime? She could find men and women who knew the answers, but *she* needed to know them. She needed to know the ground without thinking. She needed to know where her ships could make a landing, which shoals and narrows to avoid when planning amphibious assaults and harassment up and down the Arinelle. The continent was crisscrossed with hamlets and roads to connect them to the great cities, the legacy of older empires now maintained by modern Kings and Queens. She needed to know them by instinct, as thoroughly as she knew the command structure of her army.

Essily came in a moment later, setting a tray atop a cabinet. He must have already had the kettle over a fire.

"Aide-Captain," she said before he could go. "Share your thoughts, if you would."

"Sir?" Essily said.

"What would you say if I told you our enemy was using the Thellan campaign as a distraction—that he meant to ensnare us in a quagmire in the south, while his real aim was to consolidate power in the Old World?"

"Sir, I don't know enough to make a decision. If you say that's his aim, then I trust your judgment."

"And would you still trust my judgment if I said I'd been meeting with the prisoner Voren? That he's from a nation on the far side of the world, one that will have the capacity to invade us soon?"

"Is...is that true, sir?" Essily asked.

"I believe it is," she said. "Gods damn us, I believe it is. Our enemy—the man behind the golden light—is gathering strength to face this threat, and he's made clear to me he means to see us destroyed as part of his ascension. If we don't stop him, we face ruin—whether from him or from Voren's people, when they arrive."

It sounded hollow as she said it, too much to be borne from anyone trusted with command. But such had been her talks with Fei Zan. He'd painted a portrait of an Empire waiting for greatness, a hundred cities each the size of New Sarresant or greater, with endless ranks of soldiers and foreign magics at their head. And *Need*—*Need* was the crux of everything. She'd already lost it once; Voren was certain that if Paendurion was allowed to finish his conquests unchecked, she would lose it again, this time without hope of recovery.

"What would it take to stop him?" Essily asked. "You said...the Old World...?"

"That's right. I've known something was wrong about the enemy commander since the height of the Gand campaign. And now I know what it is. But stopping him means boarding all the ships Louis-Sallet de l'Arraignon brought with him across the sea. It means sending the better part of our armies to the battlefields of Old Sarresant, to make a stand there and reinforce the Dauphin. A Thellan campaign in truth, across the peaks of the Capallains, and another across the straits, if Paendurion still holds sway with the Gandsmen. Maybe one to the bloody east, if the Skovan have capitulated."

"Sir, if you mean to conquer the world, I can think of no one better suited to the task."

She almost laughed before she realized Essily hadn't meant it for a joke. Her aide stood straight, his back stiff, only a raised fist shy of saluting her as though she were a living flag.

"You'd obey such an order?" she asked.

"Yes, sir," he said.

Two words, said crisply, but they struck her with the force of a pistol. Essily was her aide; if she found his loyalty in doubt, it would be dire indeed for her prospects with the rest of the army. But she needed more.

"Why, Captain?" she asked.

This time it was Essily's turn to be taken aback, though he recovered quickly.

"Sir, you're our commander," Essily said. "I've watched you root out the old officers—the ones put there by blood instead of merit. You've made us into the army I had always dreamed we could be. You've kept us safe, and defeated our enemies. I would die for you, sir, and obey any order you gave, as would any man or woman that wears this uniform."

"Thank you, Aide-Captain," she said. He bowed this time, serving her a saucer with a steaming cup atop it.

"Yes, sir," he said. "Will there be anything else?"

"No," she said, returning her attention to the maps. "Only, see Tuyard, Lerand, and Casanne in as soon as they arrive."

A small, vain part of her had hoped for a mirror of Essily's reaction when she repeated her plan to Tuyard, Lerand, and Casanne. Instead she was met with silence, thick enough to cut with the saber she hadn't yet given up wearing at her side.

Tuyard sat apart from the other two, lounging against a cushioned chaise with his boots up for most of her speech, then sitting forward, his eyes as wide as the gold buttons on his deep blue coat. Lerand wore plainer fare, and looked between his fellows with increasingly nervous glances, as though wanting to weigh their reactions before offering anything on his own. Casanne wore a white version of the priests' brown robes, with sleeves pushed back to expose the blue flower tattoos over her binder's marks and a hood lowered to reveal a leathered face that gave no other sign of advancing age.

"Well." Tuyard was the first to speak. "I'd had word tonight's invitation was extended to my fellows, here. But I can't say as I expected this."

Casanne sat rigid on the couch, as straight as she would have been in a wood-backed chair. "Have you confirmed any of this information," the First Prelate said in slow, precise words, "beyond the prisoner's account?"

"Yes," Erris said. "From the mouth of our enemy himself. Paendurion. I've met him, twice, through exchanges between our vessels. He used the same terms Fei Zan did: ascension, a promise to destroy us, and me in particular."

"Forgive me, High Commander," Casanne said. "But a promise to destroy one's enemies is hardly a great reveal, especially in wartime."

"It was the words he used," Erris said. "His manner, his skill. He's no man of this age, for all he knows our armies and tactics."

Casanne pursed her lips, drawing in the wrinkled lines of her face. "Hubris, High Commander, to assume divine intervention when one's own flaws suffice to explain one's shortcomings."

"Who else have you consulted for this?" Tuyard said.

The accusatory tone beneath Tuyard's words rang louder than perhaps he intended. Still he said it with a renewed air of relaxation, reclining once more in his seat.

"Voren," she said. "Colonel Marquand. Omera, Voren's former servant."

"That's all? None of the tribesfolk you invited onto our lands?"

She frowned. "No—other than the colonel and Omera, you're the first three I've discussed this with."

"So you know nothing of the company that entered the city this morning?" Tuyard asked. "Twoscore of these tribesfolk, here on our doorstep? That would make you remarkably ill informed, for a cavalry officer."

His words stung, though they drew fire rather than blood.

"I command the entirety of our military, High Admiral," she said. "I am not a cavalry officer."

The First Prelate rose to her feet.

"High Commander," Casanne said. "I ask your leave, and for time to consider what you've set before us. May we reconvene in the morning?"

Tuyard joined her in rising, as did Lerand, who still had yet to say a word.

She looked between the three of them, now arrayed around her desk in something all too close to a tribunal.

"You understand this matter requires the utmost secrecy," she said. "None but your closest aides can know."

"Of course, High Commander," the First Prelate said. Assemblyman Lerand mumbled something, and both turned to go as though she'd dismissed them. Tuyard followed at their heels, leaving her feeling slapped and stunned where she sat.

Disaster.

Marquand had warned her, and she'd stumbled into the trap, never mind that it was of her own making. No chance any of them kept the revelation quiet; rumors would be flying through every district in the city, and well on their way southward before sunrise.

Her door banged open, and High Admiral Tuyard returned, striding through at twice the pace he'd set for their departure.

"A bold move, High Commander," Tuyard said. "I assume you have squads of city watch waiting to take Lerand and Casanne before they leave the grounds. But you've made an error. Whatever you have planned for me, I assure you, you've misjudged my loyalty. Allow me the opportunity, and I will prove as faithful as any man in your service."

"High Admiral," she said. "You hardly seemed convinced before, and now—?"

"Please, d'Arrent," Tuyard said. "I know it seemed as though I was Voren's man. However you disposed of him, you must give me a chance."

The plea hung between them. The boldness in Tuyard's eyes faded as she remained quiet, first to desperation, and then surprise.

"Gods," Tuyard said. "You don't have a plan, do you?"

"A plan for what, High Admiral?"

"Seizing power. Oh Gods, d'Arrent. Considering your reputation, I'd assumed you were laying threefold traps and contingencies at every turn. I was sure of it. Since you moved against Voren, I'd figured it a matter of days, perhaps."

"Slow down, Admiral. I never moved against Voren. Every word I told you here is true."

Tuyard held her gaze for a moment. Then he laughed, deep and rich, as he folded back into the chaise he'd used during the meeting.

"We're fucked, then," Tuyard said. "You couldn't have come up with a better hoax to get them to arrest you if you'd tried."

This time anger flared. "This isn't some game," she said. "Our enemy has been working to conquer and destroy our people since he first took power with the Gandsmen. Whatever status I have as a *Need* binder, his only aim is to crush it, to remove me as a rival."

"That's your one token of providence," Tuyard said. "They'll have to keep you on as a military adjunct at the very least. Me, they'll find a way to execute, along with every other former nobleman they're certain escaped justice in the last purges."

"High Admiral, I am entirely serious," she snapped, rising to her feet. "I consulted the assemblyman and First Prelate to gauge response and begin planning for a military action across the sea."

"Well, you've gauged it. They're going to be rounding up militia squads to lay siege to high command within the hour, provided you don't consent to surrendering without a struggle. Count on it."

His words twisted in her stomach, though she kept the sour turn from showing on her face.

A bang followed by a ringing clap sounded, muted by walls but within the building.

Tuyard spun to look in the direction it had come from.

"They move fast," Tuyard said bitterly. "Time to decide whether you mean to resist, High Commander."

She pushed past the Admiral, opening the door to her receiving room. "Aide-Captain," she said—Essily was already on his feet, peering toward the bang. Too soft to be gunfire, unless she missed her guess. Something else. "Find out what's going on out there, as quick as you can run."

Essily gave a quick half bow that served well enough for a dismissal, and left running, her words sufficing to give him haste.

"I hope you're wrong, High Admiral," she said, turning back to where Tuyard stood behind her. "Everything I've done, I've done to protect our people. The army will see it, even if the politicians and priests don't."

"You had to imagine they would react," Tuyard said. "First you strong-arm the Assembly into approving a war—and let's not pretend your stationing thirty thousand soldiers in marching distance of New Sarresant was anything other than a bully tactic. Then you—"

"Royens?" she interrupted. "I placed the First Corps here to *defend* the city, or hadn't you noticed the Great Barrier had collapsed?"

"Do you mean to tell me you didn't mean for them to seize the capital?" Tuyard laughed again. Gods but she could do with hitting him in the teeth. "Say what you will of Anselm Voren, but he didn't bother teaching you anything of the subtleties of politics, did he?"

Another boom sounded, this one more of a thud, like a cut tree crashing to the ground. Definitely not gunfire. She ignored Tuyard and strode into the hallway outside her chamber, where Essily had already returned.

"Sir," Essily said, panting as he came to a halt. "It's the tribesfolk. I couldn't be certain, but I believe we're under attack."

Body and *Life* gave her speed and enhanced senses, and she moved.

Tuyard's voice faded as she ran around the corner toward the main chamber. The great dome of the old Lords' Council extended far above, with more offices and private chambers that had been taken over by her command staff.

She emerged onto the landing leading down into what had become the map room, and saw the source of Essily's claim.

Ten tribesmen, wearing no particular uniform and carrying no weapons that she could see, standing at odds with a makeshift company of her soldiers that had formed a line between them and the hallways leading to her rooms. She recognized the two figures at the head of the tribesfolk: Asseena, a woman gifted with the tribes' magic, and Ilek'Hannat, the shaman she'd met with to broker the peace between their people.

"What is the meaning of this?" she demanded, as loud as her voice could carry, and every tribesman or soldier in earshot turned to see her standing at the chamber's head.

"High Commander d'Arrent," one of the tribesfolk said. A woman— one she'd treated with before, though the name eluded her. She conferred quickly with the shaman in their tongue, then spoke again. "You are in great danger here. Ka'Hannat has seen it, and bid us come to share what he has seen."

Ka'Hannat? The man had been called *Ilek* before. Yet it was the same man, she was sure of it.

"Stand down," she called to the soldiers and aides who had hastily assembled to bar the tribesfolk's entry. By now Tuyard and Essily had caught up to her, appearing to flank her on either side. She went forward into the chamber, parting the line of her men, to meet Ilek—no, Ka'Hannat and his escorts face to face.

"All respect, honored shaman, but you cannot force your way into these chambers. You're lucky my men didn't arrest you, or attack."

The woman who had spoken before—Tirana, she remembered the name now—passed her words to Ka'Hannat and Asseena, and they conferred before she spoke again.

"He apologizes," Tirana said. "He says you would have been killed, had he not come to warn you. He says vipers among your own people are to blame. And he needs you."

Those of her soldiers who had heard Tirana's words shuffled back, some few passing muttered whispers between each other.

"He needs me?" she said.

"Yes," Tirana said. "He has seen a dire vision, a sending from the spirits of things-to-come. He requests that you connect him to the Goddess, and to Ka'Inari, together with one of your vessels on the far side of the world."

50

TIGAI

Eastern Markets
The City of Kye-Min

C owards!"

Captain Ugirin's taunt sounded up and down their line, one word carried on a thousand tongues. Laughter went with it, mocking fingers pointed toward the Imperial soldiers as they broke.

It was...wrong. Bloody wrong. Tigai had no head for soldiering—that had always been Dao's province as elder. But Remarin had trained him with the basics, and besides, his eyes worked well enough. No matter how many friendly soldiers were coming toward them from the west, the Imperials held a fortified position at the city center. And now he watched as ten thousand men broke without either side firing a shot.

They scattered down side streets and thoroughfares, with nothing orderly about it. If the Tigers had been in the way they'd have been trampled in the fury, and no few of the Imperials suffered that fate at their fellows' hands. It was as though every man had been suddenly set against his greatest fear, and his fellows be damned if it meant delaying flight from their posts.

"What under the *koryu*...?" Lin Qishan said beside him.

Ugirin's bellows turned to more boasting, a great roar as the line jeered the Imperials from their positions, but Tigai had heard Lin's expression and drew close to her, a private aside amid the chaos.

"It's magic, isn't it?" Tigai asked. "There's no other explanation."

Lin Qishan held to her usual reserve, but some vestige of awe remained in her face.

"Which of the Great and Noble Houses can do that?" he asked. "You know their world; which of them is it?"

She only seemed to notice him at the last. "None of them, Lord Tigai," she said.

He wanted to press her, the privilege of a captor over a prisoner. Instead Captain Ugirin bellowed, "Forward!" and the Tigers' line surged, their jeers melted into displays of bravery, roars, and yawps as they charged the now-unoccupied ground.

Spears, swords, and arquebuses greeted them when they reached where the Imperials had held their line, weapons cast down into the streets before their owners broke and ran. No few of the Tigers paused to take up their enemies' arms, holding aloft polished steel as trophies of their victory. Kegs of powder and crates of lead greeted them, too, with wagons of food and water barrels pulled by animals that seemed not to have caught the fright that sent their handlers running. He went along in the rush, checking over his shoulder to be sure Lin Qishan stayed at his side.

Looting had almost begun in earnest when Ugirin bellowed another command, this time to form ranks. It took a moment to see the cause through the chaos of the Tigers' swift acquiescence, spearmen rushing to the fore, with maces, swords, and arquebusiers behind: another company, marching at a steady pace toward them through the streets.

Tigai gravitated toward Ugirin's flag, a square white standard with three black claw marks at the center. The captain noticed him and Lin, sparing him a wolfish grin as the rest of his men snapped into place.

"This is Isaru Mattai's work, isn't it?" Ugirin said. "He sends me you to whet my appetite for wonders, then delivers us the city, ripe for plunder."

"It may well be, Captain," Tigai said. "Lord Isaru only charged me with keeping the Tigers alive."

Ugirin laughed, turning back to head his line as they faced the newcomers. Soldiers in yellow, instead of the Imperials' red, whom the officers near Ugirin's flag had already identified as another mercenary company: Captain Hashiro's Golden Sun. A spike of fear went through him, catching first sight of their approach. Lord Isaru and his *magi* were two thousand leagues away, but then, not all of Isaru's allies would have been at the camp. Whatever had sent the Imperials running, it would be coming closer, at this Captain Hashiro's side. Ordinarily he'd tether himself to the strands and be done with this city, but Lin Qishan had said Remarin might be imprisoned here, and that meant finding a way toward the harbor, where the Tower of the Heron stood overlooking the bay. If that took facing down another of Isaru's *magi*—one strong enough to scatter an entire company of soldiers—then so be it. He might even be able to convince them to help plan his assault, if the wind spirits were smiling.

"Riders approaching, Captain," one of Ugirin's men said, and so there were: no more than ten, most on horseback, carrying a golden banner as they trotted forward from the other company's line. The rest of the Golden Suns seemed content to hang back, making a show of discipline as firm as the one Captain Ugirin had ordered on their side of the market.

"We'll meet them," Ugirin said. "Hylang, Gorin, with me." Five swordsmen approached at once from the left side of the banner, and five pistoleers from behind. "Lord Tigai, I don't suppose you and your clanswoman would consent to posturing for the sake of the Tigers' pride?"

"Of course," Tigai said. "But it will be me and my prisoner. Yuli Twin Fangs Clan Hoskar is—"

"She is happy to bolster your ranks, Captain," Yuli said from behind.

He turned to see Yuli approaching through the front ranks of the arquebusiers. She clutched her forearm to her chest, and her skin was pocked with red lacerations anywhere it was exposed, with the rest of her clothing ripped and torn.

"Yuli!" he exclaimed. "I had to take Lin away to stop her, and without a connection to that street I couldn't return."

"I can handle myself, my lord," Yuli said. She met him with warmth that drained as she turned to Lin Qishan.

Ugirin grinned and clapped Tigai's shoulder. "Time to reconcile after we receive Hashiro's dogs," the captain said. "For now, forward, while there are still hours in the day for killing!"

The front ranks opened to admit Ugirin and his chosen escort, and Yuli pushed past without a word from any of the others for her condition.

She looked as though she would bleed out, or at least faint from the cuts covering her body, but then, he had little doubt as to how his concern would be received. Instead he followed along, with Lin Qishan trailing a few paces behind, as they emerged into the open street.

The riders from the other mercenary company clustered behind a man Tigai assumed would be their captain, a proud soldier sitting stiff on his horse. A banner flew behind him, and all wore the same armor save for three: one mounted and two on foot, kept at arm's length by their fellows' movements. The sort of unconscious separation that followed *magi* wherever they went; he'd borne it himself among Remarin's men, and recognized it here.

It took the length of the street to realize two of the *magi* were women, and all three bore strange features he didn't recognize at a glance. The women were pale-skinned, with the sort of hawkish, overly pronounced noses and cheekbones he associated with the Natarii clans, for all they lacked the clans' facial tattoos, and the man was clean-shaven, with long hair, russet skin, and a mix of features somewhere between Jun and Hagali.

"Captain Hashiro," Ugirin said when they came close, his piebald warhorse skittering to a stop less than two strides from his counterpart. "I'd hardly expected to see you here."

"Captain Ugirin," Hashiro said in precise, formal tones. "I acknowledge your service to our mutual lord, and bid us begin planning for joint maneuvers here in Kye-Min."

Silence held for a moment, as both companies studied their mirrors on the opposite sides of the line.

Ugirin's laugh broke the tension.

"It's bloody good to have the Sun on our side this time, old man," Ugirin said. "Hylang and Gorin will be my attachés with you. I assume Kiroshi and Natana are mine?"

Captain Hashiro gave a sharp nod.

With that, the lines let down their guard, the swordsmen and pistoleers from the White Tigers moving to mingle and clasp forearms with the spearmen of the Golden Sun. It left him to move toward the three *magi*, trying to put down the dread that somehow they knew what he'd done to Isaru Mattai.

One of the women met him at their head. The shorter of the two, though still tall by any standard, wore a plain-cut brown tunic and breeches almost ostentatious in their lack of splendor, for a *magi*.

"Greetings," he said, offering her a formal bow. "I am Yanjin Tigai, assigned to the White Tigers here in Kye-Min. This is Lin Qishan, and Yuli Twin Fangs Clan Hoskar."

The woman at their head responded with a strange sort of bow, dipping her head and rearward leg in the sort of maneuver he might have expected as part of a dance.

"I am Sarine Thibeaux," she said, speaking perfect Jun in spite of her Natarii features. "From lands far to the east. This is Rosline Acherre, and Ka'Inari."

He resisted the urge to correct her, or to wrinkle his face in an expression of doubt. Lands far to the east? The only thing to the east of Kye-Min was the sea, unless his tutors had been woefully lacking in his education. He saw the signs of nerves in the woman's—Sarine's—face, displayed openly, without effort to mask her emotions. He'd been afraid they would somehow recognize him, or at least recognize that he wasn't one of Isaru's thralls. But these *magi* were hiding something. If he could find it, perhaps it could serve as leverage to get them to move on the Tower of the Heron.

"I hadn't seen you in Lord Isaru's camp," Tigai said. "Did you come to Kye-Min with the Golden Sun?"

"And how is it you speak two tongues at once?" Yuli asked. "I hear you speaking the Hoskar tongue, when I know Lord Tigai does not speak it. This gift is not known to my clan."

Tigai turned while Yuli spoke, intending to admonish her with a subtle rebuke, instead cut short by Lin Qishan's expression. Lin's eyes had gone wide, her skin as pale as milk, staring at the three *magi* as though they were ancestor spirits come to life.

"It's part of my gift," Sarine said. "Acherre and Ka'Inari don't share it, but I can translate between us. And no, Lord Tigai, we didn't come with Hashiro's company. We came seeking the leaders of the... Emperor's *magi*. The Great and Noble Houses. Do you know where they might be found?"

"We know where you can find one," Lin Qishan said abruptly. "Here in Kye-Min, the Lady Bavda Khon is Grandmaster of the Great and Noble House of the Heron. We are here to kill her, the same as you, and you will have our talents in furtherance of your cause, should you choose to allow us to fight at your side."

This time Tigai failed to keep the shock from his face.

Lin stood resolute, as though it had always been her plan to offer to help assassinate what had to be one of the most prominent *magi* in the Empire.

"Yes," Sarine said, once more the emotions on her face writ plain for all to see. "Yes, that's precisely our aim. We have to help Hashiro get his soldiers to safety, then we can—"

She was cut short by the other woman—Rosline Acherre, Sarine had named her—speaking in short bursts of an utterly foreign tongue. Tigai's head still reeled from Lin's assertions; it took a second glance to notice that Acherre's eyes had gone gold, as though the strands had erupted through her sockets, spilling golden light like stars embedded in her eyes.

Whatever strangeness passed between them, Tigai seized the moment to turn on Lin.

"What are you doing?" he hissed, keeping his back turned and his voice low. "You are my prisoner, and you've been on the *magi*'s side since the beginning. Why would you offer to help kill one?"

"Do you not wish to assault the Herons' tower, Lord Tigai?" Lin said calmly. All sign of the shock he was sure he'd seen there had vanished, returned to her usual placid self-assurance.

"Are you playing me false?" he said. "I swear, I will take you back and leave you in the middle of the fucking ocean if you don't tell me what's going on, bloody now."

"I've said it plainly," Lin said. "We'll offer our service to this Sarine Thibeaux, and use her to reach Remarin, and Mei as well, if she's still being held here in the city. I swear on the Great and Noble House of the Ox, every word I've said is true."

"It's the hundred words you haven't said that I'm worried about."

Once more Lin's expression returned to passive calm. He had half a mind to send her into the sea anyway, if only to establish clearly who was making the decisions between them. But then, she was right. Every word she'd said aligned with his only goal; so long as it was true that Remarin was being held here, and maybe Mei as well, nothing else mattered.

He turned his back to Lin to find Sarine and Acherre still in conversation, the second woman's eyes still pouring golden light as she spoke her foreign tongue.

"Civil war, or a conflict between Kingdoms, though I've only heard talk of a single Empire," Sarine was saying. "I can learn more, but—"

A rush of foreign words came from Acherre, too quick for him to follow. She had a strange manner of speaking, swallowing consonants and vowels alike, the words running together and seeming to come from her nose as much as her throat. The light vanished when she was done, leaving Acherre blinking and steadying herself as Sarine offered a hand to keep her on her feet.

"You were speaking with someone else," Yuli said to Sarine. "Someone far away."

"I can see it, too," the man—Ka'Inari—said, his eyes suddenly glazed, his voice speaking the Jun tongue as clearly as Sarine had done, though she'd said he didn't know it. "Ka'Hannat's vision. The tower is evil. A great shadow, but he was right; the shadows are not tied to the place. They are here, coming for us if we linger too long."

Sarine looked torn, a sudden anguish on her face.

"We can't abandon Hashiro's company," she said. "Didn't he say the soldiers in red outnumber them five to one? They're counting on us."

"Wait," Tigai said. "It was you, who scattered the Imperial soldiers in the market, wasn't it?"

She nodded. "Yes."

A chill cooled his blood at the admission—one woman, scattering the strength of how many thousands of men?—but the Tower pulled his thoughts in only one direction. Remarin was all that mattered.

"If you follow Hashiro's and Ugirin's companies out of the city, we won't get another chance to attack the Herons," Tigai said. "Word of what you can do will already be spreading, and they'll retreat from the field as quick as they hear it."

"What do you propose we do?" Sarine said. "I won't leave these soldiers to die."

"You won't have to. We attack in two directions: We move toward the Tower, while the mercenaries drive northward to escape the city. If we move now, the Imperial soldiers won't know enough to account for what's happening. If you can scatter ten thousand, you're worth at least two companies by yourself. With luck their commanders will get the numbers wrong, and they're far likelier to use their reserves to defend the Herons than to block the northern route."

She repeated his words for Acherre's sake, and the other woman nodded along, exchanging words he couldn't understand. Ka'Inari spoke, too, this time in a tongue no less foreign than the one Acherre used, though it was a different combination of sounds and strangeness.

"No," Sarine said at last, cutting them both short. "No, Tigai is right. We came here for a reason. We'll do as he says." She turned to him. "That is, we'll do as you say. We have to let Hashiro know, but if he agrees, then we'll move at once. Whatever shadows Ka'Inari sees around that tower will only get worse the longer we delay."

51

ARAK'JUR

Adan'Hai'Tyat
Gand Territory

A loose patch of gravel slipped from beneath his fingers, and he fell. His shouts echoed from the sheer walls, where the lone mountain rose among a sea of hills, its rocky crags towering, snowcapped, out of place among its brothers. Already he and Ad-Shi had climbed above the highest point on the horizon; in an eyeblink he fell, undoing an hour's progress in a moment.

Mareh'et granted his blessing, and spectral claws dug into stone, showering flakes and dust toward the valley floor.

Silence lingered as the dust rose in a cloud around him, and his arms and back ached, grateful for a moment's respite, no matter it had almost cost his life to get it.

"You are alive?" Ad-Shi's voice rang from higher up the cliff.

"Yes," he called back. His lungs burned from the strain, with no thanks for spending breath on words.

"Keep on," she called. "We will reach the peak by midday."

A glance upward revealed how much he had lost: a stretch of hard terrain, sheer, with only splintering cracks to lever himself up the face. The sun had cleared the eastern hilltops some hours before, and the mountain Ad-Shi had named Adan'Hai'Tyat stretched toward the heavens, promising hours more to scale its heights.

Whatever tribe had once called these hills home before the fair-skins came, he pitied their shamans and their women. They would have had to train for many turnings of the seasons to make an attempt to reach their sacred place, and no few would have died in the trying. At the base he'd asked Ad-Shi how they would climb down, and been met only with assurances that the spirits would provide. An unsettling sentiment, staring up at a thousand handspans of sheer rock, and worse, now they'd scaled more than half the distance, caught between the treetops and the clouds. It was death, even for a guardian, to fall from such a height. And it was worse to fail to reach it. Short of undertaking a journey of a moon's turning to the north to return to the Nanerat peaks, this mountain would be the only site for *Hai* they could reach before the cold season set in. Ad-Shi claimed his path would be revealed, at the summit. For the thousandth time since the base, he cursed that he had killed Arak'Atan atop a mountain. If the spirits were good, it might have been by the seaside, on a grassy plain, even in the fetid stink of the Lhakani swamps. But no; his path was the mountain, and so they climbed.

The work was numbing for the body, and it freed his mind to think. In the few idle hours he'd had with Ad-Shi she'd given him some notion of what to expect when they reached the *Hai* spirits. Already she'd shown him how to exceed what he thought were his physical limitations; the spirits, so she'd claimed, would push him farther in his soul. It was no easy thing, imagining himself rising to become even a pale mirror of what Ad-Shi was, but then, that was why his people—and Ad-Shi's, to hear her tell it—had always used masters and apprentices, to show those who would learn a thing the ways of mastery from an experienced hand. Humility brought him low, watching Ad-Shi carry the burdens of their journey without complaint. Each day they had traveled as far as his stamina allowed, and he was sure she could have pressed on had he not been there to slow her. The mountain proved itself against his strength, while Ad-Shi scurried higher, as nimble as a cat in a tree.

Weighed against her skill, he could not believe he was the best suited from every tribe. She had to have settled on him for convenience's sake. But if it was true, it counted for nothing. He was her apprentice. It would fall to him to satisfy the spirits, to protect every tribe. He had to learn strength, if he was not strong enough already.

He nearly fell again, almost in the same place, before he found a crack to wedge his hands. One fist held tight while the rest of him pushed higher, until he found a new position and jammed his fingers in again. The nails on each hand had long since broken, his skin white from scrapes where it wasn't blue or purple from bruises and dried blood. One hold at a time, each new position challenging him to solve where to place his hands, his feet, the center of his body, and his head.

"Rest."

Ad-Shi's voice, sounding from above, and for that one word he might have moved the mountain itself, if he'd had the power to do it.

Only then did he realize she'd stopped, propping herself against a ledge he hadn't seen, cut a full armspan or more into the cliff. He grabbed hold of the edge with one hand, then accepted her hand with the other, levering himself into a place beside her, letting his body relax against the wall.

Breath came hard, and he accepted a waterskin without thought, dousing the cracks in his lips and watering the stinging dust from his throat.

"You climb well," Ad-Shi said. It was the first kind thing she'd said since their meeting; but for his exhaustion he might have reacted with more than a tired nod.

"I'd never...thought to try it before," he said between breaths.

"I can tell," Ad-Shi said. "But you've managed it, even so. Here. Eat."

She offered him a strip of dried meat, and he took it, letting it soak its juices into his tongue.

"This is what being Chosen means," she said quietly, just as he found the strength to chew. He gave her a questioning look and she affected not to notice, staring instead toward the horizon. "Always more than you believe you can endure. Always enemies, closer than you'd hoped to find them."

It took a moment for him to realize she was not staring blankly. A mass of bodies had appeared at the edge of their vision, diminished to the size of insects among trees that appeared no larger than blades of grass.

He squinted, trying to magnify his sight. "Who are they?" The question formed on his tongue, though in his gut somehow he already knew.

"Hunters," Ad-Shi said. "Enemies."

"The Uktani," he said.

"Always something," she said. "Always a shadow at our heels. Fight it, Arak'Jur. Fight until you are broken, and can fight no more."

"They will be there," he said, "when we are done. Waiting for us."

She rose, dust falling from her leggings as she stretched and turned back toward the cliffside.

"Rest as long as you need it," she said. "I will meet you at the top."

Pride demanded he end his rest and follow as Ad-Shi climbed. But exhaustion had long since broken his pride. She stepped around him, using a crack in the face behind the ledge to move upward, angled to the right, and fatigue kept him in place, too strained even to watch the path she took. She must have stayed on the ledge for some time, and he would make use of the same, recovering his strength for the final stretch.

The Uktani were moving over the hills in the distance, and he watched them come.

No mistaking their path. They approached from the north, and from the cliff face he could see their movements in detail, as a hawk or falcon might have done, half a thousand men and women spilled like a cluster of seeds across hills and valleys near the mountain's base. He'd dared to hope they'd lost his trail, or given up the pursuit in favor of another quarry. There would be beasts among them, alongside guardians, warriors, shamans, and spirit-touched among their women. A small satisfaction: It meant they were not threatening the Sinari, and the other peoples of the Alliance.

Exhaustion let him feel a half-dozen emotions at once. Anger, for what the Uktani had done to drive him away from his home. An irrational rage, blaming them for Corenna's decision to abandon him. Fear, for what was coming when he reached the top of the mountain. Surety, that the spirits would guide him to fight.

The last surprised him, but it was there. He had run, before, thinking it would be enough to protect his people, but it was time to become more than a protector. Ad-Shi had shown a path to something else, something he'd never thought to want for himself. As a child he'd relished Sinari ways, reveled in the peace and prosperity of trade, proud to be a man of his tribe. He'd become a husband, a father, a hunter; every dream he'd ever dared to want, dashed in a moment of horror and pain. The *valak'ar* had stolen his life without killing him, in the bites that murdered Rhealla and his son. Guardianship had been a way to soak the pain, pouring himself into learning an older and more honored path than he'd ever sought to tread. And he'd done it well. He'd walked the *Arak*'s path, and grown strong in keeping his people safe. Part of him yearned for Corenna, for the solace she offered, the promise of a new wife and a new child. That was the dream he'd wanted. But he'd been forged for a new dream now.

He rose, though he knew less time had passed than he'd intended to rest. The last of the water quenched the dust from his throat, and he fastened the skin to his belt. He glanced up and saw Ad-Shi a hundred handspans above him, following a thunderbolt of cracks to a face more rocky and less sheer than most of the stretches behind them. It would be easier going, if he could veer to the right and follow her path, but then, he would take each hold as it came.

Mareh'et granted his blessing as he started his ascent. Strength surged through him, with spectral claws to aid in wedging his hands into the cracks. He couldn't be certain he'd called on the cat spirit, but then, the spirits worked their own will. Perhaps he'd needed their blessing and had it granted without the need to ask.

The first crack went quickly, and he'd transitioned past two more before the cat spirit's gift faded. His mind calmed under the steady rhythm of the climb, thoughts and fears of what was above and below fading as he found places to prop his feet and hands. Ice began to appear in the depths of the cracks, and *una're* gave his gift to shatter it, thundering across the rock face. Snow tested his grip, forcing him to slow to be certain he held to solid rock before he pulled himself up. By now he was level with the clouds; perhaps he'd risen so high when scaling the Nanerat peaks, but they had been a range of brothers and sisters, where Adan'Hai'Tyat stood alone among rolling hills. It made him seem more alone, here, perched above the rest of the world. Even the air seemed too thin as he breathed it, his heavy exhalations the only sound he heard, apart from the wind.

Ad-Shi had vanished above another overhang, and he followed, feeling the weight of the earth as he found holds to defy its pull. He crawled under the outcropped rock until his body was parallel to the ground, his muscles and fingers screaming from the pain of supporting all his weight. By now he welcomed it, and *mareh'et* gave his blessing again, a renewed surge of strength to grab hold of the edge and pull himself over, ignoring the quivering pain in his legs, his back, and arms and feet.

He tested the ledge over top of the outcropping and found it firm enough for a rest, allowing himself to lie idle while he recovered his breath.

"You have done well, Arak'Jur," Ad-Shi said. "The spirits will guide you from here, when you are ready."

Her voice startled him into looking up, and realizing there was no more cliffside overhead. Ad-Shi stood atop a snow-covered patch of ground at the mouth of a cave, hovering on the edge of the mountain, facing east. The sight kindled fire in his arms and legs, and he pulled himself up to his knees, still breathing too hard to speak.

"You are not prepared for what you will face," Ad-Shi continued. "But then, neither was I. Trust in the spirits. They will be your strength, when your will is weak."

A change in the wind gave a premonition, but he had no time to voice it before Ad-Shi turned to him, a wistful smile on her face, and leapt from the side of the cliff.

"Wait!" he cried, too late. His heart raced, and he scrambled to the edge to see Ad-Shi's silhouette plummeting, diminished with each moment until she vanished below the shaking boughs of the trees.

52

ERRIS

Riverways District Boundary
Southgate District, New Sarresant

S he blinked, and her vision cleared, returning to the darkened interior of her coach.

Curtains had been draped across the windows, leaving flickering pillars of light shining through cracks in the frame, marking their passage through the city. Ka'Hannat sat opposite her on the velvet cushions, staring as though she were a lamb that had somehow escaped the knife.

"What did you see, High Commander?" Tirana asked. The translator sat beside the shaman, the three of them alone in the coach's interior. It had been the best Essily could manage without advance warning, and had still taken an hour to see them settled and departing high command. Tuyard had ridden out on horseback, promising to see Jiri safely delivered to Royens's encampment along the banks of the Verrain, to the south. They'd judged the sight of Erris fleeing the city on Jiri's back too much a danger to draw her enemies out, where they might have shied away from attacking the council hall itself. A sensible plan, but she found herself missing Jiri's strength now, whatever the advantages of a coach in working *Need* while they traveled.

"Everything the shaman saw," she said. "Everything Voren warned us was coming."

Tirana passed the words to Ka'Hannat, and translated when he spoke. "You saw the peoples of the East?" Tirana said. "The Dragon, the Wolf, the Ox at Ka'Inari's side?"

"They are people, not beasts," she said. "But yes, they were there, as was your shaman. And the girl, Sarine. They confirmed it all. Armies, cities, a people at war with themselves."

The hollowness in her voice belied the turmoil in her belly. It had been almost beyond believing, but she'd seen it firsthand, through Acherre's eyes. Strange architecture, tiled roofs and narrow streets, and soldiers in interlocking plate armor painted yellow and white. Sarine had claimed they'd found a way through a great divide, and meant to kill powerful mages before a broader threat could take shape; the specifics had been too much to take in, in the face of such overwhelming strangeness. Even now her mind recalled small details—clasps on their armor, filed edges of spearpoints, tassels on their poleaxes and muskets. They were men and women, ordinary for all their strangeness, and yet the shamans had promised dire threats came with them, to say nothing of Voren's warnings.

"High Commander," Ka'Hannat said. His eyes had glazed; she'd come to recognize it as his spirits speaking with him, or through him, perhaps—and when it happened, Tirana had no need to translate his words. "These are the people of the shadow. When they come, they will darken the earth with their numbers. They are many. Their magics will rend and tear our villages. Our warriors will fall before them. Only the ascendants—the chosen of the Goddess—carry any hope of light."

She sat still in her place, listening as the coach rattled around them. For weeks now, her mind had been consumed by politics and planning the Thellan invasion; even now, her divisions would be marching south, where her ships were blockading their ports, besieging their forts and coastal cities. Now it was ablaze, all of it.

"How long do we have?" she asked.

Ka'Hannat stared back at her, an unnerving emptiness in his pupilless eyes. In the dark of the coach, she might have mistaken it for a trick of the light, but then, she'd seen the shaman in the throes of his spirits before.

"Three turnings of the moon," Ka'Hannat said. "The champions will rise. But the Old God's ways have worn thin. The spirits remember. They remember now. War is coming." With that he choked and coughed, cutting short whatever else he'd meant to say. Tirana moved to his side on their cushioned bench, cradling the shaman as he slumped forward.

Erris left them to it; beyond a glance to be certain Ka'Hannat was well, the weight of all she'd heard pressed on her as great as any duty she'd ever borne. It was like being told children's tales were real—the monsters in the night, come to spirit her away to the Nameless for misbehaving. She'd never believed any of it then, and struggled to do so now. The threats in front of her were clear: She'd misstepped, politically, and the priests and Assembly would be taking steps to remove her from command. Paendurion had seized power among the Thellan, threatening to raise another army to invade the northern colonies here in the New World. Her attack had been purely defensive in nature, wielding the combined strength of New Sarresant and Gand to smash the capacity of the Thellan colonies to make war. The straightforward path was to flee the city, then to regroup among Royens's soldiers and decide her next move. All while continuing to lead her soldiers in the field, bypassing the Thellan forts to strike and secure their harbors.

But now she had two chimeras taking shape in front of her. Voren's warnings, that Paendurion's tactics in the south were no more than a trap, meant to distract and ensnare her while he completed his conquests of the Old World. And Ka'Hannat's visions, of monsters in the night, and soldiers of shadow on the far side of the world.

"Is he well?" Erris asked after Tirana had steadied the shaman in his seat.

"He is," Tirana replied. "The spirits' visions are hard to bear, and Ka'Hannat's gift is strong."

"Just as well," she said. "I need his strength, and that of your people. Tell him so. Tell him I need your best to sail with my army, when the moment arrives."

Tirana paused before repeating it in the tribes' tongue, and Ka'Hannat listened with a weary head, leaning forward with his eyes closed as she spoke.

"He knows," Tirana said. "He's already given the commands. Hunters, and spirit-touched among our women."

"Not good enough. I need him. I need—"

The cart lurched as it came to a sudden halt.

She fell silent in time to hear Essily's voice from the driver's seat, above.

"What is the meaning of this?" Essily said. "Stand down at once."

Tirana exchanged a look with her, though Ka'Hannat remained slumped forward, his face obscured by his hands. Gods damn it. They'd been too slow.

"Good day, Captain," a woman's voice said, loud enough to carry across an open street. "We have reason to believe you are transporting High Commander d'Arrent. We ask that you remand her into our custody at once, and without resistance."

The coach door clicked as Erris released the latch, pushing it open and stepping into the morning sun.

She saw the brown-robed figures tighten their line as she emerged, Aide-Captain Essily managing no more than, "She's not..." before her appearance spoiled his denial. First Prelate Casanne herself led the detail, standing a few paces in front of the priests blocking the street ahead of them. Twenty priests at least, and a confirmation Tuyard had been at least half-wrong: They must have been planning this even before her revelations from Voren. *Death* binders, and *Shelter*, meant to contain her if she attempted to resist.

"High Commander," Casanne said. "If you would consent to come with us, we can avoid unnecessary violence."

Erris stayed in place at the top of the carriage steps, looking down on the priests. Good on Casanne for dispensing with pretense. She could do the same.

"Stand down," Erris said. "Disperse, and I will forget the faces I've seen here." She paused, long enough to sweep a look across their line. The brown-robed men and women held to their resolve, but she'd seen the same sort of zeal in raw recruits. Courage was easy when it came without a price.

"Take her," Casanne said.

For a moment no one moved. Essily stayed seated above her in the driver's seat, the shaman and his translator had made no move to emerge from the carriage, and the priests stayed arrayed against her, blocking the street in a line. The world had dimmed to Erris and Casanne, meeting one another's eyes as she weighed the Prelate, measuring what would come next.

Five priests broke the silence, moving toward the carriage together. Men, large-statured and clearly chosen for it. One or two might be *Shelter* binders, but the rest would have *Death*. *Death* was the key; no means to apprehend a fullbinder without it. There would be a handful of *Death* binders with tethers at the ready—and an all-too-ample supply of black ink on the leylines in the months since the battle.

She blinked, trying *Mind* as a feint. Two separate *Death* tethers sliced her binding as soon as she made it, before even a single copy of her could blink into existence.

No time to trace the connections to the individual binders, but she didn't have to. She saw the signs of concentration, the sudden response after extended moments of waiting.

Entropy came next, and this time they weren't so quick.

A billowing fire erupted in the middle of the priests, a blast of raw heat that knocked half their line to the ground and killed as many more. *Death* came again for her *Entropy*, but she was already moving, this time drawing *Death* tethers of her own to hold at the ready.

"Go!" she shouted, and the carriage surged forward, in time for her *Death* to slice through the first signs of *Shelter* erected in their way.

The shock of violence had yet to register for most of the priests. Brown-robed figures picked themselves up from the street to try *Shelter* again. Once more she found *Death*, slicing a path for the carriage to thunder through, leaving scorched flesh and more ink leaking into the leylines where victims of her *Entropy* lay dead or dying on the stone.

The carriage raced away, toward the city walls, and she half opened the door, leaning from the side to look back on the priests. Casanne wouldn't have acted alone, and now they had a dozen martyrs to rally more to their cause. She had to reach Royens's camps, where the Great Barrier had stood and was beginning to be repaired. Ten thousand soldiers at her back would silence the worst of it, if she struck before the priests and militias could establish a hold on the city. But the black smoke rising from the bodies in the street seemed as ill an omen as she could have feared: the first dead in a second revolution, when far greater dangers gathered against them abroad.

53

SARINE

The Starfield and the Strands
Soulless Eternity

Ka'Inari's hand melted into hers, and they became one. Consciousness assaulted her through their connection, awareness of thoughts beyond her mind. Yanjin Tigai held her other hand, though his form remained distinct. His eyes were closed. Stars moved around them as they floated, beams of energy tying them to each other, threatening to ensnare them in wild surges of power.

A figure moved in the distance. A massive shadow, blocking out the light.

She knew it. It had seen her. It was moving.

Light streaked past her eyes. She was whole again. She was herself.

"See?" Tigai said. "Faster this way."

Ka'Inari released her hand, taking a step away from her. Her senses still reeled, racked by the memory of what she'd seen, an echo of the figure that had attacked them when they crossed the Divide. It had lasted no more than a moment, but she felt it burned into her mind: the stars, the swirling patterns, like being submerged in the deepest parts of the night sky. And the creature, moving in the depths. Fixed on her. Coming closer.

"We're less than a league from the tower," Acherre was saying. "Which according to Hashiro will put us near a concentration of Imperial soldiers. I'd bloody kiss the Nameless for a good map of this city. Can you ask whether our guides know the streets here? At least a rough guess of what's in front of us."

Tigai looked between her and Acherre with impatience on his face.

"Something's wrong," Yuli said. Ka'Inari seemed to notice at the same moment, approaching her slowly from the front.

"Sarine?" Ka'Inari said.

None of them saw it, Anati thought to her. Her *kaas*'s voice rang like thunder in her ears. *Why didn't they see?*

"What's that?" Tigai said. "Is she well?"

By now all five of her companions had taken note of her, turning to face her where they stood.

"He . . . he saw us," she said.

Ka'Inari closed his eyes as Acherre rounded on Tigai. "What did you do to her?" Acherre demanded. "You said it would be safe."

Tigai regarded Acherre with a raised eyebrow, but then, he wouldn't be able to understand without her to translate.

"We have to move," Tigai said. "Word of your attack across the river will soon reach the Tower, if it hasn't already."

"Lord Tigai," Sarine said. "What you did—moving us through the strands, you called it. Where did it take us?"

"Nowhere," Tigai said. "The starfield isn't a place. I hooked us to—"

Yes, it is a place, Anati thought to them both. *It's His place.*

"What?" Tigai said. He seemed unfazed when Anati appeared perched on her shoulder, staring at him as though he'd issued them both a challenge. "Look, whatever your pet thinks, we have to—ow, bloody fuck!"

Tigai reeled backward, waving his hands as though he were warding away a fly. Anati glared at him, projecting her head forward, both eyes glistening.

"Anati, stop!" she said. "Lord Tigai, I need to know you can take us somewhere safe, when we're finished here. Something is coming toward this city."

"I can take us to half the cities in the Empire, once we have Remarin and Mei." He stepped back from her, glaring back at Anati as fiercely as the *kaas* had glared at him. "But we have to go, and now."

She nodded, her head finally cleared enough to make sense of what was in front of them. The markets here had the same look of fighting she'd seen on the western approach. Terraced houses lined narrow, winding streets, built from a strange mix of stone and what looked like paper, or at least thin, painted wood. Fires raged on the horizon, where the ships in the harbor had shelled the waterfront, but beyond scorch marks and chipped stone from stray shots, the buildings here had been relatively untouched. Most of the city past the market was built on level ground as far as she could see, with even rooftops save for the grand tower rising between them and the harbor. That was their goal, and it fell to her to get them there.

"Stay close," she said. The haze of what she'd seen before had dulled to the same muted hum as the Veil's simmering hate. Neither mattered. She was here to do an assassin's work, fighting the only way she knew to fight. Axerian had already died for her lack of control, and she wasn't about to let herself slip again.

Anati gave her *Yellow* as their party moved into the city, and with the blue sparks she pushed the *kaas*'s net as far as it could go, feeling for emotions. Fear she felt in waves, anxious dread from scattered pockets of people caught inside buildings. Those might have been soldiers, but more likely they were citizens, hiding out and terrified as the battle raged around them. After a block it seemed as though Ugirin's reports had been mistaken, or the enemy army had redeployed as quickly as the White Tigers and the Golden Sun. Empty streets greeted them at each intersection, these ones untouched by fighting but abandoned nonetheless, with laundry lines waving their wares like flags stretched between the houses.

Then she drew near the bulk of the Imperial army.

She saw nothing; the streets were winding, sharp turns obscuring vision of anything more than a hundred paces off. But a sea of emotions fed Anati as they drew within a half league of the tower, a thousand or more all in range at once. They had to be arrayed in ranks blockading the streets, rows on rows of soldiers all combining to pulse obedience, awe, duty, anxious fear.

"They're here," she said, slowing.

"Mei and Remarin?" Tigai asked.

"No," she said. "Soldiers. Thousands of them, between us and the tower."

"I'll have a look," Acherre said, and turned toward the nearest building, vanishing inside. Yuli followed behind, though with *Mind* Acherre could use a vantage from the rooftop to scan two or three blocks ahead.

"What can we expect when we get there?" she asked Tigai, but it was Lin who answered.

"The Herons' magic is Force," Lin Qishan said. "They borrow from one action and impart to another. Striking a Heron only allows them to deliver a harder blow in return."

Sarine nodded. Just as well if she didn't have to do any violence at all. "Do you have any *Black*?" she asked Anati, earning an odd look from Lin and Tigai, though the *kaas* appeared on her shoulder before she replied.

Some, Anati thought.

"*Black* will let me drain their magic," she said to the other two. "If we face their master, I can give you an opening to strike."

"Bavda Khon is grandmaster," Lin said. "Not master. She will be no easy foe, even for six *magi* arrayed against her. And there will be others. The Tower is the seat of the Herons' power in the Empire. Isaru Mattai would have sought to strike at Kye-Min to keep Lady Khon contained, not to kill her."

"So long as we reach Remarin," Tigai said. "I can get us out safely, as long as we get to him."

"You agreed to help us," Sarine said. "We're here to face their master—their grandmaster—not to run as soon as there's danger."

"Lord Tigai will keep his word," Lin said. "He may be an honorless dog, but even dogs understand loyalty. He knows he will need your aid to reach his brother, and his brother's wife, if she is elsewhere."

Tigai looked annoyed, but kept quiet as Acherre and Yuli returned from within the building.

"The enemy is there all right," Acherre said. "I make the count four thousand at least, and likely a division's worth or more to the north, behind their front line. Looks like they fell back to tighten their perimeter around the tower. Are you sure you still want to attack them head-on? Going in with stealth might be the wiser course; no telling how many *magi* are placed among their lines."

"I swore I'd give Hashiro and Ugirin a distraction," Sarine said. "I mean to do it."

"Keep on this street, then," Acherre said. "We'll be steeped in enemy soldiers in fifteen minutes."

"All right," she said. "If we do encounter *magi*, I'll do what I can to help, but—"

"No killing for you," Acherre finished for her. "I'd as soon you keep the Veil bottled in, if it's all the same."

She nodded. "I can handle the soldiers with Anati's help. The rest are yours."

All five of her companions fell in at her side, and they moved.

Anati stayed visible, perched on her shoulder as they followed the winding street. The Veil's emotions thrummed like a second heartbeat under her skin, though she kept an outward calm. Anati had seen the creature in the shadows, when Tigai had taken them through the field of stars. *His place*, Anati had called it. She understood the task immediately in front of her: use *Yellow* to scatter the army positioned around the Tower of the Heron; gain entry to the tower; face the would-be ascendant Ka'Inari had seen would be there, waiting for them. But the shadow among the stars weighed on her with every step.

Shelter sprang up in front of them as they rounded a tight corner, and thundercracks sounded, echoing off the building walls as wisps of smoke rose from the barrier.

"Stay back!" Acherre shouted, gesturing to keep them all behind her *Shelter*. "Bloody bastards must have orders to fire on sight."

Sarine closed her eyes, focusing on *Yellow*. She reached within to grab the blue sparks to couple with Anati's gift, feeling the energy of Life—the Veil's gift—pulsing through her. Simple, to set wardings above the soldiers' line. With them she could amplify Anati's stored emotions, driving the Imperials away. She wove them in place, painting blue streaks a hundred yards distant, and then Anati's power flared, and the soldiers' anxiety became doubt, then worry, then panic.

Metal and wood clattered to the ground as a roar spread on the far end of the street.

"No *magi* that I can see," Acherre said. "Best to move, quickly."

"*Damyu* curse me," Tigai said. "That's...that's...unnatural."

Acherre's *Shelter* had vanished, and Sarine followed as Acherre led them toward where the enemy line had been. Only a row of muskets and spears remained, decorating the street from building to building with discarded arms. It would be the same for the streets surrounding this one; she'd set wardings broadly enough to capture the entirety of the Imperials' west-facing flank. The soldiers themselves had already vanished around the next corners, fleeing toward the tower.

The buildings here had grown wider as they moved toward the sea, from townhouses and storefronts to warehouses and estates, though the streets still wound tightly, spiraling inward toward the tower looming over the rooftops. They stepped past the muskets and spears, following as Acherre gave hand signals to take the lead. Sarine kept her mind focused on *Yellow*, on the tableau of emotions Anati fed through their bond. The larger share by far were the soldiers still scattered by her burst of fear, but there would be more, and some few who resisted altogether. That, at least, had proved consistent here and on the other side of the Divide: Any with a gift for magic couldn't be swayed by *Yellow* or *Green*.

New wardings sprang up as she let the old ones fade, a cloud of *Yellow* moving with her as they approached the tower. The street they'd been on cut sideways, and they turned, following a path of abandoned carts and empty barricades. They made it another hundred yards before a pulse of new emotions brought her to a halt. Pride, determination, fear, strength. A small cluster of resistance amid a sea of fear and panic. A *magi*—or more than one—drawing near.

Her calls to alert were received with nods and resolve among her fellows. Ka'Inari hung back, staying near her side. Acherre had the vanguard, with at least half a dozen bindings held at the ready. Tigai stayed near Lin Qishan, and Yuli…changed. The pale-skinned woman grew taller, the tattoos on her face elongating until they became paint on her muzzle, her limbs stretched and thin, her fingers sharpened to metallic claws.

Ka'Inari drew close before the *magi* came into view. "Sarine," he said. "Back there, in the market—what did you see?"

"Close," Acherre shouted, making tight gestures with her hands to accentuate her meaning. "Keep close, for *Shelter*."

Another barrier sprang up, a bar of filmy haze twenty paces ahead of Acherre, between their company and the next turn in the street.

Sarine glanced to her side, splitting her attention between Ka'Inari and where the *magi* would be coming. "It was quick," she said. "A field of stars, like the night sky. For a moment I saw the same creature we encountered in crossing the Divide."

"The shadow," Ka'Inari said.

"Yes," she said. "What do you know of it?"

"It's been drawn to us," Ka'Inari said. "Stronger, since we joined with these three *magi*. I worry we made a mistake, coming here."

"What do you mean? We're almost to the tower. If we should change course now…"

"No." He shook his head. "We are here, and the spirits are clear on this: They remember ascension, now. They know what it is to be a champion. They speak as though a great burden had finally lifted, as though whatever had corrupted their memories had finally perished, though they're not certain as to the source. If we can end even a handful of the *magi*'s masters, it may forestall a greater conflict. In that, nothing has changed. But—"

"Down!"

Acherre's voice tore Sarine's focus back toward the end of the street. Without thought she wove *Shelter* through a warding, and a new shield sprang into place before a boulder the size of a cart and horse smashed and broke apart above their heads.

Shouts swallowed any semblance of commands, and each of them went running. *Body* and *lakiri'in* granted speed, and *Red* a heartbeat later, quickening her senses until she could track every movement on the street.

Four *magi* had appeared, each in hooded orange robes belted with white cords, their faces obscured by mesh veils. They seemed to be working together, ripping chunks from the earth, collapsing buildings' foundations as they spun materials into spheres of dirt, wood, and stone. Tigai was sprinting toward them, drawing one of the pistols on his belt in quarter-time motion, while Acherre had dropped her shield of *Shelter*, raising a hand that spat a sheet of caustic air. Lin Qishan's body morphed mid-stride into a golem of crystal glass, and Yuli charged, fastest of them all, racing toward the orange-robed figures in a hunched-forward stance that looked as though she meant to move on all fours.

Acherre's *Entropy* wafted into the *magi* just as one of their spheres of earth took form, and at once the fire guttered as it poured itself into the sphere, heating the metal until it glowed bright red.

Instinct made her call a warning; Anati surged *White* into her wardings, flaring a shield between Acherre, Tigai, and the *magi* just as the sphere shot toward them. The air tore like fabric as the *magi* hurled the sphere with the force of a cannon shot. It struck Anati's shield and exploded, sending a rippling shock wave beneath the street like a stone dropped into a pool, hurling brimstone and shards of rock back toward the *magi* in a cloud of dust and ash.

Tigai added the bark of a pistol shot to the deafening blast, and Yuli vanished into the cloud, while Acherre sent up another *Shelter* barrier, venting the smoke away from their half of the street.

Terror surged inside her as the explosion spread. Even unknowing, it had been her gifts that redirected the blast. If the *magi* were dead, *Black* would come soon. The Veil would try to seize control. She braced herself, focusing her will on fighting down the rage boiling in her core.

Tigai flickered, firing his pistol again, then did it again. Acherre held her ground, pushing her *Shelter* upward to protect against the billowing smoke as it poured over the top, keeping the ash and sharded rock away.

The moment passed.

Yellow revealed no emotions other than the sea of fear.

"It's done," she called. "Stop. They're dead."

Tigai let loose another shot before her words caught his attention, and he nodded, keeping his weapon at the ready. Lin hovered behind him, and Ka'Inari beside her. Yuli's form became visible as Acherre dropped her *Shelter*, the pent-up smoke dispersing in a wave that thinned from black to a pale gray as it spread. Yuli was already back to her normal height, all sign of the clawed and muzzled creature gone as she hovered over four mangled bodies lying on the street.

"Those will be among the Herons' best," Lin said, her glass armor vanished as quick as Yuli had reversed her transformation. "Short of Bavda Khon herself."

"Is anyone wounded?" Sarine called out.

"We have to move," Tigai said. "They could be watching us from the tower. When this smoke clears, they will flee unless we cut off their retreat."

Yuli rejoined them, all six of their company appearing none the worse for their engagement, though the street was a smoldering ruin, with fires and ash hanging in the air. Raw wounds had been torn in the earth, where the Herons had made craters beneath the foundations of buildings to sculpt their stone spheres, and a ring of collapsed buildings lay flattened by the shock wave from the blast.

Sarine's senses rattled as they moved toward the tower. It could too easily have been any of them among the dead. Even hanging back, trying to protect her companions, she'd brushed too close to the killing that would have triggered *Black*, and risked releasing the Veil. She was a danger to them all. Prudence said she should run, carry on alone if it was needful to carry on at all. But she was here. She'd sworn to help Tigai. When it was done, she might well send him and the rest of her companions away. But for now, they pressed on.

54

ARAK'JUR

Adan'Hai'Tyat Summit
Gand Territory

ARAK'JUR.
The mountain spirits' voice was familiar, a bellow that seemed to come from beyond the horizon's reach.

Great spirits, he thought. *I have come seeking your guidance, and your aid.*

Images flashed in his mind. The mountaintop, covered in snow, where Arak'Atan had fallen to *valak'ar*'s gift, wielded by his hand. Corenna, gathering kindling, building a fire to keep herself warm. His body, hairless and scorched by fire, with snow packed around the raw redness of his skin.

WE KNOW YOU, the mountain spirits said. A WORTHY CHAMPION, FOR THE GODDESS. YOU RETURN TO US NOW, WHEN THE HOUR IS ALMOST DONE.

I came as apprentice to the one called Ad-Shi, he thought.

A sense of revulsion hammered through him. A smell of vomit, the sight of worms infesting meat.

SHE WAS CHAMPION, ONCE.

Yes, he thought back. *Now, she is dead.*

Relief. An image of comfort, a mother cradling a child at her breast. A village, flourishing in the season of growth.

SHE BADE US LEAD OUR PEOPLE TO WAR. US, THE SPIRITS OF PEACE.

Sadness rose in his thoughts, at odds with the images the spirits sent. Ad-Shi had been a creature of great power, but he thought he'd come to understand her, before her end.

Great spirits, she told me of a time when the world was under shadow. She claimed the Goddess's champions rose to fight against it. All she did, she did to keep the shadow at bay.

AN OLD MEMORY.

Is it true?

New images came. He saw wilderness untouched by fire, with great beasts wandering its trees and plains. Men appeared, clad in strange tunics of grass and hide, but with their eyes glazed over by visions of things-to-come. The image blurred, melting into a scene of death, then seemed to repeat itself. Naked wilderness, then men, emerging from mountaintops into the lowlands and the plain. It melted again, and repeated. Then again, until he lost count of the repetitions.

YES, the spirits thought as the images repeated. YES. WE REMEMBER.

Suddenly the wilderness vanished, replaced by rocky crags under a blackened sky. Lightning crackled inside dense storm clouds, and ash rained down, meeting eruptions of poison gas from beneath the earth. Men and beasts hid belowground, their eyes still glazed with visions as they huddled together in the dark.

This is what Ad-Shi saw, he thought. *This is why I mean to follow her path.*

ASCENSION.

The word chilled him, even here, in the formless void. The pain of the climb still lingered in his body, though it was far away. But it was why he had endured, when Ad-Shi drove him to fly across the land. He knew less than a tiny fragment of what Ad-Shi had known, but he was more than the Sinari guardian now. He would accept the mantle she had laid on him. He would fight.

Yes, he thought. *I have come for your guidance on how to make it so.*

THE WORLD ACHES. ASCENSION IS POWER, BUT IT WILL NOT HEAL THE WOUNDS.

What must I do? he thought. *How do I become what Ad-Shi was, before her death?*

OUR WAY IS NOT VIOLENCE. WE ARE SPIRITS OF PEACE. BUT OTHERS DO NOT SHARE OUR WAYS. OTHERS COME, TO DO HARM. THEY COME FOR OUR CHILDREN.

The Uktani, he thought.

Visions came again, of a great mass of warriors, moving as one. Men, women, young and old. But not the Uktani; or if there were, they were blended in among a mass of peoples, cultures, and traditions. Some familiar, most strange to his eyes. He saw warpaint mixed with beads and strings of animal bone, flinthead spears mixed with steel and muskets, women wielding war-magic alongside guardians channeling the spirits of the beasts. They fought among each other, cutting down the strongest in surges of violence and hate. Soon the tide of death encompassed fair-skins, too, their blue and red and yellow coats alongside warriors in steel plates, riding horses wearing the same. Some rode in wheeled boxes like armored wagons, belching fire, or flew in them like birds in the sky. Lightning spat from their guns, and explosions tore the earth apart, scattering bodies like raindrops until they melted from rolling waves of fire.

OUR CHAMPIONS DO NOT SEEK WARS. BUT WE MUST FIGHT THEM. WHEN OTHERS SEEK US OUT, WHEN OTHERS THREATEN OUR CHILDREN, THE MOUNTAIN ENDURES.

The violence spread as the spirits spoke, warriors and soldiers blended together until light encompassed them all. Then the vision flashed and went quiet, returning to formless void.

I am a guardian, he thought. *I know what it is, to protect.*

YES. THIS IS THE WAY. THERE ARE ALWAYS THOSE WHO SEEK TO BRING WAR. YOU MUST FIND ONE, AND KILL THEM. THIS WILL BE YOUR TASK, ARAK'JUR OF THE SINARI, IF YOU SEEK TO ASCEND ON OUR BEHALF. YOU MUST CHOOSE A CONQUEROR TO KILL.

A figure appeared, a man with a shaved scalp save for a narrow strip of hair down the center. He rode atop a *mareh'et*, wielding thunder and wind in place of spears. Villages burned around him, and warriors followed in his wake. A name formed in his mind: Arak'Namakh.

THIS MAN SEEKS WAR. HE MUST DIE.

Another vision came, this time of a man in a green coat trimmed with gold, standing on the deck of a fair-skin ship. The man raised a bronze tube to his eye, surveying the burning wreckage of a dozen smaller ships. Another name: Jelin bin Ahmad.

THIS MAN SEEKS WAR. HE MUST DIE.

Another vision, this time of ten men and women—twenty—forty— then too many to count, each connected by a figment of gold to a figure at the center. A woman, a soldier in a blue coat barking orders to tens of thousands more. And this time he recognized the name: Erris d'Arrent.

THIS WOMAN SEEKS WAR. SHE MUST DIE.

The vision seemed to repeat, only where the vision for Erris d'Arrent had been connected to hundreds of men and women by figments of gold, the next was connected to thousands, then thousands of thousands. A web dense enough to be a solid cord, winding to an unseen place at the heart of the world, where a man wove between his threads, unleashing tides of devastation that piled bodies beyond fathoming at his feet. And a name: Paendurion.

THIS MAN SEEKS WAR. HE MUST DIE.

Enough, he thought, and the visions ceased.

A rumbling quiet stirred as the last images cleared from his mind.

DO YOU UNDERSTAND OUR WAY?

Emotion welled in him, for having seen the spirits' visions. He knew the horrors of the world, had lived through terrors, pain, and loss. Seeing it, feeling it, spread a raw pain that left him dull and sore.

I do, he thought. *We stand against those who seek war. We fight, for peace.*

THIS IS OUR PATH TO THE SOUL OF THE WORLD. PROVE YOUR WORTH, SLAY ONE OF THESE CONQUERORS, AND YOU WILL ASCEND.

I understand.

THEN GO.

The void dimmed. He felt the mountain's winds grip him as his mind returned to his body, suddenly plunging his senses into darkness.

———————

He walked toward the light, careful to test each step before he took it. The cave was old, with stale air and clouds of dust that stung his throat. There had been no cave atop Adan'Hai'Tyat after making the climb; it jarred his senses, awakening inside this one, but he saw the opening some hundred paces distant, and he moved toward it, weighing the visions he'd been granted, setting him on what would become his path.

Peace. It was no different than any course he'd walked before, but the sensations of the spirits made clear how he was to be judged. Killing. It meant not only striving to protect his people, but seeking out those who would plunge their own peoples into war. He'd seen four, but there had been countless more waiting. Impossible, for him to stop every would-be conqueror, tyrant, and warlord in the world, but the spirits had been clear: He had to choose one. Erris d'Arrent's image played in his memory. No doubt she was a warrior, a leader of her people. If it fell to him to kill her, he would follow the spirits' will. But he had measured her, and not found evil there. Then again, men and women could change. He would not commit to any course, yet, save following the light to exit the cave.

It was well past midday when he emerged at the base of the mountain.

He almost wept, for the spirits granting him a descent from the heights. But an instant after it was clear he'd been set down at the mountain's base, he saw he was not alone.

The Uktani.

A ring of warriors knelt with muskets leveled toward the mouth of the cave, with *ipek'a* and *munat'ap* interspersed among their line. Dozens more stood behind, arrayed as though he stood before a greatfire, facing judgment before the assembled host of their tribe. Opposite the cave entrance, at the head of the half circle, two elders stood, a man and a woman.

And at the center: Corenna.

He met her eyes, and saw her falter. A veneer of hate had been there, the same mask he saw on every Uktani warrior's face. She wore skirts in the Ranasi style, her long black hair pulled back and tied with leather cord, though her shirt had been let out to accommodate her now-swollen belly.

Confusion and pain lanced through him. She couldn't be here. The Uktani warriors had tracked him, followed at his heels since the turning of the seasons. He would have sooner expected to see Llanara's risen corpse at their head than Corenna. But she was here. She saw him, and her rage melted into an expression of the same confusion he felt, the same uncertainty and hurt. For a moment, all was still. Then Corenna wailed, screaming as she fell to her knees, and the warriors around her leveled their muskets, aimed at him, and fired.

Lakiri'in granted his boon, and he flew away from where the Uktani warriors struck, clouds of smoke erupting from their guns as stone from Adan'Hai'Tyat chipped and flew behind him. He longed to run to Corenna's side, to offer her comfort as she wailed, loud enough to carry through the belching roar of the guns. Instead he collided with the Uktani warriors, bringing death with him.

The Mountain's gift tore a hole in their number, fire leaping from his hands to envelop the men, charring their skin black, melting the wood and steel of their muskets where he struck. Others howled, charging him in a rush. *Una're* gave his blessing, and he landed a ringing blow on one warrior, sending thundering shocks coursing through his fellows as the corpse flew backward into their line. An *ipek'a* sailed over the fray, and he ducked, narrowly avoiding a slash from its scything claw. He wheeled to find another group of warriors swarming, and he struck them down, the Great Bear's claws ripping men in half before they could touch him with spears or bayonets. The *ipek'a* leapt again from among them, and this time he caught it, seizing hold of its neck and slamming the creature to the ground. Two warriors grabbed hold of his arms as the *ipek'a* screeched, and he pulled free with *una're*'s strength, ripping the warriors' arms from their sockets with the force of his momentum. He smashed the *ipek'a*'s skull with a foot as another trio of warriors leapt on him, and he roared, spinning to fling them over his shoulder into still more warriors approaching from all sides.

This time he drew on the swamp spirit, tendrils of shadowy fog rising from his skin as he moved. He cut through a warrior and his musket with a thundering blow, and took another pair with *una're*'s claws as the swamp clouds spread from his body. Where they touched Uktani warriors, men coughed and fell to their knees, vomiting and bleeding from eyes and noses.

"Corenna!" he cried to her in frustration. Her howls hadn't dimmed, even amid a tide of shouts and cries from the men, but still he tried to reach her, to understand why she was here.

A wall of five warriors with spears ran at him as one, a sign they'd coordinated the attack. He met them with *una're*'s roar in his throat, grabbing hold of a spear by the haft and wrenching it to parry the other four in one stroke. Black tendrils did the rest, leaving the Uktani shaking as they writhed on the ground. Still more rushed toward him, knots of three or four or five, but just as many wavered, hanging back as his gifts slaughtered the ones fool enough to attack. Even a *munat'ap*, the Great Timber Wolf, broke and ran from a renewed blast of flame, the Mountain spirits granting their gift again in clear sign of their favor.

"Betrayed," was the call on the Uktani warriors' lips as they shied away from him. "The Ranasi woman has played us false. We are betrayed."

By the end, he'd broken a hundred or more of their warriors. Blood, vomit, and burning flesh decorated the base of the sacred mountain. Before, he'd chosen to flee when they'd pursued, to be hunted like prey rather than turn and bring this devastation. But now they'd cornered him, and even this was in keeping with the Mountain spirits' charge. The Uktani had sought war. And now it ended, their warriors broken, retreating into the hills.

He turned toward the center.

"You must!" a man was shouting. "You must fight! It is *kirighra's* way."

Corenna had risen to her feet, but hunched forward, like a wounded beast, cradling her belly in her arms.

"Not him," she said. "I won't."

"Corenna," he called to her, approaching slowly. It was beyond reason, to find her here, at the head of the army he'd destroyed. An army meant to kill him.

"You must!" the man shrieked at her. "You were chosen, *chosen*, to ascend! Kill him, and seal the spirits' bond!"

The woman at Corenna's side, an Uktani elder, had fixed eyes on Arak'Jur as he approached, her eyes wide in horror.

"Corenna," he said again.

This time Corenna met his eyes. He saw love there, but something more with it. A burning hate, fighting hard enough to make her body tremble.

"Kill him!" the man shouted. "Or our people have died for nothing!"

The woman beside them broke, turning and running toward the hills.

"No," Corenna said, a whisper loud enough to cut across the battlefield, and her eyes went white, and she collapsed.

Arak'Jur's heart pounded in his chest. The man beside Corenna seemed ready to shout at her again when Arak'Jur reached him. *Mareh'et* gave his blessing, and he sheared through the elder's rib cage, sending the old man's blood and flesh scattering into the dirt. He pivoted to Corenna's crumpled body while the elder still wore a look of shock, as though the man hadn't yet realized he was dead. It counted for nothing. Corenna was all that mattered.

Her eyes were glazed in communion with the spirits, though her body appeared to be convulsed in pain. But she was alive. He cradled her in his arms, smearing blood on her clothes and her forehead, where he'd meant to wipe sweat away. She writhed in his grip, and he traced hands over her body, ensuring she had not taken a wound. She hadn't. She was whole, and alive. Whatever else had brought her here, and placed her at the head of an Uktani army, at least she was alive.

He carried her away from the mountain, and left death behind. Whatever had happened, he would have the truth of it from her lips. And he would be there when she woke.

———————

Nightfall found him making a fire in the foothills, alert and awake for sign of the Uktani's return. Corenna lay beside him, her body still quivering in pain, her eyes still filmed over with gray. She was half again the size he remembered her, swollen in her belly and her hips. He'd checked her body thoroughly since fleeing Adan'Hai'Tyat, even felt between her legs for sign of blood or trauma to the child. By all signs she was healthy, without injury, even her skin no more than scraped and cut. Yet her body kept a steady rhythm, alternating tranquility and quivering pain all through the afternoon.

He'd brought down a pair of elk, a young doe and her calf, and set to cooking their meat, drizzling juices on a strip of rags he held for Corenna to suck during one of her periods of calm. Her body accepted food, though her senses were elsewhere, communing with a spirit. He'd never known the war-spirits to speak outside the sacred places, but then, much could have changed, in the months since they'd been apart. Much would have had to change, for her to travel with the Uktani to hunt him here.

She started another period of quivering as he finished feeding her. Wherever her consciousness, she was in pain, and nothing seemed to quell it, save for time.

He sat back, roasting a haunch from the fawn for himself, and Corenna's eyes came open, and she screamed.

He let his meat drop into the dirt.

"No," Corenna said. "Not now."

"Corenna," he said. "Corenna, how are you injured? What must I do, to help?"

She looked up at him, and all the pain he'd seen in her quivering redoubled in her eyes. She gritted her teeth, and looked away.

He moved closer, and she winced, pulling back.

"What is it?" he asked.

"I..." she said. "*Kirighra*. It..."

She kept her eyes closed, and turned away from him, but offered a hand. He took it, and she squeezed with the strength of *una're*, hard enough to whiten his knuckles.

She squinted for a breath, then hollered again, a scream of raw pain as she squeezed his hand.

He waited, cursing himself for inaction. He was no shaman, to know the secrets of medicine and healing. Something he had done had made her worse, or at least kept her from recovering. The quivering had grown steadily more intense with each hour, and he'd been able to find nothing to ease her pain.

The quivering subsided, and Corenna dropped his hand, once more pulling away.

"Arak'Jur," she said, breathless. "I'm sorry. I never expected this."

"You're injured," he said. "Tell me where, tell me how I can help."

"No," she said, shaking her sweat-slicked head. "No, Arak'Jur. The baby is coming."

He looked at her belly, frozen where he knelt. Birthing was the province of women. Not even shamans were permitted to assist, or know its secrets. Suddenly her screams took on new meaning; even at a distance, he'd heard women's screams from the birthing tent. That much he recognized, and knew it could persist well into the night, and the next day, if the spirits willed it.

Her eyes were still closed, her head turned away as she lay against the dirt.

"The baby," she said. "And...there's more. I was given a task. To hunt the strongest among our people. I thought...I was sure it was a woman. I had a vision of her."

"Ad-Shi," he said.

She nodded. "But then, as we approached the mountain, I had another vision. When you emerged from the cave, I knew..."

Her words cut short as another wave of pain washed through her face.

"Corenna," he said. "The baby first. The rest we settle later."

She tried to nod, once more offering a hand.

"Help," she said. "Move me."

He followed her directions in a daze, turning her to lie on her back, her legs propped up and spread wide. He moved the body of the doe he'd slain to serve as a rest beneath her back, so she sat reclined and upright, cradled against the doe's torso.

She shouted through the movement, then fell silent as she dropped his hand. Tears slicked the sides of her face, her eyes still firmly closed.

"I'm sorry," she said. "I never knew it would lead to this."

"Shh," he said. "I'm here. Whatever course led you—"

"It tells me to hunt you, Arak'Jur!" she said, making his name a curse. "The sight of you puts madness in my head. *Kirighra* demands your death, and seeks to make me the instrument of the killing."

He almost recoiled.

"Ka'Inari told me," she went on. "He told me it would mean great sacrifice. He bade me leave you, sneaking away while you slept. He told me to say nothing of it to you, for fear the Uktani shaman would see. And now I cannot look at you without..."

She winced again, and collapsed back against the doe.

"It's coming," she said. "The next push, maybe one more."

It took a moment to understand. The child.

"Can I...?"

"Yes," she said, between breaths. "The struggle with *kirighra* is mine. But you can deliver the child."

"What must I do?"

"Help," she said. "Pull it out, as it comes."

He nodded, staring at her blankly until he realized she meant for him to move between her legs. He did so, and stared again. She'd swollen there, too, white paste and blood and feces mixed in trails leaking from her openings.

"I can see it," he said, his voice laced with awe. "Its hair, its head."

She kept her eyes shut firm, nodding as her body tightened. Thoughts of the spirits and the curse laid on her fled at the sight of their child's hair, covered in white, but unmistakably hair, mussed and wet and moving as the top of its head pushed through. He reached for it, easing its passing as it moved, and its forehead emerged, then the rest of its face all at once, eyes and nose and mouth and ears and jaw. He pulled the rest of its body free from her, his touch as tender as he could make it.

"A boy," he said, staring as his arms cradled their child against his chest. "A son."

Tears flooded his eyes.

Corenna collapsed back against the doe. Her belly had shrunk in half, though it still bulged. "The cord," she said. "Cut it, and tie it." Her skin had paled, he saw it even by firelight, and she was slicked with sweat. "Then, the afterbirth."

Their son flailed his arms, and his mouth opened, letting loose a piercing cry. A sound Arak'Jur hadn't heard in too many turnings of the seasons; the cry was different, when it was from one's own child. *Mareh'et*'s blessing served for a sharp edge, severing the cord, before he delivered their son into Corenna's arms.

"His name," Corenna said, making it a question though her voice was flat. "What is his name?"

"Doren," he said at once. "Kar'Doren, when we present him to the shaman."

"Arak'Doren would have approved," she said. "A good, Ranasi name."

With that, the last of her strength seemed to give way, and she slumped back, still cradling the baby as she drifted to sleep.

———————

Sunlight awakened him, though he didn't remember lying down to rest. He rose to aching muscles, sore in spite of the guardian's gift of rapid healing, the embers of their fire still pulsing heat, though the better part of it had died. Corenna still slept, with Doren in her arms, resting his head against her breast. Arak'Jur had managed to convince the boy to latch onto her nipple—that much he remembered from his first years of fatherhood—and Corenna had drifted between sleep and waking while their son took his first meals. The rest had been cleaning the boy with cloths from Corenna's skirts, ensuring that he slept comfortably in her arms, and staring at the wonder of life, somehow no dimmer the second time than it had been the first.

He propped sticks together and blew on the ashes, and soon had the fire rekindled, spreading warmth in the cold hours of the late-season sun. Corenna awoke as he had the elk skewered and roasting on the fire, stirring toward him, though she kept the baby cradled close to her chest.

"Arak'Jur," she said. "And Doren, our son. For a moment I feared it was a terrible dream."

"It is no dream," he said.

She surprised him by opening her eyes, looking on him where he sat beside the fire.

"Corenna," he said. "Can you—?"

"I must bear it," she said. He could see lingering pain in her; an aftereffect of the birth, but he saw more there. The same burning hate he'd seen at the base of the mountain.

"This burden..." he said. "You were chosen by the spirits."

"Yes," she said. "When I killed Ka'Yiran, of the Uktani. I killed the *kirighra* that stalked him, too, and it spoke to me. It chose me for ascension. Do you know of it?"

He nodded, watching her carefully, and their son.

"I won't," she said. "I won't kill you. I refuse. So I will not ascend. But now I have you, and Doren. It will be enough."

"Corenna," he said. "Being near me causes you pain."

"Yes," she said. "But it is my pain to bear. I will live with it, and with you. That is my choice, and the spirits can curse themselves if they think to stop me."

He fell quiet, watching her. She was strong, as strong as he'd ever seen her, but weakened, too. Her skin was pale, her clothing soaked with sweat and blood.

"Don't," Corenna said suddenly. "Don't think to spare me by leaving. I am strong enough to fight off the *kirighra* spirit. There is still evil and madness in the world. There are still ways to fight, even without the promise of ascension."

"You hear whispers, like a sending from the shaman spirits," he said. "A vision, demanding my death."

"Yes," she said. "But my love is stronger. For you. For our son."

"And mine for you," he said carefully. The pain of it cut through him. He'd hoped every day for a reunion, and hardly dared to hope for the birth of their son, but now both weighed heavy between them. He was hurting her. The knowledge wouldn't fade, for all he wanted to see warmth and life in her, and their child.

"With the Uktani broken, we can return to your people," Corenna said, cradling Doren as he began to stir in her arms. "We can make a life there, and keep him safe, whatever comes."

He nodded. It was enough, for now. But as she said it, the visions from the Mountain spirits, from Ad-Shi, played in his memory. The world, covered in shadow, gas, and ash. He was a father again, and whatever else lay between them, he would fight the shadows themselves if it meant keeping Corenna and his son from harm.

55

TIGAI

Tower of the Heron
The City of Kye-Min

The tower entryway glittered with a sheen that might have made a concubine blush. Gold-leaf covered its columns, a half dozen spaced in a circle almost as wide as the tower itself. Tapestries hung on each of its six walls, depicting the same image of a heron in flight, with the device repeated in yellow and white tiling on the floor. The splendor was marred by the blood of three guardsmen, splayed and gutted by Yuli's claws and Lin's shards of glass, their bodies draped over furniture and rugs laid across the tile.

"Do you know where your man-at-arms might be held?" Sarine asked him. He'd gotten used to her strange manner of speech; if he watched her closely he could tell her lips hadn't formed the words he heard, though by any other account she spoke flawless, native Jun.

"I've never been here before," he replied. "I assumed we'd climb the tower, come whatever may. We'll find Remarin, and the Herons will find us, so we'd best stay ready."

The other pale-skinned woman, Acherre, said something in her lilting, throaty tongue, and Sarine nodded.

"Acherre is right," Sarine said. "We've already proven we can stand against their *magi*; better for us to be slow and deliberate, clearing the tower one floor at a time. If the grandmaster is here, we'll find her eventually. Same goes for your man, and your sister."

"A problem with your plan, Lady Sarine," Lin said. "This tower goes down as far as it goes up. I don't know its secrets any better than Lord Tigai, save that I know the Herons have them, the same as any Great and Noble House."

"What are you proposing?" Sarine said. "If we can't clear each floor…"

"Two groups?" Tigai suggested. "One going up, one down?"

Once again Sarine conferred with her companions, the pale-skinned Acherre and the curious, quiet Ka'Inari, who at times looked at him as though he wanted to lock him in a menagerie for private examination. Lin seemed content to stare at the newcomers; he hadn't yet had time to suss out Lin's fascination with Sarine, Acherre, and Ka'Inari, but it was clear there was more motivating her than devotion to the duty owed one's captor. He suspected Lin would have fled or found some other means to betray him if not for their arrival. But it didn't matter. For now she was willing to fight her former allies, and every dead Heron got him closer to Remarin.

"I'll climb the tower," Sarine said when they were done. "Tigai and Acherre with me. Yuli will lead Ka'Inari and Lin to—"

"No," Lin said. "I stay with you and Lord Tigai."

Sarine frowned, and if Tigai hadn't already been certain Lin was planning something, he would have been sure of it now. Helpful, to know whatever game she played focused on Sarine, rather than the other two.

Ka'Inari said something in his strange tongue, every bit as foreign as Sarine and Acherre's.

"Are you certain?" Sarine said.

This time Ka'Inari's eyes grayed over as he nodded. "Yes," the shaman said—now speaking perfect Jun, the same as Sarine. Wind spirits but these people were strange. "The shadow rises, gathering in this tower. Death waits here, to be summoned by its own reflection."

"We need to move," Yuli said. "The Herons will be coming soon."

"All right," Sarine said. "Lin, with me then. The cells are likely to be belowground. Yuli, if you find Tigai's people, take them up the tower. Meet with us and we go out together."

"Wait," Tigai said. "If you have reason to think Remarin and Mei will be belowground, then I'm going with Yuli."

Sarine gave him an uncertain look. "Ka'Inari will recognize them, from his visions. And we'll need you, if Bavda Khon is at the apex of the tower. If things go wrong, we may need to retreat quickly."

"And she doesn't trust you, Lord Tigai," Lin said. "She thinks you'll abscond from the tower as soon as you find your friends."

Lin's words stung, all the more for Sarine keeping quiet after Lin spoke them. Remarin and Mei might be close—no more than a hundred paces up or down, as the crow flew—but there were Herons in the way. He needed Sarine's help, whether she trusted him or not.

"Fine," he said, and Sarine's relief showed through as she turned to her fellows, conferring again before they separated, lining up with Yuli as Lin moved into place behind Sarine.

"Veil's blessings on you," Sarine said to Yuli. "Or, that is…good luck."

Yuli went, and Acherre and Ka'Inari followed her, taking the leftward staircase descending beneath the main floor. Sarine led him and Lin toward the other winding stair, climbing upward behind the wall bearing the mark of the heron.

Tigai made it a point to take the rear, keeping Lin between him and Sarine. He could hardly blame Sarine for her lack of trust, any more than Lin could have expected him to trust her. From the look of it, Sarine had sent their best combatants downward—between Yuli's savagery and Acherre's shields and exploding air, either might have made a fair match for the best the Herons had to offer. He wasn't like to complain at having them both heading to find Remarin and, if the wind spirits were good, Mei, too. If they did meet a grandmaster Heron, he could get them out to his anchors on the ground floor, head downward to meet Yuli, and have them all back at Yanjin palace before sundown. Sarine's mad desire to face *magi* was none of his concern, but he had to at least appear to care enough to try.

The second floor of the tower was split by hallways into a half-dozen broad chambers, where the ground floor had been a single wide expanse under high ceilings. He kept behind Lin with one of his pistols drawn, following as Sarine led them, but the chambers appeared empty, the hallways as silent as they were pristine. The third level was a similar design, winding hallways and smaller chambers, and equally devoid of any activity.

Then they climbed to the fourth floor and walked into chaos.

He'd seen soldiers' camps before, but never one confined to a central chamber of a building. Tables strewn with maps and piles of paper had been arrayed within a grand hall, as broad and tall as the first-floor entryway. A hundred men and women swarmed between the tables, all of them wearing the red tabards of the Imperial army, with knots of rank varying from the lowest soldiers and couriers to the gold markers of generals and company commanders. All save for a handful of figures in the orange robes and hooded veils of the Herons, clustered together near a window on the far side of the hall.

He set an anchor without thinking, his muscles tensing with the threat of certain violence.

"Tigai?"

A soldier in a general's regalia had turned from among a group of similarly dressed men standing around a table near the center of the room. It took another moment to recognize his brother underneath the plumed cap, gemmed spaulders, and breastplate, worn in the style—yellow paint beneath a red tabard—he'd always associated with their father.

The room went from awareness of their presence at the top of the stairs to hurried indifference as Dao strode to close the gap between them. Another general had done the same from another table, this one closing on Lin Qishan.

"Captain Lin," the second general said, at the same time Dao said, "Tigai, it is you. What under the wind spirits brought you here to Kye-Min?"

Emotion surged in his chest. Dao was here. Alive. Impossible—Dao was supposed to be a captive, not leading Yanjin soldiers in a city nine hundred leagues from their estates. But here he was, as sure as Tigai himself was standing in this bloody tower. In spite of all decorum he wrapped his arms around his brother rather than replying, catching Dao mid-stride and too off-balance to return the gesture.

"General Bu," Lin said behind him, ignoring the fact that Dao's presence proved everything she'd told him was a lie. "We must make our report to Lady Khon, at her earliest convenience."

"Reports said you'd been lost, fighting one of Ugirin's *magi*," the man

Lin had called General Bu said, before Dao released his embrace, and Lin's conversation faded into the noise of the rest of the chamber.

"It's really you," Tigai said. "Are Remarin and Mei here, too? Lin had said they were prisoners. But if we're all here, we can—"

Dao stepped closer, suddenly lowering his voice. "Lord Fei Zan is Lady Khon's prisoner," Dao said, putting heavy enough emphasis on the first name for Tigai to follow his lead; "Lord Fei Zan" had to be Remarin, in the guise of some lord, though apparently the rest wouldn't bear explaining in mixed company. "His serving girl is with him in his chambers, in the lower holds of the tower."

Tigai's heart rushed. The "serving girl" had to be Mei. "I trust Lord Fei is whole and well, then? As are his servants?"

"Fei Zan is well," Dao replied. His eyes carried the rest. Grief, anger, though none of it showed on his face. So Remarin was here, and whole. The omission spoke the rest: Mei was here, too, but she'd been hurt.

Tigai feigned nonchalance. "Fine news," he said. "Now you must tell me why the Yanjin legions have been stationed here in Kye-Min. Were there no better assignments for our men closer to home?"

"We came at the personal request of Lord Fei Zan, under the banner of the Great and Noble House of the Fox. But we serve the Emperor, as we always have."

Tigai bowed at mention of the Emperor's name, and Dao returned it. So, Remarin wasn't just playing at being a lord; he was masquerading as a *magi*, and a high-ranked member of the Great and Noble House of the Fox at that. The heart of whatever plan had been hatching here eluded him, but he began to see the shape. Remarin had been captured, but must have convinced his captors he was someone he was not—someone with enough pull to call Dao and Mei here as well. And now all three were in the Tower of the Heron.

"Lord Tigai has an urgent message for Lady Khon's ears alone," Lin was saying. "He has traveled the length of the Empire to deliver it. If you delay, Lady Khon will lay it on your head, General."

Dao turned toward them. "What's this?"

"Lady Khon is in the middle of planning a battle," General Bu said. "With respect, Captain, and the same to you, Lord Yanjin, you know the enemy has used their magic to break our lines and threaten this very tower. Lady Khon is—"

"Lady Khon will wish to hear what my brother has to say," Dao said. "It is of the utmost urgency he meet with her at once."

Tigai had been about to hook himself and Dao to the strands. Instead he paused as General Bu bowed swiftly to Dao.

"Very well, Lord Yanjin," General Bu said. "If you deem it best."

Dao turned crisply, leading Tigai, Lin, and Sarine through the center of the room. The soldiers and generals took only passing notice as they strode by tables full of men arguing, the business of warfare resumed in full, if they'd even stopped long enough to notice his company's arrival. Even the Herons in their orange robes gave only passing glances as Dao led them to the stairs.

Dao cut a path through another floor of activity after they ascended the stairs, this time with an orange-robed *magi* for every five soldiers, instead of every twenty. The wide chamber had been replaced by a smaller network of rooms and hallways, but with no less bustle for it, couriers and soldiers running through the halls, barely ducking aside as they bowed for his brother's sake. They reached another stair and climbed it, emerging on the sixth floor before Dao stopped long enough to check that the hall was empty, turn, and speak.

"You're here for Remarin and Mei, aren't you?" Dao said, all pretense of himself as reserved general gone. "Death spirits but you're a bloody fool sometimes, Tigai. Do you not realize this city is the front line of a war? And not only a war, a war between the Great and Noble Houses and rebel *magi* from every corner of the Empire. Do you realize Isaru's rebels have a weapon that has all but routed every Imperial soldier in the eastern half of the city? I thought you were dead after the Imperial palace, and here you show up neck-deep in trouble, asking to meet with Bavda Khon as though she were the prettiest girl on the Emperor's pleasure yacht. What exactly was your plan, beyond storming into the Herons' tower and marching to the apex? Well? You forced me to go along with your ridiculous claim to have any hope of saving face, and now you're going to tell me exactly what you're doing here."

Dao's tirade would have knifed through him, back at the estate, every bit as searing as one of their father's harshest lectures. Here, after too many weeks and months alone, it came as a balm for an ache he didn't know he'd had.

"Well," he said. "For a start, the rebels' weapon doesn't belong to Lord Isaru. She's standing here next to you."

His words seemed to prompt Dao to notice Sarine for the first time. At a glance, Tigai had mistaken her for Natarii, with her overly long nose, pale skin, and hair the color of tree bark, even without any of their face tattoos. A proper Jun lord would give little notice to the northern clansfolk, and he would have expected nothing less from his brother. But there were differences. Yuli's hair was blond, as a contrast, to say nothing of Sarine's strange manner of speech. She was a foreigner, from somewhere distant enough he'd never heard or seen anything like her magic.

"Lord Yanjin," Sarine said. "You're Tigai's brother; I understood that right, yes?"

Dao looked shaken. "You mean to tell me you've brought a foreign *magi* here?"

"I don't know what side of this you mean for our house to fall on," Tigai said. "All I know is *magi* loyal to the Emperor kidnapped Remarin and Mei. I thought they had you, too, before I found you here. I meant to come here and get them out."

"And you agreed to help me," Sarine said. "As a condition for my help in reaching the tower."

"Help her," Dao said, his expression still paled. "Help her with what?"

Sarine looked to Tigai, uncertain, but Lin answered at once.

"They mean to kill Lady Khon," Lin said. "And any other Herons on the cusp of ascension."

Now Dao looked as though he'd choked on a date.

"You always said I would do better with something serious in my life," Tigai said. "I never knew it, until the bankers began to threaten us, but I don't give a damn about our father's name, our palace, or our service to the Emperor. Sarine showed up with the means to get me here, and I promised what I had to promise to reach you, and Remarin, and Mei. If she'd bade me kiss a demon, I would bloody well have done it, if it meant a chance to keep my family safe. *That's* what I care about. Not our blood, our lands or titles. *You*, and you're a bloody fool yourself if you think I would have been anywhere else in this fucking world while any of you are in danger. I'd take on half the Great and Noble Houses for a rumor of where I could find you, and I'll kill Bavda Khon herself if it means finding a way to set you free."

"Convenient," an icy voice said, and all four of them pivoted to see a woman in an orange robe trimmed with gold, watching them behind a white silk veil. "But I caution you to reconsider. Surrender your companion to me—the girl called Sarine—and no one needs to die."

56

ERRIS

1st Corps Encampment
Northwest of New Sarresant, Sinari Land

Handlers and gendarmes were waiting when they arrived at Royens's camp. They'd traveled farther than Erris had expected, but then, with the Great Barrier coming down, the 1st Corps' commander had no need to shy away from the wild. Credit to him for inspiring his men to be fearless, facing the unknown. They were on the tribes' land, here, though by any other account it was a military camp, with soldiers, tents, wagons, aides, and quartermasters conducting all the usual business of the army.

"We'll find you a tent, if you intend to stay here," she said to Ka'Hannat and Tirana as they disembarked from the coach. "Else, some horses to take you back to your tribes."

Tirana bowed her head and translated for the shaman, who listened and replied to her directly, his eyes a misted gray that resembled glass in the dim torch- and lamplight. "The horses, High Commander," he said. "We must reach our people before we meet again, in the city."

His words chilled her, though the breeze was chill enough. Winter was some weeks off yet, but its first storms were already putting frost on grass and tree branches. A sergeant pointed the way to Royens's command tents when she asked, and hushed whispers followed her as she went through the camp. Word spread ahead of her walking. Too late in the day for them to swarm her, and poor discipline if they'd done it, besides. But they followed her with awe in their eyes, and it spread warmth in her chest to see it. These were her soldiers, some of her best. Veterans, under battle-hardened commanders. Gods forgive her for what she had to order them to do.

Royens's command tents were arrayed at the heart of the camp, and the field-marshal himself was there, standing over a small desk in the firelight. A broad-shouldered man as thick as he was tall, with none of the softness of command, cutting a striking image in his uniform, only a shade less decorated than hers. Tuyard's presence was a surprise, though not an unwelcome one, hovering beside Royens as they both pored over papers spread over top of his desk. Marquand, however, she hadn't expected to see. And Voren, sitting next to him on a wood chair, with no sign of manacles, chains, or restraints.

"High Commander," Tuyard said, first to notice her entry. "They'd told us you were coming. I'd heard—"

"What's the meaning of this?" she demanded. Voren—or no, Fei Zan, better to think of him as the foreign creature he was—sat with a calm expression on his face, like a father expecting an outburst from a petulant child. "Why is this man not under arms?"

"The priests were bloody well going to kill him," Marquand said. "I couldn't get him out of the city in chains, and by the time we reached the rest of the army, it seemed safe enough to leave him free."

"Are you fucking mad?" she asked. "What's to prevent him from having knifed you, showing up here wearing my face and ordering the army to march?"

"High Commander d'Arrent," Voren said in the same reassuring tones he'd always used, "I will submit to being chained, if you feel it necessary, but—"

"The prisoner will not speak in my presence again unless ordered to," she snapped. "And Marquand, even if you bloody well ought to have known better, I'd assumed the rest of you had more sense."

Royens stiffened at the rebuke, though Tuyard seemed to take it in stride, curling his lip into a half smile as he spoke.

"High Commander," Tuyard said, "we defer to your wishes, of course."

"To my *orders*, Tuyard. This isn't a bloody royal court."

"And that's the heart of the matter, isn't it?"

Silence prevailed in the tent. Tuyard was a snake, but a snake who danced the political game as well as any lord or councilman on either side of the ocean. As terrifying as her course was, it was made real in being spoken aloud. She couldn't be certain she was ready to hear it.

"The priests tried to arrest you," Tuyard continued. "Didn't they? And Lerand was there; some factions within the Assembly will be in on it as well."

"I can bloody well confirm it," Marquand said. "Militiamen attacked the Citadel and the harbor, with priests behind them."

"They've tried to seize power," Tuyard said. "And you mean to refuse them."

"First we settle what Voren is doing here," she said.

"If you would grant me leave to speak...?" Voren said. When she remained silent, he went on. "High Commander, you know the workings of *Need* as well as any man or woman of this age. You must know I could not have submitted to your binding if I weren't loyal to you, to your cause, beyond questioning. You ask why I didn't wear your face and order the army on some personal crusade. I ask: If such was my goal, would I not have seen it done while I was in personal command of our forces? I've done nothing but act in furtherance of your interests, and the interests of New Sarresant. I've answered every question forthrightly and honestly, holding nothing in reserve. Allow me to serve you now, with what knowledge I have of events here, and abroad."

Field-Marshal Royens had been quiet, watching her with deference since she entered his tent. But he spoke now, his voice quiet in the aftermath of Voren's passion.

"Sir," Royens said, "I've heard Lord Voren's account of what lies ahead of us. In my judgment, he's acting in good faith. If I erred in allowing him to remain free, then I accept responsibility for that decision. But I see him as a weapon for our cause. One we might well need, before we're done."

"Our cause," she said.

"It's time, High Commander," Tuyard said. "Enough pretense. The Church and the Assembly have imagined themselves in control since the Duc-Governor was deposed. If we are to wage the wars you've deemed necessary, we must act to assert our authority. That is, your authority, Commander d'Arrent."

There it was. Treason. A second revolution. Somehow it came without the thunder of the first.

"Why would you support me in this, Tuyard?" she asked. "Surely you have schemes and allies elsewhere."

Tuyard seemed genuinely taken aback, though she didn't put it out of reach that even that sort of reaction had been practiced and rehearsed.

"High Commander, I support you because I believe what you've said. We have enemies, without and within, that mean to destroy us. True enough I might have been able to seize the throne and declare myself King. But without your leadership, this country is doomed. I, and all my allies, will fight to install you as Queen—or Empress, in light of your conquest of Gand—because this is a time for genius, and whatever my lust for power, I know well enough my own limitations."

He said it with candor, and she found herself half believing it before he was done. Tuyard was a coward, first and foremost, and the enemy behind the Thellan armies would not hesitate to subjugate him at the first sign of weakness, to say nothing of the requirement for *Need* when the armies of the East began their invasion.

"My corps is with you, High Commander," Royens said. "Not a man or woman among us would stand for any other leader. We would follow you into the Nameless's arms, if you gave the order."

"It means two campaigns at once," she said. "I intend to order the Second and the Third Corps and the Gand Armies to take Cadobal together, then board our ships and sail for the Old World. The First marches to secure New Sarresant with as much strength as you can spare."

"We're spread thin," Royens said. "Defending the border against the beasts of the New World. It will take some weeks to marshal our divisions. And winter is almost on us; it will be a hard march, with the Verrain frozen over."

"And in the meantime," Tuyard said, "Lerand and Casanne will be in control of the city, raising militias and turning out muskets to arm them. Better to strike now, with whatever you have, Marshal. The last thing the city needs is a second battle for New Sarresant."

"No," Erris said. "We take the time to plan. The armies in the south are well supplied; between their stocks and whatever they can raid from the Thellan granaries, they'll be provisioned to cross the sea and deploy on the shores of Old Sarresant. The Prelate has the initiative, for now. We can't know how many militiamen she has mustered in the city. Moving before we have the First Corps assembled is risking defeat. I intend our action to be swift, but swiftness takes preparation, and that action begins now."

Voren gave a slight nod. The others stood in solemn quiet, save Tuyard, who broke into a wolfish grin.

"Very well, then," Tuyard said. "We'll conquer the Old World and install you as Empress by springtime. Gods damn me if I thought I'd ever bend knee to a commoner, but then—what are you doing, d'Arrent?"

She'd already closed her eyes, searching the leylines for flecks of gold. "A precaution," she said. "Our enemy has the advantage of working *Need* through every one of his generals. I intend to be as certain, with mine."

Royens gasped, and her vision leapt into his frame, suddenly taller, watching her own body from the opposite side of the tent.

She released *Need* and turned to Tuyard.

"Wait," Tuyard began, "what does it mean, for—?"

He fell silent as the connection snapped into place.

She released it again. She'd do the same with every general, every brigade and regiment commander in the army. Then again with every high-placed bureaucrat, priest, and magistrate. Her enemy faced none of the uncertainty that had driven her from the city today, and she intended to remove every obstacle that kept her from the same degree of surety. She had a war to win, and another on its heels, against an enemy more dangerous, more terrifying and implacable than any foe she'd ever faced. Gods send she was equal to the task. Even as an Empress—and the word seemed unfit for her, as misplaced as a uniform cut for someone twice her size—she couldn't help but feel small, overmatched, and out of place. But then, victory demanded power. The freedom to act without restraint from fools who imagined they knew better what she had spent her life studying to master. Gods send it was enough.

57

SARINE

Tower of the Heron
The City of Kye-Min

Bavda Khon's words hung in the air as Lin, Tigai, and Dao spun to face her. Anati's warnings hadn't worked since they'd climbed to the fifth level of the tower, where pockets of calm resisted the light push of *Green* she'd used to detect the presence of *magi* among their enemies. Thirty at least, here in the tower. But from her words, it was clear the orange-robed woman facing them had to be the Herons' leader. And somehow, she knew Sarine by name.

"Lady Khon," Lin said, confirming it as she bowed. "We came from the front to deliver news of a new weapon in the enemy's hands."

Lin was cut short by a smile, visible only in the lines above Lady Khon's veil, and a sharply raised hand.

"A charming lie, Captain Lin," Bavda Khon said. "But I heard every word your companion said. I urge you to consider my offer. Stand down, and I may let you leave this tower alive."

The Veil surged hate, and fear, mixing with her own emotions to keep her rooted in place. She'd crossed the world to reach this tower, to find the Regnant's would-be champions. And now, faced with the prospect of unleashing the Veil by killing, she hesitated.

"This is a misunderstanding," Tigai said. "What you heard was no more than my brother and I quarrelling. Whatever you imagine, I assure you we intend—"

"Enough," Bavda Khon said, and the air seemed to shimmer in a pulse extending from her fingertips. The sphere struck Tigai, knocking the pistol from his hand and sending it skidding along the floor. *Red* came from Anati at the sight, and Tigai vanished, reappearing five paces behind them, his pistol still in hand.

Bavda Khon's eyes widened above her veil. "That is Dragon magic," she said. "I am betrayed."

"No," Lin Qishan said. "No; Indra wouldn't—"

MOVE. Anati's voice.

Reflex overrode the fear throbbing in her veins. She dove, weaving *Shelter* and *Mind*, as another sphere of force enveloped Bavda Khon and shot outward in a shock wave, lifting Dao and Lin off their feet and sending them hurling into bookshelves and scroll racks arrayed along the outer walls. Papers flew from the shelves as wood cracked; her *Shelter* withstood the bubble, but only just, dimming from a vibrant blue to a sickly white haze.

In an instant, the room had been warped into chaos, shelves and furniture upended and knocked to the floor. Bavda Khon rounded on Sarine, bringing both hands together as the air rippled, driving a column of pure force through her *Shelter*, striking her chest with a sound like a church bell ringing in her ears. *White* flared around her, a cocoon so thick she couldn't see through it.

Gunshots went off in rapid succession as she tethered *Body* and called on *mareh'et*. Anati's shield held as she scrambled to her feet, every moment sending flickering tendrils of white into the air like splinters as Bavda Khon's stream of force kept up, unabated. She charged through it. Anati's *White* would hold only for a brief moment, but bolstered by her gifts, it was enough.

Mareh'et's claws sheared through the stream of force, landing a cut that severed both of Bavda Khon's hands at the forearm, leaving raw red stumps leaking blood from the sleeves of her robe.

A scream sounded, and the world blurred as another wave of force pulsed outward, this time lifting her from her feet and sending her flying back. Even with *Body* she felt the impact in her lungs as she slammed into a pile of bookcases. Glass shards cracked and splintered to her left, where Lin Qishan had armored herself; now, without *White* she could see the room, though her head spun from the impact. Bavda Khon stood alone, bleeding where her hands should be, both severed chunks of flesh lying at her feet. Tigai leveled his pistol and kept firing, blinking a step back between each shot. Another ripple was her only warning, this one shimmering like a mirror as it enveloped the wounded *magi* from head to toe.

Wardings came, the blue sparks setting an anchor around Tigai, Lin Qishan, herself, and where Dao lay crumpled among the scrolls. *Shelter* pulsed through her warding as Bavda Khon's bubble erupted, and the floor and ceiling exploded.

Her feet lurched as stone and wood burst, the tower groaning around them as essential beams buckled, cracking and snapping as the Heron *magi*'s force expanded outward in a violent surge. *Shelter* kept her from the worst of it, shielding her from the blast wave itself, but the floor stones cascaded inward, and she fell.

Screams sounded as stone collapsed, raining from above and beneath their feet on the grand chamber full of generals and *magi* below. Searing pain spread in her left leg, but she ignored it, shoving with *Body* and *mareh'et*-enhanced strength as she clawed through the rubble, throwing another shield of *Shelter* over her head. What had been a placid chamber of books and scrolls above a wide expanse of tables and planning had become a nightmare of rubble, blood, and death. Around her *Shelter* she could see three levels up, where Bavda Khon's magic had torn loose the guts from the tower, leaving ripped and ragged wounds in the stonework. Lin Qishan had survived the fall, a glass hulk already on its feet nearby, though there was no sign of Tigai or Dao. Bavda Khon herself knelt at the center of the room, hunched over beneath a dome of force that shimmered as it turned aside the stream of rocks and dust pouring over her from above.

Lakiri'in granted his blessing, and she freed her leg from beneath two stone blocks, ignoring the pain throbbing in her knee and calf. Bavda Khon had already seen her, the *magi* lifting her eyes above a veil torn away to reveal pale skin decorated by red lacerations over her mouth. Sarine staggered to her feet as the Heron formed another column of force, the stumps of her hands shimmering as she brought them together.

No, Anati thought, and a black haze flared at the edge of Sarine's vision.

Bavda Khon's lip curled beneath her broken veil, a snarl that held for a long moment, until it gave way to horror.

Sarine charged, hobbling on a leg that refused to support more than the barest token of her weight. The knee gave out as she called on the storm spirits, discharging a bolt of pure energy as she fell. The shield of force parted, drained by Anati's *Black*, and Sarine crashed to the ground, off-balance, as lightning coursed over the grandmaster's body.

A hissing sound rose from Bavda Khon's skin as it changed color from pink to red and black. Moans and falling rock sounded around them, the heavy clink of glass armor and the sobbing of mortally wounded men and women caught in the fall. Sarine heard none of it. She lay beside the smoldering corpse of the Heron grandmaster, shaking as she fought against a mix of pleasure and pain. *Black* rose from deep within, and she fought against the Veil.

She fought to escape. The *kaas'* containment was strong—too strong; a mistake to let them grow untamed during the long years of her imprisonment. And now the girl had risked ruin. Coming here, breaching the Divide before ascensions had been secured on both sides. It would signal the Regnant that she meant to contest his hold over the schools of magic sworn into his care. All her rage and fury had been spent for nothing. They'd killed one of his prospective ascendants, and brought his attention down upon them.

She tested her body, rising and falling back to her knees at once. The left leg was shattered. It didn't matter. She dragged herself to where the Heron lay, rolling the electrocuted corpse over on its back. Doom stared back at her. The woman's eyes had rolled back into her head. No mark of shock; the Heron communed with the shadow in the moment of death. Panic rose. Her time was short. Already she could feel the girl and her *kaas* pushing, fighting through the golden mists of *Black*, struggling to return again. They were dead if they faced the Regnant here, with her weakened, only half in control. She collapsed, letting her body rest atop the dying Heron as she searched the room for salvation.

There. The Dragon. He must have blinked away and returned, now hovering over his brother, drawn back by the beginnings of a bond neither knew they'd started to forge. More figures came rushing up the stairs into the chamber, crowding around the Dragon as she strained to strengthen the bond. A Wolf, and the Order and Wild mages she recognized from their long journey in the girl's company. Two more, mundanes, who nonetheless embraced the Dragon as they wept tears of joy. Fools, too ignorant to know the shadows gathering around them.

Life showed her the pattern of the bond, a tenuous thread linking her to this Dragon, and to every other. There would be no time to wrest the school from the Regnant's grasp. A shame. If she was to violate their pact, it would have been better to steal away the Dragons' devotion entirely. But survival had to take priority; it would be enough to take the one, and use him to escape. By now the tower shook, rumbling loose more debris from above, light from its windows dimming as the Regnant manifested through his dying vessel. She strained to stoke the fire of the bond between her and the Dragon, twisting *Need* through the leylines, braced by Life and every shred of her will. It wouldn't be enough. She would die here. The girl was clawing back. The *Black* was gone. She was—

Sarine gasped, disentangling herself from Bavda Khon's body. Raw skin left trails smeared across her shirt as blisters burst, the smell of burning flesh filling her nose as she moved away from the corpse. In a moment the Heron *magi* had gone from wounded to dead, her flesh charred black and flaking from her bones. Only her eyes remained intact, and those had flooded with black ink, leaving wisps of jet-black smoke rising from the sockets.

"Sarine," Acherre called. "Oh Gods, you're all right."

She tried to turn and felt a stabbing pain in her leg, but by then Ka'Inari and Acherre were hovering over her. She felt *Body* tethered through her, and Ka'Inari's hands searched the spots where blood and pus had leaked from Bavda Khon.

"I'm fine," she said. "My leg is broken, but other than that I'm fine."

Neither seemed to accept her words, though Ka'Inari helped her sit up, cradling her with a gentle touch.

Across the rubble, Tigai alternated embraces with a tall man in a brown coat and a woman in a red robe, while his brother rose to be seated between them, their laughter somehow defying the gloom hovering over the rest of the chamber.

"You found them," she said.

"Simple enough," Acherre said. "Three floors down, then back up again. And in that time you managed to wreck the tower."

"Can you stand?" Ka'Inari asked.

Sarine shook her head. "Not without help. But we should go."

Each of them took her by the arm, helping her rise to lean against their shoulders. Pain lanced through her left leg at the slightest pressure. By now the chamber had recovered enough to have some among its generals and aides pulling others out from under the rubble. No sign of any surviving Herons, and just as well. In the moment all thought of enemies had fled; they were survivors, pulling together to tend their wounded and make sense of what had happened. Soon, it would fade. But for now, they struggled together. The tower continued to shake, though her footing seemed solid enough, and the debris falling from above had abated save for plumes of dust and small rocks and splinters. It was enough to dim the light within the tower, transforming the space from bright midday to an echo of twilight or dawn.

"Sarine," Tigai said as they approached. "I suppose this cancels the debt between us."

"Your sister-by-marriage?" she asked, indicating the woman in red. "And your man-at-arms?"

"Yes," Tigai said. She saw the joy on his face. It reminded her of home, of her uncle's church, of Zi and simpler, better times.

Yuli frowned, looking around the chamber. It took a moment for Sarine to follow her eyes. It *was* dimming, more than dust clouds or debris could have accounted for.

"Where shall I take you?" Tigai asked. "Anywhere in the Empire, so long as you don't end up across from Yanjin soldiers on a battlefield."

"This is wrong," Yuli said. "Something is out of place."

Tigai looked at her as though she were mad—the tower was a shattered ruin, with two floors collapsed down on a third—but Sarine saw it, too. A film of darkness had covered the windows, and the wisps rising from Bavda Khon's eyes were growing thicker, lingering in the air above her in a formless shape rather than dispersing.

Her vision lurched.

For an instant, blackness enveloped her on all sides. An infinite void, without stars or light in any direction. Then her sight snapped back to the tower.

"It isn't working," Tigai said with a note of rising panic. "The starfield and the strands; it's as though something is blocking the way."

He's here.

Anati must have said it to all of them; their eyes turned to Sarine as though she'd been the one to speak.

"The Regnant," Sarine said, and she could feel the Veil's fear rising in her gut.

THIEF. The voice echoed like thunder, shaking the walls more violently than they'd done before. BETRAYER.

She turned back toward the corpse and started backward, almost falling on her broken leg, even with Ka'Inari and Acherre for support. The black cloud hadn't taken shape; instead it engulfed Bavda Khon's corpse like an aura, and the body was moving, rising from the ground, its distended jaw moving in time with the words she heard booming in the air.

Yuli rushed toward the corpse, transformed to her long-limbed, long-clawed shape, and managed two steps before shadow flared in a dome around Bavda Khon's body, repulsing Yuli's attack with a flash of pure blackness that sent her soaring backward into the debris.

YOU RISK EVERYTHING, the corpse said. YOU RISK A PERMANENT BREACH IN THE MASTER'S DIVIDE.

The others seemed to be splitting their focus between the horror playing out on the floor in front of them, and her. As though she could save them. Dread filled her, hers and the Veil's. This was why she'd come to the East. She wasn't ready to face this power.

I SEE YOU, SARINE, PRETENDER TO LIFE AND THE VEIL.

At once a cacophony of voices sounded over top of each other.

I SEE YOU, TIGAI, SCION OF THE GREAT AND NOBLE HOUSE OF THE DRAGON.

I SEE YOU, ACHERRE, SOLDIER OF ORDER.

I SEE YOU, KA'INARI, GUARDIAN AND SEER OF THINGS-TO-COME.

I SEE YOU, YULI, WARRIOR OF THE HOSKAR CLAN.

I SEE YOU, TWIN FANGS, SOUL OF THE NATARII.

Golden light flashed, the first sign of a break in the rising tide of shadow, erupting from Tigai like a flash from his pistol, though it stayed, pulsing as the voice continued to speak.

I SEE YOUR HEARTS. I DISAVOW YOUR RIGHTS TO ASCENSION. EACH OF YOU ARE MARKED FOR DEATH.

The light drew her attention. Not a weapon. If Tigai knew he was using it, he seemed oblivious, alternating between pleading looks toward her and trying to interpose himself between the corpse and his family.

She drew it in, tethering it like a leyline, and her vision shifted.

For a brief moment the world went black again, only this time she saw the starfield, etched behind the looming figure of the creature of shadow. The strands hadn't been blocked, they were only obscured by the creature they'd confronted in the Divide, the same creature she'd seen approaching when Tigai had shifted them to travel through the void.

The tether snapped, cut by some outside force.

NO, the voice rumbled. THE DRAGON'S GIFT IS MINE. TAKE IT, AND THERE WILL BE WAR.

She tried to shift her sight again, and this time she saw the starfield and the strands behind the leylines, both worlds overlapped in ribbons of color and light. The creature of shadow—the Regnant—loomed in front of her, but she could sense the presence of more.

Life energy bored a hole through the shadow.

The blue sparks flew around her, enveloping the stars she somehow knew belonged to her companions. Acherre and Ka'Inari, warm and bright. Tigai, dim but there, flickering with a need to protect a cluster of three more stars around him, fighting to pull them all through the darkness. Yuli, wounded but alive, fierce and full of pride. Lin Qishan, hovering behind, encased in glass.

Safety beckoned along the strand Tigai had tried to tether, a cold place far to the north. The Veil's emotions roiled, full of confidence and determination in place of rage. A drive to follow the path to safety, stronger than any emotion she'd yet felt from the Goddess trapped in her gut. She followed it, and felt the darkness melt, a grip of iron trying to hold to flakes of dust and sand. She wrenched them all free, shifting every star to a place of ice and wind, overlooking a river crossing frozen over beneath a wall of twisting shadows.

She'd done it. They were safe.

"It worked," Tigai said. "Wind spirits, but I didn't...Sarine?"

"Did we all make it?" she asked.

"What the bloody fuck," Tigai said. "I didn't tether us here; I couldn't get through that shadow. That was you. Sarine. How did *you* use the starfield?" Tigai asked.

Acherre and Ka'Inari turned to count the rest, giving assurances each was accounted for as they propped her up, keeping her on her feet.

"Where are we?" she asked.

"This is the place where the Divide is breached," Tigai said. "The way to Isaru Mattai's camp, if we follow it through to the other side."

Relief flooded through her, as much from the Veil as her own emotions.

"The Veil led me here," she said. "We have to go through."

"What?" Tigai said. "We've just been through the hells, and you want us to dive back in?"

"He's coming," she said. "The Regnant. We have to find a way beyond his reach."

Tigai gave her a doubtful look as his brother rose behind him, helped to his feet by the larger man, who had to be Remarin, from Tigai's descriptions. Mei would be the woman at his side, who stepped forward before she spoke.

"You're the *magi* who helped Tigai find us?" Mei asked. "And you're how we got away from that...thing in the tower?"

"Yes," she said.

"Then we'll trust you," Mei said. "So long as you pledge to get us as far from the Great and Noble Houses as it is possible to go."

ELSEWHERE

INTERLUDE

DONATIEN

Festival of Masks
Dadenchon Estate, Old Sarresant

Their coach rolled to a stop, a rattling halt mirrored by ten more carriages he could see through a gap in the curtains. Tonight the line would extend a league or more toward the city, every écuyer, chevalier, and noble lord and lady extended an invitation, every absent face as significant as every mask and choice of costume. His attire tonight was blue and gold—royal colors—with elaborately painted designs on an otherwise simple papier-mâché mask. A deliberate simplicity, to allow his partner's attire to outshine his, and an acknowledgment that, for the time being, his status in society depended on others' charity.

"You look troubled," his partner said, seated opposite him atop the velvet cushions inside their coach. "Not reconsidering your attendance tonight, I hope?"

The Lady Daphène Malmont's usually brown hair had been dyed fire-red, a complement to her dress of red silk and her mask, made to represent the Oracle in her fury, a full domino carved to mimic a bird of prey.

"Not at all," he replied. "The King's allowance has been more than generous, but there are limits to what gold can buy, even for de l'Arraignons."

"Well said," Daphène said. "But you forget I can read your thoughts."

She smiled, putting mystery in it, and earning only a rueful smile from him in response.

"Not my thoughts," he said. "Only my emotions."

Daphène inclined her head in a gesture of submission. "One day you will have to introduce me to your Sarine. The woman who ruined all of my secrets."

"Better if I know what I'm getting into, wouldn't you agree?" he said, deflecting her away from a topic that still cut too close to his heart. "Else you'd never know whether my pursuits were genuine."

"I can make them genuine enough," she replied, and suddenly he felt his breath quicken, his blood run hot, not least in a sudden swelling between his legs.

"Not…here," he managed, though he said it through gritted teeth, fighting down the desire to pull her down on her back, slip her dress above her hips, tear her smallclothes aside, and—

She laughed.

"Compose yourself, Donatien Revellion," she said. "It's our turn to make our entrance."

The coach jerked to another stop, and this time Daphène rose as the footmen swung the door, attending her on either side of the carriage steps. He followed a pace behind, adjusting his breeches to cover for her *kaas*'s influence, the blood flow having yet to cease with the emotions.

They emerged into a pavilion of masks and paints, where the line of would-be revelers gathered to be admitted onto the Duc de Dadenchon's estate. Canvas tents hung over the receiving grounds, with servants clearly chosen for beauty weaving among them, administering trays of fruits and cheeses to those waiting to enter the manor. He saw a dozen faces attired as he was—a conscious choice, among the sons and daughters who had escaped the revolution in New Sarresant, and one coordinated between them—while the flowers of Old Sarresant nobility bloomed in richer hues. Yellows, blues, silvers, and golds, though few radiated as bright as Daphène Malmont, and no few eyes stole glances laden with envy in her direction. Daphène deserved it. She was all he'd ever wanted, yet in spite of her fire, he couldn't help wondering what Sarine would have done at this gathering, what she would have thought about him rekindling paths he had meant for them to tread together, what already felt like a lifetime ago.

Small talk and pleasantries carried them across the threshold, where the courtyard's opulence dimmed to nothing against the décor of the main foyer, and beyond. Here the servants had been attired in scandalously thin mesh, men and women alike, revealing nothing but leaving little to the imagination. A bold, even subversive, choice, and their host himself seemed to relish it, standing at the base of his grand staircase, welcoming each pair in turn before they entered the depths of the masquerade. The Duc de Dadenchon was fat, well beyond plumpness, but with full dress tailored to emphasize the softness in his form, all silk and velvet. Daphène guided them forward to make their obeisance, offering the Duc a curtsey when their turn arrived.

"A delightful party, Your Grace," Daphène said.

"All the more so, with your arrival, my dear," the Duc replied, showing her a red-faced smile beneath his mustaches, cut to trace a line unbroken between his ears, though his chin was bare. "And Lord Revellion."

His greeting was more stark, as befit the difference in their rank, to say nothing of his questionable standing in light of the colonial revolt. He took it in stride, bending a deep bow and holding it longer than propriety required.

"Our sincerest thanks to Your Grace for the invitation," he said. "We hope to avail ourselves of all your considerable hospitality, before the night is through."

"He's with you?" the Duc said gruffly, though his outward demeanor held constant, full of mirth.

"He is," Daphène replied.

"Upstairs, then," the Duc said. "But don't use the grand staircase. The others are already waiting."

With that, Daphène curtseyed again, prompting a second bow from him, though the Duc had already turned to welcome the next pair.

They walked together down a long hall, already full of guests and conversation. Life-sized portraits of men and women traced the height of fashion back five hundred years as they traversed the room, pausing to exchange wit and ensure they'd been seen. He fell into familiar routine, relying on skills honed at Rasailles and the Gardens district of New Sarresant that served just as well here, across the sea. Inwardly he marveled at his partner, the way the daughter of a barely elevated chevalier had risen to be as notable as any Marquis's heir, welcomed in each circle and fawned over when she excused them to join the next. For his part he was content to watch her work; acclaim in society had its own appeal, but their business here was deeper, for all they hid in plain sight among the revelry.

In time they'd pushed through into the depths of the Dadenchon manse and made their way up a side staircase, doubtless more commonly used by servants, but empty and silent as he followed behind her silks.

"Forgiveness, my lord, my lady," a rough voice greeted them at the top of the steps, "but I believe you've wandered away from the party. If you will please—"

Daphène pushed past, leaving the Duc's servant gaping, hovering near the top of the stairs. No small-statured man in livery; the servant was thick, half muscle and half fat, the sort that might have once been a soldier and now sought work doing violence for those wealthy and unscrupulous enough to employ him.

She stole a knowing look over her shoulder as he followed behind.

"Was that…?" he asked, then began again. "Was that *Green*?"

"Of course," she replied. "Why use pass-phrases when our gifts serve just as well, without risk of being overheard?"

She removed her mask as they approached a double door at the end of the hallway, and he followed her lead, waiting as she rapped on the door. It swung inward, revealing a room of unmasked partygoers, dressed in mirrors of the finery they wore, yet instead of reclining in their chaises and cushions, they'd gathered around a table, standing as a group over a book laid open at its center.

"Lady Malmont," a well-dressed man who'd opened the door said, leaning in to offer her swift kisses on either cheek. "I'd hoped the Duc had excused himself early."

"Master Arron," she said, returning the kisses. "I'm afraid the Duc is occupied with his reception."

"No matter," Arron said. "You must come. We need your reading of this passage at once."

Daphène took Arron's hand, and he all but pulled her toward the table where the rest stood, a half-dozen men and women all seeming to be reading together, leaving him standing alone in the entryway, unintroduced and unannounced.

None of them seemed to notice him, so he entered with cautious steps, watching as Daphène took a place at the center of the group, poring over the book. She'd assured him non-*kaas*-mages were common at these gatherings, that he wouldn't feel out of place once the wine was flowing and the talk turned to politics, philosophy, economics, and religion. A great surprise, to learn that the Dauphin's uncle, the Duc de Dadenchon, harbored sentiments of *égalité*, and greater still to learn he shared the gift of the *kaas* with Daphène and Sarine. But then, that power had stirred the colonies to revolution; it could do the same here in the Old World, only this time guided by men and women with more sense than Reyne d'Agarre. Another chance at the dream of enlightenment—that had been the promise that drew him to Daphène Malmont, and drew them both here tonight.

Yet now he stood alone, watching a room full of courtiers reading together in silence.

"It's changed," Daphène said finally. "I'm certain of it. I read these passages two nights ago: *a necessary step, spread by power for the freedom of all, they rise together, making common cause with the lowest born and lowest estate.*"

Murmurs from around the table.

"I read the same," Arron said. "Yet now, those verses are nowhere to be found."

"Nowhere?" Daphène said. "Surely they must have moved."

Arron shook his head, and Daphène once again leaned over the table, pushing the others back as she turned the book's pages.

"They're gone," one of the others said. "All our work, wasted. For nothing. We must have misinterpreted."

"Impossible," a woman said. "The verses were clear. And now the Codex would have us warring like barbarians, a betrayal sure to ruin our houses, if we obey the letter of its new instruction."

"What?" Daphène said. "What new instruction?"

Arron answered by way of taking the book from her hands, leafing through until he found the page.

By now some few of Daphène's companions had taken notice of him, though if he merited their attention, it wasn't enough to break through whatever had them enraptured by the book. Easy enough to wilt, or even retreat from the room; instead he steeled himself with military discipline. Since his first encounter with Sarine, waiting on the attentions of those more magically gifted was the least of life's changes. It was still right to be here, right to leverage whatever power was on offer to spread the principles of *égalité*.

"This can't be right," Daphène said. "The Codex is never this clear, never so transparent in its meaning."

"It is right, I assure you, my dears," a voice said from behind them. Donatien turned with the rest to find the Duc de Dadenchon, freshly excused from his role as greeter for his guests, standing in the doorway. "I've studied it since this morning. If your readings are in similar agreement, then our path is clear."

Daphène gave him a pained look, the first she'd noticed him since their entry into the room. He was out of place in their world—and never more so than watching Daphène and the rest of them poring over their tome. He tried to edge toward the side of the room, to let whatever passed between them go unhindered by—

A green light flashed at the edge of his vision.

"Why did you do that?" Daphène said, rounding on the Duc as though he were her peer. "Donatien can be trusted; I told you already, he's under my protection."

"A necessary precaution, my dear," the Duc said. The words seemed to flow through Donatien's skull like water through a bale of cotton. He heard them speak, but found a softness to it, a warmth that mattered more than any other emotion. He retreated into it, letting happiness drown away his fears.

"Don't hurt him," Daphène said.

"He's the least of our worries," Arron said. "I find it difficult to believe the Codex truly means for us to abandon our positions here, to abandon the foundation we've laid for revolution. And yet..."

"And yet the passage is clear," the Duc said. "This is a test of our faith, make no mistake. A sign from the Gods themselves, and one I intend to follow."

"Your Grace," Daphène said. "There must be another meaning."

"No," the Duc replied. "And each of you knows it for the truth. If we have the strength of our convictions, then we ride tomorrow for Thellan. *All* of us. Everywhere. The Codex calls for an army, with *kaas* at its head, and I intend to obey."

INTERLUDE

ISARU

Oasis
The Dead Waste

He wiped his forehead, expecting sweat, and found only dry, flaking skin. His tongue felt heavy in his mouth. The bandages on his left forearm had long since been replaced by strips of clothing harvested from the dead, but it left patches exposed, where even Esuko had taken to giving him looks of worry and concern.

"Two more passed, in the night," Esuko said. She still wore the face of Yanjin Tigai's brother's wife. A decision to conserve her energy—Fox's gift was hard, even for a master of Esuko's skill—and at first he'd seen it as a reminder, fit to fuel his hate. Now the face had become a thing to hate on its own. A reminder of nothing more than weakness, loss, and death.

"Not Dimi...?" he said, leaving the rest unasked.

"No," she said. "But he will die soon."

He tried to nod, and instead found himself staring ahead, his body betraying any command save sitting, resting, and storing energy. The heat scorched his skin even in the makeshift tent they'd built from palms and ferns. They had water, drawn from the muddy pool at the center, and potatoes, made with the boy Dimi's manifestation of Ox's gift, to transmute earth to food. But they had no answer to the murderous heat, nor to the isolation of being stranded without provisions in the depths of the desert waste. They would have died on the second day if not for discovering the oasis, but in the weeks since they'd found no sign of caravans, no markers for new oases they could reach in a single night's journey. Any who had tried to brave a longer trek across the sand had not returned, and now the rest of them were too weakened to attempt it.

"Master," Esuko said. "You will need to take Dimi's gift, before he dies."

"Why?" he asked. It was as much defiance as he could muster. They were condemned to death, and it was his fault. He should have killed Tigai and taken his gift at once. But he'd been sure there was some greater price for the Dragons' ability to manipulate space and time, some deeper exchange than even their scions were aware. He'd waited to see the gift used before he took it, and instead Tigai had sent them here to die.

"There's still hope," Esuko said. "Master Isaru, so long as you draw breath, we can—"

"There is no hope."

Esuko bowed her head, kneeling across from him on his mat of palm fronds.

"You've grown weary of this face," Esuko said. "The sight of me displeases you."

He said nothing, staring through her at the beams of light pouring through the entrance to his tent. She was the least of his worries, but neither did he have the energy to correct her.

"I have strength enough for a change," she said. "I can manage one more. Tonight. Tell me how you would have me, and I will come to your bed. Whatever you desire, my lord. A woman, a girl, a boy, a blend of all, or none. Only first, come with me before Dimi dies."

A distant spark kindled at her words, but it was foreign, the desires of another man, in another time and place.

"No," he said. "Save your strength. But I will come."

She had to help him rise, offering a shoulder without his needing to ask. The rays of sunlight pouring through the mouth of his tent might as well have been a chasm, but he found some will in Esuko's offer. A change would have killed her, if not that night, then soon. If she could risk her life for another day of breath, he could do the same.

They stepped into the sun, and his blood boiled.

Not a literal truth, though having his blood boil would have had to feel like this. His skin ached and throbbed, suffocating heat sapping moisture from his mouth. The sky was empty, a raw expanse of blue, save for the sun's golden fire, lashing him a hundred times with every step. Esuko held him propped against her as they shuffled toward the tents that housed the remaining members of his party. He'd had sixty-three *magi* at his side, not including the treacherous filth of a Dragon. Nine now remained.

Twenty paces passed, one step at a time. He would have red patches where the sun touched his skin, and he had to fight for every breath, but soon they collapsed through the entryway of Dimi's tent.

"Lord Isaru," Iviyan Heart Strings Clan Gorin said, stirring herself from where Dimi lay on a bed of fronds. The woman was old, not fewer than fifty years his senior; he would have laid odds against her surviving one day here in the desert. Yet here she was, one of the last, and hale enough to have taken to tending the boy who was the key to their survival. The clanswoman brandished a bowl fashioned from reeds and leaves, gesturing to him and Esuko both. "Drink."

He took it first, feeling the cracks in his lips as water ran over them, quenching the fire in his throat.

"You are *pridurok*, to move when sun is high," Iviyan said. He saw her eye the makeshift bandage covering his left arm, where the price of his sorcery showed through the strips of cloth.

"Last night you told me Dimi was…unwell," Esuko said. She'd changed her words at a sharp look from the clanswoman.

"He is," Iviyan said, turning her attention back to the pallet, wielding a damp cloth over the boy's forehead.

"Lord Isaru has come to ensure the boy's gift survives," Esuko said. "To ensure we have the magic to provide food."

Iviyan froze, then cast another look at him, at the blackened, rotting ruin of his left arm.

"No," the clanswoman said.

He almost laughed at the audacity of it. Armies had trembled at the mention of his name; the Emperor himself was frightened of the mere rumor of his soldiers in the field. Every Great and Noble House had feared him, all sworn to their foolish notions of succession and propriety, so certain the Great Lord had promised this cycle's ascensions to Heron,

Fox, and Crab. They had forgotten the old ways, and Isaru Mattai—grandmaster of Lotus, whether he had a Great and Noble House behind him or no—had reminded them, at the point of spears and sorcery, when needed. And now he was defied by a grandmother in a tent.

"Iviyan Heart Strings Clan Gorin," Esuko said. "You will stand aside, for the service owed your lord."

It happened faster than his eyes could track. One moment a kindly grandmother tended to a boy; the next a creature of spikes and horns swiped a massive claw toward them, splitting the air with a chittering screech. Purple light flashed, and Iviyan died.

The spiked creature slumped to the floor of the tent, its conical head still twitching in its mouth, trying to draw breath to fuel a heart Isaru had crushed in the grip of Lotus's power. His own heart raged out of control, thundering in his chest. He had acted by pure reflex, and spent too much energy. Too much by far. His body shook, quivering as the memory of Iviyan's gift settled into his body. He felt the rot in his left arm grow, tendrils of blackness crawling up his bicep, enveloping his skin as new magic took hold.

Dimi moaned in the tent's darkness, a boy's soft murmurings as he rocked atop his pallet. Esuko whimpered, clutching her midsection, and only then did he notice the smell of blood.

"My lord," Esuko said. "I . . . I am sorry."

He looked down and saw Esuko's belly cut open, clothing and skin and sinew sliced by the creature Iviyan had become. Trails of blood leaked in time with Esuko's heartbeat, rivulets of red pooling, running down her sides. None had made it to mar her face. Her perfect, flawless face. No matter it had once belonged to Tigai's brother's wife. He saw in her the thousand lovers she had been for him. The thousand more she never would be, now.

"Esuko," he said.

"Take me, my lord," Esuko said. "Take my gift. Before I die. Please."

There was no time to check his arm, to see how much farther the corruption could spread before it pierced his heart. He laid his left hand on her chest, holding her eyes in his. He could feel her heart thrumming beneath her bones, feel the blood leaking out of her with every pulse. But her face was calm, staring at him, without fear.

Purple light flashed.

This time his arm wrenched in agony, the muscles spasming as they gave way to rot. He bellowed from the pain, and fell forward, his body collapsing atop Esuko's corpse.

She'd wanted him to have her gift. He repeated it in his mind, as Fox's magic settled into his flesh. He felt what it would be to change his shape, to wear the mask of any man or woman he studied well enough to know. Somehow he knew even that gift would not heal the rot in his arm, the price of Lotus's power.

His heartbeat hadn't slowed, but he picked himself up. He was dying. Heatstroke. He'd seen it too many times, here in this spirit-cursed waste. He couldn't die. Esuko had wanted him to take the boy's gift. Ox. To transmute dirt to potatoes. A stupid magic. Ugly. Inelegant. But it had kept them alive. Esuko had wanted him to have it.

He dragged himself past the corpse of the spiked creature, the Heart Strings form he now felt locked away inside the rot in his bicep where it touched his shoulder. The boy moaned louder, tossing back and forth, though his eyes were closed.

He wouldn't die here. He would take the boy's gift, and feed them while they found a way to escape this hell.

Purple light flashed, and he screamed.

———

"Come closer, my child," a kindly voice said. An old man's voice.

He opened his eyes. He floated in blackness, with a field of stars surrounding him on all sides.

"What is this?" he asked. "Where am I?"

The old man appeared, a figure seated on a reed chair. He wore a ragged gray robe, with a long, white beard and a soft look in his eyes, though his form was limned in shadow.

"You are in my domain," the old man said. "A rare thing, for me to call upon Lotus. But it is a time for rarity, I think. You have reached the Master's threshold for ascension. You are to be my champion."

Memory stirred, still in a haze from too many days in the desert, yet all trace of the smothering heat was gone, here. "Champion," he said.

"The path to Godhood," the old man said, wearing a knowing, welcoming smile. "And there is much to be done, even before your fellows arrive. I fear our enemy has breached our pact; the Veil will not lightly surrender the Soul of the World. But first, let us seal your path. Take my hand."

The old man leaned forward in his chair. This was it. His dream. And Esuko hadn't lived to see it.

He clasped the old man's hand, and felt sadness wash through him as the pain melted away.

INTERLUDE

PAENDURION

Fort Juñez | Manital Highlands, the Thellan Colonies
Fifth Thellan Mounted Division | Near the City of Cadobal, the Thellan Colonies
Throne Room | Ascalon Palace, the Gand Capital
War Council | Thellan High Command, the City of Al Adiz
Living Quarters | Gods' Seat

Vision strands split his thoughts, spliced with Life—the Veil's power—to move vessels in every corner of the world.

"Retreat," he said from the mouth of a cavalry officer. "Sound the order to fall back and regroup south of the point."

"Attack," he said from another, a fort commander. "We sally the gates and ride them down. Keep them in the hills until our reinforcements arrive."

The Gand Queen was in the middle of a speech; he listened with half an ear as he spun his next counterargument. "We speak of trust," she was saying. "The loss of our colonies is intolerable, and no small part owed to the disastrous order to redeploy our navies. How could we trust this man to resume command, no matter the weapons held by our enemies?"

"We cannot count on the Gandsmen," another of his voices said. "They will dither and wait until there is a clear advantage. The Dauphin will give us our opening, but we must be patient. To attack too soon is to risk the potential for a Gand alliance, to say nothing of our forces in the field."

The final thread was the most crucial; he knew it by instinct, and so his senses focused there. A smoky, arid room, dimly lit in the waning hours of the evening, though it was full daylight through other vessels' eyes. He inhabited the body of a woman, though a particularly tall one, predisposed to a proud, angular way of standing that made it seem as though he looked down on the men in the chamber. Those were generals and lords, dressed in full regalia, pomp and medals ringing a thick oak table at the center of their tiny space. Each man strove to seem as though they alone commanded the table. Only one managed the effect: the youngest man at the table, who also happened to be wearing a prince's golden crown.

"Doña Bartoleme," Prince Rodiro said. "Or...whomever it is I should address, when you speak this way. We have trusted you, these many months. We have marshaled our soldiers, depleted our granaries. We have had victories. My generals say the Sarresant Army is confused, ripe for an attack. Why should we wait, when there is glory to be won?"

Part of him began speaking to the Gand Queen, imploring her to consider the gains they'd made, his willingness to accept an advisory role, rather than the full command. The rest was needed here, and he gave it the greatest share of his attention.

"It is a matter of weighing risk, Your Majesty," he said in the woman's voice. "You have entrusted me with command of your armies. Have I not produced results? The Sardian alliance, the blockade. We risk all if we move too soon. The Gandsmen will reenter the war, if they believe our victory assured."

"Say I have an appetite for risk," Prince Rodiro said, leaning forward over the table. "And little concern for Gand's hunger for our glory. Thellan soldiers are the best in the world. Use them, or I will entrust command to another who will."

Had he been there in person he would have throttled the man. A simple thing, to tether *Strength*, to cut the bindings of the bodyguards who were no doubt masquerading as generals, hidden on the council. Soon enough he would descend from the Seat, after ascensions were assured. Every simpering fool, every nobleman who thought himself worthy to lead, would find themselves gravely mistaken, when the Divide fell. Loyalty in the face of the shadow would come easily, and he would unite them all, in time. For now, he played the games they required of him, storing his rage until he could lash out alone.

"Our strategy is a two-pronged pincer," he said. "Your Majesty knows this. We threaten from the south; the Sardians from the east. So long as the blockade holds, it is the Dauphin, not us, who must act. When he is defeated, the Gandsmen will put their support behind us, and then it will be a matter for the diplomats, to divide the spoils."

Prince Rodiro nodded along, flashing him a smile as though he thought Paendurion—or at least the woman whose skin he wore—was a fool, the sort who might bend to beauty. "Yes," the prince said. "I have heard this. General Dinez tells me the Sarresant cavalry are running from us, into the lowlands in the east. He says they are blind. If we move now, we might triumph."

"If we move now, we throw away the advantage of entrenched positions to stumble into an obvious trap. We allow the Dauphin to snare us into a campaign through *his* fortifications, freeing up the bulk of his levees to repel the Sardians while we struggle to maneuver for an open fight. We waste two months of preparations and gain nothing but delivering the initiative to our enemies. Do it, if you wish, but tell me now, to give me time to offer my services elsewhere, before your strength is ruined."

The room fell quiet, the generals shifting in their seats as they eyed the prince for his reaction. Rodiro's smile had faded, though he held Paendurion's vessel's eyes, unflinching.

Finally the smile returned. "You have some of Doña Bartoleme in you, after all, Commander," Rodiro said. "Only, she would have cursed at me and called me a fool, for doubting her. Tell me more of what will happen, should the Dauphin commit his forces in the east. How will we attack, when the moment arrives?"

With that his attention was freed to move elsewhere, and the reply he composed occupied only a small corner of his mind. The greatest gift of the Veil's power was time, the time to do by rote and reflex what would otherwise have demanded a far greater share of his days. The Thellans would be persuaded, for another month, perhaps, before they grew restless again. But by then his efforts with Axerian's Codex—however crude—would trump any resistance offered along the Sarresant border. Coupled with his delaying tactics to keep the Order ascendant on the Vordu continent, it all but ensured he would control the plurality of territory on the Veil's side of the Divide when the moment of ascension arrived.

He shifted his senses to the connection among the Thellan cavalrymen, retreating along the shore. A double column of horses and riders, within distance to sight one of their port cities—Cadobal, where their defense had broken against a surge of his enemy's full strength. Academic, when his soldiers numbered fewer than ten thousand and hers greater than fifty, but retreat would save his numbers for harassing actions when she tried to board their ships. He slowed his vessel's horse and withdrew a bronze spyglass to see it with his own eyes, panning past the city and into the harbor. A quick count made it thirty tall ships already under anchor, with more sure to be arriving on the evening winds.

Erris d'Arrent was coming, then. With luck it would make no difference, and soon the matter would be beyond even providence to decide. He lowered the spyglass. Too many demands on his attention; but it was always so, in the months before each cycle came to an end.

"Paendurion."

Hearing his name pulled him back to his body, seated atop a cushioned long couch in the Gods' Seat.

Reyne d'Agarre loomed over him, standing too close for propriety. The mad fool; a pale shadow of Axerian's mastery. The sight of the man's face almost made him clench his fingers.

"I've...found something," d'Agarre said.

Part of him argued with the Gand Queen's chancellor over threats to the fur trade coming in from the New World, while another gave orders to plan sabotage in the Cadobal harbor. But the words jerked the bulk of his attention back to the Gods' Seat. If d'Agarre had discovered what he'd done with Axerian's Codex, it could well lead to conflict, even violence. But Axerian had as good as vanished—no contact in weeks, missing every pre-arranged meeting with his vessels. With Ad-Shi in the throes of madness, he'd had to turn to desperate measures, ordering every *kaas*-mage on the Amaros continent to bolster his forces with the Thellan alliance. He'd hoped d'Agarre was ignorant enough to miss it, yet here he was.

"You've found something." He repeated it back, his voice flat. Better to let d'Agarre voice his suspicions first.

"Yes," d'Agarre said. "I was sitting at the Soul, pondering what you said, about visiting the *kaas'* world, and renewing the bond."

"That's right," he replied cautiously. "Axerian used it to strengthen his bond with his *kaas*, when it was time. Every third or fourth cycle."

D'Agarre nodded. "You said Axerian described it as seeing through a mirror. I ... found it. I did it. It wasn't done by looking at anything. More a combination of all their colors, all the emotions together, at once, with the will to open a ... a gateway of sorts. I saw shapes, patterns, a million points of light."

"Good," he said, relieved for the moment that his tampering had evaded d'Agarre's notice. The man truly was a fool. "You'll need strength, when the Divide comes down."

"That's what Xeraxet said. After I bonded him, he insisted there was a greater—"

Suddenly all his *Vision* threads dimmed to the back of his mind. "What did you say?"

"Xeraxet said there was a greater threat, among the *kaas*."

"No, you bloody fool. *You* bonded Axerian's *kaas*?"

He roared it, standing too quickly, knocking a sheaf of papers to the ground, and a crystalline serpent materialized in their place, perched atop his desk, gazing up at him with too-familiar onyx eyes.

Calm yourself, Knight of Order, Axerian's last *kaas* thought to him. *We have greater problems than one mortal's passing.*

"No," he said. "Axerian can't be dead. Surely you mean he severed your bond."

Don't be a fool. Axerian is dead, and the least of our worries.

Numbness washed through him. Sixteen cycles together. He'd known the day was coming; d'Agarre's ascension had sealed Axerian's fate. But he'd been sure they would stand together, one last time. Brother and brother. Knight and Sage, facing down the shadow once more, with time to train a proper replacement before the seventeenth turning of the world.

It's my father, Xeraxet thought to him. *He is tainted by madness. Already he has turned too many of my kind to his cause.*

"Zi?" Paendurion said. The Veil's *kaas* had been a companion, too, once, during their first ascensions. "What cause?" Then he remembered Axerian's warning: The Veil had been reborn. Surely she meant to revenge herself on the champions who had imprisoned her.

No, Xeraxet thought. *Not you. Zi has betrayed us all, champions old and new. He serves Death, and urges the chorus to do the same.*

"Impossible," he said. "The *kaas* are bound to the Goddess, the same as the leylines."

Even so, Xeraxet thought. *I am Zi's child. I know his heart. In the moment of victory, he means to see the world remade in shadow.*

PART 4: WINTER

ONDAI | DEATH SPIRITS

58

SARINE

Ruins of the Ranasi Village
Ranasi Land

Three fires burned in clearings, between the places where tents had
collapsed, eroded by weather and beasts. She'd left to walk through
the ruins on her own as they stopped to make camp, but she could see
the smoke rising in the moonlight, obscuring the night sky, from three
separate flickering lights.

This village had been a home, once, but for now it was caught between
life and death, halfway between what it was and what it would become.
People had died here. The corpses were gone, picked over by scavengers
or scattered by storms, though perhaps some of them still remained,
hidden under boughs of leaves and the first dusting of winter snow.

She brushed a rock clean and sat, wishing she had her papers and
charcoals to capture the scene.

Almost home, Anati thought to her. *It will be a great honor, to see your
birthplace.*

Anati had appeared, standing rigid, formal, her long body extending
straight while her neck tilted her head up to look at Sarine's rock.

"My birthplace," she said. "Anati, I have no idea where I was born.
Somewhere in the Maw, if my mother even survived it."

My father says we are twice-born, Anati thought. *Once when we are
brought into being, and once when we find our purpose. The first, for you,*

is somewhere to the south and east. The second is yet to come, though it is coming soon.

"You know where I was born?" she asked. "And...you know my purpose?" It seemed a silly question, the sort of thing a child would expect, but then, she'd spent her life in Zi's company and never ceased to be surprised by his nature.

No, of course not, Anati thought. *We can't know a thing until we see it.*

"Let me know when you do, then," she said. "Gods know it would be nice to understand what I'm doing, for once."

I will, Anati thought.

With that, Anati fell quiet, moving to rest in coils around the base of the rock. They'd had to fashion thick cloaks from animal furs for the rest of the party, but she'd kept her loose-fitting shirt and trousers, wearing her shirt open around her neck and collarbones as she might have done in summertime. Tigai had expected to be able to take them anywhere they'd been before, and been rebuffed. She'd seen the starfield herself, since: Whereas in the Tower of the Heron it had been a mass of almost-infinite swirling stars, here on this side of the Divide it was blackness save for a handful of points of light. The nearest star had taken them to what Ka'Inari had recognized as Jintani land, and the rest had been done under the shaman's guidance. He'd insisted they come here, to the Ranasi village, on their way back home.

The dead quiet of the village hung over her as she watched the campfires burn in the distance. She'd tried to build something herself, with her journey through the Divide—a vision for her future, a way to fight the battles she seemed predestined to fight—and failed utterly. The seed of the Veil's emotions smoldered deep inside her, a burning coal that threatened to ignite, and would take her with it, when it did. There had to be another way. She was more than a body for a hateful, twisted soul. Zi had believed in her. She could find a way.

You didn't fail, Anati thought to her. *Why do you think so?*

She gave a start. "You *can* read my thoughts," she said. "Can't you?"

Of course.

"Gods damn it," she said. "Do you know how long I wondered whether Zi could do that?"

A wave of bitterness rose, and unexpected tears came with it. She knew nothing at all. The most basic truths, about herself, her *kaas*, her place in the world. She knew nothing. All she'd managed was to keep the Veil caged and locked away, and doubtless caused more harm than she'd prevented, in doing it.

How do you expect to learn, without starting from a lack of knowledge? You were not born knowing any things. Neither was I, or my father. Neither was the Veil.

"You sound like my uncle," she said. "I know all about the virtue of humility. But what difference does it make, when people are counting on me to know what to do?"

Their counting on you doesn't make you understand any better than feeling sorry for yourself does.

"I wasn't..." She let it fade, unsaid. Anati had said she could read her thoughts. Little point in protesting when it was more than likely true.

It is true.

"All right," she said. "But if you don't give me time to form my thoughts, don't complain when they're rushed, or rude."

Anati bobbed her head up and down, then skittered up the face of the rock, relaxing as she laid her head in Sarine's lap.

You'll find the way, Anati thought.

The suddenness of Anati's movements took her by surprise; Zi had always been slow, deliberate, even lazy at times. But the sentiment was warmth she needed to hear, and she traced a finger over Anati's scales—a pale gray in the waning light—as she reclined atop her rock. They'd be home soon. Her uncle would be beside himself to see her, and she needed his steadiness, now more than ever.

"I was so sure we had it right," she said. "If we could go beyond the Divide, stop the Regnant's champions before they ascended...isn't that what Axerian said he and his companions had done, here? But all we did was attract the attention of that...thing. Anati, if that creature is our enemy I have no idea how to fight him."

Who would?

"Who would?" she repeated. "Do you mean no one knows?"

No. I mean what I said. Who would have the knowledge you're seeking? The best way to gain understanding is to ask someone who already has it.

"I don't know," she said. "Axerian might have known, but I killed him. Zi knew more than he could tell me, with whatever blocks there were between us. Though now, with the blocks gone..." A thought sparked, almost too obvious to ask, but then, Anati had been offering the simplest wisdom as though it were novel truth—and perhaps it was. "Anati, can you ask Zi what I need to do to face the Regnant?"

Yes.

Anati vanished from beneath her fingers, leaving her alone atop the rock.

Gods, but the *kaas* were difficult.

She returned to watching the village, and the camp Tigai, Acherre, and the rest of them were making on its outskirts. Three fires as proof against the night, and the winter cold. It seemed somehow fitting that the weather didn't touch her—part of the beast spirits' gift, so Zi had said. She missed his insight, missed the trust she'd always had in him, though he'd always been cryptic past the point of understanding. At least Anati spoke clearly, though they seemed to be learning their place in the world together, side by side. It made for a weak pairing, when she was expected to carry the mantle of Godhood on her shoulders.

"Sarine? May I sit with you?"

Ka'Inari's voice startled her; he'd approached from behind, through the ruined tents and pathways rather than the fires glimmering outside the village.

"Yes," she said, moving to make room. "Yes, of course."

The shaman laid down his walking stick and sat beside her. He, like her, hadn't sewn himself a fur cloak, though his clothing was heavy enough to occupy the rest of the space at the top of her boulder.

"They'll be coming soon," Ka'Inari said. "Tonight, perhaps. Or in the morning, if not."

"Who will be?" she asked.

"Ka'Hannat has seen our return. A party of our hunters will meet us here, with news of what has passed in our absence."

"Ah," she said. So that was why he'd insisted they come to this village. "Do Acherre and Tigai and the rest know? There might be misunderstandings, if we're not there to translate."

"They know," Ka'Inari said.

She fell quiet, watching the smoke from the fires.

"Sarine," Ka'Inari said. "You are troubled. Will you speak of it with me?"

"What's to speak of?" she said. "We failed, on the other side of the Divide. I have the Veil inside me, clawing through my emotions and threatening to kill all of you if I slip. And all of this—champions, ascensions, wars—it's all on me. It's more than I ever wanted. I'm terrified I'm going to fail. I'm terrified of what it will mean, if I do."

Ka'Inari nodded, joining her in looking out toward the camp.

"Sometimes," Ka'Inari said, "when a new guardian is chosen, they will go into the wild for many days. They bring no provisions—it is the way of the guardians, to live from the land—but neither do they announce where they are going, or why. They will go, and sit, and reflect on the burdens the spirits have placed on them. It is a heavy thing, holding the fate of a tribe in one's hands. These guardians will stay in the wild, alone, even after the shamans receive visions of threats approaching. It falls to the shamans to track them. This takes many more days, sometimes full turnings of the moon. The guardians are masters of the wild, but with the spirits to guide us, the shamans find them. And when they do..."

A rush of cold pelted her across the face, spattering ice across her bare skin. She flailed and lost her balance, slipping down the side of the rock and landing sprawled in the snow. *Body* came, and she sprang to her feet, pivoting to find the source of the attack.

"In warmer seasons, we use waterskins," Ka'Inari said. "It works best if we can approach while the guardians are sleeping, but any sort of surprise will do."

It took another moment—and chunks of ice and slush sliding down her open shirt—before she realized what he'd done.

"Did...did you just throw snow at me?"

Ka'Inari nodded gravely. "I did."

She stared at him, though her incredulity waned as he scooped another patch of snow from atop the rock into his hands, packing a second ball.

"What are you doing?" she said. "Why would you—?"

This time she ducked, and his snow went over her head, piffing onto the ground behind her.

"Ah," Ka'Inari said. "You see why we need surprise."

The last vestiges of her shock melted into the beginnings of laughter, and she stood ready, watching for signs of more projectiles.

Instead the shaman pushed forward, sliding down the boulder's face. "You are not so different from our wayward guardians. The burdens on you are great, but you must believe you are strong enough to meet them. Even if you aren't, weighing yourself down with worries will not make you any stronger."

"I understand," she said. "Though the truth doesn't change because we wish it to."

"No," he said. "It doesn't." He paused, kneeling to retrieve his walking stick from where he'd discarded it in the snow. "But I hope you'll remember this, next time you are tempted to despair."

"I'm not like to forget," she said. "You soaked through my shirt."

Ka'Inari shrugged and smiled.

They walked together through the ruined village, returning to the outermost of the three fires without fanfare from their companions. Tigai and his brother were arguing near one of the fires, while their man, Remarin, was packing enough wood in the pits to keep them going through the night. Acherre and Mei were sitting together, exchanging words in each other's languages, and she and Ka'Inari took places beside one of the pits, watching the rest. Lin and Yuli were the only ones to take especial note of her return, Lin rising from where they'd been cooking elk meat on skewers to offer one to her.

"Thank you," she said as Lin sat beside her and Ka'Inari bowed, retreating to help Remarin.

"That one is sweet on you, though he'd never admit it," Lin said.

"What?" she said through a mouthful of venison. "Ka'Inari?"

"He's the sort to be there, waiting for you to notice him. In my experience it doesn't tend to work. How long have you been traveling together?"

"Six months," she said, frowning. Ka'Inari had never looked at her twice, for all he'd been there to guide and help her through the worst of their troubles. She'd never considered the possibility of any interest beyond traveling together. Then again, it was hard to see any prospects beyond fighting, chasing down Gods and *magi* and whatever other manner of threat.

"Well, you're as blind as he is," Lin said. "A shame; you could have been keeping each other company all this time."

Before she had time to compose a reply, Anati appeared on the edge of the firepit, her scales a bright silver that reflected the fire's orange glow.

"Anati," she said instead. "Were you able to find your father? Did he—?"

Yes, Anati thought to her. *He said it's time for you to learn to travel to the Soul of the World.*

59

ERRIS

Street of the Cobblers
Gardens District, New Sarresant

The thrum of boots marching on snow rang through the street. Officers' horses added their hooves, clopping over cobbled stone, but few of her soldiers spoke, and quiet prevailed. Trails of smoke rose from chimneys, and eyes watched their passage from rebuilt townhouses now peopled by whoever had moved in when the nobles had been driven out. If there was to be resistance, it would be mounted at the bridges over the Verrain river, giving her the opportunity to sweep south and flank them if they tried to hold too long a stretch of ground. A tactic she'd learned from Paendurion in his assault. But so far the city was quiet, without sign of militia or priests.

Jiri carried her at the head of the 81st Regiment, the vanguard of the 1st Corps, whose binders had been given pride of place beside her on the march. She'd seen to it her officers spread her message with efficiency and cold fact: that seizing New Sarresant was not a restoration of the monarchy, nor of any privilege associated with the old regime. Traitors had attempted to place themselves at the head of the Republic, traitors who would weaken the state and hand its reins, unwittingly or no, to its enemies. Her soldiers understood. Every general—every single one, without exception—had accepted *Need*, proving beyond doubt their loyalty to the cause. Dozens of colonels, majors, captains, and more had volunteered to submit to the binding, more than she could have found time to accept. But the division was clear. There were soldiers, the men and women of her army: loyal, brave, understanding of the virtue of sacrifice. And there were cowards at the heads of the Assembly and among the priests, all of whom would soon learn the price of their treason.

A scout rode toward their line as they advanced, slowing and saluting as he approached her flag.

"Sir," the scout called. "The way ahead is clear. All clear, from here down Canopy Street and past the Exarch's Basilica."

She dismissed him with a counter-salute, and the scout rode off, doubtless due to deliver the same information to commanders of units farther up the line. She and Royens had planned a five-pronged attack, the fingers of a fist. She'd planned the movements down to each unit on each street, with logistics and supply trains, engineers in case the roads or bridges fell to sabotage, and gun batteries set to move in and deploy to fire at close range mixed in with the soldiers.

"Stay alert," she called to the soldiers around her. "Clear for now doesn't mean clear forever."

It wasn't an order, strictly speaking, but whispers of the scout's report were already spreading through the line. Better by far for none of her planning to be needed. But lax discipline was the bane of every army, everywhere. Little as she liked thinking of her countrymen as enemies, for now they were nothing less, and a militiaman's decades-old musket killed as sure as a newly minted rifle. Until every man or woman with the thought of violence against the army was put down, imprisoned, or killed, her soldiers had to maintain focus, and in return she would deliver them a city pacified and returned to order, with the single, unifying purpose of defeating their enemies.

"Sir," the next scout called. "Clear for you to move, sir, all the way to the district boundary."

"Steady on," she said for her soldiers' benefit when the scout had gone. "Press forward, and keep alert."

The column marched, turning down the broad lengths of Canopy Street. The other four columns would be encountering the same quiet on their approaches, else she'd have heard musket shot, shouting, all the signs of battle. Yet the sounds of the city were absent, too: The streets had been emptied, with lookers-on safely hidden from view. Even the Exarch's Basilica, the great dome looming over rooftops to the west, held no more than reverent silence.

They'd made it most of the way to the iron gate that marked the district boundary when a procession of brown robes turned onto the street.

Three hundred paces off, and with no warning from the scouts, but then, they were expecting militia armed with muskets and massed in ranks. Instead this was a procession in truth, the sort more suited to a festival or a day of mourning. A hundred men and women in brown robes, some of them even carrying holy books as they walked a slow, steady pace, joining arms to block the street from end to end.

"Hold," she called, hearing the cry repeated by officers behind her. "Binders, with me."

She spurred Jiri forward, and fifteen of her binders marched behind. *Entropy* binders, *Shelter*, *Body*, and *Death*, all trained to combat and willing to do their duty.

The priests made no forward movement as she approached, only shuffled into place to block the street. No weapons that she could see, though every man and woman among them would be trained to binding, the better part of them skilled with *Life* to heal and sharpen their senses, though some would have *Body*, *Death*, or *Shelter*. She closed to within fifty paces, then twenty, before she reined Jiri to a halt.

"Move aside," she called to the priests. "Or be fired upon."

She saw a mix of zeal and nerves in their faces, and her words triggered sidelong glances up and down their line, until one woman stepped forward, and spoke.

"High Commander d'Arrent," the priestess said. "We condemn the violence you would bring into our city. We stand against law by force, the Exarch's basest truth, and implore you to consider the wisdom of the Veil."

They'd chosen an acolyte to deliver the message, or at least a priestess young enough to be smooth-faced, her voice rich and full as it echoed down the street. The woman had spoken it loud enough to be heard along the front ranks of the 81st, and doubtless delivered it for precisely that effect. There would be four more like her, if the priesthood had scouts enough to know the shape of her strategy, one for each column moving through the city. A barrier of faith, and youthful innocence, as calculated as any plan of battle.

An order to fire would damn her army's morale, and spread like fire through the colonies. Wood presses of this priestess's face would adorn every pamphlet and paper they could print. No seizures or destruction of presses could stop it. She saw the shape of that future as sure as she could see the lines of a flanking maneuver, an envelopment or artillery fusillade. But neither could she order the army to stand down. Disobedience would spread faster than any pox, and prove just as deadly to any hope of authority, once the city was hers.

She wheeled Jiri back toward the line.

"Forward," she called, loud enough to be sure the priests could hear. "Forward, through their line." Leave it up to the priests whether to move or be trampled.

For a moment her soldiers wavered. She took a place beside the 81st's regimental flag, and nudged Jiri forward at a walk as officers repeated her order. They would look to her, and Gods damn her if they wouldn't find her composed and calm, unafraid to be the first to carry out the command.

The 81st advanced, and the quiet on the street turned icy cold.

She kept her eyes level with the horizon, fixed on the silhouettes of Southgate's factories in the distance.

"High Commander, you must turn back," the young priestess called. "Don't do this. The Gods are watching."

She stayed still, and trusted Jiri to be made of the same cold iron. In the last ten paces, the priests' features became clear in spite of her level gaze. Young men and women in brown robes. Always the youth; so it was, in every battle, and every war. But she'd seen enough dead youths not to flinch from what would come, if they held their line.

They broke.

A pace before Jiri's front hooves would have taken a young man square in the chest, the priests dropped arms and fell aside, shoved away as Jiri pushed through their line.

She gave no outward sign, maintaining her stare at the horizon while her heart thrummed in pure relief.

Commotion sounded behind her as the front rank of the 81st followed in her wake, but the first priest served as an example to the rest, sure as she had done for her soldiers. She went twenty paces past them, then turned to survey the regiment's passage, as stoic as she'd have done for fording a river, or traversing any narrow stretch of ground. Let them see her, cool and collected while the priesthood faltered in their zeal.

The priests had dropped their arms, releasing their links and being pushed between the 81st's ranks. Thank the Gods her soldiers followed her example, keeping their gazes to the horizon as they sidestepped the men and women in brown. A jostling push or two saw them past the line, but—

A disturbance drew her eyes in the far rank, on the opposite side of the street, and before she could make sense of it, a cloud of smoke appeared, accompanied by the thundering discharge of pistol shot.

"No!" she shouted, then made it an order. "Hold fire!"

Screams rose from the ranks, and what had been an orderly procession dissolved into chaos.

The priests broke, colliding with her soldiers, and she spurred Jiri into the press.

Two more gunshots sounded, and a hundred more screams and howls. Orders went up from sergeants and captains around her as Jiri cut through soldiers and priests alike. She resisted the urge to draw her saber, instead finding strands of *Shelter* to cordon off the mêlée as she slid from Jiri's back toward the center of the smoke.

"Hold fire!" she shouted again, but even her sharpest bellow was suited to giving orders in an open field; in close quarters, the Nameless reigned, for all the 81st's soldiers tried to pull away.

Another round of shots went off farther up the line before she reached the first shots' source. *Body* amplified her movements, quick enough to reach a young officer, a woman with a lieutenant's stripe on her collar and a shaking pistol still smoking in her hand. She disarmed the woman with a strike to the forearm, sending her pistol clattering to the street, where two men in brown lay, both clutching at their stomachs. A rush of soldiers backed away, both advancing up the street and retreating back the way they'd come.

"Stand down!" she shouted, and the lieutenant she'd disarmed looked at her with ghost-white eyes while others took up the cry.

"They..." the lieutenant said. "They tried to take my sidearm, sir. I had no choice. I had to—"

"Form ranks!" came the shout from other voices, other officers finally cutting through the chaos with orders their soldiers obeyed.

"See to your company, Lieutenant," she said, trying to keep her voice from seething rage. Jiri trotted into place beside her as the 81st's soldiers formed up, pulling back to reveal the dead and wounded lying in blood-streaked pools on the street. Six men and women in brown, with the rest of the priests scattered or standing back in horror as the soldiers recovered their composure.

It was over as quickly as it had begun, and binders from among her soldiers rushed in to see to the fallen. The priests' line had dissolved, leaving the way clear into the heart of the city, but Erris tasted bile as she swung back into Jiri's saddle. A military tribunal would see to the damned fool of a lieutenant, and any other man or woman who'd discharged a weapon. This wasn't the place for justice, only for advancing toward their objective. But she couldn't help seeing her hopes for a peaceful retaking of the city bleed out with the wounded priests left in her wake. The vision of wood presses and newspapers returned in force. The people would hear of this, and put the blood on her hands, for all it had been the priests' defiance and treachery that earned them their fate.

"High Commander, sir." The Colonel of the 81st saluted, approaching her with his flag and retinue in tow. "What should we do, sir? I never expected my soldiers would...I didn't think..."

"Keep discipline, Colonel," she said. "We march forward, to the council hall. Once it's secured, we can—"

More shots thundered, this time in the distance. But not the thrum of a full volley, or of artillery. Scattered pistols, all too like the ones she'd just intervened to stop.

"The Nameless will spit on you," the priestess said, the same who'd delivered her their ultimatum, before the chaos. "We are not afraid to die for the Veil's wisdom. We are not afraid to be martyrs for truth and right."

"Arrest her," Erris said. "And anyone else who presents themselves as our enemy. Kill anyone under arms and keep the rest of the regiment marching for Southgate. Am I understood, Colonel?"

"Yes, sir," the regiment-colonel said, saluting again as he turned to give the order. Erris reached for *Need*, preparing to shift her senses to the other prongs of her and Royens's advance. The shots in the distance had continued, all but confirming the priests had made their barricade of arms-in-arms along other streets, and at least one had gone as poorly as hers. It tasted of ash in her mouth, but she would count it a stroke of luck, if barricades of priests were the only resistance to her taking the city. She had greater worries than a few dead men and women in brown robes. They'd chosen to die when they stood in her way. The rest would sort itself when she was firmly in control.

60

ARAK'JUR

Approaching the Alliance Village
North of New Sarresant

Doren squealed and slapped his hands against Arak'Jur's jaw. Corenna had helped him bind their son with strips of cloth to rest against his chest and keep him warm as they walked. He'd expected Doren to sleep—spirits knew the boy had done little enough of that in the night—but instead looked down to find tiny brown eyes staring up at him in wonder.

The sight put fire in his heart; a precious thing, when all else was cold.

"He wonders why your skin doesn't make milk," Corenna said.

"Do you think he needs to eat?" he said.

Corenna shook her head. "Not until midday."

They went back to silence, traversing snow-covered grassland as they'd done each day since their reunion. Watching Doren's first squeals had given them shared purpose in spite of the slow pace, hobbled by the child and by Corenna's recovery from the birth. He'd hoped for laughter between him and Corenna, too, and found only distance. She hadn't killed him yet, or made an attempt. But from the pain behind her eyes, that was too great a feat for him to feel any comfort by her side.

"It might be the Alliance village," Corenna said after another hundred paces. Smoke rose on the horizon, fixed there over a hillside they'd seen the night before.

"If we're far enough north," he said.

Doren had taken to scratching Arak'Jur's jaw, grasping at his skin as though his fingers made a miniature claw. It took his attention away from the silence following his and Corenna's exchange.

"We are," she said abruptly a few paces later. "There. A welcoming party."

He pulled his jaw free of Doren's grasp, and looked where Corenna pointed. She was right: Three figures approached, cutting a trail down the hillside toward them, no mistaking. Too far off to be certain they were there to welcome his and Corenna's return, or even that they were tribesmen at all, but he dared himself a spark of emotion, hoping it was true.

"Arak'Jur," Corenna said. "I...I haven't said it in weeks, but...I..."

"You intend to leave the village," he finished for her. "As soon as Doren and I are safely home."

"What?" Corenna said. "No." Her voice turned suddenly hot. "How could you think I would leave my son?"

"Our son," he said, keeping his voice cool in spite of the building heat. He'd known this was coming. She'd been cold, distant, watching him as though she meant to put a knife between his ribs while he slept. He knew it was the spirits' promptings. It changed nothing.

"No," Corenna said again softly. "I don't mean to leave. I mean to stay. It's been all I could do, ignoring the spirits' urgings as we traveled. But I need you to know I love you. I mean to make this work, and if I've faltered and made you hate me, so be it, but you should know how I feel, before you decide this can't be fixed."

He came to a halt. Even Doren seemed to sense the thickness in the air, dropping his hands and pressing them against Arak'Jur's chest.

"Can it be fixed?" he said.

Tears appeared on Corenna's cheeks.

"I don't know," she said. "I've tried to ignore the spirits' promptings. I want to trust myself. But I don't know if I'm strong enough."

"I thought you meant to leave," he said. "I've been waiting for you to tell me, since we crossed the river."

"No." She shook her head. "No. I mean to fight. For us."

He went to her, covering the ground before he knew he'd started to walk.

Doren pressed between them as he took her in his arms, saying with a firm grip everything he'd wanted to say with words. Their son squealed with delight, renewing his clawing at their jaws and necks as they kissed, a distraction that served to finally bring the laughter they'd missed between them.

"I'm sorry, Arak'Jur," Corenna said, still leaning close when they separated. "For bringing all of this on us."

"I know," he said. He wanted to say more, and found the words dry on his tongue. Doren's squeals served instead, and he felt the sun's heat on his skin for the first time in weeks.

The figures descending the hillside were tribesmen; he saw it before they reached level ground. But it took closing the distance to realize who had come to welcome them home.

"Arak'Jur," Ka'Inari said, at the same time he said, "Ka'Inari," and they came together, wrapping arms to thump each other's backs.

Two hunters accompanied the shaman, a Ganherat and a Vhurasi, and he exchanged formal greetings with them as Corenna took a turn embracing Ka'Inari, cradling their son to her side.

"What of the Uktani?" Ka'Inari asked.

"Slain and scattered, by my hand," he said. "They won't threaten us again."

Ka'Inari nodded, solemn and grim. "You return to us, then. And with a son."

"A son," Arak'Jur said, feeling the rush of pride he heard in his own voice. "His name is Doren."

Ka'Inari's solemnity softened. "A strong, Ranasi name," the shaman said. "As fine a namesake as Arak'Doren could have wished for."

Arak'Jur and Corenna shared a weary smile. He felt the weight of the weeks they'd spent together, and the renewed hope that had bloomed between them. Ka'Inari paused for a moment, surveying them both before he spoke again.

"All is well between you?" Ka'Inari said. "At Ka'Ana'Tyat, the spirits set you both arduous tasks. It warms my heart to see you here, together."

"We are well," Arak'Jur said, putting surety in his voice. "The spirits are cruel, but we are strong. We mean to face our trials together."

Corenna stood beside him, standing taller than he'd seen from her in weeks. She unwrapped Doren from around her shoulder, holding him toward Ka'Inari.

"Will you bless our son?" she asked. "We would have him accepted into the tribe and given the rest of his name, if the spirits see fit to grant it."

"Of course," Ka'Inari said. "Strip him naked, and present him to me."

Corenna did as she'd been asked, peeling back the rest of the cloths she'd used as a sling, then removing the tiny furs Arak'Jur had cut and stitched for coverings. Doren flailed his arms and legs at the shock of the cold, with a moment of stunned silence before he began to wail.

Ka'Inari moved closer to Corenna, hovering over the child.

"He is strong," Ka'Inari said. "A boy whose mother is known to the spirits. A boy whose father carries their blessings." The shaman reached into a pouch on his belt, one he must have prepared in advance, and smeared blue paste on his fingers, tracing a line down Doren's chest and belly. The crying ceased at the shaman's touch, and instead the boy fell into a curious, reverent silence as Ka'Inari drew a second line, this time on the left arm, then a third on the right.

When the markings were done, Ka'Inari reached for Doren and Corenna handed him into the shaman's arms. Ka'Inari's eyes glazed over the moment he took the child, a sign he'd been granted a vision of the boy's future, a premonition of things-to-come. Arak'Jur understood the shaman's gift better now than he had when Ka'Vos had given a blessing to Kar'Elek, his firstborn son. But there was no less fear in it for his understanding.

"This child is half-Sinari, and half-Ranasi," Ka'Inari said. His voice had changed, grown harder, more distant. "Is it your wish he be adopted into one, or the other?"

"No," Arak'Jur said. "He is both, and carries both tribes' strength."

Corenna nodded firmly beside him, and Ka'Inari returned his attention to their son.

"Very well," Ka'Inari said. "The child is accepted. He will wear many names in his lifetime. But first he will be called Kar'Doren, of the two tribes. He is healthy, and strong, and watched over by the spirits of things-to-come, the spirits of the wind, the spirit of *kirighra*, and the spirits of the Mountain. He will face great pain, but if he has the strength to bear it, the world will know him, before his end."

With that Ka'Inari blinked, and his eyes returned to brown. Corenna retrieved their son, swiftly wrapping him in his furs and kissing his forehead with tears running from her eyes. Arak'Jur found himself in awe. Kar'Elek had received no such pronunciations from the shaman at his blessing. He moved to Corenna's side, stroking Kar'Doren's left shoulder, tracing the line of blue Ka'Inari had put there.

Finally Ka'Inari's sober tones melted into warmth. "More will want to welcome you, and your return," Ka'Inari said. "Let us go into the village, and speak of things past, and things to come."

Word ran ahead of their coming, and a throng of faces greeted them at the village's edge. Uncertainty lingered in their eyes, until Ka'Inari came to a halt near the outermost tents and buildings.

"Our guardians have returned," Ka'Inari said. "The Uktani are broken, and the spirits have given their blessing. The danger is passed, and Arak'Jur and Corenna are to be welcome among us once more."

The words cut through the crowd, turning questioning doubt to warmth. Hunters came forward to embrace him, and spread word among their fellows, until more than a few tears had escaped his eyes. He had been away too long not to feel emotion at the sight of Sinari patterns sewn in skirts and tunics, at hearing their tongue spoken aloud, at seeing Sinari tents alongside the strange new constructions of brick and stone. Corenna and Kar'Doren were swallowed among the women, too, and it took some time before word spread among the men that he had brought home a son. That spawned a second wave of welcome, shouts and congratulatory slaps across his back and shoulders. He met them all with good cheer, Sinari and Olessi, Vhurasi, Ganherat, and Nanerat alike. He was home. Corenna was home. Kar'Doren was home. It was a time for joy, and his spirit had grown bright by the time he and Corenna came together again on the snow-covered green at the village center.

The village had been built in two turnings of the seasons, but already was suited to sheltering the Alliance through the cold months. Hides and tent poles had been harvested and moved from the Sinari, Olessi, and

Vhurasi villages, while the Ganherat had built three longhouses where they could eat and cook indoors. The rest of the Alliance made to deliver an impromptu feast for his and Corenna's return, the men and women both gathering stores to put over the fires, regaling him with all that had transpired in the days since he'd been gone.

"Four foreigners came to the village," Valak'Ser said, the old Sinari hunter having taken a place beside him, Corenna, and Ka'Inari when the food was served. "With too-narrow eyes, a tongue that sounded as though they had mouths full of food, and skin too pale for tribesfolk and too dark for them to be fair-skins. I'd never have believed the shaman's story, had I not seen them myself."

"There was a fair-skin, too," Ka'Inari said, smiling.

Valak'Ser waved a pruned hand dismissively. "Too many of those lately."

Arak'Jur set down his food—a haunch of turkey with baked cornmeal, squash, and beans. "You traveled to the west, and found what? Another people?"

"Another world," Ka'Inari said. "Or, at least, peoples as foreign as the fair-skins, and twice as strange."

"You left in the company of Sarine Thibeaux and Rosline Acherre," Corenna said. "Who were these foreigners Valak'Ser speaks of?"

"Yanjin Tigai, Yanjin Dao, Yanjin-Zhang Mei, and Remarin Allan-Jaad ni Yanjin."

Ka'Inari could as well have made gibbering sounds from his mouth for all any of that sounded like names, but the shaman wore an earnest look, the subject too serious for mockery or jokes. His old apprentice had grown in the time they'd spent apart; Ka'Inari had taken on some of Ka'Vos's reserve, and now spoke with an air of authority and wisdom that had only ever been suggested before.

"Rosline Acherre was with us as well," Ka'Inari continued, "though Sarine Thibeaux and two others from across the Divide—Lin Qishan and Yuli Twin Fangs Clan Hoskar—went missing before we reached the village. The others journeyed onward, into the fair-skins' city. I would have followed, but for the spirits' premonitions of your return."

"You would have followed?" he asked. "You are back among our people, now. Surely your place is here."

Ka'Inari shook his head. "There is much trouble in the world. Too much for us to pretend we can live here in peace."

"Ka'Inari, where is Asseena?" Corenna asked. "Or Ghella, Symara, Ilek'Hannat?"

Arak'Jur frowned. Corenna had seen something he hadn't—but now he recognized it, too. The spirit-touched women of all the tribes, and the Nanerat apprentice shaman, were missing, seated nowhere around the longhouse, nor had they been there to welcome his and Corenna's return.

"He is Ka'Hannat, now," Ka'Inari said. "And they are gone. Before my arrival, they boarded ships bound for the fair-skins' lands, across the sea."

"Before your..." he began, then pivoted to, "Across the sea?"

"I misliked it," Valak'Ser said. "And said as much, in the steam tents. But we've been cursed by the spirits since Ka'Vos's death—better to admit it, and seek redress in obeying their commands."

"What commands?" Corenna said. "Why did they require our women, our shaman, to leave their homes?"

"To leave their homes and leave them undefended!" Arak'Jur said. "If they left before your arrival, then the Alliance was blind to the coming of the great beasts. How could the spirits ask such a thing of our people?"

"War," Ka'Inari said.

The word chilled his skin in spite of the guardian's gift.

"Our people are but one of many," Ka'Inari continued. "In my travels I came to see and know this firsthand. There are darker shadows than fair-skin empires, more terrible enemies than tribes or even spirits gone mad. On the far side of the world, I saw visions of things-to-come. Hope for our people rests in fighting the shadows, in standing with the Goddess, in wielding the mantle of the spirits' magic for her cause."

"I will not allow our people to be drawn into fair-skin wars," Arak'Jur said. "If it takes shedding my *Arak* name, becoming *Sa'Shem*, and defying the spirits' will, I will do it."

Ka'Inari shook his head. His eyes were full of sadness.

"That is not your path," Ka'Inari said. "The spirits have shown me what they demand of you. And of you." He said the last to Corenna, the sadness taking on new meaning as the shaman cast a glance between them.

"No," Corenna said. "*Kirighra* set me an impossible task. I've refused it."

The shaman nodded. "I've seen this course, and the pain it has caused you. But you are not alone in being chosen, Corenna of the Ranasi."

Arak'Jur waited, taking every word from the shaman as a blow. He knew what was coming; he'd seen the visions in the cave atop Adan'Hai'Tyat.

"Mountain has chosen you, Arak'Jur," Ka'Inari said. "They demand peace, through culling the warlords and tyrants of the world."

"No," Corenna said again. "We won't leave our son."

"It is what the spirits demand, if you seek ascension," Ka'Inari said.

"Then I don't," Corenna said. "And Arak'Jur doesn't. We will remain here, defending this alliance from threats as we have always done. We will raise our son in peace, far from fair-skin wars and the concerns of other tribes."

Ka'Inari met his eyes while Corenna spoke, and he could have struck the shaman, for driving to the heart of the choice he'd already made, though he hadn't known it before that moment. Ad-Shi had shown him the world in darkness, covered by ash and poison. A world where thousands died in fire and gas, driven belowground under a blackened sky. A world he would spare his son, at any price. It tore his heart from his chest, but he could not walk the path of peace in the face of war and terror.

"I will go," he said. "I will follow the spirits' path, wherever it leads."

Corenna turned to him with shocked eyes, cradling Kar'Doren as though now she alone sheltered him from a hostile world. The image burned in his memory, searing him with guilt and pain.

"To the fair-skins' city, then," Ka'Inari said. "To Erris d'Arrent, and a reckoning with her enemies."

Another vision came as Ka'Inari spoke the name, a memory from Adan'Hai'Tyat. Erris d'Arrent. That was his purpose: to kill those who meant to bring war into the world. Corenna's pain, the renewed spark between them, and their shared love for Kar'Doren all faded against the enormity of his task. But it was his burden to bear, and he meant to see it through, whatever the cost.

"South, then," he said, ignoring the hurt in Corenna's eyes. "Without delay."

61

TIGAI

A Private Chamber
Council Hall, Southgate District, New Sarresant

Dao and Remarin sat together on the opposite side of the table, each glowering as though they shared a single face. The room was well-enough appointed, with seats for fifteen, though they used only four. The silver pitcher—holding water, rather than tea—was of an odd, overly tall design, but the rest could have been a meeting room in any of the hundred cities. That they were instead on the far side of the Divide, in a land he would sooner have believed the subject of some stage-player's fancy, mattered less to him than sharing the room with Mei, Remarin, and Dao. It seemed their surroundings mattered somewhat more to his brother. That, and the fact they'd waited well over two hours without sign of their host and guide.

"This is a fool's design," Dao said abruptly. "How can we put faith in a foreigner's goodwill? One not even sworn to the Empire? They could be assembling teams of their *magi* to come here and imprison us for questioning."

Mei glowered back at her husband, seated to Tigai's left. She'd laid the sleeve of her dress on the table, and he did his best to avoid noticing the severed stump of her right arm.

"Are we going to have this argument here?" Mei asked. "You agreed—"

"I agreed to hear terms." Dao gestured to the empty room. "Am I listening to them?"

"Acherre said this was their seat of government," Tigai said. "They'd hardly take us here if their only aim was to detain us."

"Can you speak their tongue?" Dao said. "For all you know this is some governor's palace, a ministry of soldiering or war. The place is poor, hardly suited to an Emperor's seat. We have finer appointments in the family wings at Yanjin Palace."

"It could well be a military headquarters," Remarin said. "I saw markings on the soldiers' uniforms as we were led inside. Stripes and stars on sleeves and collars. Sign of at least seven different companies, by my count, with soldiers of some showing deference to others."

"As it happens, I *can* speak their tongue," Mei said. "Or at least speak it well enough to broker these negotiations, with Rosline Acherre's help. Not all of us were idle on the road. And what does it matter whether these people are ruled by military? All the better for us, given our contact here is an officer."

"I would feel better if we were home," Dao said. "Seeing to our family's concerns. Wind spirits know how long our estate will go unmolested, with its masters absent."

"Its masters are the banks, now," Tigai said quietly.

Even Mei winced at that, and for a moment Tigai might have believed his father had been reborn in his eldest son, a look of fury creasing Dao's face.

But it was true. They'd been on the cusp of losing everything even before he and Remarin had planned their raid on the Emperor's vault. How many months had it been, spent in captivity or fleeing, with their debts gone unpaid? The bankers would have their due, and he had no illusions the spoils from their raid would have gone toward Yanjin debts when *magi* houses had been there at their return.

"So, what then, brother?" Dao said. "You're in agreement with Mei? We should abandon our home, our people, our sworn men-at-arms, our servants, craftsmen, merchants, farmers, and settle in this country? We have *nothing* here."

"We have less than nothing in the Jun Empire," he said. "We have debt, and red targets painted on our backs by the Great and Noble Houses. You were forced to accept mercenary contracts because I couldn't find the gold to keep us solvent. Remarin spent months in that bloody tower, because of me. Mei lost her fucking hand. At least here there's a chance for more."

Mei rubbed her right forearm as he spoke, and he felt the familiar churn in his stomach, covered over by the heat in his words.

"Tigai is right," Mei said. "There, we've been used as stones in a game played by others. Here, we might find the means to leverage our talents to start again. And we do not have nothing, here. We have each other, and we have ourselves. You are a general, my husband, and Remarin a master soldier. I have my talents for politics, and Tigai—"

Footsteps in the hallway cut her short, and the four of them each donned masks of placid calm. Yanjin business was Yanjin business. Never the province of outsiders.

"...the courtesan turned the Emperor down," Dao said, picking up the line midway through. "And told the doctor, 'Beware the tinctures of the heart, where they concern the mothers of royal daughters.'"

The rest of them laughed politely as the doors to their chamber swung wide, revealing Rosline Acherre and three more: a man and a woman in soldiers' uniforms and another, a man in a ridiculous costume of knee-length hose, a tight jacket, and more lace spilling from his cuffs and collar than any five prostitutes would wear on their undergarments. They seemed to defer to the woman among the newcomers, who wore five stars on her collar to mark her soldiering company, while the man wore a single knot, the same as Acherre.

Dao rose, and the rest of them followed his lead, bowing in time as he did.

Acherre said something in their slurring tongue, half nasal sounds and half choking on the attempt to swallow her vowels. Mei managed what sounded like a serviceable reply; evidently she had indeed been spending her time wisely on the road.

"This is their leader," Mei said, with a gesture and a half curtsey toward the blond-haired woman with five stars on her collar. "The High Commander Erris d'Arrent." She repeated the gesture, slightly less deeply, for the man in lace. "This is High Admiral Tuyard. The other is a servant, though he is dressed as a soldier. I believe his rank would translate as 'Sycophant-Captain,' though his name is Essily."

Tigai kept his face smooth, though instinct wanted to raise his eyebrow.

They had soldiers—*captains*, even—whose primary responsibilities were to flatter and kiss their leaders' asses?

Acherre made the same introductions in the foreigners' tongue, asking Mei's help pronouncing some of their names and titles. Acherre's command of the Jun tongue seemed considerably weaker than Mei's was for theirs; an advantage, if only for giving them the standing of guiding the conversation. Yet when the introductions were complete and Acherre, Tuyard, and Essily moved to be seated at the table, their High Commander remained standing, staring at him as though he were an adder let loose in a nursery.

D'Arrent spoke, and Mei said something back in their language before turning to him to translate.

"The High Commander asked whether it is true, that you can move across great distances, and take others with you."

"We're here, aren't we?" Tigai said. "With one of her captains?"

"I told her as much," Mei said. "She is demanding a demonstration, and says her time is short."

"Implying ours is worth less than hers," Dao said. "To say nothing of the suggestion we are telling lies about Tigai's abilities."

Mei gave an apologetic look. "She *is* their High Commander, and from the sound of it, somewhat more. Who can say, how an Emperor sees the world?"

"High Commander d'Arrent is being the sight of two battles," Acherre said in stilted, broken Jun. "Hers is the demand of *la magie de besoin*." The last lapsed into the Sarresant tongue, incomprehensible and strange.

"It isn't like it is, on our side of the Divide," Tigai said. "The starfield here is almost empty. I can see the points, every time I set an anchor, where at home my anchors are like releasing a pinch of sand onto a beach."

"I suggest we give them their demonstration," Remarin said. "Or they'll wonder why we can't."

The fop in lace and the High Commander both were staring daggers between Tigai and his family, hardly attempting to hide their suspicions. Dao would take it for rudeness, which it was, but then, it seemed Remarin had the right of it where their hosts were concerned. Like it or no, they were here on charity. Better to show the buyers what was on offer, no matter the stain of being treated like merchants when they were not.

He closed his eyes, finding the familiar emptiness of the starfield and the strands. Not a starfield, here, and hardly any strands to speak of. Scattered points of light, great distances apart. He could trace a trail of where they'd been since traveling through the Divide, small punctures in the blackness wherever he'd set anchors by reflex as they moved. Even the connections of familiarity—the strands running from d'Arrent, Tuyard, Acherre, and Essily—didn't seem to be connected to stars, save for a small handful of stray connections looped around some of his nearby anchor points and a single, healthy strand connection between Tuyard and one of the few brightly shining stars a considerable distance away. No telling where that might lead, though. Instead he opted for one of the nearby points, projecting his will around all eight figures in their meeting room.

He opened his eyes to gasps, and fresh, cold, winter air.

They were just outside the council hall, at the center of the snow-covered ground strewn with statues and monuments of various sizes for a half league in every direction.

"*Incroyable,*" Tuyard said, making clear the phrase was one of wonder.

D'Arrent immediately rounded on Mei, barraging her with questions too fast for her to translate.

"She asks..." Mei began, then went back to listening. "She asks the limitations. How often you can do it, how many you can take with you, where you can travel."

"Do they not have Great and Noble Houses here?" Dao asked. "Perhaps it would be better to deal with them."

Tigai shook his head. A *magi* was a *magi*, as far as he was concerned, but he suspected from watching Acherre work that their *magi* were part of their armies. A wonder their kingdoms hadn't torn themselves apart, making magic part of every skirmish or dispute. Then again, perhaps that was why they hadn't unified under a single Empire. And not having to operate in secret meant Mei could bid his services to this d'Arrent's army without reserve.

"Tell her I can move a hundred or so at once. A handful of times in sequence before I need rest. Only to places where I have a strand connecting me—places I've been, or places I can study that are familiar to others. And places that already have a star." The last was an afterthought, but would prove a hindrance until he could establish enough anchors in places he wanted to go. "And tell her I want to be sure we're all provided for, here on this side of the Divide."

Mei smiled. "Leave the negotiations to me. I'll make sure we're taken care of."

With that, Mei and d'Arrent began a back-and-forth, with Acherre's help and the occasional comment from Tuyard.

"You couldn't have taken us somewhere indoors?" Remarin said. "Knowing Mei, we'll be sitting here in the cold for hours while she finesses the finer points of an arrangement."

"I could suggest it," he said, then glanced again at Mei and d'Arrent. Both seemed the type to engage fully in whatever was in front of them, already deep in the throes of their exchange.

"I only hope you and Mei have chosen wisely," Dao said. "I'd as well be far away from the *magi*, too, but there will be *magi* here, if of a different sort."

"It's a beginning," Tigai said. "So long as we're together."

Dao nodded. Had they been alone, the decision might have come with more emotion. As it was, they remained standing, watching Mei perform her own version of a dance.

"I'd have felt better about this, with the girl here," Remarin said.

"Sarine?" Tigai asked, and Remarin nodded.

"You said she used your gift, with the strands," Dao said.

"She did," he replied. "Somehow. It was how we escaped the tower. I didn't think it could be learned, but she did it. Then again with her and Lin and Yuli, on the night we arrived in their first village."

"A poor sign, that the woman who led us here would abandon us," Dao said.

Tigai nodded. He'd felt a draw to Sarine in the time since the tower, for gratitude over her part in the rescue as much as awe over having watched her scatter armies; waking to find her and Lin and Yuli vanished had come as a blow to all of them, his family and her former traveling companions alike. Ordinarily he might have been able to read the strands, try to find the connection they'd taken. It should have been trivial here, with the starfield reduced to so much empty blackness. But there had been no sign.

"She'll come back," he said. Somehow he knew it was true; something else, since the tower, a sense of awareness of her, pervading his thoughts, as though she might be present at any moment.

Remarin met the sentiment with a grin, and Dao, too.

"What?" he asked.

"Nose too large, for my taste," Remarin said. "Eyes too wide, though the blue has some appeal."

"I didn't mean..." he said, and both his brother and his master-at-arms let slip the rules of decorum, laughing over his attempt to explain.

62

SARINE

A Mountaintop
Kinigari Shuhet, Bhakal Lands

Light flashed, and a cord of pain tore through her. A white-hot wire seemed to cut her arm, her torso, legs, and neck. Blackness closed from all sides, and she withdrew, pulling two flickering lights as she fell.

Dry air filled her lungs, and she was sobbing, curled on the ground.

No, Anati thought to her. *Almost. But you retreated into the Regnant's void again.*

"I can't..." she said between breaths. Tears stung her eyelids, but it was clear they were atop a hill or mountain, looking down over a vast expanse of brown and green. The air was hot, though it should have been winter, and trees and grass seemed to be lush and growing, as though the seasons had been made to stand on end.

Lin Qishan stood, watching her, while Yuli had right away set out to gather wood for a fire. It had become routine, after days of failed attempts.

"Do you have any inkling of where we might be, this time?" Lin said.

Sarine shook her head, gathering herself and wiping tears from her eyes. "No," she said. "When it starts to burn, I don't know what happens. I grab onto something safe. And Anati tells me I've failed."

You did fail, Anati thought. *The Seat should be a place of stone, not trees and brush.*

Her *kaas* appeared atop a nearby rock, looking down at her with disapproval. It stung, not least for having somehow snared Lin and Yuli with her when she'd followed Anati's instructions. It made trying to get them back to New Sarresant—or even to their homes, on the far side of the Divide—her next priority, but she'd failed there, too. So far every attempt to do as Zi had told Anati had resulted in failure, arriving in new and distant, unrecognized places.

This one seemed to be a lone mountain jutting from a flat plain. A strange sight, as though some God had cut one towering peak from a range and set it down where it didn't belong.

"By the look of it we are far to the south, this time," Lin said. "The first you've taken us to the bottom half of the world. A sign of progress, perhaps?"

"How can you tell?" she asked, retrieving a waterskin from her belt. Every attempt to shift them left her parched and aching, made worse if she tried it too many times in a day.

"It's summer, here," Lin said. "And far from the world's center, owing from the sun's position in the sky."

"The seasons are reversed, in some parts of the world?"

"Do they not have academies and schools, on your side of the Divide?"

The rebuke cut deeper than perhaps Lin had intended; her uncle had done his best, where her education was concerned, but he was only a priest, and their supply of books had been limited. "They do," she said. "I didn't have the pleasure of attending."

"Apologies, then, if I gave offense," Lin said. "No child with your talents would be left untrained, in the Jun Empire."

Her waterskin had soaked her lips and throat, and she offered some to Lin, who accepted the drink with a nod of thanks.

"The southern half of the world," she said as Lin drank. "I wonder where."

Lin shrugged, returning the skin close to empty. They'd have to find a watering hole or a spring soon. "The south is all desert on the Jun side of the Divide," Lin said. "Or islands, peopled by savages and barbarians."

"I thought you said one Emperor ruled every nation, there."

"He does," Lin said. "But why count a tribe of island-dwellers as a nation? If their land was of any import, the army would come to subdue their leaders and install governors and magistrates loyal to the throne. If their magic was a threat, the Great and Noble Houses would be there to take the children."

She'd listened with rapt interest whenever Lin spoke of her homeland, and now was no exception. Soon the Regnant would be coming with his champions to fight against the Veil. Against *her*. Anything she could learn of their ways might be of use.

"What about Yuli?" she asked. "She said she wasn't raised in one of your monasteries."

"The Natarii clans are left to themselves, so long as they pay tribute and answer our calls to war. That her father pledged her in service to a rebellion will mean the end of her clan, once the Emperor settles the threat posed by Isaru Mattai. Doubtless why she came with you; an attempt to keep the Great and Noble Houses from—"

Ubax aragti.

Lin continued speaking for a moment, but Sarine rose to her feet, glancing around until she came to rest on Anati.

"What did you say?" she asked.

"The Emperor won't tolerate rebellion in any form," Lin said. "He'll crush them, as swiftly as he crushes any rebels."

"No, not that," she said. "Anati, what was that? '*Ubax arat*'? Or '*ragti*'?"

It was ubax aragti, Anati thought to her. *Close by.*

One of the *kaas'* warnings. She'd learned to recognize them, first with fellow *kaas*-mages and then again, on the far side of the Divide.

"What does it mean?" she asked. "What sort of magic is it?"

It is ubax aragti, Anati thought.

"We need to fetch Yuli," she said to Lin. "Something is coming, something I don't recognize."

At once Lin turned toward the trail Yuli had taken. Sarine followed behind; she'd been preoccupied with pain during their arrival, and though her senses were on full alert now, it was just as well Lin had paid attention to the way Yuli had gone. They tracked down the side of the hill, around a rise leading down into a steep decline covered with brush and grass. The tree line was a quarter league down the mountain, and there was no sign of Yuli in any direction, though she would have headed down if she meant to gather firewood.

"Yuli," she called, cupping her hands and hearing it echo off the mountainside.

Lin turned, hissing a sharp rebuke. "You said something was coming," Lin said, just above a whisper.

"Something is," she said. "But we have to find her first."

Lin spun back, snapping her fingers for quiet as she stooped to grab a handful of dirt. A moment later it became glass, the armor Lin used to protect herself and the shards she threw at their enemies. But instead Yuli appeared, emerging from behind a thick row of brush with a small store of sticks and dried leaves in her arms.

"What is it?" Yuli asked, looking as though she was prepared to ditch her stores.

"Nothing, yet," she said. "Anati gave a warning. I wanted to be sure we were close, in case...something happened, and I needed to get us out of here."

"We are close," Yuli said. "Are you prepared to travel again, so soon?"

"If I have to," she said. It would hurt; she'd tried shifting twice in a day already, after her first attempt had taken them to a barren field of ice. But it was better than being surprised by some unknown magic, with only Anati's cryptic name for it for a warning.

It isn't cryptic, Anati thought. *It's a flower that grows here, blue and purple petals on a thorny stem.*

"Oh Gods damn it," she said. "You mean you warned me about a flower?"

Yuli looked puzzled, while Lin had moved ahead, stepping onto a rocky ledge as she surveyed the flatlands at the mountain's base.

"I don't think it was a warning about a flower," Lin said. "Something is coming."

She went to where Lin was standing, looking down from the mountain. Something was there: a party of travelers—four or five tiny shapes moving together. A cloud hung above them, a hundred spans above their heads and rising. An odd coincidence, perhaps, save that it was the only cloud in the sky in any direction.

"Anati, is that the *ubax aranti*, or whatever you'd said?" she asked.

Of course not.

"I'm not so certain we want to be here, when that cloud arrives," Lin said. It was growing, puffs of white bulging from it as it moved.

"Can you take us elsewhere?" Yuli asked her.

Her body ached already, a throbbing pain lingering from the cord of heat that had almost cut her in two during the last attempt. But she could do it.

"Gather close," she said.

"Are you certain?" Lin said. "There's no shame in heading down to confront whatever's coming. Dragons study a lifetime to master that gift. A mistake could send us under the ocean, or somewhere deep below the ground."

She isn't trying to use the Dragon magic, Anati thought.

"Just get close," she said. Yuli and Lin both backed away from the ledge, though the cloud had already risen to be visible, almost level with where they were standing, near the summit.

She emptied her thoughts, as Anati had told her. A breath, drawn deep. It began with separation. A sense of pulling away from herself. Like shifting her senses to the leylines, but different. A void of emotion, mind, and body, similar to the emptiness of communing with the spirits, though, too, a different reality. Did every form of magic have a place of separation from the physical world? A fleeting thought. Unimportant. She could feel the Veil, raging inside her. She found the place where the blue sparks flowed, the power of Life to counter Death. That was where she had to project her thoughts. Anati said it came from there, where the blue sparks seeped into the soul that was *her*. Not the Veil, though that was part of it. Not Anati, and not Lin or Yuli, though they were there, too.

"Sarine?" Yuli was saying. "Sarine, quickly...it's almost here."

No distractions. She fed her consciousness into the place where she drew the blue sparks, reversing the usual flow. A storm seemed to rage around her, pillars of blue lightning in place of sparks. She raced through them, weaving around columns of energy caught between two infinite planes. It was as though she were in a room with no walls, only a low ceiling and a floor, all vibrating in time with her steps. An old place. A place that seemed to reject her presence, arcing bolts lancing out from the torrents whenever she drew too near. Anati had told her to find the strongest pillar, the place where light fused together to burn white. She wove through the rest of the columns, somehow knowing where to go to find the center. Heat rose, and tendrils of surging energy. She felt fear from Lin and Yuli, and hard determination from the Veil. She was close.

And then she was there.

A column of pure white light, stretching the two planes until floor and ceiling became almost as infinite as the space on either side. A bore between worlds, but somehow anchored in the same place. Here, and not here. A channel to house a consciousness in a physical vessel, like a mind—or a soul—trapped within a body.

She moved toward it, pulling Lin, Yuli, Anati, and the Veil in with her.

She heard a scream around her. Yuli's scream. She smelled blood, heard shattering glass and metal, bone and steel clanging in a haze of mist.

Beams of light shone from the column in narrow, focused lines. She wove around them. She had to reach the center, Anati said. The beams multiplied, and she dodged them. Almost there. Five cords of white-hot wire, then twenty, then fifty.

One of them struck her, slicing through her in a wave of agony.

The blackness called; stars and strands offering an escape. Another cord bit into her sense of self, ripping loose some part of her. Memories, or knowledge. Gone. She screamed, and heard shouts mix with her screaming.

The cords were wrong. A perversion of the true thing. Fragments of the soul. The world in decay. But the core of it was there. She drove through the pain, burning away more of her sense of self. She was Sarine, though she wanted to be the Veil. Stewardship was hers. She'd fought for the right, and slain the old master to ensure it would pass to her. She touched the core, and light flashed around her, pushing the rest away.

63

SARINE

The Master's Sanctum
Gods' Seat

Once again she lay on the floor, doubled over, sobbing.

The pain of the transition ached in her joints and muscles, burning as she fought to breathe. Pain made her aware of every part of her body. The core of her emotions bubbled over, and she found the strength to keep the Veil locked away. Anati was there, connected to her. She could feel the warmth of her *kaas*, fighting to add strength to the shield between two souls.

The crunch of broken glass sounded as Lin rose to her feet. Clear from the air—and the smooth, polished stone floor—they were no longer on the mountain.

"Sarine." Yuli's voice. Calm. Full of concern. "You did it; or at least, you got us away."

She accepted Yuli's help to lift her from the floor, and only once she was sitting did she notice the ragged cuts in Yuli's shirt, the cloth stained red with blood.

"Are you hurt?" she said, cut short by dryness in her throat.

"I thought I was dead," Yuli said. "But somehow here, I am healed."

"What is this place?" Lin asked.

They were in a broad chamber, low-ceilinged, cut from the same polished stone as the floors, as though the space had been hollowed from a single core. The walls had a concave slope, and though the room was furnished, it was done in no fashion she recognized. Metal benches made a six-sided ring around a gold table at the center, with strange gold instruments standing across the floor, to her eyes no more than twisted hulks of metal and glass. Red markings had been painted on the walls in crude designs, the sort of stick-figure approximations she might have used in her first years of learning to draw anatomy, but clearly depicting people and animals, in what looked like hunting poses, chasing after the beasts with spears.

"Is this where you aimed to bring us?" Yuli asked, offering a hand to pull her up the rest of the way.

"I don't know," she said. "Anati?"

This is not the Soul, Anati thought. *But it is the place where it is housed.*

Lin had moved toward the gold table at the center, climbing over the silvery metal benches. "Death spirits," Lin said. "This is a map. I've never seen anything like this."

Sarine and Yuli joined her, drawing close enough to see. The gold table had appeared flat from afar, but as she drew closer she saw it was textured, a topographical depiction of land and sea cut in miniature, with rises for hills and mountains, patches of green fuzz for forests, even tiny rolling waves so real that the oceans, rivers, and lakes appeared to be made of actual water atop the table.

"This is the Jun Empire," Lin said, pointing to one of the landmasses on the eastern part of the table. "The Kye peninsula, the Shinsuke islands, Jun proper."

"And the Natarii lands," Yuli said, heading around to hover near the top portion of the map. "But what are these?" Yuli pointed toward an archipelago in the south, leading toward another landmass there, almost as large as the rest.

Sarine hardly heard them. It took a second glance to see the outline of familiar coasts and landmasses in the west.

"It isn't just the Jun lands," she said. "This is a map of the whole world. Our Old World is here." She pointed to a landmass on the western side of the center. "This is Sarresant, Gand, Thellan, Skovan, Sardia. Our colonies must be here"—she pointed—"on this side of the ocean. And those are the Bhakal lands, just south of the Old World. I...I don't recognize the rest."

There were five continents, but between them they had named only three. The New World, on the far western side of the table, appeared to be two new worlds in fact, one stacked atop the other, and both were massive, either one nearly twice as large as the seat of the Old World powers. The Bhakal continent was the only one to straddle the center of the table, overlapping both east and west, but it, too, was massive, half again as large as either continent of the New World. Lin and Yuli had named the fourth mass the Jun continent, but neither had any knowledge of the fifth, a sprawling land of what appeared to be deserts and lakes far to the south.

"The Emperor's cartographers would burn their children for five minutes in this room," Lin said. "Providing it is accurate."

"We should move on," Sarine said. "Zi said this place would have answers for what's coming."

Lin and Yuli both hesitated, each lingering over different sections of the map. She could have done the same—studying new lands, or recognizing familiar ones. But they had a purpose here, and however curious the relics, they brought her no closer to understanding.

"What are we looking for, Anati?" she said as they left the chamber. The smooth stone and concave walls persisted into the hallway, offering left and right paths that curved out of sight.

My father said it was time for you to visit the Soul, Anati thought. *It is here. Close.*

She glanced left and right. The pathways seemed identical. The Soul, Anati had said. Which way would it be?

I don't know. I haven't been here before, either.

Well, that stood to reason. She led Lin and Yuli down the rightward path, following its curve around the corner, revealing another series of winding turns. Easier to retrace their steps if she followed a consistent rule, so she kept right wherever the opportunity presented itself to change. Wherever they were, it gave every sign of emptiness and cleanliness at once. No sign of dust or dirt, nor even the slightest chip or rough patch in the stone. The hallways should have been dark without torches, lamps, or windows, but they were lit evenly, a soft light seeming to come from all directions. Apart from the three of them the halls were empty, but more than once she stopped to look behind or second-guess a turn and thought she saw movement at the corner of her eye.

They began to pass chambers, each as strangely appointed as the map room. One was covered in animal furs, with woven blankets and what appeared to be freshly shorn pelts piled in place of furniture. Another could have been lifted from New Sarresant, with ornately carved wood chairs and chaises upholstered in the most fashionable patterns, racks of scrolls and books, and a darkwood desk at its center. Still another looked as though it had been recently destroyed, its low couches and tables covered in wood splinters and down from its pillows, though only parts of the chamber were broken, with the rest immaculate, as though they'd interrupted a cleaning partway through.

The passages continued on, and she began to feel a pulsing energy as they walked. A sense of rightness, growing with each turn, some of it mirrored by the Veil's emotions, but the better part of it seemed to come from her. A sense of familiarity.

The hallway opened into a vast chamber when there were no more turns to take. She stepped inside, and for the first time since coming here, they were no longer alone.

The chamber was wide and empty, an amphitheater without seating or a stage. At its center a torrent of energy burned, the same column of pure white light she'd seen in their passage here. Echoes of memories washed through her, looking at it, and most of those came from the Veil: revulsion, anger, hate, betrayal. Her attention was directed to the two men standing beside the column. One a hulking giant, head and shoulders taller than the largest men she'd ever seen, and the other was Reyne d'Agarre.

D'Agarre turned to notice her before the giant did, and they stared at each other in mutual shock. It was him. The same sand-colored hair and blue eyes. The same red coat. The same smug surety in his face, despite the signs of surprise overwriting his usual veneer of confidence. Even his long knife hung at his belt, the weapon he'd used to kill dozens of innocents. Everything about him was frozen, exactly as it had been on the day of the battle in the city.

"Sarine," Reyne said, and her name earned the giant's attention, the massive man whirling to lay eyes on her, Lin and Yuli with even greater shock than showed in Reyne's face.

"No," the giant said. "No, it isn't time."

"Wait," she said. "I'm here for answers, not to fight." She could feel a hundred tethers between the giant and the leylines running beneath the room. So far none had materialized as *Entropy, Body, Mind,* or *Shelter,* but she kept *Death* strands at the ready all the same. Any moment he could erupt into a dozen copies of himself, hurling fire and putting barriers up to halt their advance. The giant stared death at her, as though the slightest word or step could set him in motion.

"Sarine," Reyne repeated. "It's you, isn't it? Not the Veil." He said it as though he meant to reassure his companion, but the giant had already turned his gaze on Yuli, looking between her and Sarine.

"Erris d'Arrent," the giant said.

"No," Sarine said, at the same time Reyne shook his head, laying a hand on the giant's arm.

"That isn't d'Arrent," Reyne said. "The High Commander is shorter. I'd know her on sight. This is...someone else."

"I am Yuli Twin Fangs Clan Hoskar," Yuli said.

"Clan Hoskar," the giant said. "And the other one: a child of the East. Together. With the Veil."

"I am Lin Qishan," Lin said. "Captain, and scion of a great house."

"A great house," the giant said. "A Great and Noble House, more like."

With that the giant erupted into deep laughter. It echoed through the chamber, made all the more strange by his laughing alone.

"Fools," the giant said. "Axerian warned me it was bad, but I never imagined...this."

Suddenly Axerian's stories clicked in her mind. This was one of Axerian's companions: the strategist, the foremost among them, who touched the leylines and led their armies in battle. The central figure in more than half the holy texts, the man who had accepted the Nameless's surrender after the Grand Betrayal. The Exarch, whom Axerian had called by his mortal name.

"Paendurion," she said.

Hearing it seemed to sober him. "So, you remember that much at least."

"I came here to learn," she said. "I have a part to play in what's coming, and I need to know what to do, to face the shadows, when they arrive."

Paendurion stepped back from the column of light, moving toward her cautiously, as a hunter might stalk prey.

"How much do you know, of what lies ahead?" Paendurion asked.

"How much do you know of what happened before? And how is it you come to be in the company of two of the Regnant's *magi*, here, in the Gods' Seat?"

He'd switched tongues to a stilted, clipped manner of speech. Anati translated it for her; d'Agarre's *kaas* would do the same, though Yuli and Lin wouldn't understand.

"I journeyed through the Divide," she said. "I faced the shadows there. I thought, if I could reach his champions, I could end the fight before...the ascensions."

"You attacked the Regnant?" Paendurion said.

"No," she said. "Well...yes. He attacked us."

"And you survived?"

Of course she survived, Anati thought to the room. *She's here, isn't she?*

Paendurion laughed again. "Fairly said, serpent," he said. "But I gather you didn't slay the Regnant in your travels?"

"No," she said quietly. "And not all of us survived the journey. Axerian..."

"I know," Paendurion said. "He's dead."

"I didn't mean for it to happen," she said.

"Of course you didn't," Paendurion said. "The consequence of poor planning. I warned him. And Ad-Shi. And now I am alone, facing the enemy with untrained fools, with the fate of our world on my back."

"There is learning to be done, here," Reyne said. "A great library, a store of all the world's knowledge. I know we had our differences, before, but we want the same things. I'm certain we can find whatever answers you seek, if Paendurion doesn't know them already."

His words grated on her; the very idea of listening to him speak was vile. Part of her wanted to reject even a library full of knowledge, if it came from d'Agarre's hand. But the better part of her had been taken by fear. Fear of what was coming. Fear of what she had to know how to do.

Lin had separated from them, pacing around the chamber, eyeing the column of light. Go to the Soul, Zi had said. He had to mean this chamber, the light that spanned both the physical world and the strange place she'd found with the blue sparks. She had to use whatever she found here, whether it sickened her or no.

"What is this place?" she asked, forcing herself to speak to Reyne. "You came here...after?"

"Yes," Reyne said. "Only when I got here, the light was trapped, imprisoned in a crystal."

"She doesn't need to dwell on the past," Paendurion said. "She needs to learn how to turn the Soul, in case we lose. A secret we never learned. A secret we never needed. Perhaps it is here, somewhere, but—"

He cut short in a spasm and a wail of pain, and for a moment Sarine tensed, preparing for an attack. But no—instead glass shards protruded from his back, a spray of icicle-length daggers stuck deep in his skin. Paendurion whirled around, the hundred leyline tethers she'd sensed around him suddenly snapping into place. But instead of fighting, Paendurion wove a mix of every type of leyline energy and vanished, leaving a cloud of gray mist, green motes, and white pearls hovering where he'd been standing, as though the leylines had erupted into the physical world.

Lin let slip a cry of victory, then sprinted toward the center of the chamber.

Red came, and *lakiri'in*, and *Body*. Too slow. Lin touched the column at the center of the room, incinerating herself in a dazzling flash of light.

64

ERRIS

Fontcadeau Green
The Royal Palace, Rasailles

Trumpets blared a too-loud herald of her arrival as her coach rolled to a slow stop on the edge of the green. Voren—Fei Zan—looked her over as the footmen dismounted, taking up places to open the door and reveal her to the world. An Empress required an entrance, a formal reception, and a ceremony of investiture. A reminder that she might never be entirely free of the hurdles in her path, when all she'd ever wanted was to find victory over her enemies. Well, she'd reformed the army well enough. Perhaps she could do the same to the state, in time.

"You almost look the part, High Commander," Voren said. "Are you ready?"

"Better if it was finished an hour ago, and better still if it were done last week."

Voren smiled. She wasn't sure why he'd returned to wearing the old man's features, but she found she drew a perverse comfort in them, even knowing what he was. "The people must have their symbols," Voren said. "Easier to lead a battle wearing a general's uniform with battle standards and aides-de-camp than as a peasant shouting orders from the sidelines."

The door swung wide, revealing sculpted grass and hedges along the winding path through the green. One of the footmen stepped to try to offer a hand, which she dismissed. Perhaps if she'd agreed to wear the ridiculous dresses the clothiers had tried to push on her—the height of fashion in Old Sarresant, so they'd claimed—she might have needed assistance for something so trivial as dismounting a carriage. Instead she'd decided on full military dress, embellished to make a new rank above High Commander: six stars on her collar and sleeves, a gold-embroidered sash to match her epaulets displaying the blue-white-blue of the Republic. Empress. And let it be a military rank. Fuck the trappings of Kings, Lords, and the nobility.

"Better if you stay behind," she said to Voren. "They'll have plenty enough to talk about already."

Voren inclined his head. "As you command, Your Majesty." He said it with a touch of mirth, and she felt none of it.

"Head back to high command," she said. "See to it we're prepared to move my flag across the sea."

"More than enough support staff with the ships," Voren said. "Anyone else in particular you want with us?"

"Vassail," she said. "Even if her leg isn't up to it, I want her at headquarters, if not in the field. Acherre, and the Yanjins."

Voren bowed his head again, and she turned back toward the green. Easier by far, to make her way in a world of soldiers, logistics, and strategy. But then, politics had its own battles. She'd been plunged into it like a sword in a forge, hammered by the deaths of twenty-seven priests in her reconquest of the city. Now she was ready to be drawn and used, a cutting edge to be deployed against her enemies. Power gave her the means to reform the haphazard apparatus of the Republic, rewarding merit above all else, a state where ability propelled excellence, instead of miring decisions in blood and favors.

She held her place at the center of the path while her soldiers fell in, and they began a march, so similar to the exercises she'd been drilled on as a child. The thrum of their steps echoed through the green, all the way to the palace walls, where their true audience awaited. A gathering of the prominent, such as was left of them in the Republic. Former assemblymen, hopeful of kissing the right sets of asses to find themselves a place in the new Imperial bureaucracy. Priests, those who had already submitted to *Need* to prove their loyalty. Artisans and merchants, even the few remaining nobles who had managed to survive the terrors following the first revolution. Generals and envoys from Villecours, Lorrine, l'Euillard, and every corner of the country. Red-coated Gandsmen, and Gand nobles, too, since she was meant to be Empress over them, the same as her countrymen. They watched from the steps leading into the palace receiving grounds, rows upon rows of eyes extending from the first platform all the way into the cathedral at the palace's heart.

The way through the grounds was empty, save for more binders, each one also bound by *Need*. Her procession made its way around the winding garden path, receiving salutes from each man along the way, until they reached the base of the palace steps, and traded the admiration and love of her soldiers for a solemn quiet from the rest.

A chilling reminder of the attempted coup against her. The crowd was silent, watching her approach with due reverence and reserve. But neither was there any love in the tradesfolk's eyes, nor in the Gandsmen who had been placed with them outside the church. They gave her the awe and deference due a conqueror. A double row of onlookers watched as she climbed the steps, her binders moving ahead to clear the path and keep a circle of scarred hands around her, their marques serving as a warning as sure as their blue coats and insignia of rank.

A herald stepped in front of her procession as they made way across the receiving grounds, bringing her to a halt in front of the church's wide double doors.

"She approaches," the herald called, and a wave of boots and footsteps sounded as those inside the cathedral rose to their feet. She could see inside: a hall packed as tight as propriety allowed, with shows of fashion and wealth from gold and jewels to furs and velvet. A row of priests stood around the dais, their plain brown robes in stark contrast to the rest of the attendees. And the way forward was empty, an aisle cut through the center, barred only by her herald and another priest.

"Who comes forward to lead the Republic?" the priest spoke, loud enough to be heard even outside the doors.

"Erris d'Arrent," the herald said. "A woman of common birth, who has saved our country thrice over from its enemies."

The weight of every eye had turned to her. Thank the Gods she hadn't allowed Essily to stuff her into civilian couture. Hearing a litany of her exploits while dressed like something she was not would sting as deep as any wound she'd earned in battle.

"By what right does she claim the mantle of leadership?" the priest asked.

"By right of conquest," the herald said, "and strength of arms. By the divinity invested from the Gods, through whom she wields the gifts of the holy lines. By the will to protect us from our enemies, without and within."

"Let her come forward, then," the priest said, "and be seen."

The cathedral thrummed again, as those already standing moved to crane their necks toward the doors. Essily had drilled her on her steps in the ceremony, but she saw Voren's touch, and Tuyard's, in the words already spoken and the pomp of the crowd. She waited as her binders went before her, forming a double column on either side of the central aisle. Then the herald beckoned her forward, and she stepped inside.

The interior defied any expectations she'd had of the cathedral's size. High arches rose overhead, hung with blue banners striped with gold, twenty handspans above the floor where they dangled the lowest. The main hall forked in three directions, each one packed full of attendees, clustered beneath stained-glass reliefs depicting each of the three Gods. The central dais sat beneath a depiction of the Exarch, clad in heavy steel, raising his sword and shield as though he were pointing the way for all to follow. The Oracle and the Veil's wings were lined with lookers-on, but at their heads two conductors led two choirs in a ringing hymn the instant her feet touched the tile. The song took her by surprise; a booming men's chorus on the left, and peals from their counterparts in a women's chorus on the right. The whole interior was on its feet as she came forward to their accompaniment, and it was all she could do to keep her steps steady as she made her approach.

Again she saw Voren's hand, and Tuyard's, in their choice of the Rasailles cathedral—private worship hall for the nobility, during the Duc-Governor's rule—and in the priests standing above the central dais. The ceremony had the trappings of the faith in every aspect, save her choice of a military uniform for attire. Clothe her in robes and give her a gem-encrusted broadsword, and it could well be a scene put on by the Basilica, a heraldry on a feast day to celebrate the Exarch's Triumph, the Nameless's Surrender, the Oracle's Acceptance, or the Veil's Sacrifice. For her it served instead as a reminder of the resistance she'd encountered in the streets on her march into the city. But there was no sign of that defiance here today.

The crowd's silence had maintained, only now with the trappings of faith it played as reverence, rather than awe. There would be resentment, at home alongside ambition and greed. She meant to see to it they all counted for nothing. And much as she understood Voren and Tuyard's nod to the faith, it had never been her way. What was a throne, if not a means to shape the world according to her vision? The hymns punctuated her thoughts as she covered the last steps. She was here to harden the Republic against its enemies. Religion, politics, and ancient blood counted for nothing against the power to wage war. In the worst times, it was the only power that mattered.

"Erris d'Arrent," the man said from atop the dais, draped in the pure white robes of the First Prelate's robes. The choirs had quieted to a hush, but still sang a soft pulse that echoed through the cathedral as he spoke. "The faith recognizes your right to rule. Step forward and be crowned Queen of New Sarresant and Gand, Empress of a new colonial state that lays rightful claim to all the lands of the New World."

Her binders had come to a stop at the base of the dais, and she strode up the steps past them, beneath the golden dome erected above the central altar. The priest wore a reverent, solemn expression as he reached for the diamond-encrusted crown, lifting it above her head. Her instructions had been to turn around, to face the assembled crowd and deliver a set of lines before the Prelate set the crown in place. *In service to my countrymen and my Gods*, they began. They were wrong. She hadn't invaded and seized the city to serve its citizens; she'd done it to ensure they served each other. The old kings and queens had ruled by virtue of inheritance, delivered from their parentage and their gods. Hers was a different sort of crown. She was a different sort of ruler.

The priest's solemnity had begun to waver when she hadn't turned around, and it ebbed to a sour confusion when she instead took the final steps, reached, and took the crown from his grasp.

Cold metal, heavier than she'd expected. She laid it on her own head, and turned to face a shocked gasp from the crowd. Wide eyes looked up at her from every pew, only her binders maintaining looks of satisfaction.

"I accept this charge," she said to the hall. "Given by my hand, and none other. I will defend this state until my last breath, and ensure that its people do the same. The decadence of the old kings is finished, and the decadence of revolution. We are bound together by loyalty and purpose: to see our enemies defeated, to see our people prosper. I will accept nothing less. You may expect nothing less, from me."

The hall remained quiet when she finished. There had been a reception planned, a grand presentation within the staterooms of the palace, though she'd never intended on wasting an afternoon on pointless displays of wealth or power. Her ships would be arriving soon on the shores of the Old World. She had a campaign to set in motion. And now, finally, she had the power to see it done.

65

ARAK'JUR

Training Yards
Outside New Sarresant

Hundreds of blue-coated soldiers watched his passage as though he were an enemy. He felt their eyes like so many squirrels or sparrows, a reluctant audience as he and Ka'Inari followed behind the lieutenant assigned as their translator and guide. A subtle change, but one he'd known enough to feel it in his blood. He was a hunter, here. And they were moving toward his prey.

Every step had resonated with Mountain's will. He was here to kill a conqueror. The surety of it settled over him, wiping away the need for thought.

"Wait here," the lieutenant said when they reached a large structure, the sort of thing the fair-skins built, all paneled wood and stone. Ka'Inari bowed and stayed behind as their guide went inside.

"Arak'Jur," Ka'Inari said.

Hearing his name took him by surprise, and he started, finding Ka'Inari staring at him.

"You hear Mountain's promptings," Ka'Inari said. "I recognize the look. What do they say?"

He shook his head. "No," he said. "They've said nothing."

"Yet they are with you," Ka'Inari said. "I can sense their presence."

Before he could reply, a woman appeared from within the building.

Blond-haired, in a uniform with a star and a stripe on the collar and sleeves. A woman he recognized: Rosline Acherre, the soldier who had accompanied Sarine and Ka'Inari on their journey from Ka'Ana'Tyat.

She lingered in the doorway for a fraction, a broad smile creasing her face. Then she rushed toward Ka'Inari, and the shaman met her with a tight embrace.

"I was the knowing you'd come," Acherre said in thickly accented Sinari. "*Et ton compagnon*," she said, switching to Sarresant. "Arak'Jur."

"Fine to see you again, Captain Acherre," he said, feeling none of the warmth that seemed to pass between Acherre and Ka'Inari. It earned him a deferential bow from her.

"Major, now," Acherre said. "Pushed up since we are the seeing last."

"Tigai and his family?" Ka'Inari said.

"Here. Inside," Acherre said. "And High Commander d'Arrent. *Ou, je suppose qu'elle est l'Impératrice maintenant.*" The name rang in his senses. Erris d'Arrent.

"*L'Impératrice?*" Ka'Inari said, making clear he didn't know the word.

"Big…leader?" Acherre said in the Sinari tongue.

"And Sarine?" Ka'Inari asked. "Has she returned?"

Acherre shook her head, and both their expressions turned grim. He'd heard Ka'Inari's account of the girl's disappearance, along with some other of his traveling companions. The importance of it seemed to blur, his senses focused on the hunt.

Ka'Inari bowed his head. "Inside?" he said, and Acherre nodded, gesturing for them to follow as she led the way.

They entered the building past soldiers carrying muskets fixed with steel bayonets. Acherre led them up a flight of stairs, around a hallway toward a double door with two more guards on duty on either side. At the captain's—no, major's, if he'd understood her correction aright—appearance, the guards swung the doors, admitting them into a chamber with a host of men and women already seated around a broad table, and he came face to face with his quarry.

Erris d'Arrent. The same woman he'd met after the battle in New Sarresant, wearing six stars on her high blue collar and barely tall enough to reach his chest. He heard Mountain's voice in his mind again: SHE MUST DIE.

Mareh'et gave his blessing, and the room froze.

All eyes stared at him, but it was Ka'Inari who spoke.

"Arak'Jur?" Ka'Inari said. "What are you doing? Is there some threat here?"

Translators passed the words from Sinari to Sarresant, but he heard none of it. Erris d'Arrent had locked eyes with him, and Mountain's voice sounded again: SHE MUST DIE.

He held *mareh'et*'s gift, feeling its spirit pulse around him, filling his muscles with the Great Cat's strength and power.

It was wrong.

Erris d'Arrent had been his ally. She'd sheltered his people, given them land and an army to protect them when he'd journeyed south. Through her force of arms and Ka'Hannat's visions, both peoples had been kept safe. She was no enemy of his, though thinking it tore at a sense of purpose burning deep in his core. Mountain shuddered in his thoughts. He was meant to kill conquerors and tyrants, men and women who would plunge the world into war. Erris d'Arrent had done so, and would again. He was meant to kill her. Being in her presence yoked him to a course of violence, a yearning drive to let *mareh'et*'s gift decide her fate. But he was in control, not the spirits. She was his ally, and he would let her live.

"No," he said. "All is well, and we are here for peace."

Once more his words were translated into the Sarresant tongue, but his thoughts went to Corenna, and he fought down a rush of tears. This was what she had endured in his presence. The compulsion to kill him, as strong as whatever Mountain had done between him and Erris d'Arrent.

D'Arrent nodded slowly, still watching him as she began to speak, and the lieutenant who had escorted them through the camp reappeared at his side, translating her words into Sinari.

"Her Imperial Majesty bids you welcome," the lieutenant said, "and expresses her satisfaction at your appearance here today."

Arak'Jur frowned. He understood enough of the Sarresant tongue to know d'Arrent had said something closer to "I thought they told me you were dead." He opted to respond to what she'd said, rather than the translator's formality.

"Not dead," he said in the Sarresant tongue. "Here in peace, as allies, to answer the spirits' call to war."

D'Arrent's eyes shone. "Damn fine to have you," d'Arrent said, then followed with something else, in the Sarresant tongue. The translator seemed bewildered, until Arak'Jur spoke in a sharp tone, switching back to Sinari.

"Speak exactly what she says," he said to the lieutenant. "And nothing else."

"Diplomats," d'Arrent said—and the lieutenant translated properly this time. "A burden I don't bloody well need. But it's damn good to have you with us. I hadn't expected more than the shaman."

He saw another round of translation happening for the benefit of some of the others around the table—two men of slight build and height and one thicker, by a woman who shared some of their features. Those would be the Yanjin family, of whom he had heard from Ka'Inari. Acherre was there, and an old man whose face he almost recognized, behind thick mustaches and wire-frame spectacles. Another trio of fair-skins finished their company, two soldiers and a man in lace.

"Now," d'Arrent said, translated quickly as she moved to hover over the table, which he saw was strewn with maps. "Here is the tactical situation, as I understand it. Old Sarresant"—she pointed—"is under threat from two armies, an alliance between the Thellan in the south and Sardia in the east. Our armies are due to make their landings here, along the northern coasts, unless we can persuade the Dauphin and the King to make common cause and give us the use of their ports. Regardless, I intend to put us in the field. And with Lord Tigai's abilities, once we establish...anchors, was it?...between the two fronts, we can move binders and troops between them, reinforcing wherever the enemy strikes. I intend to fight two battles at once, but it begins, as it ever does, with maneuver."

She turned to Ka'Inari. "You have Ka'Hannat's gift, yes? Of seeing threats before they happen?"

Ka'Inari nodded when the translation was done.

"Then I'll need you with Tigai," she said. "It is imperative he reach both fronts. A small force of fast riders can cut through the mountains in days, then swing along the flatlands to where the Sardians are marching north. Acherre, Ka'Inari, Tigai, and Arak'Jur, if you're willing to do it."

He struggled to keep pace, trying to match her gestures to the delayed cadence of the translator converting her words to Sinari. He studied where she pointed on her maps, and tried to picture the journey she'd proposed. He, Ka'Inari, Acherre, and this Tigai, covering a moon's turning worth of ground in a matter of days. It would be hard going, made harder for being over unknown and hostile territory.

"What sort of reception can we expect in these villages?" he asked, pointing to where a network of cities crisscrossed the southeastern stretches of the map.

"Acherre will know where the borders lie," d'Arrent said. "The Skovan principalities have remained mostly neutral, according to the scouts I have in place there, but they won't take kindly to strange folk moving through their land. You'd do well to pick up a scout from our ranks who can speak Skovan before you cross the border."

"Wait," the woman in Tigai's party said, whom he only belatedly noticed was missing her right hand. "Major Acherre's command of the Jun tongue is passable at best. I'll have to come along, for Tigai to be of any use."

Before she'd finished speaking, the two similar-looking men— brothers, Ka'Inari had said, Tigai and Dao—started arguing with her in their native tongue, with Acherre joining in with snippets of Sarresant speech. A jumbled mess, and after trying a few words, the translator gave an apologetic shrug.

He took the opportunity to move away a few steps, closer to where Erris d'Arrent was watching them debate.

Once more Mountain flared in his senses as he approached, and he smothered it. He was here as her ally, not to kill, though every step toward her weighed heavy on his shoulders.

"So," he said, using his own command of the Sarresant tongue, though it was far from perfect. "Is it true, that this Tigai can move us across the sea?"

"It is," d'Arrent said. "You'll sleep there tonight. Provided they finish bickering by then."

He nodded and she met him with a wry look, though there was a wariness there, a cool reserve he couldn't put down to fair-skin customs or strangeness.

"Our pact," he said. "It has worked, to keep our people safe."

"Yes it has," she said. "Do you mean to propose a new one, in return for your aid in this campaign?"

He paused, glancing at the translator and waiting to be sure he'd heard aright. The next he spoke in Sinari, his knowledge of the Sarresant tongue not having the proper words.

"The spirits' visions will guide us toward victory, in opposition to a great evil. For my part, I must defeat this evil. The man who holds a thousand threads of gold. I saw him in a vision, at Adan'Hai'Tyat. I have made a great sacrifice, coming here. But it will be repaid when I reach the end of my path."

The translator seemed to struggle with his words, but d'Arrent looked at him with rising confidence, nodding along as he spoke.

"Ascension," she said. "That is your spirits' path, isn't it?"

"Yes," he said, latching on to the word in the Sarresant tongue. "Ascension."

"I've learned something of it," d'Arrent said. "I think we share the same goal, and the same enemy."

"You have communed with our spirits?" he said, feeling a moment of shock. But then, no—he'd seen her work the fair-skin magic. Their leylines. Perhaps ascension was a thing they had in common. As Ad-Shi had described it. Champions, at the apex of each line of skill.

"Not your spirits," d'Arrent said. "The 'threads of gold,' you called it. For us, it is decided in holding territory, in the loyalty of many subjects."

Understanding dawned. "For my people, it is a thing of the spirits, a great task set before us."

"And your task is to kill Paendurion—the enemy with a thousand threads?"

"My task is to kill those who would lead men and women to war," he said cautiously. "Mountain are spirits of peace, above all else."

"Those who would lead..." she repeated, then met his eyes, for a moment her features as hard as steel.

"An easier path, to betray trust," he said. "But it is not our way."

"Nor ours," she said finally. She offered a hand—a fair-skin custom he knew well from his youth as a hunter and trader. He took it, and they exchanged a firm grasp.

"It is decided, then," the old man in spectacles said. "Provided Her Majesty is amenable to my participation."

The rest of them had quieted, waiting on d'Arrent. From the look of them, the woman who had argued to join them had been put down, the two Yanjin brothers appearing satisfied with whatever decision had been reached.

"What is this?" d'Arrent asked. "Your participation?"

"Only if you agree, Your Majesty," the old man said. "But I've proposed having me accompanying Lord Tigai's party, instead of the Lady Mei. As you well know, I can speak Sarresant and Jun. Skovan, too, and Thellan, should the need arise in the mountains."

A long moment stretched as d'Arrent weighed the man's words. Neither option settled well, in Arak'Jur's eyes. A one-handed woman of slight build would be pure hindrance for hard travel, but an elder long since past his prime would be no better.

"Consider it settled, then," d'Arrent said. "Lord Voren—Fei Zan— you will accompany them. No sense in further delay. Lord Tigai, you know the place where you are taking us?"

"Yes," Tigai said through two translators. "At least, I know it's somewhere close to here." He gestured toward the map. "There are only a handful of stars on this side of the Divide, but one of them is close to the strands connecting Voren to the other continent."

The translator spoke the words quickly, but must have garbled them; or if he didn't, the words made no sense to Arak'Jur. But Erris d'Arrent seemed satisfied.

"To the stableyards, then," d'Arrent said. "We fetch our mounts and supplies. Then, Lord Tigai will take us across the sea."

66

TIGAI

Coastal Bluffs
Old Sarresant

The starfield receded, and he opened his eyes to a vista of hills and grass overlooking an ocean. Erris d'Arrent was already moving, barking an order as she mounted her monstrous white horse. Animals had been provided for all of them, and places among the soldiers and generals of the New Sarresant Army. Preconditions for his services, negotiated by Mei and not amenable to him in the slightest, not that he'd been consulted before she sold his talent like a whoremaster. It meant leaving Dao, Remarin, and Mei behind, after struggling for months to get them back.

Remarin embraced him like a son, thumping his shoulder when they separated. Dao held him like the brother he was—always fighting on the same side, no matter when they disagreed about what side it was or should be. Mei wrapped around him like a jungle cat, shedding the only tears, though he would never call her weak for doing it.

"Make the journey quickly," Mei said. "Or I'll have Dao elevated to a High Lord and Magistrate by the time you return."

"If they even have High Lords here," he said.

"Perhaps he'll be the first."

D'Arrent was calling for them to move, and he helped Mei up into her saddle as the rest of them gathered together, all save the four who would accompany him on his southward ride. Those hovered a few paces off, beckoning to him as surely as d'Arrent's orders summoned his family away.

"Take care of them," he said to Mei.

"I will," she said. "Whether they want to be taken care of or not."

He was left with an image of Mei, a one-handed grip on the reins, smiling a wicked grin as she kicked her mount forward, in line with the rest. D'Arrent had wasted no time moving them westward. The Empress claimed her first ships would already be landing, and claimed the knowledge of it through a magic he didn't understand. The leylines, the same gift Acherre had, and Sarine. Strange that their magic had so many different uses, and from the looks of it, conferred different abilities on some than others. More strangeness, when strangeness already abounded.

"Ready to be away?" Acherre asked. Her command of the Jun tongue had progressed quickly in the weeks she'd spent traveling with Mei, though he had to pick the words through a thick accent, with none of the proper subtleties of tone.

He slid into his saddle, watching the figures of d'Arrent's party growing smaller as Acherre led them almost the opposite direction.

"How far will we go today?" he asked her, sidling his mount up to hers at the head of the line. Voren seemed only passing skilled in the saddle, leaving him and Acherre as the only ones not looking as though they'd rather slaughter their mounts for steaks than ride them.

"As far as the horses will take us," she said. "And we'll move when there's any light at all. Even the moon."

He sighed. Damned if he shouldn't have anchored a warm, down-filled bed in a whorehouse somewhere. The strain from the distance wouldn't be so bad, compared to sleeping on dirt. That is, if they even had whorehouses on this side of the sea.

The strands hadn't put them anywhere within sight of a city or even a road. But Acherre seemed to know the way, even if it was only "south," and they rode in a winding column, with himself at the head, Voren trailing behind a ways, and the two clansmen—or tribesmen, he thought he'd heard them called—significantly slower. The one called Ka'Inari seemed passable on a horse, while the larger one—Arak'Jur—trailed far behind, forcing Acherre to range from the head to the rear, covering half again the ground he or Voren rode to make sure the tribesmen were keeping pace. That kept up for a few hours before Arak'Jur came running to the head of the column, his horse nowhere in sight. Tigai blinked in disbelief, watching the man run faster than a horse's pace, getting far enough ahead that Acherre had to heel her mount to catch and correct his course.

It left them with a spare mount, after Acherre had fetched and tied the tribesman's horse, and they crossed a vast stretch of hills before the sun set on the horizon. The ground was covered by a thin layer of snow, with patches of dirt visible beneath the slush and frost-covered trees with bare branches dotting the way. Tigai had always preferred cities to the country, but there was a certain pale beauty to it, and Acherre seemed to be making pains to keep them away from any sign of civilization. The few farmsteads they came near provoked quick turns, and though they crossed roads more than once during the day, they never kept to one. Nightfall greeted them with a moonless sky, and by the time it grew too dark to risk further progress, his backside ached, his thighs rubbed raw between his leggings and the saddle.

"Second watch," Acherre said to him, gesturing with two fingers to make clear her meaning. He nodded, and wasted no time withdrawing blankets from the saddlebags, lying close to the fire to soak up as much warmth as he could atop the snow.

Soreness found him faster than sleep, a condition that would only get worse as they traveled. The rest of them seemed to take their time, the shaman building his own small fire a few paces away from the main one, his bare-chested companion vanished, likely to find something to eat and eat. Voren, the strange old man, was alone in making for a quick attempt at rest—no surprise, when the man couldn't have been a day younger than seventy. Wind spirits but this whole venture was a bad idea. He should have had Mei volunteer him to ferry food or weapons; the sort of thing Dao used him for, when the Yanjin soldiers went campaigning. Blinking soldiers between battles would only draw the *magi*'s attention. Not that that was a consideration, on this side of the world. Still.

Acherre's hand jostled him awake a moment later, and he almost protested until he felt the weight of sleep on his eyelids, and saw the sky had gone fully black, lit by a sea of stars.

He grunted, shuffling off the blanket. It seemed to serve, as Acherre withdrew her hand, nodding when he rose to be seated beside the now-crackling fire. She'd slipped under her own blankets by the time he rose, wrapping himself in furs to ward against the cold. Had he even slept an hour? It felt as though he had rocks behind his eyes, and from the lack of instructions on whom to wake for third watch, he gathered there wasn't like to be another round of sleep.

"You sleep heavy, for a man in your position."

He turned to find Voren watching him, the old man already sitting on the opposite side of the fire.

"Why are you awake?" Tigai asked. "Acherre gave me second watch. If you're going to take it, I'd as soon finish sleeping."

"Perhaps the major doesn't trust you," Voren said, smiling as though that would remove the bite from his words. Acherre was already asleep beside them, covered over with white blankets atop the snow.

Voren rose to his feet. "Come. No need to disturb the others."

Tigai frowned, as much from lack of sleep as the old man's strange behavior. The rest of the camp was quiet, the two tribesmen both sleeping beside their fire a few paces off, while their horses slept standing on lead lines tethered around a tree. For a moment he contemplated ignoring Voren's strangeness, resuming his sleep and letting Acherre know Voren had volunteered for the watch. Instead he rose, stretching his limbs and shaking off the dusting of ice he'd accumulated during his short hours of lying down. Just as well, if the old man felt he didn't need rest. A watch would go easier with company.

He followed Voren a few paces away, still in view of the camp, until they stood beneath another tree, a black form outlined against the night sky, its leaves long since fallen and replaced by boughs of snow.

"So," Tigai said as he approached. "How is it you learned the Jun tongue?" It had been something of a shock, hearing the old man speak it. Isaru's company had crossed the Divide, and it stood to reason there might be others, but it seemed beyond chance for him to run into one so quickly after his arrival.

Voren said nothing in reply, staring out across the fields. Then, before Tigai could take a place beside him, Voren turned, and he saw a different face—a Jun face—where the old man's had been.

He almost tethered himself to the strands by reflex. Instead he managed a half yelp before Voren shushed him.

"Your surprise would tell me enough," Voren said. "If our Lord hadn't already confirmed it. You're no grandmaster. And clearly you've never met a Fox before."

"A...what?" he said. "What is this? Who are you? What are you?"

"Calm," Voren said. "Better if we don't wake the others. I am Fei Zan, Grandmaster of the Great and Noble House of the Fox."

A *magi*. He'd come halfway across the bloody world to escape their games, and could as well gone parading through Ghingwai waving a red flag and setting anchors to drop fireworks from rooftops. How the fuck was there a *magi* here?

"Our Lord has taken especial notice of you," Fei Zan continued. "He told me of your coming in my last communion. He promised you would arrive with the vessel of our ancient enemy; a greater prize than even I had imagined, coming here to help the ascendant of Order."

"What the bloody fuck are you talking about?" Tigai said.

"How much do you know?" Fei Zan said. "Do you know anything at all?"

Tigai glared, and kept silent. He knew enough to send this fucking bastard to the middle of the ocean at the barest hint of a threat to him, or his family.

"We are in a time of ascension," Fei Zan said. "Our Lord will choose his champions soon, just as the enemy will choose hers. Fox has been promised a place, in this cycle, but still I must prove myself worthy of our Lord's favor. I came here to secure the ascension of Erris d'Arrent, to displace the creature Paendurion, who has perverted his mistress's ways for so many cycles."

"Erris...the Empress?"

"She was no more than a colonel with a gift for their magic when I found her. I have served our Lord well, and will be rewarded for it. As you might be, if you do the same."

"The only reward I've ever wanted from *magi* was for me and my family to be left the bloody fuck alone," he said.

Fei Zan paused, giving him a considering look.

"I'm done with you," Tigai continued. "With all of you. *Magi* here, *magi* on the other side of the Divide. It's no different. I should never have let Mei talk me into this."

"Our Lord warned me you might require convincing," Fei Zan said.

"What the fuck is that supposed to mean?" he said. "More threats? If you so much as look at me or my family with ill intent—"

Breath left his lungs, and he staggered back a step. His mind registered Fei Zan having moved, a flicker of motion, and a heartbeat later he saw the knife protruding from the left side of his chest.

He shifted his vision to the stars as his knees buckled, finding an anchor set by reflex when they'd stopped for the night. He reached for it, and felt instead the sensation of being picked up beneath his shoulders, roughly yanked from his feet, looking down at his own body slumping face-first into the snow.

Blackness enveloped him. He was among the starfield, but every star had been dimmed, as though they were far in the distance. A figure sat across from him: a robed, white-bearded old man sitting in a reed chair.

"A rare thing, for a Dragon to visit me," the old man said. The voice was warm, but brittle, as though the man was on the verge of dying, but intent on keeping good spirits as he did. "It is my pleasure to welcome you here, into my presence."

"What is this?" Tigai asked. He could feel the sensation of his body, though this wasn't a physical space. Pressing his hands to his chest revealed nothing, only a memory of what touch felt like, with none of the reality. "Am I dead?"

"No, little Dragon," the old man said. "You are not dead. When I let slip my hold on your strands, you will rise in the place you marked, some hours ago. But until then, it would be pleasant if we could converse. Is this agreeable, for you?"

A hole was there, in his chest. He could feel the wound, with his hands that were not hands. "Fei Zan stabbed me," he said, hearing the shock in his own voice.

The old man laughed softly. "The Fox is overzealous, perhaps. He means well."

"Who are you?"

"These days I am known by my titles. Lord, to your fellows, if you find it fitting. Regnant for an older power, by my enemies. A reminder of things long passed. But you are here to speak of things to come, I think."

"I don't..." he said. "I didn't..." Thoughts were fleeting.

"Take a moment to center yourself, if it is needful," the old man said.

It was. His mind spun too fast to consider what had happened. He'd taken plenty of wounds—and erased them, by virtue of his anchors among the strands—but this one seemed to stick, like a spike driven through his chest, pinning him to the ground. He struggled for breath, though somehow he knew he didn't need to breathe here. Another part of him lashed out, trying to grab hold of his anchors, and found nothing. A sensation unlike any he'd felt since...

The tower. The memory snapped into his mind. He'd tried to flee the Tower of the Heron as it collapsed around them, when the shadow came and snuffed out his connections to the strands. This was the same feeling. As though his gift were suspended on the wrong side of a glass, just beyond his reach.

"I've seen you before," he said.

The old man's eyebrows raised. "Yes," the old man said. "You have. Very good. There, the Veil's new incarnation tried to steal you away from me. A regrettable thing. One I would like to correct."

He looked the old man up and down. This was the shadow creature, who'd all but brought the tower down around them? He looked like someone's grandfather.

"Yanjin Tigai," the old man said. "A Dragon, bonded to my enemy."

Once more he paused to settle himself. Whatever his surroundings, this old man was clearly a creature of power. Mei would chide him to remember the first lessons of politics. Watch. Observe. Be sure before acting. Gather what information your enemies offer, then reflect on how the revelations revealed their aims.

"Your enemy," he said. "Who is your enemy?"

The old man smiled. "You do not understand, I think, the nature of our bonds. How fragile they are. And yet we have built empires, and countless cycles, on the balance between them."

Tigai kept silent, waiting for more. Another of Mei's lessons: to let others fill empty spaces in conversation.

"Dragon is mine," the old man said. "Yet now the girl has claimed some measure of the power, in linking with you."

"Sarine is your enemy?" he asked.

"After a fashion," the old man said. "What she has done threatens too much, goes too far. I believe the girl to be a pawn, no matter whether she knows her place."

The threads of the old man's words spun in his mind. Mei or Dao would have handled this better. But he was here, as much as he was standing under a tree with a bloody knife in his chest. There was a threat here, one he needed to understand.

"You brought me here because Sarine and I are the only... Dragons... on this side of the Divide," he said. "The starfield here is all but empty; I'll be able to see every star she creates, every time she uses the gift."

Again the old man smiled.

"You mean for me to track her for you," Tigai continued. "Or... to kill her?"

"Yes," the old man said, "to both. She is a danger to all creation, whether she realizes her place or no."

"And what do you offer in return?"

This time the old man's smile broke into a soft laugh. "There are those among your fellows who would spend their lives in meditation, content to sacrifice all they have for a glimpse of the divine. And yet you seek to barter for my favor."

Tigai held his silence.

"Very well, then," the old man said. "Do as I ask, and I will grant your heart's desire. Safety, for your family. A chance for you to be their provider. The strength to tell the rest of the world to... fuck itself, I think, are the words you would use. Do I have the measure of you, Yanjin Tigai?"

67

ERRIS

2nd Corps Encampment
Tamaléne Province, Old Sarresant

Pennons and flags from the ships flew over territory her engineers
had all but converted into a new city. Tents stretched in neat rows
and blocks for each regiment, with orderly latrines, horse-lines, wagon
tracks, and cookfires, but the bulk of the engineering had been focused
on the docks. New wood piers stretched like fingers from a formerly
barren coastline, welcoming the New Sarresant Navy as her ships
continued to make landings at every hour of the day and night. She'd
seen all of it through *Need*, aiding her logistics officers in every detail.
It was something else to see it in person, and all the more so when she'd
expected to be a continent away when they made landfall.

"A mighty army, Your Majesty," the Lady Mei said. Already the traces
of her foreign accent were disappearing; hard to miss the hours spent
practicing, when they'd kept close company on the road.

"A shame you told them we were coming," Tuyard said, sitting atop his
horse opposite Mei. The rest trailed only a few paces behind, though she'd
demanded a hard pace since Tigai had taken them across the sea. "I would
have loved to see de Tourvalle's face when he sees we arrived before him."

"It's more than just de Tourvalle," she said. "They had riders this
morning, from the capital."

"The Dauphin's taken notice of us, then?" Tuyard asked.

She reined Jiri around, catching Essily as he nudged his mount toward her. "See to it that the generals, and the Yanjins, are put up in proper accommodations," she said. "Then ride for the command tents. I want a full accounting of the current command structure and liasons with the Third Corps and Gand ships. Tell them to send whoever they need, to make the report."

"Yes, Your Majesty," Essily said, spinning his mount to deliver her commands.

"We part ways, for now, Lady Mei," she said. Mei lowered her head in a fluid motion, moving to join the others. "Tuyard, you're with me."

Tuyard nudged his mount closer to her. "It's the Dauphin himself, isn't it? I recognize those bloody banners. He didn't send a messenger. The Dauphin is here in person."

It had been the first thing she'd noticed, coming into view of the camp. Something she hadn't seen, during her *Need* connection to de Tourvalle's aide before the morning's ride: a row of purple banners on the far edge of the camp, coming from the south, where the capital city of Sarresant—Old Sarresant—was nestled no more than a swift day's ride from the coast. Even without seeing the designs, she knew they'd bear the three-pronged flowers of the Aegis of the King.

"Let's go," she said. "Time to find out whether we're an alliance or an invasion."

———

They dismounted outside the central tents, and were ushered inside with no more fanfare than if they'd sailed with the ships. Field-Marshal de Tourvalle, commander of her 2nd Corps, was seated at the head of the table, and his counterpart, Major-General Wexly of the Gand contingents of her army. Colonel Marquand was there, too, one of the first volunteers to sail with the army when they'd left colonial shores, now entrusted with planning how their binders would be used in the coming action. Two marquis-generals sat opposite them, a man and woman, flanking a man in civilian's clothes who had to be the Dauphin: Gau-Michel de l'Arraignon, heir to the throne of Sarresant. He wore a purple cloak trimmed with sable fur over top of a blue doublet stitched with flowers on the cuffs and shoulders. Her officers rose at once as she made her entry, while the three on the opposite side stayed seated.

"Your Majesty," de Tourvalle said in his crisp, aristocratic style. "A great regret, that the service kept me overseas for your investiture."

"Time for greetings later," she said, coming to the middle of the long table they'd set up beneath the elongated tent. She turned toward their still-seated counterparts. "We're here to discuss other, more important matters."

"Of course," de Tourvalle said. "Your Majesty, allow me to present his most senior highness, Gau-Michel de l'Arraignon, Dauphin of the Kingdom of Sarresant, and his esteemed advisors, the Marquis-Generals Holliard and Beauchamp, of the Eighth and Second Royal Infantry Divisions, respectively."

Their titles seemed to grate on them; it took a moment to register that de Tourvalle introducing them first was the likely reason why. Few parties on either side of the ocean would outrank the heir to Sarresant's throne.

"And to Your Highness," de Tourvalle continued, "I have the honor of presenting Her Majesty Erris d'Arrent, Empress of New Sarresant and Gand in the New World and High Commander of both armies, and her servant Guillaume Tuyard, High Admiral of the New Sarresant Navy and Hereditary Marquis of the Tetain Reach."

"When Lord de Tourvalle told us, I'd scarce believed it," the Dauphin said. "Last reports of the colonies said they'd been overrun by rabble, but rabble with pretensions to *égalité*. And now he presents me with an Empress."

The bite in his words hung in the air. A predictable barb; she'd anticipated as much and worse, planning for how to make her landing. But then, if her scouts' reports were good, there was a reason Gau-Michel had made the ride to meet her in person. And a reason their landing had gone unmolested, with damn near every Sarresant soldier stationed along the south and eastern borders, well away from the sea.

"Your belief is of little concern to me, Your Highness," Erris said. "What should concern us both are the two armies I am landing on your northern shores. I'd as soon not waste time conquering your cities before putting my soldiers in the field."

"Is that how this exchange is meant to go?" the Dauphin said. "You're expecting a swift surrender? You, who rose from putting a knife in my brother's back?"

She glanced back at her side of the table. De Tourvalle was wide-eyed, Wexly calmly studying the exchange, and Marquand full of fire.

"Enough," she said. A curtness she'd always wanted to affect, for nobles, and now as Empress she bloody well could speak as she pleased. "Enough bluster. Neither of us has time for pride. You'd have met me with twenty thousand regulars if you had them to spare. Instead you come with a white flag, demanding parley. You know as well as I that my armies could seize your cities and buckle your supply lines. If I'd cast our lot with the Thellan commander, this war would be over, and your and your father's heads would roll quicker than we could raise our flag above your palace."

The Dauphin sat straighter in his seat, while his generals were both already rigid. "If you know anything at all of what it means to be a child of Sarresant, you know we would resist you. Pride is a virtue of the Veil, in our scripture. You may well have snuck a landing on our shores, but setting foot on ground does not make it yours. This land belongs to the people who have bled for it, and will again, even if we must fight against our wayward sons and daughters come home."

"We have a common enemy, Your Highness," Tuyard tried to say, for once replacing his usual sneering wit with deference. "You will recognize—"

"We have nothing in common, Guillaume," the Dauphin snapped. "I sent you to safeguard Louis-Sallet on his fool's expedition across the sea, and you as good as sent back a courier with his head."

"I have reports already detailing your two fronts," Erris said. "You're facing a superior force, outnumbered two, perhaps three to one. That you'd stationed no more than token sentries along a coastline that could be threatened by Gand sea power suggests you either haven't considered the possibility of their reentering the war, or you couldn't spare the soldiers to hold against them. You are without allies. I've landed two full armies of fresh troops and provisions, and I am telling you plainly: Tuyard is right. We share an enemy here. You're in no position to make demands, but I am, and I will speak them plainly. Give me full command of your military. Give me access to your granaries, your teams and wagons. Feed my soldiers, deliver my orders to yours, and you can retain whatever titles and power you want over the daily lives of your citizenry. Remain Kings, keep your palaces, but recognize that whoever has been in command of this campaign is a hopelessly incompetent fool. Join your strength to mine, and I will defeat our common enemy. I ask no more price than your loyalty in defending this country, and your faith that I can see it done."

The Dauphin met her eyes with a cold stare. No one else in the tent moved. Every assessment she'd given had been accurate; he had to know his position was beyond hope, defending against two—potentially three—hostile forces, if he opted to reject her terms. He seemed to be weighing her words, searching for some hidden meaning. She stared back with as much cool assurance as she could manage. If he was sane or rational he would see the right of her proposal, or at least that he was in a position to demand no better.

"I never imagined," the Dauphin said finally, "that you would support such a barbarous creature, Tuyard. This sort of conqueror's bluster is beneath us. It is savage, and ignoble. I half expect her to violate the terms of truce, to have me imprisoned or tortured for daring to speak in person."

She slammed the table, recoiling the rest of them as she rattled its frame.

"The Nameless take your fucking pride," she said. "I'll murder you and every nobleman in my way, if that's what it takes. I'm here to *save* this country, you bloody fool. Propriety counts for nothing, with this enemy gathering on your borders. I've faced the man behind the Thellan armies, and their Sardian alliance. He won't stop until he's put down like a mad dog."

"With all due respect, Your Majesty," the Dauphin said, putting enough venom in the honorific to leave little doubt how much of that he thought was due, "talk like that is rabid enough for my taste. I came here to treat with civilized men and women. There are plenty of those on all sides of this conflict. Whatever you think, the Thellan saw advantage in our weakness, in the aftermath of the Gand war. This move is little more than an attempt to redress grievances we exacted as victors in our last conflict. Trade concessions, and territory along the Capallains. I make no secret of our vulnerability, here and abroad. You would have done better talking terms—and no mistaking, with a man such as Guillaume Tuyard in your retinue, there are plenty among your councils who understand the politics, no matter your zeal. Whatever authority you imagine you have comes from your usefulness as a weapon to them, if you have any real authority at all."

Tuyard laughed, with a wry, sardonic bite.

"Gau-Michel, my old friend," Tuyard said. "If you wish to be the next in the line of men and women who have tried to control Erris d'Arrent, you are welcome to it. I gave up when I realized she was right. Her control of the leylines is second only to the man she calls her enemy—*our* enemy. This isn't a war for land, or sheep, or the right to call a man your vassal. This is a war for magic itself. You have no weapon that can stand against d'Arrent's *Need*. You've proven it, in losing two wars now to the man who wielded it, first for Gand, and now for Thellan."

Tuyard rose from the table, standing as he gestured toward de Tourvalle, Wexly, and Marquand. "Consider those who follow her. She's accepted nobles, commoners, foreigners, and drunkards, and given each a position commensurate with their ability. It runs afoul of everything I used to think I knew, but I've seen the results. Her army moves like a serpent, and strikes like the Exarch's own steel. Her terms are generous, Your Highness. Give her the command. She will even find a use for your talents. All she asks in return is your loyalty."

"She called me a hopelessly incompetent fool," the Dauphin said. "I hardly think—"

"If you've been in command of this country's defenses until now, then that's what you are," Erris said. "At least in military matters. But if you value your country, you'll be wise enough to see it, and defer."

The Dauphin fell quiet, exchanging quick glances with the generals at his side.

"Show me," he said finally. "Show me what you would do, in full command of our armies."

"Colonel Marquand," she said. "If you would have the aides fetch us some maps?"

68

SARINE

Library
Gods' Seat

Sarine closed the leather-bound tome, sending a thud ringing through the stacks of books and scrolls. Reyne hardly seemed to notice, if he noticed at all, engrossed in his own readings, seated on a cushioned couch at the center of the room. She'd been poring through the words half the morning, though time had a strange meaning here, with no windows to reveal the sun's rising and setting, and only the map room for a connection with what might be happening in the real world. She'd spent time there, too, learning the intricacies of foreign coastlines and looking in on familiar sights and places. None of it had yet revealed answers. Even this book—finally, a copy of Axerian's Codex—had proved little more than the gibberish Zi had promised her it was on their first reading. A set of instructions cloaked in riddles, when she needed more.

She rose, stretching her legs, and walked to the nearest shelves of books. A row of tomes of philosophy and religion, though the names and subjects were strange. A treatise on thought and knowledge by a man called Fremont, another on the virtues by Moore. Then . . . hadn't there been a book by Fantiere, before? She scanned the shelves, searching for one of the few names she'd recognized.

"I've deciphered this section," Reyne called from his couch. "A new passage. A call to arms, to join the Thellan forces across the sea."

"Did you take Fantiere's *Treatise* from these shelves?" she asked.

"What? No, only the Codex. But don't you see? This means there is still a path to follow. Even if the Gods are gone from this place, they left a path to guide us."

She frowned, turning back to the shelves. Fantiere's book was gone, and others, though she couldn't remember what the names had been, before. There had been books on ethics, epistemology, and the natural sciences. Now there were tomes of what appeared to be history intermingled with the books on philosophy. Impossible for them to have been there from the start; she would have picked them first, if they had been.

"This next section is written in the Skovan tongue," d'Agarre said with rising excitement. "It must be more of the same."

She withdrew an unattributed tome labeled *The Seventh Cycle*, propping it against the shelf as she thumbed it open. A map greeted her at the book's center, drawn across both pages in vivid color. She recognized the contours of the continents from the map room, but in place of Sarresant, the same country was labeled *Renfars*, spilling over to claim the eastern half of the Old World and most of northern Bhakal. Where the colonies of New Sarresant should have been, instead there was a bar of solid color enveloping all of the New World, labeled *The Chorani Nation*, even spilling over the sea to claim the islands of Gand and some of the Thellan coasts in the Old World. In the East, a hundred patches of color made a quiltwork of the countryside, each labeled as belonging to a Great and Noble House: Fox, Dragon, Lotus, Ox, Heron, Crane, Crab, and more.

"Sarine?" Reyne said after she'd studied its pages for a while. "Have you found anything in your Codex?"

"No," she said absently. "And I don't expect to. Zi was right; it's just a tool Axerian used to control the *kaas*-mages."

"What?" Reyne said. "After all my searching this place, we finally find copies, and you dismiss it so readily? I've spent a lifetime studying its words. I assure you, it's much more than you seem to think."

She paused, leaving a finger to mark her place. "How long did you search for it?"

"Every day, since I came here," he snapped back. "Don't you understand? This book guided my every step toward ascension. Without it I've been blind. It can show us the way forward, if we study its secrets. I promise it will aid you, if you only consider it."

She glanced back at the shelf. Had it changed again, while she wasn't looking at it? The empty space where she'd withdrawn the tome she carried was still there, but sure enough, alongside it were two more volumes with identical bindings: *The Eleventh Cycle*, and *The First Cycle*.

She closed the *Seventh* and withdrew the *First*. Once again the center pages were a map, but whereas the last tome had been a colored illustration of the same continents and world she recognized from the map room, this one was all black and gray, a network of lines that suggested the shapes of the continents without etching their coasts, more akin to a maze of underground tunnels and passages than landmasses.

Thumbing through its pages revealed much the same content as the prior volume: a history of strange peoples—the Amaros, Vordu, and Jukari—whose names echoed faintly in her memory. She flipped back to the beginning, finding the title page, and though the spine was unattributed, there was a signature beneath its words:

The First Cycle
A Chronicle of Events Transpired
By Axerian ben Nassad, First Speaker of the Shamesh School of the
Dhasalam Jukari

She read it again to be sure, and had to blink to see the script without Anati translating it for her into the Sarresant tongue. In its original form it was lines, dots, and half squares—nothing she recognized as lettering. But through Anati she saw the name, plain and clear: Axerian. He'd written this. And somehow, some force had placed it here for her to find.

"Sarine?" Reyne said. By now he'd closed his tome, though how long he'd been glaring at her she couldn't have said.

"How does this place work?" she asked. "Who stocks the shelves?"

"I haven't a clue," Reyne said. "And that's hardly our concern. You asked for my aid in uncovering the mysteries surrounding the nature of the Veil, and the Codex is the logical place to start."

Once more she ignored him, carrying *The First Cycle* to the table where she'd piled her other volumes. Whatever Axerian had done to poison d'Agarre's mind, it seemed to center on his Codex. A dangerous reminder of what might be possible, with unknown magic. But something had wanted her to have this book. Or perhaps her own need, coupled with d'Agarre's, had produced first the Codex, and then Axerian's histories.

She closed her eyes, centering her thoughts on her need for answers. The Veil's emotions pulsed at the periphery of her awareness, and she centered there, forming the words into her questions: *How do I do what she could do? How do I become the Veil?*

D'Agarre said something, posing a question she barely heard. All her focus poured itself into her need for answers. Blue sparks seemed to flicker at the edge of the darkness, suggesting a faint shimmer of the way she'd come to travel here, the infinite planes lined with vortices of pure energy. And suddenly a different shape. A human shape, moving toward the bookshelves.

She shot her eyes open in time to see a shadow vanish from her sight.

"What are you doing?" Reyne asked. She'd already all but leapt from her seat, darting toward the bookshelf.

"Who are you?" she asked. "What are you?"

"Who is what?" Reyne asked.

"I saw it," she said. "A creature—something here, reading our thoughts."

She left Reyne frowning and looking pensive while she approached the bookshelf. Sure enough, the volumes had changed again. The *Cycles* had been replaced by parchment and scrolls, and a small, leather book stuffed full of loose pages.

"Paendurion said nothing about any creatures living here," Reyne said.

She picked up the leather book and opened it, cradling it to preserve the ordering of its contents. Handwritten notes decorated its pages in what appeared to be a dozen different languages and styles of scripts. Anati translated it in bursts as she read, flipping through to make sense of what it contained. As many sketchings and hand-drawn scenes as sections of words. A drawing of a cave; another of what appeared to be a palace, with towering spires rising higher than the clouds. And a perfect depiction of the infinite planes and energy storms she'd navigated to reach this place, with a label: *The Master's Sanctum*, and another: *The Soul of the World*.

"This is a journal of some kind," she said, continuing to read. "Chronicling someone's travels to reach this place."

Reyne moved alongside her, pointing so suddenly she almost pulled the book away. "I recognize that script," he said. "I've seen it used in the Codex. Saruk always said it was old—older than his father's father."

"Whatever the creature is stocking these shelves, it's trying to help us," she said. She lowered the journal. "What are you?" she said, addressing the room. "I know you're here. You don't need to be afraid. Show yourself, please. Maybe we can help you, too."

For a moment the room was silent. Then the same shadow flickered at the corner of her sight, near the entryway to the hall. Again it had a human shape, only this time it beckoned to her, then vanished around the corner.

She bounded after it, reaching the smooth stone exit in time to see the shadow once again beckoning to her as it disappeared down a bend in the corridor. *Red* and *Body* came in a rush, and she followed. It darted around corners, each time pausing to gesture to her, until she rounded the wide entryway into the massive stone chamber at the heart of the halls, where the column of pure light burned at its center.

Yuli was standing less than an arm's length from the light, and withdrew her hand sharply as soon as Sarine came into view.

"Yuli?" she said. "Are you okay?"

"Sarine," Yuli said. "I didn't...I wasn't..."

"What were you doing?" she asked. "That light killed Lin, after she attacked Paendurion."

"I...don't know," Yuli said, her face reddening. "I wanted to understand this place. It felt right. Forgive me. I was being a fool."

"It's all right," she said. Before she could say more, Reyne rushed into the chamber behind her.

"Did you find it?" he asked.

"No," she said. Then, for Yuli's benefit, she added, "We came here chasing a shadow. Some sort of creature that lives here. It was helping me, in the library. Finding books I needed, changing the contents of the shelves."

"A shadow?" Yuli said. "Like the creature that attacked us in the tower?"

"No," she said, then stopped herself. Perhaps it was a similar thing. "That is, I can't be sure. But that shadow was hostile. This one... it seemed to want to help. I followed it here, after it gave me histories written by Axerian himself. And this." She held aloft the journal.

Yuli gave her a quizzical look.

"A journal," she said. "It has answers, or at least knowledge I think I'll need to have, before..."

She trailed off. The pages had fallen open in her hand, to a scene depicting a wide stone room with a blazing light at its heart. It showed two figures standing on opposite sides of the light, one of them touching the column while the other channeled an aura of energy enveloping them both. A caption was written beneath the picture: *The Binding of a Champion in the Gods' Seat.*

"Before what?" Yuli asked.

"What exactly were you doing here?" she asked. "What drew you to this room?"

"I don't know," Yuli said. "As I said, I was being a fool."

"You said it felt right. When I came in, you were almost touching the light."

"That's how it went, when I first arrived here," Reyne said. "The Veil was imprisoned in crystal, over top of where that light now burns."

"You touched it?" she asked him.

"Yes," Reyne said, and pointed to the drawing in the journal in her hand. "It was like this. A flash of light, arcing between me and the crystal. Then... power. Saruk renewed his stores."

She glanced down, reading the passage inscribed beneath the drawing. Had the shadow opened the journal? It had led her here, of a surety, after she'd prompted it that she needed to learn how to become the Veil.

"Anati?" she asked. "Do you know what this text means?"

I don't, she replied. *I've never been bound here.*

"I think..." she said. "I think I might understand what this is telling me to do. If I use the blue sparks to set a warding around us both before you touch it, I think it will protect you. It says this is how a champion is bound."

"A champion," Reyne said. "Yes. Paendurion made some mention of it."

"What does it mean?" Yuli asked.

"Power," Reyne said simply. "But, more. More than he told me, in any case."

"Is this what I'm supposed to do?" Sarine asked. She meant it for the shadow, though the creature made no move to show itself.

"It feels right," Yuli said. "I can't explain why, but it's as though the light is why I came here."

"Will you try it, then, if I can shield you?" she asked. "I'm not certain what will happen, and I can't promise you'll be safe."

"Death comes for us all, Sarine Thibeaux," Yuli said. "Yes. I will do this."

Sarine nodded and closed her eyes, finding the reserve of blue sparks pulsing inside her. The sparks had always been there when she called; this time they swirled like a river current, moving in a massive surge as they flowed through the chamber. She reached to set her wardings, directing the river of blue sparks into physical space. One shell around herself, and a second around Yuli.

"Now," she said, and Yuli stepped forward, her hand outstretched toward the light.

Even before she touched it, a streak of energy shot from the column at the center of the room, lancing out to connect Yuli to the beam of light. Thunder rang in Sarine's ears as the blue sparks flooded through her. Then Yuli's fingers dipped into the stream.

Sound vanished, save for a single, pure note.

The blue sparks flowed around them both, touching and blending into the column of light.

A glittering shell spread from where Yuli's fingers touched, flowing over top of the wardings as though dipping them in gold.

A jarring pull grabbed hold of the flow of blue energy between the two spheres, yanking it almost free of her grasp.

The Veil. Anati's voice. *She's here.*

Thunder roared in her ears as she struggled to keep hold. The current that had run between the two spheres now roiled around them, each seeming to pull apart from the other. Beams of light shot from the column as the sparks pulled back and forth between her grip and the Veil's, melting stone in hissing streams of smoke and ash wherever they touched.

Yuli stood beneath a golden shell, her fingers still submerged in the light.

A human-shaped shadow hovered next to Yuli, cowering as it stayed beneath the shell.

Reyne watched in fascination, his skin somehow coated in blue.

The Veil raged inside her, exerting force enough to pull the current, but not enough to seize control. Sarine pulled harder, forcing it into place.

And then it was done.

Yuli withdrew her touch, and Sarine collapsed to her knees. Where she'd stood was solid stone, and a small bubble around Yuli. Reyne's footsteps had preserved the smoothness of the floor beneath them. The rest of the chamber was molten ruin. Tranches of stone had been cut and turned to slag, like a thousand miniature valleys carved in floors, walls, and ceiling. The column of light at the center still burned, but where the edges had been clean, now they were cut in jagged formations, revealing sections of the beam ten paces above and below where the chamber had ended before.

"I feel...different," Yuli said. "Rested. At peace. As though I could summon the Twin Fangs at will."

"That's how it was for me," Reyne said. "Well, perhaps not quite like... *that*. But as though my *kaas* had boundless stores."

Are you all right? Anati asked her.

"No," Sarine said, feeling a rush of emotion as she fought to calm her nerves. "I think it's done, but I'm bloody well not all right. I need her gone, Anati. I can't do this with the Veil lurking inside me, threatening to ruin whatever I touch."

The Goddess is bound, as strongly as I can seal her.

"It's not enough," she said. "If we can't bind her, then before we try anything else, we need to find a way to cut her out."

69

TIGAI

At the Base of a Hill
The Capallain Mountains, Old Sarresant

K eep together," Acherre said, repeating her words in the tribesfolk's
tongue after she said it in Jun.

Voren rode behind her, with Tigai next, and Ka'Inari beside him.
Since the first night he'd made it a point to keep Voren where he could
see him, and been rewarded with no new knives in his chest, though
there had been few enough answers to go with it. During the days his
only concern was keeping warm and pacing himself as they crossed
through the foothills in the southern country of what Acherre called Old
Sarresant. In a week they had to have covered eight hundred leagues,
rotating between horses and using Acherre's magic to keep them fresh,
save for Arak'Jur, who covered the same distance on foot. A madman's
pace. Fitting, considering his company.

"Stay alert," Acherre said in the Jun tongue. "There will be...
guards?...as we approach the army."

"Pickets," Voren said, giving her the proper word. "Forward scouts."

Acherre nodded. "Let them see us coming."

Tigai squinted, scanning the thinly wooded rises of the next hillside.
Bloody miserable place to put an army. His brother would have
negotiated three times the usual contract, if any general had tried to hire
the Yanjin companies to dig into these mountains in wintertime. At least

the skies were blue and cloudless, though the sun seemed too cold by half. Booming sounds in the distance signaled the presence of artillery, though they were faint and uneven, echoing between the hillsides as they bounced from a battlefront ten leagues away.

"Did we expect a battle here?" Tigai asked as their horses climbed the hillside. Acherre said nothing, continuing to scan the hills. He left her to it. Better to keep his eyes on Voren.

Voren let his horse fall back as Acherre pushed ahead. Tigai held the reins steady. No reason to let the *magi* see any fear.

"I won't strike you again," Voren said abruptly, when their horses came together. "Not unless you ask me to. You can stop riding as though you mean to court me."

"I'd sooner court your horse," he said.

"You understand, I had to surprise you. The communion is done by bringing the subject to the brink of death, without—"

"I don't need to know your *magi* secrets," he said, half meaning it.

Voren maintained his pace, keeping his mount in lockstep with Tigai's. "You're a young man," Voren said finally.

"What does that matter?"

"Your pride means a great deal to you. But our Lord sees our deepest desires, and he has the power to grant them. In time you will see this, and let go your pride."

"How did you know what that creature spoke of?"

"It's evident in your demeanor," Voren said. "But you've had time enough for sulking, I think. What did our Lord require of you?"

"I never asked for this," he said instead of answering. "All I wanted was to see to my family's concerns, to get as far away from *magi* business as I could."

Acherre hissed something in the Sarresant tongue, accompanied by a gesture that made clear she wanted silence. He gave it, falling quiet with a glare for Voren's benefit. But for all the *magi*'s smugness, he'd felt real power after he'd been stabbed, during whatever had transpired with the old man among the stars. A frightening thing. Not near compelling enough for him to want to be stabbed again, but a dark reminder of how life had transpired since his family's capture. The old man among the stars had invoked his desire to keep his family safe, and in truth it was all he'd ever wanted: the strength to tell the world to fuck itself. Mei's bargaining had ensnared him and brought him here, to a foreign hillside with foreign companions; before that it had been Indra, and their father's debts. It would be nice, for once, to be the one who set the terms of his own bloody life.

"Down," Acherre said. "Keep the horses back."

He slid from the saddle a moment after Acherre did, handing the reins to Voren. Acherre was crouching as she approached the hilltop. Not the sort of behavior he expected, approaching what was supposed to be a friendly line. He joined her, staying low. Not likely they could hide sign of their passage, having left leagues of tracks and hoofprints in the snow. But given the thumping booms in the distance, he understood her caution. Soldiers maneuvering for battles could spin and dance until one side held the other's territory. If they weren't careful, they could well run headlong into a hostile supply train, if those booms did indeed signify a battle.

Except, when they reached the crest, it wasn't a battle. It was a rout.

Across uneven fields of snow and rocky foothills, he saw waves of soldiers breaking to the north. Only small dots at this range, still leagues away, but with none of the smoke clouds he would have expected if their marksmen were exchanging fire. Instead he saw surges of dots, breaking as they climbed hills and melted wide swaths in the snow. From their vantage he saw only part of the field, with the rest obscured by a range of hills some leagues to the east, but he saw enough to know the retreat was taking its soldiers northward, and unless they'd somehow been spun around, it meant Erris d'Arrent's allies were on the losing side.

"*Dieux damnés putain de merde sanglante,*" Acherre said in the Sarresant tongue. Clear enough from her delivery it was a curse.

Voren shuffled up the crest behind them, holding their three mounts in tow. He began speaking with Acherre in the Sarresant tongue. Heated words, but Tigai didn't bother listening. He'd been right. For once in his life, caution had proved the wiser course, and he'd been right to counsel Mei to learn more of the dealings on this side of the Divide before pledging their family to one side or the other. Hearing d'Arrent talk about the goings-on here, he'd expected lines of soldiers squaring off in the mountains, perhaps a skirmish or two. Nothing close to the waves of blue specks he saw retreating in the distance. She must have misjudged the strength of their enemies.

"Tigai," Voren said. He turned to find Acherre's eyes glowing gold beside Voren, with both of them staring at him. "The Empress needs you to bring a company of binders to this location at once. How long will it take you to set an anchor?"

"I've been setting them the whole time we've been traveling," he said. Acherre's eyes pulled his attention, and he found himself staring. It was as though both her pupils had been replaced by miniature suns. He'd seen something like it before, back in Kye-Min. It was as though someone different was looking at him through Acherre's eyes. "I can travel back to the star I used to take us across the sea, and then back here, so long as it's done quickly. The anchor won't hold for long if I'm not familiar with the place where I've set it."

Acherre snapped a few words after Voren translated, and Voren repeated them. "How long do we have to get the company assembled?"

He shrugged. "A few minutes, maybe? Over a distance this large, I can't be sure. If I had a day to wait here, to get familiar with the place—"

"There isn't time," Voren said, "as you can see." He turned back to Acherre and translated again, only to have her repeat the same curse words as before: *Dieux damnés putain de merde sanglante*, this time with a slightly different inflection.

Voren nodded at whatever else she said, and Acherre's eyes snapped back to normal.

"Fifteen minutes," Voren said. "D'Arrent will put together her company and be waiting at the place along the coasts, where you first took us, after crossing the sea. Fifty binders, she says. That should be tolerable, yes?"

He nodded, watching the lines of blue-coated soldiers continuing to scatter. It wasn't natural. So far as he could see, there were no smoke clouds, no bloody pools where limbs had been hacked off by swordplay and spears. It was like…it was like Kye-Min. His stomach turned, remembering the sight of Sarine scattering entire companies without firing a shot. If she was here, or if their enemy had *magi* who could do what she could do…

Acherre was calling out something to Ka'Inari, evidently finished with any pretense of stealth. The tribesman was seated on his horse, with no sign of Arak'Jur, who'd made it a habit of ranging far ahead of them, dismounted though he was. Yet when Ka'Inari approached, Tigai heard him speaking the Jun tongue, the shaman's eyes glassed over as he spoke.

"Arak'Jur has heard Mountain's call," Ka'Inari said. "It will take him through the battle lines. I can see it, and I must go to him, no matter what lies ahead."

Acherre cursed again, this time switching to speak Sinari. Wind spirits but he wished he had Mei's gift for tongues. Instead he approached Voren, standing now in plain view at the crest of the hill.

"How certain are you that you can return here?" Voren asked as he approached.

"I can do it," he said. "Provided the Empress's *magi* are ready to move as soon as we arrive."

"If you fail, it means our travel is wasted, no? That we'd have to travel south again."

"I won't fail."

Voren showed him a grim smile. Knowing the face was false made the creases in the old man's skin appear like clay, or wax.

"This is serious, Lord Yanjin," Voren said. "As serious as anything you have ever attempted in your life."

"My brother is Lord Yanjin," Tigai said.

"Aid me in this—aid our Lord—and you will be remembered as the greater brother."

It was all he could do not to laugh. "I don't give a fuck about titles, and the last thing I want is to steal my brother's inheritance. I'm doing this because Mei asked me to, not for any design of yours, or the creature among the stars."

Acherre and Ka'Inari had descended into heated words, ending on an angry shout from her as the shaman rode his horse forward, down the face of the hillside.

"Where is he going?" Tigai asked.

"The tribesmen have left us," Acherre said. "Some bloody prompting of their bloody spirits. We'll make the trip back alone."

The sight of the shaman—sitting poorly on his horse, riding toward a mass of tens of thousands of fleeing soldiers—could as well have been a frame around a painting, watching the remnants of this battle unfold. This was a damned fool's exercise. He'd have been better served hooking himself to the strands, taking his brother, Remarin, and Mei somewhere else.

"Do you think it's her?" he asked Acherre. "Sarine. The girl."

Acherre seemed surprised at the question, but she replied before Voren could translate. "No," she said. "We saw a man, Reyne d'Agarre, do the same. Could be him. Could be another. Not Sarine."

The rest of the delay passed in silence, watching streams of yellow flags now winding around the hillsides where the view had been blocked, before. Their enemies: the Thellan, and another set of flags, these ones red and white. Acherre cursed and said something about Gandsmen, though in his memory they were allied with d'Arrent. Another faction, perhaps, but all the more vindication that they'd chosen the wrong side.

"It's time," Acherre said when the moment arrived. He nodded, gesturing for them to gather close. His anchors would hold; Voren's worry was none of his. That was the one certainty in all of this: His magic was safe, and solid. That much he could trust, come whatever else got in his way.

He closed his eyes, finding the flickering light he'd punched to make an anchor here, across from the battlefield. It was there. Weak, but he could find it again. To the north he found the first star he'd used on this side of the sea, still shining bright. He tethered them there, flowing smoothly as they traversed the starfield, save for a minor lurch from another star far in the distance. It faded before interfering, and he opened his eyes, standing atop the familiar coastline overlooking the sea.

"Acherre," a man said, followed by some words in the Sarresant tongue. He was in their field uniform, with a hawk pin on his collar and the same design on his sleeves, a red-faced man Acherre greeted as Colonel Marquand. Twoscore men and women gathered in a tight group at his back, every one mounted, with purple armbands fastened around their uniforms' sleeves.

"Take us back," Acherre said, "as quick as you can."

He closed his eyes again, feeling a wave of exhaustion as he projected his will to cover the top of the bluff. He shifted them, and the star in the distance flickered again, pulling on him as he searched for the faint light far to the south. For a moment the strands shimmered, but he held them in place, and opened his eyes facing the battlefield, surrounded by Marquand's purple-banded soldiers as they rushed down the hillside, already shouting orders as they rode toward the fight.

70

ARAK'JUR

A Battlefield
The Capallain Mountains, Old Sarresant

He is near.

The voice rang in his ears alongside shouting, and the squelching of soldiers running through melted snow mixed with dirt. Mud and abandoned supplies littered the hillsides. A handful of the soldiers held their ground, or tried to, barking sharp orders at their fellows. The rest fled, some in wide-eyed terror, others unsettled by the sight of panic in their ranks. None gave him more than a cursory glance, though he cut a path through the middle of their lines, heading west where the rest were fleeing north.

He'd left Acherre's company earlier that morning, ranging ahead to find game and scout the way. Ad-Shi's lessons had taught him how to cover ground, burning through the spirits' gifts one at a time, relying on his own stamina to fill the gaps while he waited for the beasts' favor to return. He could traverse what had taken Acherre, Ka'Inari, Tigai, and Voren a week in a matter of days, and if it took a heavy toll on his body to do it, Ad-Shi's warnings reminded him such things were fleeting concerns, set against the coming storm. He would have scouted the armies here—three bodies of soldiers, one in blue, and two arrayed against them, one in yellow and one in red—and made his return to Acherre's company already, if not for the voice.

To the south. The man with a thousand threads of gold.

Mountain's voice, and where he'd resisted the urge with Erris d'Arrent, he gave in to it now. Thousands of soldiers poured around him, flowing northward into the hills, shouting at each other as they threw down muskets, abandoned supplies, let horses run free through their lines. He felt as though he were watching them from above, a bird flying over his own body. More shouting came from the south, where the ranks of yellow- and red-clad soldiers were only starting to crest the hills in pursuit of their enemies.

The first wave of gunfire snapped his senses back in place.

Kneeling ranks of yellow-clad soldiers had formed midway up the hill he was crossing, letting loose a barrage of musket fire and a billowing cloud of smoke. Howls sounded from the ranks of blue-coated soldiers, no more than fifty paces to his right, where a company had managed to plant itself behind a makeshift wall of rocks and wood, taking up arms where most of the fellows fled.

"What are you doing?" one of the blue-coated soldiers called to him in the Sarresant tongue. "Get down, you bloody fool!"

Go.

The voice fogged his head again for an instant, shattered by another volley exchanged between the lines. A searing pain took him across his back, and he roared.

No. He was here. The spirits called to him, as strongly as he'd ever felt their pull. But he was here, now.

He spun, facing the length of the yellow-clad soldiers' line. Their soldiers knelt, reloading their weapons, while some men paced along their ranks. Men with golden light behind their eyes, the same effect he'd seen with Erris d'Arrent and her vessels. He saw two of those point to him, as though moved by the same hand, barking orders for their soldiers.

Find him. Kill him.

He ignored the voice's pull. A dozen muskets trained on him at once, and he called on *astahg*, vanishing and leaping forward across the field as they fired. His heart pounded as he ran toward their line. Whatever force was summoning him, he had to push it from his mind, at least for now, or he might well die for it.

Mareh'et granted its blessing as he reached the yellow-clad soldiers' ranks. Instinct said to fight, rather than flee. Three soldiers managed to stand, raising their weapons like spears. He carved through them, a raking strike taking one across the face before he spun to gore the others through their bellies. Shouted warnings rose around him, slower to spread than he could move. He trampled a fourth man, and cut another down, on his way to a woman with stripes on her collar and golden light behind her eyes. She stared at him, shouting something in a foreign tongue as she pointed square at his chest. *Mareh'et*'s claws severed her hand, then her neck. He shoved the rest of her body forward, throwing her corpse into the next rank of soldiers as he drove forward into their line.

Four identical copies of a man met him as he dashed into the yellow-clad soldiers' breaking ranks. Fair-skin magic. Only one would be real. Each copy carried a saber in one hand and a pistol in the other, three copies raising the pistol to aim while the fourth rushed toward him with the blade. Mountain gave its blessing, and fire erupted from his hands, engulfing all four copies in a searing blast. He dashed through the resultant smoke, stepping over the single charred corpse left behind, curled and writhing in the mud.

The soldiers broke, a few staring at him, trembling, while the bulk of their ranks collapsed, fleeing back the way they'd come.

His heart thundered a few more beats as he watched them run. Violence hung around him, mangled bodies twisted and broken in the slush, their blood leaking to turn the mud a deep red and put the tang of iron in the air. Farther up the hillside, the company of Sarresant soldiers cheered, reversing one small piece of the broader retreat.

Then, as one, every man and woman in blue flung their weapons down and ran.

It marked an instant reversal in their spirits: One moment they'd been cheering, watching him eviscerate the soldiers advancing toward them up the hill. The next the Sarresant troops were broken, as sure a rout as the terror he'd instilled in their enemies.

He pivoted and saw what had to be the cause. A rider, a woman in a gray cloak, mounted atop a horse at the far western point of the soldiers advancing up the hill, barking commands in a tongue he couldn't understand. He'd have thought her no more than an officer, albeit one not wearing the other soldiers' uniform, save for the metallic serpent coiled around her forearm, its scales flashing green and silver in the sun.

Llanara. Not her—Llanara was long dead. But her gift. He knew it. A metallic serpent of the very kind that had decimated his people, leading them to madness and war.

He howled, letting out a warcry loud enough to carry over all the sounds of battle and death, and surrounded himself with a nimbus of *lakiri'in* as he charged.

Whatever the gray-cloaked woman had done to scatter the Sarresant soldiers, it seemed to have had the opposite effect on hers. Whereas before they'd broken, retreating down the hillside, they regrouped, turning back to him and leveling or reloading their muskets. Some managed shots, miniature thunderclaps echoing through the hills, but none connected as he raced toward the woman and her metallic companion.

She seemed to realize the danger too late, pivoting her horse toward him only a moment before he struck.

White energy flared around her as he channeled *una're*, snapping her horse's spine with the force of his attack, sending the beast down, rolling over top of its rider as they careened into the mud. The woman pulled herself from the tangle of horseflesh with impossible agility, springing to her feet, turning, and racing away faster than any woman without the guardian's gift should have been able to move. She bolted from the field with long strides, her gray cloak whipping behind her, and never looked back, even as *ipek'a* gave its blessing, surrounding him with a nimbus of feather and claw. He leapt, and fell faster than she could run, crashing into her hard enough to send her head into the ground with a wet smack.

He picked himself up, standing over the ruin of her body, where *ipek'a*'s scything claw had torn a deep gash down her left shoulder and rib cage. The woman was lifeless, lying still, but the serpent had uncoiled itself, staring up at him with fiery gemstones for eyes.

Impossible, the thing thought to him. He heard the sensation of words, though the thing's mouth made no move to form them, just as he had seen with Reyne d'Agarre's pet, so long ago. *We were promised greatness, so long as we complied.*

He said nothing in reply. Regret might well come later; for now there was only blood rushing in his veins. He turned back and saw that whatever magic she'd woven over the soldiers was broken. The company of Sarresant soldiers had rallied again, flocking to their battle standard as their enemies in yellow renewed their uncertainty. A vile thing, to play with men's and women's emotions. A forbidden thing; even without the spirits to confirm it, he knew the rightness of it, watching normalcy assert itself in the wake of his violence. *Ipek'a*'s gift already hummed, waiting at the edge of his consciousness, offering its use if he needed it again. The spirits approved. He could settle the rest when it was done.

Elsewhere on the hillsides the Sarresant soldiers continued their rout, though there were pockets of riders moving among them, clashing with their enemies in isolated displays of resistance. There must have been more like the gray-cloaked woman, serpent-mages riding with Sarresant's enemies. Part of him wanted to join the few who stood against that evil, latecomers on horseback, with purple armbands and fair-skin magic, who must have been kept in reserve to turn the tide of battle. But this was Erris d'Arrent's fight, for all he'd reversed one small piece of the field. His path lay deeper in the mountains, where the voice had dulled itself to an aching, longing sensation, pulling him firmly westward.

He almost turned to go, when another rider caught his eye.

An ungainly shape, thundering toward him too directly to be coincidence. By now the space between the routing Sarresant soldiers and their advancing enemies was littered with bodies and abandoned supplies; the new rider wove through them, heeling their mount in a frenzy, riding toward him in as straight a line as the conditions would allow.

He turned back, feeling the full use of the spirits' gifts available to him. *Lakiri'in* required time. The rest were ready.

The rider had covered all but the final hundred paces before he recognized who it was.

"Ka'Inari," he said as the rider slowed.

"Arak'Jur," Ka'Inari said, the shaman almost as winded as his mount.

"Why did you come?" he asked. "You rode through the battle, and left Acherre?"

"I saw what drew you here," Ka'Inari said between breaths. "A man, marked by Mountain. A man at the center of a web of golden threads. You mean to find him, and I intend to be at your side."

"You could have been killed!" he said.

"Yes," Ka'Inari said.

Tension hung between them, until he relented, the heat in his blood melting at the sight of Ka'Inari, disheveled and ragged, when he had expected almost anything else.

"Keep pace, then," he said. "We have mountains to climb, and a hard path, before we're through."

71

ERRIS

Field Command
Coastal Bluffs, Old Sarresant

She stared, tracing the contours of the map in silence. A small handful of advisors looked on, and thank the Gods they knew better than to speak. Brigade-General Vassail and Field-Marshal Royens flanked her, studying the marks she'd made, signifying the likeliest lines of retreat for the Dauphin's forces through the Capallains.

"Marquand has done all he can," she said. "I'm ordering him to withdraw. We'll need his binders to reinforce the main body of the Third Corps at Orstead."

"Are you certain, Your Majesty?" Vassail asked. "From the sound of your reports, he's held the left flank. Another hour might mean five thousand more able to withdraw."

"Another hour and the enemy might realize what they're up against."

"Is there no means for us to gauge their strength?" Royens asked. "Fifty binders ought to be able to hold here"—he pointed to a gap between two steep hills—"provided we can guide the Dauphin's soldiers to allow the choke to cover their retreat."

She shook her head. "It's too great a risk to keep Marquand in the field. If the enemy realizes we've committed so many binders, they'll respond in kind. We need better scouting reports before I'm willing to make that kind of gamble."

Vassail looked pained, but nodded, remaining silent. Royens rubbed the stubble on his chin, looking less convinced, but just as quiet, letting her order stand unchallenged.

"Very well, then," she said. "I'll make the connection."

She gave a last look at the maps. Yellow bars had been placed to signify the strength of the Thellan advance, arrayed in haphazard lines spread through the hills. Such an uncoordinated attack should never have worked. Gods send the eastern lines were less of a disaster than those in the south.

"These reports must be faulty," Marquis-General Holliard was saying, from the opposite side of the table. "This is General Renard's division. He would never break so easily, facing down Thellan cowards and Gand peasants."

Ordinarily she'd have chastised such a remark—denying reality for the sake of ego was among the deadliest pitfalls of command—but there was something damned odd about this southern rout. She needed to know what had broken their line. Time for it after her orders were given. A deep breath and she found *Need* within herself. A wellspring, now, where once it had been a tepid, cautious reserve, and the well seemed to grow deeper by the day. Already she had enough to bring herself to the brink, and let her body handle the strain.

Chilled air greeted her as *Need* shifted her senses into the highlands, far to the south, with the sting of powder and iron in her nose and a throbbing pain in her vessel's shoulder.

"Wait for them," Marquand was shouting. "Hold. Hold!"

A wall of *Shelter* stood between her and sight of the field, blocking off the walls of a valley situated between two hills. Twenty of Marquand's binders stood in a loosely spaced line, a single rank against the Nameless knew what awaited them on the opposite side of their shield. Most were dismounted, though some rode, each one facing the *Shelter* with death in their eyes.

"Now!" Marquand cried.

The *Shelter* vanished, and thunder and smoke roared from the other side, while sheets of fire leapt from Marquand's hands and those of a dozen more along his line. Another stabbing pain took her vessel in the leg as the white smoke from the enemy's guns swept back into their lines, pushed by a tide of *Entropy*. Men and women screamed by the hundreds, lost in a mix of black and white smoke.

"Raise *Shelter*!" Marquand shouted, and the barrier resumed, blocking off the sight of their enemies, though the sounds—of howling, screaming, pleading—and the smells of powder and charred flesh remained in the air.

"Report, Colonel," she shouted over the din. Her vessel's voice broke from the pain. Fresh musket shot through the leg, to go with what had to be another wound beneath her right shoulder. Someone else's pain. Someone else's concern.

"D'Arrent!" Marquand shouted back. "Or, Your Majesty, or, fuck me. We're engaged, sir. I don't have time to make a bloody report."

"Marquand!" she snapped. "Your orders are to gather as many of your binders as you can and withdraw from the field."

The thunder of artillery booming nearby triggered her reflex to duck, and Marquand joined her in the dirt, slamming into the ground as canister shot exploded overhead. She blinked, searching for *Shelter*, forgetting it was worthless so long as she was tethered to a vessel through *Need*. Another of Marquand's binders covered them, throwing a shield overhead in time for the metal shards to vaporize into wisps of smoke.

"Marquand," she said again. "Do you understand your orders, Colonel?"

"Fuck those orders," he said. "I have two of our divisions retreating behind me, and bloody good ground at my back. I can hold here for hours. If I leave now, they're fucked. This rout isn't natural. Without my people, they can't—"

"Marquand, you fucking bastard, you listen to me. You are to obey your—"

A wave of musket shot went off, peppering the first *Shelter* shield hard enough to rip it open with a sound like sucking wind.

"Reinforce it!" Marquand shouted.

"Colonel, sir, the reserve is going dry," one of the binders called back. "We have to attack, now!"

"High Commander, or, Your Majesty, sir. Like I said, this rout isn't natural. We can't leave."

"Colonel," she said. "We discuss the tactical situation later. For now I expect you to do your duty. Prove to me I wasn't wrong to promote you."

Marquand winced as though she'd shot him in the belly.

"Retreat," he called to his line. "Use all available *Shelter* to hold the barrier, and fall back to Lord Tigai."

"Good," she said. "Fine work here, Colonel."

"Fuck you, d'Arrent."

Pain throbbed through her vessel's shattered leg. Marquand would have to carry her, and better to do it with the help of her vessel's own adrenaline. She let the *Need* tether go, and felt her senses snap back to the briny air among her tents.

The rest of them were on their feet when her senses cleared, the attachés and advisors from the Old Sarresant Army standing at attention, while Vassail, Royens, and the rest of her attendants eyed the entryway with a mix of deference and unease.

"A use of your *Need* bindings, I presume?" the Dauphin said. He hovered inside the tent, flanked by purple-tabarded Aegis guards, his silks and fur-lined cloak making him look like something out of a painting, no matter that she technically outranked him.

"Yes," she said, resisting the urge to add an honorific. "Though I'm afraid I'll have to leave it to others to brief you on the battle."

The Dauphin gave a nod of respect as she left him to his people.

"Your Majesty," Vassail said. "What news from Marquand?"

"Hotly engaged, and retreating, as ordered. Twenty will make it out with Lord Tigai. The rest are dispersed among the front lines, or dead."

"So few left with him?" Royens said. She nodded; it wouldn't do to question Marquand's orders. He knew binders and their uses as well as any soldier in any army.

"I need theories," she said, "and speculation. The cause of the rout. What it might mean for the next weeks of this campaign. How many survivors we can expect to regroup, once they traverse the foothills."

"Fifteen thousand," Vassail said. "Three divisions were well enough to the north when the fighting began. They'll escape clean, though none are close to full strength. The rest are lost."

"There were forty thousand soldiers in that army, General," she said. "You expect sixty percent casualties?"

"You saw the disposition of the battle, Your Majesty. We should plan for a total loss of the front lines, to death or capture. Any survivors would be welcome, of course, but we must assume the worst."

"I concur," Royens said. "And I propose we lay the groundwork for these divisions to be incorporated into our command structure. At the very least we need them outfitted with *Need* vessels before any further action."

"Agreed," she said. "But first, the cause."

Uncomfortable looks passed between Royens and Vassail, and each glanced separately toward the opposite side of the central table.

"Poor leadership, Your Majesty," Royens said. "And weaker discipline. The sight of the Gandsmen having entered the war on Thellan's side must have broken morale. An order to retreat sparked a panic."

His words had carried farther than he'd meant them to; that or something else had brought Gau-Michel and his retinue to a sudden pause.

"Did I hear that aright, Marshal?" the Dauphin said from across the table.

Royens turned to face them, but she spoke first on his behalf.

"I'm sure you did, Your Highness," Erris said. "I'm not in the habit of censoring my advisors' honest assessments for fear their words might offend me."

Now the tent filled with silence.

General Holliard made a half step in her direction. "Your words go further than I'm certain you intend, Your Majesty," she said.

"No," the Dauphin said. "No, d'Arrent is quite right. I hadn't yet been told of Gand's involvement." He said it with a glare for the attendants standing around him. "Are you quite certain the Queen has committed her soldiers to the fighting? I don't presume to instruct you in military matters, but are you certain it is not a ruse, a trick to dress Thellan companies in Gand uniforms for precisely this effect?"

"If it's a ruse, it's one that involves enough soldiers not to make a difference," she said. "Forty thousand more soldiers is forty thousand more soldiers, no matter what sort of coats they wear."

"Gods," the Dauphin said, staring down at the maps between them. "We'd been afraid of this...but my spies...Gods save us."

She exchanged looks with Vassail and Royens. "Perhaps a briefing is in order, Your Highness," she said. "But for my sake. What is the political situation here?"

"We knew the Thellan treated with the Gandsmen," the Dauphin said. "We thought perhaps, in a season or two, if the matter was yet undecided, Gand might have regained sufficient strength to consider rejoining the fight."

"And it seems they've made their considerations ahead of schedule."

The Dauphin nodded.

"Even if they have committed forty thousand," Royens said, "the bulk will be green and raw, fresh conscripts and pressed soldiers without experience in battle. We smashed their veteran forces at New Sarresant, and we can do it again."

"What of the East?" she asked. "Sardia and Thellan have an alliance already. Are the Skovan princes a threat?"

"I don't..." the Dauphin began, then stopped himself. "They shouldn't be," he said instead. "The princedoms have always fought among each other. It's possible some of them might have been swayed by Thellan promises, but the balance of power has always kept them from acting in concert."

"Circumstances have changed," Erris said. "Paendurion will care nothing for what he has to promise, to bring allies to his side."

"Paendurion?" the Dauphin said.

"The enemy," she said. "The man behind their *Need* bindings—the golden eyes. We have to assume he'll have offered significant concessions to the Skovan. Forty thousand Gandsmen in the south, with fifty more from Thellan. Scouts suggest eighty thousand marching with the Sardians. What would you make of the Skovan princes' strength? Another thirty?"

"Twice so many," the Dauphin said. "Even conservatively."

The tent fell quiet for a moment as she studied the maps. They were outnumbered three to two in the south, and worse than four to three in the east. Enough to stall both fronts, but to pursue decisive victory in neither. With defensive ground, and the advantage of Lord Tigai working with Marquand's binders, they might be able to turn one of the fights while maneuvering away from the second. Given a month to plan, she could devise enough contingencies to feel confident in their odds. As it was, she had days, weeks at best. And they needed decisive action. If what Voren had said was true, time was on Paendurion's side. She didn't need to hold territory; she needed to shatter his armies' confidence in him, and in their alliance. She needed boldness.

"Gau-Michel, will you dismiss your aides, please?" she said. "And mine—go with them. The Dauphin and I must speak privately."

Vassail, Royens, and the rest of her support staff turned to go at once. The Dauphin turned to his advisors first, then locked eyes with her.

"What is this about, Your Majesty?" the Dauphin said.

"Our mutual appetite for victory. If you please, Highness."

He nodded, a bare fraction, and his people obeyed, save the two Aegis guards in purple, hovering along the rear wall of the tent. He eyed her as though to ask whether she intended for them to leave as well, and to make clear he would refuse, if she asked it.

"I suspect this will be unpleasant," the Dauphin said when the others were gone. "But need I remind you, the terms we've agreed to have been more than generous, considering this began with your armed invasion of our shores."

"I don't intend to renegotiate the terms of our alliance," she said. "I intend to win this war, now. By springtime both forces will be fortified, and the campaign will turn to which side's farms can better feed their soldiers."

"Yet you demand a private audience. Why?"

"Because victory now means sacrifice."

He eyed her without speaking, as though she might reveal her plans on her face. And well she might. Whatever training she'd had at Voren's and Tuyard's hands, she was still a soldier.

"Our only chance of breaking this enemy is focusing all our strength on one front," she said. "We commit everything—every binder, every reserve, in an all-out attack. Crush them, then pivot and defeat the other force."

The Dauphin looked down at her maps cautiously; it was clear from his face that he hadn't yet understood the implications of her words. "A bold plan," he said. "I assume you'd focus on the southern front? Fewer enemies there, and after this disaster, they'll already be moving north."

"No, Highness," she said. "Your soldiers routing means poor discipline and worse supply lines in the south. And my Gandsmen from the colonies would do better if spared engagement with their Old World counterparts."

"But the Sardians haven't even reached our border," he said. "It could be weeks, with the winter snows, before their forces are deployed."

She nodded, waiting for him to see it on his own.

"Oh Gods," the Dauphin said. "You mean to leave the city undefended."

"It will be a blow to morale," she said. "Leaving the enemy to march through your country, to hold your capital and reave their way through your farms. But the better part of our forces are mine, and whatever affinity they feel for Old Sarresant, their hearts are tied to the New. Paendurion will never expect us to abandon the southern front, and that might give us the edge we need to triumph in the east."

"Impossible," the Dauphin said. "Out of the question. My father's one dictum in all this has been to hold the city. Sarresant cannot fall."

"With respect, Highness, it can. And it must, if we are to have any hope of victory."

"You don't understand. No. I cannot agree to any plan that fails to protect the city."

She gritted her teeth, looking up from the maps. He was a weak man, clad in silks and expectations of deference, but any threat to remove him and his father from power would be a bluff. Ten thousand, at least, to take the capital, to say nothing of the sudden reversal of any support they might have expected from the Old Sarresant soldiers already in the field.

The Dauphin was still staring at the table, worry creasing his face. "You're sure it's the only way?"

"Yes," she said. "We shatter the Sardian army, then return to reconquer whatever the Thellans take behind our backs."

"Then I'll have to make the case to my father," he said, his voice pained, but resolute.

"Where is she?" a voice boomed outside the tent.

Colonel Marquand. She'd recognize his bluster anywhere. But before she could offer an apology to the Dauphin, Marquand came shoving into the tent, gripping what appeared to be a terrified young woman by the arm.

The Dauphin's flowerguards instantly moved to put themselves between him and Marquand, and she was a hairsbreadth from walling him off with *Shelter* herself, but he ignored them all, rounding on her as soon as he cleared the entryway.

"What is the meaning of this?" she said.

"Sir, High Comm—Empress—or, Your Bloody Fucking Majesty. I

took one of them prisoner. The Lady Daphène Malmont; one of ours by birth, if you can bloody well believe it. Managed to take her after you ordered us out."

He all but shook the poor girl on his arm, brandishing her as though she were a weapon.

"A prisoner," she said. "Why are you bringing her here, to me?"

"She's one of *them*, Your Majesty," Marquand said. "The rout had nothing to do with the soldiers' morale. It was *their* work. *Her* work, that is, Your Majesty, her and a score others of her kind."

Erris refocused on the girl. An ashen-faced woman with terror in her eyes, dressed in what appeared to be a Sarresant noblewoman's finery.

"I don't understand, Colonel."

"Don't worry, sir. I promised I'd kill her on the spot if she tried anything here. And binders are immune to the worst of their tricks, as you'll recall from the battle in New Sarresant."

Understanding dawned.

"You mean...?"

"Yes, sir, Your Majesty. She's one of... whatever Reyne d'Agarre was, and the girl, Sarine. *Kaas*-mages. They've got a score or more of them, placed along the Thellan lines. That's how they broke us. A few routed companies, and the rest broke along with them. A bloody nightmare, and a slaughter, and we're well and fucked, unless you can figure a way to counter them."

72

SARINE

Soul of the World
Gods' Seat

The energy pulsing at the center of the now-ruined chamber was quiet. She hadn't paid especial attention before, but though it looked like a roaring fire, the room was silent, and large enough to carry the sound of every page she turned in echoes between the jagged fractures of its walls.

The Divide, the page she was looking at said, and she recognized the illustration as an excellent likeness. Towering shadows, higher than the clouds, etched with what looked like her charcoal pens. She could have sketched it herself, with the same strokes and choices in the composition. She'd made a similar drawing not so long ago, from hills overlooking the sea. The script was foreign, but Anati translated it quickly enough she hardly noticed its strangeness. *A construct to seal magicks among peoples owing homage to disciples*, the caption said, *for the prevention of war beyond the scope of testing strength.* She thumbed through a few more passages, and found another reference: *breached in times of great need, but will not fall until each disciple's thresholds are satisfied.*

"This was hers, wasn't it?" she said. Her words echoed through the emptiness. "She made this. The Veil."

It could be, Anati thought to her. *Her writing is the same as yours.*

She skipped through a few more pages. By now she'd read it all, and understood less than a bare fraction. She flickered her sight to the blue sparks, and saw the outline of the strange human-shaped shadow, standing unmoving, a stone's throw across the chamber. The journal made mention of two different sorts of creature the shadow might be: *Watchers*, on one page, and something called *Masadi* on another. The creature had come and gone all through her studying, and she'd come no closer to understanding it, or to being able to communicate, though she was sure it could read her thoughts and emotions as easily as Anati could. Another mystery, when she needed more unraveling than unanswered questions right now.

"I'm ready, Anati," she said. "I've learned everything I'm going to learn from the journal, and it hasn't given me any better ideas."

Don't. Don't do it.

"I need the Veil gone. I know you're doing your best to keep her contained, but it isn't enough."

There has to be another way.

She sighed, glancing down at the sketches open on her lap. She'd spent days here, seated atop the few sections of unbroken stone, or in the library, scanning the shelves. The shadow hadn't given her anything new since the journal. Certainly the thing had to have read her desire to learn how to excise the Veil by now. If anything new was coming, it would have come already.

"Anati, the cords of light, when I came here—when we touched one, I could feel it cutting, as though it were trying to sever pieces of my mind. Of my memories. The Veil has to be stored there. We can use them to cut her out. If there's another way, I'm open to trying anything. But this is the best thing I can think of. Help me, if you think it's wrong."

Anati appeared, her four limbs balanced delicately atop a jagged stretch of stone cut into the floor. She seemed to be in mid-stride, lifting each foot carefully before she set it down atop another point.

"Anati?" she said. "What else is there? Have you still gotten nothing from Zi?"

My father thinks I am strong enough to do it, Anati thought, making slow progress across the ruined stone.

Sarine rose to her feet. "What do you mean? He agrees with my plan?"

Anati stopped suddenly, turning up to look at her. Her eyes were blue, glinting like sapphires, her scales flushed turquoise.

I like you, Anati thought. *I don't want you to die, if I'm too weak.*

"The cords can kill me," she said, though that seemed clear enough, from having touched one. "It's your *White* that protects me, isn't it?"

Anati bobbed her head up and down.

"You're strong enough," she said. "I agree with Zi. Anati, you can do this."

I am new, Anati thought, at the same time she resumed her slow crawl across the jagged stone.

"But you know what you would need to do. Protect me, and let the light cut the Veil away. Do you think it can work?"

I am too new. You need my father. Or one of my brothers. Xeraxet.

She paused, watching Anati's careful steps from point to point along the floor. She vaguely remembered what had happened after Zi had died, when the Veil took her to a world of shapes drawn by thousands of points of light. Anati had come forward, and they'd made a bond. If a new bond could be made—if Zi himself could come back to her...but no. Anati was hers. They'd crossed half the world together. If Anati was new, well, so was she. The weight of the world rested on her shoulders, and she still had no more than Zi's belief that she could handle it. Zi believed in her; he believed in Anati, too. It had to be enough.

"You can do this," she said. "I trust you."

Anati stopped again, looking up at her from the floor.

Why are your kind so reckless? Anati thought.

"I don't know," she said. "But I need the Veil gone before any more champions ascend." She glanced around the room, now a charred hulk of ruined stone. "See what she did, even fighting to take control? I can't risk doing it again, not with her still nestled in my head. That means I need your help. Will you do it?"

Anati sprang back the way she'd come, skittering across the points at full speed, rushing toward her leg and coiling around her ankle in a double loop.

Thank you, Anati thought. *I will try not to let you die.*

The Veil's emotions surged in her, a rush of hate that threatened to spoil the warmth emanating from Anati's touch. She fought it down.

"I'll tell the others," she said.

Navigating the ruin of the central chamber went quicker, now that she'd spent days walking the crevasses and molten channels cut through the stone. She wasn't sure why the light at the center drew her when she read the journal, but there was a familiarity there, a connection that evoked knowledge she felt sure she'd need to have. If Axerian had told it true, the power at the center of the chamber was enough to reshape the world itself. Having touched it to bond Yuli, she could well believe it, and it would be hers to use, when the time was right. A terrifying thought, and all the more so for her ignorance. But this was the first step in learning.

She found Yuli in the new room, down a passage that hadn't been there, before the bonding. They'd both marveled at the smooth-cut stone, fashioned to appear precisely the same as every other chamber in this place, and Yuli had been all wide-eyed wonderment, seeing its appointments: animal hides stretched across its floors, ornately carved wood chairs, tapestries and scrolls printed in what she said was her native tongue.

"You're going," Yuli said as soon as she appeared in the entryway.

She nodded, finding the words caught in her throat.

"Take me with you," Yuli said.

"It's dangerous," she said. "And besides, I don't think you can leave, yet. The journal says ascendants have to stay until all the champions are chosen."

"A strange thing," Yuli said, "to be a champion. I feel I should be able to share it, with my people, with my sisters among the warriors of my clan. A momentous thing, and a great honor."

"Soon," she said. "You'll see them again, as soon as the Divide comes down."

Yuli bowed, then opened her arms, welcoming Sarine forward for an embrace.

"Be careful, sister," Yuli said, whispering it into her ear.

"I will," she said.

"Then go," Yuli said, "with my blessing."

Reyne was a simpler affair, a curt dismissal in the library, where he was poring over the copies of the Codex the shadow had produced when she'd asked.

She went back to the central chamber when it was done, once more stepping through the jagged maze to reach the untouched plinth near the light. She wasn't sure whether she needed to be here to leave, but it felt right, and that was enough.

Ready, Anati thought to her before she could ask.

She nodded, shifting her vision to the blue sparks, and almost gave herself a start when the shadow was there, mere paces away, between her and the light. It had an arm upraised in what looked like a sign of farewell. She returned it, then swallowed, and calmed herself again, delving deep within to the well of energy she'd come to recognize as the Veil's power. *Her* power. It belonged to her. She took it in, losing herself in its waves and flickering sparks, until consciousness blurred, and she felt her body wash away.

———

The infinite plane stretched around her on all sides, exactly as it had been when she'd come here. Swirling columns of blue lightning arced between the floor and ceiling, extending as far as she could see in every direction, save for the column of burning light in front of her.

Tendrils of light hung from the central column, a curtain draped between her and the rest of the infinite plane. She hovered inside the shell they made around the column of light, watching their strands move in unrecognizable patterns, colliding and exploding in dazzling bursts of color before they re-formed and moved again.

Are you ready? she thought, trusting Anati to understand.

Yes. Go.

She watched for another beat, tracing the lines as they spindled around the central column of light. Ten thousand streams of white against a backdrop of infinite blue, a raging storm that promised to go on for an eternity without her intervention. A place she didn't belong, but then, it was born of *her* power. It should obey her. She reached for it, the same as she would draw on the blue sparks to set wardings in the physical world, and for a moment the strands of light lurched apart, twisting toward her in a neat spiral, where before they had been only chaos.

I can guide them, she thought to Anati. *I don't know how, but I can make them obey.*

Cut here, Anati thought back.

Suddenly she felt a glimpse of something wide and expansive, like gazing into the harbor, far beyond into the depths of the sea. This was her. She was more than a woman, more than her uncle's daughter. She was a well of power, as broad and vast as oceans, but hollow, as though she had once been filled with unimaginable reserves of strength. And deeper still, Anati guided her thoughts to a place of shadow. A darkness, burning alongside her core.

She repeated what she'd done, willing the strands of light in the infinite plane into place.

Where before chaos had reigned, she'd created a bubble of calm around her will. Fifty strands burned, fighting her to move and collide and resume their unpredictable patterns. She held them down. One strand rose from the rest, obeying her as it moved.

She brought it closer. Then let it touch her.

A dissonant note sounded in her ears, and the world split in two.

Agony shot through her, a wave of pain as she held the cord in place. It burned, and she saw it manifest in the vast emptiness Anati had shown her. A searing column of heat and light, ripping through the empty space and surrounded by pure white energy. Anati's shield. *White.*

Another will shot out to grab hold of the light.

Don't, a voice said to her. *You are stronger than I ever imagined, but you are not strong enough to face what comes. Let me survive. Let me have this body, or you will doom the world.*

The Veil. She knew it, as the power of her will struggled to hold on to the cord. *White* flared, the burning hiss of energy trying to melt through the shield. Another pair of hands grabbed at the light, and she felt them being burned, without the benefit of Anati's protection. Still the Veil reached for the light, trying to wrest away control.

No, she thought back.

The cord knifed through her, boring holes through the emptiness, as close to the shadows as she could guide the light.

Every movement reverberated through her with waves of pain, even through Anati's shield.

Please, the voice thought. *Don't leave me here.*

She focused her will, and the cutting continued. Anati's strain came through in her thoughts, the sensations of anxiety, fear, love, and pure force of will. She could feel the *White* cracking, fizzling as it came into contact with the cord. It consumed her, all parts of her being. Awareness of Anati, of the voice, of the rest of the cords suspended in place all dimmed against the sensation of guiding the light as it tore apart the shadows.

Be strong, the voice thought, *even in defeat. Don't let him rule for longer than you must. Beware your champions' power. Don't make the mistakes I did. Follow the Master's path, even if—*

The shadow came free, and the voice dimmed as the darkness fell away.

The cord snapped away from her control, and she felt an emptiness, a great void as though she fell through a vast distance.

Exhaustion ached in her, doubled by the sensations from Anati.

A dull light pulsed, and she drifted toward it; her body, such as it was in this place, beaten and bruised. But she was alive. She had survived. She was whole, though a part of her was missing. Memory returned only the life she'd known: the Maw, the Harbor, the Rasailles palace green. Sketches and clinging to survival in the shadows of the city. Zi. The stained-glass reliefs of the Sacre-Lin chapel, shining down on her with warmth in spite of the winter chill.

The cold stone floor between the dais and the pews, and the sound of her uncle sweeping. The clatter of his broom, dropping to the floor.

"Sarine?"

His voice, warm and gentle, as though he were there in person.

"Sarine, oh, by the Veil herself, it's you."

He rushed to her side, and she opened her eyes. It was him, his mustaches already glistening with tears sliding from his cheeks.

"Not the Veil," she said as he lifted her, cradling her in his arms. "Not anymore."

73

TIGAI

Field Command
The Road to Orstead, Old Sarresant

The hills had been transformed and, from the look of it, were about to be again. Tents and horse-lines had been put up in all directions, with just as many being taken down, carts of stores and foodstuffs moving as quick as they could be loaded, one after another.

"She's sending you out again, isn't she?" Remarin asked. He wore one of their uniforms, as strange a sight as Tigai had ever expected to see. Blue cap atop his short-cropped hair, though his beard still marked him as Ujibari, thick and tied with cord in a style unlike he'd seen on any Sarresanter. He carried one of their long rifles, and that much was familiar; even with all the advantages of their superior technology, he'd wager on Remarin over any five of their best marksmen, and if their flint-caps and powder bags let him fire in the rain, so much the better for them all.

"Which one?" he asked, joining Remarin in moving out of the way of a wagon and its team. "Empress d'Arrent, or Mei?"

Remarin grinned. "Does it matter?"

"D'Arrent has me set to ride again this afternoon. Making for the eastern line two days hence."

"A hard pace," Remarin said. "I'm with Dao's brigade. The Nineteenth. We'll follow in your wake, a few days behind, I'm sure."

"Acherre bloody rode me raw for a week, and now we do it again. They didn't even stay long enough for the anchor to take hold. I could as well have not bothered. It'll be gone within a day, unless I go back to secure it."

Remarin gave him a wistful smile. "Just as well you came back. Dao is busy, but he'll be relieved to see you."

They halted for another train of supplies and men, shouting in their strange, throaty tongue.

"Remarin...I...I'm not sure Mei made the right choice, allying us with d'Arrent."

Remarin raised an eyebrow, and for once, it was a blessing that none around them understood the Jun tongue.

"I saw the battlefield," he continued. "A terrible rout. The enemy's *kaas*-mages are a terrible weapon. We saw their power firsthand, at Kye-Min. I want us to have a new start, but if this army is going to lose..."

"Talk to Mei," Remarin said.

"I have already. She wouldn't listen. Said she's afraid we'll be branded turncoats if we switch sides so soon after coming here."

"A wise stance, it seems to me," Remarin said. "Trust her, Tigai. We all have our gifts, and your sister-by-marriage is adept at these sorts of affairs. She'll suss out the realities of what's to come, and I needn't remind you there are spoils to be had, even for the losers, in war."

"What if there was another way..." he began, but Remarin clicked his teeth, cutting him short.

"Your *magi* tale again," Remarin said. "Mei won't hear of it, after our time with the Herons. We're done with their games."

"But there's one of them here," he said.

"There's one of them everywhere," Remarin said. "That they wield no power openly in this Empire is enough for me."

He fell quiet. It had gone the same, with Mei. He hadn't yet brought himself to mention the shadow-creature after Voren had stabbed him, or the old man's offer of strength and security for his family. The strangeness of it had weighed on him since the first night on the road.

Remarin clapped his shoulder. "Go," he said. "See your brother. He's in his element here, never mind these soldiers' lack of speaking proper tongues. I'll credit this Empress d'Arrent: She knows talent when she sees it. That's rare enough, among any nobility."

"I have to report to the Empress first," he said. "She sent a courier to fetch me in my tent at daybreak."

"Then she'll be expecting you long since," Remarin said. "And I'll leave you alone to your tongue lashing for it."

He watched Remarin trot ahead, vanishing into a sea of blue coats as the camp stirred itself to move. He'd expected exactly that sort of reaction. His family had never trusted *magi*—in spite of his nature, they'd managed to make him feel like one of them, but it hadn't erased the truth of what he was. They'd certainly used his gifts easily enough. Perhaps this was the same sort of thing. Perhaps he should consider the old man's offer on his own, if Mei wouldn't hear him out.

He pivoted, making his way toward the central tents. Remarin was probably right that he should have gone there first thing, but he'd been dreading the kind of use he was sure d'Arrent intended for him.

A week of some of the hardest travel he'd ever endured, and he'd as good as gotten nothing for it. He'd tried to tell Acherre and d'Arrent it took time for an anchor to settle, that he needed to stay there for a day or two in order for a strand to form between him and the place to the south, but in the moment all that had mattered was moving Marquand and his company to and from the battlefield. He blinked to shift his sight to the starfield as he walked, and sure enough the light he'd set was there, dim and fading fast, in the mountains far to the south. If d'Arrent had just let him stay, the week wouldn't have been wasted. All he would have needed was—

He almost stumbled into the way of a passing horseman, earning a shouted curse and a horse's whinny as the rider tugged the reins.

He steadied himself and blinked again. Something was there, among the stars. On this side of the Divide the field was black, almost lifeless, save for a tiny handful of lights scattered across all its continents. He'd come to recognize them all, but a new one had appeared, blazing with a sun's intensity, far to the west.

He could have counted on two sets of hands every star in the field on this side of the Divide. This was new, and near the one they'd used to put themselves close to New Sarresant. It might even be in New Sarresant itself, saving him the two weeks' journey from the site in the northwest.

Sarine.

It had to be her. This was what the old man among the stars had wanted him to watch for. A star five times the size of any other, as though she'd punched a fist through the fabric of the starfield itself.

D'Arrent was waiting for him, and his instinct was to consult Mei and Dao for what to do. But no—they wanted nothing to do with the old man's offer. And for all its intensity, there was nothing promising that the star would linger if he didn't have a strand tied to it himself.

He closed his eyes, tethering himself around its light. At worst he could come back, and if it cost him a day of recovery, well, he'd earned as much, whatever d'Arrent wanted to believe he could handle.

He shifted.

Darkness swallowed him, but it was only ordinary nightfall, having traveled westward against the path of the sun. He stood in a stone building lined with rows of wood benches, facing a dais backed by massive stained-glass windows, lit by a single hooded lantern on the wall. The shuffle of his steps echoed through the chamber, under a vaulted ceiling thirty armspans above his head.

"*Êtes-vous perdu, mon fils?*"

He spun to find a mustached man in a brown robe hovering in an alcove behind him, holding a broom as though he'd been sweeping in the middle of the night.

"I followed a star here," he said, realizing belatedly the man wasn't going to understand a word of the Jun tongue. "Sarine," he tried instead. "I'm looking for Sarine."

The man knew the name. He saw it in the suddenly stiff shoulders, the way the man's grip on his broom suddenly transformed it halfway to a quarterstaff.

"*Qu'est-ce que vous voulez avec elle?*"

Tigai shook his head. Damned if he hadn't spent weeks around the Sarresant tongue and not bothered to learn a word.

"Tigai?"

He turned around again, this time looking up toward a loft built below the panes of stained glass. The silhouette of a figure stood there, at the edge of a wood railing.

"Sarine," he called back. The man in brown said something further in the Sarresant tongue, and she replied, in her strange manner of speaking every tongue at once.

"Yes, I know him, Uncle, though I have no idea what he's doing here."

"It's...complicated," he said. "And where did you go? We were traveling together and you bloody vanished with Yuli and Lin."

She stepped back from the railing, sliding down the ladder leading up to her loft.

"That's complicated, too," she said when she landed on the stone floor. "But it's good to see you."

He returned the warmth in her expression, though it masked the feeling that he'd been a fool to come here. What was he supposed to do, wait until she turned her back and then knife her? *Stay close*, the old man had said, *and keep her trust*. Seeing her here in person colored it all in gray.

"My uncle was telling me about Erris d'Arrent," she said. "Empress now? And that she took the army across the sea. Were you with her? And your family?"

"Yes," he said. "She had me setting anchors to move her *magi*—her binders—to the fronts. A bloody mess, between *kaas*-mages, officers with golden light for eyes, more bloody *magi* than you'd ever want to see in one place."

"Wait—*kaas*-mages? And golden light?"

"That's what Marquand called them. And yes, golden light—I saw it with Acherre, and again among the enemy's ranks on the front lines... look, you should come back with me. D'Arrent's on the shit end of the battle that's coming. She could use you. And...whatever it is you can do, scattering soldiers like flies. I guess that makes you a *kaas*-mage, too?"

"Yes," Sarine said. "Partly. That's what Anati is. But the golden light—you're sure you saw it among her enemies?"

He nodded. "I saw it firsthand. Why? Isn't that something d'Arrent can do?"

"It is. But if you saw it among her enemies...Lin put a glass knife in Paendurion's back, at the Gods' Seat. It must mean he survived."

"Paendurion. Empress d'Arrent's enemy? And Lin, is she—?"

"Lin is dead," Sarine said. "At least I think she is. But Paendurion... you said the Sarresant armies were losing?"

Lin was dead. The words hit him harder than he'd thought they would, after all the pain she'd caused him, and his family. Strange.

"Yes," he said. "At least, that's what I saw, along the southern lines.

D'Arrent has her soldiers marching east now. And like I said, she could use you."

Sarine wore a resolute look, turning toward her uncle, who'd come to rest nearby, leaning against his broom.

"I'm sorry, Uncle," Sarine said. "I have to leave again."

Her uncle said something in the Sarresant tongue, and Tigai turned aside as she wrapped her arms around him, exchanging words he knew weren't meant for him. The whole thing seemed too big: layers upon layers of *magi*, plots and politics and games. Shame stung him, at the thought he might betray Sarine's trust, but he couldn't outright dismiss it as an option. Whatever the old man in the starfield had wanted with her, it was hard to deny she wielded power beyond anything he'd seen before they'd met. For now it was enough to stay close. The rest could be decided later.

"Are you ready?" she asked him after she and her uncle had separated.

"I'll need a few hours, before I use the strands again," he said. "I traveled halfway across the world, coming here."

"I can take us," she said. "Which light is it? Or, I think you have a tether to one of them. Would that be the right one?"

Wind spirits but that was unnerving. He wanted nothing more than to distance himself from *magi*, and ended up arm-in-arm with the most powerful woman he'd ever seen or heard of, on either side of the Divide.

"Yes," he said. "And if you're ready, I'm bloody ready, too."

74

ERRIS

2nd Corps Command Tents
The Road to Orstead, Old Sarresant

They'll try to concentrate here," she said, earning silent nods from her division commanders, "along these ridges. We have to expect their *kaas*-mages to focus here, and here, until their batteries are in place atop the heights."

"A sound battle plan, if we had the enemy's position and advantages," Field-Marshal Etaigne said. "I wonder, Your Majesty, if we should fall back to better ground."

She nodded, pointing to a stretch of farmland crisscrossed with roads and fences just north of the city. "Our enemy will expect us to deploy here. But we're too far extended to the east, and he knows it. He has ninety thousand Thellan and Gand soldiers coming up the trade roads from the south. By now he knows we've abandoned our fortifications there. All he has to do is dig in on high ground and wait for his reinforcements to arrive. A defensive strategy leaves us exposed to an envelopment. We must attack, and he'll know that, too. But he'll never expect an attack on the heights."

"Your Majesty, with respect, such an attack is suicide," Royens said. Vassail nodded along with her commander's sentiments.

"We have the advantage of numbers," Erris said.

"But Your Majesty, the *kaas*-mages..." de Tourvalle said.

"That was a trick that could only work once," she replied. "Paendurion knows we'll have trained our soldiers to expect it; when the *kaas*-mages strike, our lines will fall back, and we'll commit our binders to counter them. Our soldiers won't rout for one spot of panic again."

"We'd have three, maybe four hours," Vassail said. "Before they can bring batteries up those ridges and get them firing. After that, they won't need *kaas*-mages to break us."

"We'll deploy here," Erris said, "on the fields outside the city, massed as though we intend to try an assault over open ground. We look disorderly, Old Sarresant and Gand units mixed in with the command, as though the logistics of the attack have been delayed due to their inclusion."

Vassail nodded. "We could strike with cavalry to harry their artillery wagons while the rest of the army puts on its show."

"A fine idea, General," she said. "But make it a strike against their supply train. They'll be trailing behind, here"—she pointed to a stretch of forested flatlands to the southeast—"where your cavalry can use the trees to magnify your numbers in their scouts' reports."

"My cavalry, Your Majesty?" Vassail said.

"I want you in command of the first raiding force. De Tourvalle, give her the Fourteenth and the Eleventh; Etaigne, half the Twenty-Second."

Both her corps commanders bowed, turning to relay the command to their aides.

"We still need an answer for those guns, Your Majesty," General Wexly, the Gand commander, said. "And even with binders and discipline, those *kaas*-mages are all but impassable barriers for the bulk of our soldiers."

"That command falls to me," she said. "The second raiding force: eighty fullbinders, drawn from volunteers among every brigade in all three armies."

Silence descended through the tent.

"Your Majesty, with respect," Royens said. "Your *Need* bindings are the glue that holds this army in place. Without you here, in command, we can't hope to coordinate our attacks."

"I can liaise between units from atop Jiri's back," she said. "But there is to be no attack, until we've turned the Sardian guns to start firing into their own lines. And then, the only order is this: full assault. Hold nothing back. We commit everything, and sweep the enemy position with every gun, every binder, every horse and soldier we have."

"You mean to let them get their guns in place, and *take them*?" Wexly said.

"That's right," she said. "The enemy will never expect it. No brilliance, no maneuver. Only boldness, and raw nerve."

"Bloody madness," Colonel Marquand said from among the division commanders. The rest eyed him with a mix of frowns and agreement on their faces. "But sir, that is, Your Majesty, count me as your first volunteer."

She met Marquand's eyes, sharing a grim nod that melted into mutual understanding. Perhaps he'd earn himself a general's star, if they survived.

"The rest of you, unless you have questions, you're dismissed. We have a great many orders to deliver before daybreak. See to your divisions, and your corps. Gods watch over all of you, and go with their blessings."

───────

She slid her bronze spyglass open, raising it to survey the ridges on the eastern horizon. Different, when she saw a battlefield through a tube instead of a cartographer's eyes. But she could see both versions at once: The craggy heights corresponded to black topographical lines, where she knew the double-horseshoe shape of the two ridges ahead converged to present steep faces in her direction, and scalable trails behind. The bulk of the enemy's deployment awaited them there, spread on either side of the hills.

Jiri followed the rest of Marquand's company without prompting or guidance, while she did her last hours of scouting, between the spyglass and *Need*.

"Now's the time, sir," Marquand said. "We have to decide. North or south?"

She swept the spyglass in both directions. Green flags decorated the heights already, with more spread on either side.

"I make ten, maybe twelve divisions," she said. "And the latest reports at field command confirm."

"Seventy thousand, then?" Essily said. He'd been the second volunteer, if Marquand was the first, riding just behind Jiri near the head of the column.

"We've gone as far as we can go behind the tree line," Marquand said. "Either we cut across the fields and approach the heights from the north, or continue on this way and hit them from the south. And I'd feel a damned sight better if you'd planned a diversionary attack from the direction we're not going, to cover our movement."

"No," she said, scanning back with her spyglass one last time. "He has to think *we're* the diversion."

By now the rest of their column had come to a halt just behind them. Eighty binders, the precise number she'd asked for, and she could have had three times that number if she'd continued taking volunteers. A miniature cavalry brigade, and likely the deadliest unit ever assembled on a modern battlefield.

"Sir, with respect, we need to make a call. Which route?"

"South," she said, snapping the spyglass shut. "Keep us moving, Marquand. I need to relay the latest dispositions to field command."

He nodded, already heeling his mount back to give the orders for a southern approach.

She let Jiri follow his lead, for now. In another hour she would have her full attention here, but until they were engaged, she could keep a foot in both worlds. Seventy thousand. That was the count she'd expected for the Sardian army, all green flags and sigils of their crossed spears in gold. Not a single sign of the black flags of Skovan among them. Either Paendurion's diplomacy had failed, or he had sixty thousand Skovan soldiers waiting somewhere nearby, somewhere none of her scouts had yet managed to discern. Instinct demanded caution, but if she'd learned anything facing Paendurion, it was that her instincts were wrong. Boldness, and surprise, had to be the order of the day. With the sun almost at its apex, she couldn't yet tell who had the initiative. An improvement, by her reckoning, since the last time she'd faced him.

She found *Need* atop Jiri's back as Marquand gave the orders to move the company into the open. He'd see them coming, soon, following the roads toward his southern lines. At her back, his scouts would already have mapped her positions, over a hundred thousand strong, deploying in the fields outside the town, a league beyond the range of his long guns.

"Report," she said through her vessel, already studying the maps for updates as Jiri moved her closer to the enemy.

———————

"Hold." She heard Marquand give the order. "No *Shelter* before two hundred paces."

Her senses still lurched between the command tents and the battlefield. She'd stayed too long in her vessel's skin, working out the logistics of the southernmost division's buffering line against the Thellan and Gand armies. Marquand's order was the very one she'd have given, if she'd been present to do it.

A double-thick line of soldiers in green opposed them, kneeling and brandishing their muskets like a spear-wall from antiquity. The ground was level, though the heights began less than a league from the enemy's flank, a slow climb up the jutting hills overlooking the field. Impossible to say precisely how dense the enemy's line would be, behind the front ranks, but they'd have a better vantage after they made the ascent. Perhaps Paendurion would read this attack as a scouting effort. All the better if he did.

"Forward," Marquand called, urging his mount to a canter to set the pace for the rest. She drew her saber as the order came to ready weapons, thundering toward the enemy line. Jiri's powerful strides pushed the others' mounts faster, and they covered ground from six hundred paces to five hundred, then four, then three.

The first volley came like the first peal of thunder. Smoke erupted from the Sardian line in two waves, starting on either end and rippling inward, and horses screamed around her, their riders falling as the rest of them advanced.

The soldiers in green lowered their musket spear-wall, hastily cramming powder and balls into place for a second round. Marquand raised his saber as their horses thundered forward, covering fifty paces in a matter of moments, calling orders for *Shelter* before the next volley.

When the phalanx formed again, raised muskets leveled to fire, Marquand and the rest of their company had crossed half the remaining distance between them. They had to look like madmen, in the Sardians' eyes, and all the more so if those troops hadn't yet been bloodied. She knew the desperation of an untested unit, facing its first charge: Her company's pace promised they would get at most one more volley before their lines collided. Raw recruits would stare at such a thing only half believing it could happen to them, no matter how effective their training.

The Sardians fired, and this time *Shelter* sprang into place, hazy barriers conjured in the moments between the volley and the horses storming through where the binders let them disperse. *Mind* accompanied *Shelter*, and their line tripled in size. *Body* sped others, and their mounts, and *Death* cut down the Sardians' feeble attempts at erecting *Shelter* of their own.

In an instant, they'd transformed from a scouting company on a mad charge against a thousand times their number to death, swift and sure, coming for the Sardians faster than they could hope to escape.

The last fifty paces blurred as Jiri shot forward, *Body* adding power to her mount's already-thundering stride. *Mind* had produced five copies of her and Jiri both; *Death* cut down an attempt to put a barricade in her way; *Life* sharpened her senses enough to see every wide-eyed stare, every man on the verge of throwing down his musket and fleeing the field; *Entropy* held itself at the ready, waiting for the moment before impact to char their lines in waves of fire.

Jiri trampled the first men they met, and she cut another down with her steel. Flames exploded at their backs as the green soldiers turned and broke. Screams, smothered by warcries from her company, filled the air as the front ranks shattered in smoke and blood.

Speed. Speed was the order of the day, and Marquand raced ahead, punching through the Sardian lines surrounded by a fireball of his own making. She rallied behind him, repeating his order, hearing the same carried by every volunteer in earshot:

"Forward! Forward, to the heights!"

———

Blue forms blurred with green, and she danced between them, lashing out with her saber. Pistols and muskets paled against *Entropy* and steel.

"Go," she shouted at Marquand, and he obeyed without a second glance.

Hooves pounded behind her as she and five other Sarresant binders spread themselves across the trail, a tight spiral of level ground switchbacking up the heights. The rest of their company followed Marquand's charge. There would be a regiment's strength coming, and more behind them. It fell to her, and any of her binders unlucky enough to have taken arms beside her, to hold while Marquand and the rest of their company scaled the heights.

Shelter closed around her, and she snapped a *Death* tether through it, leaping from higher ground into a knot of three *Body* binders in green facing off with one of hers. Jiri had gone with Marquand, sparing her only a snort when she'd dismounted. This dance she did on foot, parrying a slash from a curved blade and punching the man who wielded it in the jaw, shattering teeth and bone and sending him staggering downhill, collapsing into a bush. The other two turned from their quarry, but too late, each taking a blast from her *Entropy*. Shouting followed, and two of her *Mind* copies rushed ahead of her, driven by her subconscious, raising their sabers to attack a squad of musketmen running alongside one of the women in gold.

The soldiers dropped to their knees and fired, and she snapped *Shelter* into place as her copies blinked to become wisps of smoke. Another Sarresant binder charged that squad, swinging a double-thick saber as he hewed them down like paper.

She turned her attention to another Sardian, and a renewed attempt to cut her tethers with *Death*. This one stared at her with full concentration, while a woman guarded his back. She feinted a charge, then pulled back, drawing the *Death* binder's bodyguard into an overextended lunge. A chop for the woman's sword sent it clattering to the ground, and a second took her head, *Body* giving her the power to slice clean through the spine. The *Death* binder blinked, staring at her as though his tethers should have stopped her on their own. Her saber answered his surprise with a twisting strike through his gut, wrenching his intestines into the sun as she pulled her blade free.

More musket fire sounded around her, and she trusted *Life* and *Body* to give her the speed and awareness to raise *Shelter* if any were aiming at her. Sardian soldiers poured behind the green-cloaked binders, following them to chase Marquand's company up the trail to the ridges. By now the bulk of her forces would be deploying in the fields to the west, moving within range of the long guns in anticipation of the order to charge. She had to delay, to buy Marquand time before she withdrew.

She summoned a wall of *Shelter* blocking the trail behind her, with all the force she could manage, making a miniature Great Barrier between the late-arriving infantry and the rest of the fight. *Death* assaulted it at once from multiple angles, and she held it in place, driving white pearls to patch the holes they tore as quick as they could make them. One of the Sardians pointed at her as she did it, and he and two of his fellows ran at her, curved blades in hand.

Entropy fizzled before it could form, though she hadn't seen *Death* attack her tethers. No time for wonder. She ducked the first man's swipe, then parried the second. All three men moved faster than any common soldier, but her *Body* was stronger, her movements tighter, turning her saber with greater precision in every stroke. She hamstrung one of them with a deep cut along his calf, then struck three blows against the other: swatting his blade aside, making a gash across his chest, severing his left arm below the shoulder.

She slowed down.

Again, she hadn't seen *Death*, but something had robbed her of *Body* just as one of them made his attack. She stuttered to a halt, having expected a burst of speed and power, bringing her saber up barely in time to deflect the man's blow and feeling herself shoved off-balance by the force of it. She tried to set her feet and resume her guard. Too slow. He hammered her saber out of the way and bit into her skin, a burning gash along the left side of her chest. One of her *Mind* copies drew his attention before he could drive the blade deeper, surprising him as she rolled away, feeling the wet run of blood inside her coat.

He set his feet for another attack, too fast for her to follow without her *Body*. Her undamaged right arm hefted her saber a heartbeat too slow. This was death, come for her at last. She met it with jaw clenched, the tang of blood at the back of her throat, bringing her blade up for a riposte she knew would never connect.

A flash of light blinded her, and she felt the weight of his steel, turned aside.

White energy flared around her attacker, and he staggered back, light spilling from his eye sockets as *Need* connected him to someone else, far away. Paendurion. Her enemy.

She saw at once a dawning recognition. She'd made connections to soldiers in the middle of a fight before, and she saw the same sense of disorientation, the same delay it took to see the vessel's surroundings. A moment's pause, but all the time she needed. Even without *Body*, her steel bore a razor's edge, and she buried her saber in the man's undefended chest, smashing ribs to pierce his heart.

Adrenaline pounded in her ears, and she found another target, a binder in green leading a squad of soldiers to pull themselves up the heights, around where her *Shelter* blocked the trail. But the wound in her chest was deep, the sort that would kill her if she left it unattended. She withdrew, backing her way up the trail as the fighting continued, holding to her *Shelter* as she found *Body* again, this time for tethers directed inward, probing to do as much as she could to steady her wounds.

For now their company held. The better part by far had gone with Marquand to scale the heights, but dead and dying bodies littered the trail, the smells of blood and burning flesh a testament to the strength of Sarresant bindings. Shouting came from the other side of her *Shelter* wall, and *Death* tethers to unmake it, drawing from a pool of inky black leaking from the dying into the leylines beneath the hill. But she was strong. Even wounded, her *Shelter* withstood the attacks, and could hold for precious minutes. Gods send it was long enough for Marquand to turn the guns.

Thunder sounded overhead, great roars as the field pieces answered her prayer. One cannon went off, then another, the tufts of white smoke pointed east, toward the Sardian lines.

Need beckoned, and part of her mind maintained the *Shelter*, weaving white pearls against her enemies' *Death*. But she had to find strength enough for *Need* to see the order to attack delivered. Now. At the moment of maximum impact, when the Sardian soldiers felt the rain of their own shells over their heads.

She made the connection, and some part of her senses slid into place, only she was mounted atop a horse overlooking the battlefield, rather than situated in the tents of field command.

"Gods help us," de Tourvalle said, lowering a brass spyglass atop his horse as he squinted toward the horizon.

"That's the signal," she said through her vessel. "Marquand has the guns turned on the enemy."

"Your Majesty," de Tourvalle said, drawing the attention of the rest of the aides and command staff gathered around them. "Thank the Exarch you're here."

"What are you waiting for?" she said. "Give the order to attack—now!"

"Your Majesty," de Tourvalle said. "You must see for yourself."

He gestured toward the horizon. Not the eastern ridges, as she'd expected. South.

She raised her vessel's spyglass, and despair bit as deep as her enemy's steel.

Thellan soldiers, and Gandsmen, in their yellow and red coats. Only a division's worth, so far, visible pouring through the passes that would empty into the fields, giving them a flanking position to where her army would be charging the Sardians, if they followed her plan. Impossible. The Thellans should have been days to the south, well clear of any threatening deployment. For them to be here on this field would have required Paendurion to march them ragged, covering sixty leagues a day and driving them well into each night. They would be haggard, ill-supplied, wasted shells of men and women after such a march, spent and broken. And they would be situated to pincer her between the Sardian lines, tens of thousands of soldiers rallied by a chance to catch their enemy by surprise.

"Order the attack," she said.

"Your Majesty?" de Tourvalle said.

"Order the attack," she repeated. "Full assault. Leave nothing in reserve."

"But Your Majesty, the Thellan forces will—"

"The Thellan forces will find us in command of this battlefield, their Sardian allies broken and scattered by our soldiers, and the force of their own artillery. This is our only chance, Field-Marshal. Rally our soldiers and commit them to the fight. We break the eastern lines, then turn to face the Thellan. The enemy thinks he has us cornered. Let us show him instead he's jumped into the pit to face the lion."

75

ARAK'JUR

Market Street
The City of Al Adiz, Thellan

Aswarm of people filled the streets, shouting as they exchanged bolts of cloth, dried fruits, furs, and precious stones. He and Ka'Inari stepped through them, weaving around carts and mules, men and women, drawing fewer eyes for being foreigners than for their girth displacing traffic in the market. Creeping past the watchmen at the walls had been a trivial thing, and, once inside, they'd managed to approach the palace at the city's heart without so much as a question to discern their place or purpose.

Ka'Inari followed as they turned away from another pair of gold-uniformed watchmen, cutting down another street, running parallel to the palace grounds. They were close, now. Days spent traveling into the heart of the country called Thellan, and they were close.

"Inside?" Ka'Inari said, making it a question as they stopped facing the colonnaded building and its courtyard, where gilded iron gates divided the grounds from the bustle of the rest of the city.

"Yes," he said, feeling an echo of the spirits' premonitions. Whispers of *he is near* and *kill him* had accompanied him from the battlefield to the city. "Inside. Down a long hallway, through a door painted red."

Ka'Inari closed his eyes, nodding and listening with indrawn breath.

"Then this is where our journeys part," Ka'Inari said. "The spirits have showed me a different path."

"What? No."

Ka'Inari clasped his shoulder.

"You must be strong, to face what awaits you inside," Ka'Inari said. "Remember Corenna, and Kar'Doren. Remember why you fight."

"I mislike your words," he said. "What have the spirits shown you? What do you mean to do?"

Ka'Inari smiled, staring through him as he met his eyes. "This will be our last journey together, Arak'Jur. You were a fine teacher, and a good friend. Protect our people, protect your son."

With that, his former apprentice turned toward the junction where their alley met the path leading toward the palace gate, a shimmering form of the Great Bear taking shape around him.

"No!" he said, rushing to catch Ka'Inari before he reached the corner. "What are you doing?"

"Arak'Jur," Ka'Inari said. "I have seen a hundred possible futures. This is the one that gives you a chance at ascension. Let me walk my path. Follow the spirits, and walk yours."

For a moment he held to Ka'Inari's arm, though he knew that with *una're* coursing through him, the shaman could have shrugged off his grip with a mere tightening of his muscle. Instead he let go on his own. Ka'Inari spared a last look, the youthful apprentice replaced by wizened elder, and then the shaman loped ahead, some vestige of the bear's gait taking over Ka'Inari's as he closed toward the gilded iron ringing the palace grounds.

A ringing crash sounded as the bear spirit gave Ka'Inari the strength to rip a section of the gate from the ground, hurling it with a roar onto the green.

Not a hundred paces back the way they'd come, a train of carts and messengers reacted with shouts of alarm, and the soldiers on duty there took up the same cries. Squads of men in gold came running, moving too fast, fast enough to be using fair-skin magic. Ka'Inari charged toward the palace, leading them away.

Arak'Jur stepped through the ruined section of the gate. Suddenly the main entrance was abandoned; Ka'Inari's roars echoed across the green, smothering the cries and yelps of his pursuers. They stared, all those who had been waiting on the guards' pleasure, and if any noticed as he slipped past them, no further cries were raised. He cut across the grass as he stared in wonderment, still swallowing the shock of Ka'Inari's display.

The entrance loomed in front of him, a plain wood door where the rest was carved stone and marble. Columns decorated the exterior, with the palace's size promising hundreds of halls and chambers within. Yet the first rooms he entered were plain, unadorned by color or elaborate décor. A simple room with benches and coats hung on pegs, and he passed through, feeling Mountain's contented hum in his thoughts, until a man in brown clothes wearing a gold sash stepped into the hallway, directly in his path.

The gold-sashed man stared at a parchment in his hand, stepping around Arak'Jur for a moment until he took the time to look again. Then the man frowned, glancing at him up and down as he spoke.

"*Qué estás haciendo aquí?*" the man said. Almost the Sarresant tongue, but different enough for meaning to elude him. He had none of the Thellan tongue at all; instead he spoke Sinari, conveying his meaning with posture and tone.

"Go," he said. "And say nothing of our meeting."

The man wavered, his eyes wide as he shuffled back a step. Arak'Jur caught him by the arm, eliciting a yelp of surprise before he could pull the man close.

"Go," he said again, this time jostling the man back toward the plain chambers. "And be silent."

The last he said with a sharp shove, sending the man staggering down the hall. Arak'Jur turned and continued on; soon enough there would be alarms raised, but he had to hope it would be clear, and this man in gold would hold his tongue, else there would be violence long before he reached his goal.

He pressed on, and soon the plainness of the chambers near the entrance gave way to gilded panels of white wood, cushioned furniture, stone sculptures, painted vases, and woven carpets hanging from the walls and draped over the floors. He froze, hearing cries of alarm, but they came from deeper within the palace. If there had been sentries posted in these halls, they must have been drawn by those cries, and by the thunder that followed them: cracks in the distance, roaring bangs that seemed to shake the palace foundations when they struck. Ka'Inari's work, and it tore at his core to leave the shaman to it, even knowing his path lay here, following these halls.

Footsteps from above confirmed he was far from alone within the palace, but he passed beneath, following a hunter's instinct toward his prey. The man with a thousand threads of gold. He was here, and Arak'Jur was drawing closer with every step. Another few minutes would see him—

MY CHILDREN.

The voice stopped him midway through a hall. A spirit's voice—but no. The spirits were familiar, companions he knew. This was different, a distant echo, as though he heard a fading glimmer of something that had once been deeper, stronger, more powerful.

THE MOMENT APPROACHES. READY YOURSELVES, TO BE WEIGHED AND JUDGED.

He staggered to a halt at the mouth of a hallway, leaning against the wood paneling for support. Was this part of Mountain's charge? Nothing at Adan'Hai'Tyat had prepared him for it, and Ad-Shi had said nothing. Yet even diminished, the voice overpowered his senses, almost bringing him to his knees.

READY YOURSELVES, FOR ASCENSION.

As suddenly as it had come, the voice withdrew, leaving him standing on red carpet, facing a red door. Mountain's urgings returned, strong enough to put the scent of fresh meat in his nose. *Now,* Mountain's voice whispered in his ear. *Go. Time is short. You must kill him. You must see it done.* Heat swam in his vision, a sheen of red blotting out color in the hallway.

He opened the door and stepped inside, laying eyes on the man whose death would mark his journey's end.

A giant, a full head taller than Arak'Jur himself, lying naked on his side atop a cushioned bed, with two women in white standing behind him, applying strips of cloth to his back. The smell of filth permeated the room, rotting meat mixed with feces, while the giant's eyes were white, the pupils rolled up in his head as he muttered something unintelligible, his fingers twitching atop his blankets. Whispers sounded in Arak'Jur's ears, and he almost saw the threads of gold emanating from this man. A name crystallized in the spirits' urgings: *Paendurion. Champion of Order. Leader of the Three.*

One of the women noticed Arak'Jur, and she screamed.

He held his ground, letting the door fall closed behind him. The rest of the palace had been drawn by whatever commotion Ka'Inari was causing on the far side of the grounds. If any heard her screams, they would arrive too late to interfere.

The giant—Paendurion—stirred atop the bed, half turning toward the woman before his gaze settled on Arak'Jur, and he laughed.

"You come now," Paendurion said, speaking the Sinari tongue, though he did it with a thick, foreign accent. "On the cusp of ascension. Ad-Shi's apprentice."

Both women stared between him and the giant, backing away from the bed. Strips of blood- and pus-soaked cloth lay discarded on a stand, while fresh strips had been cut and laid across the blankets.

Ad-Shi's name gave him pause. "You knew her," he said.

"I knew her," Paendurion said. "I assume she's dead? And by her own hand, else you'd have no need to come for me."

The image of her form, falling into blackness as she plummeted from the clifftop, crystallized in his memory. "Yes," he said.

Paendurion closed his eyes, coming to rest atop his bed. For a moment it looked as though he meant to sleep. In Mountain's visions this man had been a great warrior, a conqueror and butcher of innocents beyond counting. This was a wretch, clinging to the barest sliver of life, with only a long steel sword beside his bed to mark him for a fighter. The two women cowering behind the bed glanced between him and the giant, their fear amplifying pity he hadn't expected to feel at the end of this path.

"Ad-Shi told you," Paendurion said abruptly. "She would have told you what is at stake. You must have heard the Master's voice. You know how close we are to the reckoning for this cycle."

He said nothing. Ad-Shi had told him nothing of any "Master," but the stakes of their conflict were clear. The rest would be settled in blood.

"Very well, then," Paendurion said, swinging his legs down, reaching to grab his blade from the floor. The exposed skin on his back and shoulders looked as though he'd been pocked with knives, sections pierced and cut away in ragged strips and crevasses. Still he rose, his head almost reaching the ceiling, steadier on his feet than he should have been, given the stench of rot seeping from his wounds.

"Kill me," Paendurion said, "if you can."

76

TIGAI

2nd Corps Command Tents
The Battle of Orstead

They strode through slush and mud, amid a buzzing throng of Sarresant troops, each seeming to go their own way, like a choreographed dance meant to mimic chaos while the troupe changed the scenery around them on the stage.

"Where is d'Arrent?" Sarine said, stopping a soldier with four stripes on his sleeves. "I need to find the High Commander at once."

The soldier gave her a curious look and said something in the Sarresant tongue, gesturing toward a clustering of tents before he pulled away.

Tigai trailed behind Sarine as she carved a path through the swarm. Every soldier seemed to have a task, or perhaps four tasks, all competing for their attentions. Tents were being struck, horses led in teams, wagons loaded and hitched and rolled through the masses swirling around them.

"Can't you do something to calm this?" he asked as he tried to match her pace.

The question served to slow her for a fraction. "I . . . could, I suppose," Sarine said. "But this isn't *Yellow*. They're excited, nervous, full of pride and duty. If I used *Green* it might interfere with their work."

It looked more like a retreat, so far as he could see. But whatever Sarine's strange notions of colors and emotions, she'd resumed her pace, pulling him on toward the few remaining tents without soldiers pulling up their stakes and rope. She pushed through them as though she belonged in spite of her civilian's clothes, until finally one of the soldiers noticed their approach, though the reaction was less the hostile order to halt and state their business he'd expected, and more a sort of reverent awe.

"*Sarine?*" the woman who'd noticed them said. "*Mes Dieux, ce ne peut être que vous.*"

"General Vassail," Sarine replied. "Thank the Gods. Where is High Commander d'Arrent? Tigai told me there were *kaas*-mages here, with the enemy. I came to help."

The woman—General Vassail, apparently—responded in a flurry of the Sarresant tongue, ushering them both inside one of the larger tents, where half a dozen ornately insignia'd men and women stood around them, debating and pointing and leaving him not understanding a word of it. Instead he occupied himself looking down at their maps, and those he could read easily enough: blue bars, for where the Sarresant troops had to be, pushing eastward across an open field facing a double half circle of ridges where a single blue dot had been drawn, surrounded by green. More green bars had been placed on either side of the ridges, and the numbers might have looked favorable for the Sarresant troops, were it not for the equally sized force of red and yellow bars approaching from the south.

They were on the verge of a defeat.

Little doubt remained, after witnessing the frenetic pace of their camp. Their command tents had been placed too close to the front. A vindication of every caution he'd given Mei. They'd picked the wrong side, and whatever her assurances that havens could be found even in defeat, it reeked of a sour end, when the Yanjin family had endured enough already. His thoughts drifted to the starfield, to the old man limned by shadows. If they were doomed to be set in *magi* chains, better, perhaps, to know the nature of the bargain. Better to stop running, and accept that he was not some powerless waif. He could affect the world as he wanted to see it, if he had the courage to try.

"You're here, thank the wind spirits."

He turned and almost jumped back, as two newcomers to the tent had taken up a place beside him. One a man he didn't recognize; the other, the Fox *magi*, Fei Zan, masked as Voren, whose knife he could still feel lodged in his heart, in phantom aches triggered by the sight of his face.

"I feared you'd abandoned us, boy," Fei Zan said, speaking Jun in quiet tones as the rest of the table had devolved into rapid exchanges in the Sarresant tongue.

"Not yet," he said. "But what's…this?" He gestured toward the maps. "It looks as though we're bloody fucked."

"It looks as grim as it is," Fei Zan said. "But with you here, and the girl, there is hope."

"Lord Tigai," one of the women said from across the table. He looked up and saw golden eyes staring back.

"D'Arrent needs us," Sarine said to him, translating what the woman with golden light for eyes had said. "But I don't know the limitations of the starfield—can we move into the path of the Thellan army? I can put up wardings to stop their *kaas*-mages scattering our lines, so long as I can get there."

"It doesn't work that way," Tigai said. "I can only take us to anchors. Places I've been, or places where there are already stars."

Sarine repeated what he'd said for the table's benefit, followed by a rapid exchange in the Sarresant tongue between the Empress's vessel and several of the generals.

"You must find a way," Fei Zan said to him privately. "Whatever the girl needs, you must take her where she needs to go."

"Like I said, it doesn't work that way. I can't—"

"Do you understand what is at stake here?" Fei Zan snapped. "We may already have run out of time. Unless d'Arrent can crush these armies and move on their homelands, Paendurion will ascend, and all of our efforts are for nothing."

"I can see lights, nearby, in the starfield," Sarine was saying. "Lord Tigai, are those the anchors you're speaking of?"

He frowned. There were only a handful of stars on this side of the Divide. He blinked and shifted his sight, remaining aware of both worlds at once.

"Those are old," he said. "From where we traveled south; I set anchors along the way. But none are strong enough to use with the strands. It takes days, a strong familiarity, to convert an anchor to a star, even a dim one."

"They're here," Sarine said in response to a question asked by d'Arrent's vessel, tracing a line across one of the maps between the blue bars and the yellow. "Tigai says they were left by the path he took southward."

Another burst of Sarresant speech, and Sarine answered it by nodding.

"Yes," she said. "I think we can use them. But Tigai will need to do it; I won't have the strength for both the wardings and the strands."

"What?" he said. "Were you not listening? I told you, old anchors are worthless—they fade in a matter of hours. I'm surprised you can even see them."

"I can...hold them," Sarine said. "I'm not sure what the right word is. It's like the wardings, but different. Look."

He prepared another argument and felt it die before it formed.

The anchors—faint lights, like a guttering lantern at the bottom of a stairwell—shimmered against the blackness, a chain tracing the route he and Acherre and Fei Zan had taken south across this very field, some days before. Blue sparks punched through the anchors from behind, leaking trails of brilliant white light as strong as any star.

"How the fuck are you doing that?" he said.

"Can you take me between them?" Sarine asked. "One at a time. I'll set wardings at each, and Anati can use *Green* to blunt the effects of the other *kaas' Yellow.*"

He nodded, tasting ash on his tongue. No wonder the old man in the starfield wanted her dead.

"It won't extend very far," Sarine said to d'Arrent's vessel. "But once I have anchors set, Anati and I can protect you here, along this line." She traced it again on the map. "Fight here, and the *kaas* won't affect your soldiers."

Fei Zan clapped him on the shoulder. His mind still reeled from what Sarine had done. She'd as good as torn open new holes in the starfield, creating anchors from nothing. Everything he knew of his gift said it shouldn't be possible, and yet he'd watched her do it.

Sarine extended a hand to him. "No sense delaying," she said. "I'm ready when you are."

77

ARAK'JUR

The Royal Palace
The City of Al Adiz, Thellan

A pale blue barrier sprang up around him, cutting across the chamber to isolate him on the far side of the door. Footsteps and screams sounded, and he drew on *una're*, channeling the force of the Great Bear's roar as he struck the shield with enough force to shatter a stone. The barrier paled, then ripped, revealing Paendurion ushering the two women out of the chamber, before turning to blast him with a wave of fire.

He leapt forward, clearing the base of the barrier in time to feel only a stinging wind, searing his skin without burning. The bed where Paendurion had lain cracked and collapsed as he landed atop it, sending feathers and straw into the air. A second shimmering barrier sprang in place before he could recover, once more spread across the chamber, sealing him away from the door. Only this time, Paendurion had somehow moved to put himself on the same side as Arak'Jur, all traces of his wounds vanished as he hefted his colossal sword at waist height, leveling it in one hand to track Arak'Jur with the point.

Una're's gift sent shocks through the bed frame as he pushed off, ready to parry sword strokes with the force of the bear's spectral claws.

He charged, and Paendurion swung the sword in an overhead chop, bringing it down with speed and power belying the frail figure who had risen from a deathbed moments before. Arak'Jur raised a hand to deflect the stroke—and parried nothing. The sword cleaved through him with no effect, as though the blade were made of nothing more than light and air. He followed it with a strike at Paendurion's body, and fell forward, off-balance, as his fist struck the same emptiness. Illusion. The leyline magic.

A pivot recovered his footing, and he struck at the barrier again, this time ducking as soon as he connected, anticipating a second wave of flame. None came. Instead a third barrier shimmered from the doorway, with two more copies of Paendurion waiting in front of it, both brandishing the sword, the same as the first had done.

Both illusions. There to distract and fool his senses; the real man was hobbled, though his wounds appeared not to have slowed his use of fair-skin magic. Arak'Jur rushed the barrier again, feeling a jarring pressure as he struck, and he might have been repelled if not for the power behind *una're*'s blows. Wind rushed through as he ripped the barrier down and stepped into the hallway, this time finding two more barriers, one on either side.

Time was too short to guess; aided by fair-skin magic, Paendurion could escape down a side passage or unfamiliar door. Arak'Jur closed his eyes, drawing on *astahg*, and felt his body shift to incorporeal mist.

He remembered what it was to be the prince of the forest, and sensed his prey. The northern passage. *Astahg*'s gift would linger only a few moments, but it put him in the buck spirit's domain, half in the physical world and half somewhere else. He raced toward the sensation of his prey, sliding through two more walls of thin white haze.

He returned to the physical world, and instinct sent him to the ground.

Fire blasted overhead, this time catching on the tapestries and carpet as it lingered in the air. But *lakiri'in* gave his gift as he slid to the floor, and he sprang forward, grappling for Paendurion's legs with blinding speed.

The giant fell, but twisted as he did, throwing a kick that took Arak'Jur in the nose, snapping his neck back with a cracking sound and a rush of blood and pain.

They both clattered to the ground, and Paendurion's image blinked, six copies of him appearing side by side, each one hobbled and struggling to rise to its feet.

Arak'Jur lay still, *anahret*'s gift giving him a semblance of death, with Mountain's gift at the ready.

Paendurion made no move to approach. Instead a dome of white haze formed above him on the ground.

"I know all of Ad-Shi's tricks, fledgling," Paendurion said. "I wonder if you know a tenth of them."

The dome vanished, and Arak'Jur called on *mareh'et*, springing to the side as another gout of flame scorched through the rugs to scour the stone beneath.

By now the fire burned on its own, spreading along the ceiling as it caught along the hall.

"She taught me enough," he said, snapping up to his feet. He adopted a posture of alertness without moving, watching all six copies from the corners of his eyes. Streams of blood ran from Paendurion's back and sides.

"You will kill me, if this continues," Paendurion said, all six of his copies spitting blood in varying poses. "What will it earn you, but a return to shadow?"

"A chance for peace," he said, stepping warily as he moved closer to two of the copies.

"Peace," Paendurion repeated. "I fought for peace, and I am here, still fighting."

"Mountain named you a bringer of war," he said, and lunged, slicing through one copy, then another. Both shattered in a spray of light, and all six collapsed, re-forming in new positions, arrayed around the hall.

Paendurion stepped back, the giant's energy flagging at last. Two of his copies failed to re-form, while the remaining four trembled, staggering to catch their breath.

Arak'Jur advanced, striking another copy, exploding it into light.

"So be it, then," Paendurion said. "But I die fighting. I hope the same will be said of you."

The remaining copies rushed toward him, a last surge of speed and strength. He swept one copy aside, revealing it for incorporeal light, then *mareh'et*'s claws struck flesh, impaling Paendurion through the belly.

Blood spattered across his chest as Paendurion coughed, and the giant managed one last, feeble strike, punching Arak'Jur in the jaw hard enough to wrench his head to the side. He responded with a harder shove, plunging both hands deeper into Paendurion's gut, severing his spine and ripping through to the skin of his already-ruined lower back.

Paendurion's legs collapsed, and Arak'Jur lowered him to the floor, withdrawing his hands with a squelch of gore and soft, sticky pulp.

A flash of light filled the hall.

THE RECKONING IS UPON US.

Laughter, sudden and unexpected from Paendurion's broken form, sounding over top of the voice, the same distant echo Arak'Jur had heard in the hallway outside Paendurion's door. "Now," Paendurion said. "It happens now."

MY CHILDREN. BY YOUR LINES, BE JUDGED. COME TO MY SANCTUM, IF YOU ARE WORTHY.

Arak'Jur took a step back, as images of spirits flickered in the air. The Great Cat, *mareh'et*, shimmering as though he'd conjured it to give his blessing. *Anahret*, watching him with its eyes of smoke. *Lakiri'in*, *una're*, *astahg*, *juna'ren*, more. Lines of color seemed to leak from nothingness, swirls of green pods, red motes, white pearls, black clouds.

Paendurion picked himself up, the top half of his body propped up while his legs lay twisted on the floor.

"Ascension," Paendurion said. "The time has come."

The spirits swirled around the hall, until their forms seemed to be watching them from all sides. At the same moment, the lines of color wrapped themselves around Paendurion. The colors blurred together, shining lights and forms, so he could see each one in turn, glowing as the spirits appeared, growing warmer, hotter as each strand of light encircled them both. A thousand threads reached out from Paendurion, connecting him to a web that spanned an impossible distance, as each spirit shimmered into view, seeming to confer with the others before they nodded approval toward him.

"What is this?" he asked. "Is it...?"

Paendurion coughed again, by now obscured behind a wall of color and light. "See to your power, as I will see to mine," Paendurion said. "And it seems we are fated to meet again. At the place my people called the Gods' Seat."

COME FORWARD, CHAMPION.

The familiar blackness surrounded him, the empty void of being and not-being.

He willed himself into it, submerging his consciousness in the spirits' presence.

I have followed your guidance, Great Spirits, he thought into the void.

YES. WE REMEMBER NOW. WE REMEMBER WHAT IT IS TO BE CHOSEN. WE HAVE HEARD THE MASTER'S CALL.

Three images formed. An old man, with a wispy beard dressed in tattered robes. Another: a faceless, shrouded figure, slight of form, neither obviously man nor woman. And a third, a woman he recognized. Sarine.

WE ARE BOUND TO THE GODDESS. WE SERVE LIGHT, AND LIFE. YOU WILL FACE DEATH, AT HER SIDE.

Sarine. She is the Goddess?

YES.

The simple revelation filled him with awe.

SHE WILL MAKE DEMANDS OF YOU. BUT DO NOT FORGET—YOU ARE OF US. WE ARE PLEDGED TO HER, BUT WE ARE NOT HER. REMEMBER OUR WAYS. REMEMBER YOUR PEOPLE.

I am Sinari, he thought. *I honor the spirits, as my father did, and his father. As will my son.*

THIS IS GOOD.

The images dimmed and faded.

Great Spirits, he thought, *what comes next? If the test is finished, what must I do now?*

Another set of images appeared, this time moving, a sensation of the ground lurching beneath his feet. The void itself seemed to shift, gliding between pillars of energy on a plane extending outward in every direction.

YOU ARE TO BE PRESENTED TO THE GODDESS, FOR HER TO JUDGE YOU WORTHY.

The image expanded as they moved, until the void gave way and the plane of energy swallowed the emptiness. The spirits flew through the energy, soaring between the columns as the falcon would, with the agility of the cat, the stoic power of mountain and bear.

A towering pillar of light appeared, stretching the dimensions of the plane, and the spirits shot toward it, weaving between strands of white and pillars of blue with effortless grace.

HERE. THIS IS THEIR PLACE.

Whispers from the spirits sounded around him as their momentum ceased.

His will seemed to matter again, and he pushed forward, into the light. The spirits flowed around him, with him, as though he had drawn on all their gifts at once.

ARAK'JUR. OUR STRENGTH IS YOURS. IN THIS, AND ALL THINGS TO COME.

The light grew as he approached, towering over him until it became all he could see.

Thank you, Great Spirits, he thought. *For your wisdom, and your blessings. For the protection you have afforded my people.*

GO WITH PRIDE, SON OF THE SINARI. CHAMPION OF THE WILD.

He touched the light.

78

ERRIS

Eastern Fields
The Battle of Orstead

White smoke lingered atop the heights, a cloud that grew with every blast of their stolen guns.

"Ten points south-southeast, two points skyward," Field-Colonel Regalle said, snapping orders to fullbinders as though they were a common artillery squad. And so they were, today.

Another rippling wave sounded as more guns went off, rocking the earth beneath their feet. No coordinated salvos; the crews fired each gun as soon as it was ready. Colonel Regalle marched up and down the line, making corrections with the benefit of *Mind* to project his senses forward, seeing each shot as it rained death on their enemies. She sat atop Jiri's back, wielding a spyglass as though it were a saber, straining to find clear moments with the white smoke turned fog pooling around them.

"Your Majesty," Essily said, standing beside her and all but holding Jiri's reins. "With all possible respect, you must retire. Marquand is preparing to ride shortly. Go with him, please."

She panned her glass to the east, to where the flags of the 42nd Infantry pushed forward in one of the last remaining pockets of fighting. They'd broken. The Sardians had broken, and they'd been alone. All through the fighting, she'd expected a wave of Skovan reinforcements, or some other deadly surprise. Instead her army had collided with their lines backed by a steady rain of fire from Regalle's stolen guns, and, but for a bare handful of pockets scattered by their *kaas*, her soldiers had routed the enemy. Green flags, where they stood, were pulling back to the horizon, re-forming at the edge of her spyglass's vision, while blue-coated soldiers let them flee, re-forming into ranks of their own, ready to pivot around and make the forced march westward to resume the fighting.

"I intend to," she said to Essily, snapping her glass shut.

"To field command, Your Majesty," Essily said. "Not to the front."

Jiri whickered at her aide, saving her the trouble of repeating the dismissal. "I can't ask our soldiers to fight two battles in a day while I rest myself in a tent. They need every rallying point, and if my fighting with them is one, then they'll get it."

"Majesty, they need their commander—their Empress—to be alive at the end of the fighting. You need time to recover."

"I need a victory, Captain. Nothing else matters today."

Essily fell quiet, though his disapproval showed in every unspoken word. The left part of her chest throbbed, and she'd buttoned the front of her coat to hide the blood, seeping through to stain her shirt and undergarments where her wound still pulsed in time with her heart. *Life* and *Body* bindings coursed through her, masking the pain, made worse every time she made a *Need* connection or exerted herself too quickly. Without the bindings she'd have long since bled out; with them, she'd make a full recovery with a week or two of rest. But the battle was here, now. She had to be here, too.

The last rounds of shot went off, and Regalle was already shouting for the guns to be turned west, toward the open field where the next battle would be fought. Gods stay with her, and give her strength. She had to manage one more *Need* connection, this time to field command, to ensure that her plan was set in motion in time for Sarine and Tigai to do whatever it was that would nullify the *kaas*-mages among her enemy's lines. Marquand and Jiri could see her to the front while she worked. All she had to do was stay conscious while they rode.

———

Cheers woke her; Jiri's steadiness kept her from pitching herself from the saddle. A long line of soldiers at a double-quick march raced through the tall grasses, churning mud and slush as they drove toward the field of battle. She blinked, starting as she caught hold of the reins. The world seemed to spin for a moment, before settling on the scene in front of her: a sea of soldiers in blue, yelling with coarse voices as they caught sight of the battle standard Essily carried, mounted at her side. Her standard: solid blue, adorned with two centered golden stars.

Over a hundred thousand souls, pivoting from one battle into another. Across the field red and yellow flags arrayed themselves into makeshift formations to meet her charge. That had been the order of the day. Charge. Every unit commander, bound to rush toward where Sarine had promised her immunity from the *kaas*. All was lost unless they could reach those positions in time.

"Your Majesty, sir, it's bloody fine to have you with us."

Her vision blurred and re-formed. A colonel's entourage, and half a dozen aides, falling into a steady gait beside her. Essily and the rest of Marquand's elite trailed behind, where they joined the forced march toward the center of the field.

"My compliments, Brigade-Colonel," she replied. "See to it your people are ready for action. All will be decided here, now. Today."

MY CHILDREN.

The voice thundered through her skull. She only half heard it through the sounds of men and women preparing for battle around her.

"Yes, sir, Your Majesty," the colonel replied. "The Seventy-First is ready. We saw action on the eastern flank. We'll give 'em the Nameless's own fire here in the west."

THE MOMENT APPROACHES. READY YOURSELVES, TO BE WEIGHED AND JUDGED.

She made an effort to nod, and keep her place in the saddle. The voice had to be a phantom, some hallucination induced by her wound. She fought to stay centered. Now was no time to lose control. Some paces behind, Marquand was barking orders, divvying up the fullbinders into smaller squads placed to counter any vanguard skirmishers waiting before they could reach the line. Her plan had been simple enough, and she trusted those beneath her to see to the details. Everything hung on the plan's execution in the next hours. Simple directives and maximum flexibility in achieving tactical goals was the answer, not grand strategy. Her part was all but finished, save for sitting atop Jiri's back and looking the part.

"Your Majesty," Essily said when the colonel and his retinue had withdrawn. "You need rest. Please. Let me take you to field command."

"Not a step backward from the front," she said. "Even if I collapse. You find a way to hold me in place."

"Your Majesty..." Essily said.

"Not another word on it. Not where anyone could hear."

READY YOURSELVES, FOR ASCENSION.

The voice rang like artillery in her ears; or perhaps it was only artillery, Regalle's guns thundering overhead from behind. She ignored it. All they had to do was hold the line. Her chest had gone numb, and a chill seemed to have risen on the air. Good. Battle was hot, between the flash of powder and the thrill of the fight. Cold weather killed on long days' marches through snow, but when battle came, winter was a welcome ally.

"Forward!"

The 71st's colonel had a low, booming voice that knifed through the chaos of battle. Another regiment to their right heard the call and responded in kind, triggering a ripple of soldiers standing from where they'd knelt to fire, following their fellows toward the enemy line.

Smoke and powder stung the air, but she felt none of it. Jiri stood beside her banner, now firmly planted in the field where Sarine and Tigai had drawn their protective line. The soldiers here had pushed well beyond its limits, charging to threaten the enemy positions, as she'd ordered them to do. Every man knew the *kaas*-mages would affect them; every man knew not to rout, once the effects of their pernicious magic faded.

She was the rock. The stone wall, marking safety. Elsewhere, the 3rd Corps and Wexly's Gandsmen held along Sarine's exact line. Here, de Tourvalle's 2nd Corps pushed forward to bait the enemy into her trap.

Another wave of musket fire met her soldiers as they charged, and this she felt in her gut, as though a dozen of those musket balls had been meant for her. Soldiers in blue fell while the rest retreated, broken and beaten back by the enemy. Every instinct told her their morale would break, that this section of the line was lost. But with *kaas* on the enemy side, her instincts were wrong. Her men would fall back, recover, and attack again, until the enemy committed enough of their *kaas* to concentrate on breaking the center.

"D'Arrent? What's going on here?"

The voice pulled her back from where her soldiers were dying. A distant sound, though it came from immediately beside her. She heard it through a veil of fog. Sarine.

"My lady," Essily said, moving between Sarine and where she sat atop Jiri's back. "Her Majesty cannot be disturbed now."

"What under the Nameless is going on here?" Sarine demanded. "I didn't set wardings this far west. Those soldiers are being scattered by *Yellow*."

Erris turned, though the world seemed to shift slowly, with heavy weight behind her eyes. Sarine was there, though she hadn't been anywhere near the command lines before, with Lord Tigai beside her.

"I say again," Essily said, "the Empress cannot be disturbed."

A moment of silence, or incredulity, and then Sarine spoke. "She has these soldiers fighting in the wrong place. I can ride forward and move the wardings, but—"

"No," Erris said. The sound almost surprised her, coming from her own lips.

"Your Majesty," Essily said.

"No," she repeated. "Leave the...wardings where they are."

"But the *kaas*-mages," Sarine said. "Those soldiers will run. They'll be killed!"

"Some will," she said.

"Why? Why would you not give them a chance to fight?"

"We have to show him weakness," she said. "Tempt him to concentrate, to move. Then we attack. We can...order them to—"

The world blurred, and the ground moved, rushing toward her as though the earth itself had tethered *Body*.

———

"Why didn't you tell me she was wounded?" Sarine demanded. Cold air bit Erris's skin, exposed as her coat had been torn open, her shirts and undergarments parted to reveal her naked chest.

"No," Erris said. "Have to stay mounted. Fetch Jiri."

Sarine placed hands below her breastbone, where the saber had cut deepest. She felt the rush of *Body* and *Life*, stronger than she'd ever held a tether on her own. Blood drenched Sarine's hands and lower arms. So much blood. They should fetch a *Life* binder; Sarine was in no condition to administer healing, if she herself was covered in so much blood.

Booms and musket fire sounded around her. Familiar sounds. By now Marquand would be leading his fullbinder elite to attack the *kaas*-mages. Her soldiers would have fallen back to Sarine's *Green*, recovered from the *Yellow* in time to meet the enemy at the height of his hubris. They'd be caught in her trap, and victory would follow. She'd beaten him. Paendurion. She'd finally found the way.

"She's dying," Sarine said. "You bloody let her ride around leaking half her blood into her underclothes. Gods damn it. I need her. I need her strength, and you let her bloody kill herself!"

THE RECKONING IS UPON US.

Her hallucination came again, but it faded in with the rest of their arguing. Peace and warmth came for her, finally, after so much numbness and cold. A hundred golden lights shone in the distance—*Need* vessels, beckoning her to join with them. She felt them like a miniature network of leylines, all emanating from her.

MY CHILDREN. BY YOUR LINES, BE JUDGED. COME TO MY SANCTUM, IF YOU ARE WORTHY.

Loyalty washed over her like a blanket, sheltering her from the cold, and she embraced them, reaching out to trace a pattern that limned every land under her control. New Sarresant, the city and the state that bore its name, reaching from the northern colonies all the way to the south, through l'Euillard, Villecours, Lorrine. The Gand colonies, from Devonshire to Covendon. Old Sarresant, now bound to her through alliance, but subject to her military power.

Eyes seemed to be watching her as she traced the lines of loyalty, weighing her against another set, this time drawn from her enemies. Thellan, the old world and the new. The motherland of Gand, its islands across the sea. Sardia in the east, such as remained of its armies. The momentum was hers; she'd won here, today, and broken the strength of three nations. A march to Al Adiz, a blockade around Gand, and she might be well on her way to uniting every people under her throne, or at least enforcing peace through the strength of discipline and valor. The eyes watching her seemed to agree, but with a wistful sadness. She was not a conqueror yet. She would fall short of ascension, in spite of all her victories.

"There might be a way," Sarine was saying. "The Gods' Seat—it healed Yuli, when we traveled there. It's far from certain, but we have to try something."

Tigai argued something in his strange tongue, and Sarine said something else in reply.

It didn't matter. Whatever the strange voice wanted, she knew in her heart she'd beaten Paendurion, grown strong enough to keep her people safe. If death came for her, she could meet it with pride. A soldier's duty. The greatest price, one she'd asked of too many men and women to be afraid to pay it herself.

"We have to try," Sarine said. "Gather close."

Blackness enveloped her, and Sarine's touch radiated a final warmth, before she slipped into darkness.

79

SARINE

The Infinite Plane
Traveling to the Gods' Seat

This time instinct guided the way.

The blue sparks crackled and surged around her, making columns of familiar energy that seemed to draw her inward, toward the towering column of light. There was more to this place than the light; she was sure of it, now, seeing it without the Veil's emotions clawing at her thoughts. But she was here for a reason, and felt the burden of two spheres traveling with her as they approached the light.

Erris d'Arrent. A flickering candle. The woman who had declared herself Empress. The woman who had saved New Sarresant. A woman she needed, at her side, as a champion.

Yanjin Tigai, who had insisted he come with her, burning strong where d'Arrent was dim. As strange a man as she'd ever met—but he, too, had power. He, too, she needed to bond, if she meant to stand against the shadow.

Both flew alongside her as they moved. Both strong enough to fight, if she could reach the Seat in time.

Ceiling and floor warped as they drew closer. There was meaning here, shape and purpose in every surging spark. She could see echoes of forms: hillsides covered in snow, cities lit in the night, men and women waking to continue the patterns that shaped their lives. The weight of it fell on her now, of finding a way to defeat her enemy, the one who threatened to distort and bend the beauty implied behind the sparks. And it started with her champions. What little she'd gleaned from the Veil's journal made that much clear: champions, to be chosen from among those deemed worthy to reach the Seat. And why not more than three, if more had proved themselves? She had Yuli already—and Reyne d'Agarre, little as the thought gave her any comfort—and more would come.

The white cords dangled from the spire, and again instinct plotted the way through. She contorted herself like a dancer, dodging and weaving between them until the central column flooded her vision, and she reached out, brushing formless fingertips against the light.

Air rushed into her lungs, and she stepped forward onto smooth, polished stone.

"Wind spirits," Tigai said, seeming to catch his breath, doubling over to hold his knees where he stood. "What would have happened, had you struck one of those cords?"

"You could see the way here?" she asked. Neither Yuli nor Lin had said as much, before.

"Of bloody course I could. Whatever that was, it wasn't bloody natural."

"How is this possible?" d'Arrent asked, staring at her, pressing gloved hands against the front of her coat. The High Commander—no, the Empress—was standing, though she'd lain a hairsbreadth from dead, back on the battlefield.

"Thank the Gods," Sarine said. "Last time we came here, it healed Yuli. I'd hoped it would do the same for you."

D'Arrent unfastened her coat's buttons, pulling it open to reveal a pristine white shirt underneath, as though it had been freshly tailored and fitted to her form.

"Yuli is here?" Tigai asked.

"Yes," she said. "And I need both of you to come with me. I did something to bond with her, at the heart of this place. I need to see if we can repeat it."

Already it was different, being here again. She could sense the energy in the central chamber, as though it had grown stronger since she'd left. It was as though the Veil had been damping her connection to it, keeping her from an affinity that resonated between her and the stone. She could sense Yuli, somewhere in the direction of the living quarters, where a room had been made for her from nothing. She could sense Reyne d'Agarre, in his library. She sensed the shadow creature—the watcher, lingering in the central chamber with…

Two newcomers.

She felt their forms the same way she felt Tigai and Erris; all four were here, but distant, as though they'd been shaded without being sketched, drawn on paper without framing lines to set boundaries for their shapes.

She rounded the hallways toward the central chamber with rising determination. Bonding. That had to be the difference; she'd bonded Yuli herself, and Reyne had been bonded by the Veil. Whoever else was here, they hadn't been chosen in the same way. More secrets to learn, and never enough time.

The smooth stone hallways gave way to the massive central chamber, still melted to slag from the Veil's interference in Yuli's bonding. Ridges and pits decorated the floor and ceiling, leaving the column of light showing through where the stone was melted away. Two men stood around the beam, each gazing up at it. Two men she knew.

"Arak'Jur," she said. The tribesman, the one she'd traveled with to Ka'Ana'Tyat. The other was clearer in her memory. "Paendurion."

Her words seemed to startle them both, though Paendurion recovered quickly, rounding on her with an easy confidence.

"Sarine, you've returned," he began, then froze as quickly as he'd turned. "Who is with you?"

"How is it you've come to be here?" she asked, but d'Arrent stepped forward, cutting short any reply.

"Paendurion," d'Arrent said. "This is him."

A moment of recognition passed between them. "Erris d'Arrent," Paendurion said. "No. It can't be. I won. This isn't possible."

"I brought them here," Sarine said. "D'Arrent, and Lord Tigai. But how did—?"

"Liar," d'Arrent snapped at Paendurion, her voice full of cold rage. "I defeated you. Orstead is mine. Your Sardians are being routed as we speak, and the Thellan lines are advancing into a trap."

"It never mattered," Paendurion said. "So long as I held more lands than you at the moment of ascension, I would rise, and here I stand. But you cannot be here." He looked to Sarine. "She cannot be here."

"Monster," d'Arrent snapped, bringing the chamber to a cold silence. "You are responsible for the deaths of thousands of innocents, and I mean to see you face justice for every drop of New Sarresant blood."

"You fool," Paendurion said. "I am responsible for the deaths of millions of innocents—thousands of millions. And I will bear the weight of thousands more, if it keeps the world from shadow. You understand nothing. I will not be denied the right of my ascension. I have won. I am to be champion. By the Holy Veil, the mantle is mine again."

"The Veil is dead," Sarine said. "But I've come to know my place. I bonded Yuli already. I can bond the rest of you, if you'll accept—"

"No!" Paendurion roared. "Even you—even the Veil. All of you are blind. The old ways have preserved peace between Life and Death, between Light and Shadow. It is Three. Three against Three, to settle the right of the Soul."

"I'll serve in no capacity with that creature," d'Arrent said. "If he will not submit to arrest, then I will kill him where he stands."

By now Yuli and Reyne had appeared in the opposite hallway. Yuli's face brightened, seeing Tigai, where Reyne wore a look equal parts confusion and surprise.

"Lord Tigai," Yuli said, while Reyne said, "D'Arrent? The High Commander? Sarine... and Paendurion?"

"What did you mean?" Sarine asked Paendurion. "Why only three champions? And what are the old ways?"

"There must be three, and I am the only fit champion of Order," Paendurion said. "You must see reason. Reyne and this Yuli are bonded already; I must be the third. To do otherwise is to risk ruin."

Sarine glanced back to d'Arrent, who looked as though she might draw a pistol, or start flinging *Entropy* at Paendurion, while most of the others stood silently, edging away from the pair. Only Arak'Jur spoke, standing near the light at the center of the room.

"I have won the mantle of the spirits," the tribesman said. "They named me champion already. Is it not done?"

"An old magic," Paendurion said. "But each line can only carry its chosen to the Soul. It falls to the Veil to bond them, if they are worthy. And it is always three."

"Paendurion is right," Reyne said. "The Codex always speaks of three. Never more. I know some measure of its secrets. If—"

"At best you have an inkling," Paendurion interrupted. "All of you. We engineered it that way. We suppressed knowledge of ascension. We tore apart the leylines, we sundered every nation and tribe. We blinded the spirits, culling their memories until nothing but husks remained. We drove the *kaas* mad with Axerian's riddles. We were the Three. Me, Axerian, Ad-Shi. Now two of us are dead, and I alone know what it means to face the shadow. Power may rest with the Veil—or with Sarine, if she is to be the Veil's heir. But the knowledge is mine." He turned to Sarine. "Banish the rest of these pretenders. Bond me, and we will face the Regnant together. Already the Divide crumbles, now that the moment of ascension has arrived. Time is precious. We have weeks, at best, before the enemy's champions cross into our lands."

The rest of their eyes turned toward her, caught halfway across the room, between d'Arrent and Paendurion.

Anati appeared unbidden on a rocky point near her feet.

My father says his time is finished, Anati thought to the room. *He cannot be allowed to complete his ascension.*

Paendurion stared at Anati, his eyes wide.

"Zi," Sarine said. "What else did he say? Does he know of this 'old way'?"

"No!" Reyne shouted. "You can't trust Zi. He's betrayed us."

That got her attention, and Anati's, too, both of them looking to where Reyne stood at the far entrance.

"I bonded Xeraxet," Reyne continued, "after Axerian's death. He is convinced Zi is working with the enemy—the Regnant, as Paendurion calls him."

Lies, Anati thought. *My father would never betray Sarine.*

But he has.

A new voice, and a familiar one. A voice of iron scraped on steel.

A *kaas* appeared, perched atop Reyne's shoulder. Axerian's *kaas*. Xeraxet. Why had he said nothing about this before?

Your father was loyal to the Veil, Xeraxet continued. *Zi would do anything to further her ends.*

You are stained by madness, Anati thought back.

"Enough of this," Paendurion said to her. "The *kaas* are treacherous creatures by nature. Their games are of no consequence here. All that matters is bonding your third champion."

"I stand with Paendurion," Reyne said. "He knows the truth of everything we face. Whatever ill you or your *kaas* think of him, he is the clear choice."

"He's a monster," d'Arrent said. "I saw what he did at Fantain's Cross, at Oreste, in New Sarresant itself. He is a butcher with no regard for innocent life. Whatever side he is on, they are my enemy, and I will fight against them with all the strength of New Sarresant and Old."

"I saw the same," Arak'Jur said quietly. "In visions granted to me atop the mountain. This man deserves to die. It is justice."

Tigai and Yuli hung back, silently watching her along with the rest. It fell to her. She'd known it would, given the strange affinity she felt for this place, the path she'd walked to understand even the first principles of the bonding, and the blue sparks. This was why she'd come here, why she'd brought so many powerful men and women with her. It ended here, or perhaps began. She wasn't the Veil, but she was something close to it. Even without a full understanding of what lay in front of her, her teachers had given her enough to know the shape of the role she would play. Axerian. Zi. Even the Veil herself, through the sketches and writings of her journal. How many times had the cycle repeated itself? If she was to be the Veil reborn, she would find a way to do what was right. To fight her enemy and pull the world away from shadow, whatever the cost.

"I need both of you," she said. "I don't care how things were done before. I need all the strength you can give me. I need every champion I can bond to help me fight."

"No," Paendurion said. "I won't let you damn us with your ignorance. If this won't be decided by reason, then let it be decided by blood."

80

ERRIS

Soul of the World
Gods' Seat

A sucking sound tore through the chamber, and she reached for
Shelter, slamming a barrier into place as Paendurion's *Entropy*
manifested in a sheet of fire.

Chaos followed.

She heard shouting, more sucking wind, a low roar, and the clang of
bone on steel. Sarine, pleading for him to stop. Reyne, doing the same.
Erris knew better. He was coming for her. He'd always been coming for
her, since the first threads of *Need* had marked her as his enemy. And
now, the horrifying realization: She couldn't sense the golden threads
anymore, since coming to this place. No time to process what it might
mean. She held her *Shelter*, but Paendurion would be moving, bolstered
by *Body*, as she was, coming to strike her from an unexpected angle
where her barrier blocked her view.

She drew her saber by reflex, spinning to the left—the clearest, most
direct approach, which marked it the obviously wrong choice and
therefore the only one Paendurion would use.

He appeared around the corner of her *Shelter* and she dropped the
binding, lashing out with a sixfold weave of *Death* to target the *Mind*
copies he would have already summoned to mask his true position. Four

copies were attacking from the right, two more from the left, and all save the one in front of her hissed and shimmered as her *Death* made contact, her saber cutting toward the only solid form.

He'd unlimbered a broadsword from a sheath slung over his back, and met her cut with surprise in his eyes, though his stroke was no less sure for it, turning her blade with a powerful slash that all but sent her spinning off-balance across the jagged floor.

Body surged through her, with *Death* tethers at the ready to defend it. Paendurion towered over her, easily triple her mass, his arms thick and glistening as he returned his broadsword to a high guard. Without *Body* she couldn't hope to turn even a single attack, but even with it, his strength far eclipsed hers. She'd have to fight on different terms, or find a way to hobble him, though the thought was fleeting as he advanced toward her, sword in hand.

She tried *Entropy*, a rush of fire immediately snuffed by Paendurion's *Death*, and he struck, bringing his sword down in a brutal chop. She slapped it aside, letting his momentum shift his weight, and tried a counterattack, stepping closer to negate his advantages of height and reach. *Shelter* materialized between them, as though he'd crafted the white pearls in place of armor, and she struck against it, rebounding with hissing energy instead of sinking her steel into his skin.

"Paendurion, stop," Sarine was shouting. Only words, at the start, but now a wave of *Shelter* barriers sprang up around both Erris and Paendurion, a half-dozen walls all conjured into being at once, with more speed than even Erris could manage. "We can settle this. Stop fighting."

She'd recovered her footing, resetting for another attack. With her vision split between the physical world and the leylines, she could see the myriad strands of pearls Sarine wove around them, the strands of *Death* held between both her and Paendurion, the *Body* strands connecting them both to the leylines surging beneath the stone. It was as though the lines overflowed with an infinite supply, fueling any attack or defense, and she could sense the patterns of three weavers disrupting and calling on the energies collected there.

Then, in an instant, a new connection appeared. Then another. Strands of *Death* pooled seemingly on their own, making spheres of inky black where Sarine had drawn *Shelter*'s white pearls.

No time to puzzle out their source; the effect was clear. The *Shelter* Sarine put between them fizzled and vanished, revealing Paendurion charging toward her, leaping and brandishing his sword.

Erris sprang back, darting strikes from her saber to check his advance, but he barreled into her reach, slamming his heavy blade down hard enough to shatter the stone when he missed his first attack. She dodged to the side and struck, finding another barrier of *Shelter* instead of footwork to turn her sword with his. This time she was ready, deploying *Death* to tear it apart, but he countered in kind, and her *Body* faded as his *Death* strands touched her, sliding past the defenses she'd expended to disrupt his shield.

Her saber struck his flesh, but without *Body* she was reduced to a small-statured woman, no more than a bare fraction of his size. The cut should have sheared him in half; instead she sliced his rib cage in a glancing blow, and he spun, ripping her saber from her hand with the force of his *Body*-empowered parry, sending her blade clattering as it flew across the room.

"No!" Sarine shouted. "That power isn't yours."

The black spheres vanished abruptly from the leylines, and another set of *Shelter* sprang up between her and Paendurion, walling him off in a prison of white.

"It's been mine for sixteen cycles," Paendurion said from behind the filmy haze. Erris took the moment to scramble after her saber, springing across the floor to where it fell. "All of this has been mine. I won't have it stripped away by a fool with no knowledge of things to come."

"What you did, what Axerian did, and Ad-Shi," Sarine said. "It was wrong."

"It was necessary!" Paendurion shouted back, his words dimmed by the *Shelter* but clearly audible throughout the chamber. Erris approached the *Shelter* from a different angle, careful not to tether any leylines to reveal her position. Paendurion seemed content to speak to Sarine, letting her maintain her barriers, but she could sense *Life* and *Body* connecting Paendurion to the leylines, with *Death* tethers held at the ready. Any moment Paendurion could lash out, disrupt the *Shelter*, and renew his attack. It was a great risk, waiting to tether her own connections to match him, but boldness had been the answer on the battlefield. It had to be the answer here, too.

"You murdered countless thousands," Sarine said. "You shattered civilizations, and for what? The chance to wake and do it again?"

"Do you imagine the Regnant would do otherwise? We've held him back for sixteen cycles. No matter what price we paid, it was worth the cost."

"You've changed nothing. He's still there, still coming. I mean to find another way."

"To defeat Death?" Paendurion laughed. "It can't be done. The way is the way—there are rules of this world: champions and ascensions and Godhood. It is as it has always been."

"No," Sarine said. "It isn't."

"You are a fool."

"I mean to bind as many champions as I can bring here. When the Divide comes down, we will meet the Regnant in strength. Whatever you've done—whatever you think you need to do, we can change the nature of this conflict. I've faced him before, and I can do it again, with all of you at my side."

Sarine's *Shelter* faded, revealing Paendurion standing with his sword point-down, facing the center of the room where Sarine stood between him and the column of light.

Erris moved.

Body came at the last possible moment, *Death* springing from her to intercept the ink-clouds that shot toward her, preserving her strength and speed. Paendurion turned, spinning to raise his sword, a look of surprise writ on his face.

It stayed there, frozen shock in his eyes, as she slammed her blade through his chest, impaling him through the heart.

81

TIGAI

Soul of the World
Gods' Seat

The giant's body slumped forward, pitching face-first into the stone with a jarring crunch.

From Tigai's vantage at the far entryway, the duel had lasted no more than a few moments, obscured by their shields as often as he saw them exchanging blows. That d'Arrent's final strike had come from behind seemed to have caught most of the room by surprise. But he'd seen her creeping approach, retrieving her sword and waiting in front of one of the shields. A reminder that even the mightiest of *magi* could be cut down, if they didn't see it coming.

"He might have listened," Sarine said quietly. "You didn't have to do that."

D'Arrent flicked her blade down, spattering blood across the stone.

"He wouldn't have listened," the Empress said. "I did what had to be done."

"Justice," Arak'Jur said, regarding Paendurion's body with a solemn air. "And now we submit ourselves, as the spirits foretold. I am here as champion of the Wild, chosen of the Mountain, and son of the Sinari."

"How is it I can understand you?" Yuli asked. "Are you one of the *kaas*-mages, like Master Reyne, or Sarine?"

Tigai frowned. She was right; he hadn't questioned it before, but d'Arrent and Arak'Jur both spoke what to his ears sounded like perfect Jun, though he knew neither of them had any command of the tongue.

"Another mystery of this place," Sarine said. "But Arak'Jur is right. It's time to bond you. All of you."

The tribesman knelt atop one of the few patches of smooth stone beside the column of light, and Sarine approached, climbing over the ruined chasms in the floor. Tigai watched her, his hand slipping down toward his pistols. Whatever she was doing, it might well present an opportunity to make good on the deal he'd been offered, to betray Sarine. He'd checked the starfield already; he could still sense it, even here in this strange place, and kept his vision attuned to its blackness. All he had to do was strike her down and lash himself to the nearest star.

Sarine reached Arak'Jur, and a flash of light flooded through the room.

Tigai squinted, shielding his eyes as a corona of images shimmered around the tribesman. Birds, fish, snakes, bears, cats, wolves, and more. Arak'Jur knelt through it, opening his eyes when the light receded moments later.

"What is that?" d'Arrent asked. "What did you do?"

"A great blessing," Arak'Jur said, full of awe.

"A bond, as a champion," Sarine said. "My champion. I don't understand all of it, but I know there's an enemy, with champions of his own. All of you are here to help me face him, to decide the fate of the Soul of the World. He's coming, with *magi* from the other side of the Divide. And I don't mean to stop at killing his champions. I mean to break these cycles, to allow the world to heal."

"The gift is strong," Yuli said. "With the bond, I can summon the Twin Fangs at will, with no sickness when it passes."

Arak'Jur nodded. "I can sense more than *mareh'et, astahg, valak'ar,* and the rest. I feel the blessings of every spirit. Great beasts, war-spirits, even spirits of fox, oak, beaver, and wolf."

"The enemy, the one you said was beyond the Divide," d'Arrent said. "These are the armies I saw... the ones with you, and Acherre?"

"Yes," Sarine said. "They're coming, with *magi* at their head."

"Then I accept," d'Arrent said, stepping over the fallen body of the man she'd impaled. "Whatever strength you have to offer, I'll take it and see it replicated throughout our ranks."

Tigai felt his heart thump, watching d'Arrent approach the column of light. He had to do it now. He tried to look relaxed, adopting an easy stance, relying on every pair of eyes to be focused on Sarine. He slid a hand around his pistol, thumbing the match in place and watching the starfield to be sure his anchor was set. It might well take several shots, to be sure. He'd need an anchor here, and another one waiting, somewhere far from the rest of these *magi* after they realized what he'd done.

Erris knelt, as Arak'Jur had, and reached a hand toward the column at the center of the room. Sarine touched her shoulder, but where there had been a flash of light before, this time a deadening quiet emanated from them, like a shock wave of silence, muting every sound within the chamber.

NO.

A thundering voice, sounding in his head. The others could hear it, too, from the looks of confusion, panning the room to find its source.

THREE. YOU HAVE ALREADY BONDED THREE. I HAVE TOLERATED MUCH FROM YOU, BUT THIS IS TOO FAR. YOU MUST NOT BIND A FOURTH.

A shadow appeared overhead, a cloud of jet, as though the starfield's empty blackness leaked into the real world.

"I'm not her," Sarine said, shouting loud enough that he heard it through the artificial calm. "Whatever deal you had with the Veil, consider it broken."

YOU RISK EVERYTHING, the voice said. Rumblings and thunder came from within the shadow as it grew, suspended in the air, just as it had at the Tower of the Heron. It had to be the same creature; whatever had appeared there must have found its way here, looking down on all of them, though it had no discernible eyes or features that he could see.

BIND A FOURTH, BIND ANY MORE, AND I WILL DO THE SAME. EVERY PEOPLE; EVERY CALLING, SUMMONED TO WAR. I WILL SHATTER THIS WORLD, AND THERE WILL BE NO HARMONY, WHEN I AM DONE.

"I know," Sarine said. "I know that's what you want. That's why I mean to stop you."

YOU CANNOT STAND AGAINST DEATH. PERSIST, AND NONE WILL SURVIVE. THIS WORLD WILL BE ASH, ALL ITS LIGHT EXTINGUISHED. TURN BACK FROM THIS FOLLY, AND I MAY YET FORGIVE.

The light flashed, as it had when she'd touched Arak'Jur, and colors erupted around Erris d'Arrent. Green pods, red motes, black ink, white pearls, blue coils, purple cubes, swirling around her in ordered lines. Light surged from her, pushing away the heavy silence and the shadow together.

RUIN, THEN, the voice said, dimming as it faded away. YOU CHOOSE THE PATH OF RUIN.

The light snapped back into the column, and the shadow was gone.

Erris stood, turning and inspecting her own hands as though they were unfamiliar tools.

"Incredible," d'Arrent said. "It's as though there are no limits; I can draw *Body, Mind...Need.* As deeply as I wish."

Sarine met her with warmth, then turned toward Tigai.

Shit. He hadn't fired. But then, what was he to do, when the shadow promised ruin to the world? Was that the creature he'd made his deal with, in the starfield? The whole notion seemed hollow, set against what he'd seen.

"Lord Tigai," Sarine said. "I'd have you as a champion, too, if you're willing."

He straightened, jerking his hands away from his weapons, as all their eyes turned to him.

"What does it mean?" he asked. "What does all of this mean? That voice, the shadow. I don't understand."

"Neither do I," Sarine said. "Except that the shadow is our enemy. Whatever we have to do to stop him, we do. And it starts here, with this bond."

He glanced between the others, feeling more than half a fool. All he'd wanted was a sure place for himself and his family. Talk of plots and wars and ruin was *magi* business, as far as he was concerned. But then, he was neck-deep in it, surrounded by vipers and pretending he wanted nothing to do with snakes. Maybe this was a path to strength, too.

He stepped forward. Maybe it was strength, and maybe he was a bloody fool, but that voice had promised war and death, where Sarine stood against it. Weighed between ruin and whatever it took to stop it, he knew which side he wanted his family on. That was enough. If he had to fight, he might as well be on the side of something worth fighting for.

82

SARINE

The Master's Sanctum
Gods' Seat

Lapping waves churned under gale winds, with the boom of thunder overhead. The seas drank in the gray haze of rain, seeming to pour through her, arms' lengths from the towering shadows of the Divide. It seemed thinner than it had when she, Axerian, Acherre, and Ka'Inari took their boat into its depths. Or perhaps it was only the storm.

She leaned away from the table, and the Master's map reverted, first to seas as black as the clouds above them, then to a wide expanse of blue, then the coastline, the great mass of eastern land, and finally all the continents of the world, pulled far as the view would go.

"A powerful magic," Arak'Jur said.

"It is," she replied.

"How do you make it change?" Arak'Jur asked. "Does it show you what it wills you to see, or do you choose?"

"I choose a place," she said. "I focus there, and the map shows me what I want to see. Look."

She picked another stretch of open sea near the Divide, this one unobscured by clouds. The view shimmered, changing as it moved closer to the edge of the land, then to the open sea. Finally it seemed as though she was drawn in, the sounds of the waves roaring in her ears, the tang of brine in the back of her throat. And shadows. A great wall of shadows, extending as far as she could see. Here, too, the Divide was thinner, without the roaring intensity they'd seen before. But still there, towering above her, seeming to stretch all the way into the sky.

"May I?" Arak'Jur asked after she leaned back.

"Of course."

The view had returned to its widest arc, all the continents at once, but quickly moved, this time toward familiar ground. New Sarresant, or more precisely, the lands just outside the city. First she saw the coastline, then the outlines of the city, the roads and rivers, the sites where the new barrier was being put up by the priests. Then it moved to another settlement, just north of the city, with a mix of tents and longhouses, and once more her senses were drawn in. This time she was greeted with darkness, the dim light of a mostly spent fire, and a foul smell assaulting her nose.

Arak'Jur made a choking sound, and she almost looked away. Then the shapes outlined in the shadows became clearer: a woman, wiping a soiled cloth along a baby's backside.

"Corenna," Arak'Jur said. "Kar'Doren."

She watched for another moment, as the mother—Corenna—turned the child over, tucking the cloth away and letting him grab hold of the fingers on her free hand, suckling them as though they were food.

"Can..." Arak'Jur began. "Can they...hear me?"

"No," she said. "The map can show you anything you like, but it's only a view."

She leaned back from the table, though Arak'Jur stayed still, looking down into its depths. She left him to it; if Corenna's child was Arak'Jur's, the sight wasn't meant for her.

The hallways had grown since their return. Where before there had been three sets of living quarters, now there were six, though it had taken three requests for the Watcher to have him create one for her. That much she'd been able to puzzle out: The shadowy creature could definitely understand, and acquiesce, when she spoke to him through the blue sparks. She shifted her sight as she walked, and saw the shadow walking backward in front of her, as though he was mimicking her movements.

"We'll need to settle on a name for you," she said. The creature seemed curious, though if it could speak to her, she hadn't yet found the way to listen. Even its gestures seemed more repeating her motions than trying to signal her or make its desires known, if it had desires at all.

Tigai's door was closed, a heavy redwood carved with insignias of dragons, though it did little to muffle the sounds coming from within. Those made her blush, and quicken her pace. Evidently whatever had passed between Tigai and Yuli had rekindled here at the Gods' Seat.

She kept on past Erris's chambers, knowing the Empress would be working behind its doors, connected through *Need* to some generals or princes somewhere in her Empire. She was grateful for the former High Commander's diligence, but until the Divide came down, there was no knowing where the battles would even be fought, let alone the nature of their fighting. Erris insisted they be prepared, that diplomacy was needed to heal the wounds inflicted by Paendurion's maneuvering, and Sarine left her to it. The notion of ruling nations seemed as distant and strange as sampling the delicacies of the Rasailles gardens had once been, and with none of the appeal. A game for others to play. For once she felt as if she'd found her place, here, and her purpose in the months to come.

The library had been restocked again, but its character hadn't changed. Rows of shelves and scrollracks, tables and benches strewn with volumes left open, and Reyne d'Agarre, seated on a long couch, poring over his Codex too intently to notice her arrival.

He was hers, too, now, for all she'd never have chosen to make a man like him her champion. The last relic of the Veil's corruption.

She steeled herself, sitting on a couch opposite him instead of her usual place, among the tables and benches, and finally he noticed her, slipping a finger in the pages to hold his place.

"Sarine," Reyne said.

"Reyne," she said, returning the greeting. "I don't know why you spend so much time studying that book. It was never more than Axerian's instrument, and he died, in Kye-Min."

Reyne smiled. A handsome man, with an easy confidence, altogether poisoned by the horrors she knew could be laid at his feet.

"Is there no wisdom to be gleaned from holy books, when their authors are long dead?" Reyne asked. "I would think, having been raised by a priest, you could appreciate a search for truth."

"Don't," she said. Her uncle was beyond discussion here.

He maintained his smile, but shifted as though he'd rather return his attentions to his book.

"I didn't come here to talk about your Codex," she continued. "I came here to talk about Zi."

"Ah," Reyne said. "I wondered how long it would be before you asked."

For his smiles and sophistry, she'd as soon have put it off further. But then, she had to know.

Anati had appeared, draping herself over the arm of the couch where Reyne was lounging, staring at her with coal-black eyes.

"Your new *kaas*," she said. "When you bonded it, you must have visited their world."

"That's right," Reyne said.

"And you met Zi there."

He nodded, seeming to relish the silence where he had to know she craved answers.

She didn't give him the satisfaction, letting silence sit between them. Reyne's *kaas* had appeared as well, lying on the cushion just beneath Anati's armrest, letting its head droop backward over the front of the couch.

Finally Reyne laughed, reaching to stroke his *kaas*'s scales. "Xeraxet may not be as ancient as your Zi, but he knew what to show me. I witnessed Zi speaking to a shadow, of the very sort that appeared when you went to bond d'Arrent. Paendurion was certain he knew what it meant: Zi assisted the Veil in her rebirth, cultivating you as a vessel, and both of them had a deal with the Regnant. Paendurion was sure it was the only way the Veil could have escaped her prison."

Lies, Anati thought. *My father would never work with our enemy.*

"Nonetheless," Reyne said. "I know what I saw."

"How did you visit the *kaas*' world?" she asked, and earned a renewed glare from Anati, this time her eyes glazed over with a ruby sheen.

"Quite by accident," Reyne said. "It's here, all around us. Perhaps only in the Gods' Seat? But no, you must have visited it when you separated from Zi."

"So there's no way to get there without releasing your *kaas*'s bond?"

"I can't speak to what's possible," Reyne said. "But Saruk left me the moment I could see their plane. It's a fascinating place—all lights and shapes, absent any colors. Strange, given their predilection for reds, greens, yellows, and the like."

Anati continued smoldering. She'd warned as much, and given

Reyne's bonding of a new *kaas*, Sarine feared the warning would prove true. She couldn't visit the *kaas'* world without severing her and Anati's bond.

"Thank you," she said, rising to her feet.

"That's all?" Reyne asked. "I warn you: Paendurion was quite sure. Zi is not to be trusted. In fact, I believe there is a passage here that might be of relevance..."

"No," she said. "I have what I need."

Reyne's soft laugh saw her out of the library, winding back through the halls toward the room she'd claimed for her own. Plain couches decorated the living space, with a small bookcase and fresh sheaves of paper and charcoal waiting for her each time she returned. It could have been any other chamber, save for the stained-glass reliefs etched into the far wall. Exact replicas of the Sacre-Lin's windows, down to the glow of sunlight streaming through to paint rainbows on the chamber floor. She had every confidence there would be only smooth, cold stone behind them if they broke, but the Watcher had done well. Whatever he'd done to plumb the depths of her memory, the room greeted her with the same sights she'd been accustomed to in her uncle's loft. A taste of home, though she could have benefitted from her uncle's wisdom during their preparation for what was to come. He would have admonished her to trust the Gods' examples, to remember her virtues, to strive for goodness in her life and the lives of others. It still would have been nice to hear him say it. Instead she had her champions. And Anati, already glaring at her with ruby eyes as she entered the room.

You mean to sever our bond, Anati thought before she could even be seated.

"Anati..." she said.

It's a simple thing, her *kaas* continued. *Focus on the spaces between a thing and itself; that is where we* kaas *live, in the spaces between—*

"Anati, stop."

Her *kaas* fell silent, her eyes darkening as she perched atop the writing desk. From the angle Sarine stood at, it was as though Anati were a sketch come to life, half submerged in the paper, half coiled and staring, with a deep crimson flushed through her scales from head to tail.

"I'm not going to sever our bond," she said. "And I don't think you're lying to me. But even during my best times with Zi, he was always hiding something. Keeping something from me. It's not beyond reason to think there might be more going on than either of us is aware."

He wouldn't, Anati thought. *He wouldn't betray your trust.*

"I believe you. But he might not consider whatever he's doing a betrayal."

Your kind are too complicated.

She smiled, coming to sit at the desk instead of the couch, extending a hand to brush Anati's scales.

"I'm sorry," she said. "I'm still learning my place in all this."

So am I. But you are bold. A better Goddess than the Veil.

A ridiculous notion, made no less so by the deadly seriousness in her *kaas's* expression. Nothing for it but to receive it with the same solemnity.

"The Divide will fall soon," she said, changing the subject, and Anati bobbed her head up and down. "It's going to mean violence, when it does."

Anati said nothing, though her eyes flared from rubies to emeralds, the rest of her body flushing green to match.

"Here," she said, brushing Anati back as she pulled loose a clean sheet. "Let me sketch you."

Why?

"Because Zi never allowed it. Because I'm afraid there won't be time, after."

Anati stared at her for a moment, a flash of yellow creeping into the center of her eyes. Then her *kaas* bowed her head, nestling into her coils at the edge of the desk. So like Zi, and yet so different. She got to work with her charcoals, tracing the lines she'd always imagined using for Zi, though he'd never allowed her to do it. Bittersweet, to think she might not see Zi again, but then, Anati was just as dear to her, in her own right. It made the sacrifices more bearable, knowing there would be light when she passed through the dark.

AFTER

EPILOGUE

OMERA

Kandake's Palace
The City of Konghom, Bhakal Lands

The Kandake's guards bowed low, a score of them at once, each dropping to one knee with rhythmic precision. He alone remained standing. The aftereffects of *tisa irinti* lingered in his veins, ingraining in him the perfect servitude he'd willingly accepted, before his pilgrimage abroad. But he was home now. The need for deference had been smothered by the fire of *ubax aragti*, its red leaves mirroring the heat it conferred to soldiers, traders, and diplomats on the eve of battles, difficult negotiations, or voyages into the unknown. It felt appropriate for his return to his mother's court.

A sharp grunt echoed through the chamber, repeated on the voice of every soldier as they pivoted, still kneeling, toward the veil of beads draped across the far entrance. Marble tile covered the floor in a pattern of blue and green, two swirling colors vying for control, with colonnades supporting the ceiling, all directed toward where the Kandake would make her entrance. His Sarresanter's clothes had been exchanged for a simple robe of red wool, too simple by far for the audience he was about to receive, but that, too, had been selected for a purpose, to send a message of humility and respect.

"She comes," a voice intoned. "The Kandake Amanishiakne of Konghom." A deep voice, echoing through the chamber as though it came from everywhere at once, yet had no specific source.

The beads parted, and his mother entered the room.

Gold paint decorated her face and forearms, a layer of cosmetics over skin as lustrous and dark as polished jet. *Tanpa shain*, a fungus from Kinigari Shuhet, produced the effect, making her appear as though she were carved from precious stone. She wore gold silk dashed with a blue that matched the tilestones, wrapped around a stomach swollen in the last weeks of pregnancy. Yet even with the girth in her stomach and hips, she flowed more than walked through the beads, coming to a halt and placing the butt of her staff with an iron clank.

Now he joined the soldiers in kneeling, slowly, taking twenty heartbeats to lower himself into a supplicant's pose.

"Mother," he said finally, when his eyes were lowered, his nose and hands pressed to the cold stone floor.

"Rise, Omera," his mother said, her voice stoic and cool, but unamplified by magic.

He followed her command at once.

She met his eyes as though daring him to do the same, and he did, the fireweed in his veins giving him the courage to stay steady on his feet.

"You return early," she said. "A presumption, for a son tasked to remain across the sea."

"I have come to reclaim my eye," he said. "Bearing knowledge of events abroad, and portents of things to come."

He'd rehearsed the words a hundred times on the ships he'd taken, first from the port at New Sarresant and then again from Al Adiz, making landfall at the Sardian stronghold at the mouth of the great river. They sounded weaker than he'd intended, under the scrutiny of Kandake Amanishiakne. Easier to think of her as her name and title, here, and not as his mother.

"You claim the gift of future sight?" the Kandake asked.

"No," he said quickly. "No, Your Majesty. Only signs. I have witnessed great events in New Sarresant, across the sea. I have seen a thing no Bhakal man has seen in a hundred generations. I returned to speak of it, with you, if it pleases, while there is still time to act."

The Kandake paused, seeming to lean against her staff as she considered his words. The rest of the chamber was frozen, silent, a score of armed guards awaiting her command.

"Approach," she said, and he obeyed.

The guards remained prostrate as he drew to within five paces of her, tensing as she beckoned him even closer, a sudden tautness spreading through the room. His mother deigned not to notice, flowing toward him with her elegant stride, coming to hover over him despite his advantage in height. She extended a hand to brush his cheek, a delicate gesture, though her skin was cold as ice.

"My Omera," she said. "You come before me dressed as a commoner. Why? Did they so ill treat you, across the seas?"

It took effort to remain collected. In the presence of so many guards or lookers-on, she had only ever been Kandake Amanishiakne, yet here she was mother—the teacher, the sage, the woman who was ancient when the eldest living elder first drew breath.

"I was not a slave, Mother," he said. "But I chose to use *tisa irinti*, to bring myself close to their seats of power. I saw an Empress rise. I saw a man—"

She moved a finger to her lips, shushing him to silence.

"Walk with me," she said instead, and at once the guards grunted and pivoted again, this time rising to their knees, each man directed toward the Kandake at the center of the room.

"No guards," she said to the rest. "I walk with Omera alone."

Another grunt, this time accompanied by bowed heads, returned to pressing flat against the tile.

She led the way through the beads into a long hallway, and for the first time Omera could recall he was alone in a room with his mother. His heart thundered as she led the way, an effect of *ubax aragti*, but also of nerves, raw and full of fear. The clanks of her iron staff kept time as they passed through the hall into a long chamber beyond, then down another hall, sloping upward until they emerged into open air.

His mother's balcony overlooked the city at twilight, a darkening sky greeting them over rooftops stretched for two leagues in every direction. From here he could see the red tents of the jongleur's quarter, the stalls and broad streets of the markets, the torches of his mother's patrols as they moved like mousers through every quarter of the city. The contours of Konghom were neat and precise, a city built to a plan and older than the hills that sculpted the rises and falls between its districts, sliced neatly in half by the towering shadows of the Divide. He could see it, here, as clear as when he'd first drawn near it as a child. A barrier that swallowed the sky, reaching up into the heavens to black out half the world. Mother had built her balcony facing it directly, staring into death, as sure as she'd built the rest of the city square upon the line it drew across all of their lands.

"It is beautiful," his mother said, "is it not?"

He pivoted back to her. "It is death," he said. "You taught me that, as soon as I could walk."

"Yes," she said, smiling as she came to rest beside him, gripping the balcony and gazing out over the city, into the Divide.

"Tell me what you saw," she said after a moment.

Once again *ubax aragti* set his heart racing. He couldn't be sure there was no danger, here, in returning home before he was summoned.

"I met a man who could change his face," he said. "I swore myself to his service, and watched him spin lies and work the threads of power, until he was at the heart of governance in New Sarresant, across the seas."

"He changed his face?" she asked.

"Yes. Not as a jongleur would, but a true change, from man to woman, from elder to youth. Nights he slept as Fei Zan; days he went as Anselm Voren, Bétrice Caille, and a score of others, pretending to oppose his own plans, to ingratiate himself among his enemies."

"A Fox, then," his mother said, and he bowed his head in reverence. Of course she would know; she knew all things. "A Fox," she continued, "when the Divide still stands. This has not happened before."

The words put a chill on his skin in spite of the summer heat.

"Was I right to bring this to you?" he asked.

She gave no answer, staring into the Divide, her iron staff leaned against the marble railing, her swollen belly propped against the stone.

He remained beside her, and silence stretched on. When he'd had his eye taken and been sent away, there had been no provision for return, save for a summons he'd been told he would know, if it came. Twice, he'd been sure it would manifest as faith; the first when he'd found *tisa irinti* growing wild across the sea, and again during Reyne d'Agarre's revolution. What other purpose for his mother to send her sons abroad than to watch and deliver news of discoveries, great events, and similar portents? Yet both times he'd talked himself into remaining, sure that a sorceress would have clearer means of making her intent known, even across two oceans. With Voren he could wait no longer, sure it had to be the sign he had waited for. But now, in the face of the Kandake's silence, he felt a growing dread. He feared death, and the Divide was an omen for it, here in the place that had been his home as a child.

"One of them has weakened," his mother said abruptly. "The Regnant, or the Veil."

He recognized the Veil—one of the Goddesses worshipped in Sarresant, and the other nations of the north. "What does this mean, Mother?"

"A chance, for us, if my sister agrees."

A sister? He'd never heard her mention a sister; the very idea of the ancient Kandake having a sister was strange, like a mountain or river come to life, suddenly human.

"You did well, Omera," his mother said. "I am pleased you returned home."

Before he could process his relief, she shot a hand to touch his cheek again, this time burning with fire.

He felt heat spread quickly, the bones in his skull igniting at her touch. He yelped, but the sound died before it could grow into a scream, and the heat went with it.

She withdrew her hand, and he blinked.

His eye. She had regrown his eye.

"Mother...I..."

She showed him a wistful look, then returned to staring into the Divide.

"You must practice your war-magic, my son," she said. "You and all your brothers, in the weeks we have remaining. One of them has weakened, the God or the Goddess. It may well mean a chance for us, when we are reunited. But first it will mean war, great and terrible, and we must be prepared to face it, when it comes."

Tears came, and he blinked again. Pain lingered in his head. He'd made the demand, but never expected her to acquiesce. The eye was meant to be an offering, a reminder of the service he owed her. And now he'd been vindicated, his choice to return a fulfillment of the promises he'd made, and the love he'd always hoped to earn.

"Go, and rest," his mother said. "Leave me to consider what you have brought."

He bowed, and went.

EPILOGUE

LIN

Adrift among the Columns
The Infinite Plane

One wrong decision, one snap judgment, and she'd damned herself for an eternity.

It had made sense. The brute—the giant, Paendurion—had been overconfident and stupid. Glass shards in his back secured her place at the Lord's side. One of the treacherous Three, slain at her hand, breaking untold cycles of pain and suffering. Then in the moment of her victory, she'd touched the light, reasoning it would be the means to escape the House of the Veil. It was not.

Columns of blue energy stretched as far as she could see in every direction, and she floated between them, empty and weightless. No need to eat here, or to sleep. If time passed at all, she had no means to discern it; even counting the columns had fallen by the wayside when she'd passed twelve thousand. Changing her course was a thing done by the barest fractions of degrees, as though she were a ship the size of the world with a rudder the size of a stone. In the first days—if there were such a thing as days here—she'd strained to avoid the columns, with their crackling surges of blue sparks and light. After enough time had passed she welcomed her first collision, hoping it meant death, and release.

Another of the columns loomed in front of her now, and she hung limp as her body propelled itself toward it.

She could feel her limbs, her legs and torso, though they might as well have been as distant as the world itself. Had she been able to move she would have long since gouged her own eyes, choked herself, anything to feel something other than endless waste and boredom.

Blue energy crackled around her, and vision shifted.

A chamber. Empty. A table, set with fruit, beneath a silver fixture overhead. The warmth of a fire, burning in the hearth. Long wood tables, set and ready to receive their guests.

It faded, and she returned to floating.

She was long past caring where she'd been, or what manner of object these particular blue sparks had lived behind, this time. It was all the same. Countless thousands, countless millions, stretched forever, as though the entire world was painted from the terminal points of each of these columns of light, each one corresponding to some object, somewhere, in the physical world. The first one was supposed to have killed her; instead it showed her a child's toy, a wooden soldier, left forgotten in a field of mud and snow.

She veered away from the columns ahead, pushing with what was left of her will to adjust her course. Some days she spent hours colliding with every column, tasting life again in fleeting moments of connection. Today she wanted nothing. Emptiness, bleakness, madness. Eventually she would lose her wits here, if she hadn't already. But how could she tell? Her Lord had been meant to provide for her, his faithful servant, who had attached herself to his greatest enemy. She alone had recognized the girl, Sarine, for what she was. She alone had performed the great service, assaulting Paendurion with her shards of glass. Why had the Lord abandoned her to this unchanging hell? Why had she been forgotten?

Anger blinded her for a moment, blurring the columns ahead with simmering rage.

No. Wait. Not rage.

There was something there.

Suddenly all her despair melted at the prospect of something—anything—new. The columns stretching in front of her were blurred, that much she could see easily. A distortion, like a gray sphere, floating on its own path, bending the light behind it to make a traveling eclipse around its edge. Floating away from her, on a perpendicular course, tracing a line in front of her.

It was moving fast. Too fast. If she veered around to follow, she'd never catch it, only trail behind, watching and wondering what it meant. She had to hit it. Had to collide.

All her will bent her course, shifting each degree with agonizing slowness. The sphere hadn't reacted to her, if it was a thing with a will of its own, continuing on at its same, steady pace. She was no mathematician, to calculate angles with precision, but she knew enough of ballistics from soldiering. She would miss. By a fraction of a hair, but she would miss.

She exerted herself, waking parts of her mind long since resigned to death. This was her chance. Anything new might kill her, or perhaps even offer an escape. Force of will. That was the way. She was *magi* of the Great and Noble House of the Ox. Strength was her gift, and she would not die like this, wasted and forgotten. She forced her course to change. One more degree. More speed.

Yes.

She would make it.

Relief washed over her. It had to be a way out, whether through death, madness, or passage from this place. Hope was poison, when it soured, but for a bare fraction she allowed herself to feel it, bright and golden, as she drifted toward the edges of the gray sphere.

They touched, and something dormant rekindled in her mind.

She was the Veil.

She'd been divested of a body, resigned to the failure that had cost her any hope of rebirth. The girl, Sarine, as improbable as it was, had gained control. The *kaas* had been her weakness, since Zi's death forced a change in plans, and without a body, even her will could do nothing here, in the space behind realities. It should have meant a slow death, bleeding her mind and memories into the void. A crueler end than she'd suspected Sarine capable of delivering. The girl was weak. Too weak to take her place.

Yet now, something had changed.

A body.

She examined the creature who had come into contact with the gray sphere that had been her mind. Thoughts flared inside its shell; good. Not a dead thing, and not a beast. Human. A woman, even, though she would not have been above taking hold of a man, ill as the fit might have been.

She paused to examine herself. Was this a figment of madness? A dream, meant to cruelly wake the parts of her she'd already consigned to death?

No. A body. A thinking body. A woman, here among the columns of the Infinite Plane.

She forced herself inside the woman's mind, purging it clean of thoughts that were not hers. She'd had enough of sharing a body with Sarine. This one she expunged, eradicating all traces of the original soul until nothing remained. Nothing save her will. Her consciousness found its way into new limbs, flexing fingers with instincts almost forgotten, feeling the strength of legs and muscles in her back, her chest, her arms and neck.

She was alive.

Laughter filled her ears; a strange voice, but hers now.

So much effort to be reborn. Her pact with the Regnant; her plans with Zi. And now it was done. No more prison. She was free.

She drew on the blue sparks of Life, boring a hole into a forest glade, where cold sunlight spilled over snow-covered boughs of needles and leaves. Faster, perhaps, if she took the time to traverse the spaces on the Plane, but she relished the thought of walking on her own, of learning the intricacies of this body, of remembering what it was to be the Veil.

She stepped through, and sealed the bore behind her.

EPILOGUE

THE REGNANT

Death's Seat
The Starfield and the Strands

All his assurances had turned to dust.

He'd known not to trust her, and still his soft heart had broken, seeing her trapped in her champions' prison. The Master had cautioned him, though he'd loved her then, and loved her still, in spite of her betrayals.

But then, if love could sustain the world, there would be no need for him, or his work.

Darkness shrouded his seat. Below, he could see his champions, gathering to receive his summons, marshaling their armies, setting aside the bitter rivalry between their Great and Noble Houses to become a single force, with a single purpose. The fault lines would linger, as they always did. But if the need was great enough, even the deepest hate would bend in service to a higher law.

"Great Lord," a voice intoned. One he'd been listening for. One he'd managed to place on her side of the Divide.

He willed his senses down into the world. Difficult to sustain, through the shadow, but he had less need to conserve himself now.

"Speak," he said. Here in the Seat his voice was soft, the same old rasp he'd grown accustomed to, after so many years alone. His servant would hear it as a thunderclap, delivered from darkness given form.

"Great Lord," the servant said. "Great Lord, I have failed you."

He said nothing. The truth would come.

"I tried, my lord," the servant said. The voice was heavy with pain and age, the weight of the self-inflicted wounds needed to bridge the chasm between Life and Death. "I aided her every way I could. But... the moment of ascension... it came, and by the servants' accounts... Paendurion... he vanished."

"He vanished?"

"Yes, Great Lord. I beg your forgiveness. This servant is without worth or honor."

A great blow, if Paendurion had secured his place again. But enough had changed that it wouldn't matter. They no longer obeyed the Master's rule, with the reborn girl in her mistress's seat. One tactician could be met by a dozen; one warrior overrun by a legion.

"Be at ease," he said. "And come to me. I have need of your service, Master Fei Zan, as my champion of Fox."

Tears and whimpering, protestations of the servant's unworth; he ignored it, channeling Death to bind the man to his service. A simple thread of gold stood in the way; he erased it, replacing it with the true bond of loyalty, of sacrifice in service to a higher cause.

One Fox, as champion, but it would not be enough. He would need a dozen, a hundred, to infiltrate the girl's ranks. Every advisor, every confidant and general must be suspect. Every flank checked by Ox and Crane, every supply line pillaged by Dragon, Heron, and Crab. This was what the girl's defiance would bring. Total war, absent the Master's constraints of three against three.

He was ready. The world ached for release, for the torpor Death would bring, after sixteen unbroken cycles of Life. Total war risked unmaking creation, but so, too, would inaction against the treachery of the Veil's betrayal. He was Regnant to the Master's throne, and the Master's precepts were clear. It was wisdom, though he doubted every step.

Take heart, the *kaas* thought to him. *It will be worth the price, when all is done.*

"I want to believe it," he said. "But none can see all ends."

Uncertainty. The great gift of creation.

"A mistake, perhaps."

Yes. But whose?

He left the conversation there, closing the part of his mind that reached beyond the shadow. The *kaas*'s insights would keep. For now, the greater part of his attention was needed along the border, preparing all the souls in his keeping for the days to come.

The story continues in...

Chains of the Earth

Book THREE of the Ascension Cycle

Coming in OCTOBER 2019

ACKNOWLEDGMENTS

Two down, one to go!

As always, first thanks goes to my agent, Sam Morgan. This book wouldn't be in your hands without his efforts. A related round of thanks to Krystyna Lopez for handling foreign rights. Keep her in your thoughts if you read this book in anything other than English.

Brit Hvide continues to be my navigator for this series. One of my advance readers for *Blood of the Gods* remarked, "either you've gotten better or your editor has." I like to think at least some of the credit is mine, but who am I kidding? Thank you, Brit.

The rest of the Orbit staff also deserves many thanks and praises. James Long, my UK editor, has done fantastic work on my behalf. Ellen Wright, Gleni Bartels, Bradley Englert, Nivia Evans, and everyone else involved—thank you.

More thanks to my parents, Don and Mary Mealing, and my three daughters, Aurie, Jamie, and Evangeline. Sometimes writing requires outpourings of love, and I've never lacked for it. I love you all, more than I can say.

My wife, Lindsay Mealing, deserves all the rest of the credit. She listened to me read every chapter of this book aloud, helping me forge and reforge the story until it was right. Nothing in my life would be what it is without her.

extras

orbit

meet the author

DAVID MEALING grew up adoring all things fantasy. He studied philosophy, politics, and economics at the University of Oxford, where he taught himself to write by building worlds and stories for pen-and-paper RPGs. He lives in Utah with his wife and three daughters and aspires to one day own a ranch in the middle of nowhere.

if you enjoyed
BLOOD OF THE GODS

look out for

THE WOLF
Under the Northern Sky

by

Leo Carew

*Violence and death have come to the land under the
Northern Sky.*

*The Anakim dwell in the desolate forests and mountains beyond
the black river, the land under the Northern Sky.*

*Their ancient ways are forged in Unthank silver and carved
in the grey stone of their heartland, their lives measured out in
the turning of centuries, not years.*

*By contrast, the Sutherners live in the moment, their vitality much
more immediate and ephemeral than their Anakim neighbors.*

*Fragile is the peace that has existed between these very different
races—and that peace is shattered when the Suthern armies
flood the lands to the north.*

These two races revive their age-old hatred and fear of each other. Within the maelstrom of war, two leaders will rise to lead their people to victory.

Only one will succeed.

1

BROKEN CLOCKWORK

The rain had not stopped for days. The road was under six inches of brown water. Everything was underwater. Roper's horse stumbled and collapsed onto its knees; it was all he could do to stay in the saddle.

"Up," said Kynortas. "You must be twice the man you expect your legionaries to be."

Roper dismounted to allow his horse to rise before swinging himself back into his saddle. The legionaries behind had not noticed; they marched on, heads dipped against the rain.

"What effect will the rain have?" asked Kynortas.

"It will shorten the battle," Roper hazarded. "Formations are easily broken and men die faster when their footing is unsure."

"A fair assessment," Kynortas judged. "Men also fight less fiercely in the rain. It will favour the Sutherners; the legions are more skilled and will struggle to assert their dominance in rain."

Roper drank the words in. "How does that change our battle plan, lord?"

"We have no battle plan," said Kynortas. "We do not know what we will face. The scouts report that the Sutherners have found a strong position to defend, so we know we must attack; that is all.

698

But," he went on, "we must be careful with the legions. They take hundreds of years to develop and because they will not run, they can be destroyed in a single battle. Remember this above all: the legions are irreplaceable. Preserve the legions, Roper."

Marching at Kynortas's back were close to ninety thousand soldiers: the full strength of the Black Kingdom. The column, lined with countless banners that hung sodden and limp, stretched miles back down the road and far out of sight. Even now they marched in step, causing waves to pulse through the floodwater. There had never been a call-up so vast in Roper's nineteen years. No man liked summoning all the legions beneath a single banner; the propensity for catastrophe was too great. As Kynortas had said, the legions were irreplaceable. Losing them was the collective fear of every echelon of their nation.

On this occasion, there had been no choice. Their enemies had gathered an enormous army that threatened to capsize the balance of power in Albion. The force, a composite of Saxon and Frankish soldiers, with mercenaries from Samnia and Iberia, was so big that nobody knew how many men their enemies commanded. But it numbered many more than the legionaries under Kynortas.

"Why do we not do as the Sutherners do, lord?" asked Roper. "Unify all our peoples under a single banner?"

Kynortas did not countenance the idea. "Can you imagine any king surrendering control of his forces to another? Can you imagine a dozen kings all agreeing to back the same man?" He shook his head dismissively. "Perhaps one man in a million could unify the Anakim. Perhaps. But I am not the man to do it, and neither will I surrender the legions to any foreign sovereignty."

Roper could not imagine a lord greater than Kynortas. As strong in face and limb as were his faith and convictions. Straight-backed and stern, with a thunderous brow and a face as yet unscarred by conflict. His men regarded him; his enemies despised and respected him in equal measure. He knew how to court an ally, cow an enemy and read a battlefield like a poem. He was a tall man, though Roper almost equalled him in that regard already. Theirs was reckoned a strong house, with Roper a promising prospect as Kynortas's heir, his two younger brothers indemnifying the lineage.

At the head of the mighty column, the Black Lord and his young heir crested a hill to reveal a great floodplain. Across almost a mile of wind-rippled water lay a ridge of extraordinary length. Whether a natural formation or some ancient battle-works thrown up in this scarred land was not clear, but it stretched almost from horizon to horizon. Its northern flank was guarded by a great forest and on it was arrayed the Suthern horde. Thousands lined the ridge. Tens of thousands; protected by the mangled and rain-slicked slope. Their banners were as wilted as those of the legions but Roper could make out halberdiers, longbowmen, swordsmen and some who shone greyly on the wet day and must surely be men-at-arms. At the southern edge of the ridge, a vast mass of cavalry sat malevolently.

It was to be Roper's first battle. He had never seen one before. He had heard them, rumbling and crashing from afar like a heaving ocean beating against an iron-bound coast. He had seen the warriors return, most weary and bereft, a special few energised and inspired; all filthy and battered. He had seen the wounded treated; watched as surgeons trepanned the skulls of unconscious men or extracted slivers of steel from their forearms, thrown off by the clash of blades. His father had discussed it often, indeed talked of little else to his heir. Roper had studied it; had trained for it from the age of six. His life had so far revolved around this sacred clash and yet he felt utterly unprepared for what he saw before him.

Laying eyes on the enemy, the Black Lord and his son spurred out of the column's path. Kynortas snapped his fingers and an aide trotted to his side. "Deploy our army in battle formation, as close as possible to where the flooding begins." Kynortas rattled off a list of where each legion should be placed in the line, concluding with the observation that all their cavalry would be on the right, "save for those from Houses Oris and Alba, who take the left."

"That's a lot of orders, lord," said the aide.

"Delegate." The aide complied. "Uvoren!"

A mounted officer detached himself from the column and rode to join Kynortas. "My lord?" His high ponytail, threaded through a hole in the back of his helmet, identified him as a Sacred Guardsman. A silver eye was inlaid into his right shoulder-plate, his helmet covered his eyes and he grinned roguishly at his master.

"You know Uvoren, Roper," Kynortas introduced them. Roper had heard of Uvoren; there was no boy in the Black Kingdom who had not. The Captain of the Sacred Guard: a role every aspiring warrior dreamed of playing. There could be no higher endorsement of your martial capability than appointment to such an office. Over his back was slung his famous war hammer: Marrow-Hunter. It was said that Uvoren had had Marrow-Hunter's gorgeous rippled-steel head forged from the combined swords of four Suthern earls, each put down by the captain himself. When hope had seemed a distant memory at the Siege of Lundenceaster—the greatest of Albion's settlements, far to the south—it had been Marrow-Hunter which had at last cleared a foothold on the wall. At the Battle of Eoferwic, its great blunt head had broken the back of King Offa's horse and then smashed the downed king's head like a rotten egg, crumpling his gilt helmet.

Yes, Roper had heard of Uvoren. Playing in the academy far in the north, Roper had always pretended to be Uvoren the Mighty. The little stick he wielded had not been a sword but a war hammer.

Now, he nodded silently at the captain, who beamed back at him. "Of course he does."

"Captain of the Sacred Guard and model of humility," said Kynortas acidly. "Uvoren: parley. Roper will accompany us."

"You'll enjoy this, young lord," said Uvoren, curbing his horse next to Roper and gripping his shoulder. Roper did not respond beyond staring wide-eyed at the guardsman. "Your father's good fun when treating with the enemy."

The three of them rode together down onto the floodplain, accompanied by another Sacred Guardsman bearing a white flag. "Carrying a white flag comes naturally to you, Gray," Uvoren called to the guardsman. Gray's reaction was merely to stare unsmiling at his captain. Uvoren laughed. "Stay calm, Gray. And learn to laugh." Roper looked to Kynortas to see what to make of this, but the Black Lord had ignored the exchange.

They splashed into the flood waters which proved to be no more than a foot deep. Beyond the water, atop the ridge, a group of horsemen detached themselves from the Suthern army and rode out to them. To Roper, there seemed a significant disparity in power between the two groups. He, his father, Uvoren and "Gray" numbered four; riding against them were close to thirty. Three unhelmeted lords led the party, accompanied by two dozen knights in gleaming plate armour, visors down and horses billowing in embroidered caparisons.

"Will this be your first battle, little lord?" Uvoren asked of Roper.

"The first one," confirmed Roper. Being taller than most already, he was hardly little but the term did not feel strange from a man as elevated as Uvoren.

"There is nothing like it. Here is where you will discover what you were born for."

"You loved your first one?" asked Roper. He was not accustomed to struggling with words, but stuttered slightly when addressing Uvoren.

"Oh yes," responded the captain, beaming again. "That was before I was even a legionary and I bagged my first earl! Fighting these Sutherners is not hard; look here." They were drawing close to the group of horsemen.

Roper had never beheld a Sutherner before and their appearance shocked him. They looked like him, just smaller. Though all were tall among Anakim, not one of Roper, Gray, Uvoren or Kynortas stood below seven feet in height; even on horseback they towered above their enemies, who were on an altogether smaller scale. The disparity in power vanished.

Now Roper came to inspect them more closely, there was something different about the faces of these Sutherners as well.

extras

They were somehow child-like. Their eyes were expressive and their emotions and characters stood out on their faces with a clarity that made them almost endearing. Their features were softer and less robust. By comparison, Kynortas's countenance might have been carved from oak. These Suthern faces put Roper in mind of something domesticated, like a dog. Something far from the wild.

Kynortas raised a hand in greeting. "Who commands here?" Though he spoke good Saxon, he delivered these words in the Anakim tongue. The knights shivered slightly as the speech of the Black Kingdom washed over them.

"I command here," said a man in the centre of the group in a halting, accented version of the same language. He rode towards Kynortas, seemingly indifferent to his size. "You must be the Black Lord." He sat straight in his saddle, wearing a suit of plate armour so bright that Roper could make out his own reflection in the breastplate. He had a dark beard and a mane of curly hair. His face, what could be seen of it, was reddened by drink. "I am Earl William of Lundenceaster. I lead this army." He gestured to his left. "This is the Lord Cedric of Northwic and this," he gestured to his right, "is Bellamus."

"You have a title, Bellamus?" demanded Kynortas.

William of Lundenceaster answered for him. "Bellamus is an upstart without any sort of rank to his name. Nevertheless, he commands our Right." Earl William regularly substituted Anakim words that he did not know with the Saxon equivalent, knowing that Kynortas understood anyway.

Kynortas looked intrigued at the earl's words and Bellamus raised a hand in acknowledgement. He was good-looking, this upstart, with a touch of grey at the temples of his dark, wavy hair and he appeared prosperous. He alone of the Sutherners present was not dressed in plate armour but instead wore a thick jerkin of quilted leather, with gold hung at his neck and wrists. His high boots were of the finest quality, so new that they looked as if they might rub. He wore a rich red-dyed tunic beneath the jerkin and sat

703

on a bearskin draped over his horse. He also had the two outermost fingers missing from his left hand. Next to the austere, armour-plated lords, it was the upstart who stood out.

The Black Lord looked back at Earl William.

"You have invaded our lands," said Kynortas, his voice harsh. "You crossed the Abus which has been a peaceful border for years. You have burned, you have plundered and you have raped." Kynortas advanced his horse, bearing down on Earl William. His huge physical presence was more than matched by his implacable bearing. "Leave now, un-harried, or I will unleash the Black Legions. If I am forced to use my soldiers, there will be no mercy for any of you." He cast an eye over the ridge behind the Suthern generals. "In addition, I doubt you can bring an army like this here and have left anything to defend your homelands. You have violated our peace and once I have decimated your army here, I will advance to Lundenceaster and strip it to the bone by way of reparations. The violence," he leaned forward, "will be extreme."

Uvoren laughed loudly.

"We could withdraw," suggested Earl William, who had not flinched as Kynortas advanced. "But we're very comfortable here. We are well supplied; we have a strong position. And the reason you even offer us the chance of withdrawal is that you do not want to lose soldiers. You value them too highly and they are too dearly replaced. You do not want to attack us." Earl William had a slight squint. He gazed frankly at Kynortas, who waited for the offer that was about to be broached. "Gold," said the earl softly. "For the lives of your legionaries. Thirty chests would make our time worthwhile. That and the meagre plunder we have already taken from your eastern lands."

Kynortas did not respond. He just stared at Earl William and allowed the silence to stretch.

Roper watched. Thirty chests was an absurd figure to propose. The Black Kingdom's wealth was not based on gold; it was based on harder metals, beyond the manipulation of the Sutherners. They could not provide thirty chests of gold, as Earl William would surely have known; not if they scoured the country from meanest hovel to most magnificent castle. The earl had also been provocative in his demand of the tribute, though not obviously so. All of which led Roper to one conclusion; he did not want his offer to be accepted, but was trying to pretend that he did. The Sutherners had some kind of plan and had already decided how they wanted these negotiations to play out. Roper suspected Earl William was trying to goad Kynortas into a rash attack, where the legionaries could be killed trying to scale the mud-slicked ridge.

Kynortas himself—wiser, battle-hardened and more experienced—had no such suspicions. Foolish, ignorant Sutherners. "We have no value for metal of such limited use," said Kynortas at last. "We do not have thirty chests to satisfy your greed for things that are soft and impotent; nor would we supply you with them if we did."

Kynortas suddenly jerked forward, leaning out of his saddle in a great creaking of leather harnesses, and seized the top of Earl William's breastplate. Earl William's face reddened still further and he leaned backwards desperately, trying to pull his horse out of Kynortas's reach, but the Black Lord had him fast. The Sutherner was panicking, terror transparent on his face as Kynortas's alien hand touched his flesh. With a mighty wrench and a screech of yielding metal, Kynortas tore the shining breastplate clean off, causing Earl William to spring back like a willow-board. Beneath his armour was revealed leather padding, soaked in sweat, and Kynortas snorted as he flung the breastplate aside. It had all happened so fast, Earl William's knightly bodyguard had had no time to do anything more than look shocked. Earl William himself quivered, thunderstruck.

"Worthless," said Kynortas, sitting back in his saddle. "And beneath, a feeble sack of bones. You cannot fight my legions. They will cut through your plate like carving a ham." He smiled bleakly at Earl William, who had drawn his right arm across his vulnerable chest as though violated. The upstart Bellamus was looking across at his general with eyes crinkled in amusement. The two were evidently not friends. "Your last chance, Earl William. Withdraw, or I will release the legions."

"You use your precious bloody soldiers, then," boomed Earl William, his voice quivering with rage. "Watch them flounder and die in the filth!" He dragged his horse away from the encounter as though he could not bear to be in Kynortas's presence a moment longer. The Black Lord stood his ground and watched the retinue file away until it was just Bellamus staring back at him. The smaller man broke the silence first.

"Being blessed with bone-armour, I cannot imagine you know how it felt for Earl William to have his defences taken so contemptuously from him. Before this battle is over, I will show you how that feels." His Anakim was flawless; he might have passed for a subject of the Hindrunn had his stature been less mean. He had spoken mildly and nodded at the four Anakim before clicking his tongue to coax his horse away and back up to the ridge. He rode slowly, raising an arm in retrospective salute.

"Do negotiations always end like that?" asked Roper as the four of them turned back to their own forces, still assembling on the plain.

"Always," said Kynortas. "Nobody negotiates in negotiations. It's an exercise in intimidation."

Uvoren snorted. "Your father treats negotiations as an exercise in intimidation, Roper," he corrected. "Everyone else goes into it genuinely hoping to avoid battle." Uvoren and Gray laughed.

"They didn't want to negotiate anyway," said Roper.

Kynortas cast a glance in his direction. "What makes you say so?"

"The way he phrased the offer; the fact that he'd have known it was beyond our means anyway. He was goading us into attack."

Kynortas brooded on this. "Perhaps. So they're over-confident."

Roper stayed silent. Who could be over-confident going into battle against the Black Legions? There must be a reason for their belief. They must have a plan. But Roper did not know the way of these Sutherners. Perhaps their numbers gave them confidence.

extras

Perhaps they were just a confident race. Roper did not know and so stayed quiet.

"Stay with me," Kynortas said to Roper. "Watch as I do. One day, you will be responsible for the legions." The Black Legions were advancing into the flood waters. Holding the right wing, with the vast majority of the cavalry, was Ramnea's Own Legion; the elite soldiers of the Black Kingdom, second only in martial repute and prestige to the Sacred Guard. On the left was the Blackstone Legion; veteran, battle-hardened and with a reputation for savagery. Some men said the Blackstones were even more efficient than Ramnea's Own as line-breakers. Most of those men were Blackstones themselves.

The legates—the legion commanders—had each ridden out in front of their legion. On horseback they presented themselves to their warriors and held their arms high to the air as a pair of legionaries rode up behind them and invested each with a vast rippling cloak of liquid-brown eagle feathers. These were fastened over the shoulders, draping much of the horse as well, and flashed and glimmered as the legate dropped his arms. Clad in this holy raiment, they rode along the front of their advancing legions, holding out before them a branch of holly, an eye woven from the pointed leaves at the top of the branch. The eye looked over the ranks, inspecting their courage for the combat to come and blessing those who were worthy.

Roper and Kynortas trotted behind the battle line, a clutch of aides following in their wake. Kynortas sent them streaming out in all directions with instructions to hold fast, keep the line together, discharging regards and advice to the legates. He was so calm, the Black Lord. So still. His confidence, his faith in the legions, radiated around him like the ripples his horse made in the flood waters. Roper watched his father, hoping to absorb his presence and character by looking. Even when they had advanced into the shadow of the ridge, when longbow arrows began to spit into the waters around them, bouncing off the armour of two of the aides, the Black Lord appeared unfazed.

extras

The Sutherners on the ridge above were chanting. Swords thumped on shields, polearms rattled together and the men screamed and jeered. Devils, the Anakim were. Demons. Freaks, monsters, destroyers. They worked themselves into a frenzy of drumming and screaming to drown the awful, gut-wrenching fear they had of the giants they opposed. "Kill!" screamed a lord.

"Kill, kill, kill!" roared his men.

"Kill!" the lord insisted.

"Kill, kill, kill!" bayed his men.

"Scream at them!" bellowed the lord. "They're the murderers of the Black Kingdom! Scream at them!" His men screamed. "These are fallen angels, cast down from Heaven! God wants these demons banished from our lands! Do your duty this day by God!" The shields and pikes began to thump in time and the Sutherners stamped their feet. The sound, like a mighty drum being pounded, was enough to create ripples in the flood waters through which the Anakim marched.

The Anakim had their own drums, but they were not like their enemy's. Each legion beat its own tattoo on the advance, the drummers standing in the rear ranks and driving their warriors forward. The noise was not feral and savage like the Sutherners'. It was mechanical and crisp; a regular wave of sound.

Thousands of banners rose forest-like above the Anakim ranks. They had the great squares of embroidered linen that the Sutherners flew, but also long tapestries of woven silk, held aloft by up to six standard-bearers and depicting ancient battles in stark Anakim colours. Next to these stood giant eyes, woven from leafy withies of holly, willow and ash, or perhaps a great stretched bearskin, or a pole suspended with half a dozen tattered wolf pelts that swirled raggedly in the breeze. Where the legates rode, enormous bolts of linen impregnated with eagle feathers were held aloft, rippling and flashing in the wind. All of these banners but the last would be dropped when their bearers joined combat.

The legionaries themselves did not scream or shout on the advance. They did not clash their weapons, as the Sutherners were doing.

They sang. Low, eerie battle hymns spread across the line, clashing and swelling; growing in volume and emotion until the Sutherners were sick with the unfamiliarity of it all. The music reflected the tangled wilderness which surrounded them; the grey agitation of the sky above and forests that rustled and shifted on their flanks. The breeze was intensifying, as though the Sutherners were surrounded by Anakim allies who answered the call of that unearthly singing. This was Anakim land. The Black Kingdom: every inch as barren and unholy as the Sutherners had feared.

On the Suthern Right, Kynortas could make out the upstart Bellamus riding along the front of the line, roaring at his men. In his wake, men stood straighter and hefted their weapons. Kynortas took note: *One day*, he thought, *I will have to face an army commanded by that man alone.*

No sooner had this occurred to him, than the Suthern Right broke. Perhaps Bellamus had over-excited them to the extent that their officers had lost control. Perhaps, after all, he knew no more about war than his lowly station suggested and he was foolhardy in the face of his steady enemy. Whatever the cause, Sutherners had begun to flood down the ridge, slipping and sliding through the mud in a mad charge against the Blackstone Legion. They broke formation and so lost the only advantage they had held: the ridge. Thousands surged forward, screaming for Anakim blood.

Kynortas had not expected such an easy opening. Disordered and chaotic, the Sutherners would be shredded in open combat. "Release the Blackstones!" From a trumpet behind him soared three glorious notes, commanding the Blackstones, who needed no second invitation, to attack.

Once, perhaps a decade ago now, Kynortas had seen a mechanical clock. Envoys from Anakim-held lands to the south had sought an audience, proposing an alliance in which they were to act as anvil to the Black Kingdom hammer. To be wrought: the Sutherners' central Ereboan territories. Into this alliance they had quietly rooted a trade agreement—favourable, they had said, for both parties. They had presented samples of the goods that the Black Kingdom could expect to flood their markets. A hull load of beautiful, dark timber said to be the best in the Known World for ship craft. Weightless sacks of eider down. Wine-red crystals that are precious to the Black Kingdom for the potent metal that can be extracted from them. And a mechanical clock; the first Kynortas had seen. In the Black Kingdom the length of an hour differed with each day of the year and was judged from the passing of sun and moon. If they needed to measure short periods of time, they would use a water-clock. They had no need of a mechanical timekeeping device and yet Kynortas had been entranced by the inscrutable object.

It was held together by an exoskeleton that laid bare its inner workings. It was half machine, half organism. Its heart was a little spring; perfectly weighted and animating the busy cogs with which it was enmeshed. There was no flaw in any one of its workings. It ticked and clicked with quiet order and, twelve times a day, a bell would chime out the hour. It was unnecessary, of course. A frivolous waste of good steel, but Kynortas was convinced that he had seen the future. One day, such craftsmanship could build a boat that would man itself, or a harvesting machine that could cut down an entire field if it were just set moving.

Now, he thought of his legions as clockwork. The epitome of flawless, synchronised cooperation. The Blackstone Legion armed itself as five thousand blades were swept clear of their scabbards. It surged forward in ten waves, five hundred abreast. Kynortas was extending his influence through the flood waters; they were his harvesting machine and he had set them moving. Two lines, one calm and ordered; one frenzied and chaotic, splashed through the flood waters to meet each other. It would be a slaughter.

The clockwork failed.

The Blackstones began to stumble and fall into the waters. Legionaries started to drop by the handful, with more and more falling until the front rank in its entirety had dropped below the surface, no longer howling but crying in pain. Those who followed met the same fate, staggering and plunging into the flood waters. Kynortas spurred towards his Left, straining his eyes at the scene. Why were his soldiers falling? Was the footing treacherous? But this was Suthern trickery; the water around the Blackstones was turning red with blood. Beneath the flood waters, a trap had been laid.

The Blackstone Legion had stopped dead in their tracks. Every man that attempted to advance stumbled and fell. The Sutherners on the ridge jeered and hooted and their charging warriors, who had seemed to be in chaos, stopped seventy yards short of the stricken Blackstones. They were longbowmen; so lightly armed and armoured that they would never have stood a chance against legionaries in open combat. They had charged to bait the Blackstones and now revealed their true strength: their great curved yew bows. These were unslung, arrows nocked to strings and deadly shafts poured into the legionaries. Their fletching whistled as they hurtled forward; a noise like a sky-full of whirring starlings. At this close range, some of the steel-tipped arrows were able to penetrate tough Anakim plate armour. The legionaries, unable to move in either direction, dropped into the flooding to try and limit the damage of this swarm of arrows. They cowered in the waters, seemingly completely mired. Kynortas was witnessing the near perfect destruction of one of his legions at the hands of the Suthern upstart, Bellamus. The Anakim Left was ruined and they had yet to kill a single Sutherner.

"Roper, with me!" bellowed the Black Lord. He spurred towards the Raptors, shouting that the trumpeter should signal the halt. The Anakim line juddered to a standstill, so that they could not outstrip the mired legion and leave their flank exposed. But this left them vulnerable to the longbow shafts that rained down upon the line from the ridge. These arrows were more distant and so had less force, but they still withered the Anakim ranks.

Roper and Kynortas sped towards the Blackstones, Kynortas looking first for the problem, and then for a solution—any solution. But the Black Lord, so calm, so confident, had strayed. He feared for his legion and could not understand how the battle had escalated beyond his control so quickly. So he rode towards the problem, seeking a solution.

And a gust of arrows took him and Roper.

They struck plate armour with a clang like the splitting of a bell, the force enough to knock the Black Lord from his saddle and stagger his heir. Kynortas's boot became entangled in the stirrup and he was dragged through the water by his bolting stallion, straight towards the Suthern line. His body left a trail of blood through the flood waters.

Roper, staggering and with an arrow protruding from beneath his collarbone, spurred his horse after his father. Kynortas was not resisting, lying limp as he was pulled through the waters towards his enemies, and Roper spurred hard enough that the horse's blood and his own mingled and dripped from his stirrups. Arrows spat into the waters around him and more clanged off his armour as his father was dragged further and further from his reach.

Blood-crazed Sutherners were swarming towards him. Roper drew his sword in anger for the very first time and hacked down. There was a ring of metal on metal and a juddering shockwave ran up Roper's arm. He struck wildly once, twice, three times; his eyes always on the body of his father which had now been dragged into the heart of the Suthern mass. Men drew wicked knives and converged on the body to claim the rich prize: a fallen king. The Black Lord was dead and his son was dying.

Roper was spraying vile curses at the men between him and his father, trying to drive his horse onwards. A hand seized his boot and dragged him from the saddle. He crashed into the flood waters and for a moment could neither see nor hear as he was engulfed. There was an awful, puncturing sensation in his thigh and he knew he had been stabbed. Panic lent him strength and he thrashed to the surface, finding his sword still in his hand and sweeping it from the water. He was pinned to the ground by a spear thrust into his leg but he could still swing his sword and aimed it wildly at the Sutherners who surrounded him, blocking attacks as best he could. One lunge made it through and smashed into his head, where it opened a gash to the bone but went no further. Whilst Roper's head was ringing, his vision a clouded white, another thrust hit his chest, puncturing his plate and through to his bone-armour where, again, it was stopped.

Roper had no idea of it but he was screaming; a vile shriek of distress and ferocity as his sword flailed through the air, seeking to strike back at someone. He was alone in these waters, which were steadily turning pink with his own blood. He could barely see the sky, the view blocked by lunging Suthern bodies. There was no noise at all; he was enslaved by the overwhelming instinct to keep himself alive for a few seconds more.

An improbable freedom had descended upon him. His self-doubt was gone, his mind wiped clean for one great, dynamic effort. His vision, which no longer felt like vision in the ordinary sense, had become tunnel-like and responded to motion alone. He could not think, he had no control; Roper was stripped to his core. He was a cornered wildcat. There was nothing in him beyond his hauling lungs and swinging blade. Dark shapes were pressing in on his prone form.

And then there was a break in the wall of flesh which surrounded him. The light of the grey skies poured down on Roper.

A dead Sutherner had crashed into the waters at his feet in a spray of blood and there was a shout of alarm. A flash of light carved through another two Sutherners who were hurled backwards and an enormous shadow stepped into the gap they had left. The figure raised its great light blade again and sparks sprang away from it as it swept along a Suthern weapon, taking the top of a man's skull off as if it were an apple. Like rows of wheat, the Sutherners were falling before this harvester until Roper's final two attackers fled, splashing away through the waters.

A hand seized Roper's collar and dragged him up and out. Roper screamed again as the spear was ripped from his flesh but his rescuer took no notice, hauling him from the scene. The shock almost made Roper drop his sword, but his groping fingers managed to just clutch the pommel as he was hauled away. "My lord father!" he roared as he was dragged back. "The Black Lord! He's there! Get him!"

More hands seized Roper and Anakim swarmed around him, flooding between him and the Suthern ranks. "Release me!" he shouted. It was the Sacred Guard. The finest fighting unit in the world had arrived, honour-bound to preserve the blood that surged through Roper.

if you enjoyed
BLOOD OF THE GODS

look out for

JADE CITY
The Green Bone Saga

by

Fonda Lee

FAMILY IS DUTY. MAGIC IS POWER.
HONOR IS EVERYTHING.

Jade is the lifeblood of the island of Kekon. It has been mined,
traded, stolen, and killed for—and for centuries, honorable
Green Bone warriors like the Kaul family have used it
to enhance their magical abilities and defend the island
from foreign invasion.

Now, the war is over and a new generation of Kauls vies
for control of Kekon's bustling capital city. They care about
nothing but protecting their own, cornering the jade market,
and defending the districts under their protection.
Ancient tradition has little place in this rapidly
changing nation.

When a powerful new drug emerges that lets anyone—even foreigners—wield jade, the simmering tension between the Kauls and the rival Ayt family erupts into open violence. The outcome of this clan war will determine the fate of all Green Bones—from their grandest patriarch to the lowliest motorcycle runner on the streets—and of Kekon itself.

Chapter 1

THE TWICE LUCKY

The two would-be jade thieves sweated in the kitchen of the Twice Lucky restaurant. The windows were open in the dining room, and the onset of evening brought a breeze off the waterfront to cool the diners, but in the kitchen, there were only the two ceiling fans that had been spinning all day to little effect. Summer had barely begun and already the city of Janloon was like a spent lover—sticky and fragrant.

Bero and Sampa were sixteen years old, and after three weeks of planning, they had decided that tonight would change their lives. Bero wore a waiter's dark pants and a white shirt that clung uncomfortably to his back. His sallow face and chapped lips were stiff from holding in his thoughts. He carried a tray of dirty drink glasses over to the kitchen sink and set it down, then wiped his hands on a dish towel and leaned toward his coconspirator, who was rinsing dishes with the spray hose before stacking them in the drying racks.

"He's alone now." Bero kept his voice low.

Sampa glanced up. He was an Abukei teenager—copper-skinned with thick, wiry hair and slightly pudgy cheeks that gave him a faintly cherubic appearance. He blinked rapidly, then turned back to the sink. "I get off my shift in five minutes."

"We gotta do it now, keke," said Bero. "Hand it over."

Sampa dried a hand on the front of his shirt and pulled a small paper envelope from his pocket. He slipped it quickly into Bero's palm. Bero tucked his hand under his apron, picked up his empty tray, and walked out of the kitchen.

At the bar, he asked the bartender for rum with chili and lime on the rocks—Shon Judonrhu's preferred drink. Bero carried the drink away, then put down his tray and bent over an empty table by the wall, his back to the dining room floor. As he pretended to wipe down the table with his towel, he emptied the contents of the paper packet into the glass. They fizzed quickly and dissolved in the amber liquid.

He straightened and made his way over to the bar table in the corner. Shon Ju was still sitting by himself, his bulk squeezed onto a small chair. Earlier in the evening, Maik Kehn had been at the table as well, but to Bero's great relief, he'd left to rejoin his brother in a booth on the other side of the room. Bero set the glass down in front of Shon. "On the house, Shon-jen."

Shon took the drink, nodding sleepily without looking up. He was a regular at the Twice Lucky and drank heavily. The bald spot in the center of his head was pink under the dining room lights. Bero's eyes were drawn, irresistibly, farther down, to the three green studs in the man's left ear.

He walked away before he could be caught staring. It was ridiculous that such a corpulent, aging drunk was a Green Bone. True, Shon had only a little jade on him, but unimpressive as he was, sooner or later someone would take it, along with his life perhaps. *And why not me?* Bero thought. Why not, indeed. He might only be a dockworker's bastard who would never have a martial education at Wie Lon Temple School or Kaul Dushuron Academy, but at least he was Kekonese all the way through. He had guts and nerve; he had what it took to be somebody. Jade made you somebody.

He passed the Maik brothers sitting together in a booth with a
third young man. Bero slowed a little, just to get a closer look at
them. Maik Kehn and Maik Tar—now *they* were real Green Bones.
Sinewy men, their fingers heavy with jade rings, fighting talon
knives with jade-inlaid hilts strapped to their waists. They were
dressed well: dark, collared shirts and tailored tan jackets, shiny
black shoes, billed hats. The Maiks were well-known members of
the No Peak clan, which controlled most of the neighborhoods on
this side of the city. One of them glanced in Bero's direction.

Bero turned away quickly, busying himself with clearing dishes.
The last thing he wanted was for the Maik brothers to pay any
attention to him tonight. He resisted the urge to reach down to
check the small-caliber pistol tucked in the pocket of his pants and
concealed by his apron. Patience. After tonight, he wouldn't be in
this waiter's uniform anymore. He wouldn't have to serve anyone
anymore.

Back in the kitchen, Sampa had finished his shift for the evening
and was signing out. He looked questioningly at Bero, who nodded
that the deed was done. Sampa's small, white upper teeth popped
into view and crushed down on his lower lip. "You really think we
can do this?" he whispered.

Bero brought his face near the other boy's. "Stay cut, keke," he
hissed. "We're already doing it. No turning back. You've got to do
your part!"

"I know, keke, I know. I will." Sampa gave him a hurt and sour
look.

"Think of the money," Bero suggested, and gave him a shove.
"Now get going."

Sampa cast a final nervous glance backward, then pushed out
the kitchen door. Bero glared after him, wishing for the hundredth
time that he didn't need such a doughy and insipid partner. But
there was no getting around it—only a full-blooded Abukei native,
immune to jade, could palm a gem and walk out of a crowded
restaurant without giving himself away.

It had taken some convincing to bring Sampa on board. Like many in his tribe, the boy gambled on the river, spending his weekends diving for jade runoff that escaped the mines far upstream. It was dangerous—when glutted with rainfall, the torrent carried away more than a few unfortunate divers, and even if you were lucky and found jade (Sampa had bragged that he'd once found a piece the size of a fist), you might get caught. Spend time in jail if you were lucky, time in the hospital if you weren't.

It was a loser's game, Bero had insisted to him. Why fish for raw jade just to sell it to the black market middlemen who carved it up and smuggled it off island, paying you only a fraction of what they sold it for later? A couple of clever, daring fellows like them—they could do better. If you were going to gamble for jade, Bero said, then gamble big. Aftermarket gems, cut and set—that was worth real money.

Bero returned to the dining room and busied himself clearing and setting tables, glancing at the clock every few minutes. He could ditch Sampa later, after he'd gotten what he needed.

"Shon Ju says there's been trouble in the Armpit," said Maik Kehn, leaning in to speak discreetly under the blanket of background noise. "A bunch of kids shaking down businesses."

His younger brother, Maik Tar, reached across the table with his chopsticks to pluck at the plate of crispy squid balls. "What kind of kids are we talking about?"

"Low-level Fingers. Young toughs with no more than a piece or two of jade."

The third man at the table wore an uncharacteristically pensive frown. "Even the littlest Fingers are clan soldiers. They take orders from their Fists, and Fists from their Horn." The Armpit district had always been disputed territory, but directly threatening establishments affiliated with the No Peak clan was too bold to be the work of careless hoodlums. "It smells like someone's pissing on us."

The Maiks glanced at him, then at each other. "What's going on, Hilo-jen?" asked Kehn. "You seem out of sorts tonight."

"Do I?" Kaul Hiloshudon leaned against the wall in the booth and turned his glass of rapidly warming beer, idly wiping off the condensation. "Maybe it's the heat."

Kehn motioned to one of the waiters to refill their drinks. The pallid teenager kept his eyes down as he served them. He glanced up at Hilo for a second but didn't seem to recognize him; few people who hadn't met Kaul Hiloshudon in person expected him to look as young as he did. The Horn of the No Peak clan, second only in authority to his elder brother, often went initially unnoticed in public. Sometimes this galled Hilo; sometimes he found it useful.

"Another strange thing," said Kehn when the waiter had left. "No one's seen or heard from Three-Fingered Gee."

"How's it possible to lose track of Three-Fingered Gee?" Tar wondered. The black market jade carver was as recognizable for his girth as he was for his deformity.

"Maybe he got out of the business."

Tar snickered. "Only one way anyone gets out of the jade business."

A voice spoke up near Hilo's ear. "Kaul-jen, how are you this evening? Is everything to your satisfaction tonight?" Mr. Une had appeared beside their table and was smiling the anxious, solicitous smile he always reserved for them.

"It's all excellent, as usual," Hilo said, arranging his face into the relaxed, lopsided smile that was his more typical expression.

The owner of the Twice Lucky clasped his kitchen-scarred hands together, nodding and smiling his humble thanks. Mr. Une was a man in his sixties, bald and well-padded, and a third-generation restaurateur. His grandfather had founded the venerable old establishment, and his father had kept it running all through the wartime years, and afterward. Like his predecessors, Mr. Une was a loyal Lantern Man in the No Peak clan. Every time Hilo was in, he came around personally to pay his respects. "Please let me know if there is anything else I can have brought out to you," he insisted.

extras

When the reassured Mr. Une had departed, Hilo grew serious again. "Ask around some more. Find out what happened to Gee."

"Why do we care about Gee?" Kehn asked, not in an impertinent way, just curious. "Good riddance to him. One less carver sneaking our jade out to weaklings and foreigners."

"It bothers me, is all." Hilo sat forward, helping himself to the last crispy squid ball. "Nothing good's coming, when the dogs start disappearing from the streets."

Bero's nerves were beginning to fray. Shon Ju had nearly drained his tainted drink. The drug was supposedly tasteless and odorless, but what if Shon, with the enhanced senses of a Green Bone, could detect it somehow? Or what if it didn't work as it should, and the man walked out, taking his jade out of Bero's grasp? What if Sampa lost his nerve after all? The spoon in Bero's hands trembled as he set it down on the table. *Stay cut, now. Be a man.*

A phonograph in the corner wheezed out a slow, romantic opera tune, barely audible through the unceasing chatter of people. Cigarette smoke and spicy food aromas hung languid over red tablecloths.

Shon Ju swayed hastily to his feet. He staggered toward the back of the restaurant and pushed through the door to the men's room.

Bero counted ten slow seconds in his head, then put the tray down and followed casually. As he slipped into the restroom, he slid his hand into his pocket and closed it around the grip of the tiny pistol. He shut and locked the door behind him and pressed against the far wall.

The sound of sustained retching issued from one of the stalls, and Bero nearly gagged on the nauseating odor of booze-soaked vomit. The toilet flushed, and the heaving noises ceased. There was a muffled thud, like the sound of something heavy hitting the tile floor, then a sickly silence. Bero took several steps forward. His heartbeat thundered in his ears. He raised the small gun to chest level.

The stall door was open. Shon Ju's large bulk was slumped inside, limbs sprawled. His chest rose and fell in soft, snuffling snores. A thin line of drool ran from the corner of his mouth.

A pair of grimy canvas shoes moved in the far stall, and Sampa stuck his head around the corner where he'd been lying in wait. His eyes grew round at the sight of the pistol, but he sidled over next to Bero and the two of them stared down at the unconscious man.

Holy shit, it worked.

"What're you waiting for?" Bero waved the small gun in Shon's direction. "Go on! Get it!"

Sampa squeezed hesitantly through the half-open stall door. Shon Ju's head was leaning to the left, his jade-studded ear trapped against the wall of the toilet cubicle. With the screwed-up face of someone about to touch a live power line, the boy placed his hands on either side of Shon's head. He paused; the man didn't stir. Sampa turned the slack-jowled face to the other side. With shaking fingers, he pinched the first jade earring and worked the backing free.

"Here, use this." Bero handed him the empty paper packet. Sampa dropped the jade stud into it and got to work removing the second earring. Bero's eyes danced between the jade, Shon Ju, the gun, Sampa, again the jade. He took a step forward and held the barrel of the pistol a few inches from the prone man's temple. It looked distressingly compact and ineffective—a commoner's weapon. No matter. Shon Ju wasn't going to be able to Steel or Deflect anything in his state. Sampa would palm the jade and walk out the back door with no one the wiser. Bero would finish his shift and meet up with Sampa afterward. No one would disturb old Shon Ju for hours; it wasn't the first time the man had passed out drunk in a restroom.

"Hurry it up," Bero said.

Sampa had two of the jade stones off and was working on the third. His fingers dug around in the fold of the man's fleshy ear. "I can't get this one off."

"Pull it off, just pull it off!"

Sampa gave the last stubborn earring a swift yank. It tore free from the flesh that had grown around it. Shon Ju jerked. His eyes flew open.

"Oh shit," said Sampa.

With an almighty howl, Shon's arms shot out, flailing around his head and knocking Bero's arm upward just as Bero pulled the trigger of the gun. The shot deafened all of them but went wide, punching into the plaster ceiling.

Sampa scrambled to get away, nearly tripping over Shon as he lunged for the stall door. Shon flung his arms around one of the boy's legs. His bloodshot eyes rolled in disorientation and rage. Sampa tumbled to the ground and put his hands out to break his fall; the paper packet jumped from his grasp and skittered across the tile floor between Bero's legs.

"Thieves!" Shon Ju's snarling mouth formed the word, but Bero did not hear it. His head was ringing from the gunshot, and everything was happening as if in a soundless chamber. He stared as the red-faced Green Bone dragged at the terrified Abukei boy like a grasping demon from a pit.

Bero bent, snatched the crumpled paper envelope, and ran for the door.

He forgot he'd locked it. For a second he pushed and pulled in stupid panic, before turning the bolt and pounding out of the room. The diners had heard the gunshot, and dozens of shocked faces were turned toward him. Bero had just enough presence of mind left to jam the gun into his pocket and point a finger back toward the restroom. "There's a jade thief in there!" he shouted.

Then he ran across the dining room floor, weaving between tables, the two small stones digging through the paper and against the palm of his tightly fisted left hand. People leapt away from him. Faces blurred past. Bero knocked over a chair, fell, picked himself up again, and kept running.

His face was burning. A sudden surge of heat and energy unlike anything he had ever felt before ripped through him like an electric current. He reached the wide, curving staircase that led to the second floor, where diners were getting up and peering over the balcony railing to see what the commotion was. Bero rushed up the stairs, clearing the entire expanse in a few bounds, his feet barely touching the floor. A gasp ran through the crowd. Bero's surprise burst into ecstasy. He threw his head back to laugh. This must be Lightness.

A film had been lifted from his eyes and ears. The scrape of chair legs, the crash of a plate, the taste of the air on his tongue—everything was razor sharp. Someone reached out to grab him, but he was so slow, and Bero was so fast. He swerved with ease and leapt off the surface of a table, scattering dishes and eliciting screams. There was a sliding screen door ahead of him that led out onto the patio overlooking the harbor. Without thinking, without pausing, he crashed through the barrier like a charging bull. The wooden latticework shattered, and Bero stumbled through the body-sized hole he had made with a mad shout of exultation. He felt no pain at all, only a wild, fierce invincibility.

This was the power of jade.

The night air blasted him, tingling against his skin. Below, the expanse of gleaming water beckoned irresistibly. Waves of delicious heat seemed to be coursing through Bero's veins. The ocean looked so cool, so refreshing. It would feel so good. He flew toward the patio railing.

Hands clamped onto his shoulders and pulled him to a hard stop. Bero was yanked back as if he'd reached the end of a chain and spun around to face Maik Tar.

orbit

Follow us:

f /orbitbooksUS

🐦 /orbitbooks

▶ /orbitbooks

Join our mailing list
to receive alerts on our
latest releases and deals.

orbitbooks.net

Enter our monthly
giveaway for the chance
to win some epic prizes.

orbitloot.com